Bayou Secrets

Romance Collection

D0106753

Bayou Secrets

Romance Collection

Deborah Lynne

BARBOUR BOOKS

An Imprint of Barbour Publishing, Inc.

Print ISBN 978-1-63058-868-7

eBook Editions:
Adobe Digital Edition (.epub) 978-1-63409-333-0
Kindle and MobiPocket Edition (.prc) 978-1-63409-334-7

Published by Barbour Books, an imprint of Barbour Publishing, Inc., P.O. Box 719, Uhrichsville, Ohio 44683, www.barbourbooks.com, in association with OakTara Publishers, www.oaktara.com.

Our mission is to publish and distribute inspirational products offering exception value and biblical encouragement to the masses.

ecpa Member of the
Evangelical Christian
Publishers Association

Printed in the United States of America.

CONTENTS

Crime in the Big Easy

ACKNOWLEDGMENTS

I'd like to thank the city of New Orleans—more specifically, the French Quarter, for the perfect backdrop of my story. And to think I was born there. . .The Big Easy. There's more than Mardi Gras to enjoy in New Orleans. The streets are alive with the sounds of laughter, music, and the voices of many clusters of people walking the sidewalks, enjoying the ambiance of the city.

Again I'd like to thank my friends Emy, Marie, Marty, and Charlotte, who read, reread, and then read again my novels to help me fine-tune each book. I also thank my readers who buy my books. I love my job, and I'm glad so many people still love to read fiction.

Last, but not least, I thank Ramona Tucker, my wonderful publisher and editor. She guides me in the right direction, tightening my novel even more. I am blessed to call her my friend as well.

Chapter 1

I don't care what you tell him, Captain. Ask the chief if he wants this case solved with the real murderer behind bars." The lieutenant shifted his feet slightly as he looked anxiously around the phone at the redheaded woman sitting calmly in the chair facing the front of his desk.

Reporters. Ugh. He didn't care for them. Sure, they had a job to do, but too many times reporters got in the way of him doing his job—catching a killer.

Questions flashed, one right after the other, through his mind. He tried to pay attention to his captain's bellowing, but that woman disrupted his thoughts.

What does she want? Can she hear everything I'm saying? Does she know what we're talking about?

Sure, she appeared not to be listening or paying attention to his phone call, but down deep he knew better. She was a reporter. They had their ways of getting what they wanted.

Deadlines—that was all they worried about. Not the victims. Not the families. And certainly not the next casualty! That was how they got their stories, filled their papers or their magazines.

Who let her back here anyway? I'll give him a piece of my mind after I throw this woman out of here. I have enough to deal with around this place without adding unnecessary and unwanted interviews to my schedule.

His gaze stabbed in her direction but as quickly slid back to the phone in his hand. Lieutenant John Bradley didn't like discussing his latest case with the captain while that woman—that reporter—sat and listened to his every word, but right now he had no choice.

When she first arrived, he tried politely to send her on her way. It didn't work. As soon as he opened the door to his office, she rushed over to the empty chair by his desk and sat down. When the phone rang, he hinted for her to leave so he could take the call. He hoped she'd step out of his office.

But no. Instead, she smiled sweetly as she said, "No problem, Detective Bradley. I'll wait." Flipping a mass of red curls behind her shoulder, she crossed one leg over the other as she glanced around his office, as if she were interested in where he worked. She didn't fool him, not one iota.

John grumbled to himself, knowing she was hanging on his every word.

John should have thrown her out but didn't need the bad press. He resisted the urge, not knowing his boss would get into such a deep discussion of the two killings that had happened on the edge of the French Quarter while she sat across from him. His team was investigating both of the cases, and he was the lead detective on them. The New Orleans Police Department as a whole didn't need any more negative stories scripted in the paper or flashed across the news broadcasts. And he, for one, didn't want to add any more negative publicity to what they were already getting.

"John, do you hear me?" The captain's words silenced John's present thoughts of the reporter and brought his attention back to the matter at hand. "I'm pushing you, Lieutenant, because the chief is pushing me, because the commissioner is pushing him. Do I make myself clear? Get after it!" He barked his words loudly in John's ear. "Find something to link those two girls' deaths so you can find the killer. I'm sure they're connected." The captain's words grew stronger with each breath. The man wanted answers from his lead homicide detective, and he wanted them now.

Unfortunately, John didn't have the answers he needed. He wished he did. John only had more questions—but not for his captain, so the detective remained silent. If that reporter wasn't sitting there watching his every move, he'd tell his captain to back off. Insist the captain give John and his men some room to work. But seeing those green eyes locked on him, he didn't dare say a word she could take and print in her paper.

"We need a suspect, a name to give the commissioner. You got that, Bradley? Get me a suspect!"

John's knuckles whitened as he squeezed the receiver, pulling it from his ear. He felt daggers flying from his eyes as he glared at the phone.

Frustration will get you nowhere, man. Stay cool. Those words filtered through his mind as he tried to restrain his tongue. Oh, how he tried. For one second, then two. He even held it for three. His lungs filled with air as he held back his angry retort. Finally he could hold his words back no more, but at least he had enough sense to keep it from the intruder. Returning the phone to his ear, he turned his chair almost completely around, exposing his back to the reporter. Then in words spoken firmly but almost in a whisper he said, "Then hang it on some wino on Bourbon Street if it makes you feel better, Captain. But me, I want to get the real sicko behind bars and put him away for life. So get off my back, please, and let me do my job."

At least he controlled his impulse of slamming the phone down on the captain like he wanted. That was showing some restraint on his part, wasn't it? Sometimes this job got the best of him, but he knew he was a detective for a reason—to protect the innocent, to save people from becoming a victim, and to serve the public. When evil won out on the streets, his job was to find the guilty and put them away.

John regretted losing his cool with his superior as fast as it had happened. Instead of saying any more, he clenched his teeth together and waited for his captain's response.

In his ear came the sound of a long slow breath being drawn, and then a quick release of air followed. Suddenly, in sharp, choppy words the captain said, "I'm disappointed, Bradley. Apparently you're not listening to me."

John shook his head as he rose, and his pent-up breath released slowly, all the while keeping his back to the reporter. *Oh, I'm listening all right. I can't help but hear you.* He stretched the phone cord taut, resisting the urge to yank it out at the base. Deep within he knew he had to be straight with the captain, but he also needed some space to do his job, some privacy. That woman made it impossible for him to talk freely, so he returned to biting his tongue, almost drawing blood.

"I said find a connection. Get a lead. Something!"

John had to tell him something and make sure the reporter didn't hear a word. Swallowing hard and taking control, he spoke in a very low voice. "Sir, in the beginning the only connection we made, besides the obvious fact that both were women found strangled in the early morning hours in the same general area of the Quarter, was that they were both single. That's it. That does not connect the killings; it just gives them one more thing in common. The MO *appears* to be the same—so far—but we haven't ruled out copycat killers either. The papers gave too many details on the first one not to think a copycat was possible. And even though the fibers were a match on the rope, it is a typical material of a common rope found at any of your local hardware stores and chain stores. We must be able to do our job and do it thoroughly, even if it takes a little time." *There. I stayed calm, kept my voice low. Hopefully Captain Stewart will get the message and back off.*

"Time is something you may not have." The captain spat his words and followed it with a grunt of frustration. "So right now you have no one? No leads? No speculations?"

John sighed. "Of course we have speculations." But that wasn't enough. They needed evidence. They needed proof that backed up their speculations—not that he would share his theories now. John didn't want Miss Jaymes hearing what the department thought until they had the support to back up their speculation. The last thing he needed to see splashed across the front page of the *Morning Tribune* was Cop Suspected in Killings. The police could conjecture all they wanted, but they needed proof, the truth, and evidence to back up their theory.

"Spill it."

So the captain does know me. He paused for only a moment before responding. "Captain, I can only say this once, so please listen closely. There is a reporter sitting in my office, and I don't care to have my theory plastered across the headlines in the morning paper." John made sure his back was still to the reporter just in case she could read lips. He could never be too careful. In a hushed whisper he said, "We had thought of the possibility of someone dressing as a police officer, maybe even using a patrol car in order to pull these women over in the early morning hours. Why else would a woman, alone, stop at that ungodly hour in such a secluded area?"

"That sounds promising. Have you checked out your theory?" Hope rang out in the captain's voice.

"We're running it down now, sir," John said, still speaking very low. "Again, we have to be sure of all the facts before we start making claims. It takes time. So far every patrol car has been accounted for, so it's still speculation." Taking a moment to hold onto his composure, silence filled the airwaves for a moment or two, and then John said, "And although we haven't found anything connecting the victims, we're still looking for a possible connection there, too."

"John, you know what I'm telling you. I'm telling you to work harder and let's close these cases before the killer strikes again. You got it?"

Pulling the receiver away from his ear for the second time, he glared at it. *Oh, yeah. I got it.* Of course he got it. He got it the first time the captain said it. John wanted his cases solved as much as the commissioner, the mayor, and the governor, if not more, and for the right reasons. John wasn't up for re-election. He wanted the Quarter safe again. He didn't want to see another woman killed. John felt strongly that a madman wandered the streets of New Orleans looking for the opportunity to do it again. He had to find him quickly, and he vowed to do just that.

"That's my goal, sir." Pivoting his head slightly, he scowled at the reporter for a second, then turned back toward the wall.

If looks could kill, his certainly would do the job. Taylor watched the dark-haired detective in deep conversation with his superior. *Glad that look is for his captain and not me.* The reporter watched those expressive blue eyes dart her way and then as quickly avert in another direction in the room. He truly wished she wasn't there. Taylor smiled to herself. What better timing to be sitting in front of his desk than when he was talking this case over with his captain?

She wished she was privy to the whole conversation, but she only managed to catch snatches of the discussion. Unfortunately, the man kept lowering his voice, speaking softer and softer with every comment made. Taylor felt certain the exchange was about the killings. That was just what she wanted to hear him talk about, but to her, not his captain. As she strained to listen, trying to catch every word, she pretended to look around the lieutenant's office, trying not to appear interested in his dialogue.

Did she fool him? She doubted it. Unfortunately, the low hum of his computer as well as the rattle of the air conditioner worked as a great sound buffer, keeping his words from reaching her ears.

The detective's office wasn't as fancy as the lobby of the police station she'd entered from the Quarter less than half an hour ago. Taylor never would have known it was a police station when she first stepped inside the building had it not been for the cops in uniform. A couple officers stood behind the big long counter that divided the room and two more sipped coffee, discussing something of interest. Behind the two chained-off areas, one to the right and the other to the left, sat desks scattered in a fairly neat order, and behind most of them sat policemen and women. Some talked on their phones, holding deep conversations, while others typed into their computers. People off the street sat in chairs next to some of the desks. They were either reporting a crime or asking for help. A steady murmur of voices filled that room.

In her mind, she compared the differences between the outer room and the detective's office as she locked her ears on him, listening for any clue to the two deaths on the edge of the Quarter.

The police station's lobby had high ceilings edged with triple crown molding and intricate corners covered with elaborate carvings of small statuettes. Five crystal-looking chandeliers adorned the great room, keeping it well lit if she remembered correctly. As a reporter, she was trained to observe and remember things. Pristine white covered the walls while a sea of soft blue carpet covered the floors. Not the typical police station, but in New Orleans, especially in the French Quarter, not too many things were typical.

Detective Bradley's office, however, except for the high

ceiling, was a normal cluttered detective's workplace. Papers covered his desk, each in small stacks neatly scattered on the surface. *Oops.* Maybe it wasn't so normal after all—too neat. Her eyes rescanned the room. Several file folders stuffed with more papers were piled in one orderly stack on the corner of the desk, and an almost-empty styrofoam cup of coffee perched within arm's reach to the right side of the papers in the file folder he had open—his right side, her left. Dark gray file cabinets lined the short length of the back wall in the small office, making the room seem even smaller.

A strange neatness in this clutter made his office highly unusual in her opinion—at least by comparison to the cop shops she normally had the pleasure of viewing. Those offices always sat in disarray.

Definitely different.

Slowly Detective John Bradley pulled the phone back to his ear as he swiveled slightly back around, almost facing frontwards. In a restrained voice he replied, "Yes, sir. I understand. Yes. Yes. No, sir."

His words were still of no help. The reporter sat in the straight-backed chair across from his desk, her ears straining. She struggled hard to hear every detail of the one-sided conversation. Unfortunately it wasn't much.

Taylor knew what he was discussing—the two murders on the edge of the Quarter—and whom he was discussing them with. That subject matter was precisely why she was there. What she did hear him say, she already knew. She'd give anything to have heard what he said when he lowered his voice after he turned his back on her. Those words would have given her more insight as to what had been discovered so far.

But since she was not allowed to hear the conversation in its entirety, she wished the detective would get off the phone and give her his undivided attention.

The detective's voice returned to normal as he said, "We're checking all our leads. As soon as we have something conclusive, you'll be the first to know." Swiveling the rest of the way facing his desk, he slammed down the phone.

She heard that. The captain would be the first to know anything new. Of course. Now, however, she wanted the detective to tell her what leads they were following and what they were suspecting. . .anything she could share with her readers.

Releasing a long pent-up breath, he lifted his deep blue gaze and locked it with hers. "Miss Jaymes, what is it you want? As you can see, I'm a busy man." His jaw jerked as he stared down at the papers in front of him.

Agitation radiated from the detective. The tone he used while talking to his captain gave her the distinct impression she wasn't going to get much from this man, but she had to try. That was her job.

"Like I was saying before your phone call, Detective Bradley, I'm Taylor Jaymes, a reporter with the *Morning Tribune*. I'm doing a follow-up piece on the two victims that were found strangled in the past two weeks. Have the police determined if they were connected or not? From your conversation, what little I overheard, I gather you can't tell me that yet, but maybe you could tell me something else. You do realize it has almost been another week since the last killing? If it is a serial killer, there may be another murder in the next night or two. Now would you care to comment? Is there something you'd like to share with the public?" Taylor held her pen poised, ready to take action. She would have used her recorder to get it precise, but this lieutenant didn't allow recordings in his office. Only when he was giving his press releases could reporters record him.

The detective's inquisitive blue eyes moved slowly over Taylor's face. She felt a slight tingle as he scanned her head to toe. His dark brows drew together as a frown fashioned on his shapely lips. Taylor was torn between admiring his striking looks and figuring out what he was thinking about her as he checked her out thoroughly.

She didn't have to wonder long about that questioning look. His gaze pinned her as he leaned back in his chair. Softly, he said, "You're the reporter who almost died about five months ago when tracking that string of burglaries in the jewelry shops on and around Canal Street, aren't you?"

Taylor felt her face light up as she moved her hand gently to her chest. She loved it when someone recognized her work or her name. Of course, she would have much preferred he remembered the great string of articles she wrote instead of how she got too close and almost lost her life getting the story. "Well, a good reporter goes where the story leads and doesn't worry about the pain she must suffer to get it."

That unforgettable sound of the gunshot flashed a memory of what followed, a sharp burning pain in the right shoulder as warm blood saturated her shirt and oozed down her arm. Maybe she didn't almost die—the wound wasn't that serious even though it hurt like the dickens—but had the cops not shown up when they did, the next bullet would have hit a more vital organ. Who knows what would have happened to her and her story?

"Humph," he muttered. The frown deepened. The detective shook his head and rose. He strolled around his desk over to the door. Taylor followed him with her eyes but not with her feet. She wasn't ready to leave. Not yet. She needed a statement from him.

Detective John Bradley grabbed the knob, turned it, and said as he opened the door slightly, "Miss Jaymes, I'll tell you what I told the captain. We have no more information at this time." He glared hard as he spoke in a firm, concise voice. "When we have more information we can release to the press, you'll get it along with everyone else." Opening the door the rest of the way, he stepped back, giving her room to exit. "I'm sorry. Maybe next time."

Under his breath, she could have sworn she heard him mumble, "I hope there is no next time." If she were tenderhearted like most women, she would have taken his comment personally. But after ten years of chasing stories, her heart was made of leather. It was business, not personal.

Taylor rose, closing her pad. Pinching the strap of her handbag, she placed it over her shoulder as she made ready to leave. "Detective Bradley, I do wish you would trust me. I won't print anything you don't want the public to know. I'm just trying to do my job. I think there is more to these murders than you want to share. I think the public has a right to know. The people need to be warned before someone else becomes the next victim."

He said nothing in response, but she saw that muscle in his jawline jerk. Then she saw him talk without saying a word. His clear blue eyes narrowed, staring straight down into hers as she moved closer to him. She felt a catch in her chest. Was it the way he looked at her? Or was it her, reacting to his looks? It didn't matter. Taylor knew what he was saying. He wouldn't tell her a thing, even if he had something to say.

She stepped into the doorway. As she was about to leave, she cocked her head toward the dark-haired detective. "If you change your mind and decide you would like to tell me more, here is my card." Taylor reached into the pocket of her light linen blazer and pulled out a business card. On the back of the card she jotted down her cell number. "You can reach me anytime. On the front is my direct line at the paper and on the back I wrote my cell." In a softer tone she added as she pressed the card into his hand, "I really would work with you on this case, printing only what you want told, if you would guarantee me the final details first. Sort of an exclusive, giving me the jump on the other papers."

No verbal response came as he closed his hand around her card, so she shrugged and continued to walk out the door.

After taking a few steps down the hall, Taylor stopped. She spun on her heel, her sparkling red curls flying around with momentum and cascading down her left shoulder, past her elbow. She lifted her gaze and said with a Southern drawl, "You know I can make the cops look great, if you'd give me the chance. And right now y'all can use all the good press you can get. You haven't had much lately." She flashed a devious smile to the grim-faced detective and hoped that did the trick.

He ran his long fingers through his wavy black hair. For a moment, hope stirred her heart. He was going to give her what she came for. *Yes!*

Dropping his hand by his side, a tight smile stretched his

lips. John Bradley sighed, shook his head, and then lowered his hard blue eyes on her again. "Cops aren't supposed to look good, Miss Jaymes. They're supposed to look mean and tough. Good day!" He dismissed her by turning his back on her and walking toward his desk.

"I'll be back." Taylor threw her words at the back of his head then strode down the hall. The sad thing was, she wasn't even sure he'd heard her last remark. At the end of the hall she took the elevator down and then reentered the lobby. As she stepped into the air-conditioned room, cooler than the detective's office, she recalled his last statement: *"Cops aren't supposed to look good."*

Simmering over his words, she lifted an eyebrow. "Too bad, Detective Bradley, 'cause you sure looked good to me," she whispered to herself. Taylor remembered the wave of his coal-black hair, the clarity of his sky-blue eyes, the fit of his jeans, and the few dark curling hairs where his shirt connected two buttons down from the collar. She could feel her lopsided smile widening into a full-fledged grin.

Glancing around the lobby, she saw the two uniformed police officers behind the counter staring at her. Each probably wanted to know what she was grinning about. Both knew she had been with Detective Bradley, and most likely, both knew his reputation and opinion of reporters. The two men probably figured he wasn't too happy to see her. They may have even expected her to come running out in tears.

Too bad.

Her grin deepened even more. She'd get her story. Taylor wouldn't give up without a fight, and she fought to win.

Chapter 2

The heat of a scorching New Orleans summer day slapped Taylor in the face and engulfed her whole being as she stepped out of the police station. Drawing in a deep breath, she paused and then blew it out again. It was the latter part of June, and summer had already jumped in with a bang. This year would be a scorcher, if today's heat were any indication. The Big Easy had its own type of heat. Not only did the humidity rise unbearably, mingling with the heat, but also the wetness jammed into every inch of your clothes as the damp material clung to your body. Down in the Quarter a breeze usually helped you through the negative side of the weather.

In New Orleans, the high temperatures of the day also affected the scents in the air. And those smells weren't always pleasant. Today was no exception.

Taylor lived on Royal Street near the corner of St. Peter,

only a few blocks from the police station, so she had left her car in the small parking spot hidden within the building of her duplex for tenants only and walked to the station earlier that morning. Many of the streets in the French Quarter had no parking, making the Quarter a wonderful area for walkers to enjoy the galleries, eateries, and jazz venues that filled the city. The music was heard mostly during the nighttime.

Heading toward her apartment for her car, she experienced most of the smells that the French Quarter offered, even this early in the morning on this hot summer day.

When she passed a pile of trash bags stacked one on top of another at the curb near a place of business, the stench of dirty garbage slithered through the air, piercing her nose. Two brisk steps later, the fresh aroma of hot baked bread teased her senses, making her wish she had grabbed a bite to eat before leaving this morning. Less than a block down the street, another fragrance wafted through the air as the corner tavern's alcohol added its aromas into the atmosphere. Mixed with all those heady scents was a light hint of orange—something the Quarter's cleaning crews used to sanitize the streets every morning. What a blessing!

Taylor loved living in the French Quarter. Her mother and father failed to approve her choice of living quarters after raising their daughter in the Historical Garden District. They felt she could have chosen better, but as an artist in her own right, practicing the art of writing, the art of journalism, Taylor knew she had selected perfectly the place she called home. Mom and Dad checked on her fairly regularly. She sensed they wished she were more like her sister, Tina. The "good daughter" married and settled down right around the corner from their parents' home. And, of course, she gave them grandchildren. The Jaymes were still waiting on Taylor to find the man who would change the shape of her life forever.

That wasn't going to happen as far as Taylor was concerned. She had plans and dreams of her own that she would not give up for any man.

"Oh well, we can't all be perfect," Taylor murmured as she ducked into the hidden parking area and headed toward her car.

Pulling out the key, she pressed the button to unlock the red Mustang and climbed inside. After cranking it up, she immediately put on the air conditioner. No one in their right mind would buy a car in the South without an air conditioner in proper working order, or they would suffocate. She only put the top down in the spring and fall or on hot summer days when she took time to visit the Mississippi, Alabama, or Florida beaches. She then dressed for fun in the sun with her bikini top and a pair of cutoffs over the bottom of her swimsuit. On those few days, she didn't mind her hair whipping around in the wind, tangling more than normal. Today, the top stayed up.

Taylor drove straight to the paper. The employees of the *Morning Tribune* seemed to be bustling in fast motion. Had something new happened? Maybe. She wondered what it might be for a moment. No, she decided it was the normal hustle and bustle to get the paper ready for its next release.

Taylor sighed. She missed the smell of printer's ink that used to fill her nostrils as a young teenager when she tagged along to work with her father. Simple computers and printers had replaced the major machinery that used gallons of wet printer's ink when grinding out a daily paper—"the good old days," as some still referred to them.

Taylor had always wanted to be a newspaper reporter like her father and his father before him. It was a family tradition. She hoped one day her name, when heard, would be immediately connected with the Pulitzer Prize for investigative reporting. She received several local and state awards for some of her stories, but her goal would not be complete until she received the longed-for Pulitzer.

And she hoped that when she received that prize, offers from newspapers across the country would come flooding in. In her dream, she received offers from the *Los Angeles Daily Journal*, the *Houston Chronicle*, the *Chicago Tribune*, and the *New York Post*. If any of those papers offered, she'd be off in a flash. She loved her job and the thrill that came along with it, but those papers could help her achieve a name beyond anything she had ever dreamed.

With fast-paced steps and nods to her fellow employees, Taylor made her way through the newspaper building and to the editor's office. Passing the empty desk of his secretary, she scooted on by to his office. There was no one to announce her or to stop her from going in. She smiled.

After three quick raps on the door, Taylor turned the knob and let herself into Mr. Cox's office. It always smelled of a combination of pipe tobacco, printer's ink—thanks to a newspaper-scented candle—and leather. He, too, loved the old days and had expressed missing that smell of printer's ink. When Taylor had found that perfectly scented candle, she couldn't resist it. She had bought it for him, not trying to score extra points. No, Taylor didn't think that way. She had done it because she knew he'd love and appreciate it, which he did. On some days, one smell was more predominant than others. Today it would have to be the leather, she decided. "Morning, Chief."

A heavyset, balding man looked up at the intrusion into his peace and quiet. "Morning, Taylor," he barked in his usual tone. Everyone knew not to take exception to his gruff voice, unless of course they had done something wrong or not done anything at all. "What are you up to on this hot and sticky June morning?"

With a grin as broad as Texas, she replied, "Finding my next story." Lowering the pitch of her voice, she leaned slightly toward his desk. "The world is full of corrupt and greedy people. Ain't that grand?" Rising to her full height of five feet, one inch, she wiggled her brows, laughed, and then added in her regular voice, "Makes for good copy, don't you think?" She truly didn't like the corruption or the greed. In fact, what she loved about her job was revealing it. Shedding light on the fraudulent goings-on in the city and exposing them. Her job was to help make the city a better place to live in while she earned that Pulitzer Prize she dreamed of having one day.

Allen Cox shook his head as a smile spread across his face. He slowly rubbed his chubby hands together. "You're in an unusually good mood today, Taylor. You must feel a story coming on. You always act stranger than normal, if that's possible for you." He chuckled as his thick brows rose and fell and motioned her to sit as he tilted back in his executive chair. "Speak up. You have my full attention."

Taylor sat and crossed her legs at the ankles. With her

back rigid and shoulders straight, she felt the excitement rise within her. "I stopped at the police station this morning before coming to work, hoping Detective Bradley would be able to connect the two killings outside the Quarter by now. . .if they are connected, that is."

"Hmmph. So your senses are telling you the two murders may be connected? Did he confirm or deny? Did you get anything from him? That's the three-million-dollar question, you know." His brows rose and fell.

Chuckling at her boss's wit, she thought how lucky she was to work for such a robust man who thrived on telling the truth to all. She loved his bizarre sense of humor, too. He knew the police didn't usually confide in a reporter. Strictly the facts, after the fact—that was all they shared and on their terms, but Allen Cox loved his reporters to push, trying to get a little more than the other paper every time. The *Tribune* was always filled with facts, and he frowned on reporters who tried to slip in their own point of view on stories. After readers read the facts reported, it was left up to them to decide if the news was good or bad and how it affected their own lives. "So true. It's like pulling teeth getting anything from Detective Bradley. He's worse than most, I do believe."

The chief nodded.

"Chief, most detectives don't share much, but Detective Bradley is tighter-lipped than most. I didn't get far, but I did get to overhear the detective being reamed out by Captain Stewart. Well, he didn't tell me that was who he was talking to, nor did I actually hear the captain raising Cain, but from what I heard on Detective Bradley's end, it sounded like that to me. They are really pushing him to find the killers and close both of those cases in the Quarter quickly." She recalled the detective's expression. "I guess the commissioner is giving the chief of police a hard time. Election time is right around the corner, so the governor is probably pushing the mayor's buttons, who is probably pushing the commissioner's buttons, and it trickles on down to the detective in charge of the case. I think they call that the domino theory." She shook her head in aggravation. "You know politics. . .or, should I say, politicians." Not all, she knew, but in general this seemed to be the truth.

Mr. Cox tipped back further in his chair after he lit his pipe. Taking a puff, he eyed Taylor. "What are you sensing about this story?"

Clasping her hands in her lap, she leaned forward. "I think there's more to the story than what they're telling us, sir. Only I'm not sure if the police are keeping it from us, or if they don't know it yet. They want us to believe both killings were two separate incidents, maybe even copycat killings, but I think we have a serial killer on the loose. The way the detective talked to Captain Stewart, I think he believes the same thing. He just can't prove it yet. Plus, he didn't want to say too much with me in the room. The call came after I got there, and he hadn't managed to throw me out yet." A slight groan slipped out. She knew how much the man had wanted her out of earshot. She almost felt sorry for him but didn't dare give him privacy for the phone call. . .not that it helped her get anything she didn't already know.

Taylor swiveled toward the big window that overlooked the city. Gazing out at the clear sky, she recalled Detective Bradley's grim face. A chill swept through her body. "If it is a serial killer, that's bad news. It means another woman will be showing up dead in a day or two if they can't put a stop to the killer now. The detective knows that, too. I'm sure of it. His eyes spoke volumes, although his lips never said a word to me."

Mr. Cox nodded again. "You're probably right."

"I could tell something was bothering the detective about the murders, but he wasn't even able to tell his captain what he was thinking. Maybe it was a gut feeling and he doesn't share those with his captain. I don't know. . .but I felt something stirring the air in his office, and it wasn't the air conditioner." Taylor had a gut instinct of her own.

From the time she was small, her dad used to tease her about how great a reporter she would be because she had such good instincts. He taught her to follow her feelings. He said that was what made the difference between a great reporter and an ordinary reporter, not that he remembered today what he had preached to her as a small girl. It was like her dad had lost the vision, the burning desire that swirled in a reporter's veins when they caught their next story. She sighed.

"It sounds like you're on to something there."

Glancing back at her boss, Taylor knew she had to convince him to let her drop everything except this story. She wanted to spend every waking minute on it. This could be her Pulitzer. Taylor took a deep breath. *Here goes.*

"Chief, I finished the article on the bank embezzler and the human interest piece on the teenage boy who saved the little girl from that crazed pit bull. I need—" She looked sweetly at her boss with a smile that melted most men, leaving them putty in her hands. Unfortunately her boss wasn't like most men, and neither was that detective today. "I need my piece on the follow up of the two murders to be brief—no background remarks and no mention the police are looking for a possible link in the two killings. Not that he told me he was, but I know that he is. I'll give just enough facts to inform the readers of the updates on the police's search for the killers, but nothing to encourage them to connect the two. We don't want to give this killer any spotlight, encouraging him to go on." She bit her bottom lip.

Besides, she thought, if Detective Bradley read her report trying to downplay the murders' similarites, maybe he'd think twice and share info with her.

"There is a connection, you know, and I'm going to find it. . .if you'll give me time to really dig into this story." She was practically pleading her case through her eyes.

Mr. Cox rose to his feet and stepped around the desk. "I have always found your instincts to be correct, Taylor, but I have to think on this one for a moment." Standing over her, he looked down as he appeared to think harder.

She held her breath in that moment of silence.

Finally, he leaned slightly against his desk. "If the police can't connect them, what makes you think you'll be able to? Do you really think you'll get more than they could?"

Taylor nodded confidently. "Yes, most definitely. I'm going to dig and dig until I find something to connect those killings. Besides, I know there is a link. I know it here," she said as she pressed her hand to her stomach. "It's my gut. Remember, Dad always said I had good instincts."

"Hold on, Taylor." He shoved his hand out like a stop sign, and then shook it quickly back and forth. "Don't try to get your way by pulling your dad into it." He smiled as he spoke, though. He and Taylor's dad had been reporters together back in the day, and she'd been known to use that connection before to get her way with Mr. Cox. It worked most of the time. What could she say?

Holding both her hands up in front of her, she shrugged. "I'm not. It's just that the police haven't found the connection yet, and I know it's there. I'm going to go over my notes and my pictures from the two crime scenes. Follow the two girls' steps in the weeks prior to their murder. And do more digging. I'll find the connection. Besides, sometimes people tell reporters things they would never tell a policeman. Something will turn up. It has to, if they are connected. . .like my gut is telling me. I also plan on becoming Detective Bradley's shadow. I'll get my story," she voiced strongly.

Mr. Cox crossed his arms over his chest. "That's the spirit. With determination like that, how can you lose? And how can I refuse? Okay. I trust your instincts. You can keep your story brief."

"Chief, while you're feeling confident, I need to ask one more favor. When I said I needed more time, what I'm asking is, can you let me stay on this story exclusively, at least for the next week? That'll give me time to really follow those timelines and shadow the detective. I have to stay on it, sir. I know there is something there, something different about those killings. I just have to find it or be there when the police find it."

Taylor leaned back in the chair, dropping her hands to her sides. Mentally, she crossed her fingers, hoping to obtain the go-ahead.

Her boss raised his brows. "You think I didn't catch your unspoken request the first time? I got it. I'm giving you a week to look into it and try to find the connection. One week. That's all. If you don't come up with something good and concrete, we'll stop the intense investigation and just report what they tell us like everybody else. One week," he repeated. "Then you're back working whatever story you find or we throw at you."

Taylor jumped to her feet. "You won't regret it, Chief. I'll get the story." She pumped his hand enthusiastically and dashed out of his office, waving to Charlotte, his secretary, who was back at her desk.

At her own desk, Taylor went through her notes. Rereading the facts on the two murders, she came to the same conclusion as the detective. The two victims, Trudy Walker and Stephanie Gauthreaux, didn't seem to have anything in common other than their gender and that they were both single, with no apparent significant other.

The police had checked with friends and family to try and find someone with a motive for killing them. Unfortunately, both girls proved to be very well liked. There was no one to suspect in relation to either girl. *Could it be random?* She doubted it.

The girls each lived alone but had friends and family members Taylor could talk to again. She had to come up with some newer questions, or maybe after a few days to think about it, their friends and family would have new answers to some of the same old questions. That was a thought and a hope.

"I'll start there," she told herself as she printed a copy of the victims' background info she had in her computer file.

"Neighbors and friends might be able to give me more information now—now that the major shock had worn off. Maybe I'll even catch a neighbor home who wasn't there before." She'd find new info. She must.

Taylor decided she would spend the rest of the day trying to find out more personal information about each girl and figure the timelines for the week prior to each of their deaths. Tomorrow she would follow the detective.

After straightening her desk, she grabbed her purse and headed out of the building.

Her first stop was the public library. She found an open table with a computer in the reference department and pulled up the New Orleans and Metairie telephone directories for the past five years. Although the reports she had made listed a few friends and family members, Taylor decided to check for neighbors who lived near each girl for a while. Using the cross directories would make her search more simple. Maybe she could come up with someone there, someone new that neither she nor the police had questioned.

Taylor went back year by year, checking to see who lived in the same neighborhoods as the girls for the past five years. *Great!* They each had a few, so now to find the neighbors who knew them more personally. If they lived by one another long enough, someone was bound to know something.

In less than an hour, Taylor found three neighbors of Trudy's and four neighbors of Stephanie's who might be able to shed some light on the victims' personal lives. She had jotted down the names and addresses, along with the phone numbers, and then quickly closed her small notebook and stuffed it in her back pocket.

Next came the leg work of going to each of the homes, hopefully catching the residents there and talking to them, and even more importantly, getting them to talk to her.

Trudy, the hairdresser, had lived off the Huey P. Long Bridge in a large brick complex of apartments. Everyone's front door opened up to the same courtyard. Her neighbors were all at home and very helpful. Taylor found Trudy had worked at Mr. Jack's in the Quarter for several years and seemed to love her work creating new and wild hairdos for people. She appeared to be a likeable person. Other than not having a special man in her life, she lived a very active one. Taylor wrote as fast as the girl's neighbors spoke, making notes to review later.

Stephanie's neighbors were not as helpful, as they didn't really know her. She had lived in Metairie, a suburb of New Orleans, at the Chateau Villa. The apartments were considered very nice. The cost for rental was about three times more than the cost of Trudy's. Neighbors basically kept to themselves in this high-rise establishment. The few who knew Stephanie only knew she was an accountant at the bank on Clearlake. Other than that, they knew nothing about her.

Although both were single females, they had little in common according to the neighbors. The ladies' jobs were very different. Trudy styled hair while Stephanie managed money for clients and the bank. The bleached blond with the orange spikes lived in the lower part of town, while the redhead lived in an apartment in the high-rent district. The hairdresser came from a large family, and her education ended at the completion of the twelfth grade. The accountant, however, was an only child with a college degree in accounting.

Thinking back to her talk with the neighbors, Taylor decided Trudy's neighbors found her friendly and enjoyed having her as a neighbor. In fact, the third neighbor Taylor interviewed, Sarah Adams, seemed to know her better than the other two.

Taylor remembered Sarah had peeked through the crack in the door before she opened it. "May I help you?" Sarah asked in a timid voice.

Holding up her identification, she said, "I'm Taylor Jaymes with the *Morning Tribune*. I'd like to ask you a few questions about Trudy Walker."

As the door opened wider, a sad expression crossed the woman's face. Standing behind the screen door, Sarah said, "Such a tragic thing to happen to a sweet young girl. Come on in and we can talk," she said as she pushed the screen door open. "Would you care for a cup of coffee?"

"Thank you, but I'll pass. I appreciate the offer, though. Did you know Miss Walker very well?"

"Yes."

The woman appeared to be in her midforties by Taylor's estimation.

"In fact, sometimes she came over and had coffee with me on Saturday mornings and we talked about her week. For being such a friendly girl, she lived a pretty lonely life. I have a teenage daughter who liked to go over to her apartment some evenings to talk. My daughter probably asked Trudy for some advice, trying to get a younger person's point of view, if you know what I mean. Sherry, that's my daughter, misses her a lot." Pointing to a chair at the kitchen table, she motioned for Taylor to have a seat. "Are you sure you don't want any coffee?

How about a soda or water?"

Taylor shook her head no as she asked, "You said she lived a lonely life? So Miss Walker didn't go out much? Other reports state she dated a lot. Do you think Sherry would be willing to talk to me? And, of course, you could sit in on the conversation if you'd like. Maybe she could clear up my conflict here, since she was friendly with Miss Walker."

"I'm sure my daughter would be glad to help, but you misunderstand about Trudy's dating. She went out every weekend and sometimes during the week. Trudy dated a lot, but she always said the men she dated weren't worth the trouble. She was looking for Mr. Right, the kind she would want to settle down with and raise a family. You know what I mean?"

Taylor didn't think a man like that existed. No man could make her want to settle down and raise a family. That would involve the two C's that she avoided as much as possible—cooking and cleaning. Those were the two things Taylor hated most. Besides which, she had great plans with her career and couldn't see going any other direction. To follow her dream, she had to stay single. A man would never let her cover the stories she covered. They would be too protective of her.

Instead of giving a reply, she said, "So she dated a lot of men, but you're saying no one special, right?"

Mrs. Adams nodded. "Yes. No one special in a very long time, but it didn't stop her from looking. She was such a sweet girl. I'm sorry I don't know anything to help you, but I sure hope the police find out who killed her. That person deserves to suffer. I know her family is grieving."

After thanking her for her time and leaving a business card so Sherry could ring her later, Taylor left. One thing was for sure, Trudy had no difficulty opening up to her neighbors about her main problem. . .loneliness. She dated a lot of men, but none had been the kind of man to get serious over. So Trudy was lonely and looking for love.

Stephanie, on the other hand, wouldn't open up to her neighbors. No one knew much about her, although a couple of the neighbors had admitted to seeing one man visit her apartment frequently. They appeared to be romantically involved. Unfortunately, since the neighbors never spoke one-on-one with her, no one knew his name. Taylor got a fairly good description of the man, which might come in handy down the road. She wondered if the police had talked to the man yet. Surely he came forward when his girlfriend was murdered—unless he had something to hide.

She would ask the detective if they knew of Stephanie's boyfriend, and hopefully he would supply a name to her. Fat chance, but she would ask.

That night, while eating a chicken sandwich she had thrown together herself—her form of cooking—Taylor scanned her notes thoroughly once again. The line of work she chose left little time to slave over a hot stove in the evening, especially when she never knew if she would have to dash out on a moment's notice. Because of this, she was well known at the Court Tavern around the corner from her apartment, as well as Dante's Pizza and Pasta, which she also frequented regularly. New Orleans, especially the French Quarter, didn't lack in exceptionally good food for a person's taste buds, so why even bother to cook fancy meals? She could get those at one of the restaurants near her. . . takeout, of course. In the meantime, these smaller taverns made cleaning up after meals such a breeze.

By the time she had gone over her notes several times, even though she still hadn't talked to the victims' family members, coworkers, or close friends yet, Taylor felt she knew more about the victims than she did her own sister. Well, maybe that was stretching it a bit. Taylor did know Tina better, but she felt she was getting to know these girls more and more with each interview, which should bring an added touch to her story. Humanize it.

Standing, Taylor stretched, arching her back as she twisted slightly left, then right. A yawn escaped. Covering her mouth with her right hand, she glanced at the watch on her left arm.

"Midnight!" she screeched as she threw her hands into the air. Earlier she had planned to make an early night of it so she could beat the lieutenant to the station in the morning. Tomorrow she planned to become his shadow. . .well, today now.

Taylor heard her mother's voice ringing in her ears: *If only you were more disciplined, like your sister.* Ignoring the voice in her head, she set her alarm for five, hoping she would wake up with the first beep that sounded in the air. "No hitting the snooze," she grumbled to herself.

In no time, she showered, changed, and jumped in bed, snuggling under her covers. Taylor barely remembered putting her head on the pillow when darkness descended.

Chapter 3

An annoying ring persisted. "Shut up!" Taylor growled at what she thought was her alarm clock. She'd promised herself she wouldn't snooze, but seven more minutes. . .what would it hurt? Her hand shot out, trying to stop the noise. She pressed the snooze button, but the ringing continued. She must have pressed the wrong button. With eyes closed, her fingers danced across the nightstand, trying to find that magic button to bring silence into the air. Taylor found the button on top of her clock again and pressed it harder this time.

On the next ring she cracked open an eye and looked toward the window. *It's not even daylight yet.* Why is that stupid thing ringing? And as she started thinking her alarm was going crazy, the third ring started. Suddenly it dawned on her that the alarm clock beeped. It didn't ring.

Instantly she shot up in bed, reached past the alarm, and

snatched up her phone. Through blurry eyes, she squinted at the clock. *Four in the morning?* Early morning phone calls meant only one thing—trouble with a capital T.

"Hello," she said, then listened anxiously for a response.

"Morning, Taylor. Sorry to wake you so early." A feminine voice came across the line. "But I thought you'd want to know this. It might be connected with the stories you're working on."

Taylor flipped on her bedside lamp as she recognized the voice of the girl who worked the nightshift at the city desk. "Hey, Babs. What's up?" She grabbed the slender silver pen and black notebook that she always kept next to her bed for emergencies such as this. The good reporter was always prepared. Her father had taught her well.

"You know the two murder cases you're following? There has been another killing, and it sounds similar to those two. . .also done in the Quarter. The police are on their way now to where the body was found. Are you ready for the address? It's only two blocks from where they found the last body."

"Sure, go ahead." Taylor jotted down the information. "Thanks. I'll talk to you later."

She slammed down the phone and threw back the covers. Jumping out of bed, she pulled off the T-shirt she slept in and then dug through her dresser drawer trying to find clean undergarments.

"I've got to catch up on my washing," she mumbled as she grabbed yesterday's jeans and tugged them up over her hips. On top of the dirty-clothes hamper she grabbed her bra and slipped back into it. At least she found a clean V-neck T-shirt with a shiny finish hanging in her closet. It was one of those that fit her curves snugly. Not her first choice—in fact, it was her last choice—but at the moment she had no choice. Slapping on some baby powder, she slathered deodorant under her arms before pulling the shirt over her head.

"Later today I will do my washing," she vowed, knowing it might come to be and yet it might not, depending on her time. Work always dictated her day-to-day life. Maybe she did need to become more disciplined. No. She was disciplined where it counted. . .with her work.

T-shirts and jeans proved to be Taylor's usual form of dress. On special occasions she slipped a blazer on over her T-shirt, dressing up her jeans slightly like she'd done for her visit yesterday to see the detective. And for even fancier occasions, which she tried to avoid as much as possible, her closet held a couple of skirts with matching blazers and even a fancy dress or two. Those were gifts from her mom and Tina. Both always tried to make a lady out of Taylor. What was that old saying? "You can't get milk from a turnip?" She tried to tell her sister that, but Taylor never wasted her time on her mom. Taylor knew better. Her mother would never stop trying to make a lady out of her.

After pulling a brush through her hair and sliding her toothbrush across her teeth a few times, she was about to race out of the apartment when she remembered her vow. "I may not have time later, but I can take half a second now." Hurriedly she grabbed a laundry bag, stuffed a good bit of her dirty clothes in it, filling the sack to full capacity. "I'll treat myself today and drop these off at The Washing Well. . .after I check out the crime scene, of course."

The Washing Well offered a full-service laundry that

washed and folded the customer's clothes at a price. Sure, there were washing machines and dryers the customer could use, but when Taylor was busy, she didn't mind paying the extra fee. At the moment, she was past busy and gave in to the side of her that not only hated cooking, but cleaning as well. This was another reason she couldn't be like her sister, married to a man, having his children, and maintaining his home properly. Not Taylor's thing. As far as she was concerned, she was already married—to her career. That was enough for her.

She knotted the bag closed and threw it over her shoulder.

Taylor swiftly ripped the note out of the tablet and stuffed it in her jean pocket. Glancing at her reflection in the bedroom mirror, she frowned. "You don't look much like a reporter," she criticized, shaking her unruly curls. Blowing off her thoughts, she dropped the bag to the floor and grabbed a cap off of her dresser. She dragged her fingers through her hair, slapped the baseball cap on her head, and then clipped the back of it around a self-made ponytail. A mass of thick locks spilled out of the back of the cap as she situated it just right on her head. That was the best she could do at present to control her long red curls. Taylor grabbed the bag of clothes again, her purse, her camera, and darted out the door.

Jumping in her car, she started the motor and slipped out onto the street. It was practically empty. Taylor knew right where she was going; it was around the corner from the Quarter, actually on the edge. This body was found on Iberville, only two blocks from Canal Street and no more than a block from the Interstate. The other two bodies had been found within a five-block radius of this one. It was still dark enough for headlights as Taylor whipped her Mustang through the streets of the French Quarter. From approximately ten at night until about two or three in the morning the Quarter stayed busy, but this was the right time to slip out quickly.

Taylor was thankful for that. She should be there within a few minutes, she told herself as she turned on her radio.

Chapter 4

Have they dusted for prints inside the car yet?" John asked.

"Yes, sir," said a young policeman.

"Good. Then turn off that radio!"

The police swarmed the area, along with the crew from CSI and the detectives helping him on this case. John had called them right after he got the call. Each looked for anything they could find to give them a clue as to what happened while making sure they didn't disturb any potential evidence.

"Sir," the same young policeman who was first on the scene said to Detective Bradley, "we didn't find any signs of a struggle. . .just like the last two times. It looks like the girl wasn't aware of any danger. Her purse was open, and one of her hands still clutched it like she had been digging into it." Shaking his head, he said, "I don't understand how a girl alone could be that unaware of how dangerous it is on the streets."

"I agree with you." *Was she looking for her license?* John wondered. *Had she been pulled over by a fake policeman? Is our speculation reality?* The woman digging through her purse gave more credibility to his thoughts. He didn't say that out loud, but it was fact.

The uniformed officer cast his eyes back toward the vehicle.

John wished they had already captured this man before another life had been taken. "Okay, Nelson, we'll get the crime lab to go through the contents of her purse back at the station when they check the car more thoroughly. Make another sweep of the grounds. See if you can find any kind of strong cord or rope." The killer had never left a clue before, but there was always a first time. Would they get lucky? He doubted it, but they had to look.

"Why isn't this area taped off yet?" John shouted for whoever would listen and act accordingly. "You know it won't be long before the news media gets wind of this. They'll be destroying evidence before we can even find it."

Headlights hit John square in the face as he was talking. "Speak of the devil—" He didn't need to finish his statement. Everyone knew they were about to be covered with TV cameras and news reporters.

John glanced at his watch. *This reporter made good time. He must be listening to his scanner all night waiting for a story. They're getting too fast for me.* He stared for another moment into the bright lights.

Chapter 5

It took less than ten minutes for Taylor to reach the scene of the crime. The police were already there. Her headlights flashed on the dark-haired detective. *Detective Bradley.*

Shutting off her engine, Taylor doused her lights. She pulled her digital camera out of its small case. By always keeping the setting for flash as needed, she managed to get shots worthy of the newspaper. Taylor admitted their photographer took better pictures, but sometimes he wasn't at the scene fast enough. She'd learned a long time ago to always be prepared.

The orange and pink glow forming in the dark sky cast a soft haze over the scene. Within the next hour, the morning sun would peek out over the horizon, illuminating the full horror of the crime scene.

As Taylor walked up to the yellow sedan, she clicked off some shots of the vehicle from each angle before approaching the driver's window. At two prior murder scenes she'd managed several viewpoints, but no angle as close as she was about to take this morning for the third scene. Usually the yellow tape kept her back.

Holding her camera just right, seeing the woman's head leaning back against her headrest, her skin tinged a shade of gray-blue, Taylor held down the button for a picture. Normally the victim's body was covered by the time she got on the scene. She must have made really good time this morning.

For her next shot, she focused on the victim's hand clutching her bag. As she held down the button again, waiting for the flash, a hand caught her arm in a viselike grip and yanked downward. "What do you think you're doing? You know you can't take pictures of the victim."

Tugging her arm out of the grip, she dropped her hands to her side and swiveled toward the voice. "Well, Detective Bradley, how nice to see you, too," she said in a tone dripping with sugary sarcasm.

"I should've known it would be you." Throwing his hands up in disgust, he grumbled, "How did you get here so quickly? Did you put a bug in my car or something?"

Taylor chose to ignore his words. The fact that she planned to follow him starting today made his question a little too close to the truth for comfort—not that she would ever plant a bug in the detective's car.

Locking her gaze on him in an attempt to distract him, she spoke as her hand with the camera eased up slowly, hoping to get the right angle again—this time without him stopping her. "I'm only doing my job, Detective Bradley. I told you I'd be glad to work with you, but you haven't agreed. So, in the meantime, I have to stay on top of things for myself."

Lifting her camera a little higher, she made it even with the window of the victim's car and stole a glance as she directed the viewfinder toward the hand in the purse again. Not looking, she held the button down, keeping her arm stiff in case the detective got wise and grabbed her arm again.

The flash went off. The detective pivoted toward the camera, then glared back at Taylor. "I better not see that victim in your paper, or you will find yourself brought up on charges. Do I make myself clear?"

"No problem there."

"Well, back up and don't touch anything. Wait until they cover the body before you take any more pictures. I mean it! Or I'll take your camera. You shouldn't be so close. You could be destroying vital evidence. Besides, you know the rules." Detective Bradley stomped away.

Taylor slid closer to the driver's side. She knew better than to try and get another shot for the paper. He wasn't kidding about taking her camera. He would. His reputation preceded him. But he couldn't stop her from gathering some pictures in her mind while she had the opportunity, even though she couldn't shoot any more shots at this close an angle.

Scanning the woman's badly bruised face and slowly working her gaze downward, Taylor saw the ligature markings on the victim's neck.

"Get a grip," she told herself. Slowly she released the breath she'd been holding. Taylor had no idea what had gotten into her. She'd been to plenty of crime scenes. For over ten years she'd been chasing stories and had seen unbelievable things, more than most people. Sometimes blood would be splattered here and there, and more than one body would be lying around.

Why was this one different? Why was it getting to her? Then she remembered—usually the bodies were covered and she only saw the victims in pictures afterward from the coroner's office or old shots from family albums. This time the image had a face, and she'd seen it close up. She'd even beaten the medical examiner there. Maybe this was the break she needed.

As she eased back slightly from the car, another thought sent chills down her spine. This woman, like the other two, was close to her own age.

Too close. . .too personal.

The detective had lost interest in her and was talking to one of the men who were from the crime scene investigative unit. Thankful for the solitude, Taylor surveyed the area. The crime scene sat at the side of a main road, a business area in fact. These kinds of businesses were run nine to five, not like the French Quarter establishments that were open almost all day and all night long; therefore, there was probably no witness to the crime. . .again.

Too bad it hadn't been raining so at least mud tracks could have formed in the dirty areas, giving the police an idea of what make of vehicle to look for. There wasn't even enough dust collected on the roadside to leave markings from the tires of the murderer's car, at least not that she saw. The police probably patrolled this area more now because of the prior murders. One of the cops had probably spotted the car on the side of the road with no one else around, making it look suspicious. Surely there was no eyewitness, because, like the two before, the crime took place in the wee hours of the morning, and very few people were out roaming the business district at that time of the night. . .or morning, you might say.

The coroner arrived as she was scanning the area. When her search turned up nothing, she started questioning two of the police officers who were putting up the tape.

"Johnson!" Bradley called to one of the officers.

"Yes, Lieutenant?"

Detective Bradley took two long strides and closed the distance. "You and Brown take the evidence you gathered back to the lab and start on your report. Tell Smitty to finish putting up the tape. More reporters are pulling in. Move it, and I'll handle the press."

Johnson and Brown didn't argue. They knew better, Taylor decided. Both walked away without another word.

"Miss Jaymes, any questions you have, ask me. Leave my men alone. Now get behind the tape." The detective turned his back on her and headed toward the coroner.

"Lieutenant Bradley, I'd like to get a statement from you," Taylor called to him as he started to leave. She knew he was giving her the brush-off, but this was her job. Like it or not, she needed to get the story. He could work with her or against her. It didn't matter to her.

Well, she thought as she watched him stop in his tracks and turn her way, *I'd rather he work with me.*

Chapter 6

At the sound of her voice, John stopped and slowly pivoted, focusing his hard glare upon her. He frowned. "When I'm finished collecting all the facts, I'll be glad to answer your questions. Do you think you could carry yourself over to your car and wait there?" John figured he had enough problems without having to deal with a nosy reporter. She might look good, but that didn't get the mystery solved.

Dismissing her from his thoughts, John stepped toward the coroner. "Morning, Bob. Got anything?"

About that time another car and a van pulled up.

Just what I need—more reporters and television cameras. Great!

"John, it looks like she's been dead for about two to three hours. That would place her death between two and three this morning. That's not the official word yet, but that's what it looks like from the liver temp. I'll let you know for sure on my official report later today." The coroner pushed his wire-rimmed glasses back up on his nose, and his fingertips brushed the edge of his stringy gray hair that fell forward over his brows. Closing his black bag, he rose to his feet. "The markings on her throat look like they were made with the same rope that killed the other two girls. When the fibers are tested, if they are the same synthetic fibers as before, we'll know for sure. It looks like you won't be guessing anymore. You'll know you have a serial killer on your hands."

John blew out a gush of air. "That's what I thought." His hands brushed the rough shadow of whiskers that he'd had no time to remove this morning.

"Looks like you're dealing with a real sick person, probably a sociopath. The killer apparently gets pleasure out of killing young, innocent women. And, sad to say, he's showing no signs of remorse. All three women have been in their late twenties to early thirties." Scratching his head, Bob added, "I just don't understand how he gets to them so easily. None show any sign of a struggle. It's like they think of the killer as a friend."

"We're thinking it might be someone dressed up like a cop. You know, nowadays you can get a uniform from any costume shop in town. And if someone saw a red or blue light flashing, they might think it was a cop and pull over. If the killer walked up dressed as a policeman, most people would probably try to cooperate." John glanced at the stretcher where the body now lay covered up. "All I know is, I need to solve this case soon before he tries to claim his next victim." *And before the FBI comes in and claims it as their case. Not that*

I wouldn't welcome help, but these are my victims and my streets I need to protect.

The older man slapped John on the shoulder. "Good luck, son. You'll need it. I'll have my report on your desk before noon." On those words, Bob left. His assistant had already loaded the body on the wagon.

John watched as the tow truck hooked up to the victim's car. The investigating crew had all departed, leaving two uniformed officers to keep the news media behind the yellow tape now in place. He wanted to get out of there himself.

But as he headed toward his car, he saw that brassy redhead perched on the hood of her car. Closing his eyes, he grumbled under his breath. A couple of reporters with their camera crew were behind the yellow line filming. . .probably for the morning news broadcast. As he moved closer, some flashes went off as snaps were taken of him.

I'll make one quick statement and that should satisfy them until later today. Speaking loudly, he said, "As soon as we get results back from the coroner's office and our lab, I'll be ready to make a statement. Probably won't have anything until around one this afternoon. See you at the station." Before he could walk away, hands shot up in the air and questions showered him from everyone—except Taylor Jaymes. She stayed patiently on her car, not moving a muscle.

"Was the victim killed like the others?"

"Do we have a serial killer?"

"Did you find any evidence this time?"

"Have you gotten yourself a suspect yet?"

As all these questions bombarded him and he watched the quiet reporter sitting on the hood of her car, John held up both his hands. "No answers now. All I can tell you is we have a dead body. Not much to report yet, so you might want to wait on getting anything out, but that's up to you."

While he talked, he saw her in the background, still not moving. It was like she wasn't worried. She must have an inside source to not be at the front of the crowd demanding answers. Maybe she thought their talk yesterday gave her exclusive rights, and he was her inside source.

Well, he would put a stop to that way of thinking. Swiftly he walked past the other reporters and stopped in front of her car. "Look, Miss Jaymes, I'm tired and I need a cup of coffee. Why don't you follow me back to the station, and we can talk in the cafeteria while I drink my first cup?"

Why did I say that?

John realized he had wanted to control the situation. What was he doing? He had meant to set her straight right then and there. Be done with her and send her on her way. Maybe he thought he'd have better odds setting her straight back at the station. That had to be it. The detective had read her articles before and knew she got into her stories. Her reporting style seemed to always get her right in the middle of the investigation she reported. He needed to stop her right up front. John didn't need or want this woman in the middle of his crime scenes. He had a job to do, and she was merely a nuisance slowing him down.

Taylor slid off her car and dusted off her backside. "Great. I'm hungry myself."

After the dust was removed from her pants, she looked up at him. He could see she was studying him, but it took him a second or two longer to tear his gaze away from her. Gritting his teeth, he began to stride away.

"Lieutenant," she called, stopping him in his tracks.

His blood heated up as he faced her one more time. "Follow me in your car," he barked but low enough so the other reporters wouldn't catch wind of his meeting with her. Then they would all want one. John turned again and headed to his car.

As he passed the other reporters, he didn't even give them a glance. *They all need to wait. They want a story. I want a killer stopped.* His needs overrode theirs.

Why had he given that one reporter special permission to talk to him earlier than the rest? It had to be because he believed she had inside sources.

It couldn't be anything else, he thought as he started the car's motor and backed away from the crime scene. As he passed the area slowly, he saw the lights and cameras focused on his policemen keeping guard. John wasn't worried. They wouldn't open their mouths. He needed to get back to the station and put all the facts together on this one, combine them with the other ones and start finding connections. There had to be some, other than the obvious.

Heading back to the station, he glanced in his rearview mirror and saw the reporter's red Mustang.

Help me, Lord.

Chapter 7

Taylor turned the key. The engine of her Mustang sprang to life. She smiled to herself. The detective seemed angry, and she wasn't exactly sure why. Maybe it was the way she caught him looking at her, or was that her imagination? His eyes said one thing one moment, and then in the next, they gleamed the opposite. Total confusion.

"He didn't have to bite my head off no matter what he was thinking," she said aloud. "I didn't make him look at me."

Taylor started to complain about the detective's temper when she heard her favorite song come to life on the radio. It distracted her immediately. Instead of fussing, she cranked up the volume and started tapping her steering wheel to the beat while she sang at the top of her lungs, "Well, I got friends in low places. . ."

By the time she turned into the police parking lot behind the lieutenant and found a parking spot near him, she was in a better mood. The murder and the detective's foul temper had slid to the back of her mind. The DJ was talking about being on the lookout for the Moneyman as she killed her engine. "I should be so lucky," she said aloud as the thought of winning a quick hundred bucks made her smile grow. Who couldn't use an extra bit of cash?

She was humming as she stepped out of the car. Detective John Bradley was heading toward her. Locking the car door, she met him halfway. "One can't be too safe," she said, quirking her brow. "What better place to rob me than in the parking lot of the Eighth District New Orleans Police Department with police all around?" She flashed him a grin.

John watched as she laughed. That reporter sure was young. How could a woman as young and as innocent as she appeared to be, be in her line of business? A crime reporter had to be tough and daring. If reporters weren't careful, they wound up hard-hearted and cold. . .or dead and cold.

As his eyes studied Taylor from behind his dark shades, he walked up the steps close behind her to the front door. The scent of her perfume aroused his senses. Emotions stirred in his chest. Shaking his head, he wondered where that came from. First off, she was too young. Second off, since Jennifer's death, he hadn't even looked at another woman. He had even sworn off women altogether—especially women in a dangerous line of work. Maybe the fragrance reminded him of Jennifer.

John decided, after everyone tried to set him up with their wives' best friends or whomever, he was destined to be alone. That was when he swore off women forever. For six months after Jennifer's death, he spent a lot of time soul searching. He couldn't understand why God would take Jennifer's life, yet let him live, but then God showed him there was still plenty of work left for him to do. It was hard to accept at first, but finally John started pouring his heart out into his work and kept busy. If that was his call, then so be it. He removed his gaze from the fiery redhead and murmured, "Nope, not me."

"What?" Taylor asked over her shoulder.

That was when he realized he'd spoken his thoughts aloud. He hadn't planned to, so he chose to ignore her question.

Stopping short, she turned slightly and said, "I didn't understand what you said."

He practically ran her down when she stopped so quickly. Instantly, he scooped his hand under her elbow, turned her back around, and kept them walking toward the door. "It was nothing," he said. Once inside, he pivoted her toward the elevator.

Pressing the Up button, he said, "It's on the second floor." The double doors opened, and they stepped inside. He reached out and pressed number two. Out of the corner of his eye, he saw her staring, and it didn't matter. That subject was not open for debate. He hadn't meant to speak aloud; she didn't need to know what he had been thinking.

When they sat down to drink coffee, he would talk to her about what was going on. . .to a limit. For now, he had to make sure she stayed focused on the matter at hand. He needed her to understand she wasn't getting special treatment or inside information. None of it. She would get her information along with all of the other reporters.

Taylor watched but didn't say a word. She wondered what was going through the detective's mind. He had to break this case. The killer needed to be caught. He was the man to do it, too, she thought. Sighing to herself, she hoped he would find out she could be of use to him. Especially since, at the present, he had nothing to go on.

Once in the cafeteria line, she grabbed a tray. Her stomach growled. *Feed me. Feed me.* Grabbing a plate of beignets, she then filled her mug with hot chocolate. Glancing at the detective's empty tray, she asked, "Don't you eat?" Not giving him a chance to answer, she admired the white pastries on her plate. "This looks good. I can't believe the police cafeteria serves beignets. Mmm."

"I'm getting a cup of coffee and some toast." As he fixed his cup of coffee, a petite, yet full-busted, blond-haired woman brought him toast.

"Hey, John, I put strawberry jelly on your toast this morning. Sweets for the sweet." The waitress smiled at him. "I remembered Jennifer saying a long time ago that you loved strawberries." She flashed her lashes in his direction. Then she spotted Taylor, and her smile transformed into a tight-lipped frown.

Taylor wasn't bothered at all. She looked back at the woman without revealing her thoughts: *You're nuts! Who in their right mind would think the detective was sweet. I doubt if he has a sweet bone in his body.* Finally, the woman stormed away. Taylor's lips turned up slightly. *So much for her.*

At the table, the detective took the trays and set them aside. Pulling out his notepad, he started looking over his notes as he sipped on his coffee. She presumed it was his findings from this morning. Taylor wasn't waiting for him to share. *He probably won't, but who knows?*

At the moment, those powder-puff sensations were drawing her full attention. She figured the detective would tell her whatever he brought her here to say soon enough. Picking up a beignet, she licked her lips in anticipation.

⚬⚬⚬

While her eyes were focused on a doughnut, John studied her behind the guise of looking at his notes. He knew every word he'd written. Didn't need to read it again to discover they still didn't have much. Maybe he could use the help of the press. Maybe. He knew his team didn't seem to be getting anywhere. But how could she help him? After her last story, he knew she had some inside sources on the streets. Maybe she could get some information that could help point the police in the right direction. Evidence was what he needed.

He watched her enjoy her pastry. As she took her next bite, he eased his notepad down. "You know those things aren't good for you. You should be eating a grapefruit or something. Not all that sugar."

Taylor chewed a few more times and then swallowed. She sipped her hot chocolate before locking her gaze on him. "So you think your coffee and toast is better for the body?"

John glanced down at his toast smeared with strawberry jam. "No. You're right. Mine is no better, but I usually eat a healthy lunch and dinner. Can you say the same?" Looking at her slim, trim figure, he doubted she ate any more than her unhealthy breakfast. One meal a day and it wasn't healthy.

Her green eyes glared at her half-eaten plate of beignets,

and her fingers drummed on the table. She appeared to be trying to think of some smart answer to give him. He snickered. That would be her style.

Then she blurted, "A chicken sandwich with some chips. That was supper last night. For lunch yesterday, umm, let me think." She closed her eyes. They popped back open as she said, "Oh yeah. I remember. I had a good juicy cheeseburger and a basket of fries. I ate at the place on Canal by Macy's." Her eyes widened. "And I had a salad with it. Salads are nourishing."

He wanted to laugh. She seemed so proud of her eating habits. Instead he shook his head in disbelief. "Do you eat like that all the time?" When she nodded, he huffed. "How do you keep your figure? It's so unhealthy the way you eat. I have to say, you don't have to worry about a bullet taking you down early in life like I said yesterday. You're killing yourself now. Your veins are clogging up even as we speak."

She lifted an eyebrow. "So you think I have a good figure?"

Out of everything he just told her, that was all she grasped? John wanted to throw his hands up in the air and walk away. Instead, he sighed. Her voice had sounded teasing, almost flirty, and John didn't like it. He'd been serious. Also the little get-together they were having was business, not personal. Flirting was personal. She seemed to take everything lightly. This wasn't where he wanted to go, nor needed to go. He frowned and fell silent. John wanted her to know he was annoyed. He turned his attention to his coffee and toast. That shut her up.

Good. Now her attention seemed to be back on her food. Worked for him. After he finished his coffee, he picked his notes back up. This time he shared some of them with her as she jotted notes. He kept his tone strictly business. He finished with, "After checking every forensic lead, if we get anything concrete, we'll let you reporters know. I'm sharing these notes with you to let you know we are working every possible lead. We want the killer found. So far he's eluded us and managed to keep from leaving any clues, but these type killers do mess up. We just hope it's sooner rather than later."

"I can't believe you gave all of this to me. Thanks."

"That should do it." John slipped his notepad into his breast pocket. "If forensics uncovers anything new that I can tell you, I'll phone the paper. What I gave you will be basically the same statement I'll give the rest of the press later this morning, minus a few details. I don't want to give this maniac too much publicity. Sometimes they thrive on hearing about themselves or reading about what they have done. It spurs them on to do more. Right now, he's killing one woman a week. I don't want to make it two."

"So now you believe it's a serial killer?"

"Same man did all three, we feel sure. After the tests today, we'll know. So don't forget to call before you finish your piece for the paper."

"I'd like to ask you a question about the second girl who was killed, Stephanie Gauthreaux. Do you know who her boyfriend was? His name and address? And have you talked to him yet?"

That caught John slightly off guard. He glanced over his notes before he responded. He wanted to be sure. "We didn't know she had anyone special in her life. Where did you get that piece of information?"

"From her neighbors."

They all told us they didn't know anything about their neighbor. Everyone claimed to keep to themselves. Maybe this reporter could be some help to us after all. "We didn't know about him. But it's something to check into. Thanks for the info."

Taylor closed her notebook. "What makes people do things like what this guy has been doing?"

She's a reporter, and she's asking me that? But her question seemed genuine, so he answered. "It could be a number of things. Usually it can be traced back to something in the killer's past that hurt him or her emotionally or physically. They repress it, and then something happens to make them snap." He rubbed his face and raked his fingers through his hair. "And other times, there is no simple explanation at all."

Taylor rose, picked up her purse, and dropped a five on the table. "Thanks for your time and the information. Please think over my offer to work with you on this." She waited for a moment by the table without saying a word. Probably hoping for a response.

John rose and, starting at the top of her head, slowly looked his way down the length of her body. How could any woman as pretty as her want to put herself in constant danger chasing crime stories? It made no sense whatsoever. He admitted to himself only moments ago that she might be a help in this investigation, but down deep he knew he didn't want to bring anyone in on it. Especially her. She could get herself killed. He would handle this on his own. . .well, with the help of New Orleans' finest.

John shrugged as his eyes connected to hers. "Don't count on it."

He left her standing by the table.

Chapter 8

On the drive to the paper, Taylor scanned the city she loved so much. New Orleans, a city that truly never slept, was filled with beauty. Not so much a superficial beauty, but one that took years to achieve. The flavor of history kept it alive—the plantations of old restored to their original beauty, along with the riverboats and streetcars that ran up and down St. Charles and Canal. What a sight! The spirit of the city never died.

New Orleans stepped into the twenty-first century just like every other city in America, only without losing the history that was evident everywhere you looked. The mix was magical. In the later twentieth century, New Orleans added places like the Superdome, Aquarium of the Americas, and the Convention Center. What would they do in this century? While grand hotels were sprinkled throughout the city, the streets in the Quarter flowed with old Dixieland jazz, along with rhythm and blues. Now even country music spilled out along the streets of the grandest city Taylor knew.

The *Tribune* was located in the business district of the city; however, the spark of New Orleans was still evident on Poydras and Commerce. It didn't take Taylor long to get to the paper. Quickly she headed upstairs, via the elevator, to her workstation.

Snatching her digital camera out of her purse, she tossed her bag under her desk and sat in her swivel chair. As she touched the mouse, her computer hummed as it came to life. Instantly, a bright light lit her screen. Flipping open the bottom compartment on her camera, she extracted her memory card and inserted it into her computer. When a square screen popped up, she clicked on DOWNLOAD PICTURES. In no time, her shots were displayed in a smaller version.

Sliding the mouse to the left, Taylor directed the pointer over the first shot she had taken. Before clicking on it, she noticed a stack of messages next to her phone and tried to ignore them. But her eyes darted back to the stack, torn between looking at the pictures and seeing who had left messages for her.

I better check out those messages before I get too deeply engrossed in my pictures.

As much as she wanted to take a closer look at the pictures, she knew she needed to see what had come in after she left yesterday. Maybe someone called ready to give a statement. . .maybe a statement related to the latest killing. Glancing through the notes, she saw most were from her family—her sister once and her mother twice. "I'll have to call you both later," she said as she put the messages aside.

The last one, however, was from someone who didn't leave his name but said he would call back. "That's strange," she murmured. "Oh well, whoever you are, mister, I don't have time for you now. My love life will have to wait." Laughter bubbled from within. Her love life? That was a joke. Who had time?

She casually put that note aside with the others. But as she started to turn her attention back to the pictures at hand, she snapped the pink slip of paper back up and scanned the message one more time. "Unless, of course, you're a source wanting to give me an anonymous tip. That I'll take now," she whispered as she studied the note. "Call me. Now!"

Smiling to herself, she knew she could use all the help she could get. It wasn't like the detective was going to give her anything. Opening her bottom desk drawer, she pulled out the prints she had copied from the other crime scenes and laid them out in between her computer and her keyboard. She noticed again how isolated the areas were where both cars were found, just like this morning. There were no places of business open in those areas. In fact, the first one sat right outside the hustle and bustle of the French Quarter, a rundown and dirty area. No businesses, no houses—nothing in the background except old, empty warehouses. The second scene was close to the third one. It at least had businesses behind the car, just none that had opened yet.

Looking at the emptiness surrounding them, along with the pink skies of early morning dawn, sent chills running down Taylor's back. What possessed those women to stop for someone in those areas? Did they not realize their lives were in danger? They had to.

Although the pictures portrayed horrible scenes, excitement coursed through her veins. As she added glossy photo paper in her printer, clicked the appropriate places on the computer screen, and then hit ENTER, she waited for her new photos to print. Oh, how she hoped this would be the case that brought her closer to her dream. If she could get noted for this story and it got picked up across the wire, one of the bigger papers, maybe even *The Miami Herald*, would want to make her an offer to work for them. This would get her closer to her goal, winning the Pulitzer. The more crime she helped solve and the better stories she wrote, the more notice she got. Eventually she should get an offer from somewhere, a more noted paper with a prestigious name.

But could she leave the city she loved so much? Maybe she wouldn't have to. To get involved in the work she longed for and the stories she only dreamed of, she had to move up in her field. But did she truly have to move across the country?

Of course she did. She wanted her name known all over—national notoriety. Certainly, she would move wherever her work took her. As much as she hated the thought of leaving New Orleans, the city she loved, she loved her work more. She would move. Make no mistake about it. Her work was her life.

As the pictures printed, she started typing the article for the evening edition of the paper, telling New Orleans about Trisha McIntyre, a young female found early this morning, strangled to death. She wanted to tell the women of New Orleans to take heed, not to do anything as foolish as stopping for some strange reason in the middle of nowhere.

Tell them to use their heads. They never knew who could be lurking in the darkness. But she didn't. She also didn't mention the fact that there could be a connection to the three murders in the past two weeks. Taylor didn't want to give the pervert any limelight for what he or she had done; besides which, the police hadn't confirmed it yet.

In less than thirty minutes, Taylor had the new prints laid out with the others. As she studied them, she thought about the facts known to her. All three victims were strangled at the same early morning hour, in the same general area, and all were young single women. Well, two were—she didn't know about the new one yet.

Stephanie, the first victim, was involved with a man but not married. And as far as Taylor knew, no one had interviewed him yet. Why was he staying out of this? Why hadn't he contacted the police?

The second victim, Trudy, was single and not involved with anyone. Taylor didn't know the facts on the third victim yet, but if it was the same MO, she was probably single, too.

"Did they know one another?" Taylor asked herself aloud. "Maybe they knew each other at an earlier time in their lives."

She scanned the pictures. "There's got to be another connection." She squinted closer. Something kept drawing her to the rear shot of the latest victim's car. Finally, she pulled out her magnifying glass and studied every inch of the rear end.

"Oh my gosh!" she whispered when she found what had caught her attention. All the air in her lungs left, and she shuddered. It was the bumper sticker. Why? Because it was just like the one on the bumper of Taylor's car. The sticker revealed the girl's love for country music and the station she preferred listening to. . .just as Taylor's car bumper did. Icy fingers danced across her shoulders as she realized the latest victim had a connection to her. Grief for Trisha McIntyre's young life lost swept through Taylor.

New Orleans was noted for jazz, not country, even though a few stations had started featuring country artists. Country music had grown over the past decade, so it, too, was moving into the city a little at a time.

Her eyes glanced at the other cars, wondering if either revealed anything about their owners. Since no pictures focused closely on the rear of the cars, she had to use her magnifying glass again.

"Wow! I don't believe it! Stephanie, too?"

Astonished, she pulled the picture of the second victim's car closer to her. Studying it carefully, she leaned in toward the round object in her hand magnifying the bumper of the victim.

Her stomach knotted at her discovery, and she slammed down the magnifying glass. Part of her was excited at the thought she might have made the connection between the three women, but the other part made her nauseous. Now she, too, was connected to them. Admittedly she wasn't as young as they were, but close, and she was a single woman who loved country music. Could that be the key? It had to be.

With shaking fingers, she lifted her phone and punched out the number of the police department. "Lieutenant Bradley, please."

In seconds, she heard his gruff voice. "Bradley here. Can I help you?"

"Detective Bradley," Taylor said in a soft voice.

"Speak up. I can't hear you," he growled into her ear.

Taylor felt weak. Knowing this connection was one thing, but verbalizing it was another. Speaking it out loud would make it real. Swallowing a hard lump in her throat, she said, "Lieutenant Bradley, it's me, Taylor Jaymes. I found something you should see. I-I-I think I may have found the connection between the three victims." She stuttered as part of her fought trying not to even speak this truth into existence.

He didn't respond immediately. Taylor wasn't even sure he was still there. *Speak up, Detective. Did you hear me?* She wanted to scream at him, but fear rattled her nerves, and she seldom felt fear. "Can you meet me somewhere, or can I come to you?" She held her breath waiting for his response. Before it came, she added, "It's important."

A heavy sigh touched her ears. "I don't have time to meet you, Miss Jaymes. I have a meeting to go to. I doubt you found the connection we're looking for, but I appreciate your exuberance."

Hardheaded men! "You have to see this. I'm telling you it's important. It's the key you've been looking for. I know it. I feel it." Her voice rose with each sentence she spoke. How could he not want to know the connection? It was his job!

Silence filled the line. Then, "If you've found a connection that points to the victims' deaths, I'd like to see it." His voice was hesitant. "You can come to the station, but you have to come right now. I'm expected in a meeting with my boss and the commissioner in half an hour. Be here within fifteen minutes."

"It'll take me longer than that just to drive to the station.

Be late for your meeting. It's what you're looking for. I know it. A few minutes late won't hurt. I promise it'll be worth it."

"I'm sure it's important, but I doubt my captain will see it that way." His voice sounded like he didn't believe her anyway.

"He'll be glad you kept him waiting." He probably thought her call was just another excuse to try and convince him to let her work with him on this case. "I'll be there as fast as possible. I'm running out the door now." *But if I get a speeding ticket, you can fix it for me,* she thought but didn't say. "Wait for me." Her fear dissipated, and excitement coursed through her veins. "It's the answer you've been looking for."

"You sound pretty sure of your findings, Miss Jaymes. I can't imagine what you could have uncovered that the police department couldn't find." A fraction of a second later, he said, "But hurry on over, and I'll take a look. I really do have a meeting with my captain and the commissioner."

"I'm on my way!" Jumping to her feet, she slammed down the phone and stuffed the pictures in her purse.

In record time, she was out the door, speeding to the station. She didn't take time to enjoy the city she loved, nor did she crank up the radio and sing along. Instead, her mind stayed focused on the connection between the girls. They all loved country music so much that they stuck a bumper sticker on the back of their car to tell the world. Within the original fifteen-minute limit, she made it to the station, shoved her gear stick into NEUTRAL, and set the parking brake.

This time the detective didn't keep her waiting. The policeman at the counter said, "Go right on in. The detective is expecting you."

She walked straight to the elevator and hit the button for

his floor. As the doors started opening, she slipped out and scurried down the hall to his door. Knocking twice, she entered, not waiting for him to answer.

Without saying a word, she walked to his desk and pulled out the three photos. Sticking her hand back in her purse, she pulled out the magnifying glass and said, "Look at their bumpers."

She watched as the detective studied the prints closely. Finally he said, "I don't see how we overlooked this. We've searched prints inside and out and other items found in the cars, trying to find a connection. I guess no one got around to looking at the bumpers, for clues." He ran his fingers through his dark hair again.

Taylor noticed he did that when he was thinking. She wished she could do that to him.

Whoa. Where did that come from? Her mind was supposed to be on this case, not on some guy. "So do you think this could be the connection?"

"It's possible. It's definitely a lead." He glanced at his watch. "I really have to go to this meeting, but I'd like to talk to you a bit more when I get out, say around three or four?"

She was disappointed. She wanted to talk now. . .not later. Taylor thought he would call off his meeting and start following up on the lead she'd thrown into his lap. *Well, fine. I'll follow up on it by myself.* She sighed softly, then said, "I can't meet you until six tonight. In fact, I'm really busy, so let's just meet over dinner."

His brow furrowed, but he said nothing.

"Don't get any funny ideas," Taylor snapped. "I said let's meet at dinner because that will be all the time I can spare you. I have a busy life, too, you know."

Swiftly, she thought of what she wanted to eat tonight. Other than the pastry treats she had that morning, she hadn't eaten all day. Without giving him a chance to come up with another idea, she blurted, "Okay. Meet me at Dante's Pizza and Pasta. It's on St. Peter—not far from here."

"Don't you ever eat anything besides junk?"

She rolled her eyes. *What a dumb time to think about eating healthy. Besides, who has time to be choosey?* "Just be there. We'll discuss my eating habits another time." Taylor stood. Reaching for the pictures, she said, "I'll take those, thank you. Didn't have time to make you copies. Have a good meeting." With those words, she turned and left his office.

So put that in your pipe and smoke it, she thought. In no time she made it outside and headed to her car. Before she started following up on the lead she'd found, Taylor decided now was the time to drop off her clothes to be cleaned. Around the corner from her house was The Washing Well. It only took a couple of minutes to park in the unloading zone, drop her clothes off, and then get back on the road. What a way to do housework. "The only way," she murmured.

Even though she'd led the detective to believe she had a busy life, other than taking the next few hours locating the country bars in the area and doing a background check on the third victim, she had nothing else to do. In fact, had she not found the connection, she'd already have been through finding the background info.

Using her cell phone, she located the bars in a twenty-mile radius of where the bodies were left. She found three in the Quarter and two outside the Quarter. After leaving the detective this evening, she'd copy pictures of the three victims and go visit the bars. See if anyone recognized them as regulars. . .or even better, remembered seeing them the nights they were killed.

Next, she found the latest victim's address in the white pages on her cell. Taylor drove by Miss McIntyre's home, scoping out the neighborhood. If she had been a cop, she'd intrude on the neighbors now, asking questions, but tomorrow would be soon enough. Give them a chance to feel their grief.

A short article would be in the evening edition about Trisha McIntyre's untimely death. Taylor decided this would give the neighbors a chance to read about Trisha's death in the paper, and maybe by tomorrow they would be willing to talk about the young girl's life.

Taylor took time to run back by the paper and make duplicates of the three pictures so the detective could have his own copies. She'd give them to him when they met for dinner.

After finishing everything she had to do, she picked up her clothes, already clean and folded, and then headed home. It cost her more this way, but what she made up for in time was worth every penny. She didn't have time for mundane things.

When Taylor dressed for dinner, for some strange reason she didn't dress in her normal fashion, jeans and a pullover shirt, although her favorites were all nice and clean. Without even thinking about it, she pulled out her emerald-green short skirt and blazer and paired a paisley print silk blouse with it. Sliding into a pair of dressy, yet comfortable, black shoes with a heel, she took a few extra minutes in front of the mirror touching up her makeup and hair.

By 5:45, Taylor had already slipped out of her apartment and walked down the street to Dante's. She wanted to be sure to get them a table on the far end so their chances of being overheard would be slim. Their subject matter didn't need to be shared with anyone. Of course, in New Orleans, especially the Quarter, people didn't take time to listen to other people's conversations; they were too busy having fun.

After sitting for a while at the table, she glanced at her watch. It read 6:15. Anger started to boil within her, and her stomach roiled. She was hungry. Those beignets hadn't sustained her except for an hour that morning. Time had kept her from grabbing lunch. And by the time she had a moment, it was too close to meeting Detective John Bradley for dinner. She didn't care one bit for this guy keeping her waiting. What if he decided not to come at all? Maybe now that he had the new lead, he really didn't need to talk to her. Maybe he wasn't going to show up at all. Maybe by asking her to meet him later, it was his way of keeping her from following up on her own lead.

She wanted to be angry at her new thought, but instead, she found herself more disappointed that she had dressed up for nothing.

By 6:30, Antonio, Dante's son, called to Taylor, "Are you going to eat tonight?" She was a regular of this establishment, as well as a few others around the Quarter. "Or would you at least care for a beer while you wait?"

The old Taylor surfaced—the one before she apparently went gaga over the detective. "Forget him. I'll order now. If he shows up, he'll have to eat what I pick out. I'll take a large special with everything but anchovies." If he showed up at all, she would share it with him; if not, the leftovers would be breakfast in the morning.

Shortly after she ordered, a tall, good-looking man in a blue suit walked into the eatery. When she realized it was John, her spirits lifted. Taylor waved above the crowd to get his attention.

Yes, he made it.

Chapter 9

John spotted Taylor and headed for the table. "Sorry I'm late. That meeting lasted longer than I expected. The governor joined us."

The whole time John had been in the meeting, his mind toyed, or more like worried, over what Taylor would do with her discovery. Taylor could have rushed back to the paper and written up an article, flashing what could be the connection to the public across the front page of the evening edition of the *Tribune*. For her, that would have meant getting a front-page scoop, and wasn't that what reporters lived for? He could see the headline now: CONNECTION BETWEEN DEATHS FOUND BY REPORTER, followed by the subheading, "Serial killer loose in New Orleans. . .beware."

Those thoughts drove him crazy. It was all he could do to stay focused on the governor's words. John couldn't wait to get out of there and meet with Taylor so they could discuss what she'd found that connected the three deaths.

After all that worrying and fretting during the meeting, he surprised himself by taking time to swing by his place to shower and get a quick shave. Then he changed before dashing over to Dante's Pizza to meet with Taylor. That baffled him, but it also gave him the opportunity to glance at the cover of the evening edition. He found she'd kept her word and hadn't printed anything about what she had found—yet.

"You look tired but fresh, if that makes any sense." A crease formed between her brows. "It must have been a rough meeting. I can't believe the governor crashed it. You must really be in the hot seat now. . .at least until you crack this case. Lucky for you, I found a connection. Hopefully it will help you." Her innocent eyes rested on him as she spoke.

His gaze darted around the room before he leaned toward her and in a hushed tone said, "I did tell them that a connection may have been found, and I needed to go follow up on it. That was when they got all fired up and kept insisting I tell them what it was or give them a name of who we suspected. I don't know if the meeting was more like a roller coaster or a spinning top. We went up and down, back and forth, but mostly kept talking in circles."

She shook her head in what seemed like pity for the poor guy. And that poor guy was him. John wasn't used to being thought of that way.

With a tight-lipped smile he said, "I finally told them, when we find a suspect or two who we can link to these crimes, they would be the first to know. Until then, what we had was a theory with plenty of speculation. Thanks to you, we may have more. I didn't say that, though. Instead I said this lead may be the starting place to look for the facts we need, and they finally let me go."

Eying his dinner partner—the fiery, red-haired woman, with deep green eyes accentuated by her emerald-green suit—he wasn't sure if the green set off the fire in her hair, or if it was the flames blazing from her hair that ignited a combustible reaction in her fancy suit and his mind. He glanced away. What had gotten into him? John hadn't responded like this to a woman in years. His work had been his life and it still was. But as his gaze returned to her, he had to admit that he liked the way her eyes sparkled. In fact, he wished this dinner was for pleasure and not business.

Clearing his throat, he fumbled with the napkin on the table. "Dinner. Why don't we order—before we start talking business, that is? I think I skipped lunch today and I'm starving."

A shimmer of red splashed across her cheeks. "Oh no. What did you do?" As a police detective, he knew the look of guilt if he ever saw it.

She lifted her shoulders slightly. "Sorry. I've already ordered dinner." Holding her hands up as if to stop an onslaught of whatever the detective may have for her, she cocked a brow. "You weren't here, and I was hungry." In the silence that followed her admission, she bit her bottom lip.

"God help us. You ordered for me, too?"

She nodded.

"I know it's Dante's Pizza, but I was hoping they had other Italian dishes, like baked chicken brushed with olive oil and seasoned with rosemary, oregano, and thyme, cooked slowly, falling off the bone it's so tender, and a salad on the side. Umm. Now that I would enjoy."

With a crooked grin, she shook her head.

"I can only imagine the junk I'm about to put in my body. When I was a rookie, I lived on greasy junk food, but I promised myself when I moved up the ranks, I would eat only healthy food from then on. So break it to me gently."

He winced as he smiled on the inside. He knew already pizza was the main dish here with a few Italian sandwiches available also. Truly he was picking at her and her eating habits, which also amazed him. Joking around was another thing John rarely did, if ever. What had come over him? "No, seriously, what did you order?" he asked and then waited for the worst.

Lifting her hand in the air, she signaled the man behind the counter. "Antonio's coming. You can order yourself something to drink."

"I'll have a Coke," he told the waiter. *So she knows him well.*

"Taylor, do you need a refill?" Antonio queried. "Your order is about ready."

John watched as she smiled sweetly at the man and nodded. "Sounds good, Antonio." And then she licked her lips. Was that for the food or for the man? John wondered.

"You eat here often?" John glanced from her to the man she called Antonio. It really was none of his business, and he shouldn't have asked. This case must have thrown him for a loop, making him act so out of character. And her private life. . .what was it to him? *Change the subject.* "So what kind of pizza did you order?"

"I could have ordered the barbeque chicken pizza had I

known you had your heart set on chicken. But you'll love what I did order. Trust me. And if you want a salad, just ask Antonio for one. He'll bring it with the pizza."

Before he could talk her out of the kind of pizza she had ordered, Antonio returned with the drinks and the pizza. It smelled great, but glancing over it, John said, "Did you leave anything off? It looks like everything but the kitchen sink is on it." He tilted his head and teased, "At least you left that off."

"Don't get smart with me. It has everything but anchovies. And if you had been on time, you could have ordered for yourself." Her eyes darted to the pizza and then returned to his face. "They have different salads and great hot sandwiches. Of course, both are covered with cheese—mozzarella and/or parmesan. Your choice! Oh wait." She twisted her lips. "That's right. You weren't here to choose. So quit complaining and dig in." She threw another quirky smile at him and returned her attention to the pizza.

John found himself enjoying their banter. It was nice, relaxing over a dinner for two after a long, hard day of work. "You're right. Let's eat it while it's hot." He picked up a slice to slip onto his plate, then swiftly dropped it and blew on his fingers. "Trust me, it's hot." He blew some more and then grabbed his cold drink. "Ahh," he said as the coolness caressed his fingertips, giving him instant relief. John resolved to enjoy their little dinner and the pleasure of Taylor's company. Why not?

While they were eating, Taylor started talking business. She told him in detail how she'd discovered the connection. She swallowed another bite and took a sip of her drink. As she set her glass down, she said, "I scanned the area for country bars."

"You did what?" The detective dropped the half-eaten slice of his third piece on his plate. His jaw stiffened.

"I decided to see what country bars were near the area in which the girls had been found. Because each girl had the same bumper sticker and it was of a country radio station in town, checking out the country bars seemed like the next logical step. If their bumper stickers had been reflecting jazz music, it would have made things harder trying to trace their favorite hangout and then seeing if it was the same for each—too many jazz clubs in the Quarter. This was a plus for us."

"Us?" he questioned quickly.

"Yes. There aren't very many country bars down here. Jazz pubs are a-plenty though, so count your blessings as they say."

"You're right, Miss Jaymes. I should count my blessings, and I do every day. But, sweetheart, you getting too close to these cases would not be a blessing." With hands exaggerating what he said, John pointed to himself first and then to her. "You let me do the investigating and you do the reporting. . .but at the right time. So I'll tell you like I told the governor: This is my case, and I'll work it. And a side note to you, Miss Jaymes—I don't need civilians getting involved." His pointer finger waved back and forth in the air.

Things have been going so well, she thought. *Why does he have to spoil everything?* His gestures made it clear he didn't want her anywhere around him or his case. But must she remind him that she found the connection, not him?

Too bad he didn't want any reporter sticking their nose in the middle of his investigation. Like it or not, this nose was staying on top of things. Clasping her chin with her fingers, she rested her elbow on the table. He had seemed so friendly at the beginning of the meal. Oh well. It was nice while it lasted. In fact, that was the longest relationship she'd had in a while. She glanced at her watch. *Almost thirty minutes.* Then she laughed to herself.

Shaking her thoughts from her head, she decided to focus on the facts, not on the detective. The three victims each had the same bumper sticker on their car. That was a lead and one she would follow. She had found it. Not him, or his police department. The victims all liked the same type of music, so country bars were the starting point of this investigation. . .*her* investigation. If he were as good a cop as the word on the streets suggested, he, too, would see it.

"Call me Taylor, please," she insisted, deciding not to focus on what he had just said.

"What?" He pushed his plate back slightly. "You're trying to ignore what I said. In fact, you're trying to change the subject. Don't get me wrong. I'm glad you found a possible connection, but I don't want you to put your life in danger. Leave that for the professionals." He eyed her closely. "Okay. . .Taylor. Now, did you bring the pictures? I'd like to take a better look."

She nodded as she took another bite. Laying her slice down and wiping her hands on a napkin, she reached for her purse. "I did better than that." She pulled a red envelope marked CONFIDENTIAL out of her handbag. "I made duplicates for you. The three pictures of the back end of the cars, that is."

John reached for the envelope she offered and opened it.

He studied the pictures one after the other, his brows furrowing. Glancing up, he said, "What made you aware of the stickers? They aren't that noticeable. On one the sticker is almost faded away." He began flipping through the pictures again.

She felt the blood drain from her face as she recalled the feeling that had overcome her upon her discovery. Clasping her hands together on the table, she said, "One picture kept bothering me. At first I didn't know why. Finally I pulled out my magnifying glass and started going over the whole picture, one section at a time. Then I saw the bumper sticker and knew that was what had called to me." Taking a deep breath, trying to keep her emotions under control, she added, "You see, I have the same sticker on my car." She picked up her glass, swallowed two more gulps, and set her glass back down.

The expression on his face changed, but only for a second or two. What was he thinking? Taylor couldn't decide what that expression meant—it came and went so fast. She only knew it was different, and it only lasted a split second, maybe two. Taylor waited for him to make a comment, but he didn't. She continued. "Anyway, that made me wonder what the other bumpers said about their owners. Then I found the same sticker on the other two cars." She pushed her plate away as she finished her explanation, not bothering to finish her pizza, and then placed her chin on her cupped hands that were braced on the table with her elbows for support.

"So some things do bother you. How about that? After your great heroics on the burglaries in the Quarter that you helped our burglary division solve, it surprises me to see you affected like that by anything. I thought you were tough through and through."

Her gaze locked on him, but she made no comment. Truly, she did not know what to say. He was right. Rarely did things affect her. She was not even sure why this had. Taylor knew she wouldn't be the next victim, but the connection to those women spooked her for some reason. . .maybe just the fact that she could have been one of the victims.

His eyes brightened. "Now that I think about it, I do recall hearing the radio on in two of the three cars when we arrived. I don't recall the first car having its motor running. I'll check that out. It should be in one of the reports; mine or the first officer on the scene. We should have noticed the stickers on all three of the cars, though. I admit the one on the second car is pretty faded, but it's still there."

Taylor felt sorry for the detective. She didn't like hearing him beat himself up about not finding the connection himself. "Well, I'm a trained reporter and I overlooked it, too. . .at first. So obviously they weren't very noticeable." *Cops are human, too*, she thought but didn't dare tell him that.

"We know now, thanks to you. That's what is important." After slipping the pictures into his breast pocket, he finished off the last two slices of pizza. "That tasted pretty good," he admitted. "The spices, the tangy tomato sauce. I haven't had pizza in a long time. Normally, I cook a well-balanced meal and then save portions of the dinners in the freezer for a later date, or I go to a good restaurant near the station on my way home." His eyes glanced around the room. "Not that this place isn't good. Truthfully, I enjoyed it. I'm glad you suggested we meet here for dinner. I mean, for our business discussion."

Her heart skipped a beat. He sounded pleased. She concluded that the blond in the cafeteria at the police station might know him better than Taylor realized. He seemed to have a sweet side after all. Her gaze lifted to his face. His beautiful blue eyes were watching her. She lowered her eyes instantly. Her heart raced. She wasn't sure what caused that. Was it the way he had been looking at her, or the realization that the blond knew him so well? Either way, she frowned.

"Taylor, don't. I like seeing you smile. It makes me think there is something pleasant in this world after all."

Heat rose in her cheeks. He had complimented her again. She had to admit, she liked the feeling it gave her, but then immediately scolded herself for feeling good about it. *Don't get carried away,* she told herself. *This man is apparently taken. Besides, he's had a long day and is probably just too tired to be nasty.* "Well, Lieutenant, do you think those will help you?" She pointed toward the pictures in his pocket, where he had slipped them earlier.

He shrugged. "I don't know, but it gives us a place to start. It's a connection, and that was something we hadn't found yet." He smiled at her. "You might as well call me John. Who knows? Maybe we can be of some help to one another after all." He reached for the check.

Taylor tried to snatch it from him. "I asked you," she pointed out. "Let me pay."

He shook his head. "Not on your life. I'll get it. I think this is the first meal in over a month I actually enjoyed." He raised his brows in a quick motion and added, "Although the food tasted good, I don't—I don't think that was what I enjoyed." He smiled.

She liked the way he had trouble paying accolades, yet she had been given three in a very short time. On that thought she filled her lungs with air as her mind filled with good thoughts.

"I believe it's your happy nature that I like. It makes you enjoyable to be around. I guess you make work not feel so much like. . .work."

"Thanks. It sounded like that was almost hard for you to admit."

John pulled his billfold from his pocket and slipped out some money. "It wasn't that it was hard to say; it's just been awhile since I've relaxed a little and enjoyed myself. Your happy-go-lucky nature makes a person relax. I enjoyed this evening, even though it was business."

That was good. He kept reminding her that this dinner was business and, although he enjoyed it, it was still business. The two never mix, and she knew it. *Yes, keep reminding me that this is work. Keep me straight. Keep me in line.* She smiled to herself. It didn't work. His nice words made her feel all warm inside—and it was his nice words that kept playing over and over in her mind, not the nagging thought in the back of her mind that said he had a girlfriend. *Forget it.*

When Antonio handed John his change, he left a tip on the table. "How about I follow you home to make sure you get there safely?"

She held back a laugh. After all, he was a policeman, and he tended to think the worst of people. "John," she said, trying to call him by his first name. She liked it. Simple. Plain, yet so strong. It fit. "John, I'm a big girl now. I go home by myself all the time. You don't need to trouble yourself."

He helped pull her chair out as she started to rise. "It's no trouble. Where are you parked?"

As they exited the pizza parlor, the warm night air brushed

her skin. The humidity had dropped some, and it actually felt pleasant outside. Or was it her company that made things seem a little nicer? "I walked. I live right down the street." She pointed toward her apartment building.

"Then I'll walk you home." He took hold of her elbow and escorted her in the general direction of her place, making their way through the crowds of people roaming the sidewalks in the Quarter. "How long have you lived in the Quarter?"

She smiled at him. It was nice having a man look out for her, even though it was business. "Almost five years—fighting my mom and dad the whole way, I must admit. You would think I was still a kid the way they act. The French Quarter is no place for a single woman. . .alone." She laughed as she mimicked her parents' warnings.

John shrugged. "I've worked the Quarter for a long time, and I have to agree with them. It's the party section for the world. Everyone comes to the Quarter, and a lot goes on here."

"You sound like a cop. . .or a parent. Don't worry, Mr. Officer. I'm a big girl now, and I take real good care of myself." Stopping in front of the entrance to her little complex, she asked, "Would you care to come up for some coffee?"

He hesitated only a moment, then said, "Yes. I'd like that."

Chapter 10

Did I say yes?

*D*He watched from behind as he followed her into her building and up a double flight of stairs. She seemed strong, a self-reliant type, sure of her moves...too sure. She didn't look around as she stepped into the dark area of the entryway or the turn in the stairs. Sure, there were low lights going up the steps so no one should miss their footing, but what about things hidden in the dark corners? Anyone could be standing there, hiding, waiting to attack. Taylor just dashed up the stairs one step at a time as her hand barely caught hold of the railing, paying no attention to anything around her. Maybe it was because she knew a policeman, an officer of the law, was with her.

Then he noticed the hand that hovered above the railing appeared to shake. Was she afraid of something? That surprised him. The woman seemed so self-confident from the instant he'd met her yesterday.

Was it only yesterday?

Opening the door with her key, she led the way into her little apartment. The lights were off in the living room, but the full moon spilled in through the glass sliding doors that looked out upon her balcony. The moonlight supplied plenty of light, but she snapped on the kitchen light as she began to fill a teakettle with water.

"Let's sit on the balcony to enjoy the coffee, if that's okay with you?" she asked as she unlocked and then slid the door open. "The coffee will only take a few minutes. How do you take yours?"

"Black with a teaspoon of sugar," he said, stepping through the open glass doors. Edging near the railing, he gazed out over the courtyard. The villas and apartments in the Quarter hid such beauty. The tourists would be amazed if they saw behind the grungy stoned walls that covered most of the exterior facade. Of course, since Katrina, a lot of the buildings had fresh face-lifts.

Several of the finer hotels had remodeled after the hurricane. Their guests now saw the inside of the courtyards, like Taylor and others who lived full-time in the Quarter. Most visitors who came to the city of New Orleans visited the Quarter but spent their sleep-filled nights in the five-star hotels on and off Canal Street, the area that edged the Quarter. Daytime visitors mostly parked on the edges and walked the streets or rode through on a horse-drawn buggy. Streets were narrow with very little parking. It was a never-ending party in the Quarter with so much foot traffic. The real beauty was behind the walls, in the courtyards of the private homes and apartments. They stayed so beautiful that the city of New Orleans offered a Garden Tour. That was when the probing visitors got to see the flowers in bloom, surrounded by the brick patios with the Spanish-looking decor—a tour worth taking.

In Taylor's courtyard, the stone-covered flooring was lined with large green plants that survived on little to no sunlight. The leaves on some of those plants were huge. They offered great shade to those who sat on the black wrought-iron patio furniture. . .in keeping with the grandeur of the olden days.

John inhaled the fragrance of honeysuckle and gardenias. Raising his eyes toward the heavens, he whispered, "Thank You, Lord."

Taylor joined him on the balcony with two cups of coffee. "I decided to make instant. Quicker that way. I hope you don't mind."

"That's fine," he said, taking the cup offered him. "These apartments seem pretty quiet." *Hopefully they are also safe,* he thought but didn't say.

Taylor laughed. "Quiet? You bet. There are only four apartments and the other three have older retired people living in them. I think their bedtime is before nine. They are all so sweet, and they tend to act as my mother and father sometimes. One is a husband and wife. The other two live alone, having lost their spouses. One is a man, the other a woman. So you see, besides my own parents who smother me, I have two more moms and two more dads. So I'm pretty well looked after. You don't have to worry about me."

"I'm sure they all take good care of you."

"Occasionally, like during Mardi Gras, some have grandchildren who come visit. They get a little rowdy, but not for long." She sipped her coffee. "Oh, I almost forgot, would you like a cookie or two to go with your coffee? Ms. Sadie always bakes, and she never forgets to share with all of us. Now Martha, the married one, still cooks almost every night. She makes sure I get one to two meals a week." Patting her stomach, she said, "I know it shows, but it's a good thing, since I don't cook. First, I don't like to cook. Second, I'm not very good at it. And the most important reason, I never have the time. At least that's what I tell my mom. Chasing the next story always keeps me busy."

As much junk as she liked to eat, it was amazing she wasn't as big as a barn, but apparently she burned off all the calories she took in. "I'll pass on the cookies," he replied. "Still stuffed from the pizza."

"The sweets won't go to waste, I assure you. I'm not the only one who gets fed around here, though. Martha slips Dan, the widower, a meal or two a week also. Sometimes Joe, her husband, gets a little jealous. It's so cute. They're all in their eighties and nineties. Besides, I think Ms. Sadie has her eye out for Dan."

"Life in the fast lane here. You better watch out that you don't get caught up in the love triangle." His laugh boomed out, and she joined in. "You know, if your mom and dad sat out here, they might change their opinion of the place. It's amazing how, even though the streets are crowded, here you feel alone. The peace and serenity is awesome. How easy is it to get into the courtyard from the streets?"

"You can access it from your apartment." She pointed to the steps winding down from the far side of the balcony. "Or as a renter you can use the key, giving you access through the gate hidden behind the stairs. Trust me, the chance of my parents seeing the beauty here is nil, zip, zilch, nada. They never come to the Quarter. Never have and never will. Them be happy for me? That, too, would never happen, 'cause the only way it would is if I'd settle down, marry the perfect man, and become the perfect little homemaker. Hah! Fat chance, and we both know it." She took another sip.

"So you have no plans on taking the big step, aye? Can't say I blame you. With the business you're in, it wouldn't be fair to the man in your life."

"Oh, there's no man—" Her lips closed. "Besides, I'm married. . .to the job."

They sat out for another half hour—sometimes talking, sometimes in compatible silence. John finished his coffee and set the empty cup by hers on the little table that sat between them. He was truly enjoying their time here on her balcony—the quiet, the small talk, and the shared laughter. He found himself surprisingly delighted by her company. No pressure when talking with her. . .so easy.

Slapping his hands to his thighs, he decided he better go before he got to liking his visit too much. He rose. "Well, you're safe at home. I'd best be on my way. I have a lot of work to do in the morning. A lead to follow." He smiled at her as their eyes locked. "Good night, Taylor. And thanks again for your help." He turned to leave.

She followed him into the apartment and passed him to open the door. He stepped out into the hallway and turned back toward the door. He was about to thank her again when she said, "Well, good night, John. I enjoyed dinner and the visit on the balcony." Taylor radiated happiness, and he found himself drinking in her smile, her warmth.

He couldn't tell what she was thinking, but he felt certain she wanted to say something. Her eyes sparkled. If he didn't know himself better, he believed he actually wanted to kiss her good night. Not John. He had no time in his life for a relationship, especially another woman who put herself in harm's way and didn't think anything about it.

The corner of his lips turned up as he thought what her reaction might be if he tried to kiss her. She would probably slap his face. It might be worth the try. Instead, he managed to control his impulses.

John took her hand in his and squeezed but dropped it as quickly as he'd taken it. No harm in that. "Take care of yourself."

To his surprise, she didn't recoil from his touch. Instead, her smile stayed on her face, even grew a bit larger as she looked at him.

He didn't trust himself, so he swiftly headed down the stairs. When he reached the bottom of the top set, he pivoted and glanced back up at her doorway. She still stood, watching, and gave a slight wave. He trudged down the second set of stairs heading toward the street opening. Out on the sidewalk he strode back toward his car, one block past Dante's Pizza.

John knew leaving was the right thing. He didn't know what had gotten in to him. In the two years since Jennifer's death, John hadn't been interested in any woman, even though plenty had asked him out for the evening. His fiancée had died in the line of duty—a fellow officer, one who had lived for the work, just like he did—like Taylor did. He'd sworn off any woman willing to die for her job. He wasn't able to bear the pain of losing another love. Truth be told, Taylor, although not a policewoman, had a job that could cost her—her life, in fact. That crossed out any possibility between the two of them.

Help me, Lord. Keep my mind on the job and off of this woman.

He didn't need to think about her or yearn for a chance to know her better. It stopped here and now. Stepping next to his Bronco, he climbed in and took off. Mashing the button to lower his window, he let the fresh air blast him. Maybe the wind would blow thoughts of that pretty redhead with the explosive temper and passion for life right out of his mind. He hoped so. It seemed the harder he tried not to think of her, the more she invaded his thoughts, and the clearer the picture of her became in his head.

He had just met her yesterday. How could she consume his thoughts already?

He slammed the palm of his hand down on the steering wheel. "No. I'm not going to think of her. She could mess my life up in a heartbeat," he spat with genuine determination.

Besides, he needed to stay focused on the case.

Chapter 11

Tossing and turning all of Saturday night ruined John's sleep. His thoughts drifted to that reporter. *Get out of my head!* He smashed his pillow over his face trying to block the view.

In the past, the minute reporters were out of sight, they were out of mind. That was the way he liked it. John made a habit of talking to all reporters together, giving them the same info. Anything more than that only happened when the captain rode John to make nice with reporters— when the NOPD needed good press. But John didn't like to make nice with reporters. He didn't like telling them anything because reporters sensationalized the news, anything to sell their copy. The updated broadcasts and the newspaper stories made it harder for detectives to do their job. Unfortunately, the captain didn't agree. According to his boss, when the police department played nice with the reporters, reporters worked with the police.

Hmmph. He doubted that. Most reporters were only in it for ratings, either for the television station or for themselves. The sad thing was that they didn't seem to care about the people's lives that were destroyed by the reports they gave as news, along with the images they flashed on the screen. Some were half truths or half-substantiated reports. Whatever worked for the ratings or sold the most newspapers and magazines. John found that, with a lot of reporters, if what they reported wasn't total fact, that was okay. Their follow up story would straighten out the facts, or they would just move on to the next one.

At least that was how John saw it—although he knew he shouldn't put all reporters in one box. . .just like all cops are not the same.

Maybe Taylor Jaymes is different. Who's to say?

One thing he could say for sure: his mind refused to stop thinking about her—or the fact that *she* found the connection, not the NOPD.

Was it luck? Or was she good at what she did? Was it her investigative skills that kept her face coming into view when he closed his eyes?

It had to be. Her abilities impressed him.

Enough about her! He tossed his pillow to the side and then punched it. *Enough!*

He needed to get his mind back on the case and do his job.

There was nothing he could do tonight but try and get a good night's sleep, if it would come. After church tomorrow, he would slip by the radio station that the bumper sticker represented. Do a little background check on their employees and ex-employees. He hoped to find someone with a record or one who was fired and now had an axe to grind with the station. But instead of taking it out on the station, they were attacking the listeners. His thought process seemed far-fetched, but people reacted in strange ways.

Turning over one more time, he thought about the bars. According to Taylor, she had already started identifying the bars in the area and planned to start asking questions tomorrow night when they opened for business. She was right about them being a good lead to follow. John would start by checking out the station and their employee history. That was first on his list. Later, he and his men would hit the bars. It was their off day, but surely they would come in for a couple of hours to help him out. Police work called for that at times. Money was tight, but the job had to come first—getting the criminal off the street. They would see if anyone remembered any of the victims. . .maybe all three. They could have been regulars at one establishment, for all he knew. That would narrow down the search some.

Fat chance. He could only dream.

The French Quarter was a hodgepodge of bars, mostly jazz, as well as souvenir shops, strip clubs, and sex shows, unfortunately. And the partying never closed down in the Quarter or the bars. They stayed open until the last customer left. The activity alone kept their station working 24-7, with rotating shifts that never stopped. But as much as he hated most of the atmosphere in the Quarter, he felt that was where he was supposed to be. Now he needed some shut-eye so he could get up in the morning, refreshed and ready for the day.

Lord, I don't know what's going on in my mind or why her image keeps manifesting itself in my brain, but help me. Help me forget her and get some rest.

John knew he wasn't ready for a relationship of any kind, whether girlfriend or just a good friend. After Jennifer's death, John decided with the kind of work he did, he was better off staying single. He couldn't see putting anyone through the pain he went through with the loss of his fiancée. And if that was the case, why bother to date at all? That way of life he'd put behind him when he gave his heart to Jesus. Now he needed to keep those things behind him.

Sleep. . .help me sleep. He must have rolled around, unsettled in bed, for another half hour before finally managing to doze off.

The next thing he knew, his alarm was buzzing. Hitting the snooze button to silence it, he said a quick prayer of thanksgiving for not having another killing in the night.

Still dressed in gym shorts and a T-shirt, after the coffee dripped its last drop, he stepped out on his front porch and grabbed his newspaper. At the table John laid open the paper and started scanning the articles. After a few minutes of scanning the headlines, he released a pent-up breath. "Great, nothing about the connection. Looks like Taylor kept her word."

He poured a cup of the hot, dark brew and sat at the table again. This time he did some serious reading of the news, local and national. Time passed quickly. By the time he'd finished his second cup of coffee, it was time to get ready for church. He rinsed his cup out, placed it in the sink, and then went off to shower, shave, and change for the service that morning.

With fifteen minutes to spare, he parked his Bronco in the lot and strode toward the church doors.

"Morning, John," said the usher as they shook hands. "How are things?"

Smiling, John said, "It could be better, Timothy, but, as He tells us not to worry about tomorrow and let Him guide us through the day, that's what I have to do."

"We're thankful for men like you in this city. New Orleans is not all bad. Even in the midst of the evil here, we need a sliver of light running through so we know there is still hope for us all. You're that light, John, in the Quarter. Keep up the good work."

John thanked him. As he entered the church, he found a seat near the back. He never sat in the front—not that he didn't want to, but he never knew when his beeper would vibrate, and John needed to be where he could leave without distracting from the message.

God had anointed Pastor Larry Stanford. It showed in his actions, his life, and his messages. The church grew and grew as it reached out to the community all around it and beyond. Like the Word says, "I'll know you by your fruit." Pastor Larry's fruit was plentiful.

The message was uplifting, as usual. It helped John find strength in the Lord and comforted him with the knowledge that he would find this killer. He only had to keep looking, keep pounding the pavement, and God would lead him. John only hoped it would be before someone else lost her life. But only God knew, and all John could do was obey.

Later, down at the station, he sat at his desk. He laid the three pictures Taylor had given him out in front of him on his desk. With his fingertips, he moved his mouse, stirring his computer to action. While he waited for it to warm up so he could log on, he scanned the pictures. Instinctively, he picked up a pen and jotted notes of all he wanted to find on his computer: the country bars in and outside the Quarter within a ten-mile radius of the killings, the name of the owner of the radio station, and if any arrests listed employment at WKRN. Afterward he'd head to the radio station to see what else he could find. On Sunday he doubted someone in charge would be working, but with the right words, he should get some action. This was something he felt he couldn't delay.

In the silence of the office, John heard the *clickity-clack* as he tapped away on his keyboard. When he finished his lists, he printed a copy of each, clipped them in place inside a folder, and logged off.

First stop for him was the radio station, WKRN, the one that had been displayed on each of the victims' cars. When he arrived at the station, only one car was in the parking lot. . .probably because it was Sunday. It was what he had expected.

John entered the lobby, and the light above the inside door flashed *On the air*. He pushed the button on the side of the door and sat down. Hopefully someone would realize he was out there. He'd give them five minutes, ten tops, and then would find his own way back to the DJ on duty.

Waiting wasn't easy, especially with nothing to do. He took out his notepad and glanced over the notes he'd made at each of the crime scenes, as well as notes he had made from the ME's preliminary report at the scene. Probable COD, strangulation: petechial hemorrhaging and hemorrhaging over the back of the larynx and soft tissue over the cervical spine, along with ligature marks around the neck. Also noted were fingernail scrapings, but instead of being DNA from the perpetrator, the skin was from the victim. Each girl scratched her own neck trying to remove the rope, fighting for air to stay alive. Yet, in failing to do so, their hands fell back down on their purse, as if digging through it.

Suddenly, the door opened and a man, in radio-melodic tone, said, "Hi. Can I help you?"

John closed his pad and stuffed it in his top pocket. In the same move, he grabbed his ID and flashed it along with his badge, saying, "NOPD Detective Bradley. I have some questions I need answers to. Can you help me?"

The man's eyes grew wide as he opened the door wider. "We'll see. You'll have to come back here with me. I have to go back on the air in thirty seconds. I'm by myself for the moment. We can talk during songs. I'll put on a double play."

The detective followed him through the door to an isolated booth the size of a small office. The DJ closed the doors behind John and sat back down. He put his headphones back on, held up his hand is if to say, "One minute," and then flipped a few switches.

Suddenly that melodic voice rang out again, telling his listeners they were in for a treat. Back-to-back Alan Jackson. The man flipped a couple more switches and then removed his headset. "Now, what do you need?"

"I need to know if anyone has been fired in the past two months or if any of your listeners have filed any grievances against your station or any of your DJs."

The man's eyes widened as he sat back in his chair. "That

I'm not sure I can give to you, even if I knew it. It would only be scuttlebutt, gossip, coming from me. I just work here and listen to the talk around the station. The head honcho, Monica Williams, will be here tomorrow morning. You can ask her. She can give you all the facts our legal department will let her give."

"I need you to get Mac David, the owner, or Ms. Williams on the phone. This is a police emergency, and I need these answers now. It can't wait until tomorrow. Sorry."

The DJ nodded and picked up his phone. "Monica, darling, you need to get down to the station now. We have a policeman—" he turned toward the detective and asked, "Who are you again?"

"Detective John Bradley with NOPD homicide."

"Yeah, Sweet Cakes, it's Detective John Bradley with the New Orleans Police Department. He said he's with homicide, and he needs some answers now. It can't wait until tomorrow."

"I was told to call you or Mr. David. Do you want me to call him? I will."

John watched the man as his face gave away his enjoyment of hearing probably confusion and outrage from his superior.

"Sorry, Babe, you're the man in charge. Oops. Excuse me. Woman in charge. So you've got to come down here and help the detective, or I call Mac." His dissatisfaction for her being the boss spoke volumes in John's mind. When the DJ cradled the phone, he pointed toward the detective. "You can wait back out there in the lobby. She'll be here, she said, in fifteen minutes. But I'd count it as thirty."

John rose and was about to thank him, but the man focused back on his duties as if John was already gone. The DJ covered his ears once more with the apparatus he used to communicate with the city of New Orleans. Two quick flips on the soundboard and he was talking again in that melodic tone. John shut both doors behind him quietly and made his way back out into the lobby.

He flipped open his pad, but this time to a blank piece of paper and started jotting questions he had for the woman—Monica Williams, manager of the station. He listed a few questions on the blank paper and then left room for her answers. Flipping back to his notes on the homicides, he started with the first crime scene notes and scanned them to see if he had noted if the radio had been on in the car. He couldn't find anything on the first or the second, but he had noted it on the third. There he had Johnson cut off the radio. Of course, he wasn't first on the scene to any of these crimes. He'd have to check with each officer who had been first on the scene the other two nights. Each, John remembered, had stated in their report they had been driving slowly through the Quarter and around the exterior watching for anything out of the ordinary. According to procedure, both would have noted whether they had turned off the engine or the radio upon their arrival. Had the same man found all three, it probably would have clicked as something of importance. But to three different officers, this wouldn't have seemed important.

Taking a deep breath, he slowed his mind down. John didn't want to get his hopes up too high, but it was the first possible connection that had been found. If this wasn't the connection, where would he turn next? He hoped the sticker meant something significant.

As he was about to look at the pictures on the walls, the

outer door opened and in walked a woman clad in tight jeans and a slinky top hanging off of one shoulder. She smacked her gum as she extended long fingers with freshly polished nails, much longer than the norm. They had to be fake. She could kill someone with her fingernails alone.

John rose to his feet and grabbed her extended hand. "Mrs. Williams."

"It's Miss." She led him to her office. "Have a seat, Detective, and tell me what you need."

John took the seat she offered and flipped his pad to the questions he had listed for her. Within half an hour they were through, and he was leaving out the door when she asked, "Do you think one of these people I gave you have something to do with these killings we've had lately?"

"We're just following leads, Miss Williams. I can't tell you any more than that. Thanks for your cooperation."

He had his list of bars. Should he try to cover as many as possible right now, or wait and start fresh on these tomorrow with Brown and Johnson? John checked a few bars out on his own, but to no avail. Giving up for the night, he headed home. As tired as he was now, tonight he would make up for some of the sleep he had lost last night. . .maybe not.

Chapter 12

Monday arrived, and John woke before the alarm. At least he'd slept all night this time.

When the coffee finished dripping, he poured himself a cup and strode out onto the front porch. Letting the screen door fall back into place, he slipped over to the porch swing. Lowering his six-foot frame down onto one side of the swing, he relaxed, a cup in one hand and the other resting across the back of the swing. Gently he pushed the swing into a slow, easy rhythm. Taking a sip of the dark brew, he scanned his surroundings, enjoying the light breeze.

A sigh escaped. His neighborhood didn't have the same calming effect that Taylor's terrace projected, but he felt that sense of peace at the moment. It was only because it was still early in the morning. In the next thirty minutes, traffic would grow.

It hadn't started flowing freely yet as he sipped his coffee, so he leaned back in his seat and kept the motion of the swing going with his foot. John had a big day ahead of him. With no luck last night, he prayed today would give him insight into which way to go next.

Trying not to think about work just yet, John noted the thick green lawn that spread everywhere except around the massive roots of an old oak tree. The yard was plain and simple. He had kept it that way on purpose. With his job, he had no time to prune flowerbeds or trim bushes. His yard had one nice shade tree that seemed to reach to the top of the sky. Acorns dropped in masses into the yard. Squirrels gathered their meals and chased one another across the lawn. Watching animals in their natural habitat always brought peace to his soul.

At the corner of his lot stood a black wrought-iron lamp-post with three large round bulbs. These lights illuminated his yard from dusk until dawn. When he had the time, he sat out at night as well. Lately, that free time had eluded him.

Glancing at his home, the peaceful yard, and then the empty spot next to him on the swing, he wondered if maybe he was ready to fill that emptiness in his home, as well as in his heart. He'd thought this two years ago, when he had proposed to Jennifer, but her death caused him to slip back into his old way of thinking: single was the only way for a detective to live his life. But, again, John was tired of coffee for one and coming home to an empty house at night. Should he stay open to finding that one special woman and falling in love—a special someone to fill his free time up with love?

"*She's the one.*"

John looked around. Where did that come from? *Are You*

talking to me, God? Or is that me fantasizing? Could Taylor be that person? Could he marry a woman who lived her life in such danger? She lived a life with screwy hours, just like his. Maybe they could coexist and build something special. He knew he was drawn to her looks. He had to admit it even though he didn't want to.

He moaned. Who was he kidding? "God, if that was You, I think You need to rethink Your words."

This case, like others, stole all his free time. John needed to concentrate on that, not on a woman. He needed to find the killer and find him now, for the city's sake as well as his own.

By six he was drinking his second cup of coffee, and the noise level grew, as did the traffic. The turmoil made it hard to stay outside. With the peace gone, the pleasure disappeared as well. Time didn't allow him hanging around outside any longer anyway. Taking that last swig of the black brew, he rose and headed back inside.

Through the windows spilled the first rays of morning light, reflecting on his highly polished wood floor. The bright shine was thanks to his wonderful housekeeper, Mrs. Evelyn Brumfield. She said she kept a bright polish on his floor and furnishings because he left her so very little to do. When she came over biweekly, she wanted to earn her pay. Otherwise, Evelyn felt she was stealing his money with what little work she had to do to keep the place looking good.

He liked his housekeeper. Evelyn was a widow raising her two grandchildren on her own. John never heard the woman complain. Janie, Mrs. Brumfield's daughter, had run off with some guy who came down one Mardi Gras and never came back for her daughter and son. It broke the seven-year-old twins' little hearts, which broke Mrs. Brumfield's. So the woman simply loved them more than enough to heal their wounds of abandonment—first by their birth father, then their mother—and raised them as her own.

The house grew brighter as the sun rose to peek through the windows. John didn't like dark, closed-in spaces, so he kept no draperies or blinds over his windows, except in the bedroom. Sometimes he had to sleep in the daytime and needed complete darkness to fall asleep. On the outside of all his windows, black bars protected his home from unwanted entries, but neither the sun nor moonlight was blocked from entering freely into his home. Some windows had custom stained glass in muted colors while other panes were beveled glass. He liked the openness, yet the privacy they allowed.

Pouring another cup of coffee, he started getting ready for work. In less than half an hour he was backing his car out of the garage. His quiet corner, Bienville Street and St. Patrick, was no longer quiet.

John arrived at the office and turned on his computer. While waiting for the slow connection, he pulled out his hard files from the filing cabinet on the new murder, as well as the two previous murders, and stacked them on his desk. When his system was ready, he clicked open the large new file on his computer where he had stored all three of these killings yesterday afternoon. Today he would get the coroner's report on the latest victim. Then it should be confirmed, as he'd thought after the second, that there was a serial killer in New Orleans taking his anger and bitterness out on unsuspecting, undeserving females.

Making extra copies of the list of country bars he didn't

get to yesterday, as well as the information given to him by the radio station, he laid them next to the files on his desk as he waited for his detectives, Buford Johnson and Leon Brown, to come in this morning. Around the station they referred to Buford as "Buck."

Both were usually in by 6:30, so John made a fresh pot of coffee in the large office next door where his men and a few other detectives shared the bullpen. As he fixed himself his fourth cup—but who was counting?—his men strolled into the room, heading straight for the coffee. Leon carried a box of doughnuts that he placed on the table next to the pot of coffee.

"Morning, gentlemen. I have some new info we'll talk over while you eat your breakfast." The doughnuts were a ritual that the two had followed for as long as John could remember. They took turns bringing in the doughnuts, but that was what they ate every morning. It was a good thing they both burned up the calories they took in by going to the academy gym three times a week, when work permitted.

"Chief, did you get another lead? Someone called something in?" Buck poured himself a cup.

John smiled a half smile. "Better than that. We may have a connection between all three victims. Get your coffee and come to my office."

Opening the three folders he had stacked on top of each other, John laid them out with the pictures of the cars on top. Buck and Leon marched in, each carrying a cup in one hand and a doughnut in the other. Both plopped into the empty chairs set in front of John's desk.

"Whatcha got?" Buck asked.

"Without getting any sticky sugar on the pictures, check them out. See if you notice anything."

Instead of handling the pictures themselves, both sat up in their chairs and leaned forward to scan the pictures. Leon took another bite of his doughnut as he sat back, shaking his head. "Sir, we've looked at these before. I still don't see anything."

Buck wiped his fingers and then set his cup down, as well as his doughnut and napkin. Picking up two of the pictures and looking at the third shot still lying on top of the file, he said, "None of them seem to mind messing up their car bumpers with stickers. That's something I won't allow my wife or kids to do."

John slapped his desk as he said, "That's it."

"What? They junk up their cars—that's their connection?" Brown asked with a smirk. "And just where does that lead us? Put out an APB on all junky yards and messy houses?"

"Stow it. That's not it." John lifted a brow. "Well, it is and it isn't. Buck, you were close. I didn't see it at all. It was that reporter, Taylor Jaymes, who noticed the connection."

"That looker with the red hair?" the detective asked as he laid the pictures down. Buck snatched up his doughnut and took another bite.

John ignored Buck's comment. "They all had bumper stickers advertising one particular country radio station. WKRN."

"And that's the connection?" Brown eyed the lieutenant and then Buck.

"Yes, it is. I followed up on WKRN and paid them a visit yesterday. Found out one of their employees was terminated just over two weeks ago. . .about the time of the first murder."

That got their attention.

"We need to take a closer look at Michael Guidry. WKRN's manager fired him with good cause, right before the killings started. It seems this man has a temper and started a couple of fights at the station with his coworkers." Holding his hands up as if in surrender, he said, "I know it's a stretch, battery to murder, and to think he'd be killing women who listened to the station just because he got fired. . .but people have killed for less."

"That makes sense, sir. Did you get an address on the guy?"

"Yes, I did. We're going to pay him a visit. I also made a list of bars to check out. I printed some copies of the victims' photos for each of us. Today, I need us to pay each bar a visit with the pictures and see if anyone recognizes the faces, and if so, find out when the last time was that they were seen at the establishment. Maybe we'll get lucky. The main thing is, we now have a connection."

"So your theory of it being a serial killer is correct," Detective Brown stated, almost in a question form.

"Yes. We should get—"

The buzzing of his phone interrupted him. "Bradley," John said as he answered his phone. He heard the ME in his ear.

"I've got that completed report for you. . .well, some of the test results we are still waiting on, but you know what I mean. You want me to e-mail a copy to you?"

"Yes, please. If you could send it now, I'd appreciate it. We were just talking about it. Did everything match the other two?"

Silence hung for less than a minute. "Unfortunately, they did."

"Okay. Thanks. I'll be watching for your report."

"Was that Bob Jenkins?" Buck asked. "What timing! Almost like the ME has a bug in your office, Chief. Better look out."

Brown flicked his brows up and down and then glanced into each corner of the office as he clowned around. "Hidden microphones or cameras. Big brother is watching."

Comic relief. All stations needed it, and Brown was theirs. He kept the mood light around the station, but sometimes John didn't care for it, especially when they were working a string of cases.

"Yeah. Let me read his report before we talk further. Here's the info on Michael Guidry. You two go talk to him. See where he was on the nights in question and get a feel for his attitude toward the station."

"I listen to that station myself, Chief. I even remember 'The Crazy Cowboy Mikey,' as they called him on late-night air at WKRN. That was probably why he got fired. Being on so late at night, he thought no one cared how he talked. He got pretty wild and ugly sometimes with his callers." Detective Brown shook his head.

"That's what I was told, and it caused a few heated arguments between him and his relief. Go check him out, and call me when you finish up the interview. If you don't feel the need to pull him down to the station, we'll divide up the list of bars, and I'll help check them out."

"We're on it, Chief," Brown said with enthusiasm. "Come on, Buck."

As soon as the two left, John called his captain to let him know, as promised, what he'd gathered over the weekend.

He knew the captain already knew about the third killing, so he was prepared for some more yelling. The good news was, when John gave him the leads they were following, the captain stayed somewhat calm as he said, "Sounds like we're finally making some progress."

Glad to get that behind him, John hung up the phone. Now he could move forward, to the other things at hand. Instead, he thought of Taylor. Heading for his filing cabinet, he muttered, "This is ridiculous."

Pulling out a drawer, he flipped through the folders, found the one he was looking for, then yanked it out. He thought if he put his mind on another case while he waited for his guys to call, surely he would quit thinking about that nerve-racking redhead. The file he pulled was on robberies in the homes near Jackson Square. She wasn't the reporter involved in writing stories on that case as far as he remembered; that should make a difference. Maybe he could stay focused on the job instead of her. After flipping through the hard copy file, he turned to his computer and searched to see if similar robberies had been reported elsewhere in the city. Maybe these guys weren't just robbing in the Quarter.

Slouching down in his chair, he scrolled through the file one page at a time. Studying the list of items that had been stolen and the way the perpetrator entered each apartment, he thought he might get a clue as to who the perpetrator was. He might figure out if it was a gang of kids or a known burglar with a past history. Sometimes there was a rhyme and a reason that could link these things together or at least lead him in the right direction. They were already watching known markets for these type of stolen goods—electronics, jewelry, and paintings.

But these thieves hadn't taken flat screen TVs, DVD players, or stereo systems—harder-to-trace items for the police department. They could be sold on the streets to individuals or behind the scenes at outlets of used furniture and electronics.

The items stolen were insured by the owners but not by the same agency. John had pictures of most of the items and copies were in the computer file. An active link continued searching, should a similar piece come up for sale on a resale website. Those places were a wonderful way to unload your own items, but little did criminals realize the police department was linked in 24-7 and would be instantly notified, should a stolen piece of merchandise pop up for sale. The thieves would be apprehended within six to twelve hours of the attempt of the sale. The high-end items that were stolen were probably sold through a major fence that handled expensive jewels and pricey paintings. The burglars knew what they were taking.

As he scanned the various pictures of the jewelry that had been downloaded into the computer file, he came to a pair of ruby red earrings that sparkled with brilliance. The brilliance of the red manifested a flash of a long ivory neck supporting a mass of curly red hair twisted up and piled on a head as those dangling red earrings hung from the delicate lobes of none other than Taylor Jaymes' ears.

With more power than was needed, he clicked the arrow and moved on to the next item. It displayed a delicate necklace made of pearls and diamonds. The ivory of the pearls reflected the ivory of her skin in his mind's eye. "Enough!"

He clicked his computer off and rose. As he started pacing back and forth and then around his desk, over to the door, and back to his desk again, frustration taunted every muscle, every nerve fiber. How could she dominate his thoughts like that? He wobbled his head, trying to shove out thoughts of her. "Ooh," he muttered and then followed the same path on the floor again. Finally he gave in to his impulse.

Snatching up the phone, he glanced at her business card on his desk and punched out the number. The receptionist patched his call through to Taylor's desk. He heard the phone ring over and over again. No answer.

"Ugh," he groaned, slamming down the phone. *She's probably out somewhere stirring up trouble, digging up information for her story.*

No sooner had he replaced the receiver in the cradle than his phone started ringing. Ripping the receiver off the base, he barked, "Hello!"

"Yikes. I hope I have the wrong number," a sweet voice said tenderly. A light chuckle followed her words.

He smiled as he recognized the warm voice, full of laughter. "Always the comedian. What's that old saying? A million comedians out of work and. . .I forget the rest. But you get the message." His voice softened somewhat. "You're not funny."

He heard a soft giggle in his ear and then she said, "You're not as tough as you think or pretend to be, are you, Detective Bradley?"

John's smile fell. "I thought you were going to call me John?" He leaned back in his chair, picked up a pencil, and then twirled it in his fingers. Unfortunately nothing came to mind to say, but he found pleasure in not saying a word, just hanging on the line, knowing she was on the other end.

Yes. This is what I need.

For some unexplainable reason, this girl made him feel relaxed—when she wasn't in the same room with him getting into his business of crime. Friday night, hearing her voice across the table, had done this to him and again now. Somehow, some way, she made him feel a sense of joy. John couldn't explain it. He didn't care to even try to figure it out. It just was.

Chapter 13

Taylor laid back in her recliner as she listened to him talk. She traced her cheek as she thought of the possibility of his touch on her face.

He asked her if she had forgotten he asked her to call him John.

No. Of course not.

"I figured it was the pizza that turned your head or the excitement of the moment—you know, me finding the connection. I didn't want to chance getting chewed out for 'insubordination,' or whatever it's called." Her smile broadened as a spurt of laughter filtered through the line.

All right, he does have a sense of humor. She liked what she heard.

"Trust me. I don't say anything I don't mean."

Trust him? Of course she trusted policemen in general and the brotherhood, as well as firemen and other men of authority who risked their lives daily for the people, but him? Just his voice made her think irrationally. How could she trust him? Or was it herself she couldn't trust?

Taylor sighed but covered the mouthpiece so he wouldn't hear her. She'd have to think on that. She trusted what he stood for, but as far as the way he made her feel, she wasn't too sure. "I'll try to remember that. If you say it, you mean it. Okay. Now, for the reason I called. I was checking to see if you were doing anything with what I told you?"

The soft, friendly voice disappeared, and a hardened, clipped tone shot through the line. "Of course. That's what the city pays me to do."

She heard the tension in his voice along with the words he spat, but she couldn't complain. Taylor was the one who brought up business. "Yikes! I did it again, didn't I? I know how to push your buttons. I hope you know I don't do it on purpose."

He cleared his throat. "Sorry. I spent most of Sunday following up on the lead you gave me. Today is no exception. My men are following up on something I found yesterday, and then the three of us will be questioning some other leads. . .thanks to your insightfulness."

"I see."

"By the way, that was good detective work on your part. We hope after today to be able to narrow the bars down to one or two in the ten-mile radius of where the bodies were found. At least now we're moving forward again."

"That's good. I was going to tell you I spoke to Trudy's neighbor, Sally, and she said Trudy went out every weekend. Come Monday, she would tell both her and her daughter about some of the people she'd met and the good times she was having. By the way Trudy described it to Sally, she felt certain it was a bar or a lounge with a nice-size dance floor. Trudy talked about dancing and having fun, but Sally couldn't be positive as to which one it was. Trudy had mentioned the name in passing, but her neighbor couldn't recall it. She's supposed to check with her teenage daughter and see if she remembered where Trudy went clubbing, but I haven't heard back from her yet."

Taylor decided to keep it to herself that she had gone to the radio station Sunday afternoon. She had dropped by the station on the chance he may be there so she could update him on what she found out about Trudy's activities. He was leaving, so instead she followed him.

This morning she went back to the radio station to see what the DJ would tell her. Unfortunately, she didn't get very far, but the DJ did say a detective had been there the day before and talked to the manager. He also hinted he might be willing to talk if she would go have a drink with him after work. Flicking her brows at him, she implied she might get back in touch. Of course, she knew John had been there, so she made no commitment of joining the man later for drinks. She'd get her info from the detective, if she played her cards right. If not, then she'd contact the DJ. Taylor could keep it business, no matter what that DJ thought he'd get out of it. She knew better.

"That's good," John said. "If you ever decide to give up your writing career, you'd make a good detective. That'll help us today as we go around to the various bars in the area. Yesterday I met with WKRN's manager and got the name of a person of interest. So that bumper-sticker connection has given us two leads to follow, in separate directions. We'll see what we find."

She paused. His compliment touched her deeply. She didn't believe he was one to dole out compliments too freely. "Thank you. I'll keep that job offer in mind, but remember, to be a good journalist, you have to be a good investigator, so I'm probably where I need to be. I don't think I could carry a gun." In her line of work, she probably should learn how to shoot one, protect herself, but that wasn't on her to-do list. "While we're talking about the case, have you thought any more on what I asked you?"

He didn't hesitate to respond, so apparently he had. "You're hoping I changed my mind. I know. I hear it in your voice. You want the exclusive and all the details on the investigation."

At that moment, she thought she heard a hard snap across the line. Was he chewing gum? Or had something broken? Maybe he broke a pencil, wishing it was her neck. *Eeek!* She probably should back off and wait on him, but she wanted this story so desperately. She needed this story.

"Ah, come on, Detec. . .John." She softened her voice as she called him by name. "Give a girl a chance," she pleaded, trying to keep the conversation on a more personal level, hoping it would keep the lines of communication between the two of them open.

John tossed the broken pencil in the garbage as he shook his head. When he called her, he had planned to give her the exclusive. So why hold back now? Shaking his head, he knew.

He had changed his mind when she didn't answer his call. The lieutenant figured she was off somewhere getting into trouble, trying to get too close to his crime.

He sighed. That wasn't fair on his part to change his mind so easily. She'd earned the story. If they broke the case soon, it would be thanks to her. They'd had no leads until she discovered one. She found the connection; she deserved the story. Besides which, if he made the deal with her, he could control her words to the press. That was a plus. He would make it part of the agreement. The positives and negatives of allowing her into his investigations bounced through his head. Should he give her the exclusive, or not? Could he handle being around her so much. . .or at least talking to her on a daily basis? Could he keep a distance between them? She played havoc on his emotions, but he shouldn't make his decision based on his reaction to her. He needed to do what was best for the case.

"John, are you still there?" a sweet voice murmured into his ear.

"Actually, I've been giving it some thought. In fact, I called your office a short time ago, but you weren't there." He knew it was the right thing to do, and he urged himself forward. He would survive the daily contact. He would make sure to keep an emotional distance between them. The main thing was, this way, giving her the exclusive, he controlled what leaked to the public. For now, he needed her to keep the discovery of the connection under wraps. She found it. It was hers to disclose if she so chose, but if he agreed to give her the exclusive on the full investigation through to the final arrest, he could make her silence part of the stipulation. . .make her hold off on releasing the connection at this time.

"You called me?"

He was about to tell her the news, but her question distracted him. Her voice literally purred. Maybe it was her tone that caught him off guard.

A light laugh sifted through the line. "I'm at home. That's the beauty of being a journalist. Sometimes you're working out of your home office. It's not a nine-to-five job. Of course, sometimes it's twenty-hour days."

"Sounds like you're lucky. And yes, I'd called you. I called to tell you I'm going to give you the exclusive. By that, I mean anything major we discover, I will let you know, but you have to keep those things I share only with you under wraps until the end. . .until I say you can print the whole story. Sometimes it's those little things that help us pull everything together, and we don't want to give the killer a heads-up."

He exhaled. "And anything else you come up with, you share with us as you did earlier. But it also means when we close in on the killer, you'll be given advance warning, if possible, so you can scoop the others as well as have more details from the investigation that you can reveal in your story. For the time being, I have to ask you not to write about the connection. It might signal our perp that we're getting close and make him do something crazy."

"No problem. I promise. Thanks."

"Great. Well, I'll let you go, and I will be in touch."

Taylor sighed. As she hung up the phone, she whispered, "He'll be in touch. I wonder. . ." She closed her eyes and remembered her earlier thoughts, wondering what it would feel like to have him brush her cheek with his fingertips. Warmth spread across her face. His brilliant blue eyes came to mind. . .and the dark waves that crowned his head. Her fingers itched to feel their softness. Taylor remembered the way he had reached out and almost touched her face Saturday night, but then thought better of it.

A man in control of his emotions. Too bad.

He may not have followed through on his desires, but she saw the look in his eyes, the wanting. At that moment, she knew he'd thought about her as a woman, not a reporter.

She wished she'd said something that night and gotten him to stay awhile longer, but she hadn't. Taylor had been mesmerized into silence by that man. She laughed. What was that called? An oxymoron. Complete opposites—Taylor and silence. Taylor was never known for her silence, except when she was slipping around in the dark trying to get closer to a crime going down. . .anything to get her story.

Suddenly she opened her eyes. She was going to be working with him. That thought stirred her sanity.

Surveying her living room, she decided maybe she should pick up while she had a few minutes. Her place wasn't dirty; it just wasn't neat. Maybe she should take the time now to return her mom's call. Taylor never called her mom or Tina back—not the calls they left at work for her or the ones they left on her home answering machine. Instantly, she recalled the stranger's message at work—and then again on her home phone. There was no reason stated as to why any of them called, so what were they up to? She was assuming the three calls were connected. As busy as Taylor had been, she didn't take time to call any of them back. What were they up to? And who was that man? How did he get her home number? A fix-up? It must be, but she hoped not.

That man could have had a lead for her—but that call should have gone only to the paper. . .not her house phone. Could it have been so important that the paper gave away her home number? No. It had to be her family who passed it out freely, with hopes of finding her the "perfect man."

Glancing at her watch, she jumped out of her chair. *No time for my family now or that man. I'll call later. I need to get to the office and update the boss. What a story! Mr. Cox will be so pleased.*

By ten thirty she was in Mr. Cox's office. "He committed the story to me, Chief! I think it was because I found the connection for the victims. . .but a girl's gotta do what a girl's gotta do. The detective even went as far to say it might be the break they'd been looking for."

Mr. Cox leaned back in his massive chair, lifting his feet to rest on the edge of the desk. Pressing his fingertips together across his stomach, he said, "I knew you could do it. I had no doubts."

Taylor talked with him a little longer, explaining the connection and about the promise not to release anything yet. That was the only way, she said, that Detective Bradley would agree to give her the scoop on the story, all the little details he wouldn't be giving to the other reporters.

"I guess I'll extend that week I promised you. As long as you stay on top of it and I can spare you. Of course, you still have to submit something daily for the paper on the killings. We're not going to fall behind. There will be something you can tell the public. So do me proud."

"You got it, Chief."

Taylor left his office full of anticipation for the week ahead.

Chapter 14

She returned to her desk to find another note from that same man, Tim Robertson. This time he left his name but still didn't say what the call was about. Who was he, and what did he want? Calling her through the paper again, maybe it was about a story. But why did he call her home phone, and where did he get her number?

Picking up her phone she punched in the numbers scribbled after his name. *Beep, beep, beep* rang in her ear. *A busy signal.* "Oh well, Mr. Robertson, I can't keep trying now. I'll check you later," she said aloud. She hung up, disconnecting the call.

Instead of waiting around to hear what Detective Bradley and his men turned up, she spent the rest of the day doing a little detective work of her own. *Oh yeah, John, not Detective Bradley,* she reminded herself. That she had to work on. John's face leaped into her brain. He was good-looking—and smart.

She had to give him credit for being a great detective, too. She'd looked up his record on the force. Before now, only two unsolved cases. Who could blame him on one of them? All the evidence burned up in the fire. He cleared his cases by not giving up. If he had any unsolved cases, he held on to the files and kept returning to them in between working on other new cases, and he did it until he closed the cases. The man was relentless.

Back to the business at hand. Who knows? Maybe I'll find another link to the present case he has pending. John would like that, and so would I.

Stopping at the first country bar that was about ten miles out from the scene, but not in the Quarter, she found the cleaning crew getting the club ready for another night of business. Those guys weren't there working at night, so they would be of no help to her. She needed the bartender or a couple of waitresses to take a peek at the pictures of the vics. They'd be the only ones who might identify them for Taylor. She'd have to come back later to this one.

Next stop, she found a country bar where the band was doing a little rehearsing. They might remember one of them. Taylor sashayed over to the band with a picture of each of the girls. She managed to recover other shots of each of the victims through the paper, looking through their archives. Each girl had been involved with something in the past four years: a wedding, a wake, and a political affair. She found one for each girl. Unfortunately not all pictures were current, but she managed to zoom in on the girls in each photo and make a small replica of all three. The drummer recognized Trudy immediately.

"Yeah, I remember her. She used to come in here every weekend. I remember, because she used to flirt with me. I kind of liked it, but I have a wife at home so I couldn't follow through. Well, I could," he said and then shrugged, "but I wouldn't. So it became just light talk, but still friendly. Then, about six months ago, she quit coming in. I figured she got her a guy or found another bar she liked better."

"So when you let her know there was no possible way you'd be more than a friend, did you notice her hanging out with any other particular guy?"

"Trudy was friendly with everybody, but not in the way you're talking about."

She thanked him for his time and his candor. When Taylor left, she drove around some more and found three more bars in the vicinity of where the bodies had been discovered. After checking each out, she decided she'd have better luck at night, so she turned her car in the direction of Trudy Walker's. She figured it was late enough for Sarah's daughter to be home. Maybe she could help pinpoint the bar Trudy went to toward the end of her life. That was what they needed to find. She knew that there they would find what they needed to get a handle on the killer—their next lead at the least.

Sarah opened the front door wide and called out behind her, "Annie, that reporter I told you about is here." Turning toward Taylor, she said, "Please come in."

Taylor stepped inside and waited. There was no need to take a seat. "This should only take a few minutes."

Suddenly, rushing into the front room was a cute little blond, a younger version of her mom. She came to an abrupt halt once inside the doorway. Her cheeks blushed as she looked down and said, "Hi. Momma said I might be able to help you find Trudy's killer."

"Well, by telling me this, we might be able to help the police find the killer. I appreciate your help. Do you recall the name of the club Trudy went to in the last few weeks of her life?"

"She used to go to Mudbugs and Mustang Sally's, but lately she had been going to one she found in the Quarter. She didn't tell me the name of it, but she said it's one that bought out two businesses, side-by-side, and knocked out a wall to make the place roomy." The young girl glanced up when she finished talking and then looked away as quickly. "It's a fairly new place."

Immediately, Taylor thought of the one near Rampart and Bienville. She'd hit that one tonight. "Well, thank you Annie, for your help. And Sarah, I appreciate you sharing with me as well about Trudy. I almost feel like I know her, and that always helps when we write about victims. It adds a more personal touch. I think that's important."

When she left Sarah's, she took some time to research the third victim, like she had done with the first two: workplace, family members, neighbors, and friends. Trisha McIntyre had been recently divorced and lived in a condo in the Warehouse District. She had legally reclaimed her maiden name. Taylor noted to check out the ex. He may be holding a grudge. . . a big one. Who knew? This could be a copycat killing just to cover up another murder. When married, she was Trisha McIntyre-Matthews. The brown-haired woman had never had any children, so she was alone, just like the other two.

Next, Taylor took time to visit with some family members

of each of the first two girls. She liked to give family members a little time to grieve before detailed interviews. First off, their minds would be clearer, and secondly, she wouldn't upset them as much. Especially when she explained she was working with the police.

Trudy's mom explained they didn't know how Trudy spent her nights or where. They only talked occasionally—not that there was a rift between them, but just neither had the time to get together often, even on the phone. Boy did Taylor know how that was. She didn't have time to get with her mom and sister as much as they would like, but still they kept calling. Wasn't Trudy lucky that her mom understood?

Mrs. Gauthreaux, on the other hand, was very helpful. Although tears rimmed her eyes as she spoke, she answered all of Taylor's questions. She said, "Stephanie had recently broken up with her boyfriend, Larry David. Spelled like the boy who slew the giant, David, but pronounced *Da-veed*," she explained. "So now when she went out. . .I mean so lately when she went out, it was with the women in her office. I think they met up at the lounges. Some were even in the Quarter, but you'll have to ask her coworker, Janie Goudeaux, the names of the places they went. I have no idea."

After wiping at her wet cheeks with the back of her hand, she continued, "I never approved of her going to nightclubs, but she was a grown woman and had to make her own decisions. I wish now I had argued with her instead. Maybe she'd be alive today. You raise them, teach them morals, but today's generation feels like they need to party all the time. I don't understand it." She pressed her fingers to her temples and whispered, "I'm sorry. I don't mean to burden you with my feelings."

Taylor touched the woman's hand gently and squeezed. "I understand. I don't have any more questions right now, Mrs. Gauthreaux, but I want to say that you can't blame yourself. Like you said, she was old enough to make her own decisions. And you can't even blame her. It was the killer who was in the wrong. No one deserves to be murdered."

"Thank you."

This time, Taylor reached out and hugged the woman. *Where did that come from?* Taylor wasn't one who showed emotions. Not a hugger or a kisser. . .just a talker. She didn't even hug her own mom much. What had gotten into her? She thanked the lady for being so helpful.

"No problem, Ms. Jaymes." Mrs. Gauthreaux reached out and grabbed both of Taylor's hands and held them tightly. "I recognized your name from the paper. You have quite a reputation with helping the police solve crimes. I hope you can do the same for my daughter's murder." Another tear slipped down her cheek.

Squeezing the woman's hands, Taylor thought maybe that was why she felt connected to this woman. Stephanie's mom already knew Taylor through her writing.

Yes. "I'll do my best," she said.

"They ought to be very grateful for all the work you do to help them."

"Thank you, Mrs. Gauthreaux, for helping me get more information. It helps me to write better stories on the victims. Making them more human to the reader. Helps them know your daughter's heart."

"I don't worry about you and how you write Stephanie's story. I know it will be done well. And I hope you help the police find Steph's killer. Thank you for caring."

From there, Taylor decided to pay a visit to a neighbor of the third victim. This woman, Wendy, had the condo next door for as long as Trisha lived there. In fact, they moved in only a week apart from one another. Maybe they had connected.

"As a matter of fact, Trisha and I became fairly tight friends recently. We didn't connect in the beginning. We were both married and lived our own lives. But since each of our divorces, we kind of connected. We both had similar problems with our husbands. Mine was an emotional abuser while hers physically abused her. But the pain was the same on the inside."

"Had her ex-husband been physically abusive to her since their divorce?"

"No, not that I know of. Not physically, anyway, but it's because she wouldn't let him near her. Over the phone he played a lot of mind games on her, trying to get her to take him back. It was stressful for her in the beginning, but what could she do? Report him to the cops? For what? Not being nice on the phone? As long as he stayed away from her, she said she could handle the mind games. She planned to get rid of her house phone and go to only a cell. She'd never had one of those before. With a cell, he wouldn't be able to get her number, and it would have made it harder for him to agitate her. At least now he won't be able to torment her at all."

Taylor wondered if the police knew about her ex-husband. This again could be the copycat she was thinking of earlier. Instead of following that line, Taylor decided to stay on the track she'd been following with the other victims. "Did Trisha go to bars at night?"

"No. Usually we'd go out to places together to eat and then to the movies. Neither of us was looking for a new man in our lives and truly didn't feel like faking a good time. . .until this Friday night, anyway. I don't know what changed her, but Trisha decided she wanted to try out this new place someone at work told her about. She loved to dance and hadn't done it in years. I had a bad headache so chose not to go. She said she was going to go check it out anyway. She couldn't explain, but she felt it was important to get out again. Trisha even said it might work out better if she went alone, since it would be her first time out in a long time. She'd be around people who didn't know her, and I think she thought she could relax better. Maybe she even felt it would be a way to be free of all the past. What a mistake! I urged her to be careful, but it didn't help." Wendy's shoulders dropped as she talked about her neighbor. "Maybe if I'd gone, she'd still be alive."

"You can't blame yourself," Taylor said as she rose to leave. "Thank you for your help." Taylor handed the woman her card, and Wendy promised she'd call if she thought of anything that might help.

On the ride back to her apartment, adrenaline flowed. A good story always excited her. She thought this might be the best of her career so far. Maybe this would be the one to bring her one step closer to attaining that Pulitzer Prize she so wanted. Who knew? Wouldn't her dad be proud. . .maybe even her mom? No. The only thing that would make her mom proud would be to find a gold band on the third finger of Taylor's left hand.

"Sorry, Mom," she whispered in the car. A man was the

last thing she wanted or needed.

Suddenly she turned right. *Why not?* Since she was near the Garden District, she might as well swing by her parents and pay them a short visit before going home. She'd be busy from now until this killer was found, so she had better take the opportunity while she had the chance.

Chapter 15

Late that afternoon, after talking with Buck and Brown, Detective Bradley discovered the three girls had been seen in two of the clubs near the area. The nightclubs outside the Quarter he interviewed had seen one of the victims and another had seen the other two victims, but no one club had seen all three of the women. So this was a step in the right direction.

"Sorry to say, Lieutenant, but we couldn't find Guidry," Buck admitted. "Although his rent is paid up till the end of the month and all his clothes appear to be in his apartment, he is nowhere to be found."

"Maybe he skipped town?" Brown suggested.

"Maybe," John said, and Buck nodded in agreement.

"Or maybe he took off to clear his head or went looking elsewhere for a job. Maybe he has nothing to do with the killings." Brown sounded like he didn't want Guidry to be found guilty. Of course, if the man enjoyed the DJ, as a policeman he would want the guy to follow the law.

"But it wouldn't hurt to be sure," John reminded him. "It only takes a second to turn people's thinking around. You never know what will set someone off. And being fired from a job is at the top of that list of things that set people off."

"True," Buck said.

"Yeah, I know," Brown said as he rose from the chair with his head and shoulders drooping. "We'll check harder, Boss."

After the two detectives left his office, John wanted to call Taylor and ask her to scope the bars out with him tonight—mix a little business with pleasure. Not that he would find any pleasure in it. . .well, no, he would find plenty of pleasure in being near her. At least he had the other night at Dante's. He truly didn't mix pleasure in with business. That was the work code he lived by, and he wouldn't change it now. It would be strictly business. They would go as a couple simply to help people open up more to him. He felt certain people would talk freely if they only thought they were gossiping. Sometimes police made people nervous. Why? He didn't know. They did their job with the intent to serve and protect private citizens. Why wouldn't they want to help?

John's stomach growled. Since he'd be working tonight, he wouldn't have time to cook. He decided to run down to the cafeteria and eat a hot lunch. That should hold him through the night.

In the lunchroom, Gloria waited on him immediately, bringing him plenty of roast and gravy, along with an ample portion of green beans. "Here you go, Sugar. You don't have to wait in line. I fixed you all up. I even added a slice of that strawberry pie you love. Ponchatoula's finest."

Although John never gave her more than a few pleasant words that he could recall, she always seemed to make a bee-line to him when he entered the cafeteria. At times she appeared to be offering herself to him with her eyes. Kind of gave him the creeps, but because Jennifer had called her a friend, John tried to be polite and overlook her brash ways. "Thanks," he murmured as he took the tray and headed toward the cashier.

Before making his way to checkout, he stopped to pour himself a cup of hot tea. "I'll get that for you, Hon. Go take a seat, and I'll have it right out."

Pulling money from his pocket, John paid for his lunch and then found an empty table. He'd barely unwrapped his eating utensils and laid them down on a napkin before Gloria swished her way over to his table and set the cup of steaming hot tea down in front of him, along with a little cup of cream. The sugar was already on the table. "Here you go, Handsome."

"Thanks."

"Does that woman at your table the other morning having breakfast with you mean you're back in circulation? I thought you'd never get over Jennifer. You two were quite a pair. Glad you finally remembered you're not dead." She dragged her hand back slowly across the table as she leaned in toward John. "Glad you're back in the land of the living." Her lips curved into a smile.

Without thinking, John said, "That was a reporter, not a date. I don't think I'd bring my dates to the cafeteria."

"Ah, Sugar, didn't mean to offend you. Just you and your lady friend Jennifer used to eat in here all the time. I always hoped you'd drop her and give some of us other girls a chance."

How do you answer that? He thought they were friends. Instead of replying to her question, he said, "Thanks for the tea."

She took the hint and left without another word.

As he ate, he again pondered the idea of calling Taylor and getting her to go with him to a couple of the bars tonight to ask a few questions and snoop around. Bars were not his normal hangout anymore. He'd grown to enjoy going straight home from work, turning on a little Harry Connick Jr., Michael Bublé, or Frank Sinatra and then fixing himself a glass of iced tea. He would then relax out on the swing or in his recliner in the living room. There he enjoyed the music and the peace and quiet. That was how he spent his free time. It worked well for him.

Tonight the bars would be crowded, noisy, and the rooms full of smoke. He looked forward to none of this. Now, if he could persuade that reporter to go with him, maybe it would make the night a little more bearable.

Shaking his head, he decided against that. He didn't need to enjoy work. He needed a clear head. He needed to be able to focus. There was a purpose for his job, and he needed to be at his best. That was the only way to fight crime. He knew that was his purpose here on earth—to keep the peace and share the Word, wherever and whenever he could.

After lunch, he went back to his office and told Brown and Buck what he planned to do.

"Me and my old lady could hit a few as a couple and see

what we could find out. My sister-in-law could watch the kids for us. This would make Maddie excited about my job for a change." Buck stood, waiting for the okay.

"Lucy would get a kick out of it, too. Count me in, Boss."

That sounded like a good plan. In fact, it was what he'd thought about doing with Taylor. "Good idea."

So it was decided. Each would go to a different bar and see what they could find out. They'd meet in the morning and share the info. If anyone found something worth meeting together sooner and discussing, they would beep the other two and then all would meet back at the office.

John was the only one going alone tonight. He didn't mind. He was used to being a loner. Not that he was really alone. The Lord stayed right with him, giving John direction wherever he went. Tonight would be no different.

He ran home, showered, and shaved. His place was still clean from Ms. Evelyn's visit yesterday. With nothing to do for a couple of hours, he made himself lie down and try to take a nap. He'd need it so he could stay up as late as necessary.

Four hours later, his eyes popped open. Stretching his arms wide, he rose from the bed. The nap worked wonders, even though he didn't think he would fall asleep. At eight he was donning his jeans and a T-shirt. To hide his gun in his shoulder holster, he slipped on a dark blue blazer. It was made to dress up jeans or relax a pair of slacks. It did its job tonight. Looking in a mirror, he saw that it hid his weapon well and would help him blend in with the rest of the crowd. No one need be suspicious of him. In the movies the cop always stood out, but John always tried to blend in. He discovered more that way. People were more willing to talk.

By the time John walked through the front door of the bar, smoke filled the room. The music screamed out live and loud. The band's rendition of George Strait's "Ace in the Hole" blasted his ears.

Glancing around, he saw the place was packed, so he found a seat at the corner barstool for the time being. John wondered if Buck or Brown were at their locations yet. At least they had someone to talk to while they worked away the hours. He watched for a table to become free and ordered a Coke.

"With what? Whiskey? Gin?" the bartender replied.

"Coke over ice. Nothing extra."

"Still get charged for the alcohol whether you drink it or not."

John nodded. "I understand. Coke straight," he repeated one more time.

Looking around, he thought, *This would be so much easier if I had a woman on my arm.* Too bad Taylor wasn't with him. It wouldn't be a date. It would be business. She wanted the same thing he did—to find the killer. So why didn't he ask her to join him?

When the bartender set the filled glass in front of him, John laid three pictures on the table. Of course, these were headshots from the morgue, not a beautiful sight, but the women didn't look that bad. . .just dead.

The man's eyes rested on the pictures very briefly, one after the other, and then he looked back at John. "You a cop?"

He flipped open his wallet and revealed his badge. "Have you seen these women in here before?"

"That one," he said, pointing to Trudy Walker. "Not every weekend, but probably once a month. A friendly sort; that's why I remember her."

"What about the other two?" he asked as he handed the server a five-dollar bill and said, "Keep the change."

"A quarter. Thanks." The man glared at the five and then John. If they come in here, they don't get their drinks from the bar. Maybe they're always at the tables where the waitresses take their order. Check with them."

"I need another beer down here," a man already having had a few too many hollered to the bartender.

"Thanks," John told him, even though the man had already turned his back to go serve the other customer. Probably figured he'd get better tips from the drunk.

John sipped on his Coke as he waited for each waitress to come order her drinks for her tables. As they did, he took the opportunity to ask, "Have you seen these women in here before?"

The first two barely glanced at the pictures before shaking their heads and turning their backs on John.

What has come of this world today? No one seems to care anymore.

By the time he had a fresh cold Coke, he spotted a different waitress and approached her with the pictures as she stood next to the bar waiting for her order. "Hi, Miss. I'm Detective Bradley with NOPD, and I was wondering if you've seen any of these three women in here lately?"

She turned her head toward the dance floor, and he followed her gaze. *What is she looking for? These women are dead. They aren't in here tonight.*

"I haven't, but I'm new. They could be here now."

As she spoke, he started to look back toward her but caught a glimpse of beautiful red curls out on the floor and did a double take instead. Was that Taylor? Was she here? What was she trying to do, get herself killed? That was how she worked, if he remembered. She tried to get too close to the story. What better way than to be bait for the killer? Was she a fool?

He scanned the floor again and couldn't find the redhead, but he knew what he'd seen. He'd never seen hair so pretty before, so inviting, wanting a man to run his fingers through it. It had to be her. But where did she go?

"Sir? Did you hear me?"

Returning his stare to the waitress, he said, "Yes. Thank you for your time." John slipped back over to his stool and turned so he could watch the floor. He would find her, if it was the last thing he did.

"Ten-minute break. We'll be back soon," he heard over the speaker as the lights in the place rose to the next level, making it easier to look around.

Where was she?

Suddenly, two hands rested on his shoulders and he jumped. Swiveling, he rested his eyes on soft, shimmering red curls and luscious green eyes. "Taylor," he whispered, forgetting he was angry.

"John! I couldn't believe that was you." Excitement pealed from her voice. "I was out on the floor dancing and thought I saw you over here, but I told myself it couldn't be. You don't relax. You don't go clubbing. So what are you doing here? Are you alone, or do you have a date with you? The blond bombshell from the cafeteria?"

Remembering he was perturbed at this reporter right now, he spoke harshly. "What do you think I'm doing here? I'm working! The question is, what are *you* doing here?"

Chapter 16

Taylor slipped onto the barstool next to John and spoke in a voice barely above a whisper, so he leaned closer. "Lower your voice, and I'll be glad to tell you what I'm doing here. But the world doesn't need to know our business."

Music started up again as the band returned to the stage. He barely heard her last words as they opened with the lively tune of "Boot Scootin' Boogie" blasting through the air. John attempted to block out the band and the people around them as his gaze locked on her lips. He watched her speak more than he heard "our business." He knew by the tautness of her lips she wasn't too happy with him. Well, the feeling was mutual, so he scowled back at her. He didn't have to see his face to know what was written on it. He only hoped she got the message. Chasing a killer was *his* business, not hers.

Every cell in his being wanted to shout at her, telling her

what a fool she was to come here on her own. He knew what she was doing, trying to catch a killer. Mentally shaking his head, he corrected that. Chasing a story was what she was doing, even if it might cost her, her life.

Didn't she care? Humph! He grunted.

Why should he lower his voice? Because she said so? He was a cop. He had every right to be there and ask questions. He could yell if he wanted to, and everyone in this place had better listen to him.

Blowing out a gush of pent-up air, he admitted he didn't want them to listen right now. He wanted her to listen. In fact, he wanted her to know he was angry because she thought so little of her life. Was that the cop in him? Or the man in him that held this concern?

Seeing her pleading expression, he changed his mind. Lowering his voice, he said again, "Okay. So what are you doing here?" Taylor could have it her way for the moment. He listened for her answer, but it had better be a good one. John straightened stiffly on the barstool, giving her space.

When Taylor didn't answer him swiftly enough, he urged her along. "Well, I lowered my voice, and now I'm waiting." He watched as Taylor brushed a few strands of hair off her face. Part of him wanted to reach out and brush them away for her, but no, he couldn't do that. Averting his gaze for a second, he cleared the thought.

"I'm here working, too. The sooner we find out the bar they all three went to, the sooner we find the killer."

"That figures." John rolled his eyes as he threw his hands up into the air. "Are you alone? Or did you at least bring a date to protect you?"

This time, instead of brushing her hair back softly, she tossed that long mane that hung over her right shoulder roughly behind her back and glared in disgust. "Look, John, I don't know what your problem is. I've been doing my job for ten years or better, with no difficulty whatsoever. Tonight I'm following up on a lead. Which I'm sure you're doing as well. So what is the big deal? You're chasing a killer, and I'm chasing a story. Sure, we're going to work together—but not together, together. And to answer your question, of course I'm alone. I work better alone. I don't need a man to protect me. Besides, he'd get in my way of finding out information. And to tell you the truth, it's none of your business." On those words, she rose from the stool, turned her back on him, and started to storm away.

Rising quickly, he grabbed her by the arm and turned her back toward him. This was ridiculous. They fought like they'd known each other forever. He knew that what she did was none of his business, so why was he trying to make it his business? Regaining control of his emotions, he admitted, "You're right."

That surprised her, he could tell. Suddenly her chin came up, and a large smile started to spread. She must not be used to winning so easily. Not that she had won, but he did know he'd crossed the line. Keeping it on a business level, he said firmly, "This is my case. I am the detective. You are the reporter. I investigate the case. You write the facts." With each sentence he would point to himself, and then to her, and then back again to himself, emphasizing his every word. "If you continue to try and do my job, which may hinder my investigation, I'll pull you in on charges of obstructing justice so fast it will make your head spin. Do I make myself clear?"

She looked but never said a word. The smile wiped from her face.

"The least you could have done was brought a date with you for protection."

"Again, I don't need protecting. A date would interfere with my job. I can't snoop around and worry about keeping some man's ego happy at the same time. Without a date, I've been able to walk around, look at people, ask a few questions here and there, and got some good answers." She dropped it there, not bothering to share any information.

He balled his hand in a fist, restraining his anger. As he was about to speak, she added, "I might have gotten another lead tonight, for all you know."

"You're right. I don't know. But what I do know is that if you ask the wrong question to the wrong person, you could be the next stiff I get called to the scene for." Leaning his face closer to hers, he said, "And I don't want that." Straightening his stance once more, he said, "Stick to reporting while I do the investigating. You write the facts we give you. Don't interfere. Don't take chances that are unnecessary."

When those big green eyes started to stray from his face, he caught her chin in his hand, drawing her attention back to him, but not as roughly as he'd grabbed her arm earlier. "You're not listening to me," he said to her as her eyes still looked over his shoulder.

"John," a familiar female voice said as she rubbed his back gently.

Turning quickly, he wanted to bark, "What?" at whoever interrupted the important conversation he was having.

Instead he tightened his grip on Taylor's arm so she couldn't run away and looked down into the eyes of the woman from the cafeteria at the station. "Gloria," he said, nodding slightly.

The woman glanced at John and then looked around him at Taylor and his hand holding her. "I thought you told me you two weren't an item. That she was a. . .what did you call her?"

Great! Now what? "I—"

Before he could speak, Taylor extracted herself from his hold and reached out to shake hands with the female intrusion. "Hi. I'm Taylor Jaymes. A reporter from the *Morning Tribune*. Nice to meet you."

"Gloria." She filled in her name.

"Nice to meet you, Gloria. And don't you worry. Your man is safe from me. We're talking business here. I have no claims on him whatsoever, and he has *none* on me. Let me leave you two alone. Have a great night." She turned and smiled up at John as she said, "Nice to see you, Detective. We'll speak again soon."

And she left him there, standing with Gloria, like that was how it was supposed to be. Should he run after her?

"John, I didn't know you went to bars. I thought that went against your values."

With his back still to Gloria, John watched Taylor disappear into the crowd onto the dance floor. Finally, he twisted back around and faced the woman he had no desire to talk to, but with the question she had asked, he knew he must respond. "Yes, Gloria. You're right. I don't come to bars, except on official business. I hope you realize what is going on in our city right now and know the possible danger you are putting yourself in by going out alone to clubs. You are alone, right?"

She smiled, apparently thinking he might ask to accompany her. "Why yes, John. I'm alone. But I don't have to be."

Grabbing both of her shoulders, holding her in front of him, he looked straight into her eyes, making sure he had her full attention. "I'm telling you this for your own good, and I hope you listen. Go out in groups, if this is the life you choose for yourself."

"What are you talking about? Those killings didn't happen at a bar. Those women were murdered on the side of a street. I'm not going to stop on the side of the road for a stranger. Give me a little credit, John. You guys talk about some of the stuff you see at the tables over your lunch. I hear enough. I don't want to be the one y'all are talking about."

At least she holds a grain of sense in her head. "Well, be safe tonight when you go home. Good night."

He walked around her, heading for the door. There was no need for him to linger any longer. The waitresses had already let him know only two of the three had been seen there and neither in the past month. As he stormed for the exit, he found himself glancing over the crowd.

What was he looking for? Taylor? He knew he was, but why?

Chapter 17

Taylor made her way through the crowd and slipped off to the other side of the dance floor. Striding to the front door, she grumbled to herself the whole way. "What got into him? I wasn't doing anything wrong. Only my job. What's it to him? Our agreement has nothing to do with me doing my job." Rolling her eyes, she said, "And just think: I was beginning to like the guy." She pushed the door open.

Plodding down the sidewalk, she headed for her Mustang. Yanking the door open, she dropped inside and strapped on her seat belt. With a *click* the belt locked, and she jammed the key into the ignition. Slapping the steering wheel with the ball of her hand, it hit her. "I know where I know her from." Suddenly that blond rubbing all over John came to remembrance. "She's that little waitress in the cafeteria who kept eyeing him the other morning. She has it bad for him, and I don't think he even knows it." She laughed aloud.

"Tonight she may make her move." Putting the gear into DRIVE, she eased out of her parking space.

Edging her car into the street, she steered for home. It wasn't far. Just a few blocks down and a couple blocks over and she would be home. Passing the late-night visitors strolling in the Quarter, she didn't take time to study them, as was her norm. In the few years she had lived in the Quarter, that was what she enjoyed the most—people-watching.

Tonight her mind was on other matters—the detective and the way he reacted to seeing her tonight. You'd think he'd be grateful for all the help she gave him.

After unlocking her front door and stepping into her apartment, she tossed her purse and keys on the table and slammed the door closed behind her. Stretching and twisting, she found she was wound up tighter than a spinning top. *Why?*

Probably because of the story. She wished she'd found out more tonight, or at least gotten some important tidbit like she'd indicated to John. Unfortunately she hadn't truly found out anything. She'd alluded to it, just to make him mad. Taylor hoped it worked.

Tonight promised to be a long night for Taylor. She knew she wouldn't go to sleep if she went to bed, so she opted for rummaging through all her notes and pictures. Maybe something would jump out at her or fall into place. If nothing else, her eyes would grow tired. Then she could go to sleep. Start fresh tomorrow.

In the meantime, Taylor took out her files on the three girls and glanced over them again one at a time, not seeing anything new. As she tried to focus on the case, her mind wandered to the thorn in her side. . .the detective. Her thoughts smoldered on that devastatingly attractive man who drove her crazy. Why had he behaved that way? He told her she could work on the case with him. What was the big deal? Besides, she didn't blow his cover. Of course, he almost did with his big mouth. She was surprised no one seemed to hear his loud, irritated voice shouting at her. She sure did.

Enough about him. Think about the case, the victims. Who would do such a thing? Why these three women? And who was next? She wondered if the police had worked up a psychological profile yet. Or did only the FBI do that sort of thing? It was definitely a serial killer, so if the FBI weren't in on it yet, they would be soon. How would Detective John Bradley handle that?

She had come full circle. Her thoughts were back on him again. Not where she wanted to be.

Throwing open the top file, Trisha McIntyre-Matthews, she forced her mind to focus on the subject at hand. She had been married to Robert Matthews, but as soon as she applied for a divorce, she'd returned to using her maiden name. Had the police checked him out? Had he been cleared? Or was he a person of interest to them?

The only neighbor who had known Trisha had been Wendy. They both lived in the Warehouse District and had been neighbors for some time. Both were married to abusive husbands. Wendy's divorce was final, whereas Trisha had four more months to go. According to Wendy, Robert didn't want the divorce and was fighting it.

Three months ago, with Trisha's father's influence, Robert had been forced to leave their home. Her father had bought the condo, and it was still in his name. He wanted to make sure his little girl had a roof over her head. Part of him had never trusted Robert from the beginning, but little did her father know how much her husband couldn't be trusted. Mr. McIntyre hadn't known for a long time what went on beneath the roof he supplied. Wendy said Trisha didn't tell her parents how he abused her. Robert had made sure the marks were hidden. Their two families were friends. She didn't want her rotten husband to ruin that for her parents, whom she dearly loved. But when Robert twisted her wrists so hard, one snapped, that was the last straw. Then she told Mom and Dad everything.

At Trisha's workplace, Taylor heard a little different story, but not so different that it made Robert seem innocent. If anything, it made him look worse. According to fellow workers, Trisha never exposed her personal life to them, but within a few weeks of her marriage, her smile had gone. Trisha's joyful spirit had turned quiet, and she kept to herself. Then they noticed marks that appeared to be covered with makeup—nothing obvious, but enough for coworkers to wonder. And some days every step seemed to be filled with agonizing pain as she moved slowly, cautiously. When someone would ask if she was okay, Trisha always pasted on a smile and said, "Wonderful. Thanks for asking."

Normally the husband would be the first person the police would look at, but because of the similarities, Taylor felt certain the police were primarily focused on the work of the serial killer. She hadn't discussed details on the third victim yet with John.

Mr. McIntyre made his views clear to everyone who would

listen. He believed Robert Matthews had killed his daughter. He believed it was a copycat killing.

Taylor hoped the police had questioned Robert Matthews well and checked his whereabouts. You never knew. If nothing else, he deserved punishment for what he had put Trisha through.

Taylor wanted to talk to him herself—to see how he portrayed himself. As the suffering widower? She'd catch up with him tomorrow, she hoped. He was at the top of her to-do list.

The only possible dissimilarity between Trisha and the other two victims was the fact that Trisha was separated, not truly single. She had four months left before her divorce would be final. This was enough in Taylor's mind to look deeper into Robert's alibi. Of course, the killer might have known Trisha had split from her husband. Maybe they should look closer at men who knew Trisha well.

All of this whirled in her brain, making her feel like she was going out of her mind. She needed to talk this over with John. See what they truly knew about Robert and Trisha. What had they found out? Had they cleared him and was it with enough true evidence?

"John, I need to talk to you."

Why did they have to argue at the dance club? Pounding her fist on the table, she uttered, "John. Why does everything have to come back to you?"

She'd never needed help before. Why now?

It was late and she was tired. Maybe if she gave the whole thing a rest, tomorrow she'd have a better perspective. At least a good rest might get the thoughts of her friendly neighborhood cop out of her mind. . .she hoped.

Chapter 18

John revved the engine of his Bronco and took off. On the way home, he took a slight detour, not even thinking about it—three blocks over and two down. There he slowed his car and looked for lights in the high windows. Maybe he hadn't seen her on the dance floor when he glanced around the club because she had already left and gone home.

He hoped that was the case as his gaze lifted to her windows.

Darkness.

Disappointed and frustrated, he lowered his gaze and gritted his teeth.

John pulled over to the curb and killed his engine. He needed to know Taylor made it home safely. Sure, she'd been taking care of herself for a long time. He knew that. How could he forget? She kept reminding him. But still he had to be sure.

It's not that I'm trying to take care of her. No. He was looking out for her because now she was a part of his team. . .well, sort of. Not that he would ever admit that to her.

By peering into the darkness, into the shadows of the parking area, he could see the rear corner of her Mustang.

He grunted. That didn't prove she was home. As close as her place was to the bar, it wouldn't surprise him in the least if she hadn't walked tonight. That girl was afraid of nothing.

Either he needed to slip into the courtyard and look up onto her balcony to see if any light spilled out of the glass sliding doors or slip up the stairs and listen through the door for noise inside. The chance someone left the gates to the courtyard unlocked was slim to nil. He doubted it seriously that one of her good neighbors would do that.

What would happen if he followed his second plan of action? Wouldn't that look good? Someone see him, call the police to report a prowler, and then find him as the perp? That would be tragic. . .one of his own coming out to arrest him. How would he explain that? He'd never live it down.

"That's a chance I'll have to take," he murmured to himself as he climbed out of his parked car. Quietly, he slipped inside the hidden parkway. Squinting, he shot little daggers toward the lock on the gate and decided not to waste time trying to pick the lock. That wouldn't look good either. Stepping softly, he climbed the stairs and eased his way up one step at a time. Delicately he eased over to her front door. Pressing his ear against the wood, he listened.

Nothing. She wasn't home. *That woman!*

Then it hit him. *What if she walks up and catches me?*

He shoved that thought to the back of his mind. Otherwise, he'd have run off right then.

Finally, he heard a loud pound, like someone slamming their fist down on a hard surface. Was she being attacked? His muscles tightened. Instantly, his body made ready to kick in the door and save her, but then the pounding was followed by her voice grumbling aloud about something. Sounded like she was fussing at herself. He released his held breath.

That was good enough for him. She was home safe and sound.

Swiftly and silently, he made his way back down to his car and headed home. The short time it took him to drive the twelve miles, he tried not to think about Taylor in any way, shape, or form. To help him, he turned off his radio, lowered both front windows, and let the fresh air blow through his car. The wind sliced through as if fingers were raking his hair. Taylor's, he thought. In his mind, he heard her laughter.

He shook his head to remove that thought. Instead, a quick flash of her gorgeous smile bolted out in front of him, and he gave up the assignment of forgetting about Taylor. For the next fifteen minutes, he relived this past week with her, recalling each time he had seen her and how she made him feel.

Finally, he pulled into his garage and parked. Before killing the engine, he raised his windows.

What a night!

John unlocked his back door. As he entered his home, he hooked his key on the curved nail by the kitchen door and then made his way to the bedroom. There he slipped off his blazer and hung it on a rack in the closet, smoothing each wrinkle out before shutting the closet door.

On the ride home, all he could think about was Taylor.

Was she still arguing with herself? Had she found a better way to spend the rest of her night at home? Someone needed to talk some sense into that girl. She had to be nuts checking out the bars by herself. Taylor was looking for trouble. What if she'd run into the killer and he figured out what she was doing and why? The dispatcher would be calling him at three in the morning to come view another crime scene, this time with her behind the wheel.

Shivers raced down his spine.

Speaking of morning, it would be here way too soon. Time to hit the hay. Five would be there before he knew it. Sitting on the bed, he removed his shoes. Rising, he placed them in the closet and dropped his socks in the dirty-clothes hamper. After he laid his wallet and change on the top of his butler, he hung his jeans on the rod attached for pants. He hadn't had them on but for a couple of hours. Why throw them in the dirty clothes?

John pulled out a fresh pair of gym shorts and a T-shirt to sleep in, dressed, and climbed into bed. Feeling the need to sit up but having no energy to do so, he realized he forgot to set the alarm.

Relaxing, he closed his eyes and murmured, "No problem. I always wake before the alarm. This time I just have to make sure I get up when I wake."

No snoozing raced through his mind as he felt his body start to rest, unwinding at the end of a very long day.

Turning on his side, he released a long sigh. His nerve endings tingled as his body started to relax even more. *Help me, Lord. Lead me to this killer. We can't have another person die.* His prayers slipped out as sleep tried to overtake him.

As he sunk closer toward sleep in his mind, he saw those soft, long, red curls. His hands reached up and rubbed his eyes as he muttered, "Go away, Taylor. I'm trying to sleep here. . . ."

The next thing he remembered was waking up to a pitch-dark room, all but the red glow of his clock showing 4:45.

Time to get up.

He tossed back the covers and headed straight for the shower. The cool blast of water woke him the rest of the way. As he lathered himself with soap while water continued to pour down over his head, a glimpse of that redheaded reporter flashed through his mind.

She had dressed sharp last night. In all his anger, he had failed to take in her looks, but this morning was another matter. Tucked into those brown snakeskin boots were tight-fitting jeans. She fit right in with the crowd wearing that kind of top girls wore with the cowgirl fringes hanging across the back of the shirt. A cowboy hat would have sat perfectly on that crown of red hair, but who would want to spoil the look of those tresses falling free all around her head, down to her elbows, and around to the back. If John didn't know better, he would have believed she was all cowgirl.

Of course, he really didn't know better. In fact, he didn't know Taylor at all, except what he read written by her in the paper. And none of that spoke about her. It only showed the girl had no fear for her life.

What *did* he know about her?

His mind wandered as he dressed for the day. He knew she was a hardworking reporter. Anyone who would give up a night of relaxing at home or going out on a nice date to a movie for her job was a dedicated worker. Quickly he reminded himself how she almost got herself killed on the case of those thefts in the Quarter. How dedicated could a person be?

Suddenly he recalled her face plastered across his television set when that case had come to resolution and the criminals had been locked behind bars. His eyes had been drawn to her; he couldn't look away. She had a pull on him even then when she wasn't flesh-and-blood in front of him. He'd better be very careful now not to let the flesh rule his life. He knew better.

At the time that case was brought to a close, the police got the credit; however, the news media played her part up big. That probably wasn't good for her future incognito investigations. It had to hurt more than it helped, but it was always nice to be recognized. That he knew for a fact, even though he wished they would keep his picture out of the paper. A little good press went a long way. His name was one thing, but pictures gave criminals a heads-up on him, and that he didn't need—as he was sure Taylor didn't, either.

Knowing he was attracted to her against his better judgment, he admitted, "She is one amazing woman." He had to give her that, but he'd better watch out for himself. His attraction for the reality of her seemed to be growing too quickly. That wasn't good.

Get your attention back on the case and keep it there.

He growled, "I give up. I've got work to do. No time for you, Miss Jaymes."

Off he stormed to make a pot of coffee.

Chapter 19

Determined to know everything on this case, Taylor got up early so she could beat John to the station.

"He can call me his shadow," she whispered to her reflection in the mirror as she wiggled her brows. The good thing was, this time it was with his blessing. A smile warmed her lips as she scrunched her curls slightly at the scalp, trying to give her hair some lift and bounce this morning.

"Oh well." She gave up the battle with her hair. The red curls always won out. They did what they wanted to do.

Snatching her beeper off the dresser, she clipped it to her jeans. After stuffing her pockets with some cash, her cell phone, and her ID, she grabbed her keys, ready to hit the road. As she started for the door, her landline rang. Taylor glanced at it with the thought of ignoring it, but her steps faltered.

It might be John telling her he changed his mind. Did she want to hear that?

No.

Shaking her head, she continued toward the front door, passing the phone. It rang again. Slapping her hand against the doorframe instead of grabbing the knob and turning, she frowned. "I can't do it! I can't just let it ring. I have to answer it. It might be important," she mumbled to herself.

The inner struggle was twisting her into knots. A third ring pealed out.

Closing her fingers into fists, she said, "It might be the city desk with a breaking story they need me to cover—a rape, a missing person, another homicide."

Arghh, she groaned.

Pivoting on her heel, she took three steps and snatched up the receiver. "Hello."

As soon as she heard the voice on the other end, she regretted answering the phone. *This could have waited.*

"Morning, Sis." The cheerful voice on the other end of the line floated into her ears, so smooth, so sweet.

"Yeah, morning, Tina. I was just heading out the door. Whatcha need?"

"I won't keep you long. You sure are a hard one to track down. I've called you at work, on your cell, and on your home phone leaving messages, but you haven't called me back at all. Have you been working too hard lately? You'll never get a life if you keep doing that." Taylor's sister sounded just like her mom.

Give me a break, she thought but didn't say. Instead she rolled her eyes because she knew when her sister said she wouldn't keep her, it meant, "Sit down. This could take awhile."

"What's up?" she asked again, trying to push Tina into a response.

"You know next week is Mom and Dad's thirty-second wedding anniversary. Rodney and I thought we might throw them a little party Friday night. Invite some family and friends. I wanted to make sure you marked it down on your calendar and in your Blackberry so you'd be here." Taylor heard the command in her sister's voice.

Chewing her bottom lip, Taylor thought about it. This was probably some set-up between her mom and Tina. A blind date thing they'd cooked up. She knew them. Knew how they thought and what their priorities in life were. Number one: a husband to take care of her. Number two: a husband to love her. And number three: a husband to give her children. This all boiled down to a man in Taylor's life. She had no time for a relationship, and her career had no need of a husband. Taylor had known since she was a small child where she wanted to go in life—and it wasn't walking down any aisle to say, "I do."

Glancing at her watch, she realized she needed to get to the bottom of this phone call and get to it fast if she was going to beat John to the station.

"So do I bring a date?" This should get the truth out of her sister.

Excitement bubbled through the line as Tina said, "You mean you have a man you could ask? Who is he? How long have you been dating? Tell me the story. Mom will be so delighted. This could be the best anniversary gift you could give her."

Taylor scoffed, pinching her lips together. *I knew it. I*

knew it. "No, Tina. There is no boyfriend in my life. I was just testing you to see if you and Mom had someone lined up for me. I don't want any more fixer-uppers from you two. Do I make myself clear?"

"Yes, Sister dear, I promise. This really is for Mom and Dad. They don't even know about it. Actually, it was Rodney's idea."

Tina sounded sincere. Taylor had to give her that. Either Tina was becoming a better actress, or she was telling the truth. Taylor twisted the phone cord around her fingers as she thought of what to say. "Mom always did say Rodney was the perfect son-in-law. In fact, she wants me to find someone just like him."

"Well, you would be happy. And—"

"Don't tell me." Taylor cut her sister off as her nerves tightened from head to toe. She dreaded hearing what Tina was about to say, so she said it for her. "You happen to know someone you could introduce me to, and he's just like Rodney. In fact, you could have him come to the party. Thanks, but no thanks. If I come up with someone, I'll bring him to the party. If not, I'll be alone. You and Mom better learn to accept me the way I am. My job doesn't leave much time for socializing. And I like it that way."

By now the telephone cord had tangled so tightly in her hand it was cutting off the circulation to her fingertips. She was tired of her mother and sister playing Cupid. "And I especially don't have time to form a relationship with some man who would need me to devote myself to him. No one understands my drive for being the best reporter I can be. Only Dad has a glimmer of understanding."

Taylor heard Tina's giggle cross the line. "Dad made a comment the other day you might be interested to hear. If not, I'll tell you anyway. He said since my two little girls seem to be so much like me, he couldn't wait until you settled down and started a family. He could see a couple of grandsons, or tomboy granddaughters, running around with printer's ink staining their fingers, just like you, Taylor. You and Dad, that is."

"For your information, we don't get ink on our fingers anymore. Computers do wonders."

"I'm sure Dad was just being cute with that remark, stressing how much you are into your job as a reporter."

"And what makes him so sure my kids would be boys or tomboys?"

Tina's laughter grew stronger as it filtered through the line. "He said you wouldn't dare give him two more little sissy granddaughters. That was something only I would do."

A part of her heart broke. She felt betrayed by the one man who always seemed to understand her. Now it sounded like even her dad was going against her wishes for her life. "Tina, I really have to go. When is the party?" She listened to her sister's response and made a mental note. Later she would key it into her Blackberry.

She wasted no time getting out of her apartment before another phone call slowed her down. She climbed into her car and eased out onto the road. The only reason she drove her car to the station instead of walking was because she couldn't be sure John would allow her to ride with him. It was a police matter, and she was a reporter. The detective probably wouldn't want anyone to know they were together. With her car, she could at least follow him.

Soon she was at the station, parked, and headed toward John's office.

His office was empty, so she walked in and made herself at home in the spare chair she sat in not too many days ago. How she beat him in, she'd never know. Tina had definitely kept her longer on the phone than Taylor had wanted. After sitting and tapping her fingers silently on her lap for several seconds, which seemed like long minutes, she glared at her watch and mumbled, "It's almost nine. He must have stayed out late last night. He probably had a really good time with Blondie." She made a face as she imagined him and that Gloria woman huddled together on the dance floor.

Standing abruptly and shaking free that image of the two of them pressed together, she said, "I did enough of that last night."

"Enough of what?" The question came from the doorway.

Spinning around, Taylor discovered John's frame filling the space at the open door. Her pulse raced as she took in the dark circles under his eyes. *It must have been one night to remember for him.* She clenched her teeth, trying to restrain her first response. Asking him what kept him out so late last night was none of her business—and part of her really didn't want to know.

After holding her tongue for a minute or two, she said, "So you decided to come to work after all. I didn't know cops got to come in so late in the morning." She was satisfied at the way she approached him. "Maybe it's not too late for me to consider a career change. Your hours seem more conducive to having a life. Wouldn't my mother be proud?"

He grumbled something under his breath that she couldn't understand. "Have a seat. What are you doing here? Did you discover something new last night *in your investigation?*" Sarcasm oozed from his last words.

"I'd ask you the same thing, but I'm not sure I want to hear about you and Gloria." Taylor loved to aggravate him. She didn't know why, but she felt sure that remark would do the trick.

His face broke into a wide smile, and he started laughing.

That wasn't the reaction she'd expected. What was going on? She wasn't trying to be funny. Her intention had been to irritate him just a little, rub him against the grain.

He swallowed his laughter as he said, "So what do you think happened with Gloria last night? No. Never mind. You're too young to be thinking what you were thinking, so let's get down to business."

Taylor felt her face redden. Why was she getting angry? *You don't want to know what they did,* she reminded herself.

Then it hit her. He called her *young.* In the beginning, he insinuated she was too young and inexperienced to be getting so close to her cases. It was dangerous for her. She wanted him to treat her like a woman, a woman worldly enough to do her job well. She also wanted to be treated with the respect she'd earned over her years of experience.

"Young? You talk about me as if I'm a kid. I'm all grown up, in case you haven't noticed." She placed her hands on her hips as she punched out the words.

His eyes studied her carefully. After looking her over from head to toe, he said, "You can't be more than twenty-three, twenty-four tops. You're barely out of college. It's your job that makes you feel old." His words were said with a hint of laughter.

With a toss of her hair over her shoulders, she stood erect. "I'll have you know I'm what is known in some circles as 'an old maid.' Talk to my mom. She'll tell you. I'm twenty-eight, almost twenty-nine."

His blue eyes widened in surprise. Taylor could tell he was truly shocked. Maybe he had thought she was young and fresh out of school. Well, he was in for a wake-up call.

"You're not joking, are you?" He shook his head. "No, I can see you're not."

Taylor shot daggers at him and then sat back down in the chair in front of his desk. As he walked around his desk to sit down, she said, "I don't know whether to take that as an insult, saying I look like a baby, or assume you meant it as a compliment, saying I look young for my age."

He shrugged like it didn't matter to him one way or the other.

She reached in her blazer's hidden pocket and pulled out a pad and pen. "No comment? Just for that, I'll take it as a compliment. Let's get down to business, shall we?" She grinned as she crossed her legs. "What did we find out last night. . .anything?"

Chapter 20

John leaned back in his chair and chewed the inside of his cheek slightly as he watched Taylor swing one leg across the other. He knew he needed to reverse the direction his mind was headed.

The mind is where the battle first begins, he reminded himself.

Releasing a heavy sigh, he said, "I think you're jumping the gun here. Or maybe you just misunderstood what I meant when I said you'd get the exclusive on this investigation. I didn't mean I'd be reporting our every finding to you the moment we found something. I meant I would tell you everything we learned at various intervals, keeping you abreast of our findings. . .with the promise from you that it stays out of the paper until I give you the go-ahead. I'll contact you. You don't need to come by my office daily and hang out for the next update."

He watched her shift in the chair. "So, you see, we won't be working together, together." His hands interchangeably stretched out to her and then pulled to his chest and then back again—almost like a seesaw while stressing his point. He hoped she got the message. "Don't worry. I'll keep you filled in on the various stages of the investigation at different points along the way." He picked up his pencil and twirled it through his fingers, like a lot of people did with coins. He found this relaxed him sometimes. "You don't need to come down here as if you're going to ride along with us as we follow our leads."

A spark shot through her green eyes as they narrowed. Her back stiffened. It seemed she now understood their relationship on this investigation, but he detected a slight sensation that Taylor didn't like the way he explained the particulars.

She sat up straighter in the chair, leaned slightly forward, and as her brows lifted, she said, "You're right. I don't understand."

So much for hoping, he thought.

"Yesterday you called me to say we would work together. *Together* in the dictionary I have says 'with one another.'" She flung her hands up into the air with a confused expression. "'With one another' does not mean you by yourself." Her open hands moved with practically every word, expressing her frustration. Stabbing a finger in his direction, she added, "And then occasionally you call me?" She slapped her hand against her chest, her words choppy as she balled her hands into fists. "And then you fill me in with a tidbit here and tidbit there? That's not going to work."

"You seem very upset. Sorry." John rose and strolled over

to his filing cabinet. "Taylor, these murders aren't the only crimes in the Quarter I'm working on. I have other cases I'm handling at the same time. You and I will not be spending every day together working on this one case." He pulled out two files as the phone rang. "Like these active ones." He emphasized his statement to her by tossing the files on his desk, glancing her way, and then answering the phone. "Bradley," he said, speaking into the mouthpiece. Maybe, just maybe, she understood now. He hoped, anyway.

Buck's voice pricked John's ear as the detective said, "We found him, boss. Michael Guidry. If his story checks out, he was out of town when the first two murders took place. We're going to follow up on his alibi. See if it holds."

"Sounds good. Let me know what you find." It didn't. Not really, but he wasn't going to say that out loud. He had hoped Michael Guidry would be a strong suspect. Without giving any of his conversation or his thoughts away to the redhead watching his every move, John hung up the phone.

He didn't want to give her any more clues to chase. John looked up just in time to see Taylor slipping the strap of her purse over her shoulder. Rising to her feet, she was ready to depart from his office.

Good. Maybe she wasn't even listening to his conversation.

Guilt flooded his heart and mind. The woman worked so hard to get her story, and she had helped them so much. Without her, they wouldn't even have a lead. And this was how he repaid her? He told her they would work together, so why try to slip out the back door now and keep her out of it?

He knew why—in his heart and in his mind. He didn't need the distraction. For his own sanity, he needed to keep her as far out of his sight as possible. John's scrutiny followed her frame as she moved toward the door, proof of point. He couldn't pull his gaze away, no matter how hard he tried.

Why not let her ride along with him today when he checked on Eddie Thomas, the ex-con who was seen at two of the bars last night? His rap sheet was a mile long for physical abuse against women. Maybe he had escalated in his assaults. Maybe he needed to go further than just hurting women. Maybe he needed to see them die now. John had checked with Eddie's parole officer first thing this morning and found that Eddie was always right on time for their meetings, but that didn't make him innocent.

With her hand on the knob, pulling open the door, she turned and said, "I guess that means I continue my own investigation and tell you what I uncover. Does it mean you will show me the same respect? Or is this a one-sided deal?"

Before he could respond or even share what he was thinking, she added, "Is the police department going to tell me anything they uncover? I presume it does work both ways, right?"

"Miss Jay—" he started to say, but it was as if his answer truly didn't matter, for she was out the door, slamming it behind her.

He did hear her say over her shoulder, "You really disappoint me, Detective Bradley. I thought you were better than most." The rest of what she said was cut off when the door closed behind her, but he didn't think she really cared if he heard her or not.

"Taylor," he called out, wanting to tell her to be careful. He wished she would let him do his job instead of chasing the story herself. She could just report what he gave her. Wasn't that what a reporter did? She didn't need to go investigate on her own. It was not a game. She could get hurt.

Get your head straight, man.

He rubbed his face hard and then raked his fingers through his dark hair, trying to push his concern for her investigating on her own out of his brain. Reporters investigated and reported what they found all the time. That was their job. That was her job, so what did he care if her investigation put her in tight corners? She was a big girl. She could take care of herself. Right?

John opened the top file on his desk. *I need to get back to work. I really do have more cases than the pre-dawn murders.* Thumbing through the papers in one of the files, he muttered, "In fact, I have to be in court tomorrow to testify against this guy to make sure he goes away for a long time for his crime. That's my job!" John almost tore the page in his hand as he flipped it over and grabbed the next one in the file while completing his thoughts aloud. "Getting scum off the street."

After studying the file and refreshing his memory on the case of Donald Smith, arrested for kidnapping his son, John set the file aside, but the memory of the case lingered. The man had lost his visitation rights because of his addiction to drugs, and while under the influence, he had harmed his child. His ex-wife took him back to court, and they changed his visitation to supervised visits only. That set Donald Smith off on a tangent, yelling in court about the unfairness of it all—having some stranger hanging around him the whole time he was with his son. Security had to restrain the man.

John knew it was more than him wanting to see his son. When the man used to pick the boy up from his ex and then bring him back, he always stretched out his time with her. Smith always tried to convince her to take him back. Truth be told, Smith was only trying to hurt his ex-wife when he took the boy. The man knew the best way to get at her was through the kid, so he wanted to hold on to his rights to agitate her. . .since she wouldn't come back to him. And even if she would, he only wanted her back for a punching bag.

It broke John's heart for the boy to be used as a tool for Smith's pleasure. He remembered the sad look in the kid's eyes when they caught up with the two of them. They were at a dirty, disheveled house that Donald's mother owned and where she allowed him to stay for free. He was supposed to keep it up, but did the man care? No. He didn't care about his mom's house any more than he did about his son. All Donald Smith cared about was himself.

Sad. Do the crime, pay the time. Maybe ten to fifteen years would wake the man up to reality.

Tomorrow John had to give the facts in court. He was ready. Glancing at his watch, he decided it was time to pay Eddie a visit.

Driving over there, John didn't pay attention to his surroundings as he usually did. He was too absorbed in the guilt he felt for betraying Taylor's trust and the way he treated her. She wasn't even with him, and his mind had stayed on her. At this rate, he may as well have let her tag along.

Eddie lived in a small, one-room efficiency over on St. Phillip Street. The outside wasn't too clean, so John didn't expect much on the inside. He wasn't disappointed. When John flashed his badge, Eddie backed up and let him in. John saw dirty dishes spread around on the counter, as well as the table.

Clothes were tossed here and there. The couch covered by a blanket thrown over it in disarray didn't disguise the filth in the room. A musty odor hung in the air, mixed with the scent of stale cigarette tobacco and ashes, as well as rotted food. The stench gagged John slightly. *How can people live like this?*

Eddie rubbed his eyelids as if trying to wipe the sleep, or booze, out of his eyes. He grumbled, "What do you want? I ain't done nothing wrong."

"Just a few questions. That's all." John didn't bother to sit.

Eddie plopped down on the couch. "Go ahead. Fire away. Like I said, I ain't done nothing wrong."

John pulled out his note pad. "Where were you Friday night from midnight until 5:00 a.m.?"

"Where do you think? Right here sleeping, of course."

"You got any proof, any witnesses?"

He smirked. "Yeah. I picked up this chick and brought her home. Didn't bother to get her name, though. Who needs a name to do what we did? I paid her, and she was happy when she left."

John made a note. "Get a name, Eddie. I mean it. I'll be back to check. Another question. Where were you a week ago Saturday night?"

The ex-con squinted his eyes. Through cuss words he asked, "What are you getting at? Are you trying to pin me with those murders going on in the Quarter? Forget it! I didn't do them, and you ain't gonna lay the rap at my door. Go find some other sucker."

John knew he was wasting his time with this one. The guy wasn't smart enough to hurt someone and walk away without leaving any evidence behind. In fact, in the past, Eddie loved leaving proof that he was the one who hurt his victims. . .and he was proud of it.

"I'm not a killer! I just like to hurt those who hurt me. If I killed them, they wouldn't feel the pain."

His expression changed. It appeared he was seeing someone he was torturing in his mind's eye as a sick smile touched his lips.

John wanted to punch him in the face one quick time. If nothing else, it would make John feel better. "Come on, Eddie. Do you want to do this at the station, or are you going to cooperate and answer my questions here and now? Where were you a week ago Saturday?"

"All right, all right. Man. Let's see. . .I'm not sure. I got off work around midnight that night and went drinking. Tried to pick up some action, but wasn't lucky. Guess I was too late 'cause usually my money is good with any of those wh—"

John cut him off. He may have to work with the evil in this world, but he didn't have to listen to their foul mouths. "Who were you drinking with? Can you give me a name? Anyone who can corroborate your story?"

Nodding, he said, "Oh, yeah. Old Curtis. . .Curtis Miller. He works with me. We clean shrimp all night over by the docks. My parole officer has the info."

John closed his pad. "Your story better check out. If not, you'll be seeing me again. But next time, I won't be as pleasant. And don't forget to get me a name for the other night. Your lady friend." Stepping out, as hot as it was, John was glad to be out of the disgusting odors and rubbish all around, even though the man's air conditioner worked well at keeping his crib cool. John hated filth, and that was what surrounded Eddie.

Not wasting any time, John called the parole officer once again. He did it the minute he climbed into his car. John didn't want to give Eddie any time to contact this Curtis guy and line up an alibi. Not only did John get the exact location where Eddie worked, but the parole officer gave him some info on Curtis as well. Both were parolees.

After getting the address, John eased on over to the landing. The fish market on Decatur hired anybody who could clean shrimp and gut and clean fish. Eddie was one of the night crew, along with Curtis Miller.

John addressed the owner. "Don't you ever worry about having so many ex-cons around, Mr. Patin?" Down here in the South, the man's name was pronounced *Pa-tan*. Everywhere else, it would be said like patent leather shoes. New Orleans was Cajun country—Acadian exiles, French-speakers from Acadia.

"Not really. What's to steal? I ain't got nothing but fish and shrimp. Besides, they work cheap," Patin said. He wrote down Curtis' address and handed it to John. Patin also backed up Eddie's story as to how late he worked a week ago Saturday. Friday was his night off, so he couldn't vouch for him there.

John paid Curtis a visit. He basically told the same story Eddie had given, but in his own words. In fact, he filled in a few more details, none that John cared to hear, but he took notes and thanked Curtis for his time.

The detective decided to slip by his house and shower. Tonight he would be checking out one of the two bars left. He would see what low-life he could turn up there. With more paperwork gathering dust on his desk, John decided he would go straight from work. And since both bars were in the Quarter, if he had enough time, he'd cover both tonight. So far, all they'd come up with were dead ends. They needed another break. Hopefully tonight would give him one.

Chapter 21

Taylor followed John from one place to the next. Writing down the addresses didn't tell her who he was talking to or what the conversation was about. A lot of good it did her. These stops could deal with one of his other investigations he so proudly stuffed under her nose. How could anything take priority over these murders?

When he pulled into his own driveway, she knew it was time to call it a day. Turning her car around, she headed toward her place. Today was probably a good waste of her time.

If only Detective Bradley. . .John. . .had kept to his side of the agreement.

Tucking her curls neatly around her ear, she strategized her next step. Now that she was back to investigating on her own, she would continue checking the bars out tonight. But she needed a little time to relax before a night on the town. . .for work.

Taylor opened the french doors to the balcony, allowing a breeze to flow into her apartment. The air conditioner was on the blink again. Just what she needed! And of course the landlord would get to it "as soon as possible." It was a good thing her rent was cheap and she loved the place; otherwise, she wouldn't put up with the cavalier way he fixed things. After Hurricane Katrina, her rent had gone up a hundred a month, but it was still low compared to the outrageous prices surrounding the Quarter.

A cool shower later, Taylor slipped on a pair of cut-offs and a T-shirt. Lying on her couch, she brought the telephone with her and punched in her mother's number. It started ringing.

"Hello."

"Dad! Hi. How are you?" She was surprised but pleased to hear her dad answer the phone. Usually he let her mom get it. After retiring, he kept his distance from the outside world. That saddened Taylor. As a reporter, he was always on top of what was going on in and around the world, but when he quit working, he seemed to lose interest in the world.

"Taylor, sweetheart. What are you doing? Trailing another hot lead? I haven't talked to you in days. Tell me about it. Catch me up!"

Taylor closed her eyes and smiled. *Yes. He still loved her work. Tina probably embellished the story about him wanting grandchildren from Taylor.* She quickly told her father the story she was working on, as well as how the police department promised her an exclusive because she came up with the important link in the case. Something they had overlooked. She didn't tell him what she'd discovered. . .because she had promised John. Her dad understood the importance of not revealing certain things to the public, so he didn't press her for the details.

They talked awhile and her father praised her over and over. As they were hanging up, Taylor said, "Give Mom my love. Tell her I called and I'll see you two again soon. I promise."

Hanging up the phone, she glanced around the room as a slight breeze touched her skin. Newspapers were stacked in the chair. Paper plates and napkins sat on her desk and her kitchen table.

While I have the time, I should take a few minutes and pick up. Sighing, she closed her eyes and decided the sleep was a little more important. . . .

After almost three hours of shut-eye, Taylor woke with a start, excitement stirring within. Tonight her investigative reporting kicked into high gear as she mulled over the possibilities of what she would uncover. By the time she was dressed and walking out the door, the reporter blood in her stimulated her senses. She was determined to catch another lead. Tonight that lead would give her a name or a motive. . .something.

At nine straight up, Taylor left her apartment and walked the six blocks to the Wild Horse Saloon on Burgundy. It was a small place with a counter along the total length of the room to the right and stools cramped against one another for maximum capacity. To the left was the actual bar with more stools for the customers. The bar also ran the full length of the wall. In the middle was the dance floor, and at opposite ends were small tables with two chairs at each. The dance floor wasn't very big, but it appeared more people sat around drinking and talking than dancing. The stage for the band was smaller than the dance floor. It could be why it was only a three-piece band—keyboard, drums, and guitar.

Clad in tight-fitting jeans tucked into ankle-high black leather boots and a black and aqua blue-printed cowboy-cut shirt covered slightly with a black leather vest sporting fringes, Taylor was relaxed and comfortable, ready to dig into her work. Of course, tennis shoes would have been even more comfortable, but she couldn't have everything.

After ordering a drink at the bar, she flashed the pictures of the three girls to the bartender. He didn't recognize any of the women. Taking her drink, she made her way to the far end of the bar, where the waitresses turned in their order. While each woman waited for their drinks, Taylor showed them the victims' pictures. Two recognized one of the girls as a customer before, but they couldn't be sure how long ago it had been. Another waitress recognized all three but thought it was from the TV news and the newspapers. She didn't recall any of them being a customer, but she had a suggestion.

"What you should do, when the band takes a break, is go talk to the drummer, JR. He watches all the women." She gave a knowing smile. "If anyone noticed them, it would have been JR."

Taylor followed up on the waitress's idea. She was right.

JR pushed his hat back on his head as he studied the three pictures. "I've seen this one before. She started coming by for a while about six months ago, but I haven't seen her for at least. . .two, maybe three months."

Taylor took all this information in but made no notes yet. Pointing to Stephanie, he said, "She had just split up with some guy and was—"JR stopped midsentence. He eyed Taylor as he chewed on his words.

"Go ahead," Taylor urged.

"She was looking for a good time with no strings attached. My kind of woman, if you know what I mean." JR lifted his hat and wiped his brow with his shirtsleeve. "You're not going to tell me something I don't want to hear, I hope."

As he slipped his hat back on, she said, "No, Mr. Sneed. This is much worse. The woman was killed a couple of weeks ago. We're trying to help find her killer."

JR looked relieved, but then a little sad. "I'm sorry to hear she's dead. She was a nice woman. Her so-called boyfriend had been cheating on her. I was trying to restore her faith in men by giving her a little attention and some lovin'. The night we got together, she came by here feeling really lonely and depressed. I haven't seen her in a couple of months," he assured Taylor.

"Did she tell you her old boyfriend's name?"

"Probably. But I didn't care to listen. Sorry."

Handing him her card, she said, "Thanks for your help. If you think of anything else, please let me know." At least he sounded honest—a real loser, self-absorbed, but truthful about his encounter with Stephanie.

Downing her watered-down drink, she slipped off of the stool and headed for the door. She believed she had found all she could at this little hole-in-the-wall.

Within fifteen minutes, she made her way to Six-Shooters, the biggest western lounge in the Quarter. For a weeknight, the place was packed. Of course, more than locals visited the Quarter. People from all over the world came to enjoy the history, as well as the partying. It was known as The Big Easy, The Crescent City, Sin City, and probably other nicknames as well.

The noise level was high and the smoke thick. She doubted she'd find out much tonight, but she would give it her best shot. Taylor found a table as far away from the band as possible. *That helps some.* Maybe the distance would help her hear the answers to her questions. She hoped, anyway.

A waitress came to take Taylor's order. She flashed her press pass at her and said, "I just need to ask a few questions."

"Can't you see we're too busy for that?" She turned nervous eyes on Taylor after glancing around the room.

Taylor reached into her vest pocket and pulled out the three pictures. "I'm doing a follow-up piece on the three girls who were found dead in the Quarter. Do you recognize any of them? Have you seen them in here?"

"I've only been here two weeks. You need to speak to someone else. Look, I gotta wait on customers. Do you want something to drink or not?"

Slipping the pictures back into the pocket of her vest, Taylor asked, "Is there anyone who works here that's been here awhile?" She understood the woman was busy and doing her job, but didn't people care anymore?

"Ask her," the waitress said as she jabbed her finger toward the tall blond waiting on the next table over. Then she marched away.

Taylor hoped the next waitress would be a little more helpful with a dash of that good old Southern friendliness. Shifting her weight to her feet, she started to rise when a voice stopped her.

"I thought I'd find you here."

"What are you doing looking for me? You should be looking for the killer." She continued to rise to her feet.

"I am. That's why I'm here. I'm not looking for you, I just knew in my gut I'd find you doing your snooping around tonight."

"What do you expect? I'm not getting anything from you like you'd told me I would. So I've gone back to doing my job, on my own. I thought we were going to work together on this, but you made it plain this morning that we're not." She hoped her disappointment in the police department and in him came through loud and clear. Taylor didn't realize how much so until she started spilling her pain to John.

He lowered his eyes as he said, "I tried to stop you this morning."

Taylor almost believed he sounded sorry for the way he let her down, but she wasn't going to fall for that again. If he truly had planned to let her be a part of this investigation, he would have let her go with him today. . .or at least told her what he was doing and promise to share what he found, if anything. "I have a job to do. I'm still on this story, so I go where it takes me."

He raised his blue eyes and locked on hers. He scraped his bottom teeth, almost as if he was trying to stop the words from coming out of his mouth but couldn't. "I had every intention of having you be a part of our investigation—only not on the rough, dangerous stuff, mind you. I can't put a civilian's life at risk. But for interviews that may lead somewhere, I see no harm in you tagging along."

"So what did you find out on your interviews today?"

If what he was saying was true, he would share right now with her.

"What?"

"That's what I thought." She nodded slightly, knowing he was leading her on. *So much for sharing.* Quickly, she stepped around him and started for the ladies' room. She needed to get herself together before she started approaching the workers. Get her game face back. For some reason, John Bradley had a way of rattling her very last nerve.

John caught her by the elbow and held on tight. "If you'll calm down and sit with me, maybe we could talk about this."

Her skin tingled where his fingers touched. She wanted to walk away and leave him standing there, but she couldn't. She felt trapped, like she had to stay. Was he ready to discuss business? Was she?

"This had better be good," she muttered, as if it really mattered at this very moment. She didn't dare let him know where her mind was. It needed to be on her story. She needed to write the best investigative piece ever if she wanted to win the Pulitzer. No man was going to get in her way of following her dream. "I don't have time to waste."

John turned Taylor back to the table, then sat across from her. Leaning toward her, he looked deeply into her eyes. "How did you know what I did today?"

John saw guilty secrets shoot from her eyes, but she didn't say a word.

"Never mind. I don't want to know." She was a regular spitfire. He took a deep breath and started sharing. "I followed a couple of leads that came my way. So far, neither has panned out, but we're still looking into both men. My men have been asking questions at this bar and two others in the area. The only one that all three have been seen in is this one."

Her shoulders drooped. "I just left Wild Horse. Only Stephanie's face was recognized in there. In fact, the drummer, JR, had been intimate with her. I was just starting to ask here. I haven't been as lucky so far. I've spoken to one girl and she's new. She's only been here two weeks. Glad your guys had better luck."

John liked the way she shifted from indignant anger to work mode at a drop of the hat. Obviously, she was dedicated to her work. At least she wouldn't let her emotions interfere with her job. Maybe that meant she would be able to concentrate on what she was doing. "If you had come back when I called your name instead of storming off in a huff, you would have been with me today. You'd know the two I spoke with were persons of interest. They both had alibis we will need to corroborate. We did find one thing out today. If you'd been with me, you would have known."

A smile started to cross her lips but quickly it disappeared as she said, "How was I to know? I'm not a mind reader. You ran me off this morning. You could have said something in the beginning instead of stressing over all the work you had and that not all of it was about these murders."

Her eyes sparked. He could tell she wanted to know what he'd found out but didn't want to ask.

"Well."

Yes. She wanted him to tell her but didn't want to ask. Why was he toying with her? He knew why. He liked the way her green eyes ignited when she got agitated. And the way her cheeks grew rosy red when she tried to hold her tongue.

"Are you going to tell me or not? I thought that was what you said. You wanted to share with me the investigative results. So start talking."

Laughter tickled the back of his throat, but he held it in. Only a smile escaped. This teasing a reporter, sharing with a reporter, was not him. Open and honest with a reporter went against the grain of his makeup. Not that John was ever dishonest with a reporter. It never seemed right to share with reporters what they had found. It wasn't the thing to do—talking to a person who could ruin a case faster than anyone he knew.

It wouldn't be right to share his thoughts so openly with her. Besides, it would put their relationship on a different level than that of cop and reporter. He wasn't ready for that to happen. . .at least not right now.

"We got a match on the tire cast. It was found at two of the scenes. The first and this last one. We know the brand of tire, and it has a spot of really worn tread. Both matched. So, if we catch the killer, that will be one more thing to tie him to the killings."

He watched Taylor mull over the information he gave her. It looked like she wanted to smile but fought against it. She seemed to be deciding how to respond. As a reporter, he saw the desire to know more flash through her eyes, but then as quickly a veil covered the excitement, revealing a reserved, patient, characteristic determinination to let him spill all at his own pace. She appeared to fight every muscle in her mouth to keep it shut.

"You sure get upset easily. If you want to know more,

why not just ask? Like this morning. If you hadn't stormed out of my office, you'd already know all of this. I tried to stop you then—" Before he could defend his actions again, she cut him off.

"You could have come after me."

"I don't run after anyone."

"Then you could have told me up front that you were going to let me go with you. No. You told me I misunderstood our arrangement. You led me to believe your word meant nothing."

John reached across the table and laid his hand on top of hers. "Let's forget about this morning. Let's go someplace where we can talk."

Her hand burned where he touched her. She hadn't forgotten how her skin tingled when he grabbed her or how her heart fluttered when he said he had called after her this morning. Why was this man affecting her so? She knew it was strictly business, but something about him excited her. "What do you have in mind?"

"Could we go somewhere so we could talk without all the noise around us? Besides, we don't know who's listening."

Taylor glanced around the room. No one seemed to be paying any attention as far as she could see. "Okay. Let's go." They rose and she followed him out to the sidewalk. "Okay. Where do you want to go?"

"How about the Café du Monde? This time of night we should be able to find a quiet spot. Besides, I know you love beignets."

"Sounds good to me. You know I'm on foot."

It was several blocks back toward the river, but John took

her by the elbow and led the way. She loved the feel of the light breeze in the air. Groups of people meandered through the Quarter. It was "the city that never seemed to sleep," and Taylor loved it.

After John got his coffee and Taylor her hot chocolate and beignets, they found a table away from the crowds. To the average eye they would look like a couple wanting to be alone, but Taylor knew it was to keep their conversation private.

"At least now I know how you stay so slim. You walk everywhere you go."

"I don't walk everywhere I go—only when my story is in the Quarter do I get to do that. I'm not that lucky all the time. My job takes me all over the city of New Orleans."

John smiled but said nothing.

Taylor didn't let that bother her. Instead she turned her attention to the white powdery concoction in front of her. She smacked her lips as she lifted one and pulled it toward her mouth.

"I thought we came here to work, not eat," John quipped.

"You're the one who mentioned beignets, remember?" Taylor's gaze crashed into his. "Besides, I'm sure you had your well-balanced meal tonight, but I haven't eaten since breakfast and I'm starved." She took a bite, looked away, and sat back. After chewing and swallowing, she dared to return her eyes to John.

He was watching her.

"What?" she asked.

He smiled crookedly. "You have white powdered sugar on your nose and chin." His grin widened.

Swiping it off of her nose with the back of her hand and

then grabbing her napkin, she dabbed her chin. After tossing the white paper on the table next to her beignets, she said, "Go ahead. Tell me. What are your plans for this investigation?"

"It's simple. Since each of the three victims had been seen at Six-Shooters the night they were murdered, I suggest you and I go to the place together like a couple. We'll be able to watch without people being suspicious." John took a sip of his coffee, all the while watching Taylor. "How does that sound?"

It sounded like a date to her. She picked up her mug and swallowed a mouthful of hot chocolate. "It's a plan that might work. Count me in."

He smiled again.

Her heart raced in anticipation. The only thing Taylor didn't know was if the beating of excitement was because of the investigation or if it was the thought of being together with him every night for a while.

Maybe it was a little of both.

Chapter 22

For the next two nights John and Taylor were together from nine until one in the morning. They visited Six-Shooters both nights, undercover. Each night, they sat at a table for two tucked away in the corner so they could watch the people coming and going. They acted like two lovers, cuddled together in the corner. At times, to authenticate things, they made their way out onto the dance floor, usually barely moving to the slow numbers so they could continue to keep their eyes peeled.

Taylor found herself enjoying the play-acting. Occasionally she'd forget it wasn't real, and then she would have to reprimand herself.

When they parted Thursday night, Taylor said, "John, I'll have to meet you at the bar tomorrow night, because I have to go to my parents' anniversary party."

"Why don't I take you to the party and then we can go to

Six-Shooters from there?"

"I don't think that's such a good idea." The last thing she wanted to do was put ideas in her mom's head.

"Why not?"

What could she say? Because her mom would see them as a couple, or she would see her daughter was finally attracted to someone? She sighed. "Okay. Be at my place at seven. But watch out for my mom. She has a mind of her own. She'll have the two of us married before winter if you're not careful."

John laughed. He obviously thought Taylor was joking.

"It's not funny. I promise. I already told you my mom wouldn't be happy until she sees me, her eldest child, married. You think it's a joke. She's dead serious."

John walked Taylor to her apartment door. "I think I can handle her. I don't know too many women who want to see their daughters marry police officers. Trust me."

Closing the door as John walked away, she pondered his words. *It might not be such a bad idea. This might teach Mom and Tina both a lesson and keep them off my back—if we can pull it off, that is.* Taylor would love to pull one over on her sister and Mom, although she doubted that would happen.

That night, she slept well.

Friday came quickly. She rose and cleaned up a bit in her apartment. Not much, but at least enough not to be embarrassed should John actually come in when he picked her up tonight. By the time she was finished putting her place in order, she wished the night were over. Unfortunately, it hadn't even begun.

The afternoon started lousy with a phone call at three.

"Hello."

If she had known who the caller was and what he wanted, she wouldn't have bothered to even answer the phone.

"Taylor?" After her automatic yes, he continued. "My name is Tim Robertson. I've tried to reach you several times at work. I even left a message on your home phone. You've never returned any of my calls."

Taylor remembered the two messages left for her at work. She truly meant to return the call in case he had a lead for her, but she got so caught up in her investigation with John, she forgot. "What can I do for you?" she asked as she hoped maybe, just maybe he had something new to add to the investigation. Her heart doubled in beat.

"I'm sorry to be calling so late, so last-minute, but I wanted to escort you to your parents' party tonight."

Taylor's head snapped, and she felt her eyes bulge slightly. "You what? Where did you get my number?" She knew the answer before she asked, but she still wanted to know for sure.

"Actually, your sister gave me your work and home numbers."

She stood, one hand balled up in a fist, wanting to strike her sister, while the other gripped the phone tight. Her grip was strong enough to choke a horse. Instead, she said, "Thanks. I already have a date." Then she slammed down the phone. It wasn't his fault, but look out, Tina!

Her blood pressure rose, as the thumping grew louder and stronger in her ears. "How dare she! A complete stranger and no warning. At least in the past she usually gave me a warning. A description. A heads-up. Something."

With pent-up energy she started pacing back and forth. Taylor knew she needed to calm down. She wanted to, but just thinking about her sister plotting her life kept her piqued. Suddenly the phone rang again. She snatched it up. "You heard me. I'm not interested, so don't call back!"

As she was about to hang up, she heard, "Not interested in what?"

Recognizing the voice as John's, she instantly pulled the receiver back to her ear. His voice seemed to calm her anger somewhat. At least enough for her to be civil. "Sorry. What did you want?"

John snickered. "You think you can answer a phone like that and leave it in the air? I think not. I want to know what that was all about?" he insisted.

If she'd been smart, she would have told him it was none of his business. Instead, she fell back on the sofa. Deciding this conversation might take awhile, she made herself comfortable. "That remark, believe it or not, was meant for some man I didn't even know. He called, asking me to let him escort me to my parents' party tonight."

"Why did he wait so late to call you, and how did he get your number?"

Taylor started playing with the phone cord, wrapping it around her finger and then releasing it one wrap at a time. "My dear, sweet sister. Who else? I knew this party was a setup. I tried to make her admit it. She swore she wasn't trying to set me up with anyone. She said this was all about our parents. Tina promised she was not trying to find a husband for me. She did admit Mother would be happier if I came with a date. I told Tina if I brought someone, I would. If I didn't, they would have to live with it."

Taylor hated spilling her guts to John, but she grumbled of

all they'd done in the past two years. Blind dates unbeknown to her until—*boom*—there he was. John didn't need to hear all of her family problems, but she was mad. She needed to talk to someone. Unfortunately for him, he won the lottery—got the whole spew. The more she said to him, the madder she became. Taylor didn't even know how John was handling all of her personal stuff being dumped in his lap, but she poured it all out.

"Can I make a suggestion?" he finally said.

"Sure, but I can't swear I'll follow it." He got her attention, though. Taylor sat up to listen intently. *He thinks he knows how to get my mom and sister off my case? Great. I want to hear it.*

"We're going to this party, right?" Apparently that was a rhetorical question because he didn't wait for an answer. "Why don't we give them something to think about? You and I have been playing lovers for two nights straight, and if you don't mind me saying so, I think we've gotten pretty good at it. If we do it tonight and they fall for it, it will solve two problems."

"Two? What two?" Taylor was puzzled.

"First, it will get your mother and sister off your back for a while. At least until they figure out it was a fake date. And second, it will let us know if we're doing a convincing job at the bar for the killer, should he or she be watching. That is what we hope is happening; otherwise, we're wasting our time."

The part of his theory that caught Taylor's attention was getting her mom and sister off her back. She loved that! But could she chance playing his lover in front of them? She knew she was already physically attracted to the man. Pretending in front of strangers was one thing, but pretending in front of family was another. Part of her wouldn't be pretending, and they would see through it. When they found out later it was play-acting for their benefit, her family, at least her mom, would know the truth and would know how deeply it would hurt Taylor when the job was over.

"Come on, Taylor. Don't think about it. Just do it. It would teach them a lesson about sticking their nose in other people's lives. I know. I've been through it myself."

John sounded like he really wanted to help her. How sweet. "Okay. Let's do it."

"Now, back to why I called you to begin with. How should I dress for this party tonight? The same way I've dressed the past two nights? Casual?"

"Yes, John. By all means, dress casual. We're not fancy." What a guy! He was worried how to dress for her parents. Most men wouldn't care. "Don't forget to pick me up at seven." On that, they said good-bye.

It was almost six. Taylor hadn't eaten lunch yet, so she fixed herself a quick ham and cheese sandwich. With it she tossed back a few chips and chased it all with a glass of milk. She figured at Tina's she wouldn't have much of an appetite. Taylor ate while she finished watching an old movie on TV. By the time the credits were rolling, it was six thirty. Jumping up, she ran to get dressed.

After her shower, she dried off and dressed for the night. She wore knee-high black leather boots with jeans and a T-shirt, one with a country singer sparkling across her chest. Taylor dabbed on a bit of makeup and a quick splash of perfume, then took a minute to try and tame her wild curls. When finished, she glanced at her reflection in the mirror. "You don't look too bad." Normally Taylor would find all kinds of faults, but not tonight. She chose to bolster her morale in order to face her sister with a smile and not a .45.

That thought brought a half smile to her face. She couldn't even tell her sister how mad she had gotten today. She and John were going to play the happy little loving couple. What a joke!

Walking out of the bedroom, she heard a knock at the door. "Coming," she called. Grabbing her purse and the present she had bought for her parents, Taylor reached for the doorknob. Pausing, she said, "John, is that you?"

"No. I'm the crazy guy on the phone." He laughed.

Soon they were in his Bronco, heading toward her sister's home. "They live in the Garden District near my parents," she explained.

Glancing his way, she studied him as he drove. He sure looked good tonight. His face was clean-shaven, and he smelled heavenly. Taylor wished what they were about to do wasn't a joke.

"You up for your part tonight?" he questioned her in clipped tones.

Taylor's left brow furrowed. "Sure. I've made it through the last two nights play-acting with you. What's one more?" She knew the difference. Tonight it was in front of family, but she didn't dare let him know she was a little nervous about the next couple of hours. She continued to direct him until they pulled into Tina's driveway.

Getting out of the car, John walked around and opened the door for Taylor. As she started to step out, he reached for her hand. As she placed her hand in his, she climbed out of the Bronco. When her feet hit the ground, he wrapped his arms around her and pulled her close. Suddenly he kissed her hard, on the lips.

Taylor's heart leapt into her throat as it beat uncontrollably. As soon as she could speak, she said, "What was that for?"

Slowly he slackened his hold on her but kept one arm draped around her waist and then directed them toward the front door. "In case someone was looking out of the window. Besides, you needed to look like you've been kissed. You were too stiff-looking, almost frightened. Now"—he paused— "now you have the look of love."

She smirked. "Yeah, right." She had a hard time catching her breath but didn't want him to know how much he'd rattled her.

Her sister must have been watching, for the minute their feet touched the first step, the door flew open and Tina filled the doorway. "Taylor. You made it." Tina's voice sounded surprised.

John pulled her a little closer, making Taylor look up at him before she answered her sister. She couldn't help but smile. Taylor knew that was a warning from him to be sweet to Tina.

"Yes, Tina. I wouldn't miss this for the world. I have someone I want you to meet." They stepped into the foyer.

Tina smiled at John with open admiration. Taylor knew that look. John had better hurry up and tell them he was a cop if he knew what was good for him.

"John, this is my baby sister, Tina." After greetings were exchanged, Tina led the way to the family room.

As Taylor started to pull out of his grasp, he caught her

hand in his, keeping them touching one another as they entered the living room where everyone was seated.

Taylor's father and Rodney, Tina's husband, immediately rose to their feet. "Taylor, sweetheart," her father said as he approached her. John released her hand, giving her freedom to hug her dad. She then kissed her mother's cheek, hugged Rodney, and laid her parents' present on the end table.

"I'd like all of you to meet a. . .a friend of mine, John. And this is my family." She then called everyone by name as she pointed toward each. "Where are the kids?"

"They're upstairs. They'll join us for dinner."

"It's a pleasure to meet all of you," John said. "Taylor has told me so much about each of you these past few weeks." He gazed at Taylor. "It's only been a couple of weeks, right, darling?" Then he turned his blue eyes on her mother. "It's been the best weeks of my life. Your daughter is something special."

Needless to say, Taylor's mother ate that up. "We've always known that. It's just been hard making Taylor see it."

John slipped his hands over Taylor's shoulders and said, "I tell her that all the time—she's something special." Then he topped it by leaning down and kissing her cheek in front of everyone.

Taylor couldn't believe it. She knew her cheeks turned red. She felt the heat rise. Was he ever putting on a show! He deserved an Oscar.

Rodney interrupted Taylor's thoughts as Taylor and John sat on the loveseat. "Are you working on a new story? Dad said you were covering those murders that have been happening in the Quarter. I've seen a few of your articles, but they don't have the details you usually share with the readers. What's going on?"

"Yes, I'm covering the murders, but I'd rather we not discuss them tonight."

John took over before she could say any more. "Actually, that was how I met your sister-in-law, Rodney. I'm the detective in charge of that investigation. We're working closely on it." He smiled sweetly at Taylor. "But I'm keeping my eye out for her. I don't want anything happening to her."

Taylor's mother spoke up. "This is refreshing—a young man who wants to protect our daughter. Taylor usually won't allow anyone to protect her." She squeezed Oliver's hand, vividly showing her enthusiasm.

John smiled at Mrs. Jaymes. "I know what you mean. She gets mad at me if I put too many protective barricades between her and her story. She wants me to believe she is as tough as any man." John winked at her dad. "But I know she's as fragile as a piece of porcelain."

Oliver cleared his throat. "Well, I imagine she is that, but Taylor has taken very good care of herself, and I believe she will continue to do what is best for her."

Dear old Dad. How sweet. "You know, y'all don't have to talk about me as if I'm not here. I am, and I hear everything you're saying." Taylor nudged John in his side.

"Well, I, for one, think she's done wonderfully for herself, picking a policeman as a boyfriend," Tina chimed in to the conversation as her eyes laid to rest on John in awe.

Theresa agreed with her daughter, but neither Oliver nor Rodney voiced their opinions. Not that they didn't have one, Taylor felt certain. Her guess would be their opinions reflected their wives—so much for John's theory, them not wanting her to be with a cop.

The conversation continued and Taylor could tell her family was eating him up. They were falling for John hook, line, and sinker. Boy, had she made a mistake! Her mother didn't care that he was a policeman. In fact, she sounded like she loved it because she figured he could take better care of her daughter. Her mother was probably right, but that was beside the point. Before Taylor could pass her thoughts on to John, Tina insisted Taylor help her in the kitchen.

As they entered the other room, questions fired out of Tina's mouth, one after the other. Taylor knew it. Helping in the kitchen was merely a ploy to get her alone.

"Where have you been hiding him? He's perfect. How long have you two really been dating? He said a few weeks. Why didn't you tell us? I hate to admit this, but I did have someone I was going to set you up with tonight. Boy, would he have been a disappointment compared to John." Tina went on and on about John's perfections. His looks. His manners. His knowledge. And she didn't even know him yet.

The only way this charade would work is if her sister would learn a valuable lesson when she learned the truth. Would she? Taylor hoped it didn't backfire. But if Tina did, she would never interfere in Taylor's life again.

Tina and Taylor put dinner on the table and everyone gathered around, including the girls, Shelly and Sheila. They, too, were instantly taken with John. The food was great, but Taylor couldn't swallow a thing. It was a good thing she had eaten a late lunch.

Part of her felt bad for what she was pulling over on her

family, but the other part of her was wishing all of this was for real. Everyone liked him so much, and John fit in so well. And admittedly, she liked him, herself. Taylor hadn't heard one lull in conversation tonight. And everybody was getting in on it; everyone except her, of course.

If Taylor didn't know better, she thought John was having the time of his life. He wasn't that bad of an actor. He even had Taylor believing him.

After the presents were opened, it was getting close to nine. John said, "I hate to end this great party, but Taylor and I have something we must do tonight. It's with the case. It has been a delightful pleasure being here with you all. Thanks for including me. It was wonderful meeting everyone. I certainly see where your daughter gets her grace and charm."

Mrs. Jaymes walked them to the door and her dad followed behind. "Thank you for stopping by. The two of us have had a wonderful thirty-three years of marriage. It really is something to think about." She squeezed Taylor's arm as they walked to the door.

Her mother wasn't too obvious, was she? Taylor eyed her mom and then shook her head. Giving them another hug, she whispered, "I love you two. See you soon."

John said bye again, and the two of them left. Once inside the Bronco, he said, "Your family was very nice."

Taylor nodded. "Of course they were nice. I never said they weren't. But didn't you feel my mother measuring your chest for your tuxedo?"

"They did seem to like me, didn't they?" John's face looked surprised and yet a little self-satisfied. "And I caught that hint about marriage being wonderful. Rest assured."

Taylor rolled her eyes as she fell back against the seat. "Of course they liked you. They think you will make a wonderful husband for their wild daughter who won't settle down. You're perfect. You're a cop. You'll be able to keep me in line. Don't you see?" She huffed. "And you thought they would be turned off by your profession. I should have known better."

John remained silent for a few short minutes, almost as if he was reveling in the attraction everyone felt for him. Why should that surprise him? He was wonderful.

Taylor was worn out, and the night still wasn't over. Actually, it had only just begun. Would she make it?

She flashed her eyes in his direction. Her stomach squeezed. Tonight was wonderful, but she had to remember it was all an act. The big picture was the story, and that was where they were headed now. She had to stay focused on the prize. . .Pulitzer Prize.

Chapter 23

Friday night was no different at Six-Shooters than the two nights before; no leads, and no approaches. Toward the end of the night, in fact, the last dance of the night, as the two stepped around the floor holding each other close, John whispered in her ear. "Are you too tired for me to come by for a little while? I think we need to rethink our plan of action. This isn't getting us anywhere."

His warm breath caressed Taylor's neck as she listened intently. They might not have accomplished anything for the case, but these nights with John on his best behavior had done something wonderful to Taylor. She couldn't help but feel slightly guilty. She loved every minute of it.

Earlier tonight, Taylor enjoyed having her mother see her with a date. In fact, she delighted in the feeling it gave her to have a man interested in her, even if it was pretend.

Her heart broke a little inside as she thought about the lie she led her mother to believe, but seeing the joy on her face filled Taylor with hope. Maybe one day she could fall in love. Too bad this wasn't the real thing.

Taylor expected her mother to be on the phone first thing Saturday morning drilling her about John. Tina had her chance earlier that night. Taylor could hear her mother now. "What's he really like? Is his job more dangerous than yours? You two looked serious. Are you?" Taylor smiled at the thought of her mother's excitement. It would be nicer if their relationship had been true, but Taylor knew better than to even fantasize.

"Did you hear me?" John's voice jolted her back to the present. "May I come by?"

"Sure. That's a good idea. I was thinking the same thing myself, and time is running out before the next kill if his MO hasn't changed," she said, keeping her voice low.

In fifteen minutes, they were at her apartment. She had done her version of cleaning that morning, but as usual had left her dirty dishes in the sink after eating that late lunch. Her gaze caught the T-shirt she had slept in tossed on the chair in the living room. Not too bad. The rest of the room looked fairly neat. She swooped the shirt up and tossed it in the bedroom, behind the door. *He won't be going in there, so no big deal.*

When she turned her gaze back toward John, she realized John had noticed the few things out of order. His eyes glanced at the newspaper she'd left open on the coffee table, as well as her Coke glass from before she took off for the evening.

Flashing an awkward smile, she said, "The maid didn't make it today. Have a seat. I'll go put a pot of coffee on for you." She grabbed the empty glass and nonchalantly waltzed into the kitchen.

When the coffeemaker was set and water started dripping, she returned to the living room. The newspaper had been gathered together and left folded neatly on the coffee table, as neat as it had been when it was dropped on her doorstep. Maybe even neater, if that was possible. She noticed her throw pillows had even been straightened, along with the cushions of the couch.

"Sorry if my mess offends you." *Good*. She noticed color wash over his face as if she had embarrassed him.

"I was killing time. I thought I would help you out. Let's get down to business." He pushed a pillow out of place and leaned back against the sofa.

She laughed to herself. "The coffee will be ready in a minute. Two sugars, right?"

He nodded. As Taylor went back into the kitchen, she mumbled under her breath, "Maybe I'll throw in an extra teaspoon full. He needs it."

Taylor returned with the coffee and found no other move had been made to right her living room. In fact, John had leaned his head back against the sofa and looked to be napping.

As soon as she set the cups down, he sat up. "Smells good." As he sipped it, his smile showed it tasted as good as it smelled.

Taylor curled up in her overstuffed chair and watched him as he drank a bit of his coffee. When he placed it on the coffee table, Taylor took that moment to start their discussion. "You're right; we're not getting anywhere, and it's been another week. Any day another woman could end up dead. It could happen tonight."

⁓⊸⊘⊱

John heaved a sigh as he rubbed his whiskers and thought about his new idea. *This will put Taylor in more jeopardy, but I think it's the only way. I won't—we won't—let anything happen to her.* He leaned back and draped his arm across the back of the sofa as he said, "I know we've been watching everyone, and we've run background checks on any and everyone who appeared suspicious or even said anything out of the ordinary. In fact, we've checked out all the workers, including the band members, and nothing new has jumped out at us. We're still keeping close tabs on one of the band members, who had a record and a couple of customers we recognized with rap sheets a mile long. But we have to do something to flush out the killer—hopefully before he kills again."

John's gaze traveled around her living room, but he saw nothing. His mind was preoccupied with what this would mean to Taylor's safety. He needed to find the words to approach her about his new idea. As much as he hated it, it seemed to be the next best option.

Taylor smirked. "Let me save you the words. I see it on your face and now I know why you were so nice to me tonight. You're planning to send me packing. It's time I went back to checking out information in the light of day, and you and your men do the heavy lifting, the dangerous parts, on your own at night."

He covered his mouth, trying to hide the smile. *If she only knew how far from the truth that was. She'll know soon enough. Spit it out and be done with it.* "I think you need to go as a single woman, and I'll go keep my eye on you from a distance. The killer is not going to say anything to give himself away to a couple, but he might to an appealing single woman. And in this case, I mean a trained investigator, undercover. I must be out of my mind because I know this could be dangerous. So think it over carefully before you decide. I probably should use a policewoman, but you're more aware of what to listen for, questions to ask without sounding like a reporter or a cop. I just think you're our best bet."

Her eyes lit up.

"I knew it. The minute the word *danger* came into the picture, the light in your eyes started dancing around, doing flips. You get excited over the possibilities of danger." He raked fingers through his hair. "Maybe I'm making a mistake."

"I'm just. . .I—"

John stood. "I knew I didn't want to suggest this to you, but my gut tells me you're the one to get close. But I should really use a policewoman—not you." He shoved his hands in his pockets and walked over to the window. As he let his thoughts overtake him, he stared out into the darkness.

He was asking too much of her, and she seemed to love it. Why was he encouraging her to continue? More so, why was he putting her in a more dangerous position? Maybe this was his way of making himself lose his desire for her. He hated to admit it—it wasn't working.

❧

Taylor watched his silhouette in the window. His back faced her, but she knew he was deep in thought, regretting his plan to work with her, his plan to use her to draw out the killer.

She eased over to the window and stood behind him. She

couldn't let him change his mind. Gently she reached out and touched his back. "John," she whispered. "My eyes danced in delight, as you said, because I was delighted—excited. Not by the thought of the danger. When that thought comes to mind, which I'm sure it will, I'll shudder."

Slowly he turned to face her but said nothing.

Taylor continued. "I was delighted because you didn't exclude me from the investigation. I truly thought you were going to tell me to go back to pounding the pavement during the day and leave the night work to you." Her voice became husky as she continued. "It excites me that you realize I have enough detective instincts about me to listen and watch and discover something to help you out on your case."

Still, he stood watching, saying nothing.

She raised both her hands and shook him gently by the shoulders. "Don't you see? I know it sounds crazy, but coming from you I take that as a compliment and it makes me feel so good." She bit her bottom lip, shocked that she shared her deepest feelings with this wonderful man. When he still didn't respond, she gave up and turned to walk away.

John caught her by the arm. Turning her back around, he sat on the edge of the windowsill and pulled her in front of him, holding her still by clasping her hands in his.

"Taylor, you do realize how dangerous this will be, not to mention it's probably against every police regulation there is. I think I'm out of my mind to allow you to do this, but it feels right. . .here." He tapped his fist against the middle of his chest with her hands still in bondage.

A knot formed in her throat as she felt the beating of his heart. Swallowing hard, she whispered, "No, you're not out of your mind. It shows you have good instincts. We can work together—just not together." She smiled.

Releasing her hands so they could drop to her side, his hands gently rubbed her arms. "You have to promise me something."

Looking up, their eyes locked. "Anything."

"Three things, actually. One, you can't do anything stupid. Two, I have to be able to see you at all times—don't leave the bar with anyone." His glare hardened. "Under any circumstances. And three, you'll do exactly what I tell you, when I tell you, and I'll be watching you like a hawk. Others will be watching you, too, and what's going on around you, too. The way people react to you and so forth. Do I make myself clear?" His words were stern, but his voice gentle.

Warmth spread over her. He would be watching her every move. The only bad part? She wouldn't be in his arms anymore. She would be dancing with other men and wishing it was John. Sighing and shaking her head clear of all romantic thoughts of him, she said, "Whatever you tell me. I understand. I promise I'll listen to you."

"Listen to you. Sighing because you have to do what I say. You don't take orders well, do you?"

A crooked smile twisted her lips. He misunderstood her sigh. *Good.* She didn't want to let him know she was falling in love with him.

John dropped his hands. Glancing at his watch, he said, "Get some rest. It's late. Sleep in tomorrow. . .no. Forget that. It's already tomorrow. Be at the bar at nine thirty tonight. Look for me and try to sit near, but not too near. We don't want to give ourselves away." He smiled, lifting his brows.

"Can you handle that?" He rubbed the pad of his thumb softly over her cheek and then placed a soft kiss on her forehead. "Be careful. Good night."

Her heart jumped as his lips brushed her skin. Keeping control, Taylor murmured good night and then watched him walk out the door.

The warmth inside her was quickly replaced by a cold chill. She had felt so good when he was around, safe even. . .secure and desired. At times anyway.

But it wasn't real. . .or was it?

He stirred feelings in her she had never felt before. It scared her. And to think all this time she never believed she could find a man who was right for her.

Her career had been too important to her to even think of settling down. The story she was working on always took precedence over some guy. That was probably why nothing had ever come of any of her relationships. Would a connection come of these feelings stirring in her?

Probably not.

She still had her goal, and it was still important to her. Somehow, she thought, maybe John could fit into her life. Maybe their careers could work together. He was different. That was what made him so special.

She felt certain she wouldn't be able to sleep tonight, but within minutes, she was fast asleep.

❧

Taylor woke by ten that morning. After her morning cup of coffee and some scrambled eggs, she decided to do something she rarely did. She had an overwhelming desire to super-clean her apartment.

By three she had her place sparkling, the best it had looked in months. It even smelled fresh. Still dressed in a pair of cut-offs and a pink T-shirt, she ran down to the local market and stocked up on groceries—another thing she didn't normally do.

The desire to play homemaker really blew her away. By the time she finished shopping, she had enough food to fill her cupboards and refrigerator. Surprisingly enough, some of the food she bought was actually healthy.

"I hope I manage to eat all this before it goes bad." She closed the produce drawer after stuffing a bag of apples inside.

Feeling tired and dirty, after spending most of the day playing house, Taylor decided it was time for a shower. But as she stepped into the hallway, her doorbell rang. "Who could that be? Probably Mom checking on me." She never called, which surprised Taylor. Her mom showing up on Taylor's doorstep truly shocked her.

Before her hands turned the knob, she heard a familiar voice call out, "Taylor. Answer your door. I know you're home."

"John?" she whispered. *What's he doing here?*

Wiping the back of her hands against her cheeks, trying to remove all traces of dirt, she headed for the door. Excitement stirred within her as she reached for the knob. "What brings you here? I thought I wouldn't see you until tonight."

John's gaze slid over her head and behind her into her apartment. His brows wrinkled. "Do you have company?" As he asked the question, he took a step inside.

Taylor frowned. Looking down at herself, she asked, "Do I look like I'm entertaining company?" Backing up, she asked, "Would you like some coffee? I'm sure eventually you'll let me know why the surprise visit."

John stepped into the living room. Glancing around, he paused. Stepping back out, he looked up at the apartment number. "It is the same one. Did the good fairy come clean your apartment for you? Oh, no, I forgot. You said the maid. I guess your maid showed up today." His eyes danced around the room as he teased her. "Looks like you've been cleaning. Expecting someone special?"

"Of course not!" she snapped. "Have a seat. I'll start the coffee."

She slammed the front door shut and darted for the kitchen. What was going on? Why was he here? And did he have to be so aggravating?

Instead of returning to her company once the coffee started dripping, she chose to wait for it. When it finished dripping, she couldn't put it off any longer. "Be nice," she whispered aloud. *Remember. Just last night you had seen a different side of him.* She didn't want him to ruin the pleasant mood that he had set the night before. She poured him a cup of coffee, and Taylor fixed herself some iced tea.

John had made himself comfortable on the sofa. After placing a cup of coffee in front of him on the coffee table, she slipped into the recliner to sip her tea. "What brought you this way?"

Raising the cup, he sipped the brew and then set it back down. "I thought we should go over again what you are to do tonight. I don't want any slip-ups."

"Do you always have to sound so. . .so. . .I don't know what to call it—uncertain? Why don't you just trust me? Trust yourself for that matter? You're the one who thought I could handle it to begin with," she snapped. Calming herself, she determined to put a smile on his face. Softening her voice, she said, "I remember what you said. Stay in your sight at all times. Don't leave with anybody, and above all, don't do anything stupid." Taylor turned her lips down in a pout. "Is that right?"

John shook his head. "All right. Be smart. But still do as I told you—for your own good."

Taylor stood before he could say anything else. "I was about to take a quick shower, then eat. Have you eaten?" She answered for him. "I doubt it. Whatever happened to your good eating habits?" Before he could answer, she continued. "Relax and you can eat with me. I promise. It's healthy food."

He smiled, warming her heart. "Is this another 'Trust me' remark of yours?"

She shrugged. "Suit yourself. But if you leave, you'll miss a tossed salad and baked fish." She flipped her hair behind her shoulders and sashayed past him. "I'll be out in a few minutes."

Taylor wasn't sure if he would wait or not, but she hoped he would. Her shower didn't take long. Maybe it was because she was anxious to get back out to John. She slipped on her favorite pair of old jeans and a T-shirt.

Using the towel, she worked at drying her hair some. After combing it out and letting the curls and waves manifest themselves, she headed for the kitchen. Taylor passed through the living room and found John looking through an old photo album of hers.

"Looks like you made yourself at home." She smiled but kept heading for the kitchen.

Bending down and pulling out her casserole pan, she heard steps behind her. He followed. A grin etched in her face. "I hope you're hungry."

John sat down at the table still holding the album in his hands. "You and your dad look to be very close by these pictures."

"Uh-huh," she murmured.

John turned the page. "Your sister is always in a dress, and you are always in pants. Did you want to be a boy?"

Turning her head so she could see him, she said, "Don't try to analyze me."

He was still looking at the pictures, not paying her any attention. "You were definitely Daddy's little girl. You're always on his lap or holding his hand. Even when you got older."

"We were close, still are in fact. Just my life doesn't leave much time to go visit him, and he doesn't call often. He leaves that up to Mom. Why? Is there a problem?"

He ignored her again. "What are these awards around your father?"

He seems to enjoy snooping into my life. For some reason, though, it didn't seem hard for her to talk about her personal life with him. She smiled. "He won the Franklin Press Award and the Pulitzer Prize for investigative reporting. Every journalist wants to win that, and my dad did over ten years ago. I only hope I can win at least one major award for my writing—make him proud of me." Taylor's eyes lit up as she thought about what she was saying.

John looked up at her. "So you're trying to be like your father?"

"No. I'm trying to accomplish something in the field I

chose to follow, which happens to be the same field he chose as a young man." Taylor sprinkled the fish with garlic powder and a touch of Tony Chachere's, then poured lemon juice over it. Next, she topped it with Worcestershire sauce and a couple pats of butter, and then popped it in the oven.

Turning back to John, she pleaded, "Please don't analyze me and, above all, don't criticize me. . .just be pleasant. Is that so hard for you? You're making me sorry I asked you to stay and eat with me." Taylor turned back to the sink and started washing the lettuce.

John slipped up behind her. Leaning close to her, he whispered, "Man, you smell good. So fresh and clean." His warm breath caressed her skin.

Goose bumps covered her arms, sending shivers down her back. That was better, she thought, but didn't say a word.

"I'm glad you asked me to stay." He touched her damp curls lightly and then rested his hands on her shoulders. "I'm glad you cleaned your place for me, too."

She dropped the lettuce in the sink as she turned off the water. "What makes you think—" Her question was cut off when she turned around.

A smile spread to his lips. His hands had fallen to his sides when she turned so unexpectedly, then he started to put them back up on her shoulders, as if he was about to pull her to him and kiss her.

Placing her hands flat against his chest, she shoved him back. "What did you say?" It was a rhetorical question. She didn't expect an answer. In fact, she didn't want him to answer her at all. "I know what you said. I did not clean my house for you. What do you think I am—a slob? I clean it occasionally.

And today just happened to be the occasion: I didn't expect you here today, and you know it. You are so full of yourself!"

John dropped his hands to his sides, stepped back, and laughed. "Come on. Why is it so hard to admit you cleaned it for me? I made a comment last time so you wanted to make sure it was clean the next time I came by. Hey, that pleases me." He grinned.

"Wipe that look off your face, please. I didn't do it for you." She pivoted back to continue rinsing the lettuce.

"Taylor, why is it so hard for you to admit you did it for me?" His voice was soft and gentle. "Look at what you're cooking—fish. That's healthy. You don't eat healthy. It appears by the salad and fish you're trying to eat healthy now. I'm sure if I look," he walked over to the refrigerator, "I'll find other healthy foods inside." He opened the refrigerator door and eyed the plastic bag of apples sticking out. Pulling on the drawer, he said, "See."

Before he could look any further, Taylor stormed over, shut the drawer, and slammed the refrigerator door shut. "Get out!" She pushed him toward the living room. "Get out and stay out! You are uninvited. So leave. I did not clean for you, nor did I shop for you." Rushing around him, she stomped over to the front door. Pulling it open and holding it, she continued, "I'll see you tonight. Don't be late." Her eyes flared with anger. *The nerve of him!*

"But. . ."

"No buts. Get out! Now!" She glared him down.

John didn't say another word. Scratching his head, he left with no more arguments.

Taylor slammed the door behind him. "The nerve of that

man," she spat at the closed door. Throwing herself down on her overstuffed chair, she sat and fumed. When the fish was ready, she was no longer hungry. She had lost her appetite right after her temper.

The smell of garlic mixed with lemon wafted in the air. Taylor wrapped the entire meal and stored it in the refrigerator for another day. Then she put the dirty dishes in the sink and ran water on them. She wasn't in the mood to clean another thing today.

Choosing her outfit for the night's work, she considered her outburst with John. Why had she gotten so mad?

He was right. She had done it for him. She'd cleaned her place in case he came by so she could impress him and show him she was capable. Also all the food. . .surely she hadn't bought all of that just for her to eat.

Looking at her reflection in the mirror, she squinted her eyes. "You just couldn't admit it, could you? Although, if he had been a gentleman, he wouldn't have said such things anyway, other than maybe comments on how good it looked."

It's all his fault. . . .

Oh well. Enough of that.

The story was more important than a fight with a deadbeat cop. She'd never cared for cops anyway.

Chapter 24

What got into her?" John headed back to the office thinking all the while, *What's the big deal?*

For the next couple of hours he tried to work but found it hard to concentrate. He couldn't accomplish a thing. Tossing his pen down, he leaned back in his chair and tried to make sense of the earlier disaster with Taylor.

No matter how many times he replayed it, which he did several times, he kept coming up with the same conclusion. "There's no mistaking it. She did it for me. She had to. Didn't she? So why wouldn't she admit it?"

Had anyone come by, they would have thought he was crazy talking to himself, but right now he felt a little crazy. He threw his hands into the air. "Women! What does it matter? I didn't want to get tangled up with her anyway."

A knock at the door brought John out of his reverie.

"Excuse me, sir. Are we still staking out the club tonight?" Officer Brown asked him.

John glanced at his watch. "Darn straight we are. Thanks," he said as he jumped to his feet. "Yeah. Get in plain clothes and get on over there. Where is Buck? He knows what to do, right?"

Brown nodded affirmatively. "By the way, that was Guidry you saw at the club last night. We watched the film today, the one the club cameras produce nightly. We also spotted another known felon for sexual abuse of women, our old buddy Frank Simpson."

John remembered him immediately. Not only did he sexually abuse his women, but he also got a kick out of choking them while tormenting them sexually. He would tie a cord around their neck, then tie that same cord to their ankles and watch them try not to move and choke themselves to death while he had his way with them. Luckily for him, none of his victims died. He had been given five years in prison for what he had done. Five lousy years. That wasn't much for what those two women had suffered.

"Five years goes by fast, doesn't it?"

"Yeah. I checked his rap sheet. He's been out for five months and has stayed clean the whole time. . .as far as we know."

"One of you keep your eyes on Guidry while the other stays with Simpson. Guidry might have had an alibi for the first two killings, but the alibi hasn't been verified yet. He's still a suspect. I'll keep mine on Taylor. Between the three of us watching the three of them, and the others that come in contact with them, maybe we'll get lucky tonight."

"See ya there, Lieutenant." Brown left and John followed him out of the building.

John headed home mumbling to himself, "I can't believe how late it's gotten." He rushed in, showered quickly and changed into a fresh pair of slacks and a neatly ironed shirt. Next he slipped on his shoulder holster for his Walther PPK. The .380 was an easier weapon to hide. Then John put on his sport coat. He would stash his automatic in his glove box for backup.

Glancing around his clean home before leaving, it seemed so empty. . .so cold. "Where did that thought come from?" he asked himself before heading out the door.

On the drive to the club, he found himself thinking of Taylor again. He was running late but hoped she remembered rule number one. Don't do anything stupid. Pressing the gas pedal harder, he rushed to get there, hopefully before her. Tonight he would apologize for their squabble. Maybe she wasn't ready to admit she wanted to impress him, so he shouldn't have pushed it. Before that, though, he needed to concentrate solely on what was going on tonight.

Looking in his rearview mirror, he spotted flashing red and blue lights. His eyes darted down to his dashboard and saw the needle holding steady on sixty. Slowing down, John pulled over, came to a quick halt, jumped out of his vehicle, slamming his door, and trampled over to the police unit. "I don't need this." Flashing his ID at the policeman, he said, "I'm in a hurry here. I'm on a case."

The uniformed officer got out of his car. Recognizing the lieutenant, he started rambling apologies. He was a new policeman and apparently hadn't recognized the detective's

Bronco. "Lieutenant Bradley. I'm sorry, sir. I didn't mean to delay you. I thought you were a kid joy riding. Sorry—"

John interrupted him. "It's okay, Findley. Don't worry. I've got to go." He returned to his car and was back on his way instantly. John was late now for sure. All he could hope was that Taylor hadn't done anything foolish. He never liked using civilians for undercover operations and this was why. Unfortunately with Taylor, to him, it was a little worse.

Taylor dressed in a pair of jeans and an off-the-shoulder black fitted top. With this, she wore her black boots with the silver tips on the toes. She took special pains with her hair and makeup tonight. "All part of the job," she told herself looking into the mirror, but she knew better.

Entering Six-Shooters at the scheduled time, she glanced around. He had told her to sit near him. *Can't do that if you're not here.* She double-checked the time to make sure she wasn't early. "Right on time," she murmured to herself.

She found a stool that seemed to be in the center of the long bar down one side of the place. That looked good. She sat down and leaned over to place her order. After ordering a screwdriver easy on the vodka, she told the bartender she wanted to run a tab. Then she sat back and began looking for faces she'd seen in there on previous nights. Recognizing a couple of regulars, she started watching them, trying to catch someone's eye.

Taylor managed to get noticed by several men in the bar. She danced with a couple of cowboys who asked her, names exchanged sometimes, but not always. None made her feel like they were the one she was looking for. She dropped a few remarks, watching their response. Nothing seemed to make them react strangely. So she decided not to waste any more time on them.

The bartender stopped in front of her while she sat on her stool and scanned the crowd, looking for another one to set her sights on. "Is something wrong with your drink? You've barely touched it."

She smiled. That was nice of him to notice. She would have to leave him a good tip. "Oh, no. Everything's fine. I'm just sipping slowly."

"I noticed your boyfriend's not here tonight. Did y'all split up?"

So he had noticed her before. "Yeah, we sure did. That's the breaks. You win some, you lose some." Taylor flashed him a big smile and then took another sip of her drink. She had to get back to work. "Thanks again. I'll let you know when I need another one."

Taylor glanced around the room. She still didn't see any sign of John. She thought she recognized one of the detectives from the other day, but she couldn't be sure. Before she knew it, on each side of her sat young men dressed in jeans and western shirts, wearing boots and cowboy hats, but still no John. What could be keeping him? She turned back to the bar; giving one of her neighbors a smile in acknowledgment. That was all it took. He struck up a conversation.

John rushed to the door but slowed his stride as he entered. He didn't want to draw attention to himself.

Strolling into the club, his eyes trained for searching out small details in an instant, he spotted Taylor at the bar. Two men sitting on either side of her were vying for her attention. It was all he could do to keep his composure and walk on to a table as far away as possible, yet still in view of the bar.

Finding the right table, he took it. As soon as he placed an order, he sat back and started watching Taylor work without looking straight at her. She seemed to be getting into the swing of things, from the bar to the dance floor and back to the bar. At this rate, every man in the place would have danced with her by closing time.

After nursing a Coke for almost two hours, he found himself tired of watching Taylor dance with every dude in the room. She seemed to be enjoying it, giving him even more reason not to like it.

Ordering another Coke, he reminded himself he wasn't interested in Taylor. He was on the job, protecting her. This was a case he wanted to solve before another woman was senselessly murdered. But it was still hard to watch her dangling the bait for the killer. Especially when one of the men she danced with was Simpson—that pervert.

By midnight, Taylor felt that if she danced one more time, her feet would drop off. She at least had the satisfaction of knowing that as bad as her feet hurt from dancing, John appeared to be worse off. He looked downright miserable having to stay seated in one place all night long. He had slipped in shortly before ten, so Taylor felt safe to turn on the charm with every stranger she met after that. After all the men she danced with, shot pool with, and just talked to, she still felt no closer to finding a possible serial killer. One was very strange, but she didn't get the sense he would kill for his sick pleasure. She knew they needed to check into him, but in her heart she felt he would be a waste of their time.

Her feet throbbed. She wasn't used to dancing so much since she rarely went out. Over the past few nights, keeping up the charade, she and John only danced a few times each night. She was nursing her second drink of the night, more water than drink because she'd let it sit so long.

At the stroke of one, she called it a night. Glancing at John, making eye contact for the first time, she tried to let him know she was leaving. Since she hadn't looked directly at him all night, she hoped he got the message.

Dropping a twenty to cover the two drinks she had, she said, "Keep the change." Then she flashed a brilliant smile his way. The bartender's eyes looked at her but didn't react like the rest of the men. It didn't matter, she told herself. She was too tired to be nice, had he chosen to speak to her.

Taylor walked the few blocks home. No sooner had she walked up the stairs and let herself in, she collapsed on the couch ready to take off her boots. A pounding sounded at the door.

John, of course. She rushed to the door. Before throwing it open, she called out, "John, is that you?"

"You know it is. Open up!"

"Quiet. You'll wake my neighbors."

◈

John stepped in and quickly shut the door behind him. His temper seemed to be riding high. He knew it, and he knew why. He didn't like the way she made herself so accessible tonight.

His anger didn't seem to faze her. Taylor sat down on the

sofa and pulled her boots off one at a time.

"I'm glad you checked who was at your door before opening it." He made another attempt to make Taylor think about her own safety.

"Of course I did. I'm not going to open my door to just anyone, especially this time of night." She started to rise but flopped back down on the sofa. "If you want coffee, you'll have to get it yourself. There's instant in the cupboard if you want."

Dragging his fingers through his dark waves, he decided to speak his mind. "I don't want any coffee. You need to be more careful. Even though I wasn't the killer, I could have been one of those doting fools you left at the bar with their tongues hanging out in anticipation. You weren't supposed to be a tramp and score with every man at the bar." He moved closer and closer to the couch as he spoke. Soon he was towering over her. John wanted to pick her up and shake some sense into her. . .but then he wanted to hold her and make sure she was safe. Instead, he just stared down at her.

"You're crazy. I was doing my job. What do you think those women were doing the night they were killed? You think they had gone in just to have a drink, unwind, and go home? No. They were lonely women looking for a one-night stand probably."

That blew the wind right out of his sails. He had no idea women went looking for one-night stands. He thought only men thought that way—not that he would do that anymore. "Is that what women want? A one-night stand?"

"Some."

"Well, you did a great job sending out those signals. I'm

just glad no one followed you home to give you what you wanted."

"John. Please. I was doing my job. Hopefully you were doing yours."

She was right. What was he doing here in her apartment? He had come by to make sure she got home safely. Okay. She had.

But when he saw her, he saw all those men who wanted her tonight. He wanted her. No. Even more. He loved her. Could he let her continue this charade?

She didn't give him a chance to figure things out. Instead, she opened the door. "Go home." She glanced at her watch. "I'll see you later tonight. Don't be late—this time." With cold eyes, she dismissed him, double-locking the door behind him.

What had he done?

At 5:00 a.m. the ring of her phone woke her. It was John. She didn't want to open her eyes; she felt she had just gone to sleep.

"We have another victim. I thought you would want to be there."

Her eyes felt like sandpaper running over her eyeballs as she tried to blink them open and hold them there. Forcing them open one more time, she said, "Tell me where. I'm on my way."

Shell-shocked, confused, disoriented, and a little perturbed—all of these emotions raced through her. How could she face him so early this morning after what went down between them only hours ago—their own personal war? She had to go to the scene of the crime, though. She was tough.

This was her job. Taylor could handle it. . .herself. She would show him.

It had been a week and a day since the last victim. They should have expected another one. Actually, they had. Only they had expected the perp to follow Taylor last night, and they would have caught him.

She arrived at the scene as quickly as possible. When she stepped out of her car, the police had already roped off the area with the standard tape. The forensic crew and officers were doing their jobs. John was talking to the medical examiner. Her body chilled for a moment. No way would she let him know how upset she was over last night. How confused she was with her own feelings toward a man who probably didn't even realize she was a woman with the same needs and desires of most women. Pasting her business face on, she grabbed her camera and headed toward the detective.

John felt her presence before he saw her. Her cold expression stopped him in his tracks. Why had he behaved so stupidly last night? They were doing a job together. Why did he have to make things harder than they needed to be? He knew why he behaved the way he did. . .he was jealous. Jealous men did stupid things.

"Was she killed like the others?" Taylor asked. "I noticed the bumper sticker is on her car, too."

When John didn't respond right away, Bob answered her question. "She is our fourth. . .same MO."

"Do you have a name yet—that you can give me?" She turned to John. "I won't be printing it. I know you have to notify next-of-kin. I just thought I would get it now, to save having to come down to the station later today."

"According to her license, her name is Lisa Efferson. She lives in the Garden District." John searched her eyes for a spark of that old reporter spunk she always had before but could not find it. She was like a walking zombie, doing her job like a robot, with no emotion on her face at all or in her voice.

John felt certain she was trying to give him the impression she was fine. . .but inside he knew better. He hoped he knew better. John knew how bad he felt.

Would things ever improve? Was there anything between them? He thought so. He hoped so. Was this part of God's plan for him? He had given up on women, on love, on pain, but then Taylor swept into his life.

I didn't ever think I could feel this way again, Lord, but I do. If it's not supposed to be, shut off these feelings I have for her.

Maybe after this investigation, if it was meant for something between the two of them, they could give it a try. In the back of his mind he felt like he was setting himself up for a fall. Somewhere down the road she would get herself hurt or killed. Could he go through that again?

How do you have a life and do a job all at the same time? Was it possible? Things were simpler when all he did was bury himself in work. Since Taylor came into his life, he hadn't been able to stay on track.

He would have to decide that later. Right now he needed to crack this case wide open and get the killer behind bars.

Chapter 25

As soon as the team gathered all the information at the crime scene, John headed back to the station. When he entered, the noise level bombarded him. The building was already filling with arrestees and arrestors, as well as people filing complaints.

Heading down the hallway toward his department, John passed one culprit handcuffed, waiting to be booked and printed. John apparently was more sensitive today. Another death and he was still no closer to solving the case. His mind was so focused on what he hadn't done yet that he failed to notice the all-time high on the X-rated scale of the words being batted around the station. Criminals, loud-mouthed cops, and bad language were par for the course, so much so that most policemen let it go in one ear and out the other.

Not John. Usually he took a moment to pray they'd see the light. A lot of people had to drop very low in life before they reached out; only today John wasn't hearing the cries. He was too obsessed with stopping this killer. He had failed again. Was it because his mind had been more on Taylor than his case?

Help me, Lord. Give me direction.

Taking the victim's ID, he ran a check on her. The nearest relative he located was an ex-husband, so he called and set up a meeting with him.

The ex-husband was already waiting for him when John arrived at Tim Efferson's place of business. Mr. Efferson hadn't been sure he would be there by noon, but since John told him how important it was, he must have made special arrangements.

Tim opened the office door for John. "Come in and have a seat. Would you like a cup of coffee? There is no secretary here today, but I took a chance and made a pot. It might be a little strong."

Strong coffee? He could use some. "Thanks."

After they were both seated, John gave him the bad news in as much detail as he could share at the moment. "I realize you are no longer married to her, but you were the closest relative I could find."

The man's eyes grew wide as he stared, listening to John. When he spoke, Tim gave the answers asked of him but in almost robotic form. The reality was still trying to soak in, John believed.

"Her parents live in California. She was an only child."

"Sorry. You can give me her parents' information, and I'll gladly contact them."

The man rubbed his mouth as he shook his head. "No. That's okay. I think I'd rather let them know myself. It's going to be hard on them." Tim fell back in his chair, still stunned.

"I'm sorry to do this, but I have to ask you a few routine questions. When was the last time you saw her? Where were you last night? Do you know anyone who would want to harm your ex-wife?"

He answered one at a time as the questions were asked. Slowly but surely the veil over his eyes started lifting and when he answered the last question, he started firing off a couple of his own. "How did it happen? Did she suffer?" Tears started to form in the man's eyes. "Oh, Lisa, Lisa." Burying his face in his hands, he sobbed. "If only I'd tried harder to make it work."

When his sobbing subsided, John said, "I wish I could give you those answers, but the autopsy hasn't been completed. The best I can do is tell you that we believe she was strangled at approximately two in the morning. She was found a few blocks away from Canal Street under the interstate in her car. We're trying hard to find her killer and bring him to justice."

After several seconds of silence, Tim said, "The sad part is, she hadn't been going anywhere since we split. In fact, I think she went out last night to spite me. We had words over the phone. Now I get to live with that for the rest of my life. We had talked about getting back together, but yesterday I wouldn't make a commitment. She said she wasn't going to wait around anymore. The next call would be mine." Sighing, he added, "I guess there won't be a next call." His words choked him as sobs racked him again.

After a few more minutes, John stood. "Mr. Efferson, if you learn anything we can use, please contact me right away. Again, I'm sorry for your loss."

Taylor stopped by the *Tribune* on the way home and wrote a short article for the paper's evening edition, noting the Predawn Strangler had struck again. Then she listed the details, all except the victim's name. Before she left the paper, she called the station and spoke with Buck to see if they had any information on Lisa Efferson.

"The lieutenant is speaking with the family now. Why don't you call him back before the press release? Call him about twelve thirty or one." Buck seemed a little reluctant in helping her this time.

"I'll do that. Thanks." She slowly hung up the phone. Did she want to face him again so early. . .even if it was over the phone?

No. Tonight would be soon enough. She would have them fax her a copy of the press release. She already had the details she could release and her story written so she was ahead of the game.

After attending the crime scene this morning, she thought about what she had done wrong. Why hadn't the killer selected her? The same thought crossed her mind again, but this time the answer came with it. Her car. Taylor had walked. Tonight she would drive.

The first thought that crossed her mind was, she needed to call John and tell him. Touching the phone, about to pick it up, she shivered and then a warmth flooded her senses. "No. Tonight will be soon enough."

Taylor could not understand her emotions. Up and down. The need to see him followed by a fear of seeing him. Was this love? Had she finally, at the age of twenty-eight, found a man she could love? Before meeting Lieutenant John Bradley, she was content with life. . .even had a purpose. Now her purpose wasn't even enough to fill the void John left in her heart.

One thing Taylor learned from all this, love wasn't something you chose. It chose you. And boy did it hurt!

Later that day she received the fax confirming everything she'd stated in the article. *Great. We'd better get the killer soon before someone else loses her life.*

Several hours later, sitting at the bar in her short skirt with a brown fringed shirt tucked in, wearing soft brown suede cowboy boots, she hoped to send out the right signals tonight. She noticed John hidden in the distance and wanted to go to him, tell him she'd fallen for him.

Instead, her eyes danced around the room as she pretended to be cheerful and looking for love. After each dance with a different man, still no one seemed to make her suspect of them. Some even wanted to take her outside or home with them, but she knew the killer didn't work that way. He caught his victim by surprise—in her car. Tonight she would leave in her car. She even left her key by her purse on the bar, not too obviously letting whoever know she was driving tonight. When she left tonight, she would head toward the Garden District. Maybe, just maybe, he'll go after her tonight,

This past week she hadn't missed going to the *Tribune* every day as she normally had. She'd been too tired to think about missing the hubbub. Usually she looked forward to going in, hearing the latest news, and listening to the hum of the giant printers downstairs. Tonight she was so tired, she was heading to the ladies' bathroom to get a little rest.

Before she could push the door open, she was caught by

the arm and dragged to a dark corner of the bar. If she hadn't known John's grip, she would have screamed bloody murder, but she knew he did everything melodramatically.

"What now?" she snapped.

"That's what I want to know. Have you seen anything, or do you suspect anyone? I know I haven't seen anyone suspicious looking. Are we wasting our time?"

"Is that all?" She pulled her arm away. "Do you mean to tell me you took a chance that someone might see us and blow our cover just to find out if I saw anyone acting strange? I thought you were good at your job," she growled.

John's eyes darted around the room. "If you keep your voice down, no one will suspect a thing. I'm about the only single guy you haven't been with tonight, and I thought I better hit on you. . .to make it look good."

"For the record, the bartender recognized me as being the girl with the same man for so many nights in a row and then alone last night. He asked me if we had split up."

John squinted as he regarded the bartender but didn't say a word.

Taylor put her hands on her hips. "If you're so sure, everyone will think you're only hitting on me; then maybe they'll think I turned you down." On those words she smacked him hard across the face, but not too hard. "Now you can go back to your table and do your job." She turned her back on him and went into the ladies' room.

After taking care of personal matters, she splashed her face with cool water. John angered her just by talking to her. He had made no attempt to straighten things out between them. Had she truly fallen for him? She didn't know how much more she could take. Smacking him in the face only felt good for a moment. The joy left her as fast as it had come. She wanted to reach out and caress the red handprint she'd left on his cheek.

We are here to work. She glared her reflection down as she dabbed her face dry with a paper towel. After running her fingers through her curls and then adding a touch of fresh lipstick, she returned to the bar.

Taylor tried to put a smile back on her lips but found it hard.

"Was your old boyfriend giving you a hard time? I noticed he doesn't fit in with all the cowboys you've been dancing with. He looks out of place in here." The bartender placed a fresh drink on a napkin in front of Taylor. "I thought you looked ready for another one, Barbara." He turned away before Taylor could respond.

He called me Barbara. That's strange. I never gave him my name or a fake one for that matter. In fact, we hadn't really even spoken, other than to order a drink. Yet he just talked to me like he had known me for quite some time. That was peculiar.

A chill danced across her shoulders. She would have to tell John about him later.

Breaking her chain of concentration, another man stood next to her. "Wanna dance?" This guy looked more to be the heavy metal type, dressed in black leather and chains draping across him in various ways. *Where did he come from? And what's he doing in a country bar?* Something about him seemed familiar, but she couldn't put her finger on it.

Strange—that was what she was looking for, but would he be that obvious? She agreed to dance with him.

The minute they hit the dance floor, he practically spilled his guts to her. "I wanna be up front with you. I just got out of jail five months ago, and do you know what I came home to?"

Taylor shook her head.

"I'll tell you. My old lady left me for another man. She said we didn't like the same kind of music anymore, so I'm here trying to learn to like this junk. I was here the other night and tried to dress like the others, a little bit anyway. But tonight I thought I would be myself and try to soak up the music that way. It ain't working."

She listened with interest, asking just the right questions to keep him talking. They danced more than once. Taylor thought at first she was onto something, but by the third number, she decided this was another dead end. He was only a broken-hearted fool.

"Thanks for the dances. Good luck with your girlfriend. I hope you straighten things out." She touched his shoulder softly, actually feeling sorry for him.

A tight smile touched his lips as she left him on the dance floor. Taylor could feel the sweat dripping down her back. She was hot and tired. This had been a nowhere night—again— on top of very little sleep. It was after one in the morning, so she gave the sign and then headed out the door. Taylor hoped John would come over after he left or at least give her a call tonight. They needed to talk.

If not, she would give him enough time to get home and then give him a ring. They had to work things out if they were going to continue to work together. She also needed to tell him about the bartender so they could check deeper into his background. Something about him didn't fit. He talked a little strange, noticed weird things, and called her Barbara. If they had talked a little on the side, she wouldn't have thought much of him getting her name wrong. The way people acted and reacted was what made Taylor suspicious. He had her antennas up. This was best not to ignore.

On the out-of-the-way drive home, she didn't feel John's presence behind her. Glancing in the rearview mirror, she said, "Silly girl. You're not supposed to see him. He stays out of sight."

No one. Nothing. Finally she headed back toward her apartment. She parked her car and headed up the stairs to her place. She unlocked the door and twisted the knob to step inside. Before she could close the door, she was shoved down across the floor, and the door was slammed behind her. Falling to the floor she hit her head. "What the—?"

She didn't finish her question when she was yanked by the arm and pulled to her feet. The keys were still in her hand. Frantically she tried to feel through her keychain and find the mace. Before her fingers wrapped around the little can, the keys were knocked out of her grip. Fear rose in her throat. She wanted to scream for help. Glancing around for her purse to pull out her .22, she found it on the floor across the room. No way to get to it.

"Don't worry, sweetie," the man said as he threw her on the sofa. "I'll be gentle. I could tell you wanted to help ease my deflated ego." His mouth formed a wicked grin as he fell on top of her.

That guy, Frank, from the bar. Oh, my gosh. "No!" Taylor tried to scoot away from him. She closed her eyes and opened her mouth to scream for help. The second her scream deafened her ears, she felt the weight on her lighten.

Opening her eyes, she found the man in leather in John's grip. He released it only long enough to form a fist and smash it into Frank's gut. Then his other fist came across with a cut to the jaw. In seconds, the man in black fell to the floor.

John flipped him over onto his stomach and held him there with the man's hands behind his back. John eased his automatic out of his shoulder holster. "Move a muscle, and I'll blow you away."

When the man didn't make a move to fight anymore, John reached behind him and whipped out his handcuffs. In one easy motion, keeping the gun pointed at him, John slapped the cuffs on the perp's wrists.

Taylor sat frozen through it all. It happened so fast. If it hadn't been for John, that man would have raped her.

Her bottom lip trembled as she watched John stand Frank to his feet again. Brown and Buck were standing in the doorway. John must have given them a heads-up on the drive over. She was so grateful.

John turned Frank over to his fellow detectives and said, "We'll be down shortly, so Taylor can press charges. Thanks." Turning to Frank, he said, "I hope you enjoyed your six months of freedom, because it's over now."

The cuffed man appeared to be in a daze as he tripped out of Taylor's apartment between the two detectives. John sat next to Taylor as she continued to sit motionless. How had she let that man in? It happened so fast.

He placed a warm hand over her cold, shaking fingers. "It'll be all right." His voice sounded soft and reassuring. "You'll be all right."

Drawing in a deep breath, she said, "Thank you for saving me." Taylor rose to her feet quickly and stepped away from the couch. . .away from John. "Do you think he's the one?" She shook her head. "I didn't think so when I danced with him. I had written him off as just a man angry with life, with his ex, and with the world." Quickly she repeated the story the man had shared with her on the dance floor.

"We do know Frank Simpson has a long rap sheet. He's been convicted and served time for sexual abuse. The man's only been out of prison for six months."

"Do you know he told me that? I guess he thought it was a turn on." She shivered as she thought about him.

Rising, John moved close to Taylor and reached out.

Taylor backed away again. "I'm fine. Really. I don't need your sympathy. I'm tough—that's my job!"

John stepped back as if he'd been slapped in the face. With a hard expression, he said, "That's so true. I almost forgot. It's your job. I won't forget again." He headed toward her door. "You need to come with me down to the station and press charges. I told them we'd be right behind them."

As much as she didn't want to go with him, she knew she had to file the complaint. The man was sick and needed to be off the streets. "I'll follow you in my car."

The minute she stepped out the door, she was bombarded with her sweet neighbors' concern. Of course all the flashing lights on the police units woke them. "Everything's fine," she assured her friends upstairs. Each stood hunched close together, clad in pajamas covered by their robes. "Truly. Go back to bed. I'll tell you the juicy stuff later." Taylor figured if she made light of it, they would quit worrying.

As she made it to the bottom step, she found Mr. and Mrs. Leblanc also needing assurance that everything was fine. Giving hugs as she passed them, they accepted her quick guarantee with the promise of filling them in later. Climbing into her Mustang, she started her car and made her way out to the street.

Alone in her car she recalled how John said he wouldn't forget. Well, that was his problem. Her job was what it was and she loved it. If he couldn't handle the danger she found herself in, he didn't need to be in her life.

Earlier she refused to let him comfort her, but it wasn't because she didn't need it. She needed it all right, but she had to be tough. Normally no one was around to assure her she was okay. Now she was glad she stood on her own. Her career was her dream, and she wasn't about to give it up for anyone. No man is worth that. If he cared about her at all, he would accept her job.

Turning into the station's parking lot, she whispered, "So much for even thinking I had a chance for a real relationship. Not with my job."

Chapter 26

Down at the station, she filled out the complaint form and signed where she needed so charges could be brought against her attacker. Frank Simpson would now go back to a familiar place. Taylor hoped this time they would throw away the key. They would, for sure, if they could link him to the predawn murders.

A chill swept through her as she turned in the completed complaint form to the policewoman at the desk.

The noise level was not as loud as she remembered from her other trips to the station. Probably the early morning hour had a lot to do with it. Most arrests had already been made for the night, and a lot of people were in their beds fast asleep.

What a night! As she headed down the hall toward the exit so she could go home and get in bed herself, John stepped into the hallway and blocked her exit. "Come to my office. We need to talk."

From head to toe she tensed. "What if I don't want to listen?" Maybe he was ready to make things right between them, but she wasn't sure she was. Besides, she already knew a relationship was not going to work between the two of them.

No. He was ready to end the investigation—with me.

"You'll listen." He took her by the arm and headed toward his office, giving her no choice in the matter. Once in his office, he let her go. "Sit," he commanded.

She eyed him wearily, but obeyed.

"You'll want to hear this." John raked his fingers through his hair and sighed. "I hate to tell you this, but he's not our man."

"How can you be so sure?"

"He's worked on a barge for the last month, and it just docked here three days ago. Several people can verify his alibi."

Disappointment engulfed her. Taylor had hoped they had found the killer. She squeezed her eyes into narrow slits as she thought for a moment.

Her head snapped up as her eyes popped open and pinned John. "I just remembered something I needed to tell you tonight. . .last night. . .but with everything—"

"He's still going back to jail for what he did to you. And with his history, he'll be there for a long time."

"Great. That's good." She waved her hands in the air like it didn't really matter. What she was telling him was more important. "Listen, John, I forgot to tell you about the bartender in all the excitement." She told him her suspicions and how she had written Frank off earlier. "What Frank did wasn't typical of the Predawn Strangler. He was just a crazed idiot.

But the bartender seemed demented, like, I don't know. It was weird the way he called me Barbara."

Scratching his chin, he said, "We checked him out earlier. Let's see," he murmured as he flipped through his file searching for Jack Williams. "Here it is. No record of him ever breaking the law. His wife left him. He quit his job at the bank and has been working at the bar for about six months." John shrugged. "We didn't think anything of it, but we'll look into his activities more closely."

John glanced at his watch. "It's late. I'm going to see you home." He didn't let her argue. Actually, she didn't even try.

Once they got to the apartment, John talked her into letting him come upstairs with her. "We've got to talk about. . .us."

Taylor hesitated. She didn't think she was ready to discuss *them*, even though that was what she wanted him to say all night. It was one thing to admit to yourself you were in love with someone, but it was an entirely different story to admit it to that person. No. She wasn't ready to talk about it—with him or anyone else.

"I insist. You may not want to talk about us." He walked up behind her, pushing her gently into her apartment. "But you're going to listen, because I want to talk."

She kept walking until she reached the kitchen. She let John shut the door. "I've got to fix some coffee. It's late, and I'm very tired."

John didn't stop her. "It's just what I need." He eased over to the table and dropped down in the chair.

"Go ahead and talk. I'll listen while I make the coffee." She grabbed the glass container, rinsed out the pot, filled it with water, and then poured it into the coffeemaker. After cleaning out the filter, she filled in the coffee grounds and turned on the pot.

"I'll wait."

It started making gurgling noises instantly. Taylor pulled out the cups for lack of something to do to keep from thinking about who was with her and what he wanted to talk about.

After two cups were poured, Taylor sat across from John. "Go ahead." She took a sip of the hot brew.

John's eyes caressed her as he stared into her eyes.

That wasn't fair. She swallowed, averted her eyes, then said, "Okay. I'm ready to listen."

John took another sip before he spoke. "I think I'm sending you mixed signals. I can't help it. You have me so confused."

As butterflies swarmed her stomach, he had her attention. This was exactly what she wanted to hear—needed to hear.

"I was engaged once, to a fellow police officer. She was killed in the line of duty. I swore when Jennifer died, I would never become emotionally involved with a career woman again. I only got through her death by the help of God."

Seeing the pain shooting through his eyes, she touched his hand.

He covered hers with his. "There's more. When I saw you, I felt something that I tried to fight. But I heard a voice inside, telling me you were the one. I don't even know if you are a believer, but I am. So I was ready to see where our relationship would go—until you were almost raped because of your job."

Do I believe in God? I did pray, asking God to send John to my rescue. She pulled her hand back as these thoughts ran through her mind.

"Boy, are you a career woman or what? My head says stay away from you, far, far away, but my heart wants to know you more."

Taylor's heart pounded like a demolition ball crashing against a brick wall. He had admitted his attraction to her. . .against his better judgment. Hiding her smile, she hoped he cared for her as much as she cared for him. If that was the case, they could find the answer.

John reached out his hand. Hesitantly, Taylor placed hers in his. His thumb caressed the back of her hand as he held it. "I hope you understand what I'm trying to say. I'm scared, confused, unsure." Inhaling a deep breath, he raised his eyes to hers and she saw the fear in them.

Hope grew a little more within her.

"All day today, I kept telling myself there was a way around your helter-skelter life." Raising her hand, he pressed his lips on her skin. "But tonight told me I was wrong. Had Frank done what he wanted to you, I wouldn't be able to live with myself. Do you understand what I am saying?"

Excitement, desire, love, and plain old-fashioned lust raced through her veins. He was asking her to understand what he was saying, but how could she even think while he was touching her this way?

"My heart says yes, but my mind says no." John stood and opened his arms to her. "Right now I'm going to let my heart lead."

Taylor didn't hesitate. That was where she wanted to be, and she stepped eagerly into his embrace.

"I'm not making any promises until I know we are right for one another and we can commit to each other forever. In other words, I don't want a casual affair. I don't believe in them. I believe in until-death-do-we-part kind of love." He kissed her upturned lips gently. "Can we take it one day at a time?"

She answered with a hungry kiss. Warmth and security blanketed around her as his arms held her tight. She knew what she had to do. She had to make him forget how dangerous her job could be. Let him see most of it was fairly safe. Taylor needed John to love her like she loved him. If she could accomplish that, he wouldn't let her career stand in their way.

A marimba rhythm rang out. John's cell broke further conversation. . .and kissing. Pulling his iPhone from his pocket, he pressed it against his ear. The smile wiped clean from his face as he dropped his phone back into his pocket.

"They found another body."

Chapter 27

Not again. Taylor wanted to break down and cry. She wouldn't be so tough then, would she? "We've got to catch him, John. He can't go on killing. I really think you need to check deeper into that bartender. He looked a little crazed last night. Can't you bring him in for questioning?"

"We could, but if we do, we'd tip our hand. He'd know he was a suspect. To bring charges against him, we would need proof, evidence of some kind. Don't worry, if he's our man, we'll get him. For now, we'll keep him under surveillance. We won't let him kill another person."

"I've got to go," he said as he took her back into his arms. Holding her close, he asked, "Are you coming?"

"Of course. Do you think I would miss it? Who knows, maybe it's a copycat instead of the real deal."

"We'll see." He traced his finger along her jawline. "You really need some rest. You haven't had any."

She smiled, thinking, *What a wonderful man.* "I'm going on the same thing you're going on. . .adrenaline. I'll make it. This is bigger than any need for sleep."

He nodded. "I know. I know. Your story." He let her go. "Let's get out of here."

Taylor snatched up her camera and purse. Together they left for the crime scene.

Later that morning, still riding on caffeine and adrenaline, Taylor slipped by the paper to update her boss. When he learned she was going to be the decoy to lure the insane man out in the open, Mr. Cox wasn't too pleased, to say the least. Words of wisdom rang through her head as she recalled his fatherly advice. "Now listen and listen well. This may be your golden opportunity to write your prize-winning piece, but it's also a chance to get yourself killed. Your life is more important. Just remember that." He winked and then patted her shoulder. "Now get out there and find the rest of our story." His words were the last thing playing through her brain when she dozed off for a few hours.

The phone rang, waking her. She grabbed the receiver and dragged it to her ear. "Hello."

"Taylor. What are you doing sleeping in the middle of the day?" Her mom sounded horrified.

Taylor's eyes popped open. She didn't dare tell her the truth. Her mother worried enough about her being on the job. "Hi, Mom. What are you doing?"

"Dear, I just wanted to tell you how much we enjoyed the other night and how special it was to your father and me. I've called you several times, only you never return my calls. I know now you've been very busy with work and with John."

Her mother's voice literally purred out his name. The smile on her mother's face had to be wider than the Mississippi. "It's wonderful, honey. We're both so happy for you. Thanks again for the other night."

"Don't thank me, Mom. The party was Rodney's great idea. Neither one of your daughters thought about it."

"He's magnificent, isn't he?" her mother cooed. She didn't skip a beat when she said, "And speaking of magnificent, that young man you were with the other night seemed perfect for you. You best not let him slip away."

Taylor knew John was the real reason for the phone call. At least now their relationship was real. For that she was glad. As much as she wanted to teach her mother and sister a lesson, she hated lying to them. Especially her mom. "I'm glad you liked him, Mom. He liked y'all, too. In fact, he thinks I have a wonderful family."

"Your father even likes him. A policeman is exactly what you need. Someone stronger and whose job held a little more danger. A regular guy couldn't handle your work. Tell me, dear, are you two serious?"

By the excitement in her mother's voice, Taylor figured her mom was picking out the silver pattern. "Mom, do me a favor. Don't get overly excited. It may or may not work. But right now, we are very happy."

"Dear, you know I only want what's best for you. Sure I'd love to see you settle down and get married. Even give us a couple more grandchildren. . .but only to a man deserving of a strong woman like you. In case you don't know it, I'm very proud of you."

Tears sprang to Taylor's eyes. "Don't get all mushy on me,

Mom." With the back of her hand she wiped away the dampness. *I'm just so tired. Otherwise I wouldn't get all teary-eyed. Do I tell her how serious we've become? She's so proud now; this would shoot her over the moon.* "Okay, Mom. I'm going to tell you something. Your wish has come true. I'm head over heels in love with John Bradley." *There, I said it. Admitted my feelings to my mother, no less. Thinking it is one thing, but telling my mother?* A grin spread wide on Taylor's lips.

A squeal pierced her ear.

"Please Mom, don't get overly excited. If you do, you might be disappointed. He's attracted to me but doesn't care for the dangers of my job. I can't give up my job. So if he wants me, he has to take the whole package." Holding her breath, she waited for her mom to lecture her on how dangerous the job was and how she had been trying to get Taylor to quit the paper or start covering weddings for years.

Her mother surprised her. "Dear, if it's meant to be, it will happen. Just trust in your heart and your feelings, and you will do what is right for you. Remember, Dad and I are always here for you, honey."

A quick breath caught in her throat. She hadn't heard her mother so tender in years—or maybe Taylor hadn't been listening like she should. "Thanks, Mom. I love you. Give my love to Dad, too. I've got to go."

"We love you, too. Please be careful."

After Taylor hung up, she wanted to sit down and cry a good one, but she knew she couldn't do that. She had to be tough for tonight. Getting up, she went into the kitchen to make herself a pot of coffee.

By the time the coffee started dripping, she heard a knock

at the door. Checking the peephole first she opened it. After what she went through last night and with another killing so soon, if nothing else, this case had taught her to be cautious. "John, come in. I hope nothing's wrong."

He made himself at home on the couch after giving her a quick kiss on the cheek. "Thanks. Nothing's changed. I came to tell you what we found out about the bartender."

John looked very tired.

"You haven't gotten any sleep yet, have you?"

He shook his head. "You need to hear this, though."

"I'll listen, but you lie down on the sofa and rest while you tell me. Afterward, you can take a nap. I'll wake you in time to go home and get ready for Six-Shooters."

He did just that. She didn't have to offer twice. John was dead on his feet, she could tell.

"We haven't found him yet, but two of my men are watching his house as we speak. Hopefully he'll come home before he goes to work tonight. I've filled out an affidavit to get a search warrant, and we're waiting for Judge Peterson to approve it. We know the tire size of his van is a match, but with the warrant, we can check for that special marking we found on our mold."

"Great!"

"We want enough to put him away for good. . .without another death. He has to come home sooner or later." John turned on his side and made room beside him. "Come. . .sit by me." He patted the cushion.

Taylor obeyed willingly.

"Do you want to hear how bad his life is? Not that it's any excuse to do what he's done."

"Tell me." She brushed a curl off his forehead.

John laid his hand across Taylor's lap, keeping her close, and he closed his eyes. "His name is Jack Williams. He was married to a woman named Barbara. That's what he called you, wasn't it?"

"Yes," she whispered.

"Right. Well she left. . .for a cowboy. Jack was a banker, wore a three-piece suit every day to work. When his wife ran off with a guy that dressed in jeans, boots, and wore a big cowboy hat, Jack changed. He quit his job and started working at the bar. Apparently he watched every night for a girl that fell for the cowboy type—maybe even ignoring the guys like me, dressed in slacks. He then followed them and somehow got them to pull over for him. Maybe they recognized him from the bar and felt safe. We don't know. He's got some scam going, though. We'll figure it out, but in the meantime, we're not going to let him kill again. We're going to stick to him. . .once we find him."

Taylor stroked his forehead while he was talking. His breathing slowed down. Finally he was asleep. She leaned down and kissed him softly on the lips. Even in his sleep, his lips puckered slightly. She stayed by him for a few more minutes, allowing him to fall into a deep sleep. Then she got up and laid a light blanket over him.

A few hours later she woke him so he could go home to shower and get ready for the night. "It's a good thing you know how to get by on so little sleep."

"I do, don't I? Unfortunately, all cops have to get used to grabbing whatever sleep they can, when they can." He pulled her face down and nibbled at her lips. "I could get by on this in daily doses." He nipped at them again. "Let's make that hourly doses." He laughed as he held her close.

She kissed him long and hard, a kiss for the road. "Now get up and go." Drawing her brows together, she tried to give him a stern look but couldn't hold back the smile that filled her heart.

He sat up and stretched. As he headed to the door, he mumbled, "She kisses me like that and then tells me to go. Women. You can't live with them, and you can't live without them." He laughed as he pulled her back into his arms. Then he returned a kiss more intense, slowly, lovingly. "Mmm. Yes. I could get used to this." He smiled and then left quietly.

Leaning against the doorframe, she felt the beating of her heart. Yes, this was the real thing. She loved him, no doubt about it. She hoped it didn't take him long to realize he loved her, too. . .and that he loved her enough not to worry about her line of work. She could live with his line of work. It was part of him.

"Please, God. You told him I'm the one for him. Help him to love the whole package."

Chapter 28

Shortly after John left, he called to give Taylor the plan of action. "Remember, if you don't feel up to it, we could have Sergeant Land step in. She was trained for this sort of thing."

"But she hasn't been as close to the situation. The bartender already has a connection with me." Her throat constricted as she thought he was about to give the action to someone else. She needed to be close to the story—that made her story come alive in the paper. She held her breath, waiting for his decision.

He sighed. "Yes. You're right. Man, I wish we'd found something in his house to connect him so we wouldn't have to catch him in the act."

"I can do this, John. Trust me. When I leave tonight, I'll do like I did last night. Get in my car and head toward my parents'. Right? And you'll be right there behind him, behind me."

"Right. And don't let us lose you. Stay in radio contact constantly. Make sure your wire is secure before you leave the bar."

"Will do. Make sure you guys don't lose sight of me," she said as she clutched the phone for dear life.

Sure, she was telling John she could do it, but part of her was scared to death. As many close calls as she has had in her life, they came only because she got close to the story. This time she was smack-dab in the middle of the story. Her boss's words replayed in her mind: *Your life is more important than any story.*

"Not on your life," John promised. "Officer Lane will be by around eight to wire you up so we can hear every word that he says to you. We'll get him."

"How can you be sure he'll take the bait?"

"Trust me. He will."

On that, they said their good-byes.

When nine o'clock arrived, she was walking into Six-Shooters, wire in place thanks to Officer Lane. Taylor was ready to execute their plan. "Hey, guys. I'm sweating up a storm already. I hope I don't damage the wire. . .or electrocute myself." She said those words hoping they could hear her. The sound check earlier said they could. Taylor felt sure it was her nerves talking right now.

Drawing a deep breath, Taylor moved over to the bar and sat down. She made it a point not to watch the bartender, even though she wanted to do so. Although the police never found him today, because he never came home, he showed up tonight. Taylor hoped the plan worked. As she turned her face in his direction, about to place her order, he sat a drink in front of her.

"A screwdriver, light on the vodka."

"You remembered. Thanks." Taylor didn't linger on him. She averted her eyes to the crowd, showing him no interest whatsoever.

Several cowboy-type men hit on her throughout the night and she flirted with each of them. The closer it got to midnight, the more frightened she became. Occasionally, she caught a glimpse of John and he was always watching her, even though it didn't appear he was paying attention.

Taylor ordered a second drink with thirty minutes left, waiting for the big scene John had planned to get the bartender's attention. Between dances, she sipped on her drink that watered down more and more as the minute hand progressed.

Out of the corner of her eye, Taylor caught a glimpse of John coming her way. *This is it.*

John sauntered over and leaned on the bar next to her. Out of the corner of his mouth he said to the bartender, "Give me a beer." Turning to Taylor, he asked, "Want to dance?"

Taylor rolled her eyes. "I told you the other night, we're through. It's over. O-V-E-R." She spelled it out for him, loud enough to humiliate him in front of anyone within earshot. That was the plan. Taylor could see everyone around them staring. She even felt she had gotten the bartender's attention but didn't dare look.

"Ah, come on, Baby. What's the matter? You think I'm not man enough for you? Or should I say *cowboy* enough for you? I've been watching you every night throwing yourself all over these cowboys in here. So I'm not the blue jean type. So what?

It's the person in them that matters. I'm as much a man as any of these cowboys, and I love you. Give me another chance," he pleaded with her.

The word *love* threw her for a loop. That was what she wanted to hear from him. Although she knew this was play-acting, she wished deep down he meant it. "Forget it!" She flung her arm up as she brushed him off again and turned her back on him.

Sure enough, the man behind the bar watched the whole thing. His eyes were twitching, and beads of perspiration formed across his forehead and on his upper lip. This was getting to him. It looked like the plan might work.

She felt John lean up close behind her as he whispered loudly, "I don't think I can take another rejection. Please give me another chance. . .us another chance." Softly for her ears only, he added, "He's taking the bait. Be careful when you leave here."

John ran his hands across the fringe that draped along the back of her shirt. She turned, reared her hand back, and slapped him across the face. "Leave me alone. You're a loser. I don't associate with losers." She stormed away.

Taylor caught John's response out of the corner of her eye. Rubbing his jaw, he moaned, "Wow. What a wallop. That tiny thing packs a punch." He looked the bartender dead in the eye and laughed. Snatching his beer off the counter, his gaze darted toward Taylor and he glared in longing. "I've got to get me some of that, but I think I'll wait until she cools down." He swaggered back to his own table with the drink in hand.

Taylor waited as long as she thought was necessary and then went back to her spot at the bar. The second part of their plan went into action.

A man dressed in a pair of tight-fitting jeans strutted up to her and said, "Hey, good-looking. Want to shuffle with me?"

The music was fast-moving, and Taylor joined him willingly. The two got on the floor and shuffled around, doing twists and turns in all the right places. When the song ended, a waltz started up. As planned, they stayed out on the dance floor for the next two songs. The officer was really quite a good dancer.

When the dancing ended on the third song, they strolled hand-in-hand to the bar. Before Taylor took her seat on the stool, the cowboy turned her toward him. Holding her face gently, he thoroughly kissed her. Taylor didn't fight it. It was part of the plan.

She would be glad when this night was over. They had to get him tonight. At the rate he was killing people, they couldn't afford to mess up.

Taylor swallowed hard when he broke the kiss. The scary part was she knew she was setting herself up for the bartender to come after her later. If things worked the way they planned, she would be his next target. She hoped the fear she felt didn't show in her face.

Knowing John was watching her every move was the only thing that gave her strength. It didn't hurt to know several other police officers were there, undercover, including the cowboy who had just kissed her.

When he pulled away, Taylor reached up and traced his lips with her thumb. "Protect these. They're masterful, Darlin'." She pursed her lips at him, giving him a come-on kiss in the air.

"Maybe we can get together later tonight," he said to her, catching her hand.

She smiled. "Not tonight, Cowboy, but maybe tomorrow night," she said with promise in her voice.

"Don't let me down." He kissed her again.

"Not on your life," she promised. Taylor sat back down, catching a glimpse of Jack standing back watching their exchange. *Yes. He took the bait.* She also knew John was watching and probably felt everything was going as planned. She wished she could say something. She knew he could hear her, but so could others—and she definitely didn't want to say anything to make Jack suspicious.

Pulling out her wallet, she left the usual charges plus the tip. She noticed Jack was down at the other end of the bar talking to a barmaid. After their exchange of words, he left early.

Is he leaving for my benefit? Here we go. Taylor's heart hammered. "Here we go. I'm scared to death." Her hands were sweating as she waited, giving time for Jack to do whatever he planned.

When one o'clock struck, her usual time for leaving, she stood, strapped her purse on her shoulder, and walked toward the door. "Please stay close."

Once in her Mustang she started the engine. The radio was on, but low. Now she could talk to John. She couldn't hear him answer, though.

"I think it worked. Here goes." She pulled out on the street, heading toward Canal. "I hope you're listening. In fact, I hope the pounding of my heart isn't drowning out what I'm saying."

She was nearing the crossing of the interstate. Once she headed under it, she was an open target for the next couple of blocks. If he was going to approach her, it would be during that stretch. At every traffic light and every large building she passed, Taylor expected something to happen.

"I'm still here. Nothing yet. Wait…wait. What's this I see? There is a van coming up behind me, coming up pretty fast, I might add. It's dark, like black or navy, maybe even a very dark green. It's hard to tell. I hope you're close. I know you can't do anything until he says something you can use, or makes an attempt on me, but stay close." Her sweaty fingers tightened their hold on the steering wheel.

The lights flashed in her rearview mirror. The van was signaling to her to pull over. She slowed down but didn't stop. The van pulled beside her and the driver pointed to the side of his van. On the sideboard was a sign advertising WKRN.

She looked up and smiled at him. "So that's how he does it. John, he's pretending to be the Moneyman. His face is hidden by a large-brimmed cowboy hat, but it's him." Taylor told these things to John through tight smiling lips, so the man couldn't tell she was talking.

"This is it, John. He's motioning for me to pull over," she told John as she turned away from the van and started to ease off the side of the road. She gave him a description of the van as quickly as possible. As she slowed to a stop on the shoulder, the van pulled up behind her. She cracked her window about two inches as the man approached the car. "What can I do for you?" she asked.

"Don't you know me, sweetie? You wear my bumper sticker. You must know who I am." The voice sounded very friendly, almost like a radio personality.

"Are you the Moneyman from WKRN?" Taylor tried to sound excited.

"How right you are, Little Lady. And if you have WKRN written down on a piece of paper, you'll double your money."

Taylor glanced at her purse. She knew she didn't have it written, but she was stalling for time. Of course, that was when he choked the other girls. What should she do? She made a point of leaning away from the window when she turned toward her purse.

"I hope you can hear this," she whispered. Her stomach twisted into knots. The agony of waiting for him to make his move was driving her insane. Of course she knew her window wasn't down far enough for him to reach in, just as she had planned, but by now he should have the rope in his hands. *Come on, John. It's time for you to show up and save the day.*

She jumped when she heard him speak. "You can't find it?"

She heard his voice, then instantly heard her door being opened. How did he open it? She had it locked. "What are you doing?"

"Don't worry, Little Lady. I'm going to give you a bonus anyway." Jack reached in and grabbed her arm, dragging her out of the car.

As he was pulling her out, she was hollering, "Let go of me! What are you—?" She didn't finish her question because he backhanded her, knocking her against the car. His fist made contact with her cheek while his ring made contact with her temple. He hit her so hard Taylor barely had time to think. *Where are you, John?* Then she blacked out.

It couldn't have been more than a minute or two, but when

she came to, she found he had thrown her in the back of the van with her hands and feet both tied. In her mouth was a cloth towel keeping her from speaking. She woke facedown on the carpet, hearing the sounds of the motor humming and the tires rolling on the blacktop.

Oh, John. Where are you? Please be right behind us.

Taylor was in fear for her life. She realized Jack had treated her differently, but all she could believe was that he planned to torture her before killing her.

Maybe he figured out she was working with the police, or maybe since he called her Barbara, he thought he had his wife and was going to make her pay.

Taylor's head throbbed and her face hurt where he had struck her, but at the moment, that was the least of her worries. She fought to stay awake.

John, please save me. I need you. Where are you? She thought they would have grabbed him by now. Kidnapping and go from there. What were they waiting for?

The throb of her head beat harder and harder until she blacked out one more time.

Chapter 29

W hat happened? I can't hear anything!" John snatched the microphone on his radio. "Sound is down. Approach with caution, but whatever you do, keep that van in sight!"

Immediate response came over the radio. "His lights already disappeared. When the van lights came back into view, we pulled a little closer. It was the wrong van. A switch was made. We don't know if it was planned or luck. . .bad luck. We're heading back to the main road now."

John's fist slammed down hard on the steering wheel as his foot pressed on the accelerator. How could they have lost him? They were to follow him from the bar until the end. John was to stay at a safe distance behind Taylor so they could all be there when contact was made. She was never in his sight, but he could always hear her until the crackling started and her voice died. The wire went dead. A mixture of fury and fear took over. John had to keep his head. He hadn't seen the van pass him, and he prayed Jack hadn't made contact, although before the wire died, he knew a van was tailing her. She had described it to him. It could have been Jack. He'd know soon enough.

Driving under the interstate, he didn't even slow down for the curve. Coming out of it, he spotted the Mustang. Her car sat alone on the side of the road. His eyes raced ahead and saw the dark van picking up speed traveling away from her car.

Pressing the side of his mike, he said, "I have the vehicle in view. I just crossed under I-110 where it crosses Canal. Her car is on the shoulder two blocks down." As John passed it, he eyed it quickly but didn't lose speed. "It looks empty, but check it out. Make sure she is not lying hurt across the seat of her car." *Or even dead.* He didn't want to think those words, let alone speak them aloud, but as the thoughts came to him, he prayed that wasn't the case.

His heart pounded as fear gripped him, but then he let his police training take control. "After you're sure she's not there, radio for a team to check out her car and you two catch up with me. I'll stay close. I'm not going to lose that creep or let him lose me." John kept his eyes on the van but kept his distance. If anything happened to her, he would never forgive himself.

Minutes later he heard, "Lieutenant, the car's empty. Only her purse is in it. He must have her with him."

Bittersweet words touched his ears. For a brief second, relief flooded his heart as he knew she wasn't left dead in her car like the others before her, but almost as quickly the thought came of what his changed plans could entail. He didn't want

Taylor to be tortured.

That sick killer changed his ways of doing things. Jack Williams went from killing one girl a week to one a night—now this. He kidnapped Taylor. What was on his agenda? What were his plans for Taylor? Whatever they were, John could not permit Jack to carry them out.

Keep her alive, Lord. You're the one who wants us to be together.

As he kept on the trail, he reached into his glove box and removed his Colt. Laying it on the seat beside him, he was ready for Jack Williams. His hands tightened on the steering wheel. Had it been Williams' neck, the man would be dead.

John followed all of Jack's turns and relayed them over the radio to Buck and Brown and any other officer in the vicinity. After two more turns, John realized Williams was heading toward his old house, the one he shared with his wife. . .not the one the police had staked out, got the warrant for, and searched.

John pressed the button again. "He's heading for his old place on Magazine Street. Move it!" John relayed it to his men and then gave the information to dispatch to get more backup.

Immediately he heard the dispatcher call over the radio, "Ten-thirty-three, ten-thirty-three, all cars in the vicinity of Annunciation and Magazine, we're in pursuit of a dark van, believed to be the Predawn Strangler. He has his next intended victim with him. Approach with caution. It is believed he is taking her to 5221 Magazine Street."

He prayed they would all be there in time.

Chapter 30

Taylor felt the van come to a quick stop, causing her to roll onto her side. At least now she didn't have to smell that putrid odor of stale, wet carpet. Another minute of that and she felt certain she would be lying in a puddle of her own vomit. Her stomach churned.

The back doors flew open as the face Taylor recognized as the bartender's came into view. "It's okay, Barbara. We're home now. Safe and sound." He grabbed both of her arms and dragged her out of the van.

"I'm not Barbara," she tried to say through the cloth stuffed in her mouth. That didn't stop him as he dragged her to her feet. She leaned forward slightly, then suddenly pushed with her shoulder, causing him to lose his balance.

Caught by surprise, he fell to the ground. She tried to run away, but her feet were tied together. Tumbling, she pushed her bound hands out to catch her fall, trying to soften the landing. It didn't help. Facedown she went and slapped the ground with her whole body. "Oomph." She hit the dew-covered ground. The wetness soaked through her clothes.

Instantly, Taylor tried to roll over and stand back on her feet.

Too late. Back on his feet, he reached over and grabbed her by her elbows, hauling her erect. Headlights flashed across his face. Hastily he lifted her up, tossed her over his shoulder, and then carried her inside. Once in, he dropped her in a kitchen chair and then secured the lock on the kitchen door.

Jack left the room without saying a word. She assumed to lock any other door in the house.

A second chance to escape.

Glancing around the room, she tried to figure out the best way to go. The most obvious was right out the kitchen door, since he hadn't tied her to the chair. Like a cat she rose and lightly hopped across the floor toward the door. Turning her back to the door, she lifted her bound hands to the door-knob. Using her fingertips she turned the lock, then grabbed the knob with both hands. Awkwardly she turned it, but the door didn't budge. Surveying the door, she realized he had also locked the deadbolt.

Backing up against the door, she tried to lift her hands to the small knob that controlled the lock. Not quite reaching it, she held her breath, rose up on her toes trying to get leverage on the small knob, hoping to turn it completely to unlock the deadbolt, but she couldn't get her hands high enough.

After trying again and almost falling on her face, she gave it up. Her gaze flitted around the room and stopped on the window. If it were lower to the floor, she could make a run for it and throw herself through the glass. It would hurt badly, but it had to be better than dying.

A movement outside caught her eyes. *John? Are you here?* It had to be him. *Hold on, girl, John will save you.*

She heard a shuffling of feet coming her way. Swiftly, she jumped back over to the chair Jack had left her in and sat back down. No need to upset Jack further.

Her heart pounded ferociously as the kitchen door swung open from the hallway. Taylor swallowed hard. He was back, and he looked insane. She had to convince him to let her go. Sure, John was here, but what if he didn't get inside in time? What if Jack decided to kill her instantly?

"Jack," she murmured through the cloth. Apparently he wanted to hear what she had to say because he removed the cloth from her mouth. "Jack," she said softly.

His eyes spread wide as he looked intently into her eyes. "Barbara, I'm so glad you came back to me. I knew you would." He walked over to Taylor and traced his fingers down her injured cheek. Softly, he pushed her hair away from her face. "You've been hurt, darling. Let me help you." He spoke as he brushed the dirt away from the scratches on her face.

With every brush of his hand a pain jabbed her face, but she said nothing.

"I knew you couldn't trust that cowboy. I tried to warn you, but you wouldn't listen to me."

The thought of those hands on her face killing all those women. . .she wanted to push him away. He repulsed her, but her hands were still roped together. The only thing she could do was turn her face away from him.

"Barbara, look at me. I'm not going to hurt you. I love you."

Slowly Taylor turned back to face Jack. "I'm not Barbara. Jack, you need help. Let me help you. Or turn yourself in. The police will get help for you." Her voice was soothing as she spoke, although she wanted to scream, "Let me out of here!"

"No! I don't need any help, Barbara," he shouted as his open hand slapped her. "Shut up. I told you I'm not going to hurt you."

The slap stung, and tears sprang to her eyes, but she held them back.

"Listen, sweetheart," he said, his voice calmer. "I need you, and you need me. We are back together, and that's all that matters." He ran his hands over her hair and patted Taylor's head.

"Then cut me loose. My feet, my hands. They hurt." Her pleading made it through to his twisted mind.

Finding a knife in the kitchen drawer, he used it to cut the cord around her ankles. Blood started circulating immediately.

Suddenly she heard something. Yes. She heard the sound of vehicles arriving, seemingly surrounding the place. Now she knew she would make it. Help was all around her. John's backup had arrived. Any moment they would be rushing inside.

Of course, if she could hear them, so could Jack, but maybe he was so intent on her that he paid no attention to the noises outside. She hoped anyway.

No such luck.

"What was that?" Jack searched the room for an answer. He snatched her by the hair and yanked her head backward. "What's going on here? Did you call the police?" He slapped her again. The knife he used to cut her bindings free he now pressed against the side of her face.

"Hhhuhhh." She sucked in a gasp of air in fear as the side of her face stung from the sharp edge cutting through the skin.

At least she was still alive enough to feel the pain. Hopefully he wasn't about to end that with the blade of his knife. Her gaze stayed locked on him.

"I ought to kill you, Barbara. I thought you wanted to come back to me. Why did you call the police?" Slowly he eased the cold steel of the blade down along her cheek, running the same path his fingers had earlier. Only this time, he sliced the skin. Blood oozed out, and wetness started to run down her cheek.

Hurry, John.

A loud bang came from the living room, drawing Jack's attention. He immediately turned toward the sound. "They better not be trying to get in here. This is my home. I don't want them here." He turned his crazed eyes on Taylor and warned her through clenched teeth, "Don't move a muscle. I'll be right back."

Jack pushed open the door and peered into the next room. "They're trying to break in," he shouted as he ran to the drawer, pulled out a gun, and then scampered toward the living room. "They must be—"

"Police! Freeze!" Two quick shots rang out. The back door flew open and wood splintered, flying every which way. Brown rushed in and grabbed Taylor. Wasting no time, he snatched her up and scurried her out the opening where the door used to be.

She hadn't heard anymore, so she didn't know if John was okay. She had heard him yell for Jack to freeze. Was the first shot John's, or had Jack shot John? The waiting was more than she could bear.

In all the commotion, she had forgotten about her hands. Brown released them from their bondage. The pain was like fire, but all Taylor could think about was John's safety. The minute her hands were free, she started for the house. Maybe she could be of some help to John.

Of course there were police all around. Cars parked everywhere and lights flashed. Surely there were enough inside to help John, but she wanted to be there, to know he was safe.

Taylor didn't get far before Brown caught her by the arm. "You have to wait here."

She knew he was right, but she didn't want to wait. She needed to be inside, surprisingly enough, not for the story but for John. Her searching eyes darted from the front door to the side, breathlessly waiting to see someone—anyone.

Finally the front door opened and Jack Williams, followed by John and two officers in uniform, came out the front door. Jack's hands were cuffed, and John held him by his upper arm, directing his every step. More policemen followed out behind them.

"It's over," Taylor whispered. "Thank God."

Her knees went weak, but she managed to stay upright. Taylor wanted to run to John. As she started to pull away from Brown, he held her back. "Not yet, ma'am."

Taylor stayed back against her will but realized Brown knew what he was doing. She watched as John put Jack in the backseat of one of the patrol cars. Red and blue lights flashed everywhere in the darkness of the morning.

Hurry. I need you. Her eyes stayed focused on John's every move, waiting, longing for him to turn to her.

When John slammed the police car door closed behind the criminal, his worried eyes searched the crowd. The neighbors had started gathering, filling up the street. By now even television camera crews were arriving and news reporters.

At last she saw his eyes light on her, and she smiled. He was safe, and it was over. Yes. Now John would come to her. She was ready for him to swoop her up in his arms and profess his undying love.

With her breath held in her throat, she waited expectantly. She was ready, for she knew that was what she wanted to do to him. He had to feel the same way after all they had been through. Taylor wanted to shout it from a mountaintop. Of course, down here in Louisiana there were no mountains. A tall building would do nicely, but she would settle for standing on top of the police car and shouting it to the neighborhood. She knew it would make her feel better.

John walked toward her. His face paled. No smile touched his lips.

It's okay. It will come. I'm all right, John. No need to be afraid for me. It was all over now. He could show her how he felt. He would soon. Taylor felt confident he'd show her soon. With each stride, he drew closer and closer.

His eyes locked on hers and never strayed. He walked up to her and stopped. . .one step away, one breath away.

One more step was all that was left. Taylor started to raise her hands—to touch him—to throw them around his neck and show him how happy she was that it was over and they both were alive.

His look froze her hands in mid-air. His face never softened, his lips never curved into a smile. Instead, his lips moved as he talked—but not to her. Sure, he still looked at her, stared at her in fact, but didn't speak a word to her. He spoke to Brown. "Bring her to the station for her statement if she doesn't need to go to the hospital for her injuries."

My injuries? She squinted at him in confusion. *Forget about my injuries. What about the pain you are putting me through right now? What is going on here?*

She wanted to ask him but knew better. The cut down the side of her face was nothing compared to the knife that twisted in her heart. Her stomach convulsed.

How could he do this to her? It was over. They were both alive. He should be showering her with kisses, showing an abundance of happiness. . .but he wasn't. He turned his back to her and walked away.

She felt baffled and bewildered. What was going on?

"Come on, Miss Jaymes. You have blood on your face. Let's get you to the hospital."

"I'm okay."

"Then at least let the paramedics check you out."

Once they had her wound cleaned and stitched, Brown said, "I'll take you to the station."

The next two hours were a blur to Taylor. She gave a statement. It was recorded, typed, and given back to her to read and sign, and then a police officer brought her safely to her door.

She went through the motions, but all the while thinking

she would have been better off if Jack had stuck the knife in her chest instead of John doing it. At least then she wouldn't be feeling all this pain.

At home she went through the motions without a thought on what she was doing. Sitting at her computer, she typed her story for the paper and sent it in for the next edition, then silently made her way to the shower. As the warm water blasted her skin and soap slid over her body, she tried desperately to understand John's actions.

"How could he?" she said as her tears mixed with the water pouring over her. "If you love someone, you accept them for what they are, who they are." Maybe that was the problem. Maybe he didn't love her like she loved him.

Turning off the water and wrapping a thick towel around her body, her mind continued to organize her thoughts. She had been afraid for his life tonight, too. In fact there was a moment when she thought she might have lost him, but that didn't turn her against him. It made her realize how much she truly loved him and didn't want to spend another minute without him in her life.

Suddenly another thought occurred to her. What if he never cared for her? What if it all was an act so she would help them catch the killer by not printing what she knew for fact? What if he used her the whole time? Taylor blew out a gush of air. *Boy, was he good at playacting.* He proved it at her sister's house. What if. . .she stopped herself. If she kept thinking, *What if. . .*all day, there was no telling how sick at heart she would become. She had to stop thinking.

Taylor looked at her haggard reflection as she brushed her teeth. The bruises shone badly around her left eye from when she had fallen to the ground face-first. The cheek below had a cut slightly over an inch long with two stitches. That wasn't so bad. It may not look pretty, but she'd had worse.

Still on automatic, she padded to her bed and slipped between her sheets. Tears spilled from her eyes as she closed them, trying to fall asleep.

Maybe things would be better in the morning. With purposed thought she prayed, "Please help me. You don't know me, but I want to know You. John knows You. Are You directing him now? Are we meant to be together. . .or apart? Lead us, Lord."

A sudden calm came over her and she fell into a restful sleep.

Chapter 31

Why hadn't he called? Taylor thought for sure John would have called her by now. She loved him so much she could ignore the fact he was a cop. She had never cared too much for cops—at least never enough to get involved romantically with one. Their lives were too unpredictable, but her mind and heart wouldn't allow her not to think about becoming romantically involved with John. He was a first for her. Her heart had never opened a door to anyone.

In her mind's eye, she saw John. "Mr. Perfection," she called him. He loved everything neat, clean, and in its rightful place. Not only was he super organized, he was a health nut to boot. Taylor smiled to herself as she shook her head. "How could I ever fall in love with someone like that?" They were complete opposites.

Just thinking about him and his "bad" habits brought joy

to Taylor's heart. The only problem was he didn't love her in return.

She leaned back and closed her eyes. Beneath her lids was that perfect image of John, a house, and a white picket fence. She could even see 2.3 children. . .well, actually, two children and another on the way. . .in her dream.

Shaking her head, she laughed. "My mother would be doing cartwheels if she knew what I was thinking. I need to give her a ring. . .or Tina." After the way her mother talked to her last time, Taylor felt certain it would be her mother she would call or go see. She needed someone to talk to, someone who knew about these things. Maybe her mother could give her some good advice. If she told Tina, her sister would only be lining up another man for Taylor. Not a route she wanted to go. . .she couldn't bear it. Not now.

Taylor's eyes snapped open. "That is a defeatist attitude." She shut off the computer. She'd sent her story in earlier that morning, and it had already been proofed and posted in the online news. The paper version of her article would be out in the next issue, but at least online they had scooped the other papers with a more in-depth news story. Mr. Cox had told her to take a couple of days to recoup.

Sitting still, relaxing, had never been a part of Taylor's life. She liked to stay busy, breaking one story after another. It was how her blood flowed. Not today. What about tomorrow?

The phone rang, pulling her out of her dream world. *John.* Her heart cried out. "Hello," she whispered.

"Hey, sweetie. Dad and I were reading your story and wanted to call and make sure our baby girl was okay. Your dad seems to think this may be the one to get your name recognized everywhere. We're happy for you."

"Thanks." She sighed.

"Talk to me, Baby. Tell me all about it."

After spilling her heart out, her mom said, "I never realized how long it would take you to fall in love."

"But, Momma. What if he doesn't love me? I can't take the pain." Taylor wiped the tears from her face with the back of her hand. "Life was so much easier when I had no one."

The next few minutes Taylor's mom cocooned her daughter through tender words as tears kept falling.

Finally there were no more. "Remember I told you about his dead fiancée? Well, because of that he had sworn himself away from women like her—which unfortunately includes me. But he had gotten past all of that, and we were taking it one day at a time. It didn't last twenty-four hours. I don't understand. I don't know what to do next."

"Taylor, what do you want to happen between the two of you?"

"I want him to tell me everything is like it was before." She thought for a moment, then said, "No, not like before but better than before. I want him to tell me he loves me and can handle everything about me."

"Did you think he was falling in love with you, sweetie?"

"Yes."

"Then you're going to have to fight for what you want. If he is in love with you, the way you are with him, then it shouldn't matter what you do for a living, as long as it isn't illegal." Laughing lightly, her mother added, "That would be a little hard for a policeman to accept. You do what you have to do. Love is stronger than you realize."

"Mom, should I give up investigative reporting? Maybe settle down and follow the society section for a while?"

"Not on your life. If you did that, you would always blame him for not having the career you dreamed of since the day you walked into your father's office."

Taylor bit her bottom lip as she tried to figure out what she should do.

"Follow your heart, dear. It will lead you. I'll let you in on a little secret. I almost missed out on marrying your father because I was afraid of what an investigative reporter's wife would have to suffer. Never knowing if he would make it home from the next story, letting meals turn cold before he showed up for dinner. I wasn't sure I could handle that, but I struggled with the worry of handling life without Oliver. That was a harder cross for me to bear. Give John a chance."

A smile touched Taylor's lips. "Thanks, Mom. I love you."

"Me, too."

After they hung up, Taylor wanted to jump up and run to John. Tell him not to give up on them. Would he listen? Was it the right time, or should she wait on him? She decided she had better think things through before making a move. She only had one shot at appealing to his heart and not his head, and she wanted it to be the best approach possible. This was one story in her life she didn't want to screw up in any way.

Chapter 32

John sat on his front porch swing and watched the traffic go by. He still hadn't slept since the nap on Taylor's couch yesterday. "I'm too old for this," he muttered under his breath.

He swung back and forth as he replayed the morning in his mind. "Why did I overreact? I know her life is dangerous. I knew it before this morning went down. I put her in the situation. It was my idea, not hers, so why did I treat her the way I did?"

God, help me here. You know where I've been and where You've brought me today. You know I asked You to help me put her out of my mind and heart. You told me, she was the one. . .but clearly You see she can't be. . .right?

As the evening breeze blew through his hair like fingers gently stroking the strands, he fought his mixed emotions. Part of him blamed himself for ever falling in love with her.

Yes. He realized he was in love with Taylor Jaymes. But today confirmed her life was too dangerous, and she got too close to her stories for comfort, even though he propelled her to it. After seeing her face, the cuts, and the bruises—after his heart stopped beating while he tried to rescue her this morning—he knew he couldn't take a lifetime with her.

Her job wasn't going to change. In all investigations into criminal activities reporters took chances. Felons broke laws. Hurting or killing a reporter trying to do a story on them wouldn't deter a criminal in the least. He wouldn't hesitate to break another law. . .anything to keep from getting caught.

Could he even ask her to rethink her career choice for his own peace of mind? Would he change his career for her? John was terrified of his feelings for Taylor, but what could he do?

He stood up and stormed inside. Flipping on the television, he caught the lead into the news. Of course her face was plastered all over it, along with Jack Williams, the local serial killer finally arrested for his crimes. Her face looked horrible. Pointing the control toward the TV, he snapped it off. John couldn't take looking at what he had put her through.

Turning on his stereo, the soft music came through the speakers. Listening to it, he walked from room to room. His home was neat and clean. John always took pride in that, but he found no pride in it tonight. It looked cold and empty. Was he going to die a lonely old man? If he stayed away from Taylor, he could at least boast he never had to suffer her loss.

"She's the one for you." Those words played through his mind. "No!"

In the kitchen, he made coffee. When it was finished, he cleaned up behind himself and then sat down at the table.

What was he doing now? Was this considered suffering? He hadn't shaved. . .something John never went without. He did care what he looked like.

John sipped his coffee. His kitchen looked spotless; his home looked how he wanted it to look. But would he ever have his heart in it again?

Jumping to his feet, he threw the cup against the wall and yelled, "I don't need spotless—I need Taylor!"

Chapter 33

Taylor made her plans. She wasn't going to give up without a fight. Tomorrow morning she would beat the detective to his desk and be waiting for him. She was going to have it out, get things straight, and lay all her cards on the table. If professing her love didn't do the trick, then by golly she would think of something else. There was no way she was going to let that man walk out of her life. She loved him, and she knew he loved her. Even if she had to be the one to hammer it into his head, she would make him see their love.

After making up her mind, Taylor found it a lot easier to lie down on her sofa and rest. With the little bit of sleep she had gotten in the past forty-eight hours, and the fact she had been so upset by the treatment from John, Taylor found herself very tired. She fell asleep before seven that night...still on the couch.

Shortly after eight Taylor woke with a start.

A pounding on her door snapped her out of a deep sleep. Rubbing her sore eyes carefully, she sat up. Dragging herself to the door, she reached for the lock. Freezing in midair, she remembered the last two nights and shuddered. "Who is it?"

"Open up. . .please?"

Taylor's heart leapt into her throat when she heard John's voice. Quickly she flipped the lock and undid the chain. Turning the doorknob, she opened the door. "John, come in." Her heart hammered almost as loud as he had pounded on the door. *Calm down.* She didn't want to let him see how he affected her.

His eyebrows came together. "Oh, my gosh. Look at you! You have bloodshot eyes and bruises all over your face. I'm so sorry."

She wanted to tell him to look in a mirror. He hadn't shaved. So why was he here? Was it to see her, or did it have more to do with the case they had just worked? She couldn't let her heart run away too soon. She needed to be sure. "It's okay. What can I do for you?"

John held up his hands, each holding a bag. "I thought even if you didn't want to see me, you would at least want to see the food I brought." He raised his brows, waiting for her response.

Taylor glanced at the white bags. In the middle of each bag was a drawing of the golden arches. "Fast food? You got takeout?"

"I figured if you can't beat 'em, join 'em."

Taylor wanted to believe he was referring to her, but she couldn't be sure. With mixed emotions, part of her wanted to throw her arms around his neck and confess what she decided earlier tonight to tell him, while the other part chose caution. *Go slow. Don't make a fool of yourself.*

"Food. I can't resist. Come on into the kitchen. I'm starved." Taylor led the way. She pulled down two plates and placed them on the table.

John had already seated himself and was pulling out the burgers. "Two Big Macs and two fries. I didn't get anything to drink. I figured you could supply that."

Taylor poured them each a glass of milk. She sat across from John and watched as he appeared to be digging into his food. This didn't make sense, and she wanted to say so. In fact, she wanted to ask him what had happened to him after they caught the killer, but then thought better of it. She'd wait him out.

"Aren't you going to eat?" he asked between bites.

"Sure." She nibbled at her food. Whenever she felt him start to look her way, she averted her gaze.

After a lengthy silence passed and John had finished over half of his meal, Taylor couldn't wait any longer. Maybe if she broke the ice, he would spill it all. "You've come a long way on your eating habits, backward no less. I hope I'm not to blame."

John put his burger down on his plate. Washing this bite down with a swig of milk, he said, "Actually you are totally to blame." His husky voice broke as he spoke.

Taylor felt a wave of shock flash through her and knew it showed on her face.

John reached across the table and covered her hand with his. "I blame you for making my life better. Until you came along, I only existed, but now. . . ." He sighed and squeezed her hand. "Now I look forward to the next day. Last night, or should I say early this morning, I was scared. I saw everything in a flash, and I knew you were going to be taken from me. I knew then that I loved you and couldn't bear to lose you."

Her heart raced as the warmth from his hand penetrated hers, and she listened to his words of love. She wanted to jump into his arms and hold on forever. She started to speak, but he touched his finger to her lips. "No. Let me finish."

She stilled herself, lavishly soaking in his words.

"When it came down to Williams gunning me, I had no fear for my safety, but I knew if he got me, he would go back for you. That I feared. Sure, I had backup, cops all around me, but I wasn't thinking clearly. A man in love seldom does."

He said it again. Love. The magic word. It was all she could do to sit and not make a move for him.

"In fact, I feared more than I should have. With his shot, he missed me, but one shot and I took him down. Before he could get back up, I was on him, cuffing his hands behind him. I wanted to run to you, make sure you were okay and tell you how much I loved you."

"But you didn't," she whispered. "You said nothing to me."

Wrapping both his hands around her hand on the table, holding it tightly, he said, "When we walked out on the porch, I saw you standing behind the car, safe and alive. The joy that flooded through me, I couldn't even begin to explain, but then I saw the blood on your face. I broke out in a cold sweat and felt like all my blood had drained out of me. I decided I could not live my life in fear. Fear for your life." John stood and pulled Taylor up with him. Encircling her with his arms, he pulled her close.

His voice softened as he held her in his arms. "When I went home early this morning, my mind was made up. You and I were history." Running his fingers gently through the long strands hanging down her back, he whispered, "But I figured it out. If I can't make it twenty-four hours without you, how can I live the rest of my life without you in it? I can't."

Taylor looked up at John. She knew the love and happiness she felt had to be pouring from her eyes. John leaned down and pressed his lips to hers. A thrill of excitement shot through her veins as she kissed him back. This was more happiness than she even knew could exist. She closed her eyes as the kiss grew stronger.

Finally, he pulled back slightly and said, "So does this mean you forgive the way I acted this morning? The whole purpose in my life will be to make you happy. I love you, Taylor Jaymes, reporter and all. I'll find a way to get over my fear of losing you. I think I'll just hold on so tight, there will be no way that could happen."

Taylor held on tight. "If you're ready for me to speak, I have a confession."

John pulled back from the embrace with an expression of apprehension. "Do I need to be sitting down for this? You already have another major crime story to follow?" His face drew tight. "Maybe I'm not as strong as I thought."

Taylor could feel the tension in his grip. "Let's go sit in the living room," she whispered.

"That sounds like bad news to me."

"No," she assured him. Taylor led the way. After pushing him gently, causing him to sit, she slid gracefully onto his lap. "First let me say, you make me so very happy." She wrapped her arms around his neck and kissed him fully on his mouth. She could feel his response in the kiss. She knew he enjoyed it as much as she did.

Taylor caressed the sides of his face. "You haven't shaved lately. Poor Baby." She knew he hadn't been taking care of himself at all. It must be love. She smiled to herself.

"Don't change the subject. What is your confession?"

"I planned to go by your office today after thinking about you and your reaction last night. I thought about it all day long actually. I knew I loved you and realized, or should I say hoped, the only thing that was keeping us apart was my line of work. Then I came to the conclusion that my line of work meant nothing to me in comparison to what you mean to me. You mean everything to me. And if you want me to give up my investigative reporting, just give the word and I'll do it."

John pulled her back against him, resting her head on his shoulder. "You would do that for me?" He rubbed her cheek with his face. "I love you all the more for that gift, but Taylor, I couldn't allow it. In no time you'd regret it and hate me for it."

Taylor sat up and looked deeply into his blue eyes. "My mother said the same thing." Wrapping her arms around his neck, she hugged him tightly. "Do you know she almost didn't marry Daddy for the same reason? Of course you didn't know. I didn't know until today. And she hasn't regretted marrying him after all these years. She said if she had not married him, she would have regretted that. Do you love me that much?"

"I love you more." Pulling her face to him, he kissed her over and over again.

"John," she whispered as she kissed one cheek, then the other, "one day I'm going to want to quit my job or at least quit running around following bad guys. Do you know why?"

When he didn't respond, she kissed him again. "Because one day I want us to have children. I want to be a mamma. I don't know if I'll be good at cooking or cleaning, or even taking care of the kids, but I will sure try." Taylor gave him that same look she had given him that first day they met.

"Why are you looking at me that way?"

"Because you changed me in so many ways. . .ways I thought would never happen. I now want to be a wife, a homemaker, and a mother. I also want to have a personal relationship with Christ, like you do. I never thought I'd hear any of those words come out of my mouth—and it's all your fault." A big smile broke across her face as she spoke, hoping he felt her love.

John kissed her again. Catching her bottom lip between his teeth, he pulled gently. And then, pressing his mouth to hers, he kissed her passionately.

With her hands resting lightly on his chest, she felt the pounding of his heart.

"The wife part, we'll take care of as soon as legally possible. The mother part," he dropped kisses down her neck, "we'll start on right after the ceremony. But as far as the homemaker part goes, who cares if the house isn't spotless, as long as you're in it."

A thrill raced through her body. "You've come a long way, darling." She turned his face up, placing a warm kiss on his lips, dreaming of their future together.

Be Not Afraid
Samantha Cain Mysteries
Book 1

I dedicate this book to
the Lord
and my family in Christ.

≈∘

God has given me the gift of enjoying what I do. . .writing and sharing stories with others who love to read. My dream growing up was to be an actress. Momma and Daddy always believed I would be the new Doris Day. God had other plans, giving me a husband and a family who encourages my writing. So my childhood dream came true. Now, by writing novels, I am acting. . .only I get to play all the roles. How wonderful is that? Plus I get to share my love for the Lord, woven in to all of my stories.

ACKNOWLEDGMENTS

First and foremost, I want to thank my Lord for giving me the passion for writing. He burned this passion in my heart many years ago and has since been refining me and helping me to grow and write so that He is exalted in my stories. He's blessed me and continues to do so, and I give Him the praise and the glory. We all know He never gives us more than we can handle, nor will He ever give us something to do and not give us the way in which to do it. Thank You, Lord.

Over the years He's blessed me with critique partners: first with Elaine Grant, Sylvia Rochester, and Sharon Elliott. . .and now Emy White and Marie Barber. They have all been a blessing, trudging with me through my efforts and helping me finetune my stories. I thank each for their help.

God also put one very special lady in my path a few years ago that helped relight the flame for writing. When I was about to give up, Mrs. Lucille Montgomery, who at the time owned The Christian Book Store in Baton Rouge, Louisiana, came to me and asked to read one of my manuscripts. She was visiting our church at the time and had heard from ladies there of my writing. When I gave her a manuscript, *Be Not Afraid*, she loved it. As a bookstore owner, she felt confident she could promote my book with no problem, and she did just that with the first two novels that were released: *Grace, a Gift of Love* and then *All in God's Time*. Thanks to her encouragement, this is my third novel being released. I hope, like her, you enjoy the read.

In loving memory of my dear friend, who went on to be with the Lord on December 23, 2009.

Let not your heart be troubled,
neither let it be afraid.

JOHN 14:27 KJV

Chapter 1

A scream pierced the darkness outside the office. Samantha Cain's head popped up as she glared out the big window. She froze. Her heart pounded as an icy chill slid slowly down her back.

"What was that?" she whispered to herself as she slowly rose to her feet.

Fearfully, her eyes searched the night through a large picture window in a futile attempt to find the source of the scream. A black void filled her view as the moon hid behind a large cloud.

Standing still, Sam listened for another scream. Almost perfect silence flooded the room. Neither the hum of an occasional tugboat chugging down the Mississippi River nor the steady rhythm of a train crossing over the bridge on elevated tracks was heard. Only country music played softly in the background, barely audible over the pounding of her heart.

Was it a scream, or was it her imagination? It could have been a squeal from tires. Kids raced along the River Road all the time. A cat could have called out in the night. Possibilities flashed through her mind.

It could have been anything. Why am I reacting this way? I've worked nights too long to start jumping at every sound....

Fear comes from the devil. Peace comes from God. That wasn't a straight quote from the prophet Isaiah, but Sam got the message her mind had sent her. She took a deep, cleansing breath to calm her nerves and slowly released it.

A moment later, the scream replayed in her mind.

She shivered. That was what unsettled her nerves. It wasn't tires squealing or a cat screeching. It sounded like a human scream. . .a woman's scream.

With unsteady hands, Sam reached for the knob on the radio and turned it off. Straining, she listened again. Nothing. Silence.

Her fingertips iced over, and goose bumps lined her arms. The bitter taste of fear settled unnaturally in her mouth.

"This is silly," she scolded herself. Sucking in a gush of air, then quickly blowing it out again, hard and fast this time, she tried to shake off the feeling of alarm.

Fear not. I am with you. Words of peace crossed her mind as her heartbeat settled to a steady thump.

Maybe I just imagined the scream. To further convince herself of her strong imagination, she unlocked the double locks on the wooden door to her office. Standing in the entryway to the glassed-in lobby area, she saw first her own reflection: a woman barely over five feet tall, with long brown hair cascading down over her shoulders. Her bangs almost covered her green eyes as she leaned toward the glass door and cupped her hands around her eyes. She peered through the glass door leading outside. With the fluorescent lighting on inside, she could see only vague, indistinguishable shadows through the glass.

Pushing the front door open, she stepped out into the night air and listened again.

Still nothing.

Sam's eyes adjusted to the darkness. The one streetlight, near the gate's entrance to Liquid Bulk Transport, exposed an empty highway.

The clouds shifted slowly, unveiling the moon one slice at a time. Patches of grass-covered ground became apparent beyond the road where the levee rose to contain the flow of the mighty Mississippi. Tracing the moonlit summit of the levee in both directions, Sam saw nothing out of the ordinary.

Confident now she'd imagined the scream, she relaxed, unclenching her fists. A slight breeze stirred strands of her hair, blowing them softly across her face as she turned back toward the building. Grabbing the door handle, she was about to pull it open when she heard a rustling.

She stopped and turned in her tracks. What was that? Was it the wind? Was it something. . .or someone?

She perked her head, twisting toward the highway as she strained to listen. Then she heard it again. . .a scuffling. A couple of dogs, maybe? She wasn't sure what, or possibly who, but she knew she heard something. Sam jerked her body around in the direction of the levee. Staring hard, she tried again to find the source. Her eyes squinted, slowly tracing along the levee for something—*anything*—making that sound.

The noise stopped again. With her left ear cocked toward the levee, Sam stilled, straining to hear the sound again. Nothing.

If only it were distinct, she could find it. Identify it. Maybe then she could prove to herself it was nothing to worry about. Possibly even discover it was two dogs fighting over a bone. And, who knows, maybe a cat tried to interfere.

There it was again!

Something was out there, but what? A thrashing sound came from the direction of the levee, but she didn't dare move closer. It was louder this time. More grunting or groaning noises.

What was it? Was it those dogs she so hoped for? She didn't hear any growling. Sam stared, squinting, focusing her eyes intently toward the sound.

Finally, she saw it. Over there, on top of the levee, an eerie light cast from the moon shone upon two silhouettes, a large form locked in a struggle with a small figure of a woman. The shapes appeared for a second or two, then vanished on the other side of the levee. A woman was being attacked. Sam's heart pounded as she swiftly turned on her heel.

Running back into the building through the glass door and past the wooden door leading back into her office, she punched 911 on the telephone. As it started to ring, she glanced out the window and back at the door to the office. Oh no! She forgot to shut and lock the door behind her. Her stomach knotted as panic choked her. Her chest tightened.

There isn't time for fear, she told herself just as she heard, "This is 911 emergency. What is your emergency?"

In a rush, she said, "This is Samantha Cain at Liquid Bulk

Transport on River Road. I heard a scream and saw two people fighting on the levee. By the sizes and shapes of the shadows, it looked like a man attacking a woman. Can you get help here quick?"

"Stay calm, ma'am. I'll dispatch help right away. All cars in the vicinity. . ."

Sam listened while the operator broadcast the situation and location to deputies on duty. *What if help doesn't get here in time?* she wondered. *How can I stand here holding a phone while someone is being attacked? Can I let her be a victim, too?*

"I've been trained," she reminded herself aloud, thinking of all the self-defense and emergency courses she'd taken over the past year. She slammed the phone down on the countertop. "I can't just sit here. No way. I've got to try and help her." *Greater is He that is in you, than he that is in the world.*

With that scripture in mind, Sam grabbed her purse and pulled out a small black container of mace. *Help me, Lord,* she prayed. *I can't stand by and let him hurt her. I need to slow the man down, distract him or something, until help arrives. Please help me make smart moves. . . ."*

Now she knew exactly what she was going to do, and she knew she wasn't alone.

Racing out the door, across the graveled parking lot of the trucking company toward the levee, she didn't give herself time to worry about the consequences. She hastened toward the fight, holding the mace tightly in her grasp, ready to spray the attacker when she reached him. If nothing else, it should buy time.

As Sam rushed closer, she noticed that the woman's hands were hanging limply at her side. It appeared all of the fight had gone out of her. Sam prayed she wasn't too late.

Hold on, her thoughts whispered. Aloud, she screamed, "Leave her alone! Let her go!" Sam closed some distance between them as she started across the highway toward the levee.

The man's head snapped up, and he peered in her direction. Even from this far away, Sam saw his eyes. They blazed with a sick, detached, almost possessed look. His hands stayed locked around the woman's neck, appearing to squeeze even tighter, if that were possible. Sam knew she had to be crazy to continue toward this crazed man, but she couldn't stop now. She had to do all she could do. It took all the courage she could muster to keep moving forward and not run back to safety.

As she started up the levee, less than fifty feet away, Sam shouted again, "I said, leave her alone!"

The attacker's eyes widened as he slowly turned toward Sam, twisting the limp body still in his grasp in the same direction. The woman wasn't fighting back anymore; nor was she standing on her feet. He was holding her airborne, by her neck.

Sam's steps slowed slightly as her grip tightened on the mace.

Suddenly the attacker released his hold, and the victim crumpled to the ground like a fallen leaf. His gaze locked on Sam, and he took one step toward her.

Sam's heart skipped a beat. *I'm next. He's going to come after me now. Am I strong enough to hold him off till help gets here?* Her heart began to pound even harder.

Then she heard that still, small voice in her head: *I can do all things through Christ which strengthens me.*

There was no turning back. She gripped the can tighter and her fingertip felt for the button, ready to spray him, to stun him...to bring him to his knees.

Chapter 2

Slowly, he moved toward her. One step, and then another, his crazed gaze locked on Samantha all the while.

A lump caught in her throat. Sam tried to swallow it, to push it down so she could breathe freely. Instead, she held her breath and squeezed harder on the can in her hand.

Suddenly, a shriek of sirens filled the air. For a moment, the crazed man hesitated, looking past Sam, as if estimating the time left before help arrived.

She wanted to turn and look behind her, too. She wanted to see what he saw. . .to know help was almost there. But she couldn't. She didn't dare take her eyes off the enemy.

Flashing lights filled the semidarkness. They appeared in all the dark shadows. They were close. . .had to be.

Then, in an instant, the sick smile on his face wiped clean. His brow flicked up as he eyed her with a dare. She knew what he wanted to say. She felt it in her gut. *"Until next time,"* she heard him say, only not aloud. Then he turned and fled.

Even after he was gone, she couldn't move for a second or two. When the high shrill of the sirens sounded like they were on top of her, she managed to look toward the highway. There they were—sheriff cars and an ambulance all pulling to a stop at the bottom of the levee.

She rushed to the victim's side. The first thing she noticed was the woman's face. Eyes closed. Skin tinged blue and swollen. Blood oozing from her nose and at the edge of her mouth, with lips slightly parted. Was she dead? Had Sam gotten there too late? She prayed not. At a closer look, she detected a slight rise and fall of the chest. . .very slight. There was still hope.

Sam leaned down and touched the woman gently. "Stay with me. Open your eyes. Help is here." She stroked the side of the woman's face as she heard doors slamming and feet running. "You're going to be all right. Just hang on. Can you hear me? Help is here."

As she tried to rouse the woman to consciousness, Sam was vaguely aware of a sudden commotion around her. In a heartbeat, the help arrived and surrounded them, but something was terribly wrong. Instead of looking for the attacker, the officers' guns were drawn and pointed directly at Sam. Was this some kind of sick joke?

"Put your hands up and step away!"

"But I'm the one who called for help. I'm Samantha Cain. The guy who did this is getting away," she cried.

"I said, get up and back away. Hands on your head." The guns pointed in her direction emphasized his words.

Sam's heart raced. It was bad enough she could have gotten herself killed by a crazy man, but now—?

"Get up slowly; put your hands up where I can see them, then place them on your head. Now!" the voice barked.

Dropping the can of mace to the ground, she started to rise, lifting her arms up in surrender. For what, she did not know. "This is ridiculous," she muttered, placing her hands on top of her head, fingers clasped together.

"Step back." He waved his gun in one quick jerky motion. When she moved away, the one who seemed to be in charge, keeping one eye on Sam, leaned over the woman's body. A second later he motioned for the paramedics to approach. "She's still alive."

Not if you don't hurry, Sam thought.

After the paramedics moved in to stabilize the victim, the officer turned his attention to Sam, motioning her to move further away from the victim. It was all she could do to contain her annoyance of the men in blue. . .well, technically, green, since it was the sheriff's office that came to the rescue.

"I'm telling you, I didn't do anything wrong," she tried to explain. "I'm the one who called for help."

The officer didn't listen, nor did he seem to care. He led Sam further away from the woman on the ground. "Keep your hands up over your head. Stop. Spread your legs." He patted her down. Keeping his gun trained on her, he said to the others, "I'll take care of this one. You three spread out. Canvass the area. See if someone else is hanging around like she claims."

It's about time.

With the barrel of his gun steadily pointing at her, he used his radio and called in to headquarters. Sam was terrified. Angry, but terrified. How could they hold her here like a common criminal? All she had done was try to help. . .try to do the right thing.

"You can turn back around now. What did you say your name was?"

"Samantha Cain." Sam started to put her hands down.

"Slowly," he said.

"I told you I was only trying to help. My purse is over there." She pointed in the direction of the yellow building across the street. "At my office. I'm a dispatcher at that trucking company right there." The building sat in the midst of one very large parking lot. The lot was filled with many tanker trailers and several bobtailed tractors. And who knows, maybe by now even that sick man who hurt this woman.

"My license is over there if you need proof of who I am. I'm the one who called 911 for help."

"If you're telling the truth, you have nothing to fear."

"Only that the attacker is getting away," she mumbled slightly under her breath, "or hiding over at my workplace."

At that moment, she heard her name confirmed as the emergency caller over the two-way radio. Then the officer peered around one more time, as if scouting for trouble hidden in the darkness.

"All right, Ms. Cain. You appear to be the one who called it in. You should have stayed in your office. You could have been hurt, too." He slipped his gun back in the holster and pulled out his pad and pen. "All right. Start from the beginning and tell me what happened."

She breathed a sigh of relief. *Finally.* "I heard a scream. I saw the woman being attacked. I called for help. Then I came and tried to distract her attacker until you got here."

"Again, that was a foolish thing to do. You could have been killed. What if we had been delayed in getting here? Do you think you were big enough to take down this man you saw?" He shook his head, as if disgusted, and didn't wait for a reply. "What did the man who attacked the woman look like?"

As he mentioned the victim, Sam cast a glance at the paramedics. "Is she going to be all right?" Sam asked.

"They'll do all they can for her. Please. Give me a description of the man."

"It was dark." She shifted her feet. "I couldn't see him clearly. He was wearing a hat, kind of like a ski cap. It covered his hair and ears and even part of his face. He was tall compared to the woman. His huge hands wrapped around her throat." The whole time Sam talked, her hands were moving as if trying to do the talking for her, making her description clearer for the deputy.

"And the look in his eyes. . . ." She shook slightly as that image replayed clearly in her mind and goose bumps raced down her back.

"You said you couldn't see him clearly, yet you saw his eyes?" The tone of the officer's voice confirmed he didn't believe her.

"Yes. By the moonlight? The streetlight?" Throwing her hands up in the air and waving them around, she shrugged. "I don't know, but yes. I saw his eyes." Sam closed her eyes and tried to see his face in her mind but couldn't. All she saw were those dark eyes glaring at her and the look that said, *I'll be back.*"

Her eyes popped open, and she glanced all around her. "Have y'all found him yet?" Where did he go? Where was he hiding? She stole a glance across the street at her office. Could he have slipped over there? Would he be waiting for her? She trembled.

"What else do you remember?" the officer asked.

"They were dark. . .His eyes, I mean. And the look in them"—she shuddered as she spoke—"it was sick." Her hands tried again to emphasize what she was saying. "I believe he told me what he wanted me to know. Not in words, but in his eyes, he let me know he would be back. At least that's what I think he was trying to get across to me without opening his mouth. 'Cause he never said a word."

The officer scribbled a few more notes on his pad as he continued to question her. "Think back to before the scream. Did you hear anything then? Or see anything unusual?"

Rubbing the temples on either side of her head, she tried to think. "No. Not that I can recall." She shook her head.

Her thoughts strayed back to the attacker. The threat in his eyes was real. She was sure of it. Who was she kidding? She could have been killed. That man was ready to come after her.

He still might. *No,* she told herself. *That was the heat of the moment. He wouldn't be crazy enough to come back after me. But look at what he did. . . .*

Suddenly, overwhelmed by the reality of what had taken place tonight, her head started to spin and her knees turned to liquid rubber. All strength eased away from her. For a moment, Sam thought she was going to faint. She wrapped her arms around herself, holding on tightly, trying to stop the shaking inside of her, trying to stay upright.

"Are you okay? Hey, Joe," he called to one of the paramedics as he moved quickly to catch her. "When you get a chance, come check this one out. All the color just left her face." To her he said, "Sit down for a minute." He helped ease her to the ground.

The pounding of her heart lessened as she slowly breathed in several deep, calming breaths. *I'm safe now, and the woman is alive. I did the right thing. Thank You, Lord,* she reassured herself as she looked up at the officer.

Swallowing hard, Sam nodded. "I'm okay." She gathered up her strength and confidence. "Sorry. I guess it just hit me what happened and the fact I could have been killed. I'll be all right. Thanks."

She waved off the paramedic as the officer stepped away to converse with one of his fellow deputies. "I'm okay," she said to the paramedic. He shrugged and went back to the ones helping the woman.

After a few minutes of scanning the immediate area, the first officer came back to her. "Are you feeling any better?" When she nodded and rose to her feet, he continued. "Do you remember any unusual traffic or activity in the area tonight?"

Another siren wailed in the distance.

Beams of light from the other deputies' flashlights roamed up and down the riverbanks as the officer continued to question her. Anxiously, she watched the beams moving further and further away. "Do you think they found him yet? Would they call you on your radio—" she pointed to his two-way— "if they saw him, I mean?"

"Ms. Cain, I asked if you saw any unusual activity in the area before you heard the scream."

As the officer spoke, her mind whirled. Would they find

him? She hoped so. Sam needed to get back to work. But how could she concentrate on work? "Are y'all gonna check the yard over there? Make sure he's not hiding over there?" She glanced at the truck yard.

And what if he was over there? The pounding of her heart beat in triple time. He could have easily moved down the levee along the edge of the river and then worked his way across the highway and back down to the truck yard without being seen.

"We'll check it out. Don't you worry. In the meantime, until we catch him, I wouldn't work alone over there. You witnessed an attempted killing tonight, Ms. Cain."

A shiver raced across her shoulders and down her back all the way to her toes. She was afraid. There were no ifs, ands, or buts about it. Sam was scared to death. She knew that was her flesh, but right now, she admitted to herself, it was the part doing the thinking. And she was often alone at work. In fact, most nights after the night shift ended at eleven thirty till the morning shift started arriving before seven the next morning. Sure, drivers were in and out at various times but not constantly all night long.

She knew that, later, when she would make her way back to the office and would have time to pray, she would shake this fear. *The joy of the Lord is my strength,* she reminded herself.

A flashing red light on the dash of a small silver car caught Sam's attention. Gravel crunched below the tires as the car jerked to a stop. A man wearing a baseball cap, T-shirt, and shorts climbed out of the car and looked their way. At a glance, something about him looked familiar.

Chapter 3

Glad you made it, Detective Jefferies."

A frown covered the newcomer's face as his gaze slid over Sam.

She was right. Something about him looked familiar, but at the moment she couldn't put her finger on it.

"Langlois. Let's clear the area so no evidence will be disturbed."

"This is my crime scene, Detective. I'm the one who suggested they call you. So mind your manners. The situation is under control. Ms. Cain is a witness. In fact, she helped scare off the attacker, possibly saving the victim's life." The deputy pointed toward the beams of light. "Three of my men are canvassing the area looking for the attacker, and more help is on the way. You want to look around, be my guest, but watch where you step. The crime scene unit is headed this way also." The dour-faced detective glanced Sam's way before walking further up the levee.

Sam gave him a tight smile as she nodded. After a closer look at the detective who had just arrived at the scene and was now walking down the levee away from them toward the deputies, she asked, "You called him Detective Jefferies. Is that Matthew Jefferies, from the 3rd precinct?"

"Yes, ma'am. I asked dispatch to give him a call. This attack could be connected to a couple of high-profile homicide cases he's been working on."

Suddenly three years melted away. Now she knew why the man looked vaguely familiar. He was the man with whom Martin, her husband, had partnered just a few short months before Martin's death.

"Officer Langlois, we're going to take the victim to the Baton Rouge General Hospital," the paramedic said.

"Is she going to make it?"

"She's stable for now, but very weak."

"Could I question her?"

"She's unconscious. You'll have to try later."

The paramedics lifted the stretcher with the injured woman and carried her down to the ambulance. In minutes, the siren screamed to life again.

As the vehicle sped away, another car approached. When the car turned into the truck yard, Sam surmised it was Tim Hutchinson, one of their drivers. In no time, more drivers would be arriving for work.

"Deputy. I need to get back over there. I have work to do."

"Fine. If you think of anything else, please call me." He handed her his card.

Dare she walk over there alone? She hadn't seen any of his

men make it over to the yard yet. Sam took a few steps, leaned over, and picked up her mace. Should she ask the deputy to come with her or insist they check it first?

"Langlois! Over here," called a voice in the distance.

They must have found something. Sam glared in the direction of the other deputies. The deputy responded with a hand gesture as if saying he would be right there. Maybe they found him. Oh, how she hoped so.

"Sam," a tall, slim man sporting a cowboy hat called from the foot of the driveway near the street, "are you okay?" Tim started toward her.

"Stay there, sir." The deputy pointed as he spoke. "Don't come any closer." Then he turned toward Sam. "Ms. Cain, keep him away from the crime scene. If we have any further questions, we'll come over there. Go on back to your job. You should be safe. We are right here and will be at your place shortly."

That was probably for the best, to go back to the yard with Tim at her side. But what if the attacker was over there in the yard...waiting for her? She rubbed her hands together at that heavy thought. Her hands felt cold, just like the fear in her heart. She shook the thought away.

No one would be waiting for her. She had done the right thing calling for help and then trying to help the woman herself. She had to shake off the grip of fear that was holding her hostage. She knew it was wrong, but she also knew God understood. So much had happened to her in the past.

Had she done the right thing, though? Sam could possibly identify him, and the attacker knew that. What if he decided to come after her? Her son, Marty, was seven years old and needed his mother. And what if he went after her son to get to her? All these thoughts and questions flashed through her mind.

"Thanks. I'll stop him," she said to the deputy, then turned toward the driveway. "Wait there, Tim. I'm coming."

Before going to him, Sam stepped to the top of the levee one more time and looked in the direction Jefferies had headed to see if she could see anything. Two beams of light still hovered far down the bank of the river, while two others gathered right below her near the water's edge. Maybe they had found a crucial piece of evidence. Hopefully something to help them catch the guy.

Sam sighed.

He probably got away. In fact, it wouldn't surprise her to discover the attacker was hiding right under their noses. She didn't hold a very high opinion of the police, due to her past experience. And her perception hadn't improved over the last couple of years.

Although this precinct was a different group of officers than the ones who had disappointed her a few years ago with the investigation of her husband's death, Sam knew that police, deputy sheriffs—they were all the same in one way or another. It was a brotherhood.

As the memories of three years ago flashed through her mind, she prayed she wouldn't be subjected to the third precinct again or the press. She didn't think she could handle either. Not now. Not ever.

Sam glanced back to the foot of the levee, where Tim stood waiting for her. She took a deep breath. The victim was on the way to the hospital. Everything would be okay. She stepped back down the levee toward the highway.

"Am I glad to see you!" She stopped at the edge of the road beside Tim. At that same moment, another police car and a van pulled up behind the detective's Ford Mustang. A logo on the side of the van displayed a local news station.

"Bloodhounds," she said in disgust. "They catch it all. Let's get out of here." She remembered the media all too well.

"Hey, sweetie. Are you okay?" Tim slipped an arm over her shoulder and pulled her beside him as they started to walk across the street. "What's going on? I saw all those lights when I first pulled up and prayed you were nowhere near any of it. But then I couldn't find you. You had me worried." Tim was talking so fast, Sam didn't have a chance to answer him. "When you weren't in the office, I hollered out back and around the yard for you. You didn't answer. I thought the worst. . .but then I saw you standing on the top of the levee." Squeezing her shoulder and pulling her closer to him, Tim held her tightly to his right side. "At least then I knew you were alive. Fill me in. Tell me what happened. You are okay, aren't you?"

"I'm fine." She nodded and held on tight with her hand that she circled around his waist. Sam felt safe in the protection of Tim's arm, even if it was short-lived. "I witnessed an attempted murder."

His long stride stopped midstep. He turned her toward him. "A murder? Are you sure you're okay?"

She nodded. "*Attempted* murder. The woman is alive and on the way to the hospital. She has a fighting chance."

When they reached the glass door of the office, he slipped both his arms around her and gave her a quick squeeze. "You scared me, girl. We don't need to lose you. It's bad enough the boss makes you work the night shift. A girl alone, out on the levee road in the middle of nowhere. . .that's unheard of. "

"I'm okay. Really. Thanks, Tim," she said, grateful again for the brief hug. "I'm glad you're with me, though."

He pulled open the door and held it while she entered the building. "No problem, kiddo. And I'm gonna stay till someone else gets here, too. I'm not about to leave you by yourself. Not under these circumstances. Is the deputy gonna come over here and check out the yard? Maybe the guy's hiding out back." Tim followed her into the drivers' room.

"My thoughts exactly. He said they would. He must have figured the guy was long gone 'cause they don't seem to be in any hurry to get over here." She shrugged as she answered. But when were they coming?

Sam set her mace down and started making a pot of fresh coffee.

"You sit. I'll do that," Tim said.

"If you don't mind making the coffee, I'd appreciate it. I really do need to get back to work." He nodded as he took over. She grabbed her mace and went back to her office.

Time passed. Drivers started to come and go. Tim got on his way. The sun rose. Glancing out the window occasionally, Sam never saw them bring anyone back in handcuffs nor did she notice anyone cross the way and start checking in the truck yard.

When Pat, her replacement, arrived, she filled him in on everything. They worked to finish the last of the paperwork. Then she gathered her things up, getting ready to head home.

Officer Langlois, followed by Detective Jefferies and a few

policemen, walked up as she was heading out the door. "Ms. Cain, we need a few words with you."

Although she had met Matthew Jefferies only once prior to this, she knew his name as well as she knew her own. He was one of a group of policemen who held her to blame for Martin's death.

"Check the building and the yard," Langlois ordered the men. "Make sure he didn't slip back over here somewhere." He turned toward Sam. "Ms. Cain, Detective Jefferies wants to talk to you for a minute."

"You didn't get the guy, did you?" Now that was a stupid question. . .in more than one way.

Before the deputy could answer, Jefferies stepped closer. "I'd like you to come to the precinct with me. I need you to look at mug shots."

"The precinct? The third precinct? Now?" Sam asked, shaking her head no as she spoke. "I can't. I need to get home to my son. I need to get him off to school. Besides, I didn't see the attacker well enough. I told Officer Langlois."

"Don't you realize your life could be in danger? That man is a killer, Ms. Cain, and you saw him."

"Not good," she reminded him.

"But he doesn't know that. You need to come down to the station and try and pick him out of the mug shot books. Or at least give a description so our artist can try and sketch him."

"I'm sorry. I can't help you." No, she couldn't go there. Not to the police station. Not to the third precinct. Not now. Not ever!

Chapter 4

The detective followed Ms. Cain home but stayed at a safe distance, not allowing her to see him. Once she was inside her apartment, he found a parking place and backed into it.

Pulling his cap off, he threw it down on the seat. "What was that all about?" he grumbled. Matthew sat in his car with the motor running. He remembered the first time they had met. He believed Martin Cain was the luckiest man alive. . .to have such a beautiful wife. She seemed so sweet and loving, but the truth came out in the end.

So what was she up to? He knew who she was, so why the games? Why pretend to care for someone she didn't even know? Why pretend she had a heart?

Samantha Cain had put on a show just now, and Matthew knew it. . .almost fell for it again. Sometimes her show seemed pretty convincing. He almost believed she raced to save the woman because she cared. But Samantha Cain never cared about anyone but herself, according to her dead husband. If she cared more, maybe he would be alive today.

Maybe she hadn't killed him with her own two hands or even pulled the trigger, but she practically pushed him to his death. That was how all the men at the station saw it.

When Martin died, she tried to make everyone believe she cared about him. She said she wished she could have saved him, but she was too late. And then, like any good wife, she mourned his death. At the funeral, she looked like a walking skeleton covered with a thin pasty layer of skin. Dark circles surrounded her eyes, eyes that stared out into space in a zombie-type state.

The brothers in blue knew it was all for show. Samantha Cain's true identity was revealed day in and day out by Martin's demeanor, by little subtle remarks made by him, by his lack of enthusiasm for life. It didn't take a rocket scientist to see his life was miserable. The Captain suggested Martin go talk to their shrink, but Martin insisted things were getting better at home.

They all knew his wife was the problem, and although Matthew had only teamed up with Martin a month prior, he believed as the rest of them that the wife was the problem.

"Maybe not all of us," he admitted to himself. The supervisors of the department had apparently fallen for her game of charades. She wasn't ever a suspect in Martin's death, according to them.

As far as Matthew and the rest of the patrolmen felt, she staged his suicide. Then, she pretended to be something she was not. She played innocent. It worked three years ago, at least with the ones who made the decisions as to who was at fault. But not today. He didn't buy it. Something else brought her out there. Something or someone, but he didn't know what.

It didn't matter. Matthew had a job to do. For whatever reason, she claimed she saw the killer. If it wasn't for that fact and that there was a slim chance the man was the serial killer Matthew was searching for, he wouldn't be bothered with Ms. Cain now. However, that slim chance existed, and as a cop, he couldn't ignore it.

Somehow, someway, he would drag the description of the man from her subconscious. Matthew needed a break, and he needed it now!

Shaking his head, he raked his fingers through his dark hair. "I can't believe she even got involved." In his heart, he felt there was another reason she was outside on the levee at that time of night, technically morning, but he couldn't concern himself with that.

For the time being, he was stuck with her, and for his own purposes, he would keep her safe. Using his cell phone, he contacted Officer Shelton, then waited for him to arrive at Ms. Cain's apartment building.

"Keep a good watch on her and her apartment. If she's not inside her apartment, keep her in your sight at all times. If she leaves, follow her. Anyone suspicious hangs around, check him out. Just don't let her get wind you're tailing her."

After leaving instructions with the young detective, Matthew took off. For a brief moment, her image burned in his memory. Her soft innocence touched him somewhere deep.

"No!" he shouted. He would not let her get to him again.

She was no good and he knew it. . .even if he had to keep reminding himself.

Matthew put all thoughts of Samantha Cain out of his mind. Before returning to the station, Matthew swung by the all-night diners where the other two victims had worked and questioned the waitresses again. He knew, in his gut, that the latest victim worked at a diner, too, and he would have those details shortly and check there also. Maybe if he asked the right question, he'd get a better answer. Surely one of them saw a person who appeared suspicious, someone with dark eyes.

He was determined to close all three cases if it was the last thing he did. . .and he'd do it before another woman got killed.

Chapter 5

That evening, Sam returned to work as scheduled. A hectic pace was set and didn't slow down till way into the early morning hours. But that didn't stop anyone from asking questions, though she didn't take much time to give details. Besides, she wanted to put it all behind her and forget the whole thing—only no one seemed to want to let her. She'd heard several versions of what had happened just from the idle gossip that had spread among the drivers during that day.

Rumors spread fast in the trucking industry. Sam always knew if she wanted others to know something, she need only tell a driver. Not that they gossiped like people claim women do, but between the CB radios and the cell phones most drivers have, things spread. This story spread like wildfire. With each call, the story was embellished a little more than the version before. The guys who knew her told others out of concern, and she loved them all for caring. They were like one big family.

"So you're a hero," said John, one of the more friendly drivers, as he stood at the window waiting for his paperwork.

Sam frowned. Her hands flew over the buttons on the computer as she flashed a sideways glance at him. "Not much of a hero. The woman died, you know. I didn't get help to her in time." That was the first thing Sam had checked on when she woke up that afternoon. "She died before she even got to the hospital."

Sam pressed the ENTER key and stood.

Like a dark cloud, sadness hung over her head as she thought about not being able to save the woman. If Sam had only called right away, maybe the woman would still be alive.

"You tried. That's more than some would have done," John reassured her.

"Thanks for trying to cheer me up. I just wish I had reacted more quickly. But I didn't." Picking up the packet of papers for him, she walked over to the window between the drivers' room and dispatch office.

"You did okay. Don't be so hard on yourself." He took the clear envelope full of his paperwork with one hand, then squeezed Sam's hand with the other. "Cheer up, sweetie. Ya done good."

She knew he was trying to help her forget her problems, so she hoped her smile was convincing. "For that, I'll make you a pot of coffee." Sam unlocked the door between the two rooms, then started making a pot of black brew the Louisiana way: thick, rich, and strong.

"Thanks." John sat down at the drivers' table and flipped

through the papers in his envelope, reading his instructions on his next load.

Five or ten minutes later, after Sam had returned to her office, she heard the slam of John's briefcase, a sign he was about to leave, then the *swoosh* of the glass door being pushed open. At a glance, she saw a stranger walk into the drivers' room, keeping his back to the window, his face turned away.

"May I help you?" she asked, stepping over to the counter and looking through the window out at the stranger.

The man turned slightly, never facing her completely. "The phone. Can I use it?" he asked in a deep, gravelly voice.

She took note of his appearance. The man looked like any other stranger who came in to use the phone—dressed in jeans, T-shirt, and a baseball cap. Most of these guys were workers off the boats that docked on the other side of the levee. In cold weather, the boat workers covered their T-shirts with plaid flannel shirts and usually wore a wooly hat snugged down over their ears.

Although the stranger's face was well hidden by the bill of the baseball cap, she saw the dark stubble on his jaw. He desperately needed a shave. "If you're calling local, you can," she said. "Use line four." Sam turned to go back to the computer, noticing that John had reopened his briefcase, delaying his departure.

Most of the drivers tended to look out for her. They liked playing the protector, and Sam would tell anyone in a heartbeat she appreciated it. Especially now.

She recalled in the back of her mind what the deputy had told her. "Don't be alone." Tonight, she wasn't by herself, only the other worker was way out back on the rack. It wasn't quite what Langlois had in mind.

A few minutes later, Sam glanced up as another driver arrived. When he came through the glass door, she heard the slide of a chair on the bare floor, then the slamming of a brief-case, followed by heavy footsteps.

"See ya later, Sam," John called out as he was leaving.

"Okay. Have a good night and drive safe." She heard the mumble of words between the two drivers.

A moment later a voice called from the drivers' window, "You can't speak?" The sweet Southern drawl could sweep any girl off of her feet.

Looking over her left shoulder, Sam saw the man's wide smile, bordered on each side with very deep dimples. It was contagious, and his brown eyes lit up the room. "Hey, Jerry, what's happening? You're loaded, heading out, right?"

"Yeah, darling, and you have my bills."

Sam grabbed his paperwork and passed it through the window. Her gaze slid past Jerry to the man on the phone. The stranger sat in the dark corner. Although she couldn't see him clearly, he seemed to be staring in her direction out from underneath the bill of his cap. When she caught a glimpse of his gaze, he turned away and started talking into the receiver.

For some strange reason, the hairs on the back of her neck rose. Then all of a sudden an icy chill ran down her back, as if someone had dropped a frozen cube of ice down her shirt and held it there. Something about this man alerted her. Then, shaking her head, Sam told herself she was just being foolish because of the incident last night.

It wasn't like he was the first stranger to come in and use the phone in the middle of the night. However, she hoped

Jerry didn't ask for an advance in front of the stranger. No need to let that man know there was money around. It could entice him to hang around and rob her, even if that wasn't his original motive for walking into the building. Quickly, she motioned Jerry to go around to the locked door.

Immediately Sam unlocked it, giving Jerry access to the dispatch office. Ushering him in and locking the door behind him, she asked in a whisper, "Do you need an advance?"

"You know it, darling."

Stepping over to the drawer where the money was kept hidden, she asked, "The usual?"

He winked in response as he nodded. Sam counted out fifty for him, then had him sign for it. Leaning closer to Jerry, she whispered, "If you have a little time, would you hang around till that guy leaves? I guess I'm a little nervous after what happened last night."

He probably would have anyway, but she was more afraid than she wanted to admit. This was unusual for her. Besides learning how to defend herself, this past year she'd immersed herself in God's Word and learned to depend on Him. But to-night her eyes were on the circumstances around her instead of the Lord.

"I'll go fix a cup of coffee and keep my eye on him." Jerry stuffed the money in his wallet and then jammed it into his back pocket. "Is anybody on the rack tonight?"

"Yeah. Tom's out there."

Sam let him out, then locked the door again. She con-tinued with her work but trained her ear toward the window. Time seemed to move like a snail.

Nothing was said until the stranger finally left.

Jerry stepped over to the window. "Didn't think he was ever going to leave."

"What'd you think about him? Anything?" She stepped over to the counter.

"Strange, very strange." Jerry's lips twisted as his eyes narrowed. "The man didn't speak much for someone being on the phone. It looked like he was trying to wait me out. Maybe he knows you have money in there."

"That thought crossed my mind." *As well as the memory of the man last night,* she thought, but that she didn't say aloud this time. She tried not to give the thought any more credit than she had to. . .but the strange man sure was suspicious looking, lurking around, not saying much.

Jerry's brows drew together in uncertainty. "Maybe you should call the sheriff's office and have them pass by? Make sure that guy's not still hanging around."

Sam's gaze slid to the front glass window as she viewed the exit that let out onto the levee road. The tail lights of a dark sedan disappeared onto the highway, heading east toward the old bridge.

"Naah. He's gone now. But if he comes back, I won't hesitate. Thanks."

On that, Jerry stuck his packet inside his briefcase, picked up his carryall, and started for the back door. "I'm gonna pull my truck around to the wash rack and get a quick rinse, then I'll be on my way. See ya."

"Drive safely."

The rest of the night was uneventful. Sam completed all of her duties. Before the sun started to peek out above the horizon, she grabbed her clipboard to go outside. Locking the back door behind her, she went through the shop and into the yard to make a check of the equipment parked on the yard at her terminal—a daily procedure, one she had failed to do in the excitement of the morning before.

Circling the yard around the building, she noted the number of each tractor and trailer, including the condition of the trailers: clean, dirty, or loaded.

Lester, the mechanic coming on duty, pulled into the gate as she started on the last strip of the yard, the east side. Sam waved in acknowledgment as he honked his horn in response. Passing the east end of the wash rack, she heard the spray of the water Tom was using to clean another trailer. The stench was strong. She wrinkled her nose trying to bypass the odor of butyl acrylate.

The morning held a cool breeze in the air. It wouldn't last long, though. September days started cool but usually, as the full red circle of the sun topped the horizon, the heat would start to build. The breezes that swept through the air gave the false impression that fall was closing in. It was closer, but not there yet. Fall usually waited until October or November most of the time in the South.

People from south Louisiana didn't get to enjoy cool weather very often, not even in the springtime. It was impossible. The humidity thickened the air and intensified the heat. Clothes stuck to the skin as perspiration accumulated in the swelter. People weren't necessarily lazy in the South when they sat on their porch sipping a mint julep, like they showed in the old movies. They were just trying to get through the dense heat of the day.

Sam's eyes flitted from the wash rack to the row of tractors backed up against the fence. When she got to the end and wrote the last number down, she heard a tractor rev its engine, and then turned on her heel at the sound of a unit's tires spinning in the gravel and taking off. The truck was bobtailed, a tractor without a trailer, picking up speed quickly as it barreled toward her.

Shocked into immobility, Sam watched as it aimed directly for her. Just in time, she dashed for safety between the last two trucks on the row. The smell of burning rubber and diesel exhaust filled her nostrils.

Once she was safely out of the truck's path, she turned to catch a glimpse of the number on the passing unit. It left a trail of dust swirling in the air. The truck was theirs all right. Unit number 2478. But who was driving it?

The unit pulled out onto the highway, never slowing down, not even when shifting gears. Sam took off running for the building. Once inside, her fingers fumbled with the key as she tried to unlock the door. Inside the office, she snatched up the phone and punched out 911.

This was becoming a habit she didn't like. Quickly, she gave the person on the other end the information. The woman promised to send someone over immediately.

After disconnecting the line, she dialed the local intercom. "Lester, Tom, come up front. Please hurry." The urgency in her voice rang through her ears as she dropped into the dispatcher's swivel chair, her heart thumping madly.

Someone had tried to run her down. Who? And why? She hadn't done anything. Why would anyone want to hurt her? She closed her eyes, pressed her hands together, and leaned her face forward, touching her lips to her fingertips.

The killer! Her eyes popped open and her head rose. Her hands started shaking, and she entertwined her fingers.

Maybe it was a truck thief, plain and simple, she thought, *and he was just making his getaway.* A ray of hope slipped in. She had just been standing between the truck and the exit. The cold, hard knot in her stomach slackened ever so slightly.

Tom, wet from washing trailers, and Lester, in grease-stained clothes, came in through the door she'd left unlocked.

"My heavens, Sam, what's wrong with you?" Lester, usually laughing and making jokes, rushed in and moved quickly to her side, then kneeled down next to her. "You're as white as a sheet."

She took a deep breath, dropping her shaking hands to her lap. Lester's expression told her what she wanted to know. "You didn't see anything, did you, Lester?" When he shook his head, she turned toward Tom. "How about you?"

Tom, a new employee who was quiet and shy, never said much...until now. "Actually, I saw a truck fly by the bay opening. I thought, *Dang, that guy's driving too fast.* I figured you knew who it was and would report him today. Ain't no sense in it. He could have hurt someone."

Yes. Me. He almost did. "Did you recognize him?"

"Sorry." He lowered his head slightly and shook it. "I didn't get a very good look, and I don't know too many people around here yet. But the guy driving, what I did see of him, didn't look familiar."

"Well, someone just stole a truck and almost ran me down in the process. Lester, did you notice anyone on the yard when you drove in earlier?"

"I only saw you, but I wasn't really looking for anyone

either. After I parked my car, I went straight to the kitchen to put up my lunch." Lester rose off his knee, patted Sam on the shoulder, stepped over to the counter, then perched on the edge of it. "Did you call the sheriff? And how about the boss?"

"A deputy should be here any minute." Slowly, she stood, walked over to the big window, and gazed out. "I still need to call Ken. He's not going to be too happy, but—"

The phone rang, interrupting her sentence.

"Liquid Bulk Transport. This is Sam. May I help you?" Her hands trembled slightly.

By the time Sam finished taking an order for a load, a deputy sheriff was standing in her office. Tom and Lester had shown him into the room.

Sam exhaled with relief as she replaced the receiver on the hook and turned to the deputy. "Thanks for coming. Someone just stole a tractor from our yard." She filled him in with the make, model, and the truck company number printed on the side and back of the tractor. Next, she gave him the details of where the tractor was and how she was outside taking a yard check at the time.

"And it almost ran her down," Lester piped in.

"Are you all right, or do we need to call for medical assistance?" the deputy asked as he pulled out his pad and pen.

"No, I'm fine. I got out of his way." She stuffed her hands in her pockets, trying to hide their shaking.

"You said *his*. Did you get a look at him?"

Sam bit her bottom lip as she closed her eyes and tried to remember. "No. I didn't see him at all, but Tom saw enough to know it was a man." She turned to Tom. "I know you didn't recognize the thief, but maybe you could describe him for the deputy?"

"Great." The older man turned his attention to Tom. "What did you see, son? Tell me exactly."

"I caught a glimpse of a man driving the truck. I knew it was a man because he had stubble on his face and a baseball cap pulled down over his ears—"

"There was a man in here earlier tonight fitting that description," Sam said as she interrupted Tom. "He came in and asked to use the phone." She shrugged. "For a time I thought he was going to rob our petty cash."

The officer jotted down a short note. "Anything else you can think of?"

She shook her head.

"If you think of anything, give me a call. You said he used the phone?" When she nodded, he added, "We'll dust it for prints, but I don't know how lucky we'll get."

Sam pulled a file on the tractor and gave him the details, such as serial and plate numbers. She hoped they would find the truck in one piece, as well as the man who drove it.

The officer called in the info on the stolen truck, and he told them to send someone to take prints. "I'll go have a look around."

Meanwhile, Sam reported the incident to her boss. Ken Richardson told her to fill out the accident/incident report and then stay put till he got there. He wanted to talk to her. She agreed to wait and hung up.

Next, she called the Safety Man from the Houston Office, giving him the details, per standard procedure. Last, but not least, she called Amanda, her neighbor and friend, to let her know she would be a little late this morning. Sam asked if Amanda would mind dropping Marty, her son, off at school. Sam promised to give her the scoop later.

The deputy came back inside. "I didn't see anything out of the ordinary. I did see where he spun the tires, like you described to me. Someone will be by shortly to take the prints off the phone. In the meantime, an APB has been put out over the air, so everyone is watching for a blue and white truck fitting your tractor's description. Maybe we'll get lucky." As he started to leave, he paused. "Aren't you the woman who witnessed that killing last night?"

She didn't get a chance to answer him because Detective Jefferies strode into the room. Her eyes flew open wide as her mouth dropped. "What are you doing here?"

Chapter 6

How did you find out so quickly?" Sam couldn't believe her eyes. Confusion swirled through her mind. How did Detective Jefferies know? No one was attacked or killed, so why would he be here?

He didn't say a word. He only glared at her.

"A truck was stolen. Why did Sheriff Fletcher call you?"

"He didn't. I have my ways of knowing." He looked away from the deputy and scrutinized her closely. "I thought I told you to watch your back. I told you he would be after you."

Irritated, she sighed. "This is none of your concern. I still don't—" She cut her words off as she tried to figure how he knew so quickly. Twisting slightly to her right, Sam glanced out the window and noticed another car parked beside the detective's Mustang. She stole a glance at the detective's face, another back at the other car, then back at him again. The truth glared from his eyes. "You have someone watching me?

I don't believe it! I don't need a babysitter!"

"Apparently you do, but unfortunately my man didn't do too good of a job this morning. Otherwise, he'd be where the truck is now, and we'd have our man surrounded."

She closed her eyes and shook her head. It didn't surprise her that Jefferies had someone watching her. Nor did it surprise her that he chose to invade her privacy by having her followed. The detective was just another cop who moved up in the ranks. Did what he pleased, when he pleased, not bothering to clear it with her first. . .even though it was her life. Why argue with the man? She wouldn't win.

Releasing a frustrated sigh, she said, "Detective Jefferies, it was a truck theft—pure and simple. It had nothing to do with your serial killer."

"You don't know that. And I wouldn't be so quick to be sure if I were you." His eyes challenged her. "How often do you get trucks stolen?"

Flinching, she knew in her heart there was a strong possibility of a connection. Why she didn't want to admit it to him, she did not know. Maybe she was afraid if she said it out loud, she'd be relinquishing control to that monster. That she could not do. She had fought too hard to be in control of her life. . .to not be a victim again. Her gaze slipped from the detective to the deputy and finally back to the detective again. Her shoulders slumped. "So we don't have trucks stolen every day of the week. So what?"

"When was the last time a truck was stolen?" he insisted, apparently wanting her to admit he was right. The man was not going to leave it alone.

"Okay, okay." She held up her hands in defeat. "We've

never had a truck stolen. . .but it does happen."

"Right. And this just happened right after you saw a killer run away from a murder scene." Turning his back on her and facing the deputy, he asked, "Whatcha got?"

Sam stared in disbelief, fuming to herself as the detective seemed to take matters into his own hands as he turned his back on her. Why ask the deputy? Did he think she wouldn't answer his questions? He was right. She wouldn't, but that was beside the point. He acted as if she wasn't even there. The control thing reared its ugly head.

Holding her chin with her thumb and fingers, she tapped her lips with her forefinger. *What if it was the killer? Maybe I should listen to Detective Jefferies. He could be right. The possibility has crossed my mind a couple of times.*

Sam shook her head. No. There was still a chance it was just a thief. With the poor lighting yesterday morning, she didn't see the killer's face. Only his eyes. So why come after her? Sam doubted she would know him, even if he stood face-to-face with her.

The killer should realize that. . .right?

She closed her eyes. Just then piercing, bloodshot eyes, so dark they were almost black, stared back at her from her memory. Her heart froze. Popping her eyes open again, Sam knew. If she ever looked straight into the killer's eyes again, she could identify him. She had seen those eyes—that cold-blooded stare—an expression she'd never forget.

Quickly she had to rethink her position on the thief. She'd seen the truck thief tonight, the one she believed had stolen the truck anyway, and she didn't connect him with the killer.

"That's not true," she reminded herself in a quiet voice

that only she heard. For a second she had thought it could be the killer, but that was out of timing, not out of a visual connection, she assured herself. The man tonight was a thief, not a killer.

Truthfully, it couldn't have been the same man from the night before. She would have recognized the killer's eyes. But then, she only saw a glimpse of the man's eyes tonight. He seemed to make sure of it.

Shaking her head, she grumbled that now she was confusing herself. She didn't know what to believe anymore. Rubbing her face and her eyes, she simply wished it was all over. She was too tired to think.

When she looked up again, the detective was watching her.

"I hope you realize now that it was the killer trying to get rid of a possible witness." Jefferies spoke to Sam, but his gaze went back to the deputy, as if telling him the same thing.

"That thought crossed my mind, too," the deputy said as he agreed with the detective.

"You don't know that for sure," Sam muttered to the detective. It was the timing that convinced the detective. She was sure of it. Of course, it was the timing that made her think of it in the beginning. *But no,* she told herself again. *It's not the same man.*

"Yes, I do."

"So, if you're so sure it was him, why don't you get out there and find him!" she blurted out. Sam was tired of arguing. Tired of worrying. Tired of being tired. She wished she could go home and shut the rest of the world out of her life for now. Her nerves were twisted tighter than a spinning top.

When she heard the slight hysteria in her own voice, she winced. "Okay, I admit you could be right, although I don't believe it. The deputy has everything we know, so get it from him." She jabbed her finger in the direction of the deputy. "Maybe the truck will lead you to your killer." Pressing her hands to her chest, she continued, "But as for me, I have to get back to work. If there are no more questions from either of you, you know the way out."

The deputy glanced at his notes, then shook his head. "No questions at the moment."

"Good." She turned her back on them.

They took the hint and left the office building.

Sam glanced outside the window as all three men—Matthew Jefferies, the deputy, and her apparent babysitter—gathered in the parking lot and talked.

For her own peace of mind, she poured a cup of water, grabbed the report she had to fill out, and sat at her desk to complete it, trying desperately to ignore them.

When she looked down at the preprinted form, though, she saw instead a dark-haired, blue-eyed man with a face that could disarm any woman. It was the detective who had rushed in a few minutes ago and practically accused her of lying to him. Well, not exactly, but close enough. He did ask the deputy for the details, not her.

The same man who only yesterday, she had to admit, had stayed in her thoughts for a brief moment too long. . .until she got her head screwed back on straight. What was it about him? Although she had seen him three years ago, she had never gotten to know him. But she did remember his accusing eyes were the same as the rest of the policemen's.

Enough about the detective. Her thoughts needed to return to the report. It had to be filled out before the boss arrived. Another added distraction. Talking with the boss about anything always gave her the jitters. Somehow she felt sure all of this would end up being her fault.

The stolen truck and nearly being run over was what her mind had to focus on, not her boss's response to the situation or the devastatingly distracting detective and his interference.

Why was she thinking about him anyway? Since Martin, she hadn't even looked at another man, let alone thought about one.

As she filled in the report, she heard activity in the drivers' room. Someone from the deputy's office arrived and dusted for prints; then the official vehicles all drove away.

By the time the report was complete, an ounce of fear tried to creep into her thoughts again. Idle hands were the devil's workshop. She understood that saying all too well now. Idle hands left her mind free to think about what she didn't need to dwell on.

Finally, she admitted, she needed to face the truth, and the truth was the man in the drivers' room tonight could have been the killer. She believed, down deep, he was the thief, but was that for her own sanity? Had she been by herself, what would he have done?

Her heartbeat grew harder and louder every second—each pulsing throb more intense, more precise, like the pounding of a nail in a two-by-four. The closer the head of the nail got to the wood, the harder the hammer hit, pounding it deeper and deeper into the hardened strip of lumber.

Within the next hour, Ken Richardson, her boss, showed

up, and Sam followed him into his office.

Ken pointed toward the straight-back chair perched next to his desk. "Have a seat."

He didn't point blame or give her a hard time. *How unusual. Things must be bad.*

Together, the two decided for her own safety, as well as the company's position, it would be in their best interest if she would take a week, maybe two, of her vacation now. At least until the killer was caught.

After the decision was made, she headed home, occasionally glancing in the rearview mirror. A twinge of fear resting on the surface had her jumping at everything: every sound, every movement, every car. For a moment or two, she thought she was being followed. It could have been the policeman who had been watching her earlier. Her babysitter was probably on her tail but keeping his distance.

Shoving that possibility aside, she remembered seeing all three men—detective, deputy, and babysitter—leave together. Besides which, the bodyguard's car was gold. This one was black. Her mind jumped quickly to the chance it could be the killer following her.

Could it be? She glanced back and forth from the mirror to the highway in front of her. Another glance in the mirror, and the car turned off the highway.

What a vivid imagination she had. Shaking off the tension, Sam kept her mind on her driving. *Come on, Lord. Get these crazy thoughts out of my head.*

In half an hour, she was at home safe and sound, glad to be away from work and what was going on around there. She closed her front door, twisted the deadbolt until she heard a *click*, then dragged herself to the bathroom for a shower. It had been another long night. Thank God for Amanda, who had taken Marty to school again that morning.

When her shower was complete, Sam slipped into a short cotton nightgown and crawled into bed. Picking up her phone, she dialed Amanda's cell.

"Thanks for taking Marty to school again. You are the best."

"No problem. So what happened this time? Not more of the killer, I pray."

"No. This morning we had a truck stolen, so I had to wait for Ken to show up so we could talk. Standard procedure, more or less. Anyway, I'm on vacation now."

"Great! I'll see you tonight, and you can tell me all about everything!"

"That's a promise," Sam said.

Closing her eyes, she sighed. Sleep—that was what she needed after another rough night, and the sleep came almost immediately.

Chapter 7

After Matthew reamed Earnie Shelton out for falling asleep on stakeout, Matthew decided to work out a watch schedule. Dumping it on Shelton at the last minute like he had and expecting the man to stay sharp and awake all night after being up all day was bad planning on Matthew's part, but they all had done it at one time or another.

When Shelton had called that morning to say what had happened and admitted to dozing off shortly before the incident, Matthew's stomach knotted in fear for Ms. Cain's safety. Shelton had awakened to Ms. Cain calling for the men working in the back to come up to her office. He had heard the urgency in her voice, then listened from the back door.

No one knew he was there. In that secluded place, there wasn't any protection for those people. How could Sam dare show up for work after all she had been through the night before? Maybe she was stronger than Martin gave her credit for being.

Matthew made a rotating schedule, using Shelton and Davis in the daytime, eight hour shifts each, and took the nights for himself. The detective knew this way he could take a short nap during a portion of the day, as well as follow up on his investigation. This would also leave him free to watch Ms. Cain all night, hoping to catch the killer. He would be back. Matthew knew this.

It was no longer just a possibility in Matthew's mind that the thief was Jane Stewart's killer, as well as the other victims' killer. Why else would this man try to run Ms. Cain down?

This was the break he was waiting for, and he wasn't about to let it slip through his fingers, even if it meant being around a woman he knew in the back of his mind he should steer clear of.

For a minute, he recalled Ms. Cain declaring her independence and expressing she had no need for a babysitter. A smile touched his lips. She needed someone to watch her, all right, looking out for her well-being, whether she liked it or not, and he would make sure she had it.

Sometimes Matthew found it hard to see the woman Martin had described. She didn't come off as a flirt or a tramp when he was around her. She had never flirted with him. . .and, although he wasn't trying to puff up his own ego, he always had women coming on to him. But not her. In fact, she appeared strong and independent, with morals she held to fiercely.

Matthew shook his head. "Who knows?" Besides, it didn't matter now. She was a potential witness who needed his protection, and he needed her cooperation.

As he pulled away from the curb, he glanced at his watch. It was two thirty. *She ought to be getting up about now. Maybe I'll stop by and let her know someone will be watching her at all times. . .and maybe I won't.* His mind battled. How forthcoming should he be with her? Still, he had no trust where she was concerned. If she were anyone else, would he tell her?

He shook his head. *I don't think so.*

Instead he would address the issue of getting a description of the suspect. He needed to see if she was ready to try and describe the killer to a sketch artist. If she would do that, he could show it around at the diners. Maybe seeing a sketch of the killer would trigger the memory of the victims' coworkers. Maybe they knew something about the man that could direct Matthew toward the killer, and they didn't even know it. Maybe the killer paid with a credit card. That would get him a name and an address. If not that, maybe the man had mentioned the kind of work he did. That would point Matthew in a closer direction of where to search. He still needed that break, and he needed it now. Time was running out.

Chapter 8

S am flipped on the television. Her show had already started.

Today she found she was moving slowly, but the minute Remington Steele's face came on the tube in the afternoon reruns of the reruns, Sam thought about the real-life detective, Matthew Jefferies, and warmth spread through her.

As she smiled at the picture on the screen, a thought flashed. Her smile widened a little more.

If my life was on television, I could get the hero. But, unfortunately, my life is real, and Matthew Jefferies was part of Martin's unit. I don't want anything to do with the likes of him.

The doorbell interrupted her notions.

"Not today," she cried.

Sam didn't need any hassles with reporters. They had never called her yesterday and for that, she was grateful. She hoped the police were still keeping her name out of all of it. If not, she would stop the press before they started. She had plans today. This inconvenience was not going to interfere with her life. She and her son would go on as normal.

Killer or no killer, witness or no witness, today she was on vacation. . .so to speak, and she was going to enjoy herself.

These last two days were a thing of the past, and she would put them out of her mind. It wasn't her place to fix things or catch the killer. . .or the thief, for that matter. It was her job to be the best mom she could be. And that was her priority.

She would start fresh today by rejuvenating herself. The gym was going to be her first stop. Sam would then pick Marty up from school and spend the remainder of the day with him. Then, much later tonight, she'd fill in Amanda on all the details of how her life had been turned upside-down in less than forty-eight hours.

Amanda Thompson had been her best friend since grade school. They both knew everything about each other. Sam wouldn't trade her for a million dollars. Amanda would help Sam keep her mind off those things of the past and help her focus on today.

A knock on the door sounded before she could reach it. *I'm coming. Hold your horses.* She moved a little faster toward the door.

"Ms. Cain, it's me. Are you in there?" Matthew Jefferies' voice called through the door.

She stopped midstep.

"Please. Let me in so we can talk for just a minute." His words sounded more like an order than a plea.

Sam slowly eased over to the door. Her hand clutched the knob. At the sound of his voice, a warm feeling stirred in the pit of her stomach; her heart lurched.

That wasn't the kind of emotion she should feel right now. Aggravation should strike all the nerves in her body. How dare he just show up on her doorstep!

What is wrong with me? Excitement surged inside her, even though she tried to fight it.

Don't get interested in him. He's a cop. Martin's ex-partner. Tell him to go away! her mind screamed, but her voice said, "Wait a minute while I get dressed."

Chapter 9

If she was going to see him, the least she could do was look more presentable.

Slipping back into her bedroom, Sam put on a pair of shorts and a T-shirt, then ran a brush through her hair before returning to the door.

Knowing it wasn't smart to talk to him for her own peace-of-mind didn't stop the flutter of her heart at the anticipation of seeing him. This was ridiculous. Why was she feeling like a teenager in the midst of all this turmoil? It didn't make a bit of sense.

The more she thought about him, the more she wanted to see him. Him—a cop, no less—and that confused her even more. She sighed as she tried to control the racing of her heart.

"Now what, Detective?" she asked as she opened the door a crack and blocked his entrance with her body. She didn't dare let her true emotions show, but as her gaze settled upon his face, her pulse quickened even more. Bubbles of joy tingled in her veins at the mere sight of him. It fought against her feelings, but it seemed her body had a mind of its own.

"Good afternoon." Detective Jefferies placed his hand against the door, as if making sure she wouldn't close it in his face. "May I come in?"

She looked at his hand on the door, then back at him. The part about policemen she didn't care for surfaced—the insistence on having things their way. Part of her didn't want to let him into her home, but a battle was taking place from within. Which would win?

Finally, Sam said, "I'd rather you didn't come in. I don't know why you keep coming around. There's nothing more I can say to help you on your case. I didn't see him clearly enough to give a description to an artist. Even if the thief and killer are one and the same, I didn't get a good look at that stranger who used the phone. And again, that's a big *if* he was the thief."

And if you knew what was good for me, you'd stay away and quit making things so difficult, she added, but not out loud.

"Sometimes it helps when you sleep on what you saw," he said calmly. "More comes back to you. I also wanted to see if you gave it any more thought about the guy who used your phone. You say you didn't get a good look, but he walked into the drivers' room and you saw his shape, his size, and his coloring. All of that would be helpful, believe it or not. And if you would be willing to give that information to our sketch artist, it would help him with a composite drawing. They do wonders with computers nowadays."

He dropped his hand to his side, apparently believing she

wasn't going to close the door on him after all. "Besides, I wanted to make sure you were still okay. No repercussions from last night or the night before. Sometimes injuries don't show up right away."

Yeah, right. Like he's really concerned for my well-being.

She wished this was true but knew better. Cops, she'd found in the past, were good actors. They let you believe what they needed you to believe so they could get what they wanted out of you. There was no law against that. And, right now, he wanted Sam to believe he was a good cop.

"I didn't get injured either night. I'm fine." She shook her head. "Again, I didn't come up with anything new on his description. Sorry."

Her head knew the truth about Detective Jefferies, but her heart, for some strange reason, was disagreeing.

The battle continued. It was locking on to some goodness somewhere within him. She knew, since her attack and recovery, she had gotten closer to the Lord. By reading His Word, filling her heart with His thoughts, maybe she was becoming more Christlike and was looking for the good in humankind.

But why now? Why him—Detective Matthew Jefferies?

The detective looked at her but didn't say a word. Probably giving her more time to reconsider and invite him in. Cops. They believed too much in the power of persuasion, or maybe it was their power. Either way, she was not letting him into her home.

"I'm okay. I promise."

She squinted as a thought crossed her mind. *They've had all day to find the missing truck. Did they? And did it lead to any evidence?* Tightening her grip on the door, she met his eyes boldly. "Did y'all get anything from the prints on the phone? Did you find the truck?"

Would he tell her if they had?

The detective hesitated only a minute. "The receiver of the phone had been wiped clean. More proof he's a bad guy. Obviously his prints are in the system. Otherwise, why wipe it clean? Only the base had prints, and so far, most prints match those of drivers who are in the new system, and they all work for Bulk. He probably covered his finger with a handkerchief or something. I know you still don't want to believe that the thief and the attacker are one and the same—" his voice lowered to an almost whisper—"but I'm convinced they are. And no, we haven't found the truck yet, but we're still looking."

"I'm afraid you're wrong." That felt good. She noticed when she said it, his eyes widened, as if ready to deny anything and everything.

She could hear his thought. *Me, wrong? Truly you jest.*

Instead, he said, "I promise. We are still looking."

Shaking her head, she said, "No, you misunderstand. I believe what you said—that you're still looking. And I've come to the realization that they *are* one and the same: the thief and the killer. Only I don't believe he was there last night to kill me. I think he was just seeing if I could recognize him—to check out my reaction. But I didn't react. So I don't get why he stole a truck after that. I don't understand his motives, nor can I even speculate, but we already know he's sick or he wouldn't kill people. Personally, I hope you get him soon. I don't want to run into him anywhere. And I don't want him anywhere near my son. That's what scares me the most. I don't like being afraid, either. That was something I had to overcome and, until now, I thought I had."

Looking into the detective's eyes, she added, "I want my life to get back to normal. I'm having to take early vacation because of all that has happened. It's not fair, but I guess I'm ready for a vacation. I need a break from the tension."

Silence hung between them for a minute as they stared at one another. Then finally he said, "Aren't you going to ask me in?"

Her hold on the doorknob tightened, as did a knot in her chest. "I already said no. So I wasn't planning on it. Besides, I don't see the point."

His eyes studied her, as if trying to say something to her without speaking. But she needed to hear him say those words she knew were in his mind.

"How about if I insist?"

"Cops are good at insisting," she said through tight lips. "Why not?" She tossed her hands up in the air, as if giving up, and backed away, allowing him room to enter. "By all means. Come in. Can I get you something to drink?" Sam asked as she turned to head toward the kitchen.

Not that she wanted to be sociable. . .at least not in her mind. Her heart was another matter. She wanted to see the detective again, but not like this. Not because of criminal activities. She wished the situation could be different. Even more, she wished she could get a grip on her heart. He was not for her.

"Coffee, if it's not too much trouble. We need to talk."

Walking through the living room, she glanced at *Remington Steele* on the television, then reached for the remote to mute the sound. *So much for my television hero today.*

Chapter 10

In the kitchen, she put water in the tea kettle and placed it on the burner. "Instant is all I have." Not waiting for him to reply, she turned the burner on, then took down a cup from the cupboard and dumped two teaspoons of instant coffee into it. "Cream or sugar?" she asked, never turning in his direction.

"Black with half a teaspoon of sugar. Thanks."

While waiting for the whistle to sound, Sam poured herself a glass of juice. Better to stay busy than to look at that man. He had a way of getting into her every fiber. What was it about him? His dark hair? His good looks? No. It couldn't be that. She had seen plenty of good-looking men in her life and never had one gotten under her skin this way. It had to be because she was at a vulnerable point in her life at the moment. And, in a way, he came rushing in to save the day. . .kind of like a knight on a white horse, only his was a silver Mustang.

As she waited for the water to boil so she could pour it into the cup, he sat quietly behind her, never saying a word. But she felt his eyes on her back, watching her every move.

She took in a deep breath. Should she bring up the past and get it out of the way? Should she tell him the torture Martin put her through? None of his friends on the force knew about their past. They knew only what Martin had told them. At the time of the investigation, none of them wanted to hear what she had to say. Thank God for people higher up in the ranks who listened and saw the truth. Some truth even they couldn't see, but some seemed to understand.

The hidden scars he left deep within her by his verbal abuse, or the visible scars left by his physical abuse—maybe she should tell Matthew about those now. Maybe she should even tell him how he wounded his own son, scarring him from within.

Martin was a bully and a drunk, but he hid it well from others. He only abused the people he supposedly loved. The police could have helped her, even in the end, had they not ignored the signs.

She sighed. Maybe she should pretend the past never happened? Maybe Matthew didn't remember how they had all blamed her for Martin's death. They judged her and found her guilty without knowing the facts. . .without checking them out. Martin was one of them, so of course he was innocent. Maybe she should just let sleeping dogs lie. What good would it do, anyway? She remembered all too well the pain they put her through after his death.

After the water came to a boil, she poured it into the cup as she thought. No more pain. No more not understanding.

No more not knowing the whole truth. It was time she revealed all to one of his buddies.

Ready to confront him, she turned and placed the cup of coffee on the table before him. Then, as she moved to set her glass down and sit in the chair across from him, she opened her mouth to broach the subject.

But he beat her to it. "You seem to be doing pretty well for yourself. . .I mean, since Martin's death. Is there a new man in your life now? And your son—how is he coping with no dad?"

"I don't think that's any of your business or concern."

Now that he had brought it up, she wasn't so sure she was ready to talk about it with him after all, especially from the angle he approached it. She heard the haughtiness in his voice. He thought she was no good then, and he still felt the same way.

He sat in silence, just looking at her. He was either judging her again or didn't care one way or the other. The man was making small talk while waiting to get what he wanted from her. He needed her to help him. Otherwise he wouldn't even be hanging around; Sam felt certain of that.

Finally, she looked him straight in the eyes, as if daring him to deny what she was about to tell him. "I have my son. I don't need anyone else. And Marty is a good boy. . .doing well in school. I believe he is *coping* fine." She stressed that, because if he really was concerned, why hadn't he checked on them a month or so after Martin's suicide? Matthew was his partner, after all. New partner, she admitted, but partner no less. You would think, out of plain decency, he would have checked on Martin's son, especially since they blamed her for Martin's death. But no one did.

"That's good." Detective Jefferies nodded, then picked up his cup and took a sip of coffee. "Tastes good. Thanks."

As much as Sam wanted to straighten things out about the past once and for all, she couldn't bring herself to talk about it, about Martin, about their life. Not now. Not with Jefferies. Maybe she would have another chance later. Maybe not. At the moment, it didn't matter.

Taking a sip of her juice, she decided to get back to the present situation. "Look, Detective. The truck missed me." She raised her hands in the air, glanced down at herself, and then back at him. "As you can see, I'm fine. I ducked between two rigs as the other truck passed." Pensively, she searched his face for an agreement. "The man who tried to run me down got what he was after. If he is the killer, which I agree he could be, he found out I didn't recognize him, so he has no need to fear. So why are you here? I have nothing new to offer."

As if ignoring her words, he asked, "Did you sleep well today? Any dreams. . .or nightmares?"

"I slept fine." She wasn't sure she would tell him, even if she had experienced horrible dreams, recalling things verbatim. It would be a dream. . .not reality.

"Can you recall anything more about the man who used the phone last night? Like I said, you saw him up close in a sense. At least good enough to where you should be able to judge his height and speculate on his coloring. Do you recall enough to give a description of some sort to the sketch artist so he could create a composite of the man?"

"I already answered that at the door."

When he didn't respond, she continued, "I saw him from the back and a slight profile view. John, the driver who was in there when he came in, could probably give you a better description. The man was probably a good half foot taller than John. I did catch a glimpse of his eyes once, but it was only a glimpse, and they were shadowed by the bill of his cap. So I couldn't even say if the eyes were the same as the eyes of the killer, which I admit I got a good look at. The bill covered his eyes last night, casting a shadow over them. Besides, you can't make a drawing from eyes. He made a point of keeping his face away from the light, out of my view. That was another reason I agreed you were probably right about him and the killer being the same man."

The detective listened, never interrupting.

"With the hat pulled down, he hid his hair and part of his face." Closing her eyes, she rubbed them, then raked her fingers through her hair. Shaking her head, she opened her eyes again. "I couldn't see him clearly. However, I did notice the dark stubble on his chin. So his hair is probably dark. Judging by what I could see of his skin, arms and hands, I would say he was a light-skinned man, one who didn't get outdoors too often. He was probably in his late teens, maybe early twenties. The skin looked young, not old—you know, not wrinkled but firm, tight. Also, his body appeared to be in good shape. . .physically fit, I mean."

A strange look darted through his eyes.

He didn't ask what made her say that, but she decided to explain anyway. She could only imagine what he was thinking. "The man's arms looked like they had definition, cuts, you know, as if he lifted weights or his job was physical. I don't know if that'll help or not."

"Every little bit helps, Ms. Cain. It appears you saw more

than you realized. Besides, you'd be amazed at what we can do with computers today with only a profile description."

Scraping her top teeth across her bottom lip, she toyed with telling him she may have been followed home this morning. It had concerned her for a bit, but when the dark car turned off, she lost her worry. She doubted anyone would be interested in following her home. If she just left things alone for a while, they would cool off and life would get back to normal. Squinting as her eyebrows drew together, she thought for a moment. She could go in and speak with the artist. If it would help them catch the killer, why not? But would it make her more of a target for him to come after? She had to think of Marty now, not herself. His life, his safety was the most important thing to her. She could endure anything for her son. . .if it meant keeping him safe. *But have I really seen enough to give them a description?*

"You do realize now, even though you didn't get a good look at him, he saw you." Matthew's words rang in her head. "Up close, I might add. Twice in fact. And the second time, he studied you."

"All right, all right, yes," she admitted as she envisioned the man hiding in the shadows. "I could tell he was watching me when he was on the phone. That's why I thought the man was there to rob the place."

"You need to be careful. Be aware of what is around you at all times. He could be following you."

Now was the perfect time to tell him, but the car had turned off. Besides, she would sound paranoid. She didn't need to add more things to his list of bad things about her. "But that was at work, almost fifteen miles from here," she said. "And I won't be going back there for some time. I should be fine here at home. He doesn't know my name, so he can't find out where I live."

A short silence fell between them.

She didn't like the quiet, so she filled the silence with thoughts that had bothered her for some time. "I don't understand why some people do what they do. If all of us would just work hard for what we want, instead of taking from others, preying on the weak, this world would be a much better place to live in." She looked straight into the detective's eyes. "I guess now that you're a detective, you really get to know more about what makes these people do the things they do, like thieves, rapists, killers, and even serial killers." She shuddered. "I guess you deal with all sorts of people now. What makes people act so bad?"

"Serial killers do what they do usually for physical gratification. To them, each killing is like a sexual peak. Other killings, random killings, are usually from greed or for power. Sometimes done in the heat of passion, but usually well thought out, premeditated. For thieves, there are many explanations." He shrugged. "Some people are sick and can't help themselves, while others are lazy or greedy. Some are in a bad situation in life, while others are just in the wrong place at the wrong time."

Shivers ran unimpeded all over her body as a sick feeling consumed her. "I couldn't deal with those kinds of people day in and day out. I don't know how you do it." Maybe that was why Martin changed so drastically, but Sam had a hard time contributing it all to the job. Martin hadn't been a policeman for that long a time.

Matthew reached across the table and covered her hands with his.

Warmth crept through every fiber as silence hung between them. Sam knew she shouldn't respond this way just from his touch, his compassion—even if it was sincere—but she couldn't stop herself. Sam looked up from their hands, and her gaze lingered on his face. A soft dark lock of hair had fallen across his forehead, and Sam wished she could reach out and brush it back.

Then Matthew swiftly pulled his hands back and jammed them in his jean pockets. He looked anywhere but where Sam sat. Before he spoke again, he seemed to gather his thoughts. But Sam waited for him to speak, afraid her words wouldn't sound right even if she tried to speak them.

"It's a job. And somebody has to do it." He turned his gaze back upon her. "Back to the subject at hand. I believe someone has fixed his sights on you. Maybe I'm wrong, but what if I'm not?"

Swallowing the lump in her throat, Sam realized she had to take his words more seriously than she had so far. He could be right. Maybe she could describe the man well enough for an artist to sketch. Glancing up at the detective's face, she knew if she could keep her mind off his blue, penetrating eyes and his soft, dark hair long enough, she might be able to do it. She would at least give it a try.

Boldly, she said, "You're right. I'll try to describe the man who used the phone to your artist."

"I'll bet if you close your eyes right now and take your time, you could probably see him better than you think." His words were soft-spoken, encouraging.

For the next few seconds, she closed her eyes and thought about the man coming in to use the phone. Focusing on him, she looked past his build, concentrating on the face under the brim of that hat, and honed in on his expression when his eyes clashed with hers. Yes. He had seen her, too. Now there was no doubt in her mind. Not only could she see the cold-blooded stare she had seen the night before, but she realized the awareness in his eyes as he glared at her.

"Dark. Almost black," she whispered as she shivered slightly. "No. That was the light, or lack of it, the shadow on his face. But his eyes were dark, dark brown. Like rich coffee grounds. And sick. . .oh-so sick. The thoughts that must go on behind those eyes scare me. Wait." She looked deep into the remnants of her mind. "I've seen eyes like those before."

Chill bumps raced down her arms as she trembled. Tears welled up in her eyes as the memory that rested in the back of her mind tried to come forward. Blinking twice, she reached her hand up and wiped away the tears. She shook her head no, not ready to give in to that memory. Her conscience fought it as her mind tried to recall. Where had she seen that look before?

Her eyes popped open. The answer came quickly. She sucked in a quick gasp of air and then closed her eyes again. She laid her face in her hands as she shuddered. *No, Lord, please don't let me think on it. Don't let me go back there.*

The thought frightened her as she recalled who had that look. Her husband, Martin, the day he scarred Sam for life. . .the day he killed himself. It had to be the anger, the hate in his eyes.

"Oh," she groaned as the icy fingers of fear slipped around

her neck, clutching, holding on tight. No. He was dead. It had been three years. She refused to let it shake her so.

"It's okay. I'm here with you. No one's going to hurt you. Where have you seen eyes like those before?"

It had been a long time since she had trusted the police. Slowly, she opened her eyes. Adjusting her gaze, she focused in on the detective. *Could she trust the police? Could she trust him?*

As she questioned herself, with her fingertips she reached up under her bangs and touched the thick, rough skin on her forehead. She rubbed the disfigured skin gently out of habit. A scar left by her husband, a trusted friend, someone she loved. . .a cop. A quick reminder of where trust had taken her before it left her cold.

Dare she trust again? *No.*

"You wouldn't believe me if I told you."

Chapter 11

Tell me," he repeated. "Where have you seen those eyes before? Who are you remembering?"

Sam shrank back in her chair, afraid to speak the truth. He wouldn't believe her. Everyone at the station believed Martin was a great guy. Why bother wasting her breath? Besides, could he be trusted with the truth or would he turn that around to hurt her more? The truth was something she had always lived, so why change now? "I'm not sure I can trust you."

"Of course you can trust me. It's my duty to protect you."

"Why?" She raised her brows in question. "Because you work for the police department?"

"Exactly."

"Sorry. Not good enough." History could not and would not repeat itself. Other than Marty and Amanda, she had learned not to trust anyone except herself and the Lord. No other human. Especially the police. "Past experience keeps me from believing that to be a good enough reason to trust you. Three years ago, you all blamed me. But I was the victim. Marty and me. Martin was the guilty one. None of you could see that. You didn't believe me then, and I doubt you would believe me now."

"Let's put the past behind us and leave it there. Concentrate on today." As he spoke, his eyes probed deep within her soul, it seemed, stabbing at her heart.

"No!" She wished she could trust them. . .him. . .but she couldn't. "I mean, yes. I mean, I wish I could." Frustrated, she shook her head and then her fists in the air. She raised her voice. "I don't know what I mean! Just leave, please. Why don't you leave now! I can't help you."

"I can't leave. I need your help. Think of the victims the man has taken. Please try. . .for their sake. For the sake of future victims. I'm sure you can remember more if you would just try. Start by putting the past aside. Try to forget it."

She took in a deep breath, then continued in a calmer tone, "I don't want to forget the past, but I need to. I've forgiven the past—well, Martin anyway—but I have to remember what I've learned. I've tried to forget the pain, but it keeps coming back to haunt me. Especially now. Don't you see? Can't you understand?"

When he didn't respond to her question, she threw her hands up into the air. "I give up. You don't know what I went through." She jumped to her feet, snatched up her glass, marched to the sink, and rinsed her glass out. Slamming it down in the sink, she turned and faced him. "The past doesn't really matter, because it has no bearing on what happened yesterday, so let's drop it. Or like you said, forget it. Put it behind me. . .at least in connection with you today."

The detective watched her. His expression showed he was puzzled.

"Never mind," she finally said. "I'll come by the station while I'm out today and get with the artist. That's the best I can do."

Turning her back on him again, Sam changed her mind about more juice. Her dry mouth needed some. She picked up the glass again, poured the water out of it, snatched open the refrigerator door, pulled out the jug, and opened the lid. "I'm refilling my juice. Do you want more coffee?" she snapped.

Her fingers tightened further around the glass as she heard the strain in her own voice. She hoped he would turn the offer down. She wanted him to go. Samantha needed him to leave so she could get her senses back.

"I'll pass."

Why so much emotion? Why try to convince herself there was nothing to fear, when deep down she knew she had a lot to be fearful of? Well, not fear itself, as much as she needed to be aware of the facts around her? First off, someone was possibly after her. Secondly, the man's cold eyes looked like none other than Martin's eyes right before he attacked her. Surely, that was only because Detective Jefferies had brought the past up to haunt her. Thirdly, Marty's life could be in danger. And last but not least, the police were back in her life, and she appeared to have a fascination with this detective whom she had no business being attracted to in the least tiny bit.

All of a sudden, the room seemed to be shrinking. Sam found it hard to breathe. She didn't know why, but she knew she had to get out of that room, and fast. He drew too much emotion from her.

She took one big swallow of the juice, then set the glass down on the counter. *Escape. I have to escape.* Turning, she darted out of the room as she said, "I have to go, so you need to get out of here. Now, please."

Leaving didn't help. He followed right behind her into the living room and stopped within an arm's reach. He needed to go. She needed him to go, get out of the room, out of the apartment, out of her life.

"I didn't come here to upset you or bring up the past. I came here to get a description from you and make you realize the danger you're in. I'm here to protect you. That's my job."

"I don't need protection!" She stepped further away and then wheeled around to face the detective from a distance.

He stood in the archway dividing the dining room from the living room.

"Especially from you!" she said as she jabbed her finger in his direction. As quick as she said it, she wished she could take it back. "I can protect myself. I've trained in self-defense classes. I made sure I could protect myself. I refuse to be a victim again." Covering her mouth with her hand, she stopped herself from saying anymore. She tried to gain control of her emotions and figure them out at the same time.

Why fuss with him? Was she blaming him for the past? Was she blaming him for her being caught in the middle of her present danger? *Why? Why? Why?* she screamed in her brain. The words pounded inside her head. *Help me, Lord. Please take control of this conversation.*

In seconds it hit her like a Mack truck, or maybe an

answered prayer. It wasn't Detective Jefferies who upset her. She started getting upset when she tried to envision that man, the man on the phone, the man who tried to run her down. Not so much the man, but the look in his eyes. Intense fear had grown inside her. She had lost control.

That was it! That was the problem. Someone else was in control of her life. . .again. *Let me be your strength, your protection.* She knew she should be turning her situation over to God totally; no one was greater than Him. But right then, her flesh was in control—and scared to death.

Her bottom lip started to tremble. Control was the key. The man after her was in control.

But why take it out on Detective Jefferies? Why should he suffer for her uncontrollable feelings of terror? He hadn't done anything, except to make her wake up to reality. She was helpless *again*, and that frightened her, more than she cared to admit.

Sam's hands shook as she dropped on the couch, then cradled her head in her hands. She shuddered from head to toe as tears flowed softly down her cheeks.

Once the feelings had swept through her and settled in the pit of her stomach, she leaned back against the couch, wiped her face dry with the back of her hands, and then dropped them to her side. "I'm sorry. You're right. I'm venting my anger on you. I thought I was past all these feelings. I didn't know I could still feel so much fear. . .so much anger, so quickly. I didn't even know I was this upset. I truly thought the past was in the past."

"It's okay. I think you're more scared than anything." The detective walked over and sat next to her, looking as if he wanted to offer her comfort but not actually offering any.

Holding her hands up, she kept distance between them. She didn't want or need his pity. "You're right. I'm so used to hiding my fear, covering it up, I just couldn't see it. I work a man's job, so I can't afford to show my fear there. I have to be tough. If I showed fear, the drivers would run all over me."

"A little fear is good for you. If nothing else, it'll make you more cautious."

Cautious, huh? Like I'm not cautious enough. Sam had wrapped herself and Marty in a cocoon, guarding and protecting them from the pain of the outside world. Yes, she had learned her lesson all right, the hard way, and it had left her with a lot of emotional baggage, as well as physical scarring. She dare not let anything else happen to her son. She would protect him with her life. Her whole life, her whole world was Marty.

Since the "accident," she didn't go to parties much or out with friends. She never dated, although she had been asked by several men. Sam worked and came home. She overprotected Marty and restricted his playtime and his friends. The two of them visited Amanda, but she lived across the hall. It wasn't too scary to walk across the hall. Sometimes Sam would take Marty, and they would go visit her mom and dad, but that was the extent of her social life.

In fact, when Marty got out of school today, she was going to bring him to her parents' home to stay for a few days for his protection. She hoped that was all it took to keep him safe. Of course, she still had to clear it with her parents, but when they learned what had happened, they'd encourage both Sam and Marty to stay with them. She couldn't chance bringing danger into their home, too, so her staying was out of the question.

Another thing she did for her own enjoyment was to take time for the health club on her off days while Marty was at school. Staying in shape, preparing physically in case of another brutal attack, was her whole life, aside from Marty. Obviously she wasn't prepared enough since she had not escaped the clutches of the attacker. Not that he had attacked her per se, but, she told herself, she had never prepared for another mental assault. That was what she was experiencing now by letting the past haunt her and unnerve her while she waited to see if this man would come after her.

Sam had to face it, so she better start preparing herself all the way. Looking at the detective, she saw concern in his eyes.

"No need to worry about me now, Detective. Remember, I'm on vacation as of this morning. No more going to work until the man is caught—or at least until the excitement dies down. The boss and I both decided it was for the best."

"When they find the truck, maybe we'll know more. Just remember, he missed you this morning, but he may come after you again."

Through tight lips, she said, "Thanks for those encouraging words."

When he didn't say anything, she added, "Don't worry. You've done your job. I'm scared now, and I'll be watching constantly, so you can go."

"Sorry, but somebody had to make you see it." He paused. "I'm just glad you didn't get hurt."

"Me, too." She stood and showed him to the door. All her energy and emotion had been zapped. "Thanks again."

At the door, he stopped and turned. Reaching into his pocket, he pulled out a card and handed it to her. "Here are my work and cell numbers. Call me if you think of anything or need anything."

She took it and slipped it in her shorts pocket. "Thanks."

"Remember, be extra careful. Do you have a gun?"

"Men! Yes, I have a gun, but I don't carry it. I'd be more danger to myself than to anyone else. I haven't shot it in years. Besides, guns scare me. Trust me, I'll be okay." Sam reached for the knob to open the door and let him out.

Before he left, the detective extended his hand toward her face, but stopped halfway. His eyes studied her; then he appeared to look deep into her soul. Suddenly drawing his hand back, he said, his voice soft and tender, "Take care."

A lump caught in her throat. If she didn't know better, she would almost think he cared. "Sure," she murmured.

Sam watched him walk away, down the breezeway, till he reached the stairs on the other side and started descending one step at a time.

Confusion filled her as she thought about the emotions he stirred within her. What happened to make her react this way to this man? Why the physical attraction? Sure, he was very handsome, but looks weren't everything. She'd learned that a long time ago. If for no other reason than he had been Martin's partner, she shouldn't be finding herself attracted to him.

Sam leaned against the doorframe and smiled. It didn't matter what she told herself; her heart didn't seem to listen. It didn't have to know him to experience the feelings he awakened in her, feelings that had been dead for over three years. That was why it was called a *physical attraction*.

Stepping inside her apartment, Sam closed the door and

locked it. She glanced into the living room at the TV and noticed the end of her show. With a flick of her brows, she admitted to herself that Matthew Jefferies was worth missing Remy over. *Enough of that.* She sighed. *It's past time for a workout and to fix my mind on the here and now.*

Chapter 12

Dressed in form-fitting workout garb, Sam grabbed her athletic bag, tossed in a towel, swimsuit, hair supplies, and a change of clothes, prepared for a trip to the gym. Next, she packed a bag for Marty. In it, she packed enough clothes for a whole week's stay at her parents'—not that she believed it would take that long, but it was best to be prepared. Closing the case up tight, she headed out of his room with her gym bag on her shoulder and Marty's case in her hand.

She grabbed her purse and keys off the side table and headed toward the door. Glancing at the clock, she saw she had three hours before she had to pick Marty up at school. Could she do a quick workout and slip by the police station to give a description to the sketch artist all in three hours? She may have to skip the sauna. She would make it happen.

As she pulled the door to close it behind her, the phone rang. Sam started to ignore the ring, then thought better.

Someone from work could be on the other end with a question, or her parents could be calling to check on her. It could even be the school about Marty. Pushing the door open, she raced to answer it.

On the third ring she snatched up the receiver. "Hello."

Silence hung on the line, but it wasn't a dead line. Whoever called was still there. His heavy breathing was loud.

"Hello," she said again.

The breathing continued, sounding hot and heavy. She didn't need practical jokers at a time like this in her life. Taking a deep breath, she prayed it was a practical joker and not *him*. Slapping down the phone, she headed out the door and slammed it shut.

As she was locking the deadbolt, the phone rang again. Her hands started to tremble. No. She would not let this frighten her. Quickly, she walked along the breezeway toward the stairs.

Although she tried to fight it, apprehension stirred strongly. She slowed at the top of the stairs and glanced around. *Remember to watch your back,* she heard the detective tell her. She could do that. She had to do that.

Nothing looked suspicious, but nonetheless, she continued to look around, making sure no one was lurking in the bushes or behind cars.

Reassured with a dose of phony confidence, Sam rushed down the stairs toward her car, threw the bags in the trunk, climbed in her Toyota, and fired up the engine. The gym was near her apartment, so she didn't have far to drive, but she watched her surroundings the whole time, staying aware and alert.

"And don't forget to go by the station after the spa," she reminded herself again when she recalled her promise to Detective Jefferies. . .*Matthew*. "No," she told herself aloud. Her mind wanted to wander, but she focused on her driving.

The drive was a short trip she took often. On most of her off days, Sam would go to the spa for a workout. If time was against her, she would settle for a jog to the elementary school and back, a four-mile trek that took a little over an hour. Sometimes she did it as Marty was getting out of school, so that slowed her down a little on her return. But either way it was a good workout. Marty didn't like it so much. He would rather her pick him up in the car every time.

Upon arrival to the health club, she pulled open the glass door. Music blared. The large open room behind the check-in desk had several people lined up moving this way and that to the beat. Aerobics—her favorite. The next room was filled with equipment. There were free weights, Stairmasters, treadmills, and electronically weighted machines that made a workout easy. Every woman there appeared to be doing her best to get in shape.

After dropping her bag in a locker in the dressing room, Sam did a quick warm-up routine, then joined the women in the weight room. Next she planned to go upstairs to the track for a jog. To join in aerobics, it was best to start on time at the beginning with the slow warm-up moves before the workout and stay through the cool-down. Her timing wasn't right this time. Maybe tomorrow she'd do better.

Before leaving today, she planned to catch a swim and maybe even treat herself to a relaxing time in the whirlpool.

An hour and a half later, Sam left the spa feeling relaxed

and rejuvenated. "This is the way to start a vacation," she murmured to herself as she drove home. Her skin tingled. She felt so good, she forgot to worry, forgot to feel fear. Forgot to go by the station and give a description to the artist.

Unlocking the deadbolt, she turned the knob on her front door, pushed it open. . .and froze.

Chapter 13

The room had been turned upside-down. Stepping back, she closed the door quietly.

He knows where I live, she thought wildly. *And he could still be in the apartment!*

She wasn't about to chance it. Amanda wasn't home from work yet, so Sam ran next door to use Mrs. Gabriella's phone.

Sam knocked but not loudly. She didn't want to make the intruder aware that she was back. Mrs. Gabriella came to the door. "Hello, dear. What can I do for you?"

"Someone has broken into my apartment. I need to use your phone and call the police. They may still be inside," she whispered.

The old lady hurriedly ushered Sam in, double-locked the door, and led her to the phone.

Sam didn't have the detective's card, so she dialed 911 again. They said someone would be there in a few minutes, to stay in the neighbor's apartment.

No problem there. Sam didn't feel like trying to be a hero. No one in her apartment needed saving. Here the two of them should be safe.

Sam hid in the shadows of the curtains as she peered out of her neighbor's window, watching for the cops. While waiting, she noticed a medium-sized dark car, maybe a Ford, parked against the fence across the way. In it a man crouched down, as if hiding. Her hands started shaking. *What if it's him?*

She prayed silently that the police would hurry. Should she call Detective Jefferies? Oh how she wished she had memorized his number or even had his card with her. No. She had set it on her dresser at home and left it there. How stupid could she get?

She studied the man as she kept hidden behind the curtain. It could be someone waiting for a friend to get home, but why was he ducked down low in his seat?

Mrs. Gabriella talked nonstop. Fear does that to some people.

Sam couldn't watch any longer. Her nerves couldn't take it, so she started pacing. Back and forth she walked, as she tried to answer Mrs. Gabreilla's questions. Occasionally she glanced out the window. Time dragged by. It seemed like half an hour, but in all actuality, it only took ten minutes for them to arrive.

A strange thing happened, though, as the police car pulled into the parking lot. The man who had been hiding slipped out of his car and met the official vehicle when it came to a stop.

"What the heck?" she said aloud, the corner of her mouth twisting with exasperation. "He had someone watching me. I told him I could take care of myself. A babysitter! And a lousy one at that!" She was furious at Jefferies.

In no time, the two uniformed policemen raced up the stairs while the stranger rushed back to his car. Sam met the men in the breezeway. She put her anger to the back of her mind so she could concentrate on the moment, the here and now.

"I'm Officer Wiley and he's Dixon. Go back inside your neighbor's apartment while we take a look around yours," the young officer ordered her.

"No problem. I left it unlocked."

They disappeared inside while she waited, but she waited in the breezeway. She found herself watching the stranger in the car instead of worrying herself sick about the inside of her apartment. The man was in his own car talking on what looked to be a CB radio. Immediately, Sam knew he was calling in to report to Detective Jefferies. It had to be.

She shook her head, fuming under her breath. *It won't be long before the great detective himself shows up at my doorstep.* Although on the outside she was perturbed with him, deep inside she fought a smile that tried to form.

Did this make her happy, the thought of seeing him? She swallowed hard, trying to make that flicker of joy disappear. Then she reminded herself that she had wanted to call him almost immediately. She just didn't have his card. So, in a way, this was doing what she wanted to do all along. But she still didn't feel the need for a babysitter. At least one she didn't know about. Why couldn't he have told her he was leaving someone to watch out for her? That would have made her feel better and maybe even safer. But no, he didn't tell her a thing.

So, in short, he lied to her.

"You can come in now," called the older policeman from the front door, snapping her preoccupied mind back to the situation at hand. "You should have waited inside your neighbor's home as you were told."

"Sorry, I couldn't," she said. Looking up at Officer Dixon as he waited for her to enter the apartment, she hesitated before taking a step toward the door. When would this all be over? It had to be the same man. The one at work and the man who broke in. . .didn't it? The one who wanted to hurt her, or see her dead, and now had entered her home. Her security. Her safety net. She felt dirty and violated. How could he? Her insides were as tossed and turned as her living room.

"Look around and see if you're missing anything," instructed Wiley.

It didn't take long to discover the small bank on her dresser was gone.

"I've been robbed," she said a little too enthusiastically. "My bank that sits on my dresser is gone. I had close to five hundred dollars in bills and rolled change." Sam breathed a little easier. It *was* a normal break-in. A thief—not the one who wanted to hurt her.

Did she really believe this, or was she trying to convince herself? The thought that it wasn't the same man excited her. It made her feel a little less stressed, a little more at ease. It allowed the tensed muscles in her back to relax somewhat. But was she kidding herself?

"The burglar must have been looking for ready cash. He didn't take anything of value to pawn, since your television and stereo are both still in place." Dixon made another note in his small pad. "I doubt very seriously we'll find whoever stole your money since all he took was the cash. Nothing to trace. You might want to get a better lock on your door, though, one that can't be picked so easily."

A slow grin spread across her face as she found her head and heart agreeing in unison that it was the work of a burglar. That mattered more than anything right now. Then she overheard Wiley tell Dixon something that wiped the smile off her face immediately.

"With what Davis told us a minute ago, don't you find it a bit strange for someone to come in and tear up one room, then take some ready cash from the other room?" Wiley pushed his hat back slightly on his head, then scratched his forehead. "This could have been a warning to her. Maybe letting her know he can get at her whenever he wants."

"We go by the facts, Wiley. Cash was stolen. That's it." Dixon turned back to Sam. "We'll file a report. Again, I suggest you change that lock on the door."

After they left, she was more confused than before. Wasn't it locked when she got home? She knew she used the key. Maybe it wasn't locked, and she couldn't tell when she turned the key.

She sighed. Was it the guy or not? What Wiley said made a lot of sense to her, but Dixon, the older policeman, didn't seem too concerned. She grabbed the gold knob, twisted the lock, and slid the chain into the slot.

"That should do it for now," she whispered. "I will have another dead bolt installed. . .maybe two."

Turning around and leaning against the door, Sam realized she was slightly disappointed Detective Jefferies hadn't shown up by now. Part of her had been looking forward to him coming there. After seeing the man in the car who had been watching her, she had a spark of hope that the detective actually cared about her well-being.

Shaking her head, she tried to erase that thought. It was just a job to him. She was his job. She was a witness. Besides, didn't her babysitter watching from the car prove she couldn't trust the police? The cop downstairs didn't stop the break-in. What good was he? She could have been lying on the floor dead, and he would have never known it. Of course, she realized in the back of her mind that her "tail" had probably been at the gym with her, waiting outside in the heat the whole time.

"So much for protecting me," she grumbled. A big mess waited for her, so she might as well get started in cleaning it up. Taking a step toward the bathroom to get the cleaning supplies, her mind flashed on her grandmother's diamond broach that she kept hidden deep in her dresser drawer. The thief had been in her bedroom. That was where the money bank had been. Practically running, she rushed to the bedroom and yanked open the drawer.

She stood in shock as she stared in the drawer. Scrawled in dark red on a piece of paper she read, *I can get to you anytime, anywhere.*

A bloodcurdling scream reached her ears. It came from her lips. Fear, stark and vivid, streaked across her face, reflected in the mirror attached to the dresser.

Chapter 14

She was about to break down and cry like a baby when she heard wood splinter as her front door crashed to the floor.

No time for tears now. Searching around the room, she looked for a weapon to protect herself. Her reflexes started working. Her blood pumped ferociously. *Nothing sharp!* Sam rummaged through the drawers and around the room for something, anything, with which to protect herself.

Footsteps rushed down the hall toward her. He was coming quickly. She was running out of time. She grabbed a can of hairspray, ready to spray it in the assailant's eyes. With her finger on the button, she stood, feet slightly apart, ready. Distraught, she took aim.

As the bedroom door flew open, Detective Jefferies filled the frame. Sam's eyes widened. "Oh! It's you."

"Samantha, are you okay?" He grabbed one of her arms as

he slid his gun in his holster, then pulled her body to his and wrapped both of his arms around her. "I heard you scream and thought he had come back for you. You scared me to death."

"I scared you?" Sam wanted to laugh. His body trembled as he held her close. Or was it hers? She couldn't be sure. The warmth of his touch spread as his hands stretched across her back, holding her close. This gave her comfort. For the moment, she was safe. She closed her eyes and relished the way his warm breath felt against her cheek.

Maybe the trembling wasn't from fear, but from an aching need that consumed her at his touch. She needed protection. She needed someone she could depend on for help. She needed someone to care for her. She was tired of having to be strong and take care of herself and Marty. Yes, she had the Lord, but maybe He was giving her help.

His fingers caressed her back as he held her tight. For a few minutes, neither seemed to know what was going on between them. It was like a safety net enveloped them, keeping them from the world for a moment in time.

Suddenly, she froze in his arms, knowing this was wrong.

His hands stopped. Reality must have replaced physical reaction as he dropped his hands. They both stepped apart, leaving a space between them.

It took all the strength she could muster to move away. She wanted to feel his arms around her again, feel the safety, the warmth, the tingle, the joy.

Instead, they stared at one another, not saying a word. Sam didn't have the power to breathe, to look away, or speak. All she could do was gaze into his warm blue eyes. She watched fear, confusion, and concern flash through them but knew he felt the same thing she had.

Finally, he broke the silence. Of course, being a man, or maybe it was because he was a cop first and man second, nothing was said in reference to their moment of weakness. That was okay.

"Why did you—" Matthew didn't finish his question. He didn't have to. His gaze looked down at the open drawer and saw what had caused her to scream. "I knew it! I knew it was him!" The detective pulled out his flip phone and punched in a phone number.

As her brain took in the conversation the detective was having, her heart concerned itself over the physical reaction she had just experienced and the desires that still burned within. The need to feel his arms around her again consumed her. She wanted to tremble in his arms one more time.

Sam had never felt that strongly before. Not even with Martin. How could that be?

When Matthew slapped his phone closed and jammed it back into his pocket, she jumped. Immediately, her mind returned to the present and listened for what he had to say.

"I'm not gonna sit back and watch that nut move in on you. The captain is coming around slowly, but too slow. The note gives great credibility to the *possibility* you are being stalked by the serial killer, so he said we could keep a watch on you. . .that we are already doing. It's not enough. We tried a tail and it didn't work. *Twice!*"

He fixed his eyes on her and clamped his hands around her forearms. "You know it wasn't a simple burglary here. Right? It was the man who is after you, the man you saw kill someone. Everything has been him, and it's you he's after.

You know that now, don't you?" With each sentence, his grip tightened as he shook her ever so slightly, displaying the urgency he felt as he spoke.

Point was taken. She nodded.

"The crime scene unit is coming out for prints and possible evidence." He dropped his hands and started examining the room for other signs the perpetrator might have left. "After they get here, I'm gonna take you out of here for a time. We'll go get a cup of coffee, maybe even a sandwich if you're hungry."

Again Sam nodded.

"Great. We'll have to try to figure out what we can do to protect you. There has got to be a better way." He glanced at the drawer again. "Come on. Let's get out of this room."

Sam did as she was told. She hadn't said a word since he rushed in to help her. Maybe she was in shock, she didn't know. But talking was not on the top of her list of things to do at the moment.

"Your phonebook. Where is it?"

Sam pointed to the drawer below the phone and watched as he flipped through the pages.

Matthew pulled out his cell once again and punched in the number he had found. After a brief conversation, he hung up. "Someone will be here shortly to put up a new door for you. Sorry I destroyed it."

Sam couldn't help but smile. He had kicked the door down to rush in and save her. Her heart skipped a beat as the warmth he'd shared with her only moments ago enveloped her again.

"It will be okay," he said as he stepped near her and rested his hands gently on her shoulders. "I think you're in shock. I haven't heard you say a word, but you will be fine. Trust me."

Trust him? She believed, right now, she did trust him. If he'd known the sensations that raced through her when he touched her, she didn't think he would be touching her so readily, but he appeared oblivious to his power over her. Had she gone crazy?

"Whoever is after you is one sick man. We're going to play this a little differently from now on. Whoever is scheduled to watch you will be with you, not down in a parking lot watching from afar. That won't work anymore."

The men from the crime scene unit arrived, and Matthew told them about the note in the drawer and who he had called out to put up a new front door, then he led Sam out the opening. Quickly, he drove them to a nearby coffeehouse but watched constantly to make sure no one was following them.

The aroma of the dark roasted brew filled her senses as they walked into CC's. Matthew ordered them each a cup before they sat down. He turned with his back against the wall. He eyed everyone who came in the front and side door.

"I'm gonna run this by the shrink at work. See what she thinks about the way he is acting with you. This guy is playing games for some reason. It doesn't make sense. The doc will know, though."

Sam sat with her hands on the table as the waitress brought the two cups of coffee to them. Matthew rested his hands on hers, then squeezed slightly. "It will be okay. Sip your coffee. You're too quiet. You're starting to scare me a little. I promise you we're going to help you."

She smiled. "I'm ready for the help," she whispered. "I'm

ready to trust you."

His gaze flashed on Sam for an instant then turned back to his hot brew. Sam could tell he was amazed when she didn't argue. Maybe it confused him more than astonished him.

Chapter 15

Matthew pretended to be relaxed, but inside every one of his nerves was on fire. Here he was trying to keep his mind focused on protecting her, and she had to go and say something like she trusted him. Sure he wanted her to trust him, but not get too relaxed. Her life was in danger. She had to stay sharp. Up until now, she had done wonderfully.

He kept a keen watch on the side and front doors. His jacket hung loose, giving him easy access to his gun. Although his body stayed alert, ready for action if necessary, she kept his mind going in circles. He couldn't get over how Samantha managed herself through this whole ordeal. He saw the uncertainty in her eyes but was amazed at how she pushed past it, ready to face the problem head-on. Fear didn't slow her down.

Somehow through this whole thing, they seemed to be

carrying on a pleasant conversation. Things were different somehow. She almost appeared to enjoy his company. That was a first, and he decided he liked it. Is this what trust did to someone?

They sat for a while as he quietly asked questions about her life. Maybe this would give him some kind of lead on the case. Probably not, since she was a witness turned to the killer's next victim if that sicko had his way.

"So, besides work, where do you go? Who do you see? Name some people you come in contact with on a daily basis. Anyone who might have a grudge against you? We'll work this thing from a different angle to prove the only person after you is the serial killer." Matthew took notes of every name she mentioned, though there weren't many. She lived a very closed existence, it sounded. Again, it was nothing like the picture Martin had painted when he talked about her.

The list covered people at her work, at the health club, her best friend and neighbor, and her family. In fact, it sounded like everyone who ever had come in contact with Samantha in the last few years of her life. . .every person except Martin's family, for that matter. *I wonder why that is?* Why weren't Marty's grandparents involved in their grandson's life? That made no sense at all. Maybe she didn't mention them, assuming that was the only part of her life he already knew about, so she had no need to mention them. Or maybe because that had been over three years ago? For some strange reason, he found he was glad Martin's family had no contact with Samantha.

Matthew decided to avoid the subject of Martin. That added a strain when he was mentioned. Martin's past was something they both had in common. It wasn't a pleasant memory for him, either. That was even more a reason to bring it up, probably, but he liked the pleasantries between them at the moment and didn't want to blow it. He'd bring up Martin and his past with her later.

In the middle of her sentence, she slammed her cup down on the table. "I almost forgot. I need to pick up my son from school." Glancing at her watch, she added, "Like five minutes ago. In all the commotion. . ." She jumped to her feet. "We've got to go."

He had forgotten all about her kid being in school. "You know, it's not safe for him to stay around through all of this. He could get hurt. . .or even worse. This sick man could use him against you." He tossed his cup in the trash as he led her out the door, the whole time looking around, making sure no one was watching them.

"I know. I've already thought about that. I packed a bag for him to go stay with my parents for about a week. I hope this can be solved soon." Suddenly she stopped, and Matthew ran into her. "I left the bag in the trunk of my car."

"No problem. We'll get it."

She bit her lower lip as she reached out and touched his arm. "I'm praying you get this guy very soon."

"You and me both." He winked. "Let's go get Marty."

Chapter 16

Marty was a smart kid. Matthew watched the way he looked at his mom. He knew something was up as they drove toward his grandparents' home.

Although he listened to the interaction between mother and son, Matthew kept his eyes peeled, taking a lot of extra turns, watching for anything suspicious or a possible car following them.

"But Mom, I want to stay with you. I know you need protection. Something is going on. I could tell by the way you and Aunt Amanda were talking. Please let me stay with you."

Samantha was turned halfway around in the front seat as she spoke to her son. "I need you to be my strong boy and stay with Granny and Papaw while the detective helps Mommy find the bad guy and gets him arrested. He needs to go to jail for what he has done."

"But, Mom," he pleaded.

"I packed your slacks so you can go to church with Granny and Papaw. While you're there, pray special for me, would ya?"

Glancing in the rearview mirror, Matthew saw the boy grin at his mother. "I love you, Mommy."

What a smart boy she had raised. The boy knew something was wrong. Matthew could hear it in his voice and see it in his face, but he also had sense enough not to upset his mom. He knew when to stop begging. He seemed to be protective of her. It was almost like he was the man of the house.

The love from mother to son was obvious, too. She wanted to protect him. All the things Martin had said about Samantha were being proved wrong over and over again. How could he and the other guys have been so blind?

"I love you, too, Marty. You mind Granny and Papaw. And don't go outside without them while you're there. It won't be long. I promise."

It took a lot of convincing to get him to agree to that, but it worked. They dropped him off without any problems. The grandparents understood the dangers and begged the detective to take good care of their baby.

Matthew and Sam left to head back to her apartment.

By the time they returned, the door had been replaced, and extra locks had been placed on the new door. The CSU had come and gone.

Matthew had radioed ahead for a policeman to meet them at her apartment. He brought in one of the plainclothes officers, Officer Brent Davis. Davis pulled evening relief on this surveillance assignment. After giving him new instructions and introducing him to Samantha, Matthew said, "Now we will stick to her like glue. No more keeping our distance." The detective's main concern was to keep Samantha safe and alive. There would be no more screw ups. He was going to make sure of it. Sam could tell.

Sam eyed this Brent guy closely. He appeared young. She wasn't sure she could trust him. She had only just learned to trust Detective Jefferies. Sam also didn't know if she would like having strange men, especially policemen, staying at her place. But given the situation, she had no choice.

She didn't want to be a victim of a homicide. Maybe this time would be different. Maybe the police would do a better job of protecting her. Detective Jefferies seemed to take his job seriously.

After Jefferies left, Sam cleaned the apartment while Brent Davis stayed out of her way. But no amount of scrubbing and cleaning would take away the fear the stalker had instilled in her by letting her know how easy it had been for him to get into her apartment. He was still in control, and that was what he had been telling Sam with the strategically placed note he had left behind saying, *I can get to you anytime, anywhere.* With a guard on duty twenty-four hours a day, she hoped things would be different.

She even cleaned Marty's room. That was a feat in itself. She smiled as she realized it was probably all that nervous energy getting her apartment so clean. Well, at least something good came out of it.

She hated to admit it, but part of keeping busy was also a way to keep from thinking about the way Detective Jefferies made her feel.

After folding the last basket of clean clothes, she heard a knock at the door. Officer Davis rose immediately, drawing his gun as he moved close to the door.

It wouldn't be the killer. He'd just break in. Her hand touched the top lock, about to turn it. Thinking twice, she paused. "Who is it?"

"Me. Amanda."

"You can put that thing away," she told the officer. Unlocking the top two deadbolts and removing the solid gold bar that locked over a piece on the doorframe, Sam opened the door. "Hey girl, come on in."

"How many locks did you put on your new door? What happened here?" Amanda stared at the door and the new gold shiny pieces. "What are you protecting, Fort Knox? You even have one of those things like you see on hotel doors. Girl, this is getting serious."

"You don't know the half of it. Come in. Have a seat."

Amanda hugged her friend. "You look a little pale. I'm glad I stopped by. I think you need what I'm about to suggest. We're going to shake things up around here. Cheer you up. Get your mind off of your problems." Amanda, with her short, curly, blond hair and bubbly personality, bounced into the room. "Whatcha got planned for tonight? Any—" She stopped short. "Sorry. I didn't know you had company." Her sweet smile revealed two deep dimples.

"Hi," Officer Davis said. "Name's Brent." He extended his hand.

"Hi. I'm Amanda. Nice to meet you, Brent." She placed her hand in his for a second or two. "Oh, Samantha. You've been holding out on me." Amanda grinned from ear-to-ear as her eyes twinkled.

"It's a long story." Sam sighed as she headed toward a chair in the living room. "If you've got a few minutes, I'll fill you in."

Amanda plopped down on the sofa. The officer took the opposite end.

As Sam told her story to her best friend, she wished she was more like Amanda. Petite and cutesy, a blue-eyed beauty who never let personal problems, no matter how devastating, get in the way of enjoying life. Unfortunately, Sam, the plain Jane type, short, full-figured, with brown hair and green eyes, let her problems control her life. . .more than she should. She'd basically stopped living three years ago just to feel safe. But she knew that wasn't the answer. And now she was trying to lean on the Lord totally. The devil had a way of stepping in right when she thought she'd gotten it together.

Although Sam had forgiven Martin, she still couldn't shake the attack, the injury, or the pain. She would be the first to admit she'd left it at the cross many times, only to take it back again. She didn't want to. She prayed for strength to leave it. Still did. But she hadn't totally let go of the fear yet. Until she could do that, Sam knew she wouldn't move forward in her life.

"So, all-in-all, things haven't been too great," Sam said.

"Well, we're going to change things right now. I know you never go out anymore, but tonight is going to be different. Where is Marty?"

"At my parents'."

"Perfect. And I won't take no for an answer. You'll have your—" she winked at the policeman—"personal bodyguard. What harm could come to you? Mark Roberts just opened up a new club a couple of weeks ago. I know you don't go to bars. You don't have to drink. Besides, Mark is an old friend from school. It wouldn't hurt to show your support."

"I don't know."

"I promised him I'd twist your arm and make you come with me tonight. One night won't hurt. Besides, it will take your mind off of what you've been going through."

Mark was a guy they had gone to junior high and high school with. Even though it had been ten years, a lot of the old gang still lived locally. Only a few had gone on to other places and other things in their lives.

Sam took a seat in the chair. "I don't think I can." Part of her knew she shouldn't. She had no business going out during a time like this. She was making herself an open target.

"Well, I need to, and I need you to go with me. Since Charlie and I broke up, I haven't done much myself, and I'm about to climb the walls. Come on. It'll be good for you and me both. Whatcha say?"

Sam rubbed the back of her neck. "You miss Charlie, don't you? I thought by now you two would have patched things up."

"I did, too," Amanda confided, pursing her lips as if to pout. "I still love the jerk, but until he's ready to settle down and make a commitment, I don't need him around. He'll grow up one day. . .I hope."

Sam decided she did need a little diversion to take her mind off all the things that had happened. "Going out might do me some good."

If nothing else, it might help her quit thinking about that handsome detective. She glanced at Officer Davis. When he didn't say she couldn't, Sam said, "I guess okay. What time?"

Amanda squealed. "All right! I can't believe you gave in.

Oops." She covered her mouth. "Did I say that out loud? Didn't mean to. Anyway, I think you'll enjoy it. I'll pick you up around eight thirty."

The policeman was young, so maybe the idea sounded good to him, too. Besides, Sam saw the way he had been watching Amanda. She could have her pick of men, but she had always loved Charlie.

Sam hoped Charlie wouldn't change like Martin had. People did that. . .changed. She'd learned that from firsthand experience, but it was not something you could tell another person. Everyone had to learn it for themselves.

After Amanda left, the policeman called in and gave an update on her plans and where they would be.

"My relief comes at eleven. I needed to leave word so he knows where to meet me."

Sam smiled. "No problem." She was surprised Detective Jefferies didn't say no. That was what she had expected him to do. Maybe it wasn't such a bad idea after all.

Chapter 17

Shortly after nine, Sam heard Amanda knocking on the door. "It's me. Let's go." Amanda was never on time.

Letting her in, Sam said, "I'll drive if you'd like."

"Great."

"I'll follow in my car," said Officer Davis.

"Fine, Brent," Amanda said. "I don't plan on explaining you to any of our friends. Right, Sam? We'll introduce you as a new neighbor." Amanda looked to Sam for agreement. She nodded.

"That would be for the best," he said.

With that straight, the three headed out the door and down to the cars.

When they arrived, the place was jumping, and by ten it was packed. The people were shoulder to shoulder, and the room filled with thick smoke. That was another reason Sam didn't like coming. Besides, she preferred staying home with

Marty. He was her life.

Sam and Amanda ran into some old school friends just as expected: Brad, Mike, and Terrie. Later Sally and Dan joined them. Mark came by their table and thanked them all for coming to his club. Much later, Charlie slipped into the crowd. Before Sam knew it, they had a couple of tables pulled together full of people.

Eventually, Sam started to dance, but she stayed near their table so the officer could see her at all times. She danced with a few of the guys in their group, which helped her keep from thinking about the past forty-eight hours. . .and the detective.

Davis fit in well. He seemed to be having a good time, but every time Sam glanced his way, the policeman's eyes were upon her and her surroundings, keeping a close watch. She had to give him credit. He seemed to be doing his job. Not like the policemen in her past experience.

Around ten thirty, Sam was dancing a slow song with Brad. He was a good bit taller than Sam, all six-foot-five of him, but they danced well together. The two moved slowly with the music, keeping perfect rhythm.

"It's been a long time since we've danced like this," Brad whispered in her ear as he leaned down slightly to compensate for the difference in their heights. He had been her best friend in high school. Secretly, she had had a crush on him but told no one. In their college years, everyone told Sam to watch out, warning her that Brad had a crush on her. By then, though, Martin had already won her heart. About five years ago, everyone had even joked if Martin found out Brad was still carrying that torch, he would have punched Brad's lights out.

"It's just like old times," he continued.

Sam laughed lightly. "Yeah. Great, isn't it?" In a flash her mind whispered, *But wouldn't it be nicer if it was Matthew I was dancing with?*

Her eyes flew open in surprise, and she pulled slightly away from Brad. Her thought had even called him by first name. *Too forward. Too easy.* She had to get Detective Jefferies out of her mind, but every time she closed her eyes, his blue ones came into clear view, making forgetting him virtually impossible.

Think about the here and now, she told herself as she closed her eyes one more time. *Think about Brad and the good old days. Think about anything but Matthew Jefferies.*

Sam opened her eyes when Brad released his hold on her. The vision in her mind appeared in the flesh. There, cutting in on the dance floor, stood Matthew Jefferies. Her breath caught in her throat. She had to force herself to take in air. Blinking twice, she made sure she wasn't dreaming. As his blue eyes stared deep into her soul, he nudged Brad out of the way and pulled her into his arms.

"Sam, do you know this man?" Brad's narrowed eyes and frown showed his aggravation.

"Sure." She nodded. "Everything's fine, Brad." But everything wasn't fine. Yet she couldn't stop herself from stepping into Matthew's arms willingly. Her hands trembled as her stomach fluttered.

"What are you doing here? Trying to get yourself killed?" he said through tight lips. The words were spoken close to her ear. So close, his hot breath covered her neck. His words were meant for her ears only. "When I found out what Davis called in, I couldn't believe it. If I'd been at the precinct when he called, you never would have come."

So that was why he hadn't protested this excursion. He didn't know. Sam listened to the detective scold her for her own protection. She knew he was right, so she didn't stop him. Besides, she enjoyed being held close in his arms. She relished it way too much to protest against his words.

At the end of the song, when the last note held on, Matthew stopped scolding long enough to ask, "Where is your purse? We're getting out of here."

When she pointed, he took her by the elbow and walked her toward the table. Officer Davis was already on his feet, waiting for their return.

Sam stopped midstep. A chill rushed over her as she spotted a familiar. . .it wasn't a face so much as a familiar pair of eyes in the crowd.

"What's the matter?"

Sam turned to Matthew and swallowed hard, then looked back in the direction she had seen those familiar eyes. The face disappeared. She must have imagined it, someone who looked like that guy from the other night.

"I guess nothing," she said. "I thought I'd—" She shook her head. "Never mind."

They made their way to the table, her friends still crowding around it.

"I—" Before Davis could offer words of explanation, Detective Jefferies cut him off, saying, "We'll talk later."

Amanda and Charlie's heads were huddled together in deep conversation, oblivious to what was going on around them. Sam hated to interrupt, but she had to. The detective's grip on her elbow had not relinquished. "Amanda, are you about ready to leave? I'm kind of tired."

The couple looked up. Love seemed to be glowing from their faces. "Charlie will bring me home. If that's okay with you."

Sam nodded. "Sure, no problem."

"You'll be safe. . .won't you? He'll follow you home?" she asked, directing her eyes toward Davis.

"I'll be fine," Sam said as her gaze darted to her side at the detective hovering close.

Amanda stood and hugged her friend bye. As she did, oblivious to Sam's situation, she whispered in Sam's ear, "I think Charlie's going to ask me to marry him. He told me he realized how much he loved me once I told him to get lost. It just took him awhile to work up the courage to tell me."

Sam squeezed Amanda's arms. That explained where Amanda's mind was and why she hadn't noticed Detective Jefferies holding on so tight. "That's great. I knew you two would work things out. See y'all later."

Charlie joined them, slipping his arm around Amanda's waist. "We'll see you later, Sam. Come on, baby. Let's dance."

Saying good-bye to the others at the table, she picked up her glass of Sprite to take one last swallow to wet her dry mouth and saw scribbling on the napkin. The paper had stuck to the bottom of the glass. Her hand froze as she held the glass in midair, almost afraid to read the note, but she knew she had to.

Slowly, she peeled the napkin off the bottom of the glass and lifted it slightly to look closer at the scrawled handwriting.

I'm watching you, she read. Glancing around, she scanned

the room for that face again. Matthew must have seen her actions, because he leaned close and read the napkin over her shoulder.

He reached under his coat for his hidden revolver. Sam dropped the napkin back on the table as her hands started to shake. Using another napkin, Davis picked up the one she had dropped, and the glass, too. He dumped the drink in another almost-empty glass. He, too, had noticed the reaction and knew it was important. After covering it carefully, he slipped it in his jacket pocket.

"Let's get out of here. Now!" Jefferies said.

She yanked up her purse and scrambled toward the exit with Davis in front of her and the detective on her heels. She shivered as she stepped into the night air even though it was hot and humid outside. Apparently, it had drizzled for a short time, and now steam was rising from the heated streets and sidewalks. Another warm September day followed by an afternoon sprinkle had led to a warm, steaming night. Perspiration gathered across her forehead and at the back of her neck as she took in short, quick breaths.

The detective said to Davis, "After we get Ms. Cain safely out of here, I want you to take that evidence back to headquarters. Have them check for prints, and have them put a rush on it. The glass was probably wiped clean, but with today's technology they might lift one off of the napkin. We might get lucky."

Sam's icy fingers wrapped around the keys. She walked faster and faster to her car with Matthew on her heels. Alarm had overtaken Sam completely as she unlocked the door and climbed in. Her pale face stared back in the rearview mirror.

"Samantha. Listen to me." When her eyes turned toward the detective hovering at the side of her car, he continued. "Put on your seatbelt. I'm gonna lock you in. Give me a second to start my car. Officer Davis will stand right here until I get behind you. I'm just a car over. I'll follow you home."

She nodded. Fastening her seatbelt, she started the car and waited. When she saw Matthew's car come to a stop slightly behind her, she pulled out of her space. The officer climbed in his own vehicle. The three cars pulled out of the parking lot, forming a single line.

As the music played, she tried to take her mind off the fear growing inside. Glancing in the mirror, she saw Matthew's car following close behind and Brent Davis behind him. Without realizing it, she ran a yellow light. The detective slowed for only a second, flipped on his flashing light, and continued through the red light. A short distance separated them.

Looking down at the belt across her chest, she laughed. That was strange. Now she knew just how frightened she was, because she never wore her seatbelt, even though it was the law. Sam always had nightmares of being trapped in one and not being able to get out. Yet when the detective told her to buckle up, she did exactly that.

It wasn't long before she reached the curving road that her apartment was on. *Almost home. Matthew Jefferies is right behind me, so I'll be fine. Safety is right around the corner.*

As she made the next curve, a black car pulled out in front of her. She slammed on the brakes, throwing the car into a tailspin on the slick road. *Turn your wheel,* her mind screamed. *Which way?*

Sam couldn't remember if it was into the spin or against it. Making a snap decision, she went with it. It was either the wrong way or too late. Her car spun off the road, hit a pothole, and flipped. Her hands clutched the steering wheel tightly as the airbag released and expanded.

Her head spun like a Ferris wheel. She tried to stay focused but couldn't. The car lurched to a sudden stop as it hit a tree. Her face smashed against the bag. Unconsciousness covered her like a blanket.

Chapter 18

Slowly, Sam opened her eyes to absolute whiteness; curtains, sheets, ceiling, everything. Where was she? As her blurred vision focused, she realized she wasn't alone. With a start, she tried to sit up.

"Where am—" Her question cut off as a knife jabbed into her skull. . .at least that was what it felt like. Then a hand gently restrained her from rising.

"Don't move, Ms. Cain," the nurse said softly. "It's best if you lie still. You've had a terrific injury to your head, and any sudden movement will only make you hurt more. I suggest you move slowly."

"You're right about the pain. Where am I?" Turning her head slightly, she winced.

"You're at the Lady of Mercy. You were in an automobile accident."

The curtain was pulled back. The detective entered her

cubicle and rushed over to the other side of the bed. "Samantha. I mean, Ms. Cain. You're awake. That's a good sign, right, Miss Williams?"

"Right you are, Detective," the nurse said.

Detective Jefferies leaned forward slightly. "Do you remember what happened? When I came around the curve, your car was spinning. I didn't see what caused it."

Her mind scrambled. Thoughts, images, flashed through her mind at lightning speed. "I'm not sure," Sam whispered in a raspy voice. "It's all a blur. Not clear." She winced.

The nurse took her pulse as the detective tried again to get her to remember. "Relax. It'll come to you. The doctor will be back shortly. He talked like you'd be okay. No internal injuries, just surface wounds. One of the uniforms is in the waiting room so he can take a statement from you as soon as you're up to it." He touched her hand and squeezed it gently as his eyes seemed to search her face for the answers he was looking for. "Still no memory?" he asked.

"Sorry." Looking around, Sam realized she was in an emergency room where curtains hung on three sides of the bed and overhead the fluorescent lighting went on and on. In the distance, she heard other soft voices and an occasional ding of a bell, like the sound of an elevator stopping or an intercom system coming on or going off. Everything was in hushed tones.

Sam closed her eyes. All of a sudden, her mind's eye watched in slow motion what had happened earlier. "I remember! You were right!"

"I knew you would," he said as he leaned closer. "Hold on one minute." He rushed past the curtain and, in less than a minute, he returned with the policeman who was there to take her statement. "Go ahead. Tell us what happened."

Closing her eyes, she rewound the vision and replayed it in her mind. "I was driving home and as I turned the curve, a dark car pulled out in front of me. It was. . .it was like it was waiting for me to come around." Sam opened her eyes and looked at Detective Jefferies in disbelief. "The car was black, like the one that seemed to be following me the other night from work. Anyway, when it pulled out in front of me, I hit the brakes and my car went into a tailspin until it crashed against something, then I hit my head."

"A car followed you—never mind. That's good."

"Can you tell me the make or model of the car?" the policeman asked.

Reaching for her forehead, she winced when her fingers brushed against a bandage. An old injury splashed suddenly into her mind, and her head started spinning like a merry-go-round. Closing her eyes again, red flooded her vision.

No! She couldn't relive that now. That was then. The past. Leave it alone! She squeezed her eyes tight until the bloody mess faded into a memory. As it did, she opened her mouth to speak again but couldn't. It was too dry.

"Water. . .can I have some water?"

The nurse obliged Sam's request, then went back to writing down notes in her chart. When finished, she left the small area.

"Can you remember the make or model of the vehicle?" Matthew encouraged Sam. "Did you see the driver's face?"

"It happened so fast. I'm sorry," Sam said as her eyes were getting heavy, burning badly. She didn't want to remember.

She wanted to sleep. She wanted the pain to stop. Her fluttering eyelids closed, but she fought against the sleep that called her name. "Maybe. I'm not sure. Sleep. I need to sleep. Can I rest?"

"If she remembers anything else, you'll let me know, right?"

"No problem," the detective said.

The lids of her eyes grew so heavy, she couldn't hold them open. She couldn't stay awake, but she wanted to. She wanted to talk to the detective, not the police officer, and not about the accident. She wanted to forget that. Her memory snatched a vision of them dancing, a slow dance. She wanted to talk about that. It had been heaven. Why couldn't she stay awake and talk to the detective about that? A sigh escaped her lips as she drifted back to sleep. . . .

When she awoke, Amanda was at her side. She had no idea how long she had been sleeping, but she noticed immediately the detective was nowhere around. It was probably for the best.

"Hey, sweetie. How are you feeling? Charlie and I left shortly after you, so we saw the ambulance taking you to the hospital. Poor baby." Amanda leaned down and hugged Sam lightly. "You've been through so much. It's not fair."

"I'll be all right. Would you call my parents? Let them know what happened but tell them not to tell Marty. Let them know I'm okay. Tell them I'll call as soon as I can."

"Sure. Don't you worry. Oh, by the way, who is that cute guy you left with? He's at the nurses' station down the hall stirring up all kinds of trouble. . .about you. He's been on his cell phone for quite a while yelling at everyone, trying to get something done. The man seemed very interested in your condition and what happened to you."

Sam smiled. He was still there. "Matthew Jefferies. Detective Matthew Jefferies."

"Oh." A wicked smile covered Amanda's face. "Where have you been hiding him?" she asked as she wiggled her eyebrows.

"Be real! He's a cop! The detective on the case I was telling you about." Though she had found herself interested in the man, she didn't share it. . .not even with her best friend. Especially her best friend. Amanda knew everything Martin had put her through, and she wouldn't want to see her go through that again. Sam felt sure her friend would convince her to remember the pain Martin put her through. She'd remind her not to get involved with a cop, of all people. But right now, Sam didn't want to hear that.

Amanda scrunched her nose as she frowned. "Oooh. Misunderstood. Sorry." Shrugging, she added, "Well, all cops can't be bad. Maybe this one will be different." Amanda gently rubbed her hand. "By the look on your face, I do believe I see a little interest there. . .no matter what you're saying to me."

A doctor pulled the curtain back slightly and came in, followed by the nurse. Amanda backed out of the way, not giving Sam time to respond.

"Ms. Cain. How are you feeling?" After Sam's murmured response of not being sure, he continued. "I'm Doctor Clifton. You suffered a severe blow to the cranial, and you have a slight concussion. There is a gash a little over an inch long that runs along your hairline. It took six stitches to close it."

Another scar to add to the old one. *Just call me Frankenstein.* Oh well. At least she was alive. Maybe this one wouldn't show. Sam knew she had the worst headache of her life. It seized her head in a viselike grip and squeezed. If the pressure could just let up, she would feel better.

"I've prescribed you a mild sedative, and we'll let you go home."

"Great," Sam said, feeling a little groggy.

The doctor made a few notes on the clipboard. "I'll leave the prescription with the nurse. You'll probably feel a little sore tomorrow. By the next day you'll feel a lot better, but I suggest you take it easy for a couple more days. A little bed rest, and you'll feel as good as new. Go see your primary doctor in ten days to have the stitches removed."

"We'll give you a ride home," Amanda volunteered as soon as the doctor and nurse left the cubicle. "Charlie's in the waiting room. I'll go let him know."

"Thanks."

"No problem. That's what friends are for."

Chapter 19

When Matthew saw the blond come out of Samantha's cubicle, he rushed back in. He was worried sick about her but worked hard at convincing himself it was because she was in his protective care at the time she got hurt. He kept telling himself he had no feelings for this woman. He barely knew her. So she had been his partner's wife and he had met her only once; he knew what Martin Cain had told him about her. The man put his wife down at most opportunities, if Matthew recalled correctly. This alone should warn him not to let his attentions wander in her direction.

Martin had said a lot of bad things about her over the short period of time they had been partners, but in these past few days Matthew had seen a totally different woman than the one Martin Cain had described three years ago. That he could not explain.

It was just a case, he reminded himself, trying to dismiss the direction his mind had taken him. He cared about all of his cases. He wanted to solve them. Give all the families peace of mind. . .a safe feeling. . .nothing more.

"Ms. Cain, we need to talk. Do you feel up to it?"

Pushing the button to raise the head of the bed, she nodded ever so slightly.

He didn't want to scare her, but by now she should have already figured things out for herself, so the best approach was straightforward. "The man we presume to be the serial killer got within killing distance again tonight. We're not sure if he was out to kill you, or if he was just toying with you some more. It's like he is playing a game. He's a sick man. He hurt you bad, but I think if he had been trying to kill you, he would have. Or if he meant to, when he finds out he missed, he's going to be mad, and he'll be back with a vengeance. And next time he won't miss."

Matthew watched her eyes change from confusion to understanding before he went on. "But we won't let that happen. I'm not sure what's going on in his mind, but our psychologist believes he has twisted things up inside his head and now, instead of continuing in his normal MO, he's turned to stalking you and tormenting you. A power game. A game of control. The doc thinks the killer didn't really try to kill you with the truck, just scare you a little, letting you know he's around. Then what he did in your apartment—the note he left you—was another way to scare you and let you know he was in control. The man has a fixation on you and a need to control you. But we're not sure how long that will satisfy him. You're in grave danger."

She frowned. "My first look at him wasn't really that good. By him coming by work, he gave me a second chance at seeing him. Maybe he wants to be identified. You think?" She paused, as if thinking about what she had just said. "I hate to say it, but it didn't help—that second look I mean. Not much anyway, but when we started off the dance floor I could have sworn I saw his eyes, then his face. It was just a glance, but enough to make me think of the guy who had used the phone. Does that mean I could describe him to your artist now?"

"Yes. That would be great. I'll get you with our composite artist as quick as I can, while the killer's face is still fresh in your mind." He squeezed her hands. "Maybe he's made his first mistake. . .actually second. We got two partials off of the napkin and glass that match, so now we are running it through CODIS, hoping to get a match. . .and hoping it's not the bartender's print. If it is the killer's, his second mistake was, when you didn't recognize him, he started playing games with you, and just maybe that will work in our favor. You now have a visual in your head." Matthew stood and started pacing. "This time we'll get him."

"So now what?"

Stopping at the side of her bed, he looked her in the eyes. "Round the clock protection somewhere other than your place. I'll put you where he can't find you."

"He could be waiting outside the hospital, ready to follow me home or even waiting at my apartment."

"I know, but I have a plan, and it's already in motion."

The blond came in, and Samantha introduced Amanda to Matthew. She smiled at him, then turned her attention to Samantha. "Okay, hon, they've finished the paperwork. The nurse will be bringing in your release papers and prescription, and then we'll take you home."

"Change of plans," Matthew intervened, glancing from Amanda to Samantha and back to Amanda. "She's going with me, and it won't be back to her place."

He saw Samantha's eyes widen, but what else could he do? He had to control the situation. Not let the killer do it. That sicko was out to hurt her, and the only way Matthew knew how to keep that from happening was by keeping her with him. He had planned to take her to a safe house and guard her 24-7, but when the captain wouldn't approve the expense, since he hadn't given them anything but speculation and theory so far, Matthew decided to hide her out at his place. Marie Boudreaux, his friend and a cop, agreed to help him out. She would stay at his place, too, so the woman wouldn't feel threatened by only the two of them being there. It was for the best. Now he just had to figure out the best way to tell her without spooking her. He wasn't sure he liked it any more than she probably would, but he had no choice. He couldn't let the killer get to her again, and Matthew would take whatever means necessary to prevent that from happening.

"For what? Is she under arrest? It was an accident," Amanda said, apparently not in full knowledge of the danger her friend was in.

"She's not under arrest. It's for her protection. Her life is in danger."

"Oh." Amanda's tone softened. "Sam, are you sure you want *police* protection?"

Now that was a strange question. Who wouldn't want police protection when they were being stalked by a killer?

He watched a flash of fear in Samantha's eyes as she listened to her friend's question, then Sam glanced at him. Her eyes softened, then she looked back at her friend. "I'll be all right. Thanks for being here for me, Amanda." Sam reached out her hand to her friend.

"Well, you know my number if you need me. Call, and I'll be there." Grabbing her hand, Amanda leaned down and kissed Samantha's cheek.

When Amanda gazed at him, he could feel her sizing him up. *What is it with this woman?*

"You had better keep her safe," Amanda said in a determined voice. "She doesn't need any more pain."

"She'll be fine," he assured her. "I'm gonna keep her safe from the maniac who's been terrorizing her. Trust me."

The blond's brows rose. "I hope we can."

When Amanda left, Matthew asked, "Are you ready?"

Samantha slipped her feet off the side of the bed. "Where are you taking me?"

"To my house."

"To *your* house? Ah-ah, b-but," she stammered, "I don't think that's a wise decision. I could stay at my friend's apartment, or go to my parents." Then she shook her head. "But I don't want to put anyone in danger."

He saw fear in her eyes. . .or was it frustration? Maybe she didn't understand the gravity of her situation. "Your life is in danger. He wants to kill you. Don't you understand? This is the best answer. It'll be a safe house for you to stay at. I'll have a policewoman stay there with you. I'll be in and out. When I'm gone, she'll still be there, plus I'll have guards posted outside. It's for your safety."

She sighed. "Okay, I guess that would work. But what about the composite artist? The one who can take my information, put it in their computer, and come up with a picture?"

"You're understanding it right. And we'll do that. . .soon. I promise. First things first, and that's your safety. Don't you worry."

Chapter 20

Sam watched the detective as they traveled toward south Baton Rouge. *Matthew.* She liked his name. It fit him. The name was strong, masculine, independent, and self-assured, just like the man. Although in the beginning he had reminded her of a fictional character, a television hero, he was now a very real person with a warm, caring side that both surprised and scared Sam at the same time.

Could she trust him? He was a cop. She had learned a long time ago not to trust them. Where were they when her husband physically attacked her? Where were they when Martin committed suicide? Worse, they blamed her. After his death. . .never mind. She didn't even want to go there.

And this policewoman—who was she? Did this woman know Sam's history with the force? Would staying at his place be protection enough for them to get this killer without him getting her first?

The short of it was, in her past experience, cops had proved to be unhelpful. Yet regardless of her past, and now with her present, Sam found herself being physically and emotionally drawn to this man, this policeman. She couldn't understand it.

She couldn't help but study his rugged profile; it drew her like a magnet. Her gaze traced the contours of his face, starting with the notorious single lock of jet-dark hair that religiously fell across his forehead. She then continued her gaze down his profile to his perfectly straight nose with the slightest hint of freckles and paused momentarily at the fullness of his firm lips.

The pounding of her heart mounted. Squeezing her eyes shut, she forced that image away from her mind. The jolt of pain in her head from an action as simple as closing her eyes helped her lose concentration on him for a moment.

They were together for one reason, and one reason only. That was what she needed to keep at the forefront of her mind. She felt an additional comfort in knowing that policewoman would be at his place, too. Thoughts of him had no right in her mind, she vowed, and she would not allow them to come forward again.

He was a cop. That was all she had to remember, and she would be okay. She would repeat it over and over in her brain if necessary, but she would not—she could not—think of him in any other way.

Sam shifted her view as she fought to regain her self-control. The car turned off South Acadian onto Lakeshore Drive, following the curved road around the University Lakes.

"So what is the big plan you have in motion?"

"Another policewoman, dressed in street clothes, wearing

a brown wig matching your hairstyle, was led out of the cubicle next to yours in the emergency room. Two uniformed officers took her to a police car and slowly drove her home. All three went up to your apartment. They'll wait awhile and then she'll change back to uniform. She'll pack you a bag of your clothes and bring them to the station. Officer Boudreaux will bring your bag with her when she comes."

"Pretty smart. Maybe he'll fall for it. . .if he's watching, that is."

"Oh, he's watching."

After various twists and turns, he slowed the car down and eased into a narrow driveway. The house wasn't as large as the neighboring homes, but it was pretty. It resembled an Acadian cottage: white, trimmed with green shutters framing one big window in the front that overlooked a wonderful view of the lake. The driveway led them around to the back of the house.

When the car stopped, Sam climbed out, ready to escape the close proximity. She shouldn't have moved so fast. It made her dizzy. Her head pounded, but that didn't slow her down. She had to get away; she needed some distance between her and the detective. Turning the corner, she headed toward the front of the house.

"Samantha. Wait." He caught up to her. "Stay out of the view from the road. We'll go in the back door. I'm sure we weren't followed. I was watching, but it doesn't hurt to be cautious."

He stopped her just in time, because she had intended to put some major space between them. She had planned to take a very close look at the lake, like at the water's edge. Sam had momentarily forgotten she was in hiding. Slipping back behind the house, she followed him inside.

It was cool in his house, although the afternoon sun had heated the temperatures outside to over 90 degrees. Perspiration had gathered near her hairline, at the edge of the stitches, under the bandage. The cool air against the wetness sent a chill through her body. She shivered slightly.

"Is it too cold for you in here?" Matthew asked as he placed Sam's bag of medicines and papers on the counter in the kitchen. "I think it feels good in here, but I can cut the air down. . .uh. . .up, I mean."

"I'm fine. Thanks."

Turning on the tap water, he started to fill a glass. "Want one? Or something else, maybe? Juice or tea? I could even put on a pot of coffee if you would like. Maybe that would warm you up some."

"Water is fine," she said as she took in the view of the kitchen with its white countertops, cabinets, floors, and miniblinds. Everything was white except the black appliances and cabinet doors. This impressed Sam. The room was immaculate. At a glance through the two doors exiting the kitchen, the rest of the house appeared to be just as clean. Another positive quality.

"You do live here, don't you?" she asked as she reached for the glass of water he handed her.

Matthew scratched his chin. "Hmm. Maybe we're in the wrong house," he said with a touch of humor. "Of course I live here." He chuckled slightly. "This is my home. Why do you ask?"

Her gaze swept around the room one more time. "Sorry."

"Oh, I get it. Because I'm a guy, you thought the place would be dirty. Maybe trashed with dirty clothes thrown around, or crusty dishes stacked in the sink. What can I say? My father taught me to be neat. You might even call me a neat freak." He turned and headed for the hall door. "Come on. Let's get you settled so you can lie down for a while. I want you to make yourself at home, but there are a few rules. You can't go outside. Can't make any phone calls to your parents or Amanda or work. . .he could have tapped into their lines. I doubt it, but we want to be careful. That's about it. Other than that, make yourself at home."

"Whew. After all those instructions, I could use a nap. You wore me out," she said trying to make things light as she smiled. "No, really. I could use a short nap. I'm feeling a little lightheaded." She followed him to a corner room.

"This is the guest bedroom. It has a bathroom connected to it. In there you'll find a new toothbrush, toothpaste, soap, shampoo, and various things you might need. Boudreaux should be here soon, but for the time being, you can sleep in your clothes or use one of my T-shirts."

"My clothes are fine for a nap, but I might take you up on the offer of a T-shirt tonight for use as a nightgown, if she doesn't think to grab my nightclothes."

"No problem. I'll give you time to settle in. I hope you find everything you need. If you don't, let me know." As he started to leave, he turned back. "One more thing. Keep the blinds pulled down on both windows. Marie's taking the bedroom next door to you."

It was late morning, and Sam was very tired. Sure, she slept at the hospital, but it wasn't the same. Besides, the doctor had told her to rest. She thanked him and then looked around the bedroom. Upon closer examination of the windows, she found they were locked. "I'll be fine. Thank you. Do you mind if I take a shower? And then maybe the nap?"

"No. But if you're going to stay up a bit longer, I could put in a call to the station and have you talk to the artist. When you're through, he'll fax us a copy and you can make any corrections or additions to it. We need to get that out of the way, if you're up to it. If not, we'll do it after the nap."

"We can try." As he left her alone, she told herself, "I guess the shower and nap can wait." Sam settled for splashing cool water on her face and washing her hands. Afterward, she ran a brush through her hair, taking it slow near the stitches. Those few things took a little more energy than she thought they would, but she felt better for it. Feeling a little more refreshed, she joined him in the kitchen again.

The next half hour she spent on the phone with the artist, and then Matthew went from an office, which he'd set up in one of his rooms, to the kitchen and back again, checking out the fax as the artist made the necessary changes until it was right. By the third copy, it was what she saw in her mind when she closed her eyes. A slight chill slid down her back. The image was too close for her liking. "I think now I'll go take that hot shower. And the nap will probably be more like a half hour to an hour. I'm really tired."

"Help yourself. You need your rest. Think you could eat a light lunch before your nap? I could fix it while you are showering, if you're hungry that is. Or again, it can wait till after."

Even with an empty stomach, she didn't feel hungry, but she said, "That would be great. Thanks." The nap could wait awhile longer. Who knows? If she waited long enough, it would be nighttime and maybe she would just sleep the night through.

When left to herself, she closed the door that led to the hallway, stepped into the bathroom, and removed her clothes. The only clothes she had were the dirty ones on her, so she hand-washed her undergarments and left them draped over the shower rack to dry.

As she stepped into the shower, she thought about how much she already missed her son and the freedom to come and go as she pleased. "But I'll make it, Lord, as long as You lead me," she prayed as she adjusted the water flow and the temperature. "Keep the detective sharp and objective, so he can catch this man before he hurts anyone else, including me. Keep Marty and Mom and Dad safe, too, and don't let them worry about me." That was the good thing about prayer; it was talking to God. She could tell Him what was on her heart, and she knew He was listening. "In Jesus' name I pray, thank You."

And she was alive. She was blessed. Her life had taken her through tragedy, but the Lord had seen her through it then and He would again.

After a warm shower, Sam slipped her jeans and blouse back on. . .all part of making do. She had wrapped her hair in a towel to keep from getting it wet. That was one thing she couldn't do for the time being. Those stitches needed to stay dry. Removing the towel, she let her hair fall around her shoulders.

No need for shoes. Maybe he would loan her a pair of socks.

She sighed. How long would she be hiding out in Matthew's home? It was a beautiful home with a peaceful feeling. She liked that. Although it was neat and everything was in its place, she felt a warm glow. It was a true home, not a clinic, where you weren't allowed to touch a thing. But she wanted to go home, to bring her son home. Go back to her cocoon.

What if it took more than a day or two for them to catch the guy who was after her? Could she stand being cooped up any longer than that? Being away from Marty that long? And would she get along with Officer Boudreaux?

Sam didn't think she would last long. For one thing, she had her daily routine, and she hadn't noticed any treadmill or workout equipment in his home. Of course, she hadn't seen every room.

Secondly, and the most troubling concern, was: Could she handle being shut up in one place with this good-looking man—correction, cop—whom she found herself attracted to? Even with someone else in the house, he would still be there most of the time, she presumed.

With the greatest of care, she covered the new bandage with her bangs, which in turn hid her old scar, too. Sam had always considered her old scar ugly and cringed at the thought of what waited under the newly bandaged area. She'd know soon enough.

Walking down the hall, she zigged when she should have zagged and ended up in the living room. That was okay by her. Before going to the kitchen, she wanted to see the view of the lake. At night, she presumed it would be beautiful with the moon glistening on the water.

An afternoon view was pretty in its own right. Small

sailboats glided across the lake. People were having fun. Wouldn't that be wonderful? Sighing, she turned and found her way to the kitchen. At the door, she smelled something good but couldn't guess what it was. A growl from deep within let her know she was hungrier than she cared to admit.

"What is that? It smells delicious."

Matthew stood at the stove with his back to Sam. "Broccoli and cheese soup. Have a seat." He ladled two bowls of the hot liquid and then carried them to the table. Already on the table were two empty saucers to set the bowls on and a platter with several small cut sandwiches.

"Aren't you the perfect little chef," she exclaimed. "What an amazing guy you are. Are you sure I can't do something to help?"

"No. You take it easy. I hope this is enough food. The turkey sandwiches have sweet peppers and Philadelphia cream cheese on them."

Sam made a face. "Cream cheese?"

"You don't like it?"

She laughed. "I don't know, but I'll find out. I just figured out I'm ravenous." After blowing on the hot liquid, she sipped a mouthful of soup. "Mmm. This is delicious. I'm not a soup lover either, but I like this," she said as she washed it down with a swallow of iced tea.

"I hope you found everything you needed. It will be better when Marie gets here with your clothes." Glancing at the clock, he added, "That should be in the next hour."

"I admit, I miss fresh clothes after a shower. I can live without my makeup, but not clean clothes."

"I'm gonna give you that T-shirt I promised you, to sleep

in. Just in case."

"Thanks." She wasn't too sure it would be wise to sleep in his clothes. It might bring on some unwanted dreams—or some wanted dreams, for that matter. Either way, she wasn't looking forward to it.

At the table, Matthew kept the conversation light, which pleased Sam. She didn't feel like facing all the problems that surrounded her. Not yet anyway.

She loved the tang of the sweet peppers mixed with the cream cheese, as well as the stories Matthew told of his early days of being a cop. Nothing like Martin's early days. Martin had found nothing pleasurable in them, whereas Matthew found the joy and the thrill of good conquering bad. And the stories about his dad and his partner, Greg, kept her amused.

Taking another bite, she asked, "What is the funniest case you recall working on as a uniformed policeman?"

Matthew thought for a moment. "I know. There was a stolen horse rumored to be in hiding in Louisiana. . .of all places. I helped track him down. The jockey suspected of tampering with the horse before each race was believed to have arranged the horse's disappearance.

"The horse was our only proof. We had to find it. Besides, it wasn't just any old horse. This one had won several races, and the owner planned to race her in the Kentucky Derby. Like I said before, they had tracked the horse thief to Louisiana—to be more precise, Baton Rouge—and thus the case entered our department. The thief didn't give up easily. He went down fighting, venting most of his anger on me. I ended up in a pit of fertilizer, thanks to him."

Sam watched as Matthew made a horrible face, recalling

the incident. She didn't know talking about things involving policemen could make her smile, but somehow the detective did that very thing.

"Luckily for me, it ended well. The thief helped us put away the jockey. So everything, including the way I smelled, was worth it. I laugh about it now, but at the time, trust me, it wasn't funny," he said as he shook his head. "I didn't think I'd ever get the stench out of my hair and my skin. It took several baths. In fact, the odor was so deeply imbedded in my pores, I had to soak in a tub of vinegar and water." He laughed. "And my clothes, yuk. I gave up on them totally and threw them out with the trash."

Sam burst out laughing. "Oh. Ow. Oh," she mumbled between the bouts of laughter. She couldn't stop herself. Tears streamed down her face. "I can't believe it. Did the owner offer to repay you for your loss?"

A shocked look swept over Matthew's face. "I didn't tell him and dared the other guys to say a word to anyone." He laughed some more. "Besides, it was all in the line of duty."

Once the laughing faded, she stood and started clearing the table. "In the line of duty," she whispered more to herself than aloud.

Matthew stopped laughing. "Unfortunately, the work we do is not always funny; in fact, very little of it is. Sometimes you see a lot of death. Some cases more gruesome than others. That was hard at first." He helped clear the table.

And policemen turn hard and cold. . .and vindictive. Martin did.

"Some handle it better than others," he said.

That was for sure. Of course, Sam knew Martin's problem

went deeper than the typical reaction of a burned-out cop, but that didn't make it any easier to accept. It made it easier to forgive, but not easier to accept. According to his mother, his problems went back to his childhood. His father was an abusive man.

Enough of that. She didn't need to be thinking about Martin or her problems in the past. The past needed to be forgiven and forgotten. She had been working on it. She was sure she had forgiven, but the forgotten didn't seem to be happening. Now was a perfect time to lay them at the foot of the cross and leave them there. For Marty's sake, as well as her own, she needed to do that. And with her life in danger, she needed to be concentrating on the here and now.

"You are so right," she agreed.

Chapter 21

You go make yourself comfortable in the living room. Maybe you can take that nap you've been wanting, or go to your room for the nap. I'll do the dishes," he said as he stacked the few dirty dishes on the counter near the sink.

"But I can help."

"Go. You've done enough. Remember, you're the one who was hurt. Try and rest so you can get your strength back. It's probably time to take a dose of your medicine anyway, and it will probably help you sleep," he said as he opened the container and dropped two pills in his hand. He then handed them to her and picked up her glass of iced tea. "More tea, or would you rather have water to swallow them down with?"

She didn't argue. "Tea's fine. Thanks." It wouldn't have done her any good, and she knew it. She took the pills and then made her way to the living room. In there, she snapped on the television set. Perfect timing. With two flips of the remote control, she locked the set on *Remington Steele*.

Sam sat on the couch, leaving the recliner for Matthew, guessing it to be his favorite chair. Not realizing how exhausted she was or how quick the medicine would work, she nodded off while watching another rerun of Laura and Mr. Steele solving yet another case together.

When she woke, the room had darkened. She found herself covered with a light blanket. *How sweet of Matthew.* In her mind she called him by his given name, but then corrected herself. *The detective.* Slowly she sat up and listened for a noise in the house.

Nothing. Without making a sound, she got up and wandered around from room to room. The kitchen was empty. Cutting back through the living room, she strode down the hall, and then turned to the left this time. A light shone from the far end. She heard voices coming down the hall also, although they were kept low. She couldn't make out what they were saying, but she knew the policewoman had arrived. As she came closer to the light near the end of the hall, she noticed a clacking sound as well.

"So there you are," she said as she stepped inside. "Hi," she added, speaking in Officer Boudreaux's direction. The policewoman was sitting on a chair near a tabletop that looked almost like a sketching table but had various pictures and notecards strung across it. She immediately started turning the pictures facedown but kept her eyes on Samantha. At a glance, Sam noticed the woman was long and slender...petite in a way. How could she help protect Sam and Marty from this lunatic? But under closer scrutiny she saw the strength in her arms and the assuredness in her stature.

Matthew introduced the two. After turning over the last picture, the officer extended her hand. "Please call me Marie."

When the woman faced her, Sam also noticed the wisdom in her dark brown eyes. Her hair was short but stylish. In her line of work, it had to be easier to deal with. "Thanks for coming, Marie. This is strange for me, to be staying in a stranger's home. . .away from my son. And I'm taking you from your home. I'm truly sorry."

"Make no apologies. I'm here to serve and honored to be able to help."

Samantha thanked her before turning her attention to the detective and his room. "What are you working on?" she asked as her gaze darted around the room. His office at home looked organized—everything in its place. Not one thing appeared out of order. Behind him was a bulletin board with eight-by-ten pictures in two separate groupings. One had several pictures of women. . .dead women by the looks of them. The other group had a young girl in the middle, and other pictures circled around the one with notes below each picture.

Matthew stopped typing on his keyboard and looked toward the doorway. "We're going over the evidence, and I'm typing up a few notes."

Answering the question, yet not giving details. Good way to avoid answering her question. He seemed good at dancing around the questions. Then he tossed out a couple questions of his own. "How are you feeling? Did you get enough rest?" His fingers pressed two buttons, and the screen went black. Switching it off, he stood and walked toward her. "Can I get you something? A glass of tea? Cookies maybe? Let's all go to the kitchen."

She shook her head. He wasn't going to get out of it that easy. She wanted to know. "I'm fine. Thanks. I don't need anything. What exactly are y'all doing?" She took a tentative step into the room toward the drawing table. The notecards were still turned up. Maybe she could read a couple of them.

"Like I said, we're rehashing what we know on the serial killer. . .what evidence we do have. Noting a few observations that fresh eyes see. Since Officer Boudreaux—I mean, Marie—is going to be working closer on this case, I wanted to familiarize her with what we do have. Get her up to par on the case. And this is my work room at home. Work doesn't stop just because I'm not at the office. I keep the same pictures and notes up on my boards at home as I do at work so I can keep my mind on top of everything."

Pointing toward a wall of pictures, he continued, "This is another case I'm working on right now. A young girl was murdered, and I'm closing in on the killer. The way I work, putting everything out in front of my eyes, helps me solve the case, but please don't get close to them. You don't need to be seeing some of this stuff. Even the pictures involving your case. Let us do our job, and you just get well."

"Go back to whatever you were doing, and I won't bother you," Sam said. Glancing around, she wondered what all he had on that serial killer. What had he learned about him through the other crimes? Did he have anything on the man who had been following her? She knew that, before her, no one had lived to give a description. But had they found other fibers with DNA, like the crime shows on TV talked about?

She saw a copy of the description she had given the artist in view on the board with the dead women. Dread swept through her. Turning away, she realized she really didn't want to see anything in relation to her case right now.

"That's okay. We need to take a break anyway." He yawned and stretched as he rose. Quickly, he walked Sam away from the room and steered her down the hall. Marie followed closely behind them.

"There is something I learned today that I need to share with you, but I've been putting it off."

Did she want to listen, to hear something on her case? She took a staggered breath. Yes. She wanted to get her life back, and if he found more to get her life back to normal, she was ready. "Great. Let's sit in your living room. Okay?" She liked the comfort of his sofa. She'd sit there and hold the blanket across her knees. Maybe she could hold on a little longer to that feeling of peace as she listened.

"Great." They made their way toward the living room as he said, "One of my snitches told me he heard a guy at one of the bars bragging about chasing some woman and putting the fear of God in her. He said the man wasn't very old himself and claimed to be taking out some kind of revenge on her. My snitch says his whole face lit up with pleasure as he spoke about it."

Sam stopped midstep as nausea threatened her. Spinning on her heel, she said, "How sick! He brags about it?" It would take more than a comfortable sofa and a warm blanket to feel safe from that sick man.

"I showed him our sketch of the guy." Matthew touched her shoulders lightly as he turned her back around and eased her again down the hall toward the living room. "My snitch said it could be the same guy."

"You left for a while today?" She had slept thinking she was in his safe protection, and he wasn't even there.

"Not even an hour. And it was after Marie arrived. Your nap was almost four hours long. And don't worry; the house was watched, front and back. You were safe and sleeping like a baby." His eyes searched Sam's eyes. Worry crossed his face as he glanced in Marie's direction.

Maybe it was a sign from him for her to leave the room because almost immediately she said, "I'm going to take you up on that offer and go pour me some tea, if you don't mind. Either of you care for any?" Both Sam and the detective shook their heads, so she left them alone in the living room in pursuit of her tea.

For some reason the fact he had left bothered Sam. Since she was staying at his house, she presumed they would be together constantly. She presumed when he said he was going to be protecting her, he would be around her all the time. But of course that couldn't happen. The detective wouldn't be able to do his job if he stayed with her constantly. Besides, he had told her that was one of the reasons Officer Boudreaux was staying there. The other, of course, was because he was a moral man or at least knew she would feel better with another woman around. Anything to keep her safe from that sicko.

She grimaced. She didn't even want to think about that crazy man or her situation anymore. Not now. Not at this moment anyway. She shivered as she walked over to the big picture window and gazed out upon the peaceful lake. She needed a change of thought, a change of scenery, to disperse the coldness she felt inside, to combat the fear that threatened to consume her. *Give me peace, Lord.*

"It's pretty impressive. The view that is," he said softly as he stopped directly behind her.

With low lighting in the room, she felt safe and out of sight. The scene displayed in front of her took her breath away. It was better than she had imagined earlier. The moon sparkled on the water, throwing a pathway of diamonds in front of her. It was quiet and serene, allowing peace to settle over her. An answered prayer.

Maybe she could put her trust in this cop, this man, and in Officer Boudreaux. Marie didn't seem to have prefixed feelings of dislike for Sam. Maybe the woman hadn't been around three years ago and didn't know Sam and Martin's history. *Lord, You brought them into my life for a reason, and I'm going to trust them because I trust You.*

"Do you like it?" The detective's question came almost in a whisper.

She nodded without turning her head. "It paints a picture of serenity. In your type of work, dealing with crooks and killers, the bad side of life, I imagine it helps you to stop along the way and get your bearings."

"This view was the reason I kept the house after my father died. When I'm stuck on a case, I find myself standing here thinking, and before I know it, pieces start to fall together. It puts my mind at ease, helps me get my sense of direction."

"I wish it would give me the missing pieces right now. The who and why." She sighed.

"We'll figure out the who. The why is because you saw enough to put him away for a long time."

They both stood a moment or two in a comfortable, compatible silence. Then she broke it. "If I didn't know better, I'd say the world was at peace at this very moment. Too bad it can't last."

Matthew laid his hands gently on her shoulders. "It is, for now anyway, but you probably shouldn't stand in front of this window."

Marie walked in, clearing her throat at the time. "Sir, Ms. Cain, you sure neither of you want some of this tea? There's more hot water in the kettle. I can go make another cup or two."

Sam shook her head.

Matthew said, "No thanks. Let's sit." He led Sam to the sofa, and Marie sat at the other end. Matthew took the recliner but didn't lay back in it. When they sat, he asked, "Tell us about your job. What exactly does a dispatcher do? Shouldn't a man work the late shift?"

Her claws threatened to show themselves, an automatic reaction of hers, especially when the question was asked in the tone he used. She glanced at Marie. Surely she, as a woman, had dealt with these same caveman feelings before. Men are big. They handle the tough jobs. "Why? Do you think a man would do a better job?"

Marie smiled but said nothing as her eyes rested, amused, on the detective. It was like she couldn't wait to see how he handled Sam's question. Good. Marie was on her side. Sam had figured as such.

"No, not a better job. I just thought at night like that, with the creeps in this world, it might be safer if a man worked that shift."

Marie interrupted. "I think Ms. Cain has been through this type of discussion before. Am I right?"

"Yes. And please, call me Sam." Her claws slid back into place as she said reluctantly to the detective, "Possibly true, but you won't get me to admit it. Besides, I've worked the night shift for a couple of years now and haven't had a problem I couldn't handle. . .until now," she added.

"I believe that. How about you, Boud. . .uh, Marie. I'm gonna have to get used to calling you by your first name. Sorry. But Samantha, I didn't mean to offend you. I'm a cop. That's how I think. I believe people should always do things a certain way, and of course," he glanced from one woman to the other and then finished his sentence, "that way is my way."

They all laughed.

Shaking her head, she backed off on her attitude. "I'm sorry. I don't mean to get so defensive. I've already argued this with Martin in the beginning, my parents, and with several drivers who believe a woman's place is in the home."

"For the record, Marie, her husband was a policeman. He died a few years ago."

"Sorry. I didn't know." Marie smiled apologetically in Sam's direction.

Matthew leaned back against the chair. "So you don't think a woman should be at home, playing Mama?" He tossed his head slightly in the policewoman's direction. "She probably agrees with you."

Sam shrugged. "I didn't say that. But no, I don't think that's where a woman has to be. Sure, at some time in her life a woman might choose that, but while she's working, she should do whatever she wants to do. If she can manage a family at the same time and wants to, great. But most homes today need the woman to work."

"She got you there, sir." Marie laughed. She was clearly enjoying watching them volley remarks back and forth.

"Think about this. If a man had been in the office the other night, right now you wouldn't be in danger, and you wouldn't have to hide out here to be safe."

"Back at you, Sam. He's right there." Marie's grin seemed to be growing by the minute.

Sam looked away as her mind stated, *And I wouldn't have gotten a chance to know you.* Immediately she shook that idea out of her head. "It would just be him instead of me."

"I doubt that," Marie said.

"A man wouldn't have even noticed the scream, or if he had, he would have thought it was a cat fight and forgotten about it," said Matthew.

Marie shook her head in agreement with the detective.

"We don't know that for sure. Besides, it was your idea for me to hide out here," Sam reminded him quickly. "You're the one who said I needed protection and decided to take it on yourself. I don't have to stay." Her whole body stiffened. She wanted to get up and run out of the room. The last thing she wanted to be for anyone was a burden.

"That's not what I'm saying. I know you're not here because you want to be. What I'm saying is that if you hadn't gotten involved, you wouldn't be hiding out, and it wouldn't be necessary for me to keep you safe. Why did you go across the levee? Did you truly think you could save her?"

"Well, yes and no. Although I've taken several self-defense classes, I knew I couldn't hurt that big man, but I thought I could slow down the process at least long enough for help to get there. And as far as you having to keep me safe, nobody asked you to become my protector." She jumped to her feet; her head spun slightly at the sudden movement. "I can take care of myself," she threw at him as she stumbled around Marie's feet, then fled the room. Sam didn't need his help—or anyone else's, for that matter—nor had she asked for it.

By the time she reached the bedroom, Matthew was right on her heels. "I think you misunderstood me. . .again."

"I think I read you loud and clear," she said as she stepped into the bathroom. Sam snatched her underthings off the shower curtain rod, balled them up, then stuffed them in her pants pocket. Her bag was on the bed, so she grabbed it. Now to call for a taxi.

When she turned to head to the kitchen, the dizzy sensations tried to overcome her. She spared not a glance at him as she started to walk around him, standing in the middle of the bedroom that was to be hers for the duration of her stay. Maybe Marie would take her home. She'd ask her.

"Samantha," he pleaded as he took her by the shoulders, stopping her from leaving the room. Turning her to face him, he slipped her hands in his to prevent her from pulling away. "Look at me. I wasn't complaining." His expression had softened, but that was beside the point.

She looked down, trying not to take in the emotion she saw in his face. "You could have fooled me. It sounded that way." She kept her eyes averted to the floor, not ready to look him in the eyes, especially this close.

When she didn't look up, he dropped her hands and lifted her chin toward him. Cupping her face in his hands, he said,

"I'm glad you're staying here. I know I shouldn't admit that, nor should I say it. But had it not happened when it did, we would have never met. . .I mean, gotten to know each other better. I'm just sorry your life had to be put in danger." Lowering his voice to a whisper he added, "I'm also scared something could happen to you. I don't want that."

Sam didn't say a word. He was doing it again. Her pulse raced. The throbbing at the base of her neck was about to explode. His clear blue eyes flashed silver sparks. Had his words been a slip of the tongue, or was he really glad they had a chance to get to know one another?

What did it matter? She had to quit being sidetracked by his looks, his personality, and his so-called concern for her.

"You do realize the guy may be ready to end your life? Sure, he's toying with you now, but death could be at the end of his plan." His eyes seemed to caress her as he moved ever so slightly closer. "I can't let him get near you. The next time you might not be so lucky."

Sam swallowed hard. Her gaze darted to his eyes, then to his lips and back again. Her mind had been heading in this direction for the past couple of days. . .and now it was there. She wet her lips. She wanted him to kiss her. Her breath caught in her throat as she waited what seemed like an eternity.

Gently his hands cradled her face; his thumbs brushed her cheeks. "I shouldn't. . .I shouldn't be doing this."

She closed her eyes.

"But I want. . .I want—" His lips came down on hers.

The wonderful pressure of his mouth against her lips weakened her knees. She couldn't resist and kissed him back.

What was she thinking? She didn't do this. Kiss a man she

barely knew. Kiss a man period. . .let alone a cop. Then it hit her. She was scared, scared for her life.

As if he heard her question, Matthew stopped kissing her and pulled away slightly. "I'm sorry. I shouldn't have done that. I'm supposed to be protecting you, not taking advantage of you."

She looked him in the eye, swallowed hard, but didn't say a word.

He couldn't tell her she had been a distraction to him from the first moment he'd laid eyes on her. Sure, he knew who she was and what she was supposed to be like, but nothing she had done since they met backed up anything Martin had told him over three years ago.

His thoughts flashed on what might have happened, had he not stopped them. What if Martin had been telling the truth? What if she was setting him up? He exhaled. He didn't know the truth. Confusion twisted in his gut. He shoved his hands through his hair again as he remembered what had become of Martin. He didn't need to get involved with this woman. He only needed to protect her so he could get close to the killer. So why tempt fate?

"You're right. This shouldn't have happened. I haven't even kissed a man since Martin. I'm sorry. It didn't mean anything. I know that. I've been so scared these past couple of days."

He thought for a moment. If Martin had been telling the truth, it meant something. It meant she was up to something, trying to manipulate him just like she had done Martin. "All that matters right now is that I'm on a case, and my job is to protect you, not become involved with you."

He looked deep into her eyes, watching, wishing he knew what she was thinking. Was the past the truth? Or was she a different person than Martin had painted? Matthew just couldn't be sure.

But he did know that he had a job to do, and that was what he had to keep first and foremost in his mind. "I'm a cop. Let me do my job," he said, backing away slightly.

Matthew's words brought Sam back to reality, like a slap in the face. It was just a kiss. What had gotten into her? She thought earlier it was fear, but she wished she knew.

"Good idea. Go do your job."

He reached out and touched the side of her face. "Don't worry. You're safe. I'm not going to let anything happen to you. And I won't kiss you again. Sorry. That shouldn't have happened. It sounds like Marie turned on the television. Let's go watch a little TV. Then maybe you'll be able to get some more rest. I'll go get your medicine. It's time to take some more."

She turned away, putting space between them. "I'll get my medicine. You just do your job."

His words had sounded sincere, but down deep she knew they were not the words she really wanted to hear. As much as she told herself she didn't want a cop around, didn't need a cop, she knew, this man, this cop, had moved into her heart, and there was no getting him out now, whether she wanted to or not.

Chapter 22

The next morning, Matthew left Samantha with Marie so he could check with Jake, another one of his informants, and see if he picked up on anything new. Matthew had officers staked out in the front and back of his home, still making sure no one could enter. She would be safe.

Driving slowly through downtown and along the river, Matthew watched for any sign of Jake. It wasn't long before he found his snitch begging on the streets.

"It's always women you beg from Jake," Matthew mumbled under his breath as he eased into a parking spot along the curb. Maybe his informant believed women felt more pity, which was probably true. And his looks and youth didn't hurt when he turned his charm onto these older women who visited the city.

Matthew didn't wait for Jake to finish panhandling as he bumped his horn a few times, catching the snitch's attention.

When Jake gave up and walked over to the car, Matthew pushed the passenger door open. "Get in. Didn't mean to interfere with your work," he said with a touch of sarcasm.

The snitch pulled a handful of cash from his pocket, spread it out, and waved it in front of him like a handheld fan. "That's okay. I'm doing good today. Whoever said the South was full of friendly people knew what they were talking about." Jake slipped the wad back into his pants pocket. "I guess you're here to find out if I got any information for you."

Matthew nodded.

The bum wet his lips in anticipation and, with a greedy glint in his eyes, rubbed his forefingers against his thumbs. "So, what's in it for me?"

"As long as people continue to give you handouts, you're never going to try to get back in the game of life, are you?"

Jake smirked. "Why work when you ain't got to?"

Matthew realized Jake found his new life too easy. In fact, it wasn't even new anymore. The man had been on the streets for two years. Matthew almost felt sorry for his snitch but knew deep down the man had quit caring. He had lost his job, his home, and then his wife and children. Swallowing what little pity he had left for the man, Matthew said, "Tell me what you found out, and I'll pay you what it's worth. I've always been fair."

The bum shrugged. "Okay. It's like this. The guy you're looking for stays at one of those run-down motels a few blocks from here. Not sure which one, though. Rumor is, he has family here but for some reason doesn't associate with them. His boat is scheduled to pull off at the end of the week, but last night he claimed he had unfinished business to tend to before he left town again. Sometimes the guy hangs out at the bars downtown. That's where he's been mouthing off anyway, at The French Door and The Moonlighters."

"Why didn't you call headquarters when you saw him last night?" Anger started to burn within Matthew at the missed golden opportunity.

"Wasn't sure how long he'd stay and whether I had time to leave and go call you. Besides, I didn't have a quarter. I made all that money you saw today."

Squeezing his fingers around the steering wheel, Matthew tried to control his temper. Once he felt he had it under control, he continued. "What did he look like? Can you ID him? Did you find out his name or what boat he worked on?"

Scratching the stubble on his dirty face, Jake said, "Last night they called him Buddy or Bobby. Something like that. I'm not sure." He shrugged. "Never got a good look at him. The bar was dark. He's bigger'n me. I saw that."

That wasn't saying much, because Jake was small for a man. "How much bigger is he?"

The snitch shrugged. "About a head and a half taller. He's probably about six foot. But that's a guess. Could be more. And the boat he works on, who knows? There're so many. All I know is, he's gonna do something before he leaves Friday night."

Matthew wished Jake had more information, but at least he could have the two bars staked out and check the ships scheduled to leave at the time Jake had said.

"Okay, Jake." Matthew pulled out two twenties and one of his cards. On the back, he jotted down his cell number. "If you hear anything, I mean *anything*, or see him, call me right away.

If I'm not at the station, you can reach me by my cell. Here's a couple of quarters. Don't spend them. Save them to call me. Time is running out."

Jake's eyes widened at the two twenties. "Sure. Thanks." He stuffed the money and the card in his shirt pocket, then dropped the coins in his pants pocket. As quick as he could, he opened the door and jumped out of the car.

Matthew watched as Jake disappeared around the corner. Rubbing his jaw, Matthew thought about his next move: finding Freddy, the derelict, who slept in front of the old motels downtown. Sometimes, the bum even found a way to slip into one of the rooms for a full night's sleep. Maybe Freddy knew more than Jake.

As Matthew drove around slowly, looking for Freddy, he remembered bits and pieces of last night. The confused look on Samantha's face focused clearly in Matthew's mind.

"Oh, Samantha," he murmured.

Once again he tried to fight his attraction to Samantha. He reminded himself what she had put Martin through and where he had ended up. If Matthew was smart, he wouldn't want the problems that came with knowing that woman. . .that is, *if* what Martin said was true. Doubt jolted through him.

He tried to brush off his attraction to Samantha Cain as pure physical attraction, but he knew it was more than that. Every time he turned around, something about her touched his heart. The way she handled herself with the drivers. The way she cared for the woman over her own well-being. The way her friends rallied to her side. That was the kind of woman a man could fall for easily. If he let himself. . .but he wouldn't.

Not him. Even if Martin had totally lied about her, look at her. Her life was in jeopardy now. Three years ago it was a mess. She could be the one causing all the problems in her life. She was the one who ran out and straight into trouble. How many people run toward a scream? Most run away. And even if she wasn't causing the problems, Matthew reminded himself, if he focused on his feelings for her, he would be putting her and her son in a constant state of possible danger. And that would be his fault. That was the reason he steered clear of serious relationships with women in the past. Why change now?

Closing his eyes, he realized he couldn't bear it if something happened to Samantha. Not now. Not ever. He could tell himself until the cows came home that Martin knew her better than he ever could, but Matthew knew that wasn't true. Knowing how he would feel if something happened to her told him something he didn't want to know—or admit. He had already fallen for her.

What did it matter? He knew he wasn't good material for any woman looking for a serious relationship anyway, because his job was such a dangerous one, plus it had the odd hours. No woman in her right mind would get mixed up with a cop. Not much free time. No regular hours. Go whenever the case demanded. Basically, he was on twenty-four hour call.

This morning over breakfast they had eaten in strained silence. The only one who had really talked was Marie, and she tried to force conversation throughout. None of them had spoken of what had happened the night before. Marie didn't know the whole situation, and Matthew would keep it that way. As for him and Samantha, they probably needed to talk, but right now that couldn't be his number-one concern. Now he needed to concentrate on keeping her alive and catching the man who was after her, the man who had already killed three women. . .three that he knew of. There could have been more elsewhere. He was checking into that, too. The guy could have started these attacks years ago and worked up to murder. Who knew? That was what he intended to find out.

"Safety," he said. "That is what I'll do today. I'll take her to the firing range. Let her practice shooting."

He caught up with Freddy at the old Capitol-Heights Inn, which was closed down, badly in need of repairs. With the casinos on the riverfront, old hotels were being remodeled and made like new. It was only a matter of time before this one would be fixed up as well.

Freddy was in one of his drunken stupors, so he was of no help. Next, Matthew ran down some information on another one of his cases, then slipped by the station. He managed to get more copies of the sketch made and passed around at the station. Every once in a while he caught himself looking back at that sketch. Something about it, about *him*, felt familiar.

Matthew discussed the new developments of the case with Davis and Shelton. After much deliberation, he and the two assisting officers arranged a stakeout at each of the bars downtown and organized a follow-up on the boats to interview the deckhands scheduled to leave port on Friday at midnight. With the aid of a computer, they ran a comparison of those boats with the dates of the incidents and determined which ones were docked at the time and which weren't.

A list of workers scheduled to go out on the boat, along

with the sketch of the assailant, would give them a list of possible suspects, and then a team of officers would be dispatched to pick up and bring them in for questioning. In that group, they should find the pervert.

Satisfied he'd done all he could for now, Matthew headed home, watchful of his surroundings, making sure he wasn't being followed. Pumped and alert, his adrenaline soared. Each moment drew him closer to catching the killer. Time was near. His nerves tingled with anticipation. He was about to catch his killer. Matthew couldn't wait to get the crew members in for interrogation. The rap sheets alone could probably single out the man.

"Probably not," he corrected himself, mumbling. The serial killer had been very careful so far.

Matthew turned into his driveway, still scanning the neighborhood for anything out of the ordinary. *Nothing. Good.* Using his cell, he checked in with both officers and relieved them so they could go back to the station.

The back door was locked, so he unlocked the door and let himself into the kitchen. Intense quiet filled the room as an odd feeling crept over him. He set his briefcase down on the counter.

Samantha, where are you? And Marie, where are you? Your car is still here. He wanted to scream their names out loud but restrained himself. Instead his eyes sharpened as his gaze darted around the room, and his ears honed in on the slightest sound in the house.

His training and experience took over. Quietly he slipped his gun out of his shoulder holster and released the safety. Without making a sound, he slipped in and out of each room, searching them quickly. Had she taken off? Decided she couldn't trust him after all? Or had the nutcase found her? Fear ate at his gut. How could his men not have seen her slip out, or the killer slip in? No. Marie wouldn't have let her. This made him more nervous. What if the killer had slipped in unnoticed? Taken Marie down by surprise? He would have Sam to himself. He could be toying with her now, torturing her. Matthew took a deep breath. This killer was sick, not smart. He wouldn't have been able to slip in unnoticed, Matthew told himself as he continued from room to room.

The rooms were empty. No noise came from any part of the house. No television sounded, nor did he hear a stereo playing. He didn't even hear the sound of running water.

In her room, the bathroom door stood open a good foot or two. No one was in there. His senses heightened, he glanced in Marie's room. It appeared to be in order.

Down the hall, Matthew peeked into his office, thinking maybe she was snooping around at his notes and the pictures while Marie studied the case file more. He wouldn't like that, well the part about Samantha looking into the case more. . .seeing the brutality the killer used on those women, but he almost prayed that was what she was doing. It beat the alternative.

Nothing. His anguish intensified. Where were they? Quickly, he glanced in his room as he passed it. No one was in there either. He moved to the back room of the house. Opening the door slowly, he peered around the doorframe, then breathed a sigh of relief.

There they were. Samantha was exercising with earphones covering her ears and Marie was walking the treadmill with pictures spread across the front. Her eyes darted up, and her hand drew her Glock instantly. He clicked the safety back into place on his own weapon and then slipped the gun in its holster.

Marie lowered her weapon. "Gheeze, Louise. You took a chance coming in so quietly. Why didn't you say something, sir? I could have blown you away."

He shook his head, thankful nothing had happened to either of them. "Samantha!" he bellowed.

She stopped midstep, her face flushed. "You're back early," she said as she removed the headphones from her ears. "I thought you said you'd be in late this afternoon. I hope you don't mind. I borrowed a pair of your gym shorts I found on top of the dryer. Marie didn't know I'd be up to a workout so she didn't bring any of my workout clothes."

"She said the doctor told her she could go back to her routine activities if she felt up to it. I hope you don't mind we helped ourselves to your workout room."

Words caught in his throat. He wanted to yell and scream at both of them, especially Samantha for scaring him so badly, but couldn't. No words formed. Mixed emotions stormed within. Glad she was safe. Well, glad they were both safe, but angry that they had put him through unnecessary worry, unnecessary torment—not that Samantha had even known what she had done. Marie, on the other hand, had seen him enter with his gun drawn and probably read the look on his face. But not Samantha. He would keep her in the dark as far as how she made him feel.

"What's wrong?" she asked as her eyes searched his face. "You look as if you've seen a ghost."

Matthew swallowed a lump in his throat before speaking. "I thought for a second or two you had gone. Decided to protect yourself." He didn't tell her any more than that. Didn't let her know the real fear he had felt and hoped she couldn't read his emotions.

The look on her face, an expression of guilt, told him more than he wanted to know. He realized immediately she had thought about leaving. That thought was like a sharp stab in the heart, but he didn't try to understand why. He didn't want to know why that knowledge hurt. He pushed that reality, the fact she wanted to leave, to the back of his mind.

Suddenly, looking at her standing there, glistening in sweat and perspiration, another thought took the place of his last one. She might have thought about leaving, but she didn't.

That touched him, but he didn't dare let her know. No. Some things he had to keep to himself. He had to get a handle on his feelings before even a hint of what he might be feeling was made evident.

"I got through early and decided we are going to the firing range if you're up to it. Obviously, if you're exercising, you must feel pretty good."

"Working out helps me think clearer." Sam wiped the sweat off her neck and face and then tugged at her bangs. "Besides, it makes me feel better. I promise, I'm not overdoing it. You'd be amazed how much energy was zapped out of me. By the way, I made a long-distance call. I'll—"

"What? You're not supposed to let anyone know you're here. You're hiding out, remember!" Anger started to build in him as his fists tightened into two balls. Was she trying to get herself killed? Why couldn't she follow simple instructions?

"It was my folks. Don't worry. I didn't tell them anything, only that Amanda and I were heading down to New Orleans for a couple of days so they wouldn't worry about me. And I didn't stay on the line but a minute. I remembered what you had said. Marie, tell him. I did it the only way she would let me."

"She did good, boss. Don't worry."

"Oh." He ran his hand through his hair. Maybe no harm was done. He hoped. Scratching the back of his neck, he added, "Do you feel up to practicing your shooting?"

"I learned how to shoot a gun a long time ago. My daddy took me out to the country and made me learn. However, I believe a gun is dangerous in the hands of those who don't know what they are doing. So I keep mine in the top drawer of my dresser, tucked out of sight."

"Well, I'm going to see that you know what you're doing," he said as he arched his brows. What was he going to do with this woman? "You may not care to use a gun for protection, Samantha, but with your job, as well as the odd hours, it wouldn't hurt to know a little bit more about how to protect yourself with a gun. At least enough to feel confident with a gun."

"Besides, it could come in handy in the situation you are in now. Wouldn't you rather know you could protect yourself if you needed to?" Marie asked.

"I can defend myself." Sam turned the radio off and placed it on the shelf behind his weight table. "I've taken courses to be sure I could. Maybe not with a gun, but—" She couldn't continue. Turning worried eyes upon him and lowering her voice to a whisper where only Matthew would hear, she said,

"Truthfully, I'm afraid of guns. Martin killed himself with his own gun. Since then, guns are something I make a point of staying away from."

Choosing to ignore the remark about Martin, he said, "I didn't think you were afraid of anything. Well, no problem. I can help you overcome that fear. I'm going to take you to the firing range." He turned his back on her and walked down the hall.

"I guess that means we're going. You're in charge, and I follow your lead." There was a slight sarcasm in her voice, but only slight, Matthew felt sure.

"Hey, boss. While y'all go there, I think I'll run over to headquarters and finish up some paperwork I need to do. . .if that's okay by you."

"No problem, Marie. That should work out great. I'll give you a ring when we get back to the house. Do either of you want lunch first?" he called over his shoulder. "All that exercise should have built up an appetite."

"I'll catch a sandwich at headquarters."

"I'm not hungry, but I do need to clean up first," Samantha said.

The old Sam was back. He heard it in her voice. He liked the fighter in her, and right now she needed to stay that way.

Chapter 23

In no time at all, they were at the public firing range. Very few people were there, probably because it was the middle of the day. That was fine with Sam. She didn't like guns or the noise they made, but she could use the distraction. The range master took their money and handed them ear protectors.

"Wear these," Matthew said as he put his on. "Your ears will thank you later. Let's go." Matthew led the way.

Placing two guns down on the booth in front of them, along with ammunition, he said, "We're going to start easy and refresh your memory on how to shoot with this .38."

He showed her the proper way to hold a gun, how to aim, and then squeeze the trigger. "Take your time and you can hit your target. Squeeze the trigger slowly." Matthew set up a human silhouette as her target.

"Are those legal?" she asked. "I can see a deer maybe, but a human?"

He gave her a disgruntled look, then placed the silhouette fifteen yards away.

That didn't seem too far to Sam. She shouldn't have any trouble. Sam had seen people shoot on television often enough. It seemed fairly simple when she had been a teenager, although time had passed slightly by since then. She had hit the can her father had set on a tree stump. Of course, it did take about six tries, if she remembered correctly.

She held her arm out straight, took aim, then squeezed. Her hand jerked upward. Sam knew immediately she had missed the target entirely.

So much for what it looked like on television. They practiced for the next couple of hours. By the end of that time, at least she was hitting the flat piece of cardboard. Sam knew of one more thing she hated about guns—the smell that lingered in the air. Gunpowder left a stench that was hard to describe, but one thing was for sure, it stunk worse than a cap gun.

"I'm going to move it in to ten yards now."

Sam read his lips more than heard his words but understood what he told her.

For another hour, she practiced. Only this time, he didn't let her take aim. Instead, he had her hold the gun by her side, safety off. At the drop of his hand, she was to raise the gun, fire three times at the chest, and then they checked to see if she reached her mark. Matthew set up a new silhouette for this exercise.

When he brought the silhouette to them for the last time, he said, "You're getting better. Not bad, in fact."

Matthew's words brought a swell of pride to her chest. It

didn't last long though. His next words ruined it.

"But if you had to use the gun right now to save yourself, I'm not sure what the outcome would be."

Her brows drew together as a frown formed on her lips. She didn't mean to pout but couldn't help herself. "I thought you just said I was doing good?"

"Not bad, really. But we'll have to come back for more practice. Can't learn it all in one day, you know." With thumb and forefinger, he raised her chin and added, "Don't worry. You'll be fine. I'm not going to let anything happen to you." He hesitated as he looked deep into her eyes. "I promise," he whispered.

Sam bit her bottom lip as it started to quiver. His touch alone was enough to make her fall apart, but for him to sound concerned over her well-being, and that voice, so deep and sincere—it was more than she could bear. She thought he had made himself perfectly clear the other night. She wished he would quit confusing her.

Matthew dropped his hand. "You've watched me fill the clip and change it; now I want you to do it." Matthew dropped the clip and emptied the few bullets that were left in it. Handing the empty clip to her, he said, "Give it a try."

Grabbing the black piece of hard plastic and several small bullets, she attempted to do what she was told. By the time she had slid five bullets into the clip, she found it becoming harder with each one. After filling the clip, Matthew showed her how to load it into the gun and remove it. Next, he pointed out the safety and explained the purpose. He taught her to load the first bullet into the chamber. She had to pull the slide, and it automatically fell into place.

To practice this, he had her drop the clip, remove the bullet from the chamber, and start over. After several practices, she did it one more time, set the bullet in the chamber, then put on the safety.

Matthew and Sam picked up their spent casings, then Matthew put the guns safely away into the holsters. Sam watched as he paid the man for the extra targets they used, then turned to her and said, "Let's go."

Sam rode in exhausted silence as Matthew drove toward his home.

"Stay in the car till I signal you to come in. I have to be sure no one has gotten into the house."

She watched as he checked for the tiny piece of thread he'd left in the door at knee level. Matthew had told her about it as they left to go shooting. He said no one ever thought to look down low for something that really wasn't visible. If it was still in place, no one had been there. However, if the thread was missing, someone had opened the door.

In an instant, he whipped his gun out of its holster and glanced around the back yard. It didn't take a genius to read his expression.

"Not again," she cried out to the empty car she was sitting in.

Quickly, with the gun pointed downward, he ran back to the car. "Look in that case on the backseat and pull out the .38. Remember it's loaded."

She nodded.

"Take the safety off and wait. Somebody went in my place, and they might still be here." He peered around the back yard.

Fear rose in her chest. She only hoped it didn't show in her eyes.

"You'll do fine," he reassured her. "Just hold on to the gun while I'm inside checking things out. Do you remember how to hold it?"

She nodded.

He saw her innocence mixed with fear and hated to leave her by herself but had no choice. He never should have let Marie go back to the station. "Good girl. Don't forget to take the safety off and just sit tight while I look around." He leaned through the window and gave her a quick kiss on the lips. Why, he didn't know. "Just don't shoot me when I come back out." He tried to give her a smile of encouragement. On that, Matthew headed back to the house.

As quietly as possible, he opened the door and moved silently from room to room. Nothing seemed disturbed. Matthew checked all the closets, the shower stalls, and anywhere else someone could be hiding. Nothing. Great. Maybe Marie had come back. Maybe she had forgotten something. He'd give her a call and find out.

After a quick phone call to the station, he found out Marie had been there the whole time. "Well, someone came in to the house while we were gone. I'm going to have to move Samantha. I'll give you a call when we settle, and you can come to us. But when you do...make absolutely sure you are not followed. Do you understand me?"

"Yes, sir. No problem. I'll be waiting for your call."

Returning to Sam's side, he said, "Come on. You're going to throw your things in your bag and I'll pack some of mine.

Grab a change for Marie, too. We're going to go somewhere else to stay the night."

She didn't question him, just did as he said. The fear was still strong in her eyes. Her enlarged pupils pulsed as she searched for hidden answers. Her head darted this way and that, not trusting a soul. He wished he could remove the fear from her eyes. . .from her heart.

Before leaving, Matthew grabbed his charger for his cell phone and packed it, too, just in case. He didn't dare miss Jake's call.

When they were both packed, he put the bags in the trunk and got the two of them out of there fast. He drove around, making sure they weren't being tailed.

After riding around for twenty minutes, Sam finally broke the silence. "It looks like we're going in circles. Where are you taking us?"

"I'm making sure we're not being followed." Matthew pulled into the parking lot of a bank and, using the drive-thru ATM machine, withdrew some money from his savings account. Her eyes were full of questions as she watched him put all that money in his wallet.

Before she could ask, he answered her unspoken question. "We don't know how long we'll be staying at a motel, and I don't want to charge the room. That's too easily traced. . .in case he's smart enough to know you are with me."

His eyes continually glanced to the left, to the right, then to the rearview mirror. "I'm making sure no one is tailing us, especially a small black car."

She didn't like seeing the concern in his eyes. It meant she was in danger. He was, too, but she had put him there.

It wasn't fair. Automatically, Sam slid down in the seat, and her eyes darted around, looking for any sign of that black car. How long would they be driving around? *Please find us a place soon. I feel like a sitting duck.* Sam knew Matthew would drive as long as he deemed necessary to keep her safe. "I'll pay you back the money you are spending," she assured him.

He flashed his white teeth at her in a reassuring smile, yet never taking his eyes off the road or their surroundings. "Don't you worry about it. The department will reimburse me."

"If not, remember, I pay my way, and since this is all for me, I will pay back every cent."

He finally pulled into the parking lot of the Red Roof Inn. While he went in to get the rooms, Sam stayed low and waited in the car, again holding the gun as he'd instructed her to do.

He was back in minutes. "Our room's in the back. That way no one can sneak up on us."

She started to question *our room*, but he didn't give her a chance. Nor did she get to ask if Marie would be joining them.

"You'll be safe. No one can trace us here. I signed us in as Mr. and Mrs. Tom Jordan. I told them we would be here for a couple of days."

She wanted to ask why he didn't get each of them a room, but he'd parked the car and was exiting it before she could form the words.

He unlocked the door to the room, and they went inside. *Good.* Her gaze fell on two double beds. At least it wasn't as bad as she thought it would be at first. But in this small room, with no other place to go except the bathroom, could she keep her distance? Surely she wouldn't want to be rejected a second time by this man she had no business even thinking about to begin with.

Yes. Of course she could handle it. She had no choice.

Chapter 24

The minute they were in the motel room with the door closed, Sam found she didn't have to worry about Matthew's intent. He immediately pulled his cell phone out of his jacket, flipped it open, and started punching numbers.

Apparently, making advances toward her was the last thing on his mind. He also made sure she couldn't overhear his conversation by turning his back on her and keeping his voice low.

"Humph," Sam mumbled under her breath as she made a face, shrugged, and turned away from him. Why couldn't he let her hear? It was her life that was in danger.

She sighed. Maybe it wasn't about her. He was the professional. Leaving everything in his hands, she decided to go get cleaned up. It was going to be a long night.

She scooped up her shampoo, conditioner, underclothes,

one of Matthew's T-shirts and her robe, and took them into the bathroom with her. He'd told her to stuff some of Marie's clothes in her bag, too, so the policewoman must be planning to join them. That was good. It would give her someone to talk to, because right now she didn't feel like being sociable to the detective. Turning the hot water on, she waited for the steam to rise before adding cold water to adjust to a perfect temperature.

"A good hot shower. I need that tonight." As the water blasted, she directed the stream of water on the lower part of her face, careful not to hit the stitches. *Yes. Rinse away all that pain and the problems I seem to have in my life. Let me go back to those boring days I used to complain about.*

What she wouldn't give to be living that old routine of life again. But, if she were back into her old life, she wouldn't have gotten to know Matthew Jeffries, nor would she have felt the tingle of excitement that rushed through her when his voice called her name. She would have hated to miss the sparkle in his eyes when he spoke of his work. Sam loved the dedication he showed in his job. Matthew was everything she dreamed a good man would be. Everything she had hoped Martin would be. Sam had stopped believing one existed. . .until now.

The past few years had tarnished her view of men. First Martin and the pain he put her through, then his fellow men in blue and what they had put her through, suspecting her in his death. And, she had to admit, there were a few men she worked with who lived for the day, never worrying about tomorrow. That wasn't what she believed a man or woman should do. Not that she would worry, but she would plan, work for a future for her and her son. God's Word said to worry about nothing and pray about everything. Those words had gotten her through many a tough week.

The problems of today are large enough to worry about, she thought, *but I won't. I'll trust the Lord.* After all, He had sent Matthew and Marie into her life to help save and protect her. Matthew had a good head on his shoulders, and Marie seemed to be in better shape than Sam had given her credit for. She'd noticed when they were working out, Marie had strong biceps and her legs were taut with muscles. She would trust the Lord—and trust Matthew and trust Marie.

Matthew Jeffries seemed different than all those other men. He lived every day to clean the crime out of the city and make tomorrow a better, safer day for the citizens. He believed the world was worth fighting for.

She sighed. Slowly, she washed her aching limbs with soap and water. Pain shot down her arms to the tips of her fingers every time she moved. It was bad enough the headache she already had from the accident, but now, due to all that practice today, her whole body hurt.

Sam didn't remember her hands and arms hurting like this when her father first taught her how to use a gun. But then, she realized, it hadn't been a matter of life and death. When her dad showed her, it was just the basics, and he wasn't worried if she perfected her aim. However, the aftereffects from today left a great deal of strain and pain in her body. Hours of practice had done that to her, but at least now, if necessary, she felt confident she could pull out the gun, fire it, and hit what she was aiming at.

Sam stayed under the spray of water until it turned cold.

The time had come to climb out of the shower and face the detective. Better yet, she would face her attraction to Matthew Jefferies. She should face it and fight it. Yes. She would fight it. . .she hoped.

After drying and dressing, she wrapped the towel around her hair and marched out to face her fate. To her surprise, he wasn't there. Only Marie. Her heart sank. So much for good intentions. But that was a good thing. "Where did he go?"

"He just left. He said he'd be back in a few minutes. Of course, I just got here myself," Marie said.

Frowning, Sam toweled her hair as dry as possible, then started combing the tangles free.

"How did the shooting go? Did you learn more?"

"I think so," Sam said. "I know I hurt in my arms and fingertips. But I'm sure that will pass soon enough."

Marie laughed. "Yes. You'll feel better by morning."

They talked about hair next. Marie told her how she used to leave hers long and hanging, but once she became a cop, she had started braiding it. But it was such a hassle that last year she'd whacked it off and never looked back. She said it saved hours of combing, drying, and fixing. She called it her wash-and-wear do.

By the time the last tangle was out, Sam heard a key turning in the lock of the door. Her heart stopped. She froze. She didn't even try to run for cover in the bathroom. There wasn't enough time. Besides, Marie was right there, and she had already pulled her gun out and had it aimed straight at the door. The woman was fast.

The door opened, and Matthew stepped in. Marie slipped her gun back into her holster.

Sam blew out the breath she had been holding. "You scared me to death." As she started to fuss, her stomach let out a big growl, and her nose knew instantly what was in the bags in his hand. "Food. All right!"

Marie laughed. "You change your moods faster than anyone I know."

Matthew closed the door, locked it behind him, then set the two bags on the dressertop.

"Oh, that smells wonderful. I'm starving."

"I'm glad to see your appetite is back," Matthew said with a smile. "I wanted to wait and see what you wanted to eat, but you took so long in the shower, I gave up and decided to please myself. Marie ate earlier so she's not hungry like us, so she said anything would be fine. I hope you like Popeye's fried chicken."

"Perfect." Sam smacked her lips in anticipation as she sat down on one of the beds, waiting for him to pass her a bag of her own. "Let's eat."

He pulled three boxes from one bag and passed her one, and then Marie. Next, he reached in the other and pulled out a couple of drinks. "I hope you all drink Coke. Forgot to ask you, Marie, before I left. Sorry."

She shrugged. "Fine by me."

Before he sat down with his food, he took a moment to place his cell phone in the charger on the nightstand next to his bed. Seconds later he shrugged off his sport coat, revealing his shoulder holster and gun. He removed them and laid them next to his cell phone. Last but not least, he got his box of food and drink and sat on the side of one of the beds, with his gun in reach.

Matthew turned on the television and started flipping channels. About the time Sam figured out what show they were watching, Matthew changed the station.

"Make up your mind, would you?" she said.

"Yes. Please. You're making me dizzy changing it so fast," Marie said.

"What do y'all want to watch?"

"I don't care. I'm going to take my shower when I finish eating." Marie bit into her chicken without another word.

"It doesn't really matter to me either, but if there's a good cop show or detective. . .never mind." They probably had no desire to watch what they lived every day. "Anything is fine. A comedy. Whatever. Just make a decision, please."

Chapter 25

Matthew hid a smile. She was something else. The more Matthew was with Samantha, the more he liked her, no matter how hard he tried not to. Martin must have had something wrong with himself. Everything the man had ever said about Samantha was proven over and over again to be untrue. She was open and honest, always trying to be fair with everyone around her, even though it was *her life* in danger.

"Here," he said as he tossed the control to her. "You pick. I have some things to go over when I finish eating anyway." He watched the expression on her face change instantly.

"What things?" she asked as her eyes grew big with curiosity. "If I can ask, that is."

Matthew took a bite of a biscuit and washed it down with Coke before answering. "I got word that the sheriff's office called today with some results. They found the truck that was stolen from your yard and lifted some prints." He took a bite of his chicken and started chewing. "Mmm-mmm. Popeye's. They make the best chicken. Spicy. . .just right."

"Don't change the subject. So they found the truck?" All thoughts of food seemed to disappear as she pushed her food aside and rose from the bed. "Great! So now what?"

He hated seeing her get so excited. There was news, but no leads to the perp yet. "The prints matched the set they lifted from your apartment connecting the two crimes, just like I had thought all along. They are all one and the same: the attacker, the thief, the stalker, the psychopath killer we're trying to catch. We have probable cause to get a search warrant requesting fingerprints of the boat workers from the local shipyards, the two that are scheduled out Friday night. If they keep prints of their employees, maybe we'll get a name and a face so we can catch this guy. Apparently, he's not in the system. It doesn't mean he's never done anything wrong until now. It only means he's never been caught. But we will get him."

"Great," she said quietly, then dropped back down on the bed. The enthusiasm left her voice as color drained from her face, and her eyes glazed over.

Which was worse? Too much faith in believing everything was coming together, or finding out the police didn't seem to be any closer to catching the perpetrator? "Finish eating. We'll talk about it when we're through." Matthew watched her as she stared right through him. What was she thinking?

"He didn't look like a killer, you know," she mumbled. "I mean, the guy who had been at work the other night. I didn't really see him good, but you know what I mean. How could I have been so close and not known?"

"The majority don't look like killers," Marie said. "But who is to say what a killer looks like?"

Matthew frowned at Marie and then said to Samantha, "Eat. We'll talk later."

"I think I've lost my appetite."

They sat in silence as Matthew tried to eat his dinner. Marie finished her meal and threw away her empty box and cup. He noticed Samantha was true to her word, because she didn't eat another bite.

After he finished, he cleared his mess and set Sam's aside. She seemed to be in a trance.

"I'm going to shower." Marie disappeared behind closed doors.

When Matthew finished washing his hands, he walked over to the side of Sam's bed and sat across from it on the other one. "Samantha," he spoke, his concern strong, "you've known all along they were one and the same—the truck thief, the burglar, and the killer. I've been telling you that from the beginning. Now we're getting closer to proving it. That's all. Nothing has changed, except we are getting closer."

She sighed but didn't say a word.

"You have to be brave a little while longer. Don't give up on me now. We're going to catch him. I promise."

Sam's bottom lip quivered as she ripped out his heart. *She is so strong. . .so warm. . .so loving.*

Her green eyes looked up at Matthew. "But what if you don't? I can't spend the rest of my life running. I have a son to raise. And I need to be with him." Tears rimmed her eyes. "I can't believe I didn't know. That man sat in the driver's room watching, waiting. Why didn't he do something to me then? He had opportunity. Why put me through torture now?"

Matthew shrugged. "I think that's all part of his game. Who knows? Or maybe there were too many people around?"

A single tear trickled down her cheek. Matthew did the only thing he could do. He wiped it away with his thumb, but then another followed. Feeling compelled, he moved to her bedside and pulled Samantha to his chest and wrapped his arms around her. Holding her tight while she cried, he said, "I'm glad he didn't, 'cause he could have killed you." Matthew ran his hands gently over her back, trying to comfort and re-assure her. "We won't let him get you. I won't let him," he whispered. "I promise." He rocked side to side, holding her close.

Tears streamed down, soaking the front of his shirt.

"Now that the chief is finally in full cooperation with us, we should be able to close in on him quickly."

"The more I think about what this man has done, the more confused I am. If he knows where I live, why only tear my place apart?" Her voice choked back sobs as she questioned the man's motives.

He wished he knew. The man had plenty of opportunities to kill her; had he wanted to do so, she would be dead.

"Why didn't he wait for me to return and. . .kill me? Why?" Her breathing was jagged, her words broken. "Why?"

"He's a sick man who enjoys making you afraid and delights in your fear." Tightening his embrace, Matthew wished he could console her, make her forget the killer was after her.

Samantha's body shook in his arms as her sobbing grew stronger.

"With the other women, our psychologist believed he was taking out his frustrations against his mother. But when I told the doc I suspected him of following you and making attempts on your life, she said that was a bad sign. Once a psychopath changes his normal routine of doing things, it only gets worse. I know you don't want to hear that, but the good thing about it is that's when they start making mistakes. And he's done that. And we will get him. I promise you that." Gently, he ran his hands down the softness of her hair. "I'm sure it gives him some sort of sick perverted pleasure, scaring you like he has."

She didn't say anything else. Samantha settled into a soft, steady cry, and Matthew didn't try to stop her.

Finally, her crying abated, and the short gasps of air softened to a steady rhythm. Matthew noticed the evenness of her breathing.

She puts on a good tough fight. But where does this woman get her strength? Her body has worn itself out. Maybe she'll rest well tonight. He continued to stroke her hair gently.

He wished she wasn't a target. He wished he wasn't committed to staying unattached. It would be easy to fall in love with Samantha, but he couldn't. Mostly for her sake. He had to be strong. He had to do what was right, what was best for Samantha and Marty.

When Marie came out of the bathroom dressed in sweats and her hair sticking out all over her head, Matthew looked up. "She got scared and started crying. First time," he whispered. "She cried herself to sleep."

"That's a good thing. I noticed she was always trying to be tough through this. Crying means she has truly accepted her situation. We'll get him, sir. I know that."

"You're right, Boudreaux. We will. Do me a favor, and pull back her covers," he said as he scooped Samantha up in his arms.

Marie pulled back the covers and fixed the pillow, then slipped out of the way.

He settled Samantha into the bed and pulled the spread over her. Before turning the light out, he glanced at Marie. She had her back to him, facing a mirror combing her hair. Quickly he bent down and gently pressed his lips against Samantha's.

"Sweet dreams," he whispered.

Chapter 26

The next morning, the sun peeped through the curtains and woke Matthew. He had slept in the chair all night. Well not much, but some. He had dozed off about an hour before the sun rose. Since he had given the other bed to Marie, it didn't leave him much choice but to sit up all night. He had done it before and could do it again.

As he turned his attention toward Samantha, he found she was sitting up in bed. "How long have you been awake?"

"Not long," she said softly.

"Do you want some coffee now, or can you wait for breakfast?"

Marie started to stir as Samantha said, "I can wait."

Throwing back the covers, Marie climbed out of bed. Her sweats were crumpled, but she looked comfortable as she said, "Well, I can't. I have to have my morning coffee. I'll start the pot," she said as she marched over to the counter in the dressing area. There sat an empty coffee pot, unopened cups, and a pack of coffee grounds.

"Good. Make you some coffee. Samantha, maybe you could get dressed while I go take a quick shower."

"Matthew. I'm sorry about last night. I mean, the crying. I don't normally do that. Air my emotions like that."

Matthew noticed the smile that touched Marie's face before he turned back toward Samantha. "Don't worry. I think you needed it. I'll be ready in a few minutes."

When he returned to the room, Samantha was combing her hair as best she could and Marie sat in the chair he slept in the night before. "I'm almost ready," Samantha said.

"Where do you think you're going?" It wouldn't be safe for her to be running around the city this morning. He couldn't let her go. He wouldn't take that chance.

Samantha's eyes opened wide. "I'm not staying here. Besides, you were very careful, remember? No one followed us. And I'm hungry. You said breakfast, remember."

Matthew slipped on his shoulder holster, secured it, and then covered it with his lightweight sport coat. The look in her eyes betrayed her. She wasn't going to give up. He glanced at Marie for help in persuading Samantha to stay put.

"Don't look at me. I'm hungry, too."

He sighed. "I guess we can go right across the street to McDonalds." As a warning, he added, "But we sit with our backs to the wall, as hidden away as possible. Do you have a pair of sunglasses, Samantha?"

Looking in her travel bag, she pulled out her purse, dug deep, and held up a pair of sunglasses. "No problem."

"She's a woman always prepared, boss." Marie winked at Sam.

"You sound like you feel better today." Her eyes looked a little puffy from the good cry she'd had last night, but he wouldn't mention that. Matthew watched as she slipped on the glasses and stared at her reflection in the mirror.

"I can still see your eyes. You have a pair she can wear, Marie?" As the woman shook her head, he said, "I guess those will do."

"Good. Then I'm ready, 'cause I'm hungry!"

"Me, too," Marie echoed as she headed for the door.

Matthew stepped behind Samantha. Their reflection in the mirror shone like a family snapshot. Their eyes met, and Matthew winked at her, "That's my girl." He liked her *nothing can get me* attitude. "Let's go get something to eat," he said, grabbing his phone and sticking it in his pocket. Marie had opened the door and headed out and down the stairs. He stepped out the door and saw Marie scanning the area. He looked around for his own peace of mind, then let Samantha leave the room.

"Stick close to me." They walked around the backside of the motel and crossed the street to McDonalds. When their order was filled, they took the food to a corner table in the back where they would be unobserved. Marie and Matthew sat facing the room, and they had Samantha sit with her back to everyone. During breakfast, Matthew and Marie constantly looked around, making sure no one watched them, but they did it very nonchalantly.

"So what's on our agenda today?" Samantha asked between mouthfuls.

Matthew almost choked on his coffee. "Excuse me? Did you ask what *we* were doing today?"

"It's not like we're at your house where I can move around, work out, watch television. You know. Keep myself occupied. The motel room is small. Marie and I can't stay tucked up there all day. I'd rather be a sitting duck at home."

"You're not going to change my mind. There is no 'we' today. 'We' aren't doing anything. I am. You two are going back to the room and wait." He took a bite of his eggs.

"I thought this was my case," Samantha said with a pouty expression.

He saw Marie hide her smile behind her coffee cup.

"I mean, I'm the prime target now. Even your chief admits it. And you're going to leave me and Marie in a room with no back exit? Doesn't sound like much safety in that. No offense, Marie, but I know I won't feel very safe. I know you know your job, but what if he comes through the front. While you're trying to stop him, I won't be able to run for my life. No back way out. What I am to do?" She shook her head and said, "Not safe at all."

She was trying to get his pity. That was a card she hadn't played before. In the time he had known her, she'd usually played that tough guy role.

He took another bite of his eggs, trying to ignore those eyes, that voice. He was not going to give in to her. Seeing this side of her almost made him laugh, and he would have, had it not been such a serious situation. Of course, that didn't stop Marie. She laughed out loud but tried to cover it with a cough.

Samantha leaned over the table, moving closer to him,

practically putting her face up next to his. In a firm, hushed tone, she questioned, "Why can't I go with you? I don't want to stay in the small motel room. Please," she begged.

Matthew wiped his mouth with a napkin, took another swallow of coffee, then sat back against the booth. Looking at Samantha in all her innocence, he was so tempted to reach out, pull her into his arms, and protect her from the ugly world outside. But he had to resist.

He shook his head as he waved her back. "No. You almost got me," he said, pointing at her. Shaking his head, he said, "But no. Sorry. You can't go with me. Marie will be with you in the room, and I'll have a man right outside your room, only you won't be able to see him. He'll watch your room like a hawk. You'll be safe inside. I promise."

She stuck out her bottom lip, pouring on the pity-me picture.

"Don't think that's going to change my mind. Samantha, you can't go with me. Right now, you'd be safest if you stay put, out of harm's way."

Samantha took a deep breath, then said, "Whatever you say." She turned her attention back to her breakfast.

That was too easy. Matthew didn't like that quick answer, nor the tone in which it was spoken. It probably meant he should handcuff her to the bed if he wanted her to stay in the room, but he couldn't do that, although the thought was very tempting. Marie would see to it she didn't leave the room. He could trust her to take good care of Samantha.

After breakfast, he saw them safely back to the room. Looking out the window for the officer assigned to protect Samantha, Matthew said, "I see him now. He's out in the parking lot dressed as a telephone repairman. It's Guidry," he said to Marie. "If you need him, just signal or call the station and they will send him in right away." Looking at Samantha, he added, "Just stay in and watch some soap operas or something. That shouldn't be too difficult."

Samantha rolled her eyes. "You don't know me at all."

Anger permeated her face, and Matthew knew she was agitated with him. He hated leaving her like this, but he had no choice. Quickly, he closed the door behind him.

In no time, Matthew was whipping in and out of traffic, making good time to the station. He knew the sooner he started talking to the boat hands, the faster he could get back to them.

Johnson met him at the interrogation room. "We narrowed it down to two boats and pulled in ten men who fit the description. Unfortunately, the ship had no prints of their deckhands. We're checking to see if the search warrant covers taking these guys' prints as we question them. In the meantime, the sketch eliminated four of them. There are still a couple of the men we couldn't find. Davis and a couple more of our men are out looking for those guys. Do you want to split this group of men in half for interrogation, or both of us cover one at a time?"

"Quicker if we split the job. Did you pull a rap sheet on any of them?"

Johnson nodded. "Two of the six had a record."

"Fine. You take those. I'll take the other four." Matthew saw Johnson's brow furrow, trying to understand his reasoning, but he knew better than to ask. Sam's assailant's prints were not on file, therefore, Matthew wanted the possible suspects with no prior record.

Matthew took one from his group at random and Johnson took one from his. Each pair went into separate interrogation rooms.

The questions asked were basically the same, and their answers were being recorded. They asked each: "Where were you on the dates of the killings? Can that information be verified? What about family? Do you have any? And are they still living? Is there any special woman in your life?" And they watched each man's response.

By the time they finished questioning all of them, Matthew and Johnson met at Matthew's desk to go over the results. They each concluded that neither found a prime suspect, but to be safe, Matthew instructed a couple of uniforms to follow up on each person's alibi, making sure they could be verified. Besides, none of them had those dark eyes that Samantha described. Sure, they all had brown eyes, but not *dark*.

"We need to find those other two fast! I feel it in my gut, one of those guys is our man," Matthew snapped as he pushed his hands through his hair.

"We're working on it, sir." Looking wearily at Matthew, Johnson swiped his eyes. "I'm tired. Last night was a long one. It took several hours to find the ones we could find. The night ended pretty late." Glancing at his watch, he said, "Why don't you bring Ms. Cain back with you this afternoon. We should have the others by then. That way, while we ask them questions, she could be looking them over and give a positive ID."

He didn't like the thought of Samantha coming down to the station where the killer could see her. He refused to take that chance. "She's hidden away for a reason," he snapped.

Matthew's voice had a curt edge to it.

"Okay, okay! I just asked. I thought it would be a good idea. We'll find those two. We'll page you and meet you back here, okay?" Johnson said as he headed for the door.

"When we have the killer locked up, with no chance of seeing her, or following her, then and only then will I bring her in to identify him."

"Got it."

Matthew closed the folder on his desk as Johnson left the room. Nerves were on edge around here and Matthew knew it. Everybody was working nonstop to get this maniac before he struck again. Matthew stuck the file in his desk drawer and got up to leave.

A familiar voice said, "Well, where the heck have you been?"

His gaze jerked in the direction of the voice. "Greg, you old son of gun." His father's old partner, Greg Singleton, came in and plopped down in the chair next to Matthew's desk. Matthew slapped him on the shoulder. "It's good to see you, old man. What are you doing here?"

"Give me some of that nasty coffee, and I'll tell you."

He poured Greg a cup of coffee, then sat back down in his chair. "So. What are you up to?"

Taking a sip, Greg said, "I stopped by your place yesterday. I let myself in the back door. Remember I still have the key your dad gave me? I waited over an hour. When you didn't show, I had to leave. I should have left you a note but didn't have time."

The rest of his words faded into the background as Matthew thought about what Greg had said. *So Greg was the reason for the scare. No one had broken in. Sam's safe there, and we can go back home. Great!*

"Did you hear what I said?"

"Yeah, something about the governor. What?"

Greg sat up in his chair. "I said I'm working for the governor's office now. They have me on the payroll. I guess you could say for security reasons. Kind of a cushy job if you ask me, but I don't mind. I'm almost sixty. I need something easy." He laughed.

"That's great. Look, I don't mean to rush you, but I'm on a case right now that won't wait. Why don't you come by for dinner one night soon? I'll cook."

"I never turn down a free meal." Greg stood. "Do you still cook like you used to? Of course you do," he answered his own question. "I wouldn't miss it for the world." As he started to walk away, Greg turned back and asked one more question. "Is there a little woman in your life yet?"

Matthew raised his brow, giving Greg a stern look. "You know how I feel on that subject."

"Sure I know. But I thought by now you would have figured it out. Let's see, how does that old saying go? Oh yes. It is better to have loved and lost, than never to have loved at all. Look at me. I'm living proof. Me and your dad. He might have been unhappy after your mom died, but trust me, he was always happier than me. Katherine was the best thing that ever happened to him, and he wouldn't have changed a minute of his life with her. Except maybe he would have made it last longer if he could have. But like Tad always said, look what they made." Greg's eyes rested on Matthew. "He had you and his memories to keep him company. I never had anything."

"Now don't go get all teary-eyed on me. I haven't changed my views, and I don't plan to." Matthew paused, his gaze looking past his old friend and out the window. "If I did, though, I know who I'd grab up in a minute."

"I see the sparkle in your eyes just thinking about her. You better do it before it's too late! You might not have another chance. Look at me. Still alone at fifty-eight. What a life. It stinks." Greg slapped Matthew's shoulder. "Well, I'll let you go. Call me. And make it soon."

Matthew walked out with Greg because he wanted to get back to Samantha as quickly as he could. It was great seeing his dad's old partner, and now Matthew's friend. Maybe he should take heed to what Greg had said. No. He had seen the way his dad missed his mom. He didn't ever want to go through that pain and suffering himself.

When he parked in the motel parking lot, he checked with Guidry. Everything seemed fine so he relieved him of duty. Matthew ran up the stairs taking two at a time. He couldn't seem to stop his feet from flying. Where had this extra energy come from?

Was this what it felt like to come home to the same woman every night? To come home to Sam every night?

All excited, maybe even feeling a thread of hope for the future, thinking of the possibilities, he swung open the door.

Matthew stopped dead in his tracks. "What do you think you're doing?"

Chapter 27

Startled from the sudden loud voice at the door, Sam looked up and glared at the man who filled the space. She turned her head away with a quick snap. *Do I explain or not?*

The bathroom door slammed open at the same time and Marie jumped out with her gun pulled and ready to fire. "Dang it, sir." She lowered her weapon. "Are you trying to get yourself killed?"

"At the tone, the time will. . . ." Sam let the words she heard fade into the background as she made her decision. She would teach him a thing or two. . .or at least give him something to overreact about. "I can't talk now, Amanda. I have to go. But I'll call you back soon."

Annoyance consumed her. What did he think she was? An idiot? Maybe this would teach him a lesson. She knew she was in hiding in this secluded motel room for a reason.

Of course she wouldn't call someone and give away her location. . .if for no other reason than to keep from putting her friend in jeopardy.

Slamming down the phone, she jumped to her feet and turned, jammed her hands on her hips, and faced Matthew. "How dare you talk to me like that! Who do you think you are?" Sam glared at Matthew in defiance.

"Detective, don't—" Marie started to call out but Sam interrupted her.

Sam held her hand up toward Marie and mouthed, "Don't." She hoped the woman could see what she was trying to say without having to say it. *Don't protect me. I know you know, but he should have had sense enough to know I wouldn't do such a stupid thing. Let me handle it my way.* That was what she wanted to say and hoped her eyes said it all. Marie shut her mouth and slipped her gun back in the holster. Shaking her head, the woman went back into the bathroom and closed the door behind her. Probably to handle the matter she went in to handle to begin with. . .before Matthew pitched a fit.

Without a word, he shut the door to the motel room. "I shouldn't have yelled, but you don't seem to understand how dangerous it is to let anyone know where you are. Please, sit down."

"I will not," she snapped, still irked by his attitude.

Matthew closed the distance between them, holding her gaze like a magnet. His eyes held a glint of an indefinable emotion. Was it concern? Compassion? She wasn't sure, but one thing she was sure of, he was too close. So close, she had to sit just to give herself room to breathe.

"You do realize you're in protective custody for your safety?

What if he had tapped your girlfriend's line? He could be on his way here right now." He quirked his brow. "That *was* your friend, Amanda, right?"

She practically bit a hole in her bottom lip, trying to keep quiet, not wanting to out and out lie.

"He could be on his way here right now! Lucky for us, we can get out of here. Get your things together. We'll finish this discussion in the car. Hurry up, Marie. We're going."

Matthew turned and left the room again. Sam assumed he was going downstairs to check them out of the motel, just as he assumed she would do as she was told. "Men!"

The bathroom door opened and Marie stepped out. While drying her hands, she said, "He's just thinking of you, Sam. He's trying to protect you and at the same time catch a killer, in addition to the other cases he is working on. The man has a lot to think about. Just remember that when you try to understand him."

That took some of the steam out of Sam's sail, but not all of it. In a huff, she tossed her things in her little black bag. She wanted out of there as much as he did, so of course she did as she was told. And Marie's words did help her to understand him a bit more, but she wished he would have trusted her and known she had the smarts not to do something so stupid.

"Good girl," he said when he returned, then grabbed the few items he had unpacked and threw them in his bag. "I'll get these down to the car. You two double-check that we aren't leaving anything and come straight down," he commanded as he zipped his bag closed, grabbed hers, and headed out the door.

He was always giving orders. Sam wanted to scream.

Instead, she stepped over to the door and slammed it behind him. "I wish your head had been in it!" she said in irritation at the closed door.

"Feel better?" Marie asked as a smile spread across her face. "He always gives orders. He's used to that. He has men working for him all the time. Don't take it personally."

"Humph. I admit, that felt good." A small smile played at her lips also. "To have been such a sweet, wonderful man last night, he sure is a demanding ogre today."

"Just remember. He's doing his job."

Yes. He's doing his job, and I'm work to him. No more. No less. Running her fingers through her hair, she said, "Well, if we want out of here, we better start searching."

Finding nothing left behind, they ran down to the car. Matthew had the motor running, yet stood outside the car with the passenger door open, waiting while keeping a sharp eye out. Sam got in as Marie climbed in her car.

Sam said nothing to the detective, although she was curious where they were headed now as she climbed in and he closed the door behind her. Something changed his mind about having to stay hidden. But she wouldn't dare ask. He would have to volunteer the information.

Maybe they were going back to his house. That would be wonderful. She didn't know what changed his mind and his attitude, but she was very grateful. Another hour in that room, and she would have gone stark raving mad.

Minutes later and miles down the road, Matthew broke the silence. "For the record, my house wasn't broken into by the killer. It was an old friend of my father's. The one I told you about yesterday. Greg. He has a key and used it but forgot to leave a note."

Inside she smiled at that, excited to know his house was a safe hideaway again. She loved his place, warm and welcoming, but didn't dare let him know how happy it made her. She hoped as far as he was concerned, he believed she was still agitated. She planned to keep up the silent treatment.

Out of the corner of her eye, she saw Matthew glance her way, so she quickly averted her eyes.

"Do you want to know what we did today on the case? We made some headway."

Of course she wanted to know, but she couldn't tell him that and keep quiet at the same time. Finally, acting as if it didn't matter one way or the other, as they pulled to a stop at a red light she said, "If you want to tell me."

When he didn't respond, she turned her head to look at him. His gaze was locked on her. Obviously, her eyes betrayed her. He apparently saw the excitement there, because she saw his smug expression. Shrugging off his self-satisfied attitude, she thought, *Big deal. So he knows me better than I thought.*

"Okay. Okay. I want to know. Tell me," she said, giving in to his victory. "What did you find out? Are you close to catching him? What?"

"I knew you'd break. I'm a cop. I know these things."

"Ha, ha, funny," she said, sarcasm dripping from her voice. She hated that smirk on his face, but she had to know now. "Okay. Okay. So you win. What? Tell me." She punched him lightly in the arm.

His lips turned up in a half grin as pure delight penetrated his eyes and he wiggled his brows. "One of my informants tracked down some information, so now we know the killer works on a boat that's pulling out midnight Friday night. We ran a check and found two boats scheduled to leave at that time."

"How do you know your information is correct?"

He huffed. "We don't. But we have to use whatever we get and try to go from there. Anyway, we pulled in a few men from the crew that fit the description you gave and came close to the drawing the sketch artist made. We managed to question them. Unfortunately, none of those were him, but we still have a couple more to locate. When we do, we should have our man."

Matthew sounded very confident, which gave her an idea. She touched Matthew's shoulder lightly and said, "Why don't you bring me in and let me look through one of those hidden windows, or whatever, to see if I can spot him?"

"No!" he barked.

She jerked her hand back at his gruff reply. "Why not?" she asked, confused. "I thought you wanted to catch him?"

"I do." Matthew slowed the car down as he turned onto his street. Curving around the lake, he pulled into the driveway. "But it would be too dangerous for you. After we get him and arrest him, then we'll have you look at him. But not until then."

Sam sat back on the seat and looked out the side window. Sometimes she didn't understand him. It seemed to her that if she could point him out of the few left to interrogate, it would help. She closed her eyes as she tried to let Matthew's response sink into her thoughts and maybe make some sense.

None of it made sense. "Matthew, why won't you let me come in? Sure, it might be dangerous, but wouldn't it help you get the killer faster? The sooner the better. I'm in danger until you get him. Didn't you just say a minute ago you would do whatever it took? I'm willing to take that chance. Do my part."

In a very quiet voice Matthew said again, "No."

"But—"

"Samantha," he said her name in a whisper, interrupting her question. Matthew pulled the car around to the garage and put it in park. Turning in his seat, he faced Sam.

The solemn look on his face softened Sam's heart along with the way he called her name. Although she wanted to, she couldn't feel anger as she waited for his next words.

"I can't let you go down to the station and put your life in jeopardy. I. Me. Matthew Todd Jefferies. . .the man, not the cop."

He reached out and cupped her face. Wetting his lips, he added, "I have to do this without putting your life in more danger than it already is. Can you understand that?" His thumb caressed her cheek.

Sam's heart pounded like a big bass drum. She thought it would beat right out of her chest. At least now she knew he wasn't just using her to catch his man. If he had been, he would let her walk into the station and try to pick him out of a lineup.

"Do you understand?" he whispered as his fingers stroked the side of her face.

Leaning into his hand, she closed her eyes and let the pleasure devour her. Her heart raced as breathing became hard to do. "I'm not sure, but it sounds like you care what happens to me."

"I told you, you were a smart girl." Matthew reached his other arm out to her and drew her to him. Sam fell into his embrace. His lips found hers with no problem; like a magnet they drew together.

The warmth of his mouth covered hers. Her hands found refuge in the softness of his wavy hair.

Down deep she wanted to hear him say he wouldn't, couldn't put her life in danger because he loved her, the magic words that would make everything all right, the words her own heart had been working up to. Yes, she admitted to herself, she had fallen in love with this man.

The pressure of his hands on her back shot pleasure through her. He pulled her closer to him. One more inch was all that separated her from being totally in his lap.

The horn blasted, shattering the silence around them and scaring Samantha out of her mind. They both jumped.

Sam quickly pulled back to her side of the car. Her heart beat triple time. Heavy breathing was still coming, and she couldn't slow it down. Her eyes flashed on Matthew. What were they doing? Acting like schoolkids. At that same moment, Marie's car pulled in beside his.

It took Matthew almost as long as it did Sam to regain composure. "Let's get inside. We shouldn't be out here like this anyway."

Of course, always the cop thinking about correct procedure. You don't make out with a possible witness in your car. She wanted to laugh, but it wasn't funny. So much for the magic words she wanted to hear.

As they got out of the car, Matthew grabbed their bags and brought them in with him. She and Marie followed him inside. In the kitchen, she watched him place the bags on the counter. She knew what was next. He would tell her to go to her room. Rest, relax, she needed it; after which, he would add an apology, swearing it would never happen again. He had made a mistake.

She stood, head held high, feet apart, ready for Matthew's onslaught of words.

"Samantha." His tone was as soft as it had been in the car. Holding up his hand, as if to say wait a minute, he then turned his eyes on Marie. "Can you give us a minute here?"

Marie's eyes widened as she glanced back and forth. Sam was sure the woman didn't know what to do. It looked like part of her wanted to stay and defend what Sam had not done but been accused of, but part of her didn't want to disobey her immediate boss. She shrugged as she looked at Sam one more time and then said to the detective, "No problem, boss." And with that, she left the room.

Surprised at him asking Marie to leave them alone, Sam just stared at him. Maybe she wasn't ready for what he had to say. She trembled.

Matthew sighed. "I'm not doing the proper thing. I know you should go down to the station, point him out, make a positive ID, but I can't let you."

She held her breath, waiting. Still, the promise to keep his distance was coming. . .that was his way.

Instead, Matthew closed the space between them, wrapped his arms around her, and pulled her head to his chest, holding her lovingly in his arms. "I can't let you do it, because if something happened to you, I would never know what love was." He kissed the top of her head. "I think I'm falling in love with you. The thing is, I don't want to fall in love with you, but it seems I'm not the one in control. And now I can't take a chance of losing you. Can you understand?" His brow furrowed as he asked her that.

Sam pulled her head away from his chest but stayed wrapped in his arms. The magic words had been spoken. He was falling in love with her. She was at a loss for words herself. Swallowing hard, she moistened her own lips. "You sure know how to sweep a girl off her feet."

Chapter 28

His lips came down on hers and he kissed her soundly. "Don't wake me if I'm dreaming," she whispered. "Trust me, you're not dreaming. Unfortunately, the ugliness of the mess we are in is all around us. It will catch up to us soon, but in the meantime we will deal with it. . .together."

Sam gently caressed the side of Matthew's face. "I don't know what happened to you today, but it's wonderful. Don't change."

His lips came down on hers again, this time in a long, sensuous kiss. This man thought he was falling in love with her, and she knew she loved him. Could it get any better than this? Her hands wrapped around his neck, pulling him closer.

When they pulled slightly apart, he looked into her eyes as his hands moved slowly down her back in slow circular movements. "Samantha Cain, you just don't know what you do to me."

Sam kissed his mouth and then buried her head in his chest as he continued to hold her close. She sighed. They stayed locked in an embrace for a long, long time.

Finally, Matthew hugged her one more time and kissed the top of her head. "As much as I'd love to stay like this forever, we need to put some space between us so I can get my mind back on work. As you can see, once I start thinking about you, I can't seem to stop."

"I haven't noticed, but I'll keep my eyes open." She winked. "I don't know about you, but I'm hungry."

He pecked her on the lips. "That's not a bad idea. You set the table, and I'll whip us up something after I toss our bags in our rooms. And I'll let Marie know it's safe to come back in here. I just didn't want to share my feeling for you for the first time in front of someone else."

This was a new side to Matthew, one she loved even more. He dropped all of his barriers. Would it last? She hoped so. She hoped they weren't rushing things, and she prayed they were thinking with their heads as well as their hearts.

He returned within seconds and started pulling things out of the refrigerator and cupboard. "Marie is on the phone in the office. She'll join us shortly she said."

"What are you making us?" she asked.

"Ham and cheese omelets. Do you like omelets?"

Yielding to temptation, Sam walked up behind him and wrapped her arms around his waist. "He cooks. He cleans. I think I've found me the perfect *little woman*." She chuckled. "Thank You, Lord." Leaning her face into his back, she placed a light kiss between his shoulder blades. He laughed as his masculine scent teased her nerve endings. She then released him so she could do her share. She pulled plates down from the cupboard and silverware from the drawer, then quickly set the table as he placed a plate of bacon in the microwave and pressed a couple of buttons, then pushed down a couple slices of bread in the toaster.

"I didn't know love could be so wonderful. Here I've been fighting it all my life. Was I crazy or what?" Matthew said as his blue eyes caressed her lovingly. When the bread popped up, he put two more in and slapped some butter on the toasted ones.

"No way. You were just waiting for me and don't you forget it. You can't just fall in love with anyone. Only that certain someone. And I'll tell you now. I'm it. I hope you believe in God. I know He's been there for me these last few years. And I know He brought us together." As she rambled on and on. she realized he hadn't said he loved her. At least not, "I love you" specifically. He had said he thought he was falling in love, and then just now said love was wonderful. But that was pretty darn close, and enough for her at the moment. She blew him a kiss, then grabbed two glasses. "Milk or orange juice?"

"Juice. I've never really thought about it before. I know about God, because of my father. He made sure he continued to take me to church after Mom was killed. But eventually his job got in the way. I'd like to know more. Sometimes with the job, it's hard to believe there is a God."

"Don't worry. There is, and I will share Him, the Gospel, with you so you can have your own relationship with Him. You'll be even happier then." This told her Matthew needed to know and accept the Lord for salvation. This was evidently one of the reasons they were brought together, so she would make it a priority to share the Gospel with him. "One thing I'll say right now is, to have a good relationship as a couple, God has to be in the middle of it. For Marty's sake, as well as mine and yours, I will definitely tell you all about Him and salvation." As she poured them each a glass, she remembered just a short time ago they were fighting because he thought she had put their hiding place in jeopardy. And now she was witnessing to him. Sam needed to tell him the truth. "I have a confession to make."

He turned and looked at her. "Oh no. The look on your face tells me I'm not going to like this."

She shrugged. "Yes, you will. Earlier, when I was on the phone and you walked into the motel room, I was checking the time because I was worried about you. Marie suggested I call time."

"So she knew? Why didn't she tell me even though you wouldn't?"

"Because I asked her not to. She started to, but I shook my head no, and she understood what I was saying. I guess you could say it was a woman thing."

He smiled. "Good confession. I'm glad. I thought you were smart enough to know not to call your friend."

"You should have trusted your instincts about me. Because it didn't sound like it when you came in the room."

"I panicked." He pulled a chair out from the table. "Sit. Let's eat." Grabbing the pan off the stove, he stepped back to the table, cut the omelet in thirds, and scooped out part on her and Marie's plates, and then the rest on his and placed the pan back on the stovetop. "Marie," he called, "come and get it before it gets cold."

Sam sniffed the aroma. "Smells wonderful. There is one more thing. I would like to set straight with you about what really happened three years ago."

Pulling the bacon out of the microwave and placing the strips on a plate, he then put it on the table. "I've learned in these few short days that your husband told many lies. I don't have to know everything, but it would probably be for the best if you told me what went down on the last day." He grabbed the saucer with the stack of buttered toast and added it to the table.

Lifting her hand to her bangs, she brushed them aside. She had quit wearing a bandage when she showered at the inn, never replacing the old. "Do you see this?" she asked as she revealed her old scar.

He stood fast, staring. He frowned. "Martin did that?"

"Martin did that to me the night he shot himself. For some time he had been accusing me of infidelity and some other morbid things, but that night he'd lost all control. When I came home, he was waiting for me. He was drunk. After shouting accusations at me, he grabbed me by the back of my neck and dragged me over to the mirror. Yelling—" Her voice cracked. She swallowed hard. She hadn't realized how painful it would be to tell the story, a story she had kept secret for so long.

Matthew touched his lips to her scar and whispered, "It's okay. You don't have to say another word."

She shook her head. "No. I have to finish. For my own sake, if not for yours." Sam continued the story. "Martin yelled at me to look at the tramp in the mirror, slamming my face against it over and over. The mirror shattered, but he kept slamming me against it. Finally, I blacked out. When I came to, he was gone. Blood was everywhere. I was weak, but I knew I had to get to the hospital. By the time I was stitched up and released, I drove myself home. Martin's mother was waiting for me. She told me Martin had called and told her he couldn't put me through what his father had put her through, and she rushed right over. The front door was unlocked, so she had let herself in. She saw the blood and broken mirror but didn't know what to think.

"Together we went out to the garage and found him. He had told her earlier, he couldn't be like his dad. That was why he took his life that night. She swore me to secrecy, because neither Martin nor his mother wanted to tarnish the image everyone had of his father or his grandfather. I didn't like it, but I did it out of the love I once felt for Martin, the Martin I had known in the beginning. Plus Marty. He didn't need to think ill of his father. We had managed to keep it from him so far. One day, maybe, I'll tell him the truth."

"Oh, baby. I'm so sorry. The department treated you unfairly. Everyone assumed you had pushed Martin to his death, but in the end he did what he did out of the love he felt for you. In a sick, twisted way, he saved your life." Matthew pulled her up into his embrace and held her close.

They stayed that way for a few minutes, and then she kissed his cheek. "Enough pity. I'm just glad it's over, and you know the whole story. Let's never talk about it again."

"That's all right with me."

Slipping out of his embrace, she sat back down. "Let's eat. Soup's getting cold." She smiled.

"We had that—" Matthew cocked his head slightly, interrupting his own words with silence, and looked questioningly at the ceiling. "Was that yesterday? No the day before. Today it seems like we've been together forever. Doesn't it?"

"With many more to come." Sam sniffed the food in front of her again. "Maybe," she added. "Do I smell onions?"

He pulled a face. "You don't like onions?" He clicked his tongue behind his teeth three times. "That will never do. I put onions in practically everything I cook." He shrugged. "Oh well, I guess that means you get to do the cooking after all."

"Not on your life. I'll learn to love them." She took a big bite. As she started chewing she said, "Mmm. This is wonderful. Onions and all!"

Matthew smiled as he took his first bite. "It doesn't take much to make you happy, does it?"

"It takes one big cop, with dark wavy hair, steel-blue eyes, and a warm heart." Sam never believed she would fall in love again. "Do you know anyone who fits that description?"

Matthew smiled. "It better be me," he said, and they both laughed.

Marie walked in. "Am I too late? Smells good, and I'm starved. Glad to see you two made up. You don't know how much pressure you put on me when the two of you aren't getting along."

"I think we'll all do fine. Thanks for your understanding," Matthew said. "Help yourself to juice or milk. Your choice."

"What understanding? I just like everyone getting along," she said as she poured a glass of milk. "Keeps the stress level down and makes it easier for me to do my job." She smiled at Samantha. "You know what I mean?"

The three of them finished the meal with very little conversation. The food took their complete attention. Everyone seemed to have worked up a big appetite.

As he took his last bite, he glanced at his watch. "I've got some more work to do." He stood up and started cleaning up the dishes.

"I'll get that. Don't you worry. I do know my way around in the kitchen, I promise," Sam said, then added, "Just not much as a chef."

"I'll help her, unless you need me to do something, too, boss."

"Great. You help her. I have to go to the station for what I need to do. I hate to eat and run, but I have to. It's almost two." Matthew made his apologies as he stood to leave.

Sam followed him to the back door and walked outside with him. "Hey. Can I have just one kiss before you go, to prove to me I'm not dreaming." Sam met him halfway. One long, wonderful kiss and he was gone. Going back inside, she locked the door.

Walking on air, she helped clean the kitchen.

"I can see you two have come a long way," Marie said. "I've never seen the detective so happy. Glad y'all worked things out."

"Me, too. I didn't think I would ever find love again. But I was content, because I had my son and he means the world to me. When we finish here, I'm going to go for a workout. Want to join me?"

"Of course. That's what I'm here for. To stay by your side and keep you safe. Besides which, my passion, when not being a cop, is to work out. I want to stay in top shape. When you started talking about men and how they treat you in the workplace, I understood. Been there. . .done that, as they say."

"I figured as much. I'm going to go slip on those gym shorts and a T-shirt, and I'll meet you in the back room.

She made another stop in the bathroom. In the mirror, even with the bruises, her face seemed to glow. "I am in love," she told her reflection. After brushing her teeth, she continued to her original destination.

In the weight room, she adjusted the weights on the machine and did a few warm-up exercises. Marie was already running a steady pace on the treadmill. Sam started a slow workout. She did steady reps working out her arms and upper torso and then reps that worked the lower portion of her body. Half an hour of the weight machine was enough for her. She grabbed the jump rope that hung on the wall and started jumping. Fifteen minutes later, she moaned, "Enough." Returning the rope to its rightful place, she did cool-down exercises.

"Do you only do the treadmill?" Sam asked Marie. "I've never seen anyone run steady for almost an hour."

"It's endurance. I have to keep my endurance up. You never know when you'll have to be on a foot chase. I don't want to be the one to lose my perp because I lost my energy." Marie laughed as she continued to run steady.

When finished with the cool-down exercises, she dragged herself from the room. "I'm going to shower."

"I'll be right outside your room. No problem." Marie stopped the treadmill and followed Sam out of the room.

Sam strolled to the bathroom and stripped for a shower. The water streamed over her body pounding, massaging all the right places. Sam let the water do its magic, then washed and rinsed from head to toe, keeping a washcloth over her stitches. After drying, she wrapped the towel around her and went to her room.

Opening the bedroom door to the hall, she saw Marie sitting outside just as she said she would be. "I'm going to lie down and take a nap. . .I think. I know I'm going to lie down anyway."

"That's probably a good idea. You get some rest. I'll be out here."

Closing the door again, she slipped on a pair of shorts and T-shirt and then lay across the bed, listening for Matthew's return. As she waited, her thoughts recalled his kisses. She closed her eyes, reveling in the afterglow. Before she knew it, she fell asleep, taking that much-needed nap so her body could continue to heal.

Chapter 29

Where is the other one?" The cops finished interrogating the man they had found, which told Matthew what he already knew. "It must be him."

"I have to agree." Johnson said. "We couldn't find him, though. We searched everywhere."

"We've got the bar staked out. And the patrol car is keeping an eye out at the motels downtown near the river," Davis added.

Before Matthew could respond, his phone rang. "Jefferies," he said into the receiver.

"This is Officer Holmes, from the Cincinnati Police Department. We received an inquiry on a set of prints you are looking for an ID. We've got it. Eighteen years ago, we arrested a sixteen-year-old for the death of his mother. He was tried as an adult and convicted, sentenced ten years to life at a state penitentiary for the criminally insane."

"Is he still in prison? What's the story?"

"Six years ago he was released after serving his ten years. He'd also been pronounced cured at the time of his release. It was a long, sad story with a lot of years of sexual abuse. The doctors found out his mother had sexually abused him, and when the kid finally thought he was old enough or man enough to put a stop to her, he refused to play any more of her sex games. If we'd had the technology then that we have today, he probably would have gotten better help and truly recovered. But you apparently can connect him with a crime down in Louisiana."

"Yes. We have three dead women we believe we can connect him to."

"That's too bad. He was one sick kid, but it was hard to blame him after what the doctors had found."

"What do you mean?" Matthew questioned.

"In the beginning, his mother would leave him locked in a room when she left to go to work at night. Sometimes he'd slip out and wander the streets. As he grew older and she took notice of his body maturing, she found pleasures with him, and instead of locking him up before leaving, she would tie him up, leaving just enough slack for him to stand up and use the pot she left for him to relieve himself in. She told him it was for his own protection. And for years he believed it. But, like I said, he grew up. As he grew, he wised up. That's when he strangled her to death."

Matthew interrupted, "Those three women we believe he has killed are all middle-aged women. Maybe he thinks they are his mom, and he's killing her over and over. Did she work nights at a diner?" Matthew asked.

"As a matter of fact, yes."

"He sexually abused the first two after they died. He would have done it to the third one, but a witness stopped him. Our psychologist ascertained he was rebelling against something in his early life and determined it was probably a form of abuse by his mother. She was right. It's sad what he went through, but it doesn't give him the right to do what he's done. We have to catch him and lock him up. For good this time. What's his name?"

"Robert Thomas Howard."

"Thanks for the information. Please fax me a copy of the complete report along with the most current picture you have, if you don't mind." Matthew gave him the fax number, then hung up the phone.

"We've got him now. Check the lists. See if there is a Robert Howard or a Thomas Howard. Or anything similar."

Johnson's face lit up. "Lieutenant. It's Bobby Howard. And that's the one we are looking for now."

Pounding the desk with his fist, Matthew shouted, "We got him. Now all we have to do is find him."

"Don't worry. We will."

Matthew wished he could stop worrying. Instead, he would only worry more. Samantha was the woman he loved. Everything Martin had said about her had been a lie. Now that he found her, he couldn't lose her. He wasn't his father. He couldn't make it through life without her. Of that he was certain. She was a breath of fresh air in his once very drab life.

He was robbed of ever knowing a mother's love. He didn't want to be robbed of ever knowing a wife's love. *Yes. When this is all over, I'm going to ask her to marry me. I'm not afraid anymore. . .of love, of her, or of a commitment.*

"Sir, did you say something?" Johnson asked.

A smile forced its way to Matthew's lips. He didn't think he had said anything aloud, but who knows? Buck Johnson must think Matthew was going over the edge. "You get the APB out?"

Johnson nodded.

"Then go home and get a good night's sleep, Johnson."

"Yes, sir."

After Johnson left, Matthew, overwhelmed with a feeling of elation and hope for the future, picked up the phone and called Greg. After inviting him for a spur-of-the-moment dinner, he said, "Yes. Tonight. I know it's last-minute. Can you make it or not? I have a surprise for you."

"How can I say no to that? Of course, I'll be there. Seven okay?"

They agreed on the time. Matthew made a few more calls to the right people, picked up the fax on the Howard case along with the picture, set proper wheels in motion, then called it a day. On the way home, he stopped and picked up a few ingredients to a special recipe he planned to cook that night. All the way home, he was very careful not to be followed. Nothing was going to ruin their future together.

"Samantha, I'm home," he called when he entered the kitchen. "Marie, where are you?" Neither answered him, and he heard no television or anything. *Déjà vu.* This time he wasn't going to panic and think the worst. They were probably in the back room again, working out.

Samantha missed her routine. He hoped she got back to it soon, only doing it from his house instead of hers. He hoped she and Marty both would feel at home in his house. *A complete family.* He couldn't hold back the grin that covered his face as he worked his way through the house. He was actually thinking about marriage. This was definitely new to Matthew.

As he stepped into the living room, Marie entered from the hallway. "She's in her room, boss. I didn't want to holler out loud and wake her. But she's fine. . .taking a nap. Since you're here now, I'm going to go shower, if that's all right with you. We worked out after you left, and I'm really in need of soap, if you know what I mean."

He laughed. "By all means. Go take your shower. We're having company tonight for dinner. I think you'll enjoy him. A retired cop."

"Great," she said as she headed to her room.

He made his way to Sam's bedroom and knocked lightly. When she didn't answer, he opened the door and peeked inside. He smiled. "Asleep again." She had found peace in his home with all the turmoil that was going on around her. He was so glad. The last rays from the sun filtered through the blinds and shone directly on her sleeping torso.

Matthew leaned over the bed, dropping tiny kisses on her face as he whispered, "Samantha, wake up. I'm home." He kissed her again and again.

Her lips puckered toward the kisses until her eyes popped open. "What a way to wake up. You have my permission to do this anytime."

Running his fingers through her long brown hair, he nuzzled in the softness. "Woman, you drive me crazy. How can you sleep when the sun is still shinning?"

"Mmm, that feels good." She turned her head, giving him easier access to her neck. "All I can say is, I never used to take naps in the late afternoon. But sleeping while the sun is shining is not a problem. Remember, I work nights."

He nibbled at her earlobe. "Wake up now. I have a surprise for you. Someone's coming over for dinner."

Pulling out of his embrace, she sat up quickly. "And you want me to whip something up? You must be out of your ever-loving mind. I'm going back to sleep. I wasn't joking when I said I didn't cook very well."

Matthew started laughing. Not a small laugh, but a huge, robust laugh. "You're wonderful."

"Even if that's so, I still won't cook your dinner. Sorry," she pouted as she placed her hands on her hips.

"Come here," he said in a low growl. Pulling her to her feet and close to him, he lowered his head as his lips claimed hers. After one long hard kiss, he eased away. "Mmm, nice. *I'm* doing the cooking. Do you remember asking me what happened to make me change earlier and admit my feelings for you?"

"I remember everything about today. Why?"

"Because you're going to meet the reason tonight."

She looked suspiciously at him. "A person changed your mind about how you feel about me?"

"No, silly. My mind didn't have to be changed about how I feel for you. I think I've loved you since the first time I laid eyes on you. Well, second time actually. It just took me awhile to understand it and believe in it. Anyway, my father's old partner and best friend made me realize how I didn't want to chance losing you without ever loving you.

He made me open my eyes and my heart."

Sam murmured as she snuggled close, "Thank you, Daddy Jefferies' friend." Raising her face, she pressed her lips to his.

Chapter 30

Later, in the kitchen, Matthew took items out of the grocery bag, pulled some things from the refrigerator, grabbed a couple of pots and pans, and got busy doing what he did well. Sam and Marie busied themselves setting the table.

"When we finish here, I'll help you with the cooking. I don't mind helping," she added, remembering the hard time she had given him when he first mentioned the meal. Changing the subject as quickly as she brought it up, she said, "I can't wait for you to get to know Marty better. He hasn't had a man, other than his grandpa, around him in a long time. You will be a very good influence on my son's life."

"You might end up with another cop in the family if you're not careful," Marie said jokingly. "Of course, you can't ask for a better teacher than Detective Matthew Jefferies."

He stopped dicing onions. His eyes sent a warm, loving

look in Sam's direction. "I know she's joking with you, but seriously, I can't wait to get to know him better. You've raised a wonderful son. He's a smart boy."

"Thank you. What's the matter? You look a little. . .I don't know, worried maybe?"

He sighed. "I think I'd better remind you what you're letting yourself and Marty in for. It's only fair. Who knows? You might decide it would be best not to get involved with me, with my life."

"My father was a policeman and I turned out fine," Marie said. "In fact, my dad knew your dad. And I have two brothers on the force. My baby brother works for the FBI. I don't think that's too bad coming from a cop's family. So don't put it down, sir."

"Don't get me wrong. I'm not. I love what I do, and I love that my father before me did it, too. I'm proud to be the son of a policeman. But I also know the danger the family can be placed in, and I wanted Samantha to think it over before it was too late."

It was already too late. He was in her heart, and she couldn't just rip him out. A tiny knot caught in her throat. Sounded like he was having second thoughts though, and that frightened her a little.

"Don't look like that. It's you I'm thinking of right now. I know I love you and want to be with you and Marty, but it won't be as easy as it sounds. Cops lead horrible lives. We're practically on call twenty-four hours a day. Sure, we have set times to go into work and times to head home, but the case doesn't always allow us to stay on schedule. It means phone calls in the middle of the night and me rushing out at odd hours, not able to explain a thing to you."

Sam moved closer to him as she watched his blue eyes soften. "I'm sure I'd get used to it. . .if you're sure you are not having second thoughts about me."

"Unfortunately, the job is dangerous. He's right there," Marie said.

"Not only dangerous for me, but for you and Marty as well. Your lives could be put in danger. Those nuts out there, you never know what they plan to do next. They wouldn't mind using you to make me play it their way. . .that's what they did with my mom. That's why I've always avoided getting close to anyone."

Sam reached up and gently touched the side of his face. "So what exactly changed your mind? I know Greg, your dad's partner, but what did he say that changed your mind so completely?"

Matthew stopped stirring the pot for a minute and focused his full attention on Sam. Bending slightly, he kissed the tip of her nose, then brushed it slightly with his. "Greg let me know that even though my father suffered a lonely life, in the end, he always had his memories of Mom to keep him warm. Greg said the only thing that has kept him warm at night was a blanket and maybe a bottle of whiskey. Not much comfort in that."

Sam wrapped her arms around his waist and whispered, "Greg sounds like a smart man. I can't wait to meet him."

"We best all stop talking, or I'll never get the meal cooked. And to respond to your earlier offer, thanks, but no thanks. You two would probably help me most if you'd leave the kitchen. Not that I don't want you around. You either, Marie. I'm kind of getting used to having two women underfoot. But I think more clearly when Samantha is not around to distract me."

"We'll go in the other room, but when you get it going, I'll come in and sit with you while it cooks if you'd like."

"Deal. Or I'll come join you two in the living room."

Flipping channels from one to the other, she realized she was as bad as Matthew. "Anything special you'd like to watch?"

"Not really. I don't usually watch much television."

Finally, Sam stopped on a movie. A great detective show. Her kind of film. They watched the movie in silence. After getting halfway through the flick, she heard her name being called from the other room. She liked the feeling of being loved and feeling at peace with the world. Even though danger awaited her out there in the dark of night, she knew she was safe with Matthew. "Thank You, Lord, for bringing him into my life," she whispered as she let out a sigh of contentment.

By the time the dinner was almost finished cooking, Matthew had joined them in the living room. He got Marie to sit in his chair and he sat by Sam. The doorbell rang a short time later. Matthew rose and answered the door. Sam stood slightly behind him, and Marie stayed seated.

"And this must be that special woman that makes your eyes dance with delight," Greg said as he walked into the house.

Sam felt her cheeks go warm as she thought about making Matthew's eyes do anything. His eyes made her do everything. Sam reached her hand out to shake Greg's as they were introduced. "It's a pleasure—"

"You don't get off that easy," the older gentleman said as

he swooped her up in a big bear hug. "I'm family."

The three laughed as they walked back into the living room. Marie rose from her seat. "I'm not," she said as she stuck out her hand. "I'm Marie Boudreaux. It's a pleasure to meet you. I've heard some stories about you and Jefferies...ugh, the older Jefferies I mean, from my dad. Mark Boudreaux. Captain Mark Boudreaux."

Greg laughed some more. "So he's Captain now. I can only imagine the stories you've heard."

"Marie is here on special assignment helping me keep Samantha safe. It's a long story and we've got all night. Let's go in the kitchen and sit at the table so we can really talk."

"Something smells wonderful. Matthew, my boy, did you cook this, or did you?" he asked Samantha.

Sam had to laugh to herself but didn't bother to share the joke with Greg. He must know Matthew loves to cook. Matthew was a gift sent from God. She never was much good with the stove. She could nuke with the best of them, reheating leftovers or heating carryout from a good restaurant, but that was pretty much her limit. The meals she prepared were very simple but healthy.

The four sat down and enjoyed a wonderful meal of salad, french bread and shrimp fettuccine. The thick, creamy sauce was seasoned with onions, celery, bell pepper, and garlic. The food was delicious and the conversation, light. Greg told old war stories of the police force from when he and Tad patrolled together. And Marie chimed in with a few of her own: some about her, some about her dad. Matthew spoke up occasionally himself. Sam sat back and enjoyed hearing the stories and watching everyone laughing as they enjoyed talking about their jobs.

"My compliments to the chef," Greg said as he lowered his fork and eased away from the table.

"Here, here. That was good, boss. Best I've ever had."

Matthew took his praises graciously, and they all retired to the living room. Sam and Matthew sat together on the sofa as Greg made himself comfortable on the recliner and Marie took the overstuffed chair.

"I'm glad my boy found him a woman like his mother. He never got to know her, but I did. Trust me, you have a lot of her qualities," he said as he glanced at Sam. "One of them being," he darted his brows up and down as he paused in his statement, "you don't cook, do you?"

She laughed.

Matthew considered her with a curious expression. "I've never tasted anything she's made, come to think of it," Matthew admitted as his gaze darted toward Samantha. "She admits to not being the best in the kitchen. . .but can't cook?" Still not sure, he added, "I can tell you the last few times I saw her at her house, she was about to eat something. She must cook a little. Her son, Marty, looks healthy. So my guess is she can cook a little. Jump in there, Samantha. Tell the man you can cook. . .right?"

Marie and Greg both were laughing.

Sam smiled and raised both of her hands in the air. Shrugging, she said, "I'll never tell." For now, that would remain her little secret.

They talked most of the night. Greg shared secrets from the past. . .some of Matthew's well-kept secrets. Now Marie would know, too. How long before the whole force would know?

After a couple stories were told and Matthew's worried eyes darted to Marie, she said, "Don't worry, boss. Your childhood stories will remain a mystery at work. My lips are sealed." She pinched her fingers together, then slid them across her lips, as if zipping her mouth shut.

Some of the stories were priceless. Sam would treasure them forever; others, more humorous escapades, made the night an enjoyable experience. She loved Greg immediately.

Sam watched Matthew as he reminisced with his old family friend. His eyes sparkled whenever it was a story including his father or mother or both. Matthew listened excitedly whenever Greg told a story about Matthew's parents, Tad and Katherine. She could tell he never got tired of hearing about his mother. Matthew missed out on a lot there.

She smiled to herself as she thought about her mother and how she would eat Matthew alive. Diane did not have a son and would love being able to treat him as one. Her mom had never trusted Martin, and her worries had turned out to be true. How do mommas know these things? Sam couldn't wait to share Matthew with both of her parents and Marty.

Later that night, after they said their good-byes and Greg left, Matthew put his pager on the counter and his cell phone in the charger. Marie said good night and went off to her room. As he double-checked the locks on the doors and windows, Sam headed for the spare bedroom. Pulling out the T-shirt she slept in, she sensed Matthew's presence at the doorway. Looking up and finding him watching her, she smiled. "Good night," she whispered.

"Good night."

His eyes were waiting, wanting. She eased herself over to

the door as he opened his arms to welcome her in them.

"Samantha, I don't tell people I love them, but I told you, and I meant it. I love you. You are the best thing that has ever happened to me. When all this is through, and your life gets back to normal, I want to be a part of it. Of yours and Marty's life. I hope you realize this."

Sam's heart leapt out of her chest. "Yes," she squealed. That was pretty close to a proposal. She knew it hadn't gotten to that, but. . . . "Thank you. I want it, too."

"Sweet dreams," he whispered as he bent and kissed her lightly on the lips, then turned and went down the hallway toward his room.

She watched his back until he disappeared behind the door. "Good night, sweetheart," she said softly as a smile spread across her lips. In all her days, Samantha could not ever remember being happier.

The next morning, Sam awoke to the ringing of the phone. Glancing at the clock, she saw it was early. Slipping on her robe, she ran to the kitchen. By the smell of the coffee, Matthew had been up for a while.

"Jefferies," Matthew said in the phone as she entered the kitchen.

Sam couldn't hear what was being said, but she saw his reaction. Marie, too, walked in while he was on the phone. His body stiffened as he listened. Something was wrong. Was there another murder?

"Who was it?" he asked. Silence as he listened. "Where? Was he told anything?"

More silence. Sam wanted to know what was going on,

but she had to wait, then he said, "I'm on my way."

"What happened?"

"Oh baby. I don't know how to tell you this." He hung up the phone and moved around the counter closing the space between them.

"What happened, sir?" Marie asked.

Sam's heart stopped beating as she held her breath, waiting for what he couldn't tell her. The killer found Marty? Was he okay? Were her parents okay? "So tell me. What? He's killed another woman? Please, tell me. You don't know the thoughts that are running through my mind." As bad as that would be, another woman being killed, it would be worse to her if it was her son. She couldn't lose her son. Her stomach twisted.

Matthew reached out to take her hands. "It's Amanda."

Sam gasped as her knees started to buckle. Matthew grabbed hold of her and held her upright. "Amanda? Is she all right?"

"She's alive but in bad shape. This guy has gone off the deep end. I'm heading over to her place now. Marie, you stay here. . .no. On second thought, Sam, he has no idea where you are. Right now, I'm going to bring Marie with me so she can maybe help with Amanda. Being a woman, she might be able to get a few more details from Amanda than what she might tell me."

"I have to go with you! I need to be there for her, too."

"No." Matthew shook his head. "You can't. Don't you see that's what the killer wants? He's trying to flush you out, and he knows she's your best friend. He figures you'd rush to her side to help her. That's got to be what his plan is, and we can't fall into it. We'll go to Amanda and make sure she gets all the help and protection she needs. But you can't. You have to stay here. Promise me," he begged. "Promise!" he said again sternly when she didn't answer right away.

"Okay, okay. I promise. But hurry. Get to her. Help her, then let me know she'll be okay. I'll be waiting for your call." Her hands shook like crazy. What was she going to do while she waited? The slow passing of time was going to kill her.

Sam followed them to the back door and watched as they each jumped into their own car and started backing out of the driveway. Quickly, she locked the door and ran to the living room. She peered through the picture window as taillights disappeared and they raced to Amanda's aid.

Seconds later, Sam dropped to her knees by the couch. "Oh, dear God," she prayed, "let her be okay. Please don't let her die because of me. She just found happiness in her life. Please don't take it away from her." She prayed and cried until there were no tears left to shed.

Chapter 31

Matthew arrived with sirens blasting and lights flashing. Marie pulled in right behind him. Police cars were everywhere. Amanda's apartment was a mess with furniture upside down, drapes pulled off the wall, the phone ripped out of the socket, smashed to pieces, lamps turned over, and shattered remnants of figurines everywhere.

"What a mess!" Glancing at Officer Johnson, Matthew asked, "Where's the victim? Is she okay? Do we have any witnesses?" He knew who had done this, felt it in his gut, but had to ask. The more evidence they had when the killer was caught, the deeper they could bury him.

"The victim is on her way to the hospital. Been beat pretty bad, but they talked like she would be okay. We have the boyfriend, Charles Chambers," he said pointing toward the man who was being kept in the middle of the breezeway. "He wants to get to the hospital, so you might want to talk to him first. And the neighbor across the breezeway, Maria Gabriella. She called 911."

"I think I better let him breathe a little first. Give him a couple minutes to calm down some." Matthew nodded in thanks. "Marie, find out which hospital and get on over there. See what, if anything, you can get from Amanda. Johnson, grab another uniform and you two go door-to-door to see if anybody heard or saw anything suspicious last night or in the past few days. We need to canvass the area. We have his picture, a few years old, I admit. But use it along with the sketch and see if anyone saw him. We'll get enough to put him away for life. . .when we get him."

"I'll get right on it. Don't worry, sir, we'll get him."

"And I'll get back with you as soon as I know anything from the hospital," Marie said as she left.

"Thanks," he said to her and then to Johnson, he added, "I know we will. I'll go talk to Chambers and Ms. Gabriella." Matthew walked toward the two, flashing his badge toward Charles. "I'll be with you in one minute, sir, if you'll wait over there." Matthew pointed to the other end of the breezeway.

"Please hurry, though. I need to get to the hospital," Charles said.

"I understand, sir. They said she was going to be fine, so try to relax so you'll be able to answer my questions. You'll be more help that way." Matthew turned his attention to the neighbor. "Ma'am, what exactly did you hear, and did you see anything?"

The older woman fiddled with the lapels of her robe. "This morning, I heard a lot of commotion through the wall, and then when I was putting on a pot of coffee for Joe, my husband, I heard the neighbor scream. And when I say scream, she screamed. That was around five thirty this morning. I immediately called 911. After what happened to Samantha's place, I didn't know what else to do. Joe was in the shower, or he could have gone to see if he could help her. But me, what could I do? Nothing. So I stayed inside till the police got here."

The older man standing near Amanda's door trying to sneak a peek must be Joe. Matthew found it hard to believe the woman wasn't curious enough to look out a window or something after calling for help. "And you didn't see a thing? Didn't look outside at all?"

She looked down at her feet.

That proved it to Matthew. She was not telling him the whole truth. "Mrs. Gabriella, in order to catch the bad guy, we need to know everything. Did you see anything? I need your help, ma'am. All you can give me. You never know what's important."

"Okay." The older woman looked nervous. "I admit it, but I was watching for the police. I wasn't being a busybody like everyone thinks I am. While I was watching for them, I saw a dark-haired man go running away from our building and jump in a little black car. He sped off in the same direction the police came from."

"Had you seen him before? Do you know the kind of car he drove off in?"

When she shook her head no, Matthew said, "I'll have an officer take you down to headquarters so we can get a written statement from you." He glanced at her attire. "As soon as you're ready," he added.

Matthew left her, gave instructions to Officer Myer, who was standing guard outside Amanda's door while the Crime Scene Division worked inside. Next Matthew walked over to talk to Charles Chambers. "Mr. Chambers, let's take a walk. You look like you could use a little fresh air."

The boyfriend's eyes were red, as if he had been crying. Feeling sorry for the guy, Matthew knew how he would feel if it had been Samantha. "My officer said Amanda is going to be all right. Really. She's lucky you got here when you did."

Charlie was shaking his head. "Don't you see? It's all my fault. She wanted me to stay over last night, but I was mad. It's so stupid now! I was mad because she wouldn't consent for us to live together for a year and then get married. I wanted us to get married and told her so, just not right now. First I wanted to get my degree. That's a year away. I went back to finish school for her...so I could do great things, give her the world."

Matthew let the boyfriend talk out his grief. He needed to get past it so they could get on with the investigation.

"I was so determined that she wouldn't support me in any way, 'cause all you ever hear about is how men use women to get their law degrees, then run off with their secretary later. I didn't want to ever be one of those statistics. If I hadn't pushed so hard or been so pig-headed, we would have been together at her place or mine, and this wouldn't have happened to her."

Matthew stopped them at a cement bench out in the courtyard. "Have a seat, Mr. Chambers."

Charlie sat down, dropped his elbows on his knees, and rested his face in his hands. The man looked drained; his eyes threatened to tear again.

"Mr. Chambers, listen to me. I'll tell you like I told

Samantha, Amanda is going to be all right. Because of you, we got help to her in time. That nut didn't kill her. In fact, I don't think he planned to kill her. I think attacking Amanda was meant to be more of a warning to Samantha, another way to scare her and pull her out of hiding. It scared her, and she wanted to be here. But I wouldn't let her come."

Charles was a friend of Samantha's, so Matthew knew he could confide in him, which in turn hopefully helped in calming him down some so he could be of some use to the investigation.

Using the backs of his hands, Charlie rubbed his eyes. "Sorry. Call me Charlie. From what Amanda told me, I think we might all be good friends in the future." He then extended a hand toward Matthew.

Matthew shook it, then started his questioning. Charlie gave a detailed report of the guy. The description fit Robert Thomas Howard all right. The attacker practically ran Charlie over in the doorway as he fled from the scene.

"Instead of running after him, I went in to check on Amanda. I just knew that guy had raped her or even. . .killed her." His forehead furrowed as he drew his brows together in a frown. "Thank God he hadn't. Not yet anyway. But he had slapped her around and had been choking her when I unlocked the door and started walking in. The noise of the key turning in the lock or jingling in my hand must have stopped him. I think he wanted to kill her."

Matthew wrote as Charlie spoke. Sounded like Matthew had been wrong in his earlier assessment of the situation. He had thought this was more of the same, like when he had broken into Samantha's apartment and tore it up, putting fear into her and trying to scare her out into the open. But it wasn't. It sounded like the guy had flipped right off the deep end.

From all accounts, once a serial killer changed his pattern, it started the wheels in motion, and he went completely out of control. All along, Matthew had known Samantha was being stalked because of the killer's fear of his crime being witnessed, but maybe that was just the beginning of his change. Now the man was going to be more determined than ever to get to Samantha.

Noting everything Charlie told him, Matthew said, "We need you to drop by the station later today so we can get a written statement. I know right now you want to get to the hospital and see for yourself Amanda is all right." And Matthew wanted to get back to Samantha as quickly as possible.

"Thanks, I sure do." Charlie shook his hand.

"Do me a favor. Tell Amanda as soon as it's safe, Samantha will get in touch with her, but right now her life is in extreme danger, as you both know. Watch your back, and drive safe."

"Will do and we understand. I'll see you later," Charlie said and left for the hospital.

Matthew walked back over to the apartment. The Crime Scene Division was finishing up collecting physical evidence, and they were about to leave. Another policeman stood watch at the door. Myer had left to take Maria Gabriella to the station.

"Sir, this call is for you." The uniformed officer handed the walkie-talkie to Matthew.

"Come in," Matthew said, speaking into the black apparatus in his hand.

"We have two possible witnesses over here. Do you want

to talk to them before you leave?" came the voice across the walkie-talkie.

"Be right there." He handed the black object back to the policeman. "I'll check back in over here, before I leave."

One more thing he needed to do before interviewing those two witnesses. Call Samantha. He went to pull out his cell phone.

"Dang it!" He didn't have it. He'd left his phone at home. Matthew retraced his steps to Mrs. Gabriella's and asked to use her phone. Amanda's phone was out of commission.

He heard Samantha pick up the phone. She sounded like she was breathing hard.

"Working out your worry?" he asked.

"I hoped it was you. I almost didn't answer the phone, but I decided to take the chance. How is she?"

"Amanda will be fine. I told Charlie to tell her you'd call her as soon as it was safe for you. He understood and promised he would. But listen. This man has gone over the edge. Whatever you do, don't leave the house. Stay there. He has no idea where you are. Do you understand me?"

He heard a big sigh. "I understand."

"I don't know when I'll be home, but I'll get there as soon as I can." He wanted to stress one more time not to go anywhere, but hopefully what happened to her best friend would frighten her enough to keep Samantha inside. She had a strong determination, always trying to prove she could handle any situation.

For now he had to put Samantha on the back burner of his mind. She was safe at his house. He had too much to do to be distracted by his thoughts of her and not much time to do it in. He headed for the two witnesses.

Chapter 32

His phone call about Amanda had caught her by surprise. She had spent the morning working out trying to keep from worrying. After she'd done all she could, she started cleaning his home from room to room. There was that nervous energy at work again. Her friend would be fine. That was the important thing.

A smile touched her lips. Her friend would be fine and Matthew took time to call her and give her the update. With all that was going on, he thought of her needs and worries and made that phone call.

After they hung up, Sam peeked into his office thinking about cleaning in there. "The only room I haven't touched," she said out loud. Stepping in, she glanced around, and then decided not to touch a thing. He probably had everything right where he wanted it.

She couldn't help herself as she glanced at one of the

bulletin boards, and then stepped closer to it. The pictures covering it were of the three bodies. They were not a bloody mess like you would see in the movies. This was real life, she reminded herself. Each woman's face was puffy, with eyes bulging and bruises around the face and neck. They were sickening. Sam had to turn and leave. She couldn't think about them right now. All she could see was Amanda's face, thinking Amanda could have been one of those victims.

Thank You, Lord, for protecting her and for not allowing the man to hurt my best friend. It's me he wants, Lord, but I pray You help them catch him before he can harm me or anyone else. Please let this nightmare end.

Shivering, not from cold, but from the eerie feeling of being in the room with those pictures of dead women, she left. She wasn't afraid. She knew the Lord would look out for her. She only prayed she would hear His direction.

Walking back in the kitchen, she decided to make a fresh pot of coffee. As she reached to grab the Mr. Coffee pot to fill it with water, her hand froze midair. Her eyes noticed Matthew's cell plugged in to the charger. He had left his phone. And laying next to it was his pager.

"Great." *How could he forget so much today?* She half smiled to herself, remembering what he had said to her only yesterday. *You make me forget everything.*

"That could be a bad thing. It must be bad, because now you've gone off and left something I know you need. I hope you didn't forget your gun." As that thought crossed her mind, a dash of alarm gripped her heart. No. He couldn't have left that, too. *He'll be okay. He knows what he is doing.*

She had to quit worrying. Things would be all right. *Trust in the Lord. You've asked, you've prayed. Quit worrying. Start be-lieving and receiving,* she told herself.

Sam filled the pot with water as she had planned at first, poured it into the well, and then pulled out the section to hold the grounds. Placing a filter inside, she scooped up two large dippers full of Community Dark Roast, then added another half scoop. "There. That ought to be perfect." Putting it in place, she turned on the coffeemaker and sat back to wait.

Chapter 33

Matthew made his way to one of the witnesses waiting for him.

The elderly gentleman said, "I saw a man sneaking around that apartment." With arthritis-stricken fingers, the old man pointed toward Samantha's apartment. "That was several days ago but weren't none of my business. With young folks today, you never know what they're up to."

Matthew shook his head as he wrote down the old man's statement, which included a description that fit Howard.

Next he turned to an older, full-figured woman who had been out walking her dog. They had kept them about fifteen feet from one another. "What did you see?" Matthew asked as he walked up to her.

"I saw a young man, dark hair, average height, run out of that building and jump in a black car, and then he took off." She turned to a Labrador retriever and said, "Sit." Turning back to Matthew, she added, "The next thing I know the police are swarming the place."

The same thing Mrs. Gabriella had said. "How young? A teenager? A young man in his twenties? What?"

She squinted her eyes as she appeared to think. "I'd say in his early or mid-thirties. Nowadays, you never can tell. I'm almost ninety-one. Bet you didn't know that, did you, young man?"

He smiled, shaking his head, then thanked her. Walking her toward the older gentleman he said, "I need you both to drop by headquarters to give a written statement and look at a few mug shots. If you need a ride, we'll have an officer escort you to the station." They both agreed, so Matthew made the arrangements with the policeman standing nearby, then returned to Amanda's apartment.

With every witness, every fiber, he was building a case. There was no way Matthew would let this guy slip through his fingers. . .or the courts for that matter.

Chapter 34

The coffee smelled heavenly as it filled the pot. The black murky water was just what she needed. Pulling down a cup, she started pouring coffee into it. His cell phone started ringing. *Should I? It could be important.* After several more rings, she flipped open the phone. "Jefferies' residence, may I help you?"

"Matthew Jefferies," the caller said.

"I'm sorry, but he isn't in right now, could I take a message?" Sam tried to be helpful.

"Look lady! This is a matter of life or death. He told me I could reach him anytime at this number, if he wasn't at his desk at the station. Now let me talk to him."

Sam chewed on her bottom lip. What should she do? *A matter of life or death,* he had said. *Whose?* Should she take a message, try to reach Matthew and get him to call the man back, or what? "I'm sorry, sir. He truly isn't here right now, but if you care to leave a message, I'll see that he gets it."

"Jefferies told me—aw, never mind! Take a message, but make sure he gets it right away. Jefferies told me to call if I hear anything. Tell Jefferies I got the man's name and where he's staying. I'll be waiting for him outside the Arts and Science Center downtown near the Kidd. I'll be sitting down near the river, on the levee, trying to stay out of sight. Don't want to take no chance of being caught. I'll wait half an hour. If he ain't there by then, I'm out of there, and he'll be sorry. Tell him to bring some money if he still wants this information. You got that?"

Sam was writing as fast as she could. "Yes. I do. You've got some information he wants. You'll be waiting for him, right? He's got half an hour." She glanced at her watch noting the time.

"Yeah, you got it." The line went dead.

Sam's hands were shaking. She punched in Amanda's phone number to get him the message immediately. It rang and rang. No answer. That was strange. Maybe they'd left. Sam tried calling him at the station. "He probably isn't back yet," she mumbled to herself.

His number rang a few times, then someone else picked up. "Homicide, Guidry" came the voice on the phone.

"Oh, Officer Guidry, this is Samantha Cain. Could I speak to Detective Jefferies, please?"

"I'm sorry, ma'am, but he's not here. He's working a case right now. I'll try to get word to Detective Jefferies, if it's important."

Sam breathed a sigh of relief. "Yes, it's very important. It's urgent. Tell him it's a matter of life or death."

"Is something going on there? 'Cause if you think someone is breaking in, I'll send a unit right away."

Thankful, Sam said, "That won't be necessary. It's not here. It's not me. I'm fine, but he has to meet someone—" she glanced at her watch—"in twenty-five minutes. Can you get a message to him right away and have him call me?"

"No problem. I'll get word to him."

Sam waited for what seemed like eternity, but in reality it was only a few minutes. When he didn't call her back right away, she doubted Matthew could get there in time. "I wish Marie was here. She would know what to do, but no. I'm glad she is there for Amanda. Maybe I should go and stall the man. That would help." Looking up the number for a taxi service, she ordered one right away. Sam was close; it shouldn't take long.

As she waited, she thought, *Boats, river, levee.* Could it be connected to her case? She doubted it, but it was important to another case, so she would do what she could to help him. And she would do it with the utmost care.

In the corner room, where her things were still sitting, she rummaged through her black bag for the .38. Matthew insisted she keep it with her at all times. That was as close as she had come to having the gun with her.

Sam switched from shorts to a pair of jeans, stuffed some cash in one pocket, and then, after double-checking the safety on the gun, slid it in the other pocket.

Grabbing the pad she had written the note on, she tore off the top piece of paper and shoved it in the pocket with the cash. Then she swiftly scribbled another note for Matthew and stuck it under a magnet on the refrigerator where she knew he would see it when he got home, in case the police didn't talk to him first.

A yellow cab was there in less than ten minutes. "Arts and Science Center please, and hurry."

She didn't mean to sound so desperate, but the driver turned around and gave her a strange look before saying, "Look, lady, I drive the speed limit. If that ain't good enough, get out and call for another one. I don't play those cloak-and-dagger games."

"Sure. I didn't mean speed. Sorry." Sam sat wringing her hands. She tried to rehearse in her mind what she would tell this guy. How would she know him? She never met the guy and didn't think to ask his name, and then she thought, he would be the one trying to stay hidden. Sam knew she wasn't trained to talk to an informant, but how hard could it be?

Glancing at her watch, she saw the time for Matthew to get there had almost run out. She was doing it for him and that was all that mattered. Like he had said before, you do what you have to do.

Back to the man she was looking for, Sam realized if he was trying to stay hidden, there was a good chance she wouldn't even see the man, but she had to try. For Matthew's sake. And, of course, he was not going to show himself, since he was expecting a man, not a woman.

When the taxi stopped, she paid the driver the price he asked. Slipping out of the yellow car, she stood frozen in place as she looked up and down the sidewalk. It looked deserted. "Shouldn't be hard to determine who he is," she whispered. "He should be the only one here."

Carefully, she moved toward the steps leading to the levee.

Chapter 35

Sir, this call is for you." The uniformed officer caught up with Matthew and handed him the walkie-talkie. "It's headquarters."

Matthew was about to leave. Everything was wrapped up at the scene. Only thing left was to go back to the station and complete his report.

"Come in," Matthew said into the black box.

"You had a call from Miss Cain," said Officer Guidry. "She said it's urgent you call her right away. We beeped you and called your cell phone, sir, but when we got no response I radioed you at the scene."

"Is she all right?"

"She said she was fine, but it was very important that she give you a message right away."

"Got it. I'll give her a call right away." Matthew handed the walkie-talkie to the uniformed policeman. "Loan me your cell. I'll get it back to you as quick as possible."

No questions asked, he gave Matthew his phone.

"Thanks." Quickly, Matthew called. No answer. He ran and jumped in his car. Starting his engine, he strapped himself in and pulled out in a hurry. He turned on his siren and flashing lights. They cleared a path for him as he raced toward home.

He punched in his home phone again. Still, there was no answer. The phone rang and rang. "Come on Sam. Pick up. It's me. Take the chance."

No answer.

In no time, he was there. He rushed inside. It was empty, but he found the note hanging by the magnet. Scanning it quickly, he crumbled it in his hand and muttered, "She didn't. How could she be so foolish?"

Racing out the door and back into his car, he fled toward the river. *Samantha is gone. She is trying to help me.* What she didn't know was that the snitch who called was following up on the killer who was after her.

"Dear God, please keep her safe. Help me get there in time." This was new to Matthew, but Samantha believed in Him. *It's her God. She loves Him. He must love her.*

The closer he got to his destination, the more he questioned what was about to happen. Had the killer slipped some false information to Matthew's snitch to turn the tables? Was it a setup?

He let dispatch know where he was going, just in case. Taking corners practically on two wheels, he sped to make the meeting in time. Hopefully, the information was for real and it would be enough to help catch the killer and put him away for life and not some sick plot by Robert Thomas Howard, aka Bobby.

Less than a block away, he cut off the siren, remembering it could be a setup. If so, Jake wouldn't be aware of it, but gut instinct told Matthew it was probably more than a meeting with his snitch. He had to get there in time to save Samantha.

Matthew's adrenaline heightened as he anticipated what was about to go down if his instincts were correct.

Chapter 36

The steps to cross the highway were steeper than she recalled. At the top she crossed over to the other side, and then took time to catch her breath. Sam looked out over the levee in search of the man. Buildings had been added around the downtown area along the river since the last time she had been there with Marty to watch the fireworks display. The July after Martin's death. She had tried to get his mind off of his father. Now, because of the legalization of gambling a few years ago, they had cleaned up downtown and added shops and hotels.

With careful strides, Sam raced down the steps and headed toward the concrete structure of seats along the levee. A massive cement area had been added along the levee, as well as benches for lovebirds to cuddle on. Flower beds planted here and there added to the view. She wished she was there to enjoy it.

Searching to the right, she saw the USS *Kidd* docked down at the end of a long pier. Glancing around, she noticed one man walking away from her, going back over to the highway area. Could that be him? Probably not. He was supposed to be hiding. He had a sleeping bag tucked under his arm. The homeless slept anywhere they could find to feel safe, as long as officials didn't run them off, and the number had increased after Hurricane Katrina.

Docked on the edge of the water further down, she could see the two floating casinos, but because of the distance, she could barely hear the music and noisy people.

Swallowing hard and taking a deep breath, she murmured, "Here goes." She walked along the concrete path in the direction of the pier to the *Kidd*. Her gaze traveled first one direction, then back the other way, searching the levee for a man. . .hiding. She didn't see a soul.

This was an excellent view of the muddy Mississippi River. The current was rough, even though there was no wind and no bad weather approaching. It was said, if something went in the river, there were doubts it would ever come out again, or if it did, it would be miles downstream. Due to the undertow, there had been many bodies never found of people who jumped over the side of the bridge, committing suicide.

That thought sent shivers down Sam's spine. She shook slightly, feeling as if a ghost had walked over her grave.

Since the man was hiding, she decided she needed to take a closer look around the pillars holding up the pier. This would be a perfect hiding place. When she started her descent, she didn't go down the wide cement stairs that had been built like bleachers for people to sit on to enjoy the fireworks display on the fourth of July. Instead, she went down the concrete slope. It was easier. This way she could move down toward the water and not have to watch her footing.

As she neared the bottom of the cement, she noticed a person sitting, huddled over, almost next to the water under the walkway to the ship. His body leaned slightly against the large cement structure bracing the pier.

"Maybe that was what he called being hidden," she said under her breath as she started toward the man.

When the cement ended, which was two-thirds of the way down the levee, the ground became hard-packed dirt mixed with loose gravel. The level of the river was down. No grass grew on this section of the levee at all. She walked down the decline toward the man, toward the water's edge. Moving very cautiously, she eased closer and closer to the hunched-over body.

The closer she got, the more she didn't like it. He hadn't moved a muscle. He should have noticed her approaching by now. He should have turned and looked in her direction. Maybe it wasn't the one she was looking for after all. She hoped not, now that she was less than ten feet away. He still sat with his head bent over. Maybe he was drunk and had passed out in a drunken stupor. Yes. That was why he hadn't noticed her approach.

Step by step, Sam moved closer. When she was almost up to him, she slipped on some gravel that rolled beneath her feet. She started to fall but caught herself. Straightening up, she took the last five steps, placing her right next to the man.

Sam squatted by his side. "Mister," she said as she touched his shoulder lightly. He still didn't move. If he was asleep, he was one heavy sleeper, if drunk. . .dead drunk.

A slight breeze stirred off the river. At that moment, Sam got a whiff of whiskey. She was right. "The man's drunk," she mumbled aloud.

Looking closer, she saw marks on his neck, red marks along with some bruises. Suddenly, she remembered where she had seen those types of markings before, on the victim's bodies in the pictures hanging on Matthew's bulletin board in his office.

Was he dead, too? Panic rose within and pin needles pricked her body. She had to get out of there. Every nerve stood on end.

A wire wrapped around her throat before she could turn. A horrifying scream broke the silence around her. Sam's scream shattered the stillness as her hands reached up and caught hold of the wire starting to close tightly around her neck.

The man is dead, not drunk. And I'm next!

Those thoughts flashed through her mind as she screamed and fought for her life.

Chapter 37

Matthew whipped up to the curb in front of the Arts and Science Center. As he was coming to a stop, he called in for backup.

He leaped out of his car and slammed the door shut. As he turned toward the levee, he heard a scream. He would know Samantha's voice anywhere.

"Samantha!" he screamed as his mind shouted, *Hold on, baby! I'm on my way.*

His heart pounded as he rushed around the building.

Another scream sounded, but the distance seemed further. He was not going to lose her—or the killer.

There was no time to waste.

Chapter 38

Sam pulled with all her strength till the wire cut into her fingers. The warmth of the blood oozed around the wire and trickled down her hands. "He's not going to get me," she swore under her breath. She had too much to live for: Marty, Matthew. God had just blessed her with a future for her and her son; she wasn't going to lose that without a fight.

Be not afraid. You can do all things through Christ. Strength started to flow through her veins as those words came to mind.

She couldn't knee him in the groin; he was behind her. She had to do something, anything. Quickly and with all her strength, she lifted her right foot up and pushed backward into his knee. She hit it so hard, she heard a pop.

"Aaahhhh," he cried out.

On target. The wire dropped from around her neck, giving Sam the opportunity to run as fast as she could. She didn't know how badly she had damaged him, but she wasn't going to hang around and find out. Sam took off up the levee, across the loose gravel, and away from the water's edge, toward the cement incline. It was much slower running uphill.

For a second, she stopped and looked around for help. No one. She had to hide. The floating casinos were too far, and she knew the streets were deserted. Hiding on the *Kidd* was her only chance. It was closer. She had to make it to the ship and hide until Matthew found her. Hopefully, he would get the message and be there soon.

Quickly, she ducked under the linked chain that stretched across the beginning of the pier, and then ran toward the USS *Kidd*. Just ahead, a locked gate stretched across the walkway. The gate's bars looked like a jail, only the bars extended out one foot on both sides of the railing.

The gate was too high to climb over, and the slits were too narrow to slip through. Without wasting any time, Sam threw one leg over the side railing and eased along the edge of the pier. Step by step, she slipped her feet in the openings between the bars, working around that extra distance. She made it from one side, back down the other side, and then reached the rail. Holding on tight, she crossed her right leg over the railing onto the other side of the locked gate and pulled the other leg behind her. She made it, one movement at a time.

Once on the other side, Sam ran as fast as she could. As she ran the last few feet on the pier and crossed over onto the ship, she paused for only a second to see how far behind she had left him. He was limping after her. At least she had slowed him down, and she had a lead.

This scum wasn't going to catch her. She could pull the

gun out and shoot him, if she thought she could hit him, but Sam didn't trust herself under these real circumstances. Better to keep the distance. Hide—that was what she needed to do. She doubted she could shoot a person. It was one thing to shoot at a target. It was another to shoot at a real human being. She couldn't do it. Matthew would get there and save her. She needed only to hide out and wait.

In the distance, near the building, she saw a moving shadow but didn't have time to stop and be sure. *Let that be Matthew. Please, Lord, let that be him.*

Hurrying around the deck, she ducked through a portal and ran down a flight of stairs, moving as quickly as possible and scanning for any feasible hiding place.

Running down a short narrow hallway and taking every turn, she saw plenty of doors to run through. She even opened a few, hoping it would throw the killer off or at least slow him down some more.

Unfortunately, it didn't seem to. Before she knew it, she heard his feet dragging down the hallway in her direction. She hadn't lost him at all. Sam ducked into one of the small rooms and glanced around. She had to hide.

There it was. A great place for her to crawl into and hope he didn't find her.

She crossed the room. Along the back wall was a storage area for lifejackets. Sam lifted one of the seats, crawled into the big box-looking thing, squatted down in the bottom, and curled up into a fetal position, then let the lid close over her. The gun handle poked in her stomach while the barrel pushed into her leg.

Her heart pounded in her chest, the beating so loud she

was afraid he might hear it. Sam tried to slow down her breathing so she could ease the hammering of her heart. Just when she had it almost under control, she heard a bang. The metal door clanked against the wall as he threw it open and stepped into the room. Listening very closely, she managed to hear his feet. The first step slapped as it hit the metal flooring and the second one dragged behind it.

He wasn't even trying to be quiet. The man wanted Sam to hear him, she decided. This was part of his plan to scare her to death. She swallowed hard. It was working. *Be not afraid,* she reminded herself.

"I've got you now," he called to her.

I'm okay, she told herself. *Stay calm.* Sam's body shook all over. She couldn't fall apart. She had to be strong. She had to be tough. Sam didn't want to be another statistic for this sicko. She was not alone. The Lord was with her, and Matthew was on the way.

She wiped the sweat off her hands by rubbing them against her jeans. Her hands slid across the hard object in her pocket.

The gun! She had no choice now. She had to get ready, maybe even use it. Trying to straighten herself a bit so she could slide the gun out of her pocket, she eased her hand in the pouch, touched the cold steel, then cautiously, trying not to make any noise, pulled the gun out of her jeans.

Her hands were still shaking and now they held a gun. She had told Matthew about the danger of guns when the user didn't know what they were doing. Now she was afraid she fit that description perfectly.

Think! she yelled at herself in her mind. Matthew had gone over this with her to be sure. *Remember.*

Feeling with her hands, because she was in total darkness, her fingers found the safety. Clicking it off, she took hold of the gun with her right hand in firing position, and held it steady with her left. Aiming it straight up, she sat waiting and ready.

The killer's feet were still moving around in the room. "I know you're in here, and I'll find you."

She could hear him opening cupboards and knocking things around as he called to her, warning her. Next she heard him lifting the seats one at a time, and then letting them slam shut. Sam's heart clamored as it banged up against her ribcage. *Oh God, oh God, help me, please,* her thoughts cried out. She could hear the whacks and crashes getting closer and closer.

Finally, she heard him next to her as he grabbed the handle on the lid above her. Sam sat waiting. . .but ready.

"Are you in here?"

A flood of light filled the box as the seat was lifted open. Sam didn't breathe. She waited. Her eyes adjusted. He still had to look down in to see her. She knew this and counted on it. The box was deep.

Her hands shook more and more with each passing second. His shadow covered her first, and then she saw his head. As he bent over to look in, she fired the gun twice in quick succession. Sam saw him fall backward.

She scrambled up and out of the box, holding the gun tightly in her right hand. She looked over at him, afraid to run around him. There he was, laid out on the floor.

A small puddle of blood stained the floor next to his face. A moment of relief washed over her, and she started to ease around him and head toward the door.

As she made her way past the body on the floor, the killer caught her by the ankle. "Oh, no you don't!" he hollered.

His hands wrapped around her foot as she tried to pull away. He pulled her foot right out from under her.

Sam landed with a thud on the floor. She lost her air but not the gun. Her hand held on tight. Her bottom hurt, but she didn't have time to think about it. She had to shoot again. Sam turned the gun on him. As she started to pull the trigger, he knocked her arm up into the air. The bullet rang out, but missed the target.

The killer knocked Sam flat on her back and covered her body with his, holding her arm out, keeping the gun out of his face. A stale odor of sweat invaded her senses as they struggled. His cold eyes, which she remembered all too clearly, stared down at her. The dark stubble on his tanned face didn't hide the etched lines of pain and anger shadowed beneath the facial hair.

Sam's hand was still wrapped around the gun tightly as she gagged from the smell of his body odor. *Oh Matthew, where are you? Please Lord, let him get here in time,* she cried out in her mind.

She wasn't going to give the gun up, or her life for that matter, without a fight. Sam pulled her arm in and pointed the gun toward his chest. Just when she thought it was right to pull the trigger, he twisted it back toward her.

Sam never thought in a million years she would be doing this. She should have waited for Matthew, or been more prepared. She should have practiced shooting more, worked out more, and built up her strength. *My strength comes from the*

Lord, she reminded herself as she twisted the gun one more time in his direction.

Her heart cried out to Matthew again, but still, he wasn't there. Her finger squeezed the trigger. The sound reverberated in the metal room.

Chapter 39

Matthew followed the sounds and knew he was close. As he worked his way down another flight of steps and eased around the corner, he caught a glimpse of a man entering a room at the far end. Sprinting down the tiny hallway toward the shadow he had seen, he heard shots ring out. Matthew reached the room, stepped through the door, and simultaneously fired his weapon. The man was on top of Samantha. Both Matthew's and Samantha's shots rang out at the same time. Everything seemed to freeze. The killer still sat astride Samantha, but Matthew knew he had hit him. In another instant, Matthew saw the killer snatch the gun out of Sam's hand, and he turned it on Matthew as he turned his whole body around and off of Samantha in one quick motion.

Matthew fired off two more shots at the perpetrator, straight to the chest. When the bullets hit, the killer, Robert

"Bobby" Thomas Howard, dropped the gun and fell backward across Samantha.

Immediately, Matthew pulled the perp off of her, turned him over, and laid him on the floor. Squatting down, he twisted the killer's hands behind him and slapped the cuffs on him. Samantha lay perfectly still. At a glance, she looked to be fine. "Samantha," he called as he rose to his feet.

No answer.

Matthew sank down close to her. Blood was on her blouse. "Samantha, talk to me. You're okay." He wasn't sure, but she had to be. The blood soaked a large area. She had been hit, but Matthew wasn't sure where. Thank God it wasn't the heart, too low for that.

"Samantha, Samantha, hang on! I'm here! We're going to get help! Hang on!" he said to her, hoping she was listening to him. Punching buttons on the borrowed cell, he called the station. Backup had already been sent. Now on his words two ambulances were being dispatched.

Matthew turned to Sam. Careful not to move her since he didn't know the extent of her injuries, he leaned down near her face and whispered, "Hold on, baby. Help is on the way. You're going to be okay. Hang in there. Stay alive. Don't you dare die on me now." He kissed her lips. "Stay with me, baby."

When the first cop appeared through the door, Matthew barked orders at him, "When the ambulance arrives, get them up here ASAP!"

Another policeman on the scene inspected the killer. "He's alive, but barely. He's losing a lot of blood."

"There is one coming for him, too. Don't let him out of your sight. Not for one minute. Go with them to the hospital and stay with him."

She still hadn't said a word. Could it be shock? Her eyes had opened, but she just lay there. He didn't know what was going on, but he knew she was alive. "Hold on. Help is on the way."

A short time later, the ambulance attendants carried Sam up top, and Matthew followed her all the way to the emergency vehicle.

"Take good care of her," he told the men and watched in despair as they drove away, siren screaming and lights flashing.

Keep her alive, Lord. Give us a chance.

Chapter 40

At the station, Matthew talked to the chief, giving him all the details, then rushed through the necessary paperwork on Robert Thomas Howard. Anything that wasn't mandatory would have to wait. He needed to be with Samantha.

Howard was in critical condition, still under tight security at the hospital. By the time Matthew's report was completed, he had received the details of Howard's mother's death, which gave him a better understanding of the man's warped mind. Not that it excused anything he had done, by any means.

Matthew turned in his completed report, gave a statement to the press, then left for the hospital. When he arrived, he found Samantha was in surgery. The bullet had done some internal damage that the doctors were attempting to repair.

"She's in good hands. Have faith," the nurse told Matthew

as he stood next to the desk. "You can wait in the waiting room. Drink some coffee and relax. As soon as she comes out of surgery, we'll let you know."

The first thing Matthew did was get word to Charlie and Amanda, then asked if they would contact Samantha's parents. After that, time dragged by.

Matthew poured a cup of strong, nasty coffee that hospitals were famous for having. It might not taste good, but he knew he needed something to keep him going. Right now he wanted to fall completely apart worrying about what could be happening to Samantha.

Marie walked into the waiting room and went straight to the detective. "How is she, sir?"

"She could die during surgery, and it would be all my fault." If he had caught the killer earlier, she never would have become involved in Howard's sick story. Matthew also realized the only reason a gun had been around for her to get shot was because he insisted Samantha relearn how to use the gun and keep it with her for her own protection.

She had tried to tell him it would be more dangerous in the hands of someone who didn't know what they were doing. She was right. A one-time practice at the firing range wasn't enough to make her proficient with a gun. Sure, under normal circumstances, the practice would have helped. But hers were nothing near normal. It was all his fault.

Had she not had the gun, she might be fine right now. He had heard her scream and when he heard that, she had been just on the other side of the levee. Somehow, she managed to get away from the killer long enough to run to the USS *Kidd*. On the *Kidd*, she managed to stay out of his clutches, probably by hiding, up until right before Matthew caught up to them. He had seen the killer climbing around the locked gate and fled after him, knowing in his gut, the killer was chasing Samantha.

Without the gun, she would have only been fighting with Howard when Matthew arrived. He was that close behind the killer. Matthew could have overtaken him, and Samantha would be safe at this very moment. It was all his fault.

"Sir, if I had stayed with her, maybe she wouldn't be there fighting for her life. So it's just as much my fault as it is yours."

He knew Marie Boudreaux was just trying to make him feel better, but it wasn't working. He wouldn't be better until Samantha was perfectly fine again.

"Her friend, Amanda, is fine, sir. She had to get a lot of stitches and she is going to hurt like the dickens, but everything he did to her will heal. That will make Sam happy when she learns this. In fact, they are coming here when she gets released from the emergency room. Which should be soon."

He heard her speaking but really didn't hear what she was saying. His mind stayed on Samantha. Marie went and poured him a hot cup of coffee when she poured herself one, and then came back and sat in silence but waited with him. Time crept by.

Amanda and Charlie finally arrived. Her bruises were ugly, and her stitches were many, but she was all in one piece. No broken bones, and he hadn't raped her. She would heal.

Samantha would be glad to hear it.

Quickly Matthew gave them the news on Samantha, then

told them that the killer was in the hospital fighting for his life but under lock and key.

The doctor came out to the waiting room. "The damage has been repaired and Samantha is in recovery. Everything went well."

Shortly after, Samantha's parents arrived and were introduced to Matthew and Marie. Amanda gave them an update on Samantha's condition.

"Where's Marty?" Matthew asked.

"We left him with our neighbor. We didn't think he should see her right now. When she's better. . ." Sam's mother tried to smile, but Matthew could tell she would rather cry.

"I'm sorry your daughter is going through this. It's all my fault. I should have gotten to her sooner. I should have—"

Diane grabbed Matthew's hand and held it tightly. "Son, don't blame yourself. She'll be okay. She's in God's hands." Reaching into her purse, she pulled out a small Bible and shared some scripture with him. "So you see. We only need to trust Him. He's in charge, and He'll see her through."

"But what if she doesn't make it?"

"She'll be with Him in heaven. Either way, she wins, and we'll get through. But, I believe, He'll bring her through this. He's given me peace."

"I hope you're right."

They all sat in silence, waiting. It could take a couple of hours for the drugs to wear off. When they did, she would be fine. Matthew had to keep reminding himself of that. Marie left to go back to the station. Matthew promised to call as soon as they knew something.

Matthew swallowed a big swig of cold coffee from his

fourth cup, then tossed it into the trash can. Time passed slowly, but finally a nurse came into the room. "She's waking up."

"How is she?" Matthew asked as he rushed to the nurse's side.

"She's weak at the moment, but her vitals are stable. She should continue to strengthen."

"When can I see her?" Sam's mom touched the nurse's arm. "When can we see her?" she added as her gaze moved to her husband.

"We can let you in for a minute or two and only a couple of you at a time." Her gaze moved to each one of them as she spoke.

Running his hands through his hair, Matthew said, "Thank you." He wanted to go. He needed to go. But Matthew knew he wasn't blood. Her parents only knew him as the cop who had saved their daughter. Matthew looked at Amanda. He knew he was pleading with his eyes and hoped she got the message.

"Let's let Matthew go back there first," Amanda said as she slipped her arm through Diane's and held her gently. "Remember what I told you? I believe he would be the best medicine for Sam right now."

The mother hesitated, but her husband laid his hands gently on his wife's shoulders and whispered, "Come on, honey. Amanda said she loves the guy. Let's give her what she needs right now, not what we need."

Diane nodded in agreement. Everyone returned to their seats and waited it out.

"Tell her we're here and give her our love," Diane said.

"Mine and Charlie's, too," Amanda called out.

Matthew nodded as he rushed out of the room.

Would she be all right? The doctor said he repaired all the damage. What if he missed something? Would she ever forgive Matthew for not getting there sooner? Could he forgive himself if Samantha didn't make a complete recovery? Could they get past this and make a life together for themselves? For the three of them?

He loved her, and if he couldn't have her, his life would be meaningless.

Passing through the double doors into recovery, Matthew followed the nurse into Samantha's section. Quietly, he entered her room.

His heart dropped to his stomach as his gaze fell on Samantha, her face so pale, her body so limp, just lying there. Her eyes were closed, and machines were hooked up to her. Matthew's eyes scanned the monitors. Looking at the needle in her arm, he winced. His gaze traveled up her arm to her face. The loss of blood left her weak and pale, the paleness emphasizing the bruises to her face.

Stepping to the side of the bed, he said, "Hi, sweetheart." He bent down and kissed her cheek. "Welcome back to the land of the living. I'm so glad you're going to be all right."

She opened her eyes and looked at him but didn't say a word.

"Amanda and Charlie are here. They called your parents, and they are here, too. Marie was even here for a little while. I promised her I'd let her know how you are doing. You kind of grew on her. You have a way with people." He touched the back of her hand gently. "Everyone is waiting to see you, but I pushed to get to see you first. Hope that's okay." Gently, he brushed a few strands of her hair to the side of her face.

"Marty. Where is Marty?"

"He's with one of your parents' neighbors. Your mom said they would bring him up later. When you're in your own room."

Her fingers jerked as she asked very softly, "Is it over? Did you get him?"

"Yes. I wish I'd been there sooner to protect you, sweetheart. But I promise, I won't let anything happen to you again." Looking down at her, he whispered, "I love you."

Her eyes fluttered closed. When he saw her even breathing, Matthew realized she had fallen back to sleep. Since the doctor had said that was what she needed, he slipped quietly out of the room. Besides, he needed to give her parents a few minutes with her, too.

"She looked great, but she's fallen back asleep again," Matthew said.

Her mom had to see Samantha for herself. Matthew understood that. She promised not to wake her.

When her parents came back to the waiting room, Matthew said, "You ought to go get Marty and bring him back. She asked for him. He would be the best medicine for her. By the time you get back, she should be in a room."

"That's a great idea. We'll stay here with the detective," Amanda agreed.

"Matthew, please. Call me Matthew."

Her parents left to go get Marty.

While they sat in the waiting room, Amanda and Charlie talked over old times they had shared with Sam. Matthew listened and enjoyed hearing the stories of Samantha as a child and some of the escapades she and Amanda had been involved in. Some of the stories even included Charlie and Martin. Amanda then went on to mention the hard times Sam had these past few years taking care of herself and Marty, but her son made everything worth it.

Matthew took a lot of it in but mostly stayed focused on his desire for her to be totally well and his need to be near her.

About the time the nurse came out to let them know what room Samantha was being transferred to, Marty and his grandparents came walking in.

As a group they went to the fourth floor and headed to the room. When they got there, Samantha was already sitting up. Everyone walked in and gathered around the bed, giving Marty the closest spot to his mom.

"Momma! Oh, I'm so glad you're okay. Don't ever do this to me again. Granny and Papaw told me you are going to be all right, but I was scared." Tears were running down his face as he held his momma's hand, squeezing it tightly.

"Oh, baby. Momma didn't mean to scare you. You kept me strong through this whole ordeal. Thank you for being my big man for me." She smiled at her son as a tear trickled down her cheek.

Matthew felt such joy. He was going to be a part of that family. A proud feeling swept over him. *What a lucky guy I am. Thank You, Lord. Samantha was right. She said to trust You.*

"Guys, do you mind stepping out in the hall. I need to talk to Matthew for a minute."

He smiled and thought good thoughts till everyone cleared the room. Samantha turned her eyes on him. The smile from her face was gone. What was she going to say? Why the look? Everything was over. Only the best could possibly happen now. What was she thinking? Matthew wasn't sure he wanted to know, but he braced himself.

Chapter 41

How would she tell him? What words could she possibly use that would make him understand? As she was about to speak, Matthew bent over the bed and placed a warm, loving kiss on her mouth.

Her heart raced as the warmth of his lips pressed against hers. Love swelled inside her as her heart drummed out of control. Joy mixed with fear raced within her. Could she do this to Marty? Could she do this to herself?

She attempted to raise her head off of the pillow so she could sit up. A pain shot through her side and stomach, and she groaned.

"Aren't you supposed to stay still?"

She nodded. "Probably."

"Please do what they say. I'm so glad you're going to make it. You sure had me worried." Matthew kept his face close to hers. His eyes peered into hers.

She had to tell him. Again before she could form the words, he leaned over and brushed his lips gently against her cheek. "I was so scared. My life would be nothing without you."

She swallowed hard. "I don't know if I can go through this again."

"What do you mean? I thought you understood it was over. We got him. You don't have to worry anymore."

Sam didn't know what to say, but she had to continue. "What about your next suspect? What if the fears you've had all your life come to pass and they go after me to get to you? Or even worse, they go after Marty. Use him against you. I don't think I can take that chance with my son."

He breathed a sigh and then smiled.

She watched the changes on his face. Why wasn't he afraid? A thought flashed through her mind. *Everything happened for a reason. At least I'm alive. My son won't lose another parent.* Where did that come from? She couldn't stop the thoughts, but she still knew what she had to do. Yes, everything happened for a reason. This happened to make her see clearly, she couldn't put Marty through it.

"I understand what you're saying, but you are wrong. I was wrong then. In fact, today I blamed myself for what happened to you. If you had died, I would never have forgiven myself. I insisted you use the gun." Matthew caught her hand again and held it tightly. "Marty could have lost his mom. . .but he didn't. You were right. No one should handle a gun if they don't know exactly what they're doing. If I had listened to you, or at least let you listen to yourself, you wouldn't have been shot.

"Unfortunately, I wasn't thinking like a cop. Shoot, I wasn't thinking period. I just wanted you to be safe. Thank God, you're all right now." He squeezed her hand tighter. "I prayed. I knew God loved you, so He would listen to me, even though I don't know Him...yet."

Yet? This might be the good that will come out of what has happened, but I can't take a chance and marry a policeman for my son's sake. Matthew will have to understand. I love him, but I love Marty, too. And I have to put him first.

"Samantha Cain. Are you listening to me? I love you, and I will never let you go. It's you and me and Marty together forever. I want you to marry me. Will you marry me?" he asked, his voice strong and clear.

She looked into his eyes and watched as the love poured out of them. Against her will, tears started to form in her own eyes. *What do I do, Lord? I love him, too. Sure I want to marry him, but I can't. It wouldn't be fair to Marty. It wouldn't be fair to Matthew.*

"Samantha!" Matthew's voice started to rise. "Why aren't you talking to me?" He dropped her hand. "You hold me to blame for what you're going through, right? That's it." He paused, and then added, "You're right to do so. I can't blame you, because I know I did this to you. But it won't happen again. I'll keep you safe. You and Marty both."

"You can't promise that. Well, you can promise it, but you don't control things. You can only try."

Dragging his fingers through his hair, he groaned, "You are right. I don't control it. Your God does. And He allowed us to meet again and fall in love. Don't you think He had a purpose in that? Don't you think He could have stopped that if we weren't meant to fall in love? He's your God. I only know what you've told me and what my dad tried to tell me as a young man. And let's not forget your mom."

She couldn't take her eyes off of Matthew. He was the same but different. Sam was worrying about the future instead of living for the day. *What does the Word say? Worry about nothing, pray about everything.*

"We could have a beautiful life together, no matter what the outcome." He went on. "We were meant to be together. I've waited my whole life for you. I love you. Please, don't make me go on without you. I couldn't do it."

A look of horror crossed his face when she did not respond to his open admission of such an overpowering of love. He shouted, "You do still love me, don't you?"

"Yes," she whispered as she closed her eyes and lifted up a silent prayer. *Help me, Lord. Show me the answer.*

Calmness filled the room as a smile spread across his face.

"That's all I needed to know." Snatching her hand again, he leaned down to her face. "Say yes to marrying me," he whispered before his lips covered hers.

Sam savored his kiss of love. She wanted it to go on forever. Life would be grand if it didn't matter that their lives would be in danger, but Sam lived in the real world. Things do happen, even to good people. She couldn't put her son in jeopardy like that. She had to say no.

When Matthew ended the kiss, he caught her bottom lip with his teeth and eased away, slowly releasing his hold as he moved back. Her tongue touched her lip, spreading the warmth he had radiated within her.

"Samantha, I'll let you know now, I won't take no for an answer."

Her gaze rested on his loving face. From it she drew courage she never knew she had. God put them together for a reason. A moment ago, she knew it was to save Matthew's eternal life. But could it be more? He loved her and she loved him. What more could she ask for? He made her believe they could face anything together.

"Your parents shared a word from the Bible earlier in the waiting room. It talked about trusting God and fearing not. That is what being a Christian is all about. Trusting God. Knowing He is in control. You need not fear. He sees the big picture. Your mom said you'd be okay because you are in the Lord's hands. I even asked, but what if she dies? And do you know what your mom said? She said then you would be right next to Him in heaven. How could you lose? How could Marty lose? How could I lose? It's a win-win situation." Matthew stood up straight and grinned from ear to ear. "How can you argue with God?"

With a peace in her heart, she fixed her stare on his beautiful blue eyes and said, "Yes. I'll marry you."

Looking up, he said, "Thank You, God." Catching her face in his hands, he leaned down and kissed her hard on the mouth. After the kiss, he pulled back slightly, his voice almost in a whisper, and said, "Girl, you scared me. For a minute there, I thought you were going to say no."

"I almost did," Sam confessed. "In fact, I meant to."

As he dropped his hands from her face, she automatically reached out for them, catching them in her grasp. He squeezed gently, then rested her hands back down by her side.

A joy deeper than she ever thought possible overwhelmed her and she shouted joyfully, "There is no arguing with God's Word. Thank you for reminding me."

"We'll both thank your mom, too."

Her eyes held Matthew's gaze as her shaking hands covered her mouth. Water rimmed her eyes. Tears of joy rushed down her cheeks. She whispered, "Bring the family in. Let's share the news."

"It will be my pleasure." He rushed to the door and swung it open. Marie had joined the family out in the hall. Everyone was waiting, and their eyes all rested on Matthew as he opened the door.

"Come in. . .everyone. We have some great news to share with you all." He rushed back to her side as they were filling the room.

"I love you," he whispered, for her ears only.

She laughed. "I love you more than anything in the world," she said a little louder than intended.

"More than me?" Marty cried out. Samantha winked at her son and said, "As much as you. Everyone, Matthew asked me to marry him." She looked back at Matthew. "For the record, Matthew, I could never tell you no."

"Truly?"

"Never. . .about anything."

"That's my girl," he whispered as his lips pressed against hers.

And all the people in the room cheered, including Marty.

Testimony of Innocence
Samantha Cain Mysteries
Book 2

I dedicate this book to
my critique partners, Emy and Marie,
who have believed in me for a very long time.
Thank you for your encouragement along the way.

And, as always, God and my family.
Without them, I am nothing.

ACKNOWLEDGMENTS

The Samantha Cain series has been a dream of mine for almost twenty years. If it wasn't for my friends and family who believe in me, it would probably still be a dream. I look forward to many books to follow and hope everyone enjoys them!

Charlotte and Marty, thanks for your help in the final stages of *Testimony of Innocence*.

Emy and Marie, I can never thank you enough for your love, support, and critiquing, but I'll keep trying.

Ramona Tucker, my editor, thanks for believing in me. You're the best editor anyone could ask for, and you really live your faith. I'm proud to be part of the family at OakTara.

Last, but not least, I thank You, Lord, for calling me to write fiction and for giving me the ability to share Your love in every one of my books.

∾

"I have told you these things,
so that in me you may have peace.
In this world you will have trouble.
But take heart! I have overcome the world."
JOHN 16:33 NIV

Chapter 1

Three hard knocks sounded on the front door, awakening Samantha from her short nap on the couch after working the night shift.

She stirred. *Open your eyes.*

Forcing her eyes open, Samantha glanced at her watch.

Umph. Nearly time for her to wake her son, Marty, for school.

Three more raps pounded on the door.

Who could that be at this early hour?

Instantly, an image from six short months ago flashed through her mind. Two police officers stood at her apartment door with bad news: Matthew Jefferies, her fiancé, had been killed in the line of duty.

Her insides coiled as she rose. Ice tipped her fingers as she stared at the door, her feet frozen to the floor.

The demanding knocks came a third time. Against her

better judgment, she moved in the direction of the front door. Taking a cleansing, reassuring breath, she slowly reached out for the doorknob. The cold round ball matched the chill within. Only bad news came this early in the morning. "Give me that extra strength, Lord," she whispered.

A single thought allowed her a moment of cheer. Maybe Greg, Matthew's dear friend and now hers, or Amanda, her best friend for many years, decided to drop by to say hello and check on her and Marty. But that pleasing idea vanished almost as fast as it had come. She knew better. Emptiness gnawed at her heart as she released the breath she'd held and forced herself to open the door.

Morning light spilled inside the door, revealing two strange men standing on the front porch. Both were dressed in off-the-rack suits: one brown, one blue. Glancing behind the unexpected men, she saw a dark blue government-issued car parked in the driveway and realized the men were plain-clothed police officers, detectives of some sort. This reality intensified the grip on her insides as she tightened her hold on the doorknob.

Not again. She bit her bottom lip, trying to retain control of her emotions. What could they possibly want with her?

"Hello. May I help you?" Her tone surprised her. It sounded calm, almost peaceful, as if she were glad to find them standing on her front steps.

But voices, she knew, could be deceiving. In her heart, she wanted to yell at them to go away. It had only been six months since Matthew died—a week before their wedding. You'd think after that tragedy she could handle anything that came her way. But she was still grieving.

"Samantha Cain?" The man in the brown suit flashed his badge.

"Yes."

"I'm Lieutenant Jones, and this is Sergeant Barnett. May we come in?"

As the first man spoke, the man in blue also exposed his badge, as if making sure there was no misunderstanding that both were police detectives, there on official business.

She opened the door wider. "Please come in. Take a seat. I'll be back in a minute. I have to wake my son for school."

Shivers raced through her as she walked out of the living room. She wanted to run and hide. What was this about? Her heart tightened.

At least her son—the most important thing in her life— was fine. She planned to keep him safe and guard him from the ugliness of the world. In the first eight years of his life, Marty had already lived through too much. First, his father, who took his own life, and then the death of Matthew, who planned to be his future father—truly his daddy.

What more could possibly go wrong?

Sam also knew her parents were fine. She had spoken to them last night.

What else was there?

Who else was there?

She sighed. Whatever it was, she would handle it. Life would still go on, day after day.

Knocking on Marty's door, she stepped into the room and slipped over to his bedside. "Hey, baby, it's time to get up. Get ready for school," she whispered, shaking him gently. "Rise and shine." She stepped to the window and rolled the plastic pole slightly with her fingertips, opening the blinds a crack. Sunlight spilled into his room.

"Aw, Mom, do I have to?" His little body stretched as he tried to open his eyes. Twisting under his covers, he hid his face from the light and tried to go back to sleep.

The boy knew the answer before he asked, so she didn't bother to respond. He would get up. That she also knew. He loved school—the learning and the playing.

"We have company, so I may not get to make you breakfast," she told him in a matter-of-fact tone. "You can fix yourself a bowl of cereal, or better still, tap on Ms. Margaret's door. Tell her I have some company and ask her if she'll fix you something this morning. Tell her I'll explain later. Right now, I'll go put on the coffee pot for her." She ruffled her son's dark reddish hair. "Get up now. Be a good boy."

Taking another route back to the living room, she slipped through the kitchen and turned on the coffeemaker. Margaret always pre-cleaned and set the machine with grounds and water the night before. The woman was such a blessing in Sam's life.

Next Sam walked through the swinging door separating the kitchen from the living room. The floor plan of Matthew's home, now hers and Marty's home, was laid out exceptionally well. The house was warm, cozy, efficient.

Matthew had listed Samantha as his beneficiary, leaving everything to her, including his house. At first it had been strange and unsettling living there without him in it, especially since that was where they had planned to live once married. After a short time she realized the blessing. Living there now kept his image, his scent, her memories of him, and the time they'd spent together closer to her and to Marty. Matthew had been a strong influence in her son's life, even though the time had been short. Already his home felt like theirs, with only great memories hidden in the shadows.

"Now, gentlemen, what can I do for you?" Masking her insecurities, she perched on Matthew's favorite chair across from them. Matthew may not be there for her now, but she felt his presence in his things.

"We have a few questions for you," the lieutenant said as Sergeant Barnett pulled out a pad and pen.

"About what? What questions could you possibly have for me? You two are detectives, right? From which precinct and which division?" As a former cop's wife, Sam knew there were several divisions, such as robbery, homicide, burglary, and even a general investigations division. But she had no idea what they could possibly want with her.

"When was the last time you saw your boss, Ken Richardson? And what did you two talk about?"

"My boss?" Them asking questions about Ken had never entered her mind. She had to think on that one—for two reasons. One, she didn't get along that well with her boss and tried to keep her distance from him as much as possible; and two, she worked the night shift, which gave her little, if any, contact with him. He left every day at four thirty on the dot, and she worked the night shift, 6:00 p.m. to 6:00 a.m.

"Is Ken okay?" For the two of them to come to her door, something had to have happened to Ken. But still, why come to her? She only worked for the man. Sam only knew him as a boss.

"Answer our questions, Ms. Cain. When was the last time

you saw or spoke with Ken Richardson?"

"I don't understand why you'd be asking me about my boss. What's wrong? Did he do something wrong or did something happen to him? No one mentioned anything about him last night at work when I went on duty. And no one called about him during the night. I was there all night. So why are you asking me about my boss this early in the morning?"

Sam hoped he was okay. Even though she didn't get along very well with the man, she didn't want to see anything bad happen to him. As a person, a family man, he was great. . .just not as a boss.

"Ms. Cain, please. Answer the questions. We can bring you in to the station if you'd rather answer our questions there."

She pulled in a quick breath. *Bring me down to the station?* Shivers slid across her shoulders. Sam didn't want to go there.

This is ridiculous. Why ask me about Ken? They should talk to Dorothy.

"Again, when was the last time you saw your boss?"

She shrugged. "I'm not sure. The last dispatch meeting we had, I guess. And that was over a month ago."

"You guess?" Jones questioned, his brows raised, his eyes burning a hole through her. Then a smug look crossed his features. "Why are you asking if he's okay? What do you know about him?"

"I don't know anything. I'm asking because you're asking me questions about him. And you came to my house to do it. That tells me something is wrong. So what happened? Where is he? Is he okay?"

"Please, Ms. Cain. You need to answer my questions." His growl shook her to the core. "You said the last time you saw him was at a dispatch meeting, but then you said *you guess*. Did you or did you not last see him at that meeting?"

"You misunderstand. I'm sure I saw him at the last dispatcher's meeting. He runs them, and I was there. I just can't be sure if I've seen him *since* the meeting. I don't see him very much since I work nights. He's gone before I come on duty. The only time I see him is when we have a dispatcher's meeting, or when he calls me in for a private meeting—to question me on how I handled a particular incident. I don't think that's happened since the last dispatcher meeting. . .but I'm not positive. Give me a second." Squinting, she glanced from one man to the other.

As much as she tried to concentrate on the last time she saw Ken, the fact the detectives were at her house talking to her about him would not let go of her brain. Finally she said, "I still don't understand why you are asking *me* questions about Ken, unless something has happened to him. And then, still, why ask me? I don't know the man outside of work." She shook her head. "Something's got to be wrong. Please tell me he's okay?"

Ignoring her plea, Sergeant Barnett wrote as the lieutenant continued his interrogation. "Where were you last night between midnight and 4:00 a.m.?"

She rolled her eyes. *Do they not listen when I speak? Didn't I tell him I was there all night? Keep your cool.* Drawing a relaxing breath, she took a second to control her tone. "At work, like I said. I work the night shift, six at night to six in the morning, four nights a week. Sunday nights through Thursday mornings."

What was going on? No hints, no clues were given so she

asked again, "Why are you here? Is Ken okay? Please tell me at least that much." Her nerves tightened like strings on a guitar as the tuning pegs are twisted. Why couldn't they answer her questions? She answered theirs.

"We'll get to that, ma'am. Did you talk to Mr. Richardson last night from work? Did you call him? Or did he call you?"

Something doesn't feel right. Uneasiness crept through her. *Maybe Ken got arrested for something.*

"Has he done something wrong? Something illegal? At least tell me that." Tired of this one-sided conversation, Sam tried to stand her ground. "I want to know what's going on before I say anything else to you—not that I like the guy or anything, and I'm not out to protect him, but I don't want to be the one accused of getting him in trouble either." She had to look out for herself. Since she worked for the man, she was the one who would have to put up with any repercussions from this interrogation. No one else would protect her—not anymore.

Besides, she knew if she got Richardson in trouble, there would be payback later. . .although she had to admit he had been nicer to her since her engagement to Matthew. Even since Matthew's death, Ken had remained a decent guy to her, and she for one would like to keep it that way.

A frown creased Barnett's forehead as he glanced at Lieutenant Jones.

"Please, ma'am," Jones said, even though the tone didn't say *please*, "we need the answers to these questions. If you don't want to answer them here, like I said before, we can take you down to headquarters."

"This is absurd." She shifted, straightening her spine.

She hadn't been to the station since the day after Matthew's funeral. They had brought her in to give her his belongings from his desk, things they had cleared out. Other than that, she had handled all her dealings with the police station through the lawyer Matthew had used when he drew up his will. That was more contact than she cared to have with the police station. . .then, now, or ever.

Her insides quivered at the thought of going back down there. *No*. She wasn't ready. Blinking her eyes rapidly, she held back the tears that threatened as memories washed over her like a sudden downpour of rain. Her shoulders sagged. "Okay. What was the question again?"

"Did you talk to Ken Richardson last night while you were at work?"

Keeping her voice steady, she replied, "As I said earlier, no one talked to me about him, nor did I talk to Ken last night."

"You didn't call him from work around midnight last night?"

"No. Most definitely not." Lifting both her hands, palms out as if giving up, she waved them vigorously. "Trust me." Then thrusting her thumb toward her chest, she said, "I would have remembered if I'd called and had to wake him up at that time of night. He likes us to handle all situations. We only call him in extreme emergencies."

"And he didn't come by the office during the night?"

"No," she said decisively.

Barnett's gaze jumped from Samantha Cain back to his partner.

Jones eyed her suspiciously. "Did anything strange happen at your place of business last night?"

Sam dragged her fingers through her long brown hair, still in disarray from her short nap. She restrained from the desire to pull her hair out; they were driving her so crazy. *I have rights. . .don't I?*

Locking her gaze on the lieutenant, she lifted her chin boldly. "Look, I demand you tell me what this is all about. I have a right to know. I've answered your questions. At least let me know he's okay." She folded her arms across her chest, ready to keep her mouth shut and say no more, even if it meant going down to the station.

If he was in trouble, that was one thing, but if something happened to him, she wanted to know. Dorothy, his wife, may need someone to talk to. The woman had been there for her when Matthew died. Sam wanted to be there for Dorothy, if needed.

Apparently they got the message, because the lieutenant glared straight into her eyes and said, "Your boss was found dead on the floor of his office this morning."

Chapter 2

A gasp escaped Samantha Cain's lips as she jumped to her feet. "What?" Her eyes opened wide with real shock. "Ken, dead?"

She wasn't acting; Mark Barnett sensed it in his gut. The woman didn't know her boss was dead. Her head shook, as if not wanting to believe this had happened nor understanding how this could have happened. Blood drained from her face. Her strength seemed to suddenly slip away as her knees wobbled and her body drifted slowly toward the floor. The sergeant leapt to his feet and grabbed her by the elbow, trying to steady her.

Samantha yanked loose from his hold and held on to the nearby chair arm with a viselike grip, her knuckles turning white. After a moment, she settled into the seat. "How could this be?" she asked almost in a whisper, but it didn't sound like a question directed to the detectives.

"Are you all right?" Mark asked, trying to keep his tone business-as-usual but wanting to offer support in her time of distress. Jones might not care, but Mark had known Detective Jefferies and how much he loved this woman. He could see the appeal—strong yet fragile, plain and simple yet beautiful. And that long, straight, silky brown hair that fell around her shoulders. . .what's not to like? He had heard rumors of her first marriage and the tragic ending, and then the poor woman went through the death of her fiancé. Samantha Cain deserved a little respect and sympathy in his opinion. He didn't want to put Detective Matthew's fiancée through this torment. She didn't deserve it.

But his superior seemed to enjoy the misery he was putting her through.

"This can't be," she whispered. "Ken, dead?" Doubt filled her eyes. "He can't be dead. I don't believe it." Suddenly the cloudiness in her eyes vanished. Turning her gaze first on Jones and then on Barnett, she asked, "How? And you said he was found upstairs? In his office? This morning?" Slowly she leaned back into the chair. "That couldn't be. I never saw him last night."

"Okay. So you were there last night, well, early this morning. Did you hear or see anything?" Mark tried to encourage her to think and give an answer that would throw suspicion off of her.

Jones probably didn't like his question, but Mark didn't care. He had to give the woman a chance. Wasn't it innocent until proven guilty? They were supposed to ask questions to see if she heard or saw anything, not questions trying to incriminate her. Mark eased back down on the sofa and picked up his pad and pen again, ready to write should she respond. He regretted his swift glance at the lieutenant's face. No doubt Jones would give him grief when they got in the car. Oh well. Mark would deal with it then.

~⊚~

Staring but seeing nothing, Sam rubbed her temples. Reality started sinking in. This had to be a bad dream. Who would kill Ken? Well, he had plenty of enemies, but to kill him and be found dead at work? While she was at work, no less!

"I can't believe it. I just can't believe it," she mumbled over and over to herself. Pivoting toward the detectives, she looked straight into Jones' eyes. "Ken wasn't there last night. He would have come into my office and spoken to me had he been there. So how could he be found dead in his office this morning? It makes no sense." Confusion and disgust filled her with frustration.

I'd know if he'd come in last night. I would have seen him enter the front door. Surely he'd have said hello and then gone up to his office. Why sneak in the back way and not reveal his presence to me? And be dead? Who? How?

To the detectives she had stated it like fact that the man never came to the job last night, but then in her brain she had to convince herself of those same words. In truth, she wondered, would he have spoken to her? He barely did whenever they came face-to-face. But why not at least make his presence known to her?

So how did he end up upstairs this morning. . .dead?

Closing her eyes, she frantically tried to recall anything strange—a sound, footsteps, a large thump in the night— that might suggest he was upstairs in his office while she worked downstairs. Admittedly, he could have slipped up the back way without telling her, but why would he? It made no sense. . .unless he was hiding something. . .or someone? Someone he didn't want her to know was there with him.

That thought confused her even more. He wouldn't do that to Dorothy. Would he? But neither did it make sense that Ken was dead. She blew out a rush of air.

Lieutenant Jones threw the next question at her, and it hit her like a sucker punch in the gut. "You were the only one at your place of business last night, right?"

"Yes. At times. I mean, the guys in the back worked until 11:30. That's two mechanics and a rack-man. After that, a few of the drivers came in to leave out on a run. That was from about 3:00 a.m. on through the morning. Other than that, I thought I was there by myself." Her teeth scraped her bottom lip as her mind whirled in wonder.

How could I not have heard him upstairs moving around? A man that size couldn't be too quiet, could he?

"So from 11:30 p.m. until 3:00 a.m. you were alone?" Jones' question sounded more convicting than questioning.

She clasped her fingers together while thinking hard. "I thought so, but apparently I wasn't." Dropping her hands to her sides, her fingers formed tight fists as the lieutenant's expression told her he'd found the guilty party.

Then she remembered. "Wait," she said, pointing her finger in the air. "I also had a driver come in around 2:00 or 2:30, but he was coming in off the road to go home. Maybe he saw something." She grabbed onto the hope.

"We'll need his name, as well as the others who were coming and going," the sergeant stated, sounding almost gentle. "You're right. They may have seen something."

Sam couldn't help but glance his way. With the way the lieutenant was questioning her, her heart longed for someone to believe in her. She gave him a tight-lipped smile, hoping it reached her eyes. That was her way of saying, "Thanks for sounding like you believe in me." He didn't seem to be accusing her like Jones was. Relief slid through her veins as some of the tension slipped away from her shoulders and neck.

"Sure. No problem. Maybe one of them saw something." She hoped, anyway. Sam studied the lieutenant, trying to read his thoughts, hoping they would reflect Barnett's words.

Oh well. One maybe believing her was better than no one believing her.

Returning her gaze to Sergeant Barnett, she asked, "What happened to him? I mean, how did he. . .die? When did he die?"

Could she have saved him? She wondered. Sam covered her mouth with her hands and then gently slid her fingers away as these questions hit her full force. Swallowing the hard lump that had formed in her throat, she whispered, "Sorry."

She hadn't even seen Ken come to the yard and go upstairs, let alone to the building—or anyone else for that matter. Sam couldn't recall any cars driving in during the night. Of course her back was to the entrance when she worked logs, and when she keyed things into the computer updating the loads and deliveries. Sam always used the computer facing the drivers' window so she would know when someone was standing there, waiting for her help. She rarely paid attention to traffic out on the highway, even at midnight or 1:00 in the morning, for that matter. Over the years she'd learned to ignore outside intrusions. Usually it was a driver coming in to go out, or someone dropping him off. Occasionally, it was a drunk and he'd lost his way. But even those interruptions didn't disturb her anymore.

The last time anything bad had happened was a little over a year ago, when a serial killer had strangled a poor woman and Sam had tried to save her.

Truth hit her. Of course she couldn't have saved him. If she couldn't save that little woman last year, how in the world could she possibly think she could have saved her boss, a big man of six-foot-six? Anyone hurting him had to be as big, if not bigger.

"We don't have the coroner's report yet," Jones cut in before Barnett could answer, "so we're not sure of any specific details at the moment. I have a few more questions for you, though. Other than drivers and the men who were working with you till 11:30, did you see anyone else enter the parking lot or the building?"

"No stranger, if that's what you mean. Besides, Ken Richardson wasn't even there last night. I would have seen him, I tell you. He would have said something to me had he come by there last night. I'm sure of it."

Sometimes Mother Nature called, she reminded herself but didn't share that with them. Surely they knew no one could watch twelve hours straight for intruders while performing their work duties without some sort of break.

Hoping to explain things a little better, she added, "It's the same routine every night—well, Monday night through Friday morning. He leaves before I get there; locks his office upstairs before he goes. The only one having a key to get in his office besides him is the shop foreman. I never see my boss. And I surely don't understand why someone would want to kill him. Sure, there are times I wish he wasn't around, but I would never kill him."

Jones watched Sam intently. His eyes sparkled with delight, as if she had made a full confession.

Sergeant Barnett said quickly, "We didn't accuse you, ma'am. We're merely asking you questions."

"I know. I didn't think you were." She didn't, but now she wasn't so sure.

The way the lieutenant had perked up and then the way the sergeant jumped on that statement made her think that maybe they *were* accusing her. She wondered if earlier she had only wished someone believed in her. Now she questioned her hope in Barnett for believing in her. She'd noted the lieutenant had watched her reaction with a keen eye, but that she expected. He was a cop. But the way Sergeant Barnett stated so swiftly they weren't accusing her, though, alerted her senses. She had seen enough crime shows on television to know police don't always mean what they say.

Second thoughts made her wonder. As kind as the sergeant seemed only moments ago, maybe he wasn't condemning her but warning her to watch how she spoke. She had better watch her step and keep a tight lid on what she said. She might be a suspect in Ken's death after all. Oh, how she wished Matthew was here with her to counsel her, to protect her.

Obviously they asked her questions for a reason. "Questions for a person of interest," Matthew used to call them. Maybe these two truly thought she did it, since she was the only one there most of the night. But really, truly, would she be that dumb? Would anyone kill him at the office where he or she would be the only suspect? Not to mention she'd never kill him. . .or anyone else. . .for that matter.

She nearly laughed to herself. At six-foot-six, Ken had weighed close to 300 pounds. She was a mere half an inch taller than five feet, weighing 140 pounds. He would squash her like a bug. In fact, her boss used his size to intimidate her and others—and it worked most of the time.

Since Sam had been engaged to Matthew, Ken hadn't antagonized her as much. And since Matthew's death, Ken continued to keep his distance from Sam. She guessed in the beginning it was because Matthew was a police detective. Richardson probably figured out the law might be on her side. Smart thinking on his part. Or, after Matthew's death, it could have been out of respect to the dead that he never returned to his old ways of torture.

"So do you have any more questions, or are we through? I need to get my son off to school so he won't be late."

"Are you sure you didn't call him last night around midnight?" Jones blurted.

"Positive. Anything else?" She was ready for them to leave.

"Not at this time, Ms. Cain, but we need a list of names from you of everyone you remember passing through the terminal last night, including the men who worked in the shop." Jones' voice seemed cold, and his smugness made her antsy. "And who did you say had the other key to his office?"

"Our shop foreman. Otto Thomas."

As she began to give the names of the drivers and workers who had passed through or worked during the night, Barnett flipped his paper over, giving himself a clean sheet to write on.

After Sam named everyone she could remember, she said, "You can call the office, too. I'm sure they will give you these guys' cell numbers or addresses so you can reach them for questioning also."

When finished writing the names given, the sergeant smiled slightly and thanked her for her time.

"We'll be in touch," Jones said sharply. On those words they left.

After shutting the front door, Sam's first reaction, besides shaking all over, was to call Greg.

Greg Singleton was Matthew's father's partner years ago and a dear friend to Matthew. Greg had come back into Matthew's life when he was working on catching the serial killer that roamed the Baton Rouge area last year. As Matthew and Sam's relationship grew, so did a friendship between her and Greg. After Matthew's passing, Greg had been there for them, and now she considered him to be her and Marty's friend for life. The man had retired from the force a few years back and now worked as a special agent assigned to protect the governor.

Clutching the phone, she punched out his phone number and then pressed it against her ear, listening as it rang.

After two rings she heard Greg's voice say, "Hello. You've reached 555-1418. I can't come to the phone right now, but if you'll leave your name and number, I'll get back to you as soon as possible."

She hated speaking to machines, but at the moment she was glad he had one. "Greg, it's me. My boss is dead, and I think the police think I had something to do with it. Please call me right away." Desperation resonated in her voice. She couldn't control it. A tight-fisted grip snagged her heart.

Dropping the phone into the cradle, she knew Greg would get back to her right away—as soon as he heard the message anyway. She just prayed it was in time.

A sigh slipped through her lips. Now to tell Margaret without alerting Marty to the fact that anything was wrong.

Chapter 3

Slipping on a smile to mask the lines of stress, Sam strode toward the swinging door to the kitchen. Marty was a smart kid. He'd be full of questions. And Margaret? She'd read the concern in Sam's eyes in no time. So Sam did her best to conceal her eyes by lowering her head as she entered. "Good morning, everyone. Thanks for filling in this morning for me, Margaret."

Marty's back was to her, but Margaret locked eyes with Sam over Marty's head. In one instant, the wise woman clearly saw through the lowered lashes. Margaret's hazel eyes told Sam she'd kept Marty busy, but as soon as he was off to school, she wanted all the details.

Glancing back at her son, Sam saw he was drinking the last of the milk in his cereal bowl. "Okay, Marty. Go brush your teeth. It's time for school."

"Who were those guys, Mom?" He put down his dish and

turned curious eyes her way. "What did they want, and why did they come so early?"

"Nothing concerning you, big boy. Now go get ready." She flashed him a smile with raised brows, hopefully conveying she meant business.

He grumbled but jumped down from his chair and hustled out of the kitchen.

Margaret rose and stepped next to Sam. "Okay. You sit and tell me quickly. I'll fix your coffee. Who was that at the door this early in the morning? And what did they want? I know it doesn't concern me either, but tell me what you can so I can be here for you." Margaret squeezed Sam's hand. "Really. Sit. I'll get you a cup of coffee."

Appreciating her friend, Sam did as she was told. She sat at the table, clasped her hands, and leaned forward. Her insides were a jumbled wreck. She didn't understand what was going on...and couldn't believe what she had been told. What happened to Ken? How did he die? And how did he end up at the office without her knowing? She didn't want to share all of her concerns with Margaret. The woman was a dear and very helpful over the past six months. Every day she was becoming more like a friend, but Sam didn't want to burden her with everything. "My boss was killed last night," she murmured.

Margaret's eyes widened. In slow motion, she set a cup of coffee in front of Sam. Still moving at a snail's pace, she returned to her seat. "Killed? How?"

"They found him this morning at my job site." Sam started wringing her hands. "The sad thing is, I think they think I had something to do with it. I'm waiting for Greg to call me now. So when he calls, if I'm asleep, please wake me."

Sympathy poured from Margaret's eyes as she reached across the table and covered Sam's twisting hands, helping them stop their movement and relax. "It will be okay, Ms. Sam. You know I'm here for you and Marty. I love you both like family already. Whatever you need, I'm here for you. And don't you worry. Mr. Greg will take care of you and this misunderstanding." Her eyes were steady as she spoke in confidence.

When Marty raced back into the kitchen with his backpack, Margaret released her hold.

"I'm ready, Mom. Let's go." The little boy who didn't want to wake up for school this morning was now replaced by a child excited for another day of learning. . .or was it the playing at recess that excited him so?

Sam smiled thankfully at Margaret and, turning in her chair, opened her arms to her son. "Okay, let's go." He rushed into her arms and hugged her tight before heading out the back door. Rising to her feet, she said to Margaret, "If only I had half that amount of energy." Laughing, she followed him out the back door and to the car.

Keep me strong, Lord. I think the madness in my life is about to start all over again.

≈⧞

That night, the buzz at the office was unbelievable. Sam wished she'd heard from Greg before she had come to work, but she hadn't. He must have been on a job that took him out of town. Those usually lasted a few days.

Sam rubbed her temples, trying to make the headache she'd had all day go away. Sleep barely touched her eyes today so she felt certain tonight was going to be a tough one—trying to stay wide awake and handle all that went on in a normal night. Hopefully, there would be no problems. Unfortunately, by the gossip around the shop and drivers' room, it didn't sound like it would be a normal night. Everyone had his two cents to add to the situation.

The main office had already sent a temporary fill-in boss to keep the terminal running smoothly. Did it really help? She doubted it. Each person had a different idea on how Ken died, and everyone wanted to talk about it. All of a sudden, every driver, every wash-rack hand, every mechanic was his best friend and knew all about his private life. Of course, all anyone really knew was that he loved his family and loved to fish. To hear the guys talk now, they each knew who would have wanted to kill Ken. Of course, each of their suspects had different reasons for wanting the man dead, and they all sounded like pretty solid motives. Some maybe even the police would follow up on. . .she hoped anyway. Sam had no idea where they were getting their information. Who was to say if any of it was really true?

The first thing she'd learned years ago working at a trucking company was that you couldn't believe everything you heard from a driver and only half of what you saw. Sure, most of the rumors held a grain of truth, but by the tenth person passing on the story, not much of that truth was still in there—but it made a wonderful tale to keep the tongues wagging.

It was strange working tonight, knowing her boss was dead. Sam wanted to call Dorothy and tell her how sorry she was for her loss, but maybe Ken's wife wasn't ready to hear from the people at work yet. Sam would wait a couple of days. At the funeral, she would talk to her.

Testimony of Innocence

Yellow tape stretched across the bottom of the stairs leading to the boss's office, which left a constant reminder that something horrible had happened in the building. Not that anyone needed reminding with all the talk floating around. The doors leading up the stairs were closed and locked behind the tape; however, that wasn't unusual. Only the bright yellow reminder made things odd. Oh, and, of course, the policeman hanging around the drivers' room in front of the double doors. That added to the peculiarity of it all.

I wonder if he'll be here all night.

According to the gossip, there had been cops in and out of the building all day long. At that moment, Sam was glad she worked nights and not days. Out back she saw that the yellow tape stating *CRIME SCENE—DO NOT CROSS* also ran across the bottom of the stairs out in the shop. These steps led up to a storage facility as well as to the main entrance of Otto Thomas' office. Through there was another door leading to the boss's office. At the bottom stood another policeman on guard. Since Richardson and Thomas held the only keys that unlocked the door that separated the two offices, only they could unlock the door. Sam guessed they kept it locked, but she wasn't sure.

Back in the earlier days, when she was the secretary, that door was kept wide-open most of the time. Of course, it was a different boss and different shop foreman then. The only time she recalled it being closed was when a meeting was going on in either office—but that was over five years ago.

Richardson liked his privacy. The day he started working at their terminal was the first day that door stayed shut between the two offices.

By midnight, her brain was so tired of listening to all the scuttlebutt, she couldn't wait to get out of there. The foot traffic in the office died down as the hour grew late. Most everyone was home in bed by now or already rolling down the road in the direction of his consignee, the point of delivery for his load.

Since Greg hadn't returned her call, she knew he had to be on duty with the governor. Otherwise he would have called Sam's cell number, even if he'd gotten back late. Under contractual obligation with the governor, he was not allowed to talk with friends and family during his time on the job. It usually lasted no more than a couple of days at a time. She felt sure she'd hear from him soon. If only he could listen to the message sooner, Sam believed he'd find a way to get in touch with her.

Truth be told, she hadn't listened to the news lately, so she had no idea what was going on with the governor. Greg could be out of town protecting him for a week right now, for all she knew. Sam hoped he'd call soon. His advice was much needed.

"Hey, Sam. Have you been fingerprinted yet?" Ronnie called from the drivers' window, snapping her out of her thoughts. He'd slipped in without her noticing, but again, that wasn't unusual.

Tonight of all nights, after what happened last night without her knowledge, she should have been paying closer attention. But a cop was standing at the bottom of the front stairs and another at the back stairs. Surely they'd be watching the comings and goings of everyone. She had other things to handle. Besides, Sam had a hard enough time concentrating on work with so little sleep.

Her office was kept separate from the drivers' room as well as the entrance to the building. The policeman standing guard at the bottom of the stairs inside would see someone immediately when they walked in the glass door to the trucking company. The separation of the dispatch office from the entranceway had been added several years ago when a fight broke out between one of the drivers and a dispatcher. The angry driver had leaped over the short wall that originally separated the two rooms. In a matter of moments, that driver yanked the dispatcher up from his chair and was choking the life out of him.

The full-sized wall added since then had a window cut into the middle with a shelf built on the dispatch side. The structure kept a distance between the two parties without cutting off communication altogether. A thick clear plastic window filled the area from top to bottom. An opening about ten inches across and four inches tall allowed paperwork to be passed from dispatcher to driver and vice-versa. Also a small hole, about the size of a fist, was cut into the middle of the window about five feet up from the ground. This allowed conversation between dispatcher and driver.

The terminal's front, back, and side doors were double locked, making it difficult to exit or enter the offices of the building. Safety loomed all around them, except when the night dispatcher had to unlock one of the doors to get a cold drink or snack from the machine in the drivers' room, to put logs in the drivers' boxes, or to walk out back to the lunchroom and heat up his or her dinner in the microwave. During this time, anyone who wanted to could slip in quietly and hide in the office to catch the dispatcher off guard later.

That scenario only occurred to Sam when she first started working nights and saw how dark and secluded the building and grounds were late at night. At that time, she locked the door behind her coming and going. In a short time, she got past her moments of concern and rarely locked the back door when going to heat up her dinner. The extra time spent on putting her dinner down to lock or unlock the door, along with the fact that the phone would sometimes ring at just that moment, caused her to eventually quit locking it behind her most nights. Sam's faith was in a mighty God who took care of her. She only had to learn to listen to Him closely. He urged her at the right times when to lock the door.

"No, I sure haven't been fingerprinted. Why?" As she asked Ronnie, her mind wondered for a moment why her prints weren't taken. And then as quickly she remembered that last year her prints had gone into the system during the time the police were trying to solve the killing across the highway. The killing she had tried to prevent but failed. The police didn't need to take them again she thought as she added, "Have you?" She reached for his packet of paperwork that was held in a wall file with all the rest of the packets for loads sitting on the yard, waiting to be delivered.

Ronnie was a driver she considered to be a friend. They had both worked for the company for about the same length of time, and there was almost as much love lost between him and the boss as there was between Sam and the boss—even though she didn't like the fact someone had killed Ken. In fact, not too many workers cared for Ken Richardson, although several took credit earlier in their gossip session for being one of his best buddies.

"Yeah. They caught me this morning before I headed out to go load. In fact, they said they were requesting all employees' prints. Like we really had a choice." He glared for a minute, then laughed. "It's more than my little BB-brain wants to think about anyway. I guess they'll get to you sooner or later. It's really weird, isn't it?"

Sam decided not to remind him of last year's catastrophe when they got her prints. She decided to leave it alone. Ronnie was right about one thing. Whoever they wanted to print would do it or look guilty, one of the two. She passed him his paperwork through the window and then they spent the next fifteen minutes talking about what might have happened to their boss. All the while the policeman listened in. . .Sam felt certain. It didn't matter. One thing both Ronnie and Sam agreed on was they doubted if anyone who worked there killed him.

"We didn't love the guy and we all wished we had a different boss, but none of us would kill him. We didn't want to see the man dead," Ronnie said. "Richardson was a pain, but a pain we'd learned to live with. Besides, none of us are killers. We're just hardworking stiffs who make the government richer by pouring in our tax dollars." He flashed a grin, but not of delight.

"Ain't that the truth?" she said with a chuckle to his remark about the tax dollars. They weren't laughing at the situation. It was a sad state-of-affairs right now. Who would kill Ken? And why?

"They said it happened last night here while you were working. You didn't see or hear anything?" Ronnie dropped his paperwork into his briefcase.

A laugh slipped out of her mouth—not a funny, ha-ha laugh. It was more like hysterical type of laugh you'd hear from someone who was about to go crazy. "Give me a break, Ronnie. You sound like those two policemen who came to my house this morning. But you're right; you'd think if there had been a struggle upstairs, I would have heard something. I mean, I can hear the rats run around upstairs at night. You'd think I would have heard a big man like Ken struggling for his life." She pointed toward the ceiling. "I admit his office is over the drivers' room, not our office, but still, you'd think I would have heard something. But I didn't. And I didn't see anything either. I never sit and watch out the window. At night you can't see much anyway, except headlights when they come into the yard. But again, I'd have to be looking that way to notice. So many of y'all come in and out at night, I don't even pay attention anymore."

"The police came to your house?" Ronnie asked when she finally quit talking.

Sam slapped the heel of her hand against her forehead. "Aye-yi-yi." Throwing her hands out in front of her like two stop signs, she shouted, "Yes! Now, let's change the subject. Please." She dreaded any more talk on the matter. It was too depressing.

Ronnie, being the friend that he was, did as Sam asked. Before he left, he smiled, told a corny Thibodeaux and Boudreaux joke, and then said as he was walking toward the exit, "Keep your chin up, girl. Remember, this won't matter ten years from now." That was Ronnie's favorite line about any problem that arose.

Admittedly, there had been times lately that Sam told

herself the same thing. "Yeah, right." The only reason those questions about not hearing or seeing a thing bothered her earlier today was because she was here when it all happened. In her own mind she felt partly responsible for not doing anything to stop Ken from being killed—only she didn't know it was going on at the time. She truly never heard a thing.

Sam knew, no matter how she felt about her boss, she would have done everything in her power to save the man, no matter how poorly he had treated her in the past. She loved him through Christ and that gave her reason to always try to do her best for the man as well as always be there for him.

As the door snapped closed after Ronnie's exit, another thought crossed Sam's mind, bringing a smile to her lips. *Around here everyone says if you don't like the way things are going, hang around a bit and they'll change.* Of course, when the change happened, it was usually for the worse, but she simply chose to ignore that part of the saying. *Think positive* was always her motto to live by anyway.

By the time the minute hand neared the twelve as the hour hand closed in on the six, she felt better and better. Maybe today the police would discover something to help them find the true killer or killers. Too bad Matthew wasn't on the case. He'd solve it in no time.

Twelve hours had slipped by slowly that night, probably because there wasn't much to keep her busy. At least now the night was almost over and she would be off for the next three days.

Pat, her relief dispatcher, walked in to take her place. "You look tired, Sam. Rough night?"

She crinkled her nose as she thought how to answer his

question. "Work-wise everything is fine. But I'm still a little down about Matthew. I'm not sure how long it will take to get over my loss. And now, with what's going on around here. . ." As her words faded, she shook her head, not even trying to complete her sentence, but the message was clear.

"I know what you mean. But at least you didn't have the circus around you last night like we had yesterday," Pat grumbled. "If it's like that today, I'm going home sick. It's worse than last year. . .probably because that murder was across the street on the levee. We had our fair share of cops in and out of here then, too." He smiled as he rubbed his dark beard. "I guess you don't need to be reminded of that time either. Sorry."

As Pat sat in the chair Sam had vacated, she patted him on the shoulder. "Cheer up. It probably won't be as bad today. Besides, most of the stuff should be going on upstairs. Hopefully after they get all their evidence, the policemen won't be hanging around all night again."

"Did they give you a hard time last night?" he asked as his gaze moved toward the policeman still out there by the bottom of the stairs.

"No. They stood at their post and walked around a little. Occasionally, they talked to one another at the back door of the drivers' room, but they kept it open. That's how they took their bathroom and lunch breaks, too. When one couldn't stand at their post, the other watched both from the open door."

"That's good."

Squeezing his shoulder, she added, "All you'll have to deal with today are the reporters and TV crews." She laughed as he turned, giving her the evil eye.

"You better hope not. If they show up, I'll give them your home address, telling them you were the one on duty. Go ask Sam for the details." He wiggled his dark brows.

"You wouldn't dare."

He smiled a somewhat sinister grin.

She laughed as she backed away, pointing at him. "I'll tell them you did it, so watch out," she warned.

Both of them laughed until the drivers started gathering at the window wanting to know what was so funny.

"Come on, guys, give us something to laugh about, too," Jerry said. "Our day is just starting, Sam. We're not going home like you are."

"My heart bleeds for you, Jer." She patted over her heart with both hands, like fluttering wings.

"Come on, Sam." Jerry's eyes twinkled and his deep dimples beckoned her. "Besides, I just made a pot of coffee. Come have a cup and talk to us. Me and John want to know the straight and skinny. We know you'll tell us the truth."

She shook her head. "Not this morning, guys. I'm tired, and I'm going home." Turning back to Pat, she said, "On that, I'm out of here. Have a good day." She grabbed her purse and headed for the door.

He hollered bye to Sam as she walked out the front door. She even heard him say, "Drive safe."

Unfortunately she didn't make it to her car. Lieutenant Jones and Sergeant Barnett walked toward the door, blocking the path to her car.

"Morning," she said as she started to go around them. They had another man with them today, carrying what looked like a laptop with a handle.

"Got a minute?" Jones asked.

"Do I have a choice?" Sighing, Sam turned around and walked back inside and into the dispatch office with them.

From the drivers' room she heard one of the drivers holler, "I thought you were leaving?" Sam didn't bother to answer them.

To Pat she said, "I didn't make it. Sorry we're doing this in here, but it shouldn't take but a minute."

"No problem," Pat said, even though it didn't sound like his heart was in on his answer. He then turned his back on the group and continued to do his work.

Lieutenant Jones took charge, turning his dark eyes on Sam. "Simon is going to take more prints today. Those guys you mentioned are coming in this morning. We've taken about half the employees' prints and we'll get more today. We'd like to take yours now. But if you refuse, we'll gladly come over in a couple of hours with a court order and get them. If we need to do this the hard way, we can do that. No problem." The lieutenant's hard gaze spoke volumes.

"What's wrong with the ones you got last year?"

Neither seemed to know about what happened last year or didn't care to acknowledge it, and Sam didn't feel like explaining, so she simply shrugged. "Whatever. Go ahead and take them. I have nothing to hide. I've been in Ken's office before, but my guess is it's been a long time."

"Unless someone wiped them clean, they'll be there. But we're not interested in the prints around the room, only the prints we lifted off the clothes the victim wore."

"Great. Still no problem. Just, can you take my prints first?

I've worked all night and need to get home and see my son off to school." *Not counting the fact I didn't get any sleep yesterday after you two came to my house.* That she didn't say aloud. When her eyes flicked to Barnett, she saw his crooked smile, and her natural response was to smile back.

Jones even seemed nicer today, or maybe it was because he was asking other people questions, too. Not just her. The fingerprint technician was the one who took care of Sam.

"Hi. I'm Simon Roth. It won't take me but a minute. Computerized," he said as he lifted his machine slightly.

He laid his case on the empty desk back against the inner wall, opened it, and touched a button. A light came on. After he cleaned the glass, he said, "Lay your hand on top of that piece of glass." It was like a scanner on a copier. A purple beam started at the tip of her middle finger and moved slowly down and past the heel of her hand. He pressed a couple of buttons on his keyboard, wiped the screen clean, and then said, "Other hand, please." The light did the same thing again as her left hand laid on the glass.

It took less than a minute and no mess. Modern technology was wonderful. She guessed he was through because he thanked her for her time. Although it was clean and easy, she didn't like it any better. It made her feel like a criminal. She was glad it was over.

Glancing at the detectives, she was glad when they both nodded as if to say, they too were through with her. That made her day. She needed to hurry home. "Bye, again," she said to Pat as she raced out of the dispatch office.

When she passed the bottom of the stairs, she noticed the doors leading to Ken's office were open, and she peered up. A chill rushed down her spine. Ken would never be climbing those steps again.

Swallowing the knot in her throat, she headed out through the glass door to her car.

Chapter 4

In less than half an hour, Sam was home. The light on her machine was flashing. Yes, she who hated talking into machines—even more than she hated listening to the owner say the same spiel before she could leave a message—had one of her own. At least she didn't play a long clip of music before the caller could leave a message. Sam left her messages short and to the point: "We're not in. Leave a message." She couldn't make it any shorter.

Watching the blinking light, she hoped Marty hadn't heard the phone ring or the message that was left. In her heart, she felt certain it was Greg calling back. Hearing the silence in the house led her to believe both Marty and Margaret were still fast asleep.

Sam and Margaret had prearranged, should Sam ever have to call, that she would let it ring once, hang up, and call right back. That way Margaret didn't have to answer every call that came into the house. . .not that many people called. Usually the calls were telemarketers. This way those unwanted callers would get the machine. Most hung up without leaving a message. Now *that* was a great thing.

"Hi, Sam. I didn't call you last night 'cause I knew you were at work and couldn't truly talk. I'm already up waiting for your call now, so please call me as soon as you get home."

She didn't have to be told twice. Quickly, she punched in his number.

"Hello." A deep, groggy male voice crossed the line and filled her ear.

"I didn't mean to wake you, Greg. I thought you said you were up."

"Morning. I guess I dozed off while waiting. Sorry."

"It's good to hear your voice." She twisted the cord, wrapped it around her finger, then released it, only to start over again. "Thanks for getting back to me."

"You sound scared. What happened? Not another killing across the highway I hope."

"Not across the highway. This time at the terminal. They found my boss dead in his office. And I think the police believe I did it."

"Sam, you've got to be kidding! What have you gotten yourself into now? Your boss is dead, and they think you did it? Why would they think you killed him?"

"Beats me." Hastily she tried to explain. "The only thing I can figure is because he was killed on my watch. I was there working the night shift, and he was killed in his office." Pulling on the cord, she stretched it out again and wrapped it around her fingers one more time. "Of course, I was downstairs. And

I swear I never heard a thing. They talk like I should know something, and I'm covering it up." She blew out a gush of air. "Greg, I honestly don't know if they suspect me or not. It's not like they've accused me. But yesterday when they came to my house and were asking me questions, I got this strange ache in the pit of my stomach, if you know what I mean. And this morning when I was leaving work, they had me stay so they could take my prints. I mean, I don't feel threatened by them, because I know I'm innocent. But the way Lieutenant Jones looked at me, it's like he suspects me even if Sergeant Barnett doesn't. I don't know. I'm not sure. But I get this horrible feeling when they question me."

"You said they took your prints? Did they Mirandize you first?"

"No. We were all asked to volunteer our prints. They said it would help eliminate prints so they could find some fingerprints that don't belong there—and we were supposed to buy that. Well, actually they told the drivers that. When I said my prints are in his office so you will find them, Jones said they are matching prints on him, his clothing, not prints found in the office. Personally, I don't have anything to hide, so I don't need to feel guilty. But they make me feel so uncomfortable." She trembled all over. "So dirty."

"Well, girl, you get some rest. I'll see what I can find out for you. I'll also find you a good criminal lawyer, just in case."

Iced air swooshed through her, as if she were standing in the doorway of a freezer and it was opened and slammed shut. "So you think they suspect me, too? I was hoping you'd tell me not to worry—that they are only following procedure."

"I don't think they necessarily think you're guilty." His

voice sounded reassuring and the pitch came across strong and sincere. "But I believe in being prepared. As you said, you were the only one there when he was killed. . .as far as they know. And I've heard the way you talk about him, so I'm sure one of your friendly drivers have told them how you two don't get along. Besides, it won't hurt to be prepared."

The grit of what felt like sandpaper slid over her eyeballs as she closed them tightly. Sam was so tired. It had been almost thirty-six hours with maybe a one-hour catnap in between. "Greg, I don't know how to thank you. I know you've been busy, probably working on a job for the governor, but I need your help. I don't know where else to turn. If Matthew—"

"Don't you worry. I'm here for you, Sam. Matthew loved you, and he would kill me if I didn't try to help you. Besides, girl, I think a lot of you and Marty both. You're like family to me. . .almost."

"Thanks, Greg. Sorry I woke you. So you better get some rest, too."

"It's been a long three days, but after a shower, I'll be as good as new. Now you get some rest and I'll come by around two. Let Margaret know I'm coming and ask her to wake you—just in case you're still asleep when I get there. That woman watches over you and Marty like a prison guard." He chuckled.

Greg and Matthew both were glad when Sam had found such a wonderful woman to care for Marty. With the odd hours Sam worked, it wasn't easy, but God had brought her this special woman who was now a dear friend, too. Margaret had moved in with Sam and Marty at their apartment.

Sam couldn't help but think again that, had she and

Matthew been married before his death and living at his place, then maybe he'd still be alive. Maybe he would have been more alert when he was attacked. She worried the extra drive from her place to his every night with the hours he worked might have been a distraction for him. Why had they waited a whole year to get married when six months would have been enough? Shaking her head, she remembered. She had wanted to make sure marrying Matthew was the right thing for both Marty and her. She sighed and said aloud, "Thanks again, Greg."

"What are you thinking? I hear it in your voice. Talk to me."

She smiled to herself. Greg almost knew her as well as Matthew knew her. "I was just wishing Matthew was still here."

"You and me both, kiddo."

"I know you're going to watch out for us, but. . ." Tears formed in her eyes, but if she allowed them to fall, she wouldn't be able to turn them off. Sam couldn't cry—not now—not when Marty might find her. She would save her tears for the shower. Her son had been through so much in his short life, she didn't need to add to it.

"That is a fact, so don't you worry, hon. Go to sleep and dream about him. That way he'll be with you. Right now I've got to shower and go see some people."

"Thanks, Greg," she said one more time before hanging up the phone. Yes, she could dream about Matthew, and he would reappear. In her dreams she could still find him. The only problem with that was when she woke up, he would be gone, and she'd have to deal with the heartbreak all over again. Sam wasn't sure she could make it through the next time. Caring for Marty was her stronghold, keeping her mind and heart busy. She thanked God for the time she did have with Matthew, but now she had to concentrate on her son and his needs.

Greg was a good man. He'd help her through this new crisis—if she needed it. Hopefully she was jumping the gun and assuming things that weren't true to fact. Maybe the police didn't think she had anything to do with it.

She sighed. What had happened to the positive attitude she usually had? She needed it now more than ever.

Lately, Sam admitted, she hadn't done too well staying so positive. *Lord, help me. You are my strength.*

Her purpose in life came running down the hall, all smiles and full of energy. "Morning, Momma. I'm so hungry. Can you make biscuits this morning?"

A smile crossed her lips as she soaked in the image of her baby growing up. *He'll be nine next month. They grow up so quickly.*

Chapter 5

Greg didn't like the way that sounded. Were the police investigating this crime or had they already decided Samantha's guilt?

"Don't worry, buddy. I'm not going to leave your woman in the lurch." Greg talked as if Matthew sat in the same room with him, but Greg knew better.

To himself he said, "First things first." Greg flipped open his cell. Scanning the names in his contact list, he found who he was looking for, an old friend still on the force. Lieutenant James Draper chose to spend the last of his days before retirement working a desk job. After the injury to his leg a year ago, he could have taken an early retirement with a reduced pension. Instead, James decided to ride his time out behind a desk. It wasn't the real grunt work of police procedure, but it kept him on the force full-time so he could retire in another three years at his full pension. Now Greg hoped James, Jimmy to his friends, hadn't changed his mind. For all Greg knew, the new position behind a desk all day bored him to no end. His old buddy might not be willing to share the info Greg really needed, but he had to try.

Tapping his friend's name on his phone, the man's cell number appeared on the screen, and Greg tapped it, too. Instantly the phone keyed in the number and a ringing tone sounded.

"Lieutenant Draper. May I help you?"

"Hey, Jimmy, old boy. It's me, Greg. I hope you can help me." Greg hoped more so that he would *want* to help him. Greg knew Jimmy could get his hands on most of the information in the case, but it was against policy to talk to anyone outside the force about the facts of an ongoing investigation. "Can you spare me a few minutes? I need to come see you right away."

"You sound serious, Greg. Is the governor giving you a hard time? Are you thinking of coming back to the force?" Adding a little merriment to his voice, Jimmy said, "I'll tell you what. Bring some doughnuts and we can talk."

"You're on. Do you still like the powdery ones filled with strawberry goo?"

"I may be a gimp, but I still have my taste buds. Bring 'em on."

By the time Greg picked up the doughnuts and drove to the precinct almost forty-five minutes had passed. The doughnuts were hot and fresh since that had been his last stop before reaching the precinct. That should score him a few extra points. Greg nodded at some of the officers as he passed and made his way toward Jimmy's desk. That was the thing most policemen didn't like about a desk job. Everyone was in a large room with several desks, and you had very little privacy, if any. But with the noise level of the computers, copiers, and faxes all humming, as well as the low chatter from various desks, no one paid much attention to all the conversations going on at the same time. So, in a way, they had privacy.

As Greg reached Jimmy's desk and was about to drop the box in front of him, the tall thin man rose and stuck out his right hand, welcoming the intrusion. "I don't care what you need. I'm just glad to have the break in the monotony of taking complaints of noisy neighbors or reports of cats stuck in trees. Good to see you, Greg." Jimmy shook Greg's hand almost off of him.

"Hey, old man. Glad to see you, too. You're looking good. No stress lines across the face. The desk job might be boring but at least it lets you go home at night not worrying about catching some perp before he kills again. Right?"

"You got that right. My wife is grateful for that."

Pulling his hand back, Greg grabbed the chair next to the desk and dragged it a little closer before sitting down. "I've got a big favor to ask of you."

Plopping his skinny self back in his chair, Jimmy rolled closer to his desk again and opened the box of doughnuts. Smacking his lips, he said, "Whatever I can do for you, buddy." He glanced up at Greg and then back at the doughnuts. "You name it." His fingers plucked a confection-covered delectable out of the box and raised it to his lips. "Mmm," he moaned in delight before taking a big bite.

Greg set his elbow on the corner of the desk and leaned toward Jimmy. "You remember Matthew's fiancée, Samantha Cain?"

"Uh huh," he mumbled as he chewed.

"Well, her boss was killed, and it sounds to her like the police are suspecting her."

Jimmy swallowed his mouthful of doughnut and gulped a little coffee behind it. "Really, man! Isn't that how Matthew met her to begin with? Wasn't she in some kind of trouble after a killing happened over by her workplace?"

"Close enough." Greg didn't want to go into details and remind him she was the widow of a fellow officer who took his own life and Matthew was that policeman's partner at the time. Jimmy didn't need to be reminded. So many of the men in blue weren't very friendly toward her in the beginning, according to what Matthew had told Greg.

"Problem is, she didn't do it, even though it's a well-known fact she didn't get along with her boss," Greg said. "She was at the place where his body was found. So to me, it sounds like the police may have motive and opportunity wrapped up with a ribbon on top. Too simple. Too easy. I don't know about means. Sam isn't even sure how the man died, just that they found him dead in his office the morning after she worked the night shift. She never saw anyone come or go. She had no idea he was upstairs dead when she left to go home after a night on the job. Unfortunately this makes her a prime suspect."

Jimmy finished off the first doughnut and was going for the second one when he said, "It sounds like she might be in a little trouble." His gaze drifted from the doughnut box to Greg. "Again."

"Exactly. That's what I'm hoping you can check out for me. See how much. Take a look, ask around, and see if they are set on her, or if they are still investigating. It seems to me all the evidence against her is circumstantial." He shrugged. "Actually sounds like someone planned it that way."

Swallowing the last of his second doughnut, Jimmy took time for another gulp of coffee. With a thoughtful look he said, "I'll see what I can find out, but I'm not promising anything. Understand?"

Rising, Greg stuck out his hand and they shook. "I appreciate whatever you can do. Sam has been through so much. Remember, Matthew was killed a week before their wedding, and the woman is still grieving deeply. Not to mention her son, Marty. He loved Matthew like a dad. I don't think he needs to have his mother arrested for something she didn't do."

Jimmy rose and clapped Greg on the back of his right shoulder. "I gotcha. I'll get back to you right away." With a limp, Jimmy started walking through the room around the desks with Greg.

"Thanks again, Jimmy. You have my cell. Call me any time, day or night." They shook hands one more time before parting ways.

Back in his car, Greg started the engine, fastened his seat belt, and pulled his cell out of his top pocket. Slipping it into the holder, he pressed the button to speed-dial Sam's home number, and then clicked on SPEAKER.

"Cain residence. May I help you?"

"Well, good morning, Margaret. Don't you sound all peaches and cream this morning?"

"Oh, Mr. Greg. Hush yourself." She giggled.

"I can see you blushing without being there, Margaret.

And quit calling me Mr. Greg. It's plain old Greg. Do you hear me?" Greg gritted his teeth when he realized he was flirting with Margaret while Sam was waiting for some news—preferably good. "Is Sam awake?" He decided to keep his mind on business.

"She's napping but told me to wake her when you called. Have you found out something that will help her? Are you coming over?" Margaret's interest was made clear on the phone. She cared so much for Samantha and Marty, it was upsetting her to see them go through more tragedy. Greg knew without a doubt, Margaret had a huge heart.

"I'm on my way. I don't have much to tell her yet, but I thought I'd come over and we could discuss the situation more, face-to-face." He slid the gears into reverse and backed out of the parking space. "I'll be there in about ten minutes or so. . .if that's okay."

"I'll put on a fresh pot of coffee, wake her up, and start cooking some breakfast for both of you. When she gets up, she'll stay up. Ms. Sam's off for the next three days. She rarely sleeps more than four hours anyway when she's coming up on the long weekend. And under the circumstances, the hour and a half sleep she's had will probably be all the sleep she'll need today. That way, tonight, she'll be back on track with Marty's schedule."

"Margaret, you know they say the way to a man's heart is through his stomach, and woman, you are on the fast track to mine." He did it again. What had gotten into him? Every time he got near that woman he acted like a schoolboy. Greg thought his flirting days were over.

"Oh, Mr. Gr—I mean, plain old Greg." She chuckled.

"You quit that. Come on over. Ms. Sam will be up when you get here."

After a quick laugh, Greg pushed the gas pedal a little harder. "I'm on my way, woman."

Chapter 6

Sam heard a light tapping on her bedroom door. As it opened slightly, she heard, "Sorry to wake you so soon, but Mr. ah. . .Greg is on his way. He'll be here shortly. I brought you a cup of coffee to help you wake up." Margaret moved toward the bed and set the cup on the nightstand.

As Sam opened her eyes slowly, Margaret's words started to sink into her sleepy brain. Her eyes popped open. Suddenly she felt wide-awake and sat up in bed. "Did he give you any idea of what he found?" Hope fluttered in her heart as anticipation climbed. Glancing at the numbers glowing on her digital clock, she realized not even two hours had passed since she'd talked to him that morning. "Wow. That was quick. I hope it's good news."

"Sorry. He hasn't found anything out yet, but he wanted to talk face-to-face and get some details. I'm sure he's been checking into things already this morning. As much as possible, anyway."

Tossing back the covers, Sam eased over and sat on the edge of her bed as she took the cup from the nightstand. "You're right. I'm sure he's doing all he can. And I'm grateful." Sipping cautiously on the hot brew, she looked up. "Thanks."

"I'm making breakfast for you and Mr. Greg. . .uh, Greg, so hurry and get up. Now let me get back to cooking." Margaret scurried from the bedroom.

Sam rose from her bed sipping more of her coffee. Oh, how she wished Matthew was still around to hold her and assure her everything would be all right, but he wasn't. She shook her head, trying to remove those thoughts. The sooner she accepted that she was on her own, the sooner she could move on with her life. Instantly her heart assured her, *You're not on your own. The Lord will never leave nor forsake you. And look at the great friends you have. And most of all, remember Marty needs you to be strong and there for him. You will never be alone.*

"I just miss you, Matthew. You were my rock," she whispered upward for a moment. *And now,* her mind shouted at her, *get busy. Get dressed before Greg gets here.*

Padding to the bathroom connected to her bedroom, she yawned and put her cup on the counter. Sam leaned over and splashed the cold running water on her face. She needed all the help she could get to wake up quickly. With the little sleep she'd had in the last two days, it would probably take a little miracle. She'd take that, too, a miracle. A grin touched her lips as the reflection in the mirror showed her face dripping in water. Snatching the hand towel off the rack, she dabbed her face dry. "That helped."

After two more gulps of coffee, she stripped and showered.

Wrapping a towel around her, soaking up any drops she might have missed when toweling dry, she stepped back into her bedroom and dressed. Once her teeth were brushed and her hair was combed, she felt ready to face the world. . .well at least face the day.

"Something smells good," she said as she entered the kitchen with her empty coffee cup. Margaret had set the table for two. When the doorbell rang, Sam said, "If you don't mind letting Greg in, I'll pour myself another cup."

"Sure," Margaret said as she rushed through the swinging kitchen door.

Sam glanced at the door, still swinging, with curiosity. Margaret's face had flushed when the doorbell chimed and then she raced to answer it. Was something stirring between Margaret and Greg? Sam smiled, deciding to take better note of the two in the future.

To Sam's ears, the conversation in the living room seemed to be of a jovial nature. Even more reason to believe that Margaret's blush had a reason for being there. After the last twenty-four hours, Sam was glad to hear someone laughing. In that instant, she realized she need not concern herself as much as she had with the situation surrounding her life. Her existence was in God's hands, and He wouldn't give her any more than she could handle. That was a promise from Him. Sometimes Sam believed God gave her a little too much credit, but she knew the fire she walked through with God's help only refined and strengthened her. The Word told her so. Besides, she'd lived through enough to know God was in control. Not her. His way was higher than hers.

The kitchen door swung open and stayed. Greg held it

that way, allowing Margaret entrance. Both were smiling brightly. Greg sniffed the air. "My stomach hears you, dear, loud and clear. What did you make for breakfast?"

"Nothing special. I promise. I whipped up a couple of egg, cheese, and onion omelets, then sliced some of that ham I baked the other night. I warmed it up in a skillet."

"You don't have to tempt me anymore. I'm ready to eat." He rubbed his stomach. "I'm famished."

"I'm guessing that's a good thing, Greg. It looks like Margaret's got it all ready for us. You better be hungry. Look at all the food."

Margaret scurried over to the oven and lifted a pan. Quickly, she slid her spatula under one omelet and laid it on a plate. As she was doing the same thing with the other omelet, she said, "You two sit down and eat before it gets cold." A plate of hot, lightly browned ham sat in the middle of the table and beside it was a stack of buttered toast. "Do you want milk with your breakfast or just coffee?" The question, although she didn't call them by name, was addressed to both.

"Coffee's enough for me," said Sam.

"If it's not too much trouble, I'll take a glass of milk with my breakfast and then I'll drink a cup of the coffee for dessert." Greg slipped into the chair with his back to the outside door and his face toward the living room. "You spoil me, Margaret."

A rosy glow spread across her cheeks again, and her eyes twinkled.

There goes the blushing again, and look at Greg. He lit up while talking with Margaret. Maybe there is something going on. Wouldn't that be nice?

Sam blessed the food, then said, "You are going to join us, aren't you, Margaret? Greg is going to give us an update on what he's found out."

"Please do, Margaret," Greg said as he pointed to a chair to his right, across from Sam. "But I hate to say, I really don't have anything yet. Sam, I want you to give me details on what exactly went down at your place of work for the last couple of days." Stuffing a bite of the egg creation into his mouth, he emitted a low murmur of pure pleasure as he started chewing and closed his eyes. After several seconds ticked by, he swallowed slowly, appearing to savor every last flavor of the morsel. Opening his eyes, he said, "Margaret, this omelet is very tasty. Thanks so much for including me in the breakfast feast."

"Thank you," Margaret whispered.

"Greg is so right. Margaret, this is delicious," Sam said as she cut another bite off her slice of the ham. "And Greg, don't worry. I knew you didn't have anything. Margaret told me when she woke me up a little while ago. I'm still a little groggy, but I'll catch up. I think it's called sleep deprivation." Sam slipped another bite of the ham into her mouth and enjoyed the flavor of honey and ham.

Margaret fixed herself a cup of coffee and joined the two at the table.

As Sam ate, between bites she rehashed the last two nights of trauma at her job. She finished her breakfast long before she had replayed all the details. "I don't understand how they could think I would kill my boss. I wouldn't kill anyone, unless maybe Marty's life depended on it. My dad told me a long time ago, you never know what you'll do until you're put in a situation where you have to react fast, so never say never." Sliding her chair back, she rose and stepped over to the coffee pot to pour herself another cup. "Are you ready for your dessert, Greg?" She chuckled. "Margaret, may I fix you another cup, too?"

"Don't mind if I do, please," said Greg as he handed his empty cup over to Sam.

"I've had enough coffee for now, thanks anyway," Margaret said.

As Sam placed a cup of the brew on the table near Greg, he said, "I wish I had some answers for you. I'm not even sure why they are looking so closely at you. I understand you were the only one there most of the night, but most people wouldn't believe you did it given his size alone. So why do they? Why do you think they are focusing on you?"

Sam shrugged. "Beats me."

"One good thing I can say, I did get to talk to my old buddy, Jimmy, who is still on the force. He promised to see what he could do to get some information for me—share what he can without crossing the line. An ongoing investigation is usually kept close to the vest."

Margaret rose and picked up the empty plates from the table. As she carried them to the counter, she said, "I've seen her boss before. He is one big man. Unless Sam shot him or drugged him, I don't see her getting the upper hand on the man. How was he killed, anyway? Did your friend know? Besides, don't the police have to have motive, means, and opportunity to arrest someone? This whole thing makes no sense to me." Margaret's curls bounced as she shook her head.

"When I left Jimmy, he was going to check into any and everything he could find out about the case. Then he said he'd let me know what he could. We'll see what happens."

Sam helped clear the table as Margaret started rinsing the dishes and loading them into the dishwasher. While moving the glass and silverware from table to counter, Sam's gaze slid over Greg. "I hope your friend can help, but I realized a short time ago I shouldn't be worrying. God is in control. I'm glad He has given me two wonderful people who care so much about me to help me step in the right direction through this whole mess—"

Greg's phone chimed six quick successive dings, repeating over and over, cutting Sam's words short. He reached in his pocket and pulled out his phone. The dings stopped as he said, "Singleton here."

Sam and Margaret both turned and waited. Sam pinched the edge of the table with her fingers as her eyes stayed glued on Greg's face, while Margaret seemed to be holding her breath. Seconds turned into long minutes, more than Sam wanted to wait. As soon as Greg pressed the button to end the call, she said, "What'd he say? What'd he find out?"

Greg rose. "I have to go back down to the station, but he said it didn't look good. He suggested you get yourself a good lawyer."

Sam's heart stopped beating as Margaret gasped. When Sam found her breath, she whispered, "Get myself a lawyer? But I didn't do anything." She snatched hold of Margaret's fingertips and held on tight.

Catching Sam's upper arms in a tight hold, Greg said, "Hang in there, girl. It'll be okay."

The phrase *innocent until proven guilty* flashed through her mind. But then she remembered Christ was innocent, and they still hung Him on a cross. Then she thought how foolish to even compare her life to Christ's. He had a great purpose. God had a plan. Without Jesus suffering on the cross, we would not be saved for eternity. *So what purpose is there for them to find me guilty when I'm not?*

Suddenly a peace washed over her as she remembered, *God is in control.* She hadn't been found guilty. The police were checking out her story. Whatever lay ahead, she would get through it with the Lord on her side.

Taking in a deep breath, she stood straight. "Thanks," she whispered to Greg and then walked him to the front door as Margaret followed along with them.

Chapter 7

Mark Barnett looked over his notes of all the interviews they'd conducted in the last thirty-six hours and studied the pictures of the crime scene.

The interviews of the workers all kept to basically the same story. Each employee started out as a strong defender of their boss's reputation, but in the end admitted to the fact that not too many people cared for the way he handled the terminal. Richardson wasn't a very well liked man. Now when it came to what they had to say about Samantha Cain, it was nothing but glowing words for a wonderful coworker.

The drivers loved the way she looked out for them. Her fellow dispatchers liked the way she did her job and that she was always willing to help them when they felt overwhelmed with work. Since she'd been working the night shift, they missed her personality. . .and help. . .on the days. Some immediately shared how the boss treated her so poorly. Ken apparently didn't like having a woman as a dispatcher. Some employees they had to pry it out of, but in the end, the story was still the same. None understood how Sam put up with Ken's treatment of her. She didn't deserve it, but Ken Richardson didn't seem to care. In fact, most said he hoped she would quit.

Studying the pictures one at a time, he felt he was missing something. He felt a churning in the back of his mind. . . as if he'd noticed something, but his rational thoughts hadn't connected it yet. What was it? Something missing? Or something there that shouldn't be? He sighed, wishing he knew.

Sitting back in his chair, he glanced across his desk at his partner. He'd love to share his thoughts, knock some ideas around, but, to Ben Jones, the case was already solved. He wanted to hang Samantha Cain out to dry.

Mark sat up slightly and leaned forward a bit, eyeing his partner. Something was going on over there in Ben's mind. What, he didn't know. The lieutenant's mind was fixed on something. "Share partner," Mark said. "What are you looking at so intently?" *Let's try to act like partners.* Jones appeared to be staring through his computer screen. This got Mark's full attention.

"We just got the results on all trace evidence, including all the prints we had taken. Guess who's on top?" Jones pressed a button on his screen, and the printer hummed as it kicked on automatically.

Jones had the biggest smile, so Mark didn't have to guess who was on top. The man never smiled. He shook his head as he said, "It must be Ms. Cain's. You wouldn't look so happy otherwise. What do you have against her? You're like," he lifted both hands in question, "I don't know, man. You're convicting her before you get all the evidence. I don't get you, Ben. In fact, I've never seen you act like this on a case before. What gives?"

Jones pulled the report off the printer and dropped a copy on his partner's desk. "Check it out. See where her prints were found."

Mark picked up the paper and scanned the names of the prints found in the office and where they were found. "Gimme a break." He tossed the paper back down on his desk as if it was of no consequence. "We knew we'd find her prints on the letter opener. It belonged to the dispatchers. Remember? I'm sure her prints weren't the only ones found."

The smile broadened as he cocked his head. "Think again."

"That's too easy." Jumping to his feet, Mark snatched his blazer off the back of his chair, hooking it with his finger. "Let's go do some real detective work. Like finding out more about our victim and who would want him dead. Then we can talk to other possible suspects. And then let's wait until all the facts and evidence are in before making an arrest. Let's wait on the results on the hair sample for one thing. Besides, we really do need to find out a little more about this man and his life. Listening to all the coworkers, it's not like he was an innocent man. It sounded like he was one of those men who did some jobs under the table. I'm sure we'll find more people who didn't like him, besides just the people who worked with him."

"Yeah. But will we find their prints on the letter opener, the weapon used to stab him in the heart? The weapon we found tossed out back in the big garbage bin?" Another smile, this time more of a smirk. "Let's go chase some other possible suspects. I don't want to be accused of focusing only on her when we do finally get to go and arrest the woman." A bellow of laughter escaped as he pulled the car keys from his pocket. "I'm ready."

If they hadn't been partners for the past five years, Mark wouldn't have known what a truly good detective Jones could be. Right now Mark wanted to smack him upside the head. Maybe that would knock some sense into him.

What does he have against Ms. Cain? Matthew, a fellow detective, had thought the world of her—had been ready to marry her—yet Jones thought she was a killer. Mark would have to work harder at finding other viable suspects before Jones hung her out to dry.

As they were about to leave, his partner's office phone rang. Stepping back over to his desk he snatched up the receiver. "Jones here." His eyes widened as he listened to whoever was talking to him. His gaze seemed to brighten with every word.

Mark's heart tightened. Jones' expression could only mean bad news for Samantha Cain. Mark stood waiting for Jones to hang up the phone so he could crow a little more. At least that was the impression Mark received from the look on Jones' face.

"Thanks." Jones slammed down the receiver. "Let's go. The ME has something else for us." He jabbed his fist up into the air. "Yes. Maybe this will be the clincher I was hoping for." Then he drew his fist in and downward in one smooth motion.

All Mark could do was follow the man downstairs, dreading what the medical examiner was about to share with them.

Chapter 8

Three hours passed before Greg returned, and he wasted no time joining Sam and Margaret at the kitchen table. He took a seat and laid a file on the tabletop. Opening it, he revealed some printed papers along with photos. Sam couldn't help but try to tilt her head slightly to see the photos.

Shocked, she pointed to the one on top. "That's mine." The police had a picture of her necklace. . .her misplaced necklace. "Matthew gave that to me. Who's holding it, and what's it doing in a folder you brought back from the police station?"

She didn't understand. How could someone have her necklace? Even more, why was it in that picture? Since Matthew had given it to her, she'd worn it all the time, only taking it off at home at night when she went to bed. Every morning she had put it back on until a few months ago. Sam couldn't even say how long it had been. With the loss of Matthew, her mind was on other matters these past few months, but she knew it would turn up one day safe and sound in her own home. Truth be told, she figured it had dropped behind her dresser. One day she planned to pull that heavy thing out from the wall and look behind it. That, like other things, had been put on her list of things to do when she moved on in her life. Since his death, she had concentrated on caring for her son and working. That was about it, and that was how she got through one day at a time.

"That's the bad news, hon. Ken Richardson was found clutching it tightly. The ME had to pry his fingers loose. That was what the report said." Flipping through the papers, Greg pulled the report out and laid it in front of her. "So it seems, according to the response from the detectives, he snatched it off the killer's neck. Look at the clasp. It's broken." He picked up the pictures and laid them out. "These are copies of the crime scene photos. Look at this close-up of the chain—snapped in two. Obviously they don't know it's yours yet, but they are asking questions. As soon as Jimmy heard the buzz, he thought I'd want to know, so he added it to the file he was making for me. I thought I recognized it when he showed me that picture. I wasn't sure if it was yours or not. I never said a word to Jimmy. Just thanked him for his help."

"Oh no!" she cried out. The tight squeeze on her heart crept up to her throat, choking off her oxygen supply. "How did he get my necklace? It disappeared a few months ago." She laid her hand on her chest and dragged in a deep breath of air, forcing her lungs to expand and then, just as quickly, released it. "I figured I misplaced it one night before going to bed or it fell behind furniture, or something. I knew one day it would show up again. I wasn't worried. It's not like I ever took the necklace off anywhere except here at the house...well, and at our apartment before we moved here. I presumed one day it would show up down in the couch or behind a dresser or somewhere. But here in our home, not there."

Margaret reached over and patted Sam's hand. "It will be okay, Ms. Sam. Greg will help you figure this out." Her eyes shot a glance toward Greg, and then she lowered her lashes.

Sam fastened her gaze once more on the photos, wrestling with worry, fear, and confusion. She wasn't sure which emotion described her feelings best as she soaked in each picture, each shot. Seeing Ken lying on the floor, looking at peace, his hands balled up into fists at his side twisted her stomach. He was dead. That big man, who stopped others dead in their tracks with a look or a word, was lying there lifeless. So not like Ken Richardson. The close up of his hand holding the necklace, apparently taken later by the ME, and then various shots of the necklace, close-ups of the body, close-ups of the necklace, followed with pictures of the rest of his office in its entirety left her wordless. Finally with raised eyes she said, "What do we do, Greg? What do I do?"

"Margaret's right. I'll help you. We both will help you, and you'll get through this, too. First thing we're going to do is find you the best defense attorney there is—not that you'll need him or her. Somehow the police will find the true killer and if they don't, we will! You're not taking the fall for this, kiddo. Trust me."

Sam couldn't believe this was happening again. Maybe it wasn't the same thing. It wasn't like a killer stalked her again like last year, but now—now she might be snatched away from her son. For murder, no less. That could mean life in prison. Sam knew her parents would step in and raise Marty if it came to that, but that wasn't the point. She wanted to raise her son, watch him grow up, be with him his entire life. Besides, Marty had already lost his father and his soon-to-be stepfather. He shouldn't have to lose his mother, too.

"Thank you, Greg and Margaret. You don't know how much you mean to me. I appreciate your help so much. Let's get started. The sooner we clear me, the sooner we can get on with our lives." She started to rise, but Greg laid his hand on top of hers, stopping her actions.

"Let me make a few calls." Greg padded over to the counter where the house phone sat. He pulled out the phonebook that rested under the handset and carried it to the table. Flipping through the white pages, he found who he was looking for and started punching the numbers into his cell phone. "This should only take a minute."

Margaret stood and then in a soft voice said, "While Greg takes care of finding you the perfect person to protect you, I'm going to pick up the house. You know I'm here for you, and if you have to go anywhere with Mr. ah, with Greg, don't you worry about Marty. I'm here, and that's where I'm staying." She wrapped her arms around Sam's neck, gave her a quick squeeze, and then left the room.

Sam fixed herself and Greg another cup of coffee. By the time she finished and sat back down, Greg was finishing his call. His eyes locked with hers and he said, "We've got an appointment." He glanced at his watch. "We need to be there in about one hour. Finish this cup, then go get ready. My buddy gave me a great attorney's name earlier. She used to work for the DA so she should be sharp and know all the angles. She should be able to tell me what we can do to help the police find the real killer instead of settling on you as the scapegoat. That's all you are, you know. An easy, *let's close this case and put it behind us,* answer for the cops. We're not going to allow that to happen, Samantha. Don't you worry! Matthew wouldn't let it happen, and neither will I. I'll make sure we find the true killer." Greg slapped the table, pitched her a crooked grin, and then picked up his cup and took a swig of coffee. Winking, he said, "Trust me, kiddo."

"I do." Sam's shoulders relaxed a little as she took another swallow of her coffee. "I do," she repeated and then set her cup back down on the table.

An hour later, Sam and Greg sat in the waiting room of Claire Marie Babineaux, Attorney at Law. They didn't wait long before the receptionist said, "Ms. Babineaux will see you now." She rose and stepped around her desk and then led them to her boss's door. Opening it, the woman stepped back, giving Greg and Samantha room to walk in, and then the receptionist closed the door behind them.

The lawyer was already moving toward the door to greet them. Extending her hand, she said, "How do you do? Please, have a seat." She motioned them toward the two chairs facing her desk.

As they sat down, Greg said, "You came highly recommended by a friend of mine from down at the courthouse. This is Samantha Cain, the lady I spoke of on the phone."

"Tell me again what you've been charged with," Claire said, directing her question toward Samantha.

"Oh!" Sam's hands flew up as if in surrender. Her voice in

a higher pitch than normal squeaked as she said, "I haven't been charged yet. And hopefully I won't." Her heart raced at the thought of being arrested.

"We're trying to be a little proactive here," Greg explained as he clamped a hand down on Sam's shoulder and patted her gently. "It's okay," he whispered. "I used to work for the police department and a friend of mine on the force gave me a little heads-up when I started asking questions. Sam, tell Ms. Babineaux what happened."

Sam gathered her thoughts. "Okay. Two homicide detectives came to my house yesterday morning after I had worked the night shift. I'm a dispatcher at a trucking company. The detectives asked all kinds of questions and then finally let me know that my boss, Ken Richardson, was found dead in his office that morning. I worked the night shift and was basically the only one there most of the night."

"So this is a case of being in the wrong place at the wrong time?" Claire asked. "Is that what you're telling me? Police usually have a pretty strong case before the DA tells them to make an arrest. Why—besides the fact you were there the night he apparently was killed—did they pick you?"

Greg handed Claire the file folder. "Inside you'll find pictures of the crime scene, as well as some of the notes made by the first officer on the scene. I don't have anything the detectives have said, other than the note made after the ME's picture of the necklace found in his hand, but that was enough to make me feel we needed to take action. Samantha is innocent."

The lawyer's eyes were noncommittal as she glanced at Samantha before looking down at the file in her hands.

Sam watched the attorney scan the statements made by the police officer at the scene. She wanted to speak out in her own defense but knew now was not the time. Next the woman's eyes scrutinized each picture one at a time. "I see they mention you being there all night long and that you heard no one upstairs where the body was found. Is this true?"

"Yes, but I didn't do it." Sam wanted to shout but forced herself to remain calm. "Some drivers came in and went out, passing through, you might say, during the night—but I never heard anything from upstairs. Not that I can recall, anyway. Besides, upstairs is always locked at night. The only part anyone can get into is the upstairs storage section out back. Some of the major parts for our trucks are stored there. Other than that, the shop foreman and the boss both have offices upstairs with separate entrances. There is a door, however, that separates the two offices. The boss's office you enter at the top of the stairs on the side of the drivers' room and the shop foreman's office you enter from the back stairs in the shop. For all three doors there is a key. Three different keys. Keys only held by Ken, the boss, and Otto, the shop foreman."

"And you say you didn't hear anything upstairs?"

"No, I didn't. I reminded the homicide detectives that Ken's office was over the drivers' room, not the dispatcher's. Besides, I don't have a key to any of those doors I mentioned."

"And you told them that? So why are they still focusing on you?"

Sam looked at Greg, not sure what to say next. She had no true idea why they would focus on her. She was there all night. Yes, it was true they didn't get along. But she would never kill him. Besides the fact he was so big, how would she ever get the upper hand on that man even if she wanted to?

He nodded. "Tell her everything. You know—how he treated you different."

Whoosh. A long slow gush of air released. "Okay. First, because I was the one there—opportunity. Second, because the boss and I didn't get along too well over the past couple of years. Motive, I guess? Third, because his wife said he came to the office because I called him...but I didn't. More opportunity. Lastly, and they don't even know this but we do, that necklace he's holding in his hand is mine. When they find that out, they really will be circling the wagons for me." Her hands made two fists. "I know I sound guilty—with all that, I mean. How can they not help but think I'm guilty? Wrapped up with a pink bow and ready for slaughter." Sam wanted to cry. Pressing her fingers against her lips, she tried to hold back the sobs that threatened to escape. After she said all of this to the attorney, how could the woman not think she was the guilty party, too? Discouragement hung like a cloud over her head.

"And the preliminary report stated he died from a stab wound. They discovered a bloody letter opener out back in the shop in the big garbage can. The weapon had a partial print. It matched Sam's fingerprints," Greg added.

"Means." Sam's voice was low, and her shoulders drooped. They had enough to put her away for life. She didn't want to go to jail. She couldn't; she had to be there for her son. Locking her tear-filled eyes on the lawyer, she said, "But that's the dispatcher's letter opener...all the dispatchers. Not just mine. We keep it in the dispatch office in the pencil holder. All the other dispatchers who use it should have their prints on it as well," Sam added in her defense. "I noticed last week the opener was missing."

"Did you tell anyone? Or did anyone else notice it and tell you?" asked Claire.

"I left a note for the secretary, asking her to get us another one. I told her someone must have walked off with it. That happens all the time with our pens and paperclips, so she was used to ordering things again for us. We've even had staplers walk off over the years." Sam wrung her hands in her lap.

"One thing stood out to me when I glanced over the police officer's notes. When he went to notify the wife of her husband's death, on his follow-up questions he wrote that the wife stated you called him out to work," Claire said. "And you said a moment ago that wasn't true. Did you tell the detectives you never called him that night?"

"Yes, I did. I told them emphatically that I did not call the boss! I try to never call him at night. Only in case of a bad accident would I disturb him at home."

"So why is his wife lying?"

Shaking her head, Sam said, "She's not. Not Dorothy. She wouldn't do that. She and I have always gotten along well. Maybe Ken told her I called, using me as an excuse to slip out at night. I don't know what that man does away from work. There is no telling what he does or who he sees." Frowning, she added, "Not that I've ever thought he was unfaithful to his wife before. Don't get me wrong. I'm not trying to give the man a bad reputation or ruin his memory. I'm just trying to give you a reason why she might think I called."

Silence filled the room as Claire Babineaux glanced over the paperwork one more time and then the pictures one at a time. Sam watched in silence but finally turned her eyes on Greg, hoping to get an inkling of an idea of what he thought the lawyer might be thinking. She needed something good to cling to before she went home to Marty. She couldn't have him go through another major ordeal in his life.

Please, Lord, give this woman wisdom to clear my name of this charge, should they bring it against me. After lifting a prayer to the Lord, she glanced at Greg again.

He was studying the lawyer but then, seeming to sense Sam's eyes on him, turned in her direction. He gave her a half smile and a reassuring nod.

There was the hope. She waited longer for the lawyer to break the silence.

Finally Claire said, "I think I can help you. And I agree in jumping on this right away. My thoughts are that the DA isn't far from making an arrest. All this evidence the officer speaks of seems pretty good. But I'm sure they will get with you on some of these things to see if you can explain any of them. They'll want to be sure. Some of it is circumstantial, but when they discover that necklace is yours, they'll really feel good about their evidence. So remember, the next time they want to talk to you, don't do it without me. Here's my card. Put me on your speed dial." She rose as if she was saying good-bye at the same time.

Sam stood as she took the card. Greg rose as he said, "Remember, Ms. Babineaux, I was a policeman for many years. I want to help do any detective work I can. . .help point the police in the right direction. Sam is not the killer, so the best defense should be the police finding the true killer, even if they need me to point them in the right direction."

Claire smiled. "I do have an investigator, you know. I've been doing this job for some time. First as an Assistant DA and then I stepped out on my own. But I felt led to help the innocent. Working for the DA for ten years like I did, I believe, helps me be a better defense attorney. Not bragging, just stating a fact." She pulled another card out of her business card holder and held it out in Greg's direction.

"That's why we came to you. We need the best." Greg took the card and then shook her hand.

Sam swallowed hard as Ms. Babineaux extended her right hand in Samantha's direction. Shaking it, she said thank you to the lawyer, but to the Lord she said, *Here we go again. I'm so sorry, but lead me in every step of the way. Help me prove my innocence. Lead Greg and my lawyer in all the right steps also.*

Could things get worse? She prayed they wouldn't.

Chapter 9

Sam climbed in Greg's car. Her back erect, rigid while she waited for him.

He clambered in, put the key in the ignition, and turned it. The motor purred to life.

"Now what?" she asked. "Do we go home and wait on the lawyer to tell us our next move?" The harder she thought about the next move, the less she could think straight. Was there hope for her? Could she get out of this mess? She was innocent, but how could she prove it?

Slipping the gears into reverse, Greg said, "No. We need to try and gather a little information about Ken Richardson. You only know Ken the boss. We need to find out what and whom he was involved with away from the job, as well as things that might have gone on through the job that you wouldn't know anything about. We'll go back to your place and you can make a list of the friends' names you do know. Hopefully, through them, we can get some leads to start tracking."

Shaking her head, she said, "I can think of some of his friends he brought around the office or who called, but they were his friends. They didn't want to kill him."

Darting his eyes in her direction, Greg said, "Kiddo, I know you think the man was well liked by everyone who didn't work for him, but obviously someone didn't like him. They didn't like him enough to kill him. That's a pretty strong dislike."

"You're right." She concentrated. "There are two local friends and an old buddy who calls him pretty regularly from Alabama. Well, they did when I worked the day shift."

"That's a start. We'll see what we can get from them."

"But Greg, those are his friends. Do you really think they'll give up information to us that easily? Especially if they know I'm a suspect. Wouldn't they try to cover up things they knew about their buddy? I mean, anything negative about him. You know, to protect his memory." Sam clasped her hands together to keep from wringing them. Oh, how she wished this wasn't happening, even though she believed in her heart all would end well. Surely God would not let her be found guilty of something she didn't do. She was innocent. Ken's friends probably wouldn't tell Sam anything, but she needed to help find the information. Somehow, someway. Sam didn't want to wait around while the police and Greg did all the work. She wanted—needed—to do her part.

"First the list, and then we see how they respond to me. I think it's best you're not with me when I question his best friends. They may already realize you are a person of interest to the police, so they probably wouldn't want to help you. I don't have to let them know I'm working on your behalf." He flashed her a bright smile.

"But I can't sit around doing nothing."

Greg spared her another glance, then returned his observation to the road ahead. "Don't you worry. After we make that list and I go find addresses on his friends you don't know, you'll have plenty to do. In the meantime, try to take a nap. Get caught up on some of that sleep you've missed. Maybe by tomorrow, I'll have enough info that the two of us can start following leads, together. Remember, you may have a long road ahead of you proving your innocence, and you need to be rested and ready for it."

"But I—"

"Listen, honey. You need to rest and then you need to give Marty some kind of heads-up as to what's going on. You need a clear head to say the right things to him. So please take my advice this time." He tried to give her an encouraging smile. "When do you have to go back to work?"

"Not for three more days."

Greg patted her clenched fists. "It will be okay. Maybe by that time, everything will already be cleared up. Let's hope for the best. Do you trust me, Sam?"

"You know I do," she said.

A small dimple appeared in his right cheek. "Then know you'll get through this. I promise."

Worrying her bottom lip, she realized he was right. She needed to tell her son what was going on. *But how? And what do I tell him? And how much should I tell him?*

There was no reason to upset Marty or make him worry if it turned out they didn't come after her. Her words needed to show strength and confidence, which she didn't have. If she let her fears seep out through her words or in her actions, Marty would latch on to them for himself. She didn't need to do that to him; he didn't need to sense fear. The scripture in Second Timothy about the Lord not giving man the spirit of fear but of power and of love and of a sound mind whispered in her spirit.

Hold on to that, girl, she told herself.

The car turned into the driveway but stopped suddenly, snatching her out of her deep thoughts. Blocking the car's path was another nondescript dark sedan.

"Not again!" she cried out.

Greg caught her by the elbow. "It'll be okay. Remember, we're prepared for them."

Her stomach twisted as she stared in disbelief. "I know we are, but not now." Her words tumbled from her mouth. "Not so soon. It's not fair."

Greg killed the motor. "Don't panic."

She tried to draw on his strength.

"Take a deep breath. Two of them, in fact; then release them slowly," he commanded.

Focusing her eyes on Greg, she did as she was told. Tears wanted to form, but she could not show weakness. She had to be strong, for Marty's sake, for her sake. *Fear is not from the Lord. Fear is from Satan. Don't grab hold of it. Breathe. Breathe. You have power. You have love. Power. Love. Power.* She breathed in and out with each word. Fast at first, but then down to a normal intake and exhale.

"That's better. Now remember: if they want to bring you in for questioning or even if they want to ask you questions here, you can't say a word without your attorney present. So let's walk in confidently and see what they have to say. They don't have a police car with them so it doesn't look like they're here to make an arrest. Most detectives, although they can and do make arrests, usually have an officer in a squad car with them to carry the prisoner back to the station when it's preplanned."

Sam's heartbeat went wild—double time, triple time. *So much for calming down.* How would she get through this? What was going to happen? She still hadn't told Marty anything. Would he come home to the detectives still here questioning her? Or to an empty house, and his mother in jail?

Lord, please don't let that happen. Please don't let them arrest me. Again she thought those words—*power* and *love.* The quick, shallow breaths she took with each word slowed as a veil of peace slid over her, and her heart rate returned to normal. *I can do all things through Christ who strengthens me.* The words *I will never leave you nor forsake you* touched her spirit as the calmness warmed her being.

Letting a tiny smile tinge her lips, she told Greg, "Okay. I'm ready."

He got out and hurried around the car to open the door for her.

Sam turned in her seat as the door opened, ready to face her fate. She knew she was not alone.

Chapter 10

Margaret swung open the front door and came tearing down the steps. She reached Sam and Greg before they moved three steps from the car. "Ms. Sam, it's the same two men who came yesterday. They insisted I let them in. I'm so sorry."

Grabbing Margaret's hand, Sam gave it a squeeze, turned her around, and headed them all toward the house. "No problem, Margaret. It will all work out. I know you and Greg are here for me, too. We'll make it through." The three of them proceeded up the walk together, Greg bringing up the rear.

"Hello, gentlemen," Sam said as they stepped into the living room. Both detectives rose to their feet.

"Ms. Cain," they said in unison.

The lead detective took charge immediately. "We have a few more questions."

"Greg, these are the two detectives I was telling you about.

Lieutenant Jones and Sergeant Barnett." Sam pointed at each as she said their name and smiled as she spoke. She refused to let Jones intimidate her.

After acknowledging the introductions, Greg turned her way and gave her a slight nod with a half smile.

Suddenly she realized what his smile meant and said, "No problem, Lieutenant." Now was the time to do as Ms. Babineaux had instructed. "Just let me make a quick call to my lawyer before you begin your questions. I'd like her to be present this time when you ask me whatever you need."

"Why?" Jones stammered, apparently taken off guard. But then he swiftly added, "Do you need a lawyer? We're only asking for some more information. Or do you have something to hide?" He smirked. His eyes revealed that he didn't trust Sam. Clearly he was a cop who trusted no one, believed no one, and liked no one. A cop with a bad attitude.

Sam hadn't liked him from the time they'd met, and those feelings hadn't changed. He reminded her too much of her dead husband, the kind of abusive man who gave policemen a bad name.

The sergeant spoke in a more appealing tone as he said, "It's just a couple of follow-up questions, ma'am. Surely you don't need a lawyer for that." His eyes seemed genuine, but dare she chance it? She thought not.

Pulling the card Claire Babineaux had given her out of her purse she said, "I wish I didn't have to call one. But for my protection, I feel I must."

As she grabbed for the phone sitting on the end table next to the couch and started to lift it, Lieutenant Jones said, "Tell your lawyer to meet us at the station. We'll bring you in for questioning there." He moved toward her, pulling out his cuffs.

His scare tactics worked. Sam panicked and wanted to shout, "It's working," but didn't. Instead she pinned her eyes on Greg, hoping he had a way of slowing this man down. Did he have the right to force her downtown? And did he have to handcuff her? Sam pleaded silently with her eyes for Greg's help.

"Lieutenant, are you arresting her?" Greg stepped over, blocking Lieutenant Jones' path to Sam.

The detective cocked his head toward Greg, surveying him head to toe. "I wasn't planning on it, but it sounds like that's the way she wants it."

"I'll tell you what, Lieutenant. I'll bring Ms. Cain to headquarters. We'll call her attorney right now to meet us there. Since you aren't arresting her, there is no need for handcuffs, nor a need to ride with you to the station."

Jones' dark eyes smoldered as he continued to study Greg. With a sour look at his partner, he said, "Let's go. We'll ask our questions at the station."

Sam stood frozen, watching this entire scene unfold.

As Greg led the detectives outside, Margaret grabbed Sam's arm. "It's okay, honey. Call your lawyer. Greg is going to take care of you. I'll be here when Marty gets home. Don't you worry! He'll be fine. You'll be fine. Just hold your head up high, and remember you've done nothing wrong."

She's right. Do what you have to, Samantha Cain. You're not alone.

In almost robotic moves, Sam punched in the attorney's phone number. By the time Greg came back inside, Sam was ready to go with him. "Ms. Babineaux said she would meet us there."

Turning back to Margaret, she hugged her. "Thank you so much. I don't know what I would have done all these months without you, and you're still here helping me. One day I'll make it up to you."

"You've become family to me," Margaret murmured, "so there's nothing to make up. I'm grateful to be a part of yours and Marty's lives."

Smiling at Margaret, Greg rested his hand gently on her shoulder. His eyes were thanking Margaret as his lips said, "Come on, Sam. Let's head down to the station and get this over with."

With friends like these two, how could she miss? She headed out the front door.

Chapter 11

The noise level and commotion as they stepped into the third precinct was so high, Sam almost couldn't hear herself think. Greg did the talking as they approached the main desk. Her gaze drifted around the room.

She didn't want to be there. Anywhere but there would have worked for her. Such horrid memories. First with Martin's suicide and the whole precinct believing Sam was responsible. Well, almost everyone. Then last year's hunt for the serial killer where she was the only living witness, which brought her to the station several times. The only good memory was her short time with Matthew. He did soften the hearts of most of the officers toward her, helping them see the truth. Sure, she knew there were good cops, but unfortunately the few bad cops like Martin and now Jones plagued her memory.

Let's get this over with. She concentrated on the officer speaking to Greg as he told them where to go. Homicide detectives had their own bullpen area, located on the second floor. Once they were there, a plainclothes detective led them to an interrogation room and told them to have a seat. The room was almost empty. It contained a table with a few chairs gathered around it. No light poured in from any window. It was a dim, depressing place with subdued overhead lighting.

Dread swept over Sam as a quiver of alarm sliced through her. She felt trapped, almost imprisoned, even before the door was shut. "This is not good. It's not good at all." Sam knew instantly if she couldn't take it in this small room she would never make it in prison. *Help me, Lord.*

"It'll be okay, Sam. Relax."

Pulling out a seat, she nodded and then lowered herself in the chair, trying to revive that sense of peace. Placing her hands on the table, she crossed one hand over the other, preventing the shakes.

"Trust me, Sam. It will be okay. They won't ask anything until your lawyer is present. And remember, I'm here with you." He patted her hand as the door swung open and slammed against the wall.

Her gaze shot over to the door. There, filling the empty space in the doorway, were the two homicide detectives. She focused on the lieutenant with an attitude. *Jones, what a creep! And what a way to make a grand entrance!* He was just a man, she reminded herself. . .a man with a badge. But she had done nothing wrong, so she need not worry.

Once all eyes were upon him, Lieutenant Jones marched to the table and plopped himself down, dropping a large file on the table as he sat. Sergeant Barnett followed him into the small room but seemed not as sure of himself as Jones. Or was it Jones he wasn't so sure of? Sam noticed the way the sergeant's green eyes studied the lieutenant.

Jones filled up what little space was left at the table in that small room as Barnett took the empty seat next to Jones but sat slightly away from the table. One lone chair sat in the corner by itself. Presumably, that would be pulled up to the table for her lawyer's benefit.

A knot formed in her throat but Sam forced it down as she glanced at Greg. He gave her a quick nod of assurance.

"While we wait on your lawyer," Jones said in a slow, dramatic melody, "I'll let you in on a little secret." He slapped the folder open on the table, then looked at Samantha with haughty eyes. The stiffened muscles on his face screamed of his smug, complacent attitude.

What kind of secret could he tell her? She wondered. There couldn't be more evidence against her. She hadn't done anything. Everything was circumstantial, so what possible secret could he have? And why would he share it with her if he were going to use it to take her down?

Jones whipped through the first several pages of his file folder. He stopped when he came to a stack of pictures, eight-by-tens. Sam watched as he picked up a handful of the pictures and dropped them one at a time in front of her—facing her—so that she saw all five very clearly.

A gasp slipped out as her eyes were drawn to the third picture laid out for display. Greg had shown her some of these at her own kitchen table, but this wasn't one of them. And at home she didn't feel as threatened.

In this picture, her boss lay out on the floor in his office, his eyes open in a dead stare. She wanted to cry out, "He can't be dead." But she didn't. She knew Ken was dead. Poor Dorothy. How would she get through all of this? Sam remembered not so long ago looking into the face of the man she loved, lying cold and dead on a gurney. She had made the positive ID for the medical examiner. Her heart broke for Dorothy having to go through the same thing.

Before Jones flipped over the next picture in his hand, Claire Babineaux strutted into the room. "I hope you haven't started questioning my client without my presence, Lieutenant Jones. Hello, Samantha and Greg." The woman stepped over to their side of the table. Greg rose instantly and pulled the empty chair next to Samantha. Claire sat down next to her client and laid her hand gently on top of Sam's. "We both know that's a no-no, Lieutenant."

Sam, cocooned between the two, felt her lawyer's strength flooding the room and Greg's protection penetrating deep into her emotions. She drew on both, feeling stronger almost immediately. Inhaling a deep breath, she pulled her eyes away from that horrid picture and looked at her lawyer. A slight smile touched her lips as she said, "Thanks for coming."

"And what are you showing my client? Crime scene photos? I thought you brought her here to ask questions. Do you have questions for my client, or was this one of your little scare tactics you use on innocent people?"

Jones grumbled under his breath as Barnett regarded Sam's lawyer with what almost appeared to be admiration.

"I was waiting on you, Claire. I didn't want to overstep my boundaries. Ms. Cain, does anything look out of the ordinary to you in these pictures?" He flashed his gaze on the lawyer as he said, "That is my first question. I assure you." He laid a couple more pictures over the first five he'd dropped in front of her. All were angles of her boss's office with the body lying in the midst of each shot.

"Do you mean, besides my boss laying there dead in the middle of the room?" Sam glared at the man. What a foolish question! Everything looked out of the ordinary when a dead man lay in the middle of it all.

"Of course, I mean besides your boss being dead. Take your time and look around the room. Do you see anything that should be there that isn't? Or anything that is there that shouldn't?" Jones glanced at his partner and flicked his brows as if to say, *Watch this. I've got her now.*

Sam's eyes flashed on her lawyer.

Claire nodded. "Go ahead. See if you notice anything out of the ordinary." Claire turned her eyes toward the detectives and added, "But let me remind you, Lieutenant, this isn't her office, so I'm sure she doesn't know everything in or about his office."

With an annoyed expression Jones demanded, barely moving his lips, "Just look at the pictures, Ms. Cain."

Quiet filled the room as Sam studied the photos one at a time. His fishing trophies all seemed to be displayed prominently on his credenza and his mounted fish hung on the walls. Papers were stacked in his in-box file, as well as his out-box file. The photos of his children and grandchildren stood angled on the bookcase. The high polish on his furniture seemed to be glowing as usual. Everything appeared to be in place.

After a few minutes passed, Sam raised her eyes and looked at the detective. "I don't see anything out of place. At least not to my knowledge," she added softly. "It looks like his office did the last time I was in it."

"You're sure? You don't see anything new?"

Sam skimmed over the photos one more time. "No. I'm sorry. I don't. It would probably be better if you asked Otto. He is in there more than anyone. He would know if anything was out of place. I so seldom go into Ken's office, working nights like I do."

Slapping another picture down on the table, right on top of the other three she had been studying, he said, "How about now? Do you see anything out of the ordinary now? Look at this close-up shot of your boss's hand." He jabbed his thick finger at it as he tapped the picture over and over. "Tell me if what's in his hand belongs in his office."

This was the picture taken by the ME after he wrenched her boss's fingers open—a picture of her necklace. Her mouth grew dry. Her eyes flicked from the picture to Greg and then to Claire. *What do I say now? How do I answer this?* Her eyes begged her lawyer to step in and save the day. Obviously the police knew it was hers—not that she would deny it—but how did she tell the detective the necklace belonged to her?

"Ms. Cain. Do you recognize that necklace? Does it belong in his office?" The close-up of Ken's hand held a slim gold chain. On the chain was a heart encrusted in diamonds.

Claire again gave a slight nod. "Go ahead, Sam. Tell him."

She gulped, then said, "The necklace is mine." Pinning her eyes on the lieutenant, she said, "My fiancé gave it to me. I thought I'd misplaced it about a month or two ago somewhere in my home. I haven't been able to find it." Shaking her head, she added, "But I have no idea how it got in Ken's hand."

"You mean it didn't come off in a struggle between you and your boss the other night? You were the only one there. He was found dead after you left. He was clutching your necklace in his hand." His mouth twisted in a sneer. "Surely you can come up with a better excuse than 'I lost it.'"

Sam sat straight in her chair. "Lieutenant Jones, I'm not giving you excuses. I'm stating a fact. That necklace is very special to me. I only take it off at home, so I assumed it would show up sooner or later at my house." Lifting her pointer finger of her right hand and shaking it slightly, she said, "Not in the hand of my boss. I have no idea how it came to be there. But I guarantee not he nor anyone else snatched it off of my neck! That I would know."

Jones glared at her as Barnett sat quietly back. The smugness faded from Jones' face, and a slight smile edged the sergeant's lips. Not big, mind you, but enough for Sam to feel a little satisfaction creep into her joints. *Maybe the sergeant is on my side.*

"Is that all the questions you have for my client, Lieutenant? If so, we'll leave. If not, ask your questions."

"I have enough to arrest her right now. First, she didn't like her boss." Using his right hand he held down one of his fingers on his left hand. "It was a well-known fact in that office. Gives me *Motive*. Second, she was the only one there when he died. *Opportunity*."

"Well, Lieutenant. You have circumstantial evidence at best. And I don't hear any means." Her lawyer rose. "I think we're through here."

Jones reached into his file, shuffled through a couple more pictures, then pulled one out and slapped it down on the table.

"The letter opener that was found in the garbage but used to stab the victim in his chest had her prints on it." He stabbed his finger viciously in the air toward Samantha. Turning his gaze on Claire and holding up three fingers, waving them a little, he announced, "The third and final—*Means!*" The smugness returned.

"She already told you that was the dispatchers' letter opener that went missing. They all used it, so of course her prints would be on it," Greg said as a matter of fact.

Claire laid her hand gently on Greg's as she said, "Was it the murder weapon? Is that how he died, Lieutenant, from a stab wound? Even if so, it's still all circumstantial. Come on, Samantha, Greg, we're going."

Both stood to their feet, ready to follow Claire out of the room.

The detectives followed suit, but Jones threatened, "Ms. Cain, we *will* get more evidence. You will not get away with murder."

"But—" She turned to plead her innocence.

Claire interrupted. "She's innocent, Jones. Give it up. Come on, Sam. Let's get out of here."

Sam wanted to stay and defend herself to that wretched man, but Greg steered her out of the room and Claire followed. Once they made it out the front door, her lawyer looked at Sam. "You don't need to defend yourself. He needs to prove your guilt. Don't you worry. Just continue on with your life."

That would be great. Sam wished she could—and that the whole mess was behind her. Suddenly she heard the words of James 1:12 in her mind: *Blessed is the man who perseveres under trial, because having stood the test, that person will receive the crown of life that the Lord has promised to those who love him.* She knew she loved the Lord; she just wished He didn't have so much faith in her to endure all these trials and tribulations. But she also knew the Lord loved her and would see her through.

One day at a time, she reminded herself.

Chapter 12

Opening the front door and about to step into her home, Sam heard a squeal and jumped, her nerves not quite under control these days.

"Momma!" Her son shot to his feet and scampered to the door. He wrapped his arms around her waist. "Momma. Are you okay? Is everything all right?"

Margaret rushed through the swinging door from the kitchen and mouthed, *I'm sorry.* She shrugged and raised her arms in a questioning motion as she continued lip talking. *I didn't know what to tell him.* Then she said aloud, "I explained to Marty that the detectives had a couple of questions they needed to ask you, but they needed to do it at the station for some reason. He was worried. I told him not to worry. You would be back soon. And here you are." She fixed an exaggerated smile on her face for Marty's sake.

Greg eased Sam and Marty into the living room so he

could squeeze the rest of the way into the house and then closed the door behind him. "Why don't we go sit at the kitchen table and talk about it? I'm sure Marty would love to hear everything—if that's okay with you, Sam. Unless you want to speak to him in private."

"No. No. That would be great." She gave her son an extra tight hug. "We can all tell Marty what is going on with the police and why they've come to the house a couple of times."

Marty dropped his arms from around his mom and rushed past Margaret toward the kitchen. "Oh boy," he said as he pushed on the door. Even with his deep concern for his mother, the boy still embraced the excitement of a child when it came to cops and robbers. It was part fantasy for him, so she knew he didn't truly understand what was going on in the real world, even if he did know more reality than most kids his age should know. She hated having to tell him his mother was being accused of murder. *Not yet,* she reminded herself. But after all he'd been through, she hated telling him anything.

Margaret pulled three cups down from the cupboard and set them on the counter next to the coffee pot. "Coffee is fresh. Y'all had perfect timing," she said as she started pouring the hot black liquid in each cup.

"You are reading my mind, dear." Greg tossed a smile her way as he stepped closer to the countertop. "Thanks."

"Marty, would you like milk and cookies, or a soda?" Margaret asked, always thinking of everyone else.

"Mmm. Are the cookies homemade?" His innocent eyes rounded as they looked in anticipation.

"Sorry, sweetie. Store-bought."

His brow furrowed. After much consideration, he smacked

his lips. "I guess that's still good. Thanks Ms. Margaret." He grinned as he scrambled into a chair at the table.

Sam watched the buzz in her kitchen as everyone did his own thing. When Greg finished fixing his cup of coffee and took a chair next to Marty, Sam slipped over and stood by Margaret. The dear woman poured two cups and started to add the cream and sugar for Sam. "Margaret," Sam whispered, "you don't have to wait on me all the time. You've become like family in the months you've been living with us. So please. Two things. Quit waiting on me hand and foot. And quit calling me Ms. Sam. Just call me Sam. Okay?"

The curls on her head bounced as she nodded. "Thank you so much." She paused and then said, testing the waters, "Sam." Smiling, Margaret grabbed her black coffee and took the chair on the other side of Marty.

This left the chair straight across from Marty available for Sam. This way she was able to look straight into his eyes as she spoke, giving him the confidence that he needed to feel.

Sam stirred her coffee and joined them all at the table. *Lord, please give me the right words to say to Marty. He needs to know the truth but not so much that he becomes afraid.*

All eyes were upon her as she took a sip of her coffee and then set the cup on the table.

Marty took a bite of his Oreo cookie. As he crunched on the dark chocolate, he said, "I'm ready, Mom. Tell me. What's going on this time? I'm not going to have to go to Granny and Papaw's, am I?"

Poor child remembers the problems last year. "No, sweetheart." She smiled into his eyes. "Marty, do you remember my boss, Ken Richardson? You've met him before at some of the holiday gatherings at the terminal."

"Sure I remember him. He's that giant man." Marty peered up to the ceiling, waving his hands at the giant, and made a grunting noise as he exaggerated Ken's height slightly. "I've never seen anyone as tall as him." Marty took another bite of cookie and followed it with a gulp of cold milk.

Everyone couldn't help but smile at Marty's response. To a boy not quite four feet, a man over six feet tall would seem like a giant. "That's him, son. Well, something bad has happened to him. Someone killed Mr. Richardson."

His face grew solemn. "Oh no. Like Matthew?" His bottom lip began to quiver. "I'm sorry, Momma. I'm so sorry." He put his cookie down and dropped his head toward the tabletop. "I bet his kids miss him, too."

Sam didn't know about Greg and Margaret, but Marty's view on Ken's death choked her. It was all she could do to hold back the tears. He equated Ken's death to Matthew's death and how hard it had hit him. His little heart showed concern for Ken's kids—even though they were all adults now. How sweet. "I'm sure they do, sweetie. His wife, his kids, and his grandchildren are all going to miss him. It's a very sad thing."

"I'm sorry, Momma. Why do the police keep asking you questions?" He paused and then asked in a very small voice, "And why do people have to die?"

"The police think I might know something because he was found in his office early one morning and I had worked the night shift. In fact, they are hoping I know something—

but unfortunately I don't." She reached out and grabbed her son's hand, holding it tight. "Baby, I wish I could give you a better answer on why people have to die, but it's just part of life. We live and we die. The important thing is how we live our life while we are alive."

"Like Matthew? He was a good guy. He loved helping people."

She fought back the tears. It was getting harder by the moment. Finally she said, "That's right, honey. He loved us and he loved others, always trying to help them."

Sam glanced at Margaret, whose eyes were rimmed with tears, and then to Greg, whose gaze was locked on Marty. She wished they would add a pearl of wisdom.

Lord, help me.

"And he loved the Lord. God is love, Marty. And Jesus tells us the most important thing for us to do is love others. Not just your friends, but even the people who are hard to love." She halted, believing the Lord Himself had prompted those words.

The boy looked up with bright eyes. "Do you love the man who killed Matthew, Momma?"

A heavy blow to the gut caught Sam off guard. She gasped as she tried to form the right words.

Greg stepped into the conversation, saving her. "Your momma loves everybody through Christ, Marty—even the bad man who killed Matthew. That was his job, to catch bad men and put them in prison so they couldn't hurt anyone. Unfortunately, this guy killed Matthew before he could arrest him. Your momma hates that the man killed Matthew, but she loves him through Christ and hopes that, during his time in prison, he finds the Lord."

Greg said it perfectly. *Thank You, Lord.*

Marty regarded Greg for several seconds, then finally said, "Okay. That makes sense." He bobbed his head up and down. Suddenly, his brows scrunched together and he peered sideways at Greg. With a slight hesitation he said, "And one day Momma will be happy again, right Uncle Greg?"

"You got it, buddy. One day." Greg lifted his hand for a high five, and Marty slapped it to him.

"All right." Marty snatched up his cookie and took another bite. "So, Ms. Margaret, what's for supper?"

Samantha sat back in her chair, unable to stop her amused grin. She watched as the three people she loved the most in the world rose from their chairs, seemingly content with the world. She loved her mom and dad as much, but they weren't there at the moment. Sam would catch them up on things in her life soon. Hopefully they would take it as well as Marty.

The three started moving around, all chattering with one another as they continued on into the living room. Oh, how she wished it were that simple.

One day, Lord, I will move on. But right now I still miss Matthew so much. Please let me hold on to him and my memories a little longer.

Her son appeared satisfied with the explanation she'd given him for what was going on as things in their lives were turned upside down again for the third time. If only she could explain it to the police simply enough to help them believe she had nothing to do with her boss's death. What should she do to clear her name? What could she do?

Wait on the Lord. He would direct her.

In the meantime, she needed to stay calm and safe in His arms.

Chapter 13

*T*wo *more days.*

That thought crossed Sam's mind the minute she opened her eyes the next morning. Only two days left before she had to go back to work. Only two days left she could possibly use to help solve the mystery encircling her life. How could she use those days to help Greg turn the investigation away from her? On Sunday, she would return to work that evening, so she had better get busy!

After the big talk at the table with Marty yesterday afternoon, Sam sat down with a blank piece of paper and listed names of people she knew were friends of her boss. It wasn't a very long list, mind you, but it provided Greg with a starting point. He said he would begin the investigation right away and, as soon as he could, would bring her in on it. But she knew being around Greg in the beginning would only hinder the talks he planned with each of Ken's friends. . .especially if they knew she was the prime suspect, according to Detective Jones.

Of course, when Greg talked to TJ Roberts, the terminal manager Ken replaced, she could go with Greg. Sam didn't list him as a friend but as someone who may know something about Ken's reputation. She and TJ had gotten along well. Samantha had been his secretary and promoted to dispatcher on his watch. She hated it when the main office ran TJ off.

He stood up for his drivers. In fact, TJ went out of his way to take care of his people. That was what the main office didn't like about him. . .at least that was what she believed. And the customers loved TJ. They knew if he said he would do a job, it was going to be done. Some of those same customers only used her company as a backup now because they didn't trust Ken. They claimed he always billed them for more than they hauled, but no proof could be given. The tickets always matched what Ken said. Although the old customers didn't like it, they couldn't prove the weight tickets were wrong and that was what they were billed from.

She could also go with Greg to talk to Dean Smith, the present chief dispatcher. He, too, wasn't a friend like the others listed. But since Ken made him chief dispatcher over guys with more seniority, everyone felt there was a special something about their relationship no one knew about but suspected. However, Dean did a fine job, and Sam had no complaints during the short time she was on days when he first started working for the company. Since she'd been night-shift dispatcher, she hadn't had much dealings with him but assumed he still did a good job. Like the boss, she only saw Dean at the dispatcher meetings. Sam felt certain he would talk freely around her. She would get with Greg this afternoon and see when he planned on talking with those two.

What can I do today? Maybe I should go pay my respects to Dorothy.

The funeral had been delayed since the ME hadn't released the body yet, but Sam knew for certain the woman already felt the loss and pain—just as she had felt when Matthew had been killed. It wasn't easy even now to go through each day. Thank God for Marty, giving her a reason every day to focus on him and live each day God blessed her with.

Dorothy and Ken's children were in their twenties and thirties. None lived at home anymore. Pity swept Sam's heart as she thought how lonely Dorothy's life had become overnight.

Sam slipped out of bed. Glancing at the clock she realized how early it was, so she pulled her hair up into a knot and clipped it. After taking a quick shower and dressing for the day, she made her bed and then padded down the hall to wake up Marty.

"Rise and shine, buddy. It's time to get up." She took a moment to observe her beautiful son's reaction as he moaned a little, then squirmed, twisting and turning under his bedsheets. Finally he grabbed his covers and dragged them over his head.

A small chuckle escaped her lips as she stepped over to his bed. "Come on, Marty." Leaning close, she whispered in a melodic tone, "It's Friday. The best day of the week. Get up, sleepy head." Slowly she eased his covers down, revealing his face one inch at a time. And then quickly she put her lips on his forehead, making a loud smooching sound, exaggerating the kisses.

"Aw, Mom!" The little boy wiped the sloppy kisses off his face and peeked open one eye. "I'll get up. Give me a few more minutes. . .please?"

She ruffled his reddish brown curls. "Okay, buddy. I'm going to go start a pot of coffee and then start mixing some pancake batter. If you get up and are dressed in time, you can have some for breakfast. If not, it will be a banana on the run for you. Don't sleep the morning away."

Smiling to herself, she left his door slightly ajar. If nothing else, the smell of bacon would bring him to his feet in a heartbeat. The boy loved bacon and pancakes. Tiptoeing down the hallway toward the kitchen, she paused at Margaret's bedroom and knocked softly on the door. In a quiet voice she said, "I'm putting on the coffee and then making pancakes if you want some." Sam didn't wait for an answer. She knew Margaret would come if she wanted to. . .or not. On Sam's off days, she made it a point of being the one who took care of Marty, so when Margaret joined them, it was like she was a part of the family. In the past few days she'd realized just how much Margaret felt like family to her. What a blessing!

Sam stood with her back to the kitchen table, stirring the batter while the dark brew dripped into the pot, filling the room with the aroma of the freshly roasted coffee. She savored the peace and quiet. With the mountain of worries that should concern her, she didn't dare ponder them. Sam had given them to Christ, and she didn't dare try to take them back—at least not at this moment. She hoped she'd left them with Him. Sam knew for a fact that He would lead her if she kept her faith in Him.

At the patter of little feet running into the kitchen, she

pivoted and watched the whirlwind swoop up to the table. "So, my little man, you decided to come eat? Just in time. No banana on the run for you today."

He laughed out loud, dragged a chair from the table, and jumped up in the seat. "I wouldn't miss pancakes and bacon for anything in the world, Mom. You know it's my favorite." He rubbed his hands together. "And I'm ready to eat!"

Sam flipped his pancake and then grabbed the plate of bacon. Placing it on the table, she said, "Let's say a blessing. Your pancake is almost ready."

"Let me! Let me!" Enthusiasm bubbled over as he waved his hand in the air. She nodded so he began. "Dear Lord, thank You for my favorite breakfast. Bless it and the cook. Thank You for my mom who cooked it for me 'cause she loves me. Please, Lord, take care of her. In Jesus' name I pray. Amen."

"A-men." A voice from the hallway boomed out loud and strong, which was followed by Sam's "A-men." "I couldn't have said it better, young man." Margaret smiled at both Marty and Sam as she entered the room. "I'm ready for mine, too."

"Coming right up." Sam quickly poured more batter in the skillet and waited a couple of minutes. As the batter formed little circles, gelling the mixture, she knew when the pancake was ready for flipping.

While Margaret fixed a cup of coffee, Marty busied himself with spreading butter and watching it melt. Sticking a piece of bacon in his mouth he chomped down on it. "Um-um," he said, "this is so good. Thanks, Mom."

As swiftly as Sam scooped out the pancake and slapped it on a plate for Margaret, Sam wasted no time fixing her own and joining them at the table. There wasn't much talking going on this morning. It seemed everyone was too busy chewing.

When Marty took his last bite, he pushed his chair out and jumped to the floor. "Gonna go brush my teeth and then I'll be ready." As fast as the whirlwind rolled into the kitchen, it blew back out again.

"He is such a good boy." Margaret's voice oozed with pride. "You've done a wonderful job raising him."

"I hope I'm in it for the long haul. . .raising him, I mean." Sam laid her fork down and picked up her glass of milk. Two swallows emptied the remains. Setting it down, she said, "I can't see God letting Marty suffer more than he already has."

"He has been through a lot, but the Lord saw him through it all. And He will continue to take care of Marty. Don't you worry."

Marty came running back into the kitchen with his school bag slung across his back.

"Looks like I finished just in time." Sam rose from her chair and hugged her son when he barreled his way into her.

"Breakfast was great, Mom. Thanks again." He hugged her waist and then kissed Margaret on the cheek. "See you this afternoon." And then Marty dashed toward the back door. "Come on, Mom. We don't want to be late."

"Coming, Son. I'm right behind you." She tapped Margaret gently on her shoulder as Sam passed. Snatching her keys off the hook in the kitchen and grabbing her purse off of the drain board, she reached for the back doorknob. "I'll be back in a few minutes," she said as she stepped outside.

In the car Marty chatted nonstop. "Today is going to be a great day, Mom. For me and for you. Don't you worry about a thing. I already prayed about it, and God told me not to worry.

It's in His hands, and you know how big they are." The puffed out-cheeks shadowed his smile as he spoke with confidence.

What a wonderful son. . .and his faith.

To be so young, her son knew so much.

Thank You, Lord, she whispered in her head. She loved her little boy so much and would do anything for him. As fast as that thought came, she heard a quiet voice inside say, *"And you're My little girl. I'll do everything for you."* Sam's heart caught in her throat. *Out of the mouth of babes.* The comfort her son gave her was unexpected, yet so powerful.

Turning into the horseshoe drive at school, she rolled slowly to a stop. As Marty opened the door to leap out, Sam said, "I love you, Son. Thanks for being my big man. You'll never know how much you mean to me."

"Aw, Mom." He flashed a smile at her and jumped out of the car.

Sam laughed to herself as she drove off.

She returned home to find the kitchen already cleaned to a sparkling shine and Margaret sitting at the kitchen table sipping on a cup of coffee. "Margaret, you shouldn't have. I'm off work for a couple more days. I can do these things, too, you know." She gave the woman's shoulder a squeeze, then grabbed the pot to pour herself another cup.

"Sit down and join me, would you, Sam? I have something I'd like to talk to you about, if it's okay." Margaret lifted her cup to her lips to take another sip, never taking her eyes off of Samantha.

"This sounds ominous." Sam sat at the table, not knowing what to think or how to take that statement. "Please tell me nothing happened while I was gone. Detective Jones didn't call the house or anything, I hope."

Margaret's soft curls bounced a little as she shook her head. "No. Nothing's happened, not today anyway." Seriousness filled her eyes. "Something did happen the other day, sort of. I need your advice. . .and ah. . .your opinion." Margaret's lips tightened into a fine line, and a slender line of concern formed between her brows.

"It will be okay, Margaret, whatever it is. I promise." Sam touched the older woman's hand. "What? Tell me all about it."

"Okay. Here goes." She took a deep breath. "Mr., ah. . ." She paused on his name and then smiled as she said sweetly, "*Greg* has been very friendly toward me lately."

"He likes you. So do we."

"I know that, but I don't mean like that." Margaret held her hands up, palms facing out as if trying to stop every thought that might sidetrack her. "He sort of. . .flirted with me. I'm in my late fifties, so I'm not sure if he's just joking around and that's how he treats all women, or if he is truly flirting with *me*." She pointed at herself. "The thing is, I like the man. When I met him months ago I thought he was handsome. I've been a widow for so long and never before have I ever looked at a man and thought that." She stared into Sam's eyes like a little puppy, pleading for attention. Only Margaret wanted guidance.

"Really?" Joy touched Sam's heart. She couldn't help but smile as she took another sip of her coffee. Putting the cup back down on the table, she lifted her left brow. "Sounds like maybe you have a crush on him. I mean, to notice him when you really haven't been finding any interest in any other man since your husband's passing. And to tell you the truth"—

she paused, drawing Margaret's total attention even deeper—"I've been watching the two of you the past couple of days. I see the way he looks at you when you're skirting around the kitchen preparing dinner or breakfast, or whatever you're doing. I've seen the way you blush when he calls you 'dear.' I think it's so sweet. And I think maybe it's a two-sided interest."

A wide grin filled Margaret's face. Clasping her face in her hands, she whispered, "Truly?"

Sam gave a slight shrug. "I admit I've only known the man about a year, but from the way Matthew used to talk about him and what I've seen, he used to chase women all the time but never got serious with any. Ever. And in the last few years he quit chasing any and seemed to find contentment just living his life, such as it was. He even told Matthew how he regretted never finding that special woman he could love and settle down with. I believe that was the conversation that made Matthew realize he didn't want to wait any longer for letting his feelings for me be known. That was the night Matthew told me he had fallen in love with me. At the time we met, Matthew was a confirmed bachelor, believing he would never marry." She choked on those last words.

"I'm so sorry, Sam. I didn't mean to bring up such sad memories."

"My memories aren't sad. It's only the loss of him that's sad. The remembrances are wonderful." She relished the memories. "Matthew never married, and that was my fault. I put it off a bit too long. Don't make that mistake if Greg shows interest in you, and you are interested in him. You go for it, woman. You have a lot of life ahead of you. Live it."

"Oh, Sam, thank you." Margaret rose and hugged Sam.

After their shared embrace, Margaret backed away and apologized for taking up so much of her time.

"Don't be silly. I love that you felt open enough to share this with me. I love Greg, almost like a big brother, and I love you. What wouldn't be better than to see two people I love so much find they are perfect for one another? The only thing is, I'd hate to lose you. . .well, you know what I mean. You mean so much to Marty and take such good care of him."

"Let's not get carried away here. The man hasn't even asked me out or anything. Besides, you two are my new life, and I would never leave you. I love caring for Marty. He's come to be like a grandson I never had."

They laughed.

"Sorry. I tend to do that sometimes—think down the road a ways. By the way, I'm going to freshen up a bit and go pay my respects to Dorothy while Marty is at school. See if I can do anything for her. You know what I mean?"

"Do you think you should? What if the police have her believing you did it?"

Sam shook her head. "Surely Dorothy knows me better than that."

"She should. Well, be careful. I'm here if you need anything."

Sam grinned. "That's the thing I was talking about. You are always here for Marty and me. I'm spoiled."

"That won't change. Go do what you have to do."

On the drive to Dorothy's house those words Margaret said played over in Sam's mind. *What if the police have poisoned Dorothy's thoughts? Surely Dorothy wouldn't believe them. She's known me for several years.*

Sam paused before turning into their big horseshoe drive. Several cars were parked along the curb, so she pulled up behind the last one.

Maybe now wasn't a good time. It looked like others had the same idea, dropping by to pay their respects. Sam's heartbeat doubled as she opened the car door and stepped out.

"Give me the right words of encouragement for Dorothy through this time. Thank You, Lord."

Climbing the few steps leading up to the front door, she held her head high, pressed the doorbell, and waited.

Chapter 14

The door opened wide, revealing a young woman dressed in a black silk button-down blouse tucked into black linen slacks. A few strands of blond hair fell loosely around her face. The rest was swept up, twisted, and secured on top of her head with two black shiny sticks stuck through the knot of hair. It was a stylish hairdo. Sam recognized Ken's oldest daughter immediately. "Dana. Hi," she said, extending her right hand. "I'd recognize you from your pictures anywhere. Your dad was very proud of all of you kids."

Dana slipped her hand into Sam's but gazed back with questioning eyes. Obviously, Sam wasn't as well known to Ken's children as they were to her.

Of course. That makes sense.

"Come in. . . .please." The words spoken were almost robotic. Apparently they had already had a steady stream of visitors. The postponement of the funeral had to make things awkward for the family and friends.

"Pictures of you and your sisters and the grandkids cover his credenza and bookshelves in his office. Ken always spoke proudly of each of you. I've even met your two sisters at the crawfish boil last year. I don't believe you've come to any of our lunches at the terminal, though, so we've never met."

Releasing the grip of their hands, the young girl snatched hers back as if she'd been burned. Her eyes widened with recognition. Still blocking the entrance to Sam, Dana said, "You must be—"

"Samantha. Come in, dear. Dana, let her in." Dorothy sauntered over with both hands outstretched.

The daughter obeyed instantly, and Sam found herself in a warm embrace. Dorothy didn't listen to the police, obviously. She knew Sam was innocent. Relief flooded Sam's emotions.

Holding Dorothy in her arms, Sam whispered, "I am so sorry. I know how hard this is for you." Enhancing the hug, she tried to let her love surround the woman. Tears formed in Sam's eyes. She couldn't hold them back. Even though she didn't get along with Ken, her tears were for Dorothy and her loss. "I'm here for you if you need me, Dorothy. Anything."

The older woman squeezed Sam one quick time and then broke their contact. "Thank you, dear. Come with me. Meet some of our friends and family who came to pay their respects." Dorothy reached out her hand and Sam caught hold of it.

In the great room, so many people had gathered. Some were sitting, while others were gathered in groups. Sam recognized Susan and Cathy, the other two daughters of Ken and Dorothy, right away. Both girls turned their gaze upon Sam as she entered the room and then quickly looked away.

Sam gave herself a mental shake. *What is wrong with his girls? I understand they are upset, but why do all three of them act like I have done something to them?*

Reality struck. Apparently the chief detective on the case had shared his opinion with them, and they had chosen to believe it. *Maybe I shouldn't have come.* But at least Dorothy wasn't treating her poorly. Hopefully that meant Dorothy didn't believe Detective Jones' theory.

"Attention, everyone. This," Dorothy said as she placed her hand at the small of Sam's back and edged her forward, "is Ken's number one dispatcher."

Sam almost laughed out loud, but she held it in. Why would Dorothy introduce her that way? Surely Ken had complained about Sam to Dorothy many times over the years. Maybe not. Oh well, she wasn't going to be the bearer of bad news to this woman. Maybe Ken didn't bring his bitterness home and poison his wife's opinion of her. Great.

Over the phone and on her occasional visits to the office, Dorothy had always been pleasant to Sam. Of course that was when Ken first started working for the company. He didn't wait long to stick her on the night shift.

Sam smiled timidly and nodded slightly to the group of people.

"I'm not going to call your names, but be sure and introduce yourself." Squeezing Sam at her waist, Dorothy said, "Ken probably told her stories about most of you. And some of you may have spoken with her on the phone when you called him at work. Introduce yourself to her as she makes her way around the room. Maybe she'll share a story or two from the terminal."

Scanning the faces from left to right, Sam knew no one. But the way Dorothy introduced her, Sam felt beholden to walk around the room and extend her condolences to each one. So as much as she didn't want to do it, she started on her left, with the oldest woman in the room. This was probably his mother. If so, Sam had spoken to her sometimes late at night when she had tried to reach Ken at home and got no answer. She figured Sam would know where he was. The sweet woman didn't want to disturb her son in the middle of anything important by calling his cell. She always checked with the people who worked for him, believing they knew his every move. The man never shared his private life with anyone. . .at least not with Sam.

On the nights his mom called, Sam could never tell her where he'd gone. She had paged him, leaving his mom's number as the call-back number. Whether he called her or not, Sam never knew but figured he had since Mrs. Richardson called her several times over the years for Sam to connect her to her son. The woman always took a few minutes out to share pleasantries, making Sam wonder how such a caring woman could raise such a hostile son.

The woman smiled brightly as she extended her trembling hand. "Oh, how wonderful to finally meet you in person, dear. Your smile always came across the line when I spoke to you on the phone. I thank you for always being willing to help me get in touch with my son."

Sam took the wrinkled but soft hand and covered it with her own. "Mrs. Richardson, it was always a pleasure talking with you. I'm sorry we're meeting under such sad circumstances."

Mrs. Richardson's eyes rimmed with tears as they chatted. The older woman's hands quivered as they held tightly to Sam's.

"Your son loved you very much. He told us tales of his youth, and how he gave you a lot of grief. He also told us how you always whipped him in line." Sam hoped those words gave the woman some comfort.

A tear slipped down her cheek, and she sniffed. "Thank you, dear. Thank you so much." Mrs. Richardson inhaled a quick gasp. "Your children aren't supposed to die before you. No parent should have to bury her child, no matter how old. It's not fair." Tears began to fall in a steady stream.

Sam knelt before the older woman and whispered words of comfort. As the sobs slowed down and tears dried, Sam rose to her feet. "Take care, Mrs. Richardson. One day at a time the Lord will see you through."

"Thanks, dear." She touched the tissue under her eyes one more time.

Sam bade her good-bye and moved on to the next group of people. She didn't stay as long there as she had with Ken's mom. In fact, with each group she made her stay shorter and shorter. As much as she wanted to be there for Dorothy, she had no intention of getting to know Ken's family and friends in one swift walk around the room.

All three daughters hovered around Dorothy, almost like a shield. Her earlier thoughts had to be true. They had to have heard the talk from the detectives. All three regarded her with condemnation—all but Dorothy. Drawing a deep breath, she strode over to the group to say good-bye.

Before she could, the middle daughter, Susan, stepped out of the group, blocking Sam's way. "You've got nerve." Her voice, though whispered so others weren't aware of the evil tone, stopped Sam cold.

She swallowed a lump in her throat. *Help me, Lord.*

"I'm sorry, Susan. I'm here to pay my respects to you and your mom. I'm not ashamed of anything. Please let me say good-bye to your mother, and I'll be on my way."

Susan stood firm and tall, towering over Sam's five-foot, one-inch frame. As the daughter's eyes shot daggers and her mouth opened to fire more words at Sam, Dorothy caught her daughter by the elbow. "Susan, sweetheart, go see if Grandma wants another cup of coffee."

"Mother," she said strongly, trying to tug free as she pleaded.

"Go. Now. Everything is fine." Dorothy released her daughter's arm and the girl stepped away. Extending her hand, Dorothy said, "I'm sorry. Emotions are a little tense around here. These girls don't seem to know what to do with their grief."

Sam wanted to deny Susan's allegations, or at least her insinuations, but decided now wasn't the time. Dorothy knew Sam would never hurt her husband, even if she could have. It wasn't in Sam's nature to hurt anyone. Grasping Dorothy's outstretched hand, Sam stated, "I'm truly sorry for your loss. I'm still grieving over my loss of Matthew, so I do know how you feel. Again, if I can do *anything* for you, let me know."

The elegant woman squeezed Sam's hand. "I will, dear. Thank you for coming and sharing your heart with my family and me. We appreciate it very much." Dorothy dropped Sam's hand and placed her hand at the small of Sam's back as she directed her toward the front door.

Did Dorothy want her out of there, too? Did she blame Sam for her husband's death? Oh, how Sam hoped not.

Driving home, Sam prayed for the Lord to comfort the family. She reminded herself that everyone grieves in their own way. The kids needed someone to blame, and she seemed to be an easy target. But Sam knew the truth. She had not done a thing. The only thing she wished was she had heard the scuffle upstairs that led to his death, so she could have prevented it. But she hadn't, and she couldn't change the past.

Help us, Lord, to find the truth. Lead Greg in the right direction since the police seem to have fixated on my guilt.

Where to go now? What was the next step? She knew she had to trust the Lord to prove her innocence. If there was anything He needed her to do, He'd let her know. In the meantime she would go wherever she felt His leading.

Waiting was the hardest part. But that was the next step. Maybe Greg would have something for her to do when she got home. Sam pressed the accelerator in expectation as the car rolled a little faster down the road.

Chapter 15

Detective Barnett couldn't understand why Jones, the lead detective, was so convinced that Samantha Cain killed her boss. Jones' misconception had Mark baffled. How could he even think such a thing? She was so small, and her boss was so big. Sure, little people kill big people all the time, but usually signs of a struggle would be present. Or in some cases the ME would find drugs in the bloodstream, giving reason why the smaller person could bring down the larger one without using much force. Neither held true in this instance. . .at least not in the preliminary report. There wasn't even blood spatter around the room showing an attack with the letter opener. One solid hit. . .and very little spatter. Maybe the drug had been undetected in the first test, and Richardson lay still on the floor as Cain slammed the knife in his chest, piercing the lung and causing asphyxiation. That was the only thing that made sense at the present. If

Jones was correct, maybe Samantha Cain had sedated him in some form that the ME had not uncovered yet.

Detectives couldn't solve cases merely on conjecture, though. They had to study all the facts, all the evidence. The evidence they'd collected spoke clearly to Mark. Not clear enough to exonerate Samantha Cain, but clear enough to know Jones was headed in the wrong direction. To the young sergeant, it was plain someone was setting Ms. Cain up. No one in their right mind would kill someone where they would be the only suspect. Everything was circumstantial and too obvious at that.

The office was found with only a small pool of blood around the wound and very little spatter, so his heart was still beating when stabbed, but Richardson didn't fight back. The thrust penetrating his body had not been substantial. The room itself was found clean and neat. No overturned furniture. Not even papers out of place. That ruled out a struggle for sure. Mark felt there was a chance the body had been placed there.

But still it didn't explain why Samantha Cain didn't hear or see anyone that night. How could that have happened?

A toxicology report would come in sometime today. Maybe that would clear up some things, but no matter how he looked at this case, read the evidence, or listened to the people interviewed, in his gut Mark could not believe this little woman killed anyone, especially a man of Ken Richardson's stature.

Across the desks, Jones was munching on doughnuts and slurping down coffee. Mark lowered his gaze to the folder in front of him. There had to be more to the man's death than merely a disgruntled employee. They needed to push his friends and coworkers harder, even check more into his family life. Everyone painted this man as a saint—everyone except some of his employees. Others made it sound like he was their best friend. Probably trying to look good for the next boss. There had to be more, and it was his and Jones' job to find it.

Frustrated, he rubbed his clean-shaven face and pulled his keyboard over in front of him. There were other ways to find out things about people in today's world, the world of the Internet.

Tapping the keyboard, he filled the search bar with Richardson's full name. In seconds over ten hits appeared. There were too many for his liking, but Mark scanned the various links. Speed-reading the text, he found a lawyer, a doctor, and eight other professionals on one link all living in New York City, another man in Georgia, and someone's link on Facebook with no personal profile included.

"Aha," Mark whispered as his fingers went back up to Google and typed in Facebook. There were so many social media networks for him to search; he was bound to find something else on the victim. . .using the computer. Today some of the older generation hadn't caught on to using high-tech gadgets. To people like Jones, it was a bother to have to use the computer. That was one of the reasons Jones liked having Mark as his partner—he keyed in all their reports. The only thing Ben Jones did on the computer was read his e-mails and play games. Nothing too technical, of course.

Forty-five minutes later, Mark found a lead. On one of the networks Richardson had a page. It didn't look condemning on the surface, but some of the typed chatter, the wording patterns, led Mark to believe there was more behind the innocent conversations the victim had with his social media pals. Don't people realize anyone could find them if they thought to look? And once their words, pictures, or videos were in the airwaves, there was no taking them back.

After copying and pasting several postings, he would see if one of their computer geeks could crack the code, as well as figure out to whom the IP addresses Richardson communicated with belonged.

As his list printed, another thought surfaced—texts on the victim's phone. Sure, they didn't find anything incriminating on the phone calls or the texts left in full view for anyone looking at the vic's phone, now in evidence lockup. But when the customer deleted a message, the phone company still had a record of that message. He would get a warrant and then secure a copy of the last six months of texts to and from the victim. Maybe someone other than the obvious disgruntled worker had threatened Mr. Richardson—and maybe he would find out more about the man's life. . .something suspicious.

Mark scanned the printed page of what he had saved and then folded it, sticking it in his back pocket. Picking up the phone, he started to call Kevin from IT but realized he didn't want Jones to hear him. Instead he sent an e-mail requesting Kevin to check out what he had copied and pasted, as well as the victim's social media page, and see if he could determine if there was a hidden code. At least the man could trace the messages back to IP addresses and try to locate the true names and addresses for him so Mark could speak one-on-one with each of them.

An hour and a half had passed and his partner hadn't said

a word to him. Mark wondered what Jones was doing at his desk. Surely he'd finished his breakfast by now. Glancing over, he found his partner reading over something on his computer. Maybe the old man got wise and decided to do a little digging himself.

Negative. Jones was probably reading his e-mails. That was the majority of the old man's Internet knowledge.

"Hey, Ben, I think I found us another possible lead," Mark said across their desks. They faced each other, making it easier for the two as partners to communicate to one another as they discussed a case they were working on.

Jones stuck his left hand up in the air with one finger sticking out, never taking his eyes off the computer screen, as if to say, *Wait one minute. I'm in the middle of something.*

Mark clamped his mouth shut against the words he wanted to say. Why didn't Jones want to know whom else could possibly be blamed? That remark should have gotten his partner's full attention, but he was so fixated on bringing Samantha Cain down, he probably didn't even want to hear what Mark had to say.

"We got her!" Jones slammed his hands together with one loud clap and then jumped to his feet, almost dancing a jig as he stomped around bobbing his neck back and forth and pumping the air with his fists, like he'd just scored a touchdown.

Shaking his head, Mark said, his voice growing louder with each word, "Ben, did you not hear what I said when you told me to wait? I said I found another lead."

Jones stopped his dancing and frowned in Mark's direction. "What's with you, partner? You've been so fixated from the beginning that it wasn't Ms. Cain. Why, when it's so obvious she did it?" He stood motionless, staring at his partner in disbelief.

Trying to keep calm, Mark sat back in his chair.

Enough! Slapping his hands to the arms of his chair, he stood in disgust and aggravation. With his eyes penetrating, burning a hole through Jones', Mark said in a harsh voice, "And why is it you've already tried and convicted Ms. Cain? You've got some stick—"

"That's enough, Barnett," Jones interrupted. "Let's roll. You young people will never learn." He grabbed his crumpled suit jacket off the back of his chair and stepped to the printer. Pulling a piece of paper off the machine, he folded it and stuck it in his breast pocket. "I'm the lead detective, and I've got a new piece of evidence. One that explains how that little woman did the dirty deed. Even you'll have to believe it."

I doubt it, Mark thought but knew better than to speak aloud. The sneer on his partner's face caused Mark's stomach to churn. What was his problem?

Getting irrefutable evidence would be the only way to change Ben's mind. And he would do it. Mark would follow his own lead on his own time without sharing his findings with Jones, until he could tie it up in a bow, so to speak. Mark hoped he found facts to back up his possible theory soon. Then he'd clue Jones in. The man didn't really want to hear anything that would exonerate Ms. Cain. So Mark would keep it to himself for the time being.

Right now he wanted to refuse to go with the detective, but he couldn't. Ben Jones was the lead on this and every case they worked together. Mark may have to follow Detective

Jones, but he didn't have to agree with the man. He would go so he could keep himself abreast of what Jones was plotting against Samantha Cain. Maybe that was the best way to handle this case, this time. He hated going behind his partner's back, but what choice did he have?

"We're going to slip by the DA's office and get a warrant to search Samantha Cain's home. If my gut is right, we'll find all the evidence we need."

Mark grabbed his suit coat and followed Jones to the elevator.

We'll see.

Chapter 16

Sam saw Greg's black Accord parked at the curb of her house when she turned into the driveway. She hoped he had good news. After that visit to the Richardsons' home, she could use a little uplifting.

Parked around back, she killed the motor and stepped out of her Toyota. By the time she walked over to the back steps, she heard laughter from the kitchen. Greg must be telling one of his many stories. She was glad Margaret found things to smile about again. When the woman first came to work for them, she'd maintained a serious countenance. After a few months, Marty had her smiling most of the time. Matthew occasionally made her laugh, but never a full belly laugh. That was Greg's doing, and it sounded wonderful. He'd even worked hard to make Sam at least smile since Matthew's death.

He'd been successful—until now. Unfortunately now her mind stayed too busy to laugh. Too busy to smile. She tried not to worry because she'd given her problems to the Lord, but she couldn't help but ponder the situation. *I guess the spirit is willing but the body is weak.*

Sticking the key in the knob, she unlocked the door and then opened it. The aroma of onions and garlic simmering on the stove assaulted her senses the minute she stepped inside. "Um, um, um. Something smells delicious in here. What are you cooking?"

"Steak and gravy. I hope that's okay by you."

Greg's chest puffed up slightly. "It's my favorite. She said there was enough for me, too. Hope you don't mind, but I'll be joining you all for supper." Greg glanced at Sam, smiling as he spoke, but when his gaze turned to Margaret, his smile deepened. If Sam wasn't seeing things, she believed Greg's eyes even twinkled.

"Sounds good to me—supper and you're staying. The smell sure has my stomach calling out." Dropping her purse and keys in their usual spot on the counter, she pulled a cup out of the cupboard.

"Would you like me to fix you a snack? Dinner is a few hours away. Knowing you, you didn't bother to grab lunch while you were out today, did you?" Margaret knew her so well.

With a slight chuckle, Sam said, "Don't mother-hen me, Margaret, but you're right. I didn't eat lunch. I—"

"Oh. That reminds me." Turning on her heel, Margaret announced, "Your mom called and she wants you to call her back. I can't believe I almost forgot to tell you."

"You didn't tell her anything, did you?"

"Of course not."

A sigh of relief escaped Sam's lips as she set the cup on the counter.

"It's not my place," Margaret said, her eyes flitting from Sam to Greg and back again to Sam. It was like a neon sign flashing *Guilty* over and over.

So did she tell her parents anything? Sam wasn't sure. "Margaret?" she questioned softly. "What are you hiding? Or what did you say?" Sam knew that look on Margaret's face meant something.

The older woman raised her brows. "I promise I didn't say anything to your parents." Dropping her gaze to the floor, she whispered, "But. . ."

"Out with it, woman."

"Oh my," Margaret murmured. She tapped her fingertips to her lips. Pausing for another second or two, she glanced again at Greg for what appeared to be direction or a spot of encouragement. He gave her a supportive nod and the woman continued. "But I was just telling Greg that I thought you needed to share this with them. I know you don't want to worry your parents, but they want to be there for you. I think if they find out another way, it would hurt them deeply. They love you so much, Sam."

Sam gathered her long strands of hair into a form of ponytail, dropping it over her left shoulder. The longer her hair got, the more she routinely repeated this action. Her anxious fingers continued to play with her long strands as she thought. Finally, she nodded. "You're right. I'll call them now."

Sam slipped to the bedroom to make the call. She wanted a little privacy because she had no idea how her mother or father would react. Besides, Marty didn't need to hear the worry that would probably pour from her voice. Glancing at her watch, she saw she had over an hour before the bus dropped him off in front of the house.

Her mother answered on the second ring. "Hello." Her parents still lived the old way, no caller ID or anything to tell them in advance who was on the other end of the line.

"Hey, Momma. It's me."

"Oh, sweetheart. I knew it. I knew it. I hear it in your voice. I told your father Margaret sounded upset even though she tried to hide it. What can we do? And what is going on? Please tell me you're okay—and Marty. Dear, don't keep us in the dark." She called in the background, "Honey, it's Samantha. Come quick."

"We're okay, Momma, but something is going on. But I don't want you or Dad to be upset. Tell Dad everything is okay."

"One second. He'll be here in a moment."

Sam could see her mother's gaze in her mind's eye, flitting back and forth from the phone to the doorway, anticipating her dad's arrival. She waited in silence as she imagined her mother's every move.

"Okay, dear. He's here. Go ahead and tell us."

Sam knew they both put their ears up next to the phone, waiting to hear what Sam had to say. A smile touched her lips. She loved them so much. "First let me say, everything is okay. The sad thing is my boss was killed the other day, and they found him in his office early the next morning. Unfortunately I was the one who worked the night shift before the body was found, and I seem to be the police's number one suspect."

Her mother, Diane, had drawn in a deep breath when she

heard about Ken Richardson's death, but when she heard the police suspected Sam, a squeal escaped.

"It's okay, Mom. I didn't do it. Greg is helping me find proof since the police...well, not all of them." She didn't want to paint the wrong picture for her mother. "There is one detective who seems to believe in my innocence. Or, more to the point, he doesn't seem as strong as his partner in thinking I'm the guilty party."

"Hold on, Sam," her father said.

Her father didn't give her a choice. She heard the clank of the phone hit the counter and then the dragging of a chair on the floor. Sam wished she could see in their kitchen and know what was going on. "Dad. Daddy, can you hear me? What's happening?"

"Samantha, it's okay. Your mom needed to sit down for a minute. This is a little much. How can the police think a person as sweet as you could possibly kill your boss—even if he is a monster to you?"

"I don't know, Daddy, but I do know everything will be okay. I know God is taking care of things and He's surrounding me with people to help me and Marty."

"Well baby girl, keep us posted," her dad said. "And if we can do anything, let us know. Marty can come stay with us again. Anytime. You know we'd love to have him."

"I do. Thanks, Daddy. Give Momma a hug for me, and you two don't worry. Before, Marty's life could have been in danger. That isn't the problem this time, so I'd rather not interrupt his schooling. Margaret is here for him every day when I'm not. We're keeping him in the loop but not by telling him everything. He's almost nine now. I can't treat him like a baby.

And you'd be so proud of him."

"We are, dear. We'll be praying for you both. Take care. We love you. Give our love to Marty."

Sam said her good-byes and they hung up. She glanced at her watch and hurried to the kitchen. They needed to talk before Marty got home. She wanted to tell them what happened when she visited Dorothy's home without Marty hearing the details. Sure, she had shared the circumstances of what was going on to a degree with her son, but there was no need for him to hear everything.

After pouring a cup of coffee, Sam added cream and sugar and then joined Margaret and Greg at the kitchen table. "Margaret, you can rest your mind now. Mom and Dad know everything. Thanks for suggesting I call." She quickly updated them both on her visit to the Richardsons' home, paying her respects.

Margaret shook her head in sorrow.

Greg said, "You probably shouldn't have gone there, but at least you've let them see you're not afraid. Maybe that alone will be enough to have Mrs. Richardson suggest the police check other avenues. I'm sure they talked to her a good bit in the beginning of the investigation, trying to find out all they could about her husband. Well, we hope they did, anyway."

She agreed with him. "Now, Greg, did you find out anything today that might help divert the investigation away from me?"

"Turns out your perfect boss had a couple of flaws." He gave Sam a half smile.

A moan of expectation burbled up from deep within. Her heart expanded as it filled with hope for the truth. "Really?

Great! Tell me more."

"He likes to gamble and chase women."

"Wow," Sam said, shocked. "That I wouldn't have guessed in a million years. I knew he wasn't perfect, but I truly thought he was faithful to Dorothy. And the way he takes care of his family, even though they've all grown and left the house, the man is. . .*was*. . .very generous, almost to a fault."

"That's something else I need to look at closer. Thanks."

Sam raised a brow in question.

"The kids and their dependency on him. Parents do some crazy things when it comes to their kids. Helping them out of trouble, which only allows them to make bigger mistakes, and then assuming Daddy will bail them out again. . .that could lead to some powerful enemies, if you know what I mean." He shrugged. "I want to cover all bases."

Queasiness gnawed at her stomach. Sam hated that she and Greg were digging into Ken's past and his family affairs. It seemed too personal to her.

"Don't fret, little lady. This is your life we're talking about. And if it takes opening some of their closet doors to expose other possibilities, then that is what we'll do. Right?"

Sam sat in silence, thinking what an awful thing they had to do.

When Sam didn't speak up, Margaret did. "Right. Besides, if the man's a gambler, he may have a few enemies who would want to kill him. So don't you worry! Greg will get the police looking in the right direction." The woman stepped over to the coffeemaker. After refilling her cup, she offered more to Greg.

"Thanks, Babe, I don't mind if I do." He held his cup up so

she could pour more in the empty mug.

"Sam?" Margaret turned the pot in her direction. After a slight nod, Margaret topped off Sam's cup and then grabbed the sugar bowl and cream pitcher, moving them to the table.

While everyone tended to his or her coffee, a thought emerged. *Didn't bookies like gamblers? That was how they made their money.* And as much money as Ken seemed to have, she doubted he owed anything to them. Sam felt certain he paid all of his debts. "So how will this help? Surely if Ken gambled, he won more than he lost. And when he lost, I'm sure he paid what he owed. The man was loaded and making great money. Sometimes we, his employees, believed he even made a few deals under the table, if you know what I mean."

"Nobody wins all the time," Greg assured her. "And the man may not—"

A loud pounding on the front door interrupted his words.

Rolling her eyes, Sam rose to her feet. "It's them again. I know it. They never ring the doorbell. It's like pounding on the door is more powerful. And that big detective loves pushing his power."

"Let me get it." Greg headed toward the living room.

"No," she said, stopping him in his tracks. "I don't want them to think I'm afraid, 'cause I'm not. This will work out in the end. I just have to be strong. You two stay in here. I'll call you if I need you."

"If you're sure." Greg stepped back.

Margaret's gaze darted from the direction of the front room to the stove. Making a snap decision, she stepped over to where the steaks were stewing in the gravy and turned the knob. Instantly the fire went off from under the pot.

"Good idea. Thanks. I'd hate for them to burn our supper, too." Sam pushed through the swinging door. As she moved toward the front door, she glanced through the big picture window and called out in a hushed tone, "I guess you better come on in here after all, Greg. They brought police cars with them." Although she had planned to be strong, her cracking voice revealed a smidgen of fear. The backup troops with the detectives could be the cause of that. She knew what it meant. Trouble. It looked like they were here to arrest her. But why so many cars?

As she opened the front door, Greg and Margaret rushed through the swinging door and then stood back. They were there if she needed them but not hovering so the detectives could see her strength.

"Well, well, if it isn't my two favorite detectives! And look, they brought some friends with them." She kept her tone sweet until her eyes met the convicting ones of Detective Ben Jones.

"What do you want now?" she asked without pushing open the screened door. Sam didn't want to invite them into her home again. Although she hadn't meant to be disrespectful, she was getting tired of the smugness on that man's face. Her annoyance spilled into her words.

Holding a paper up, Jones opened the screen door. "Step aside," he said in an authoritative manner. "We have a warrant to search your premises."

"For what?" She backed up, allowing him entrance as she took the paper. "I don't understand. What are you looking for here at my house?"

"It's on the warrant. I suggest you read it."

"I'll call Claire." Greg whipped out his cell from his pocket and started dialing.

Fighting tears, Sam murmured, "This can't be happening to me. Not again." Inside she screamed, *Why, Lord? Why me? Why so much? I know You don't give us any more than we can handle, but I think You just believe a little too much in me. Stop this insanity. . .please.*

Margaret rapidly moved to Sam's side. "It'll be okay. Hang in there." Her hands enveloped Sam's forearms, pouring courage and strength into her veins.

Sam surveyed the other detective as he stepped through the door. An expression of what appeared to be regret flashed in his eyes. Was he regretting or apologizing for the intrusion? Or was he apologizing for his partner? Either was greatly accepted and soothed her frustration slightly.

The men dressed in uniform followed the detectives and immediately dispersed in every direction. As they scattered, Greg hung up his phone. "Claire's on her way. She said just stand back and don't say a word."

Sam sighed. *Wait. Of course.*

What else could she do?

Chapter 17

If you three will take a seat and stay out of our way, we should be out of here soon." Jones wasn't asking. He was telling. "Detective. Stay here with them. I'll go see what the men are finding." His partner gave a nod as he stood with his back to the wall and his arms folded across his chest.

Sam wasn't sure if she could talk to him or not. Her lawyer had said to wait for her. But surely that didn't include being impolite to the one man she thought might be on her side—Jones' partner. He never looked in a negative way at Sam. He always seemed to be the one who tried to help her see that he and his partner were only doing their job.

Sighing, she decided to be herself. "Detective Barnett, is it?"

He nodded and revealed a partial smile.

"Can I get you a cup of coffee?"

"Thanks, but no thanks, ma'am. We'll be through here in

a short time. Sorry for the intrusion."

"Tell me, Barnett," Greg said, as he looked the detective up and down. "You don't seem as pushed to lock up Samantha Cain as your partner. What is it with that man? Why is he out to get Sam instead of doing his job and searching all the possibilities?" Greg stepped closer to the detective.

"And you are?"

"I'm Greg Singleton. Retired from the force five years ago. I was Detective Singleton, with Homicide, for over twenty years." He extended his hand, and Barnett returned the greeting. "I was partner to Matthew Jefferies' dad. Did you know Matthew Jefferies? He was Samantha's fiancé."

"I knew of him, sir. And," glancing at Samantha, he added, "I knew Ms. Cain was engaged to him before his death. Sorry, ma'am."

Samantha and Margaret both watched as the two exchanged words. When the detective acknowledged Sam, giving her his sympathies, a chord touched her heartstrings.

"Like I said, it's been awhile since I've been with the force, but I'm sure police procedure is still the same. Follow the evidence. Her necklace in her boss's hand—everyone knows was planted. If she had wanted to kill him, surely she wouldn't be dumb enough to kill him where she would be your first and only suspect. Give the woman a little credit."

The detective raised his brows and glanced toward the two doors exiting the living room leading to other parts of the house. Then he said quickly, almost as if he didn't want to be overheard, "I understand you completely, sir. We—" He cleared his throat. "We are looking into all the evidence, sir, ma'am. You can count on it." His gaze slipped from Greg to Samantha as his eyes revealed sincerity.

The doorbell chimed and Sam looked to the detective for permission to answer the door. He gave her a nod, letting her know she could. Opening the door, Sam said, "Oh, Ms. Babineaux, thank you for coming so quickly."

Greg stepped beside them and handed her the warrant. Greg could have scanned it, but Sam felt sure he was more at ease letting someone in the legal world be certain of its contents.

Claire's gaze skimmed over the papers and then said, "This warrant entitles them to look throughout your home and storage and any buildings on the premises, as well as your car."

"What are they looking for?"

"According to this warrant, Ken Richardson was not killed by that single stab to the chest that they thought in the preliminary report had penetrated the lung. Their finding now states death by poison."

Margaret jumped to her feet. "So they're looking for poisons? Oh, no." Her gaze jumped from one person to the other. Then, as fast as she'd said it, she looked like she wished she could have pulled the words back into her mouth.

But everything happened for a reason. Sam knew if they had poison around the house, it was for a good reason, and it wasn't to kill anyone. Greg stood and slipped over to Margaret's side. He seemed to give her comfort as he hugged her, and then helped her back onto the sofa. He squeezed in next to her. Sam heard him whispering, "It'll be okay. Don't worry. Relax. What are you thinking that's upsetting you so?"

The lawyer stared in Margaret's direction, never letting her eyes waver. Finally Claire said, "Yes. That is exactly what they are looking for. So what is it that's upsetting you so, ma'am? And who are you?"

"That's Margaret. She lives with us. She takes care of my son and me. She's almost like family." Sam tried to assure Margaret as well as Claire Babineaux.

Margaret reached out to Sam. "I'm so sorry." Avoiding the detective's glare, she turned her eyes on the attorney. "We have rat poison in the shed out back. I know, because I bought it. Ms. Cain is not even aware of it. At least I don't remember ever telling her." She shivered. "I'm so sorry," she whispered again as she eyed Samantha with a soul-wrenching look.

Sam stared at her friend. "My heavens. Poison? What on earth for? We don't have any rats, do we?"

"As a matter of fact, we did, but we don't anymore," Margaret explained. "One night, while you were working, I heard skittering across the ceiling. Years ago we had rats in the attic, and I remembered the sound all too well. So I went to the hardware store the next day and purchased a large bag of rat poison pellets and scattered them up in the attic."

"I don't remember ever smelling a dead rat," Sam said slowly. "I know when we've killed them at work with poison, the stench is deadly when those things crawl into the wall somewhere and die. That's a smell you don't forget."

"I know what you mean. But the kind of poison I bought was supposed to make them run away and find water. It makes them thirsty. And living across from the lake, I felt sure they'd run across the road and crawl into the lake and die. Never heard them again, so I believed it worked. Anyway, because there's a small child in the home, I felt led to put the remainder of the package of pellets outside in the storeroom under lock and key. I didn't want Marty to accidentally find it and there be a horrible mishap."

Sam moved over to the couch and wrapped her arms around Margaret. After giving her a hug, she released her and looked into her eyes. "You are the best. Thank you."

"I hope you're not in trouble for something I did," Margaret said.

"It'll be okay. Don't you worry!"

"The ME's report indicated the type of poison. Rat poison wasn't the killing aid. It was potassium cyanide," Claire said as she read the warrant.

"I don't even know what that is," Sam stated as a matter of fact.

"It's a poison that makes it appear someone died of a heart attack. But in this case, the preliminary report had stated stabbed to death. Apparently the final report came out today, and Detective Jones hurried over here to try and find the poison."

Greg turned cold eyes onto Detective Barnett as he said, "Jones decided Sam was guilty from the get-go. I've worked enough crime scenes and with enough detectives to know when someone sets his mind and then tries to find the evidence to match his decision."

Detective Barnett looked like it was all he could do not to speak up. Would it be for his partner, or would it be to agree with Greg? Sam wondered. In her heart, she felt this detective was trying to follow evidence. He didn't seem to be on the same page as Detective Jones.

Thank You, Lord.

All of a sudden the voices moved into the kitchen. It sounded like they were tearing the place apart. Making balls with her fists, it was all she could do to sit, be quiet, and stay calm. It would all work out in the end. She knew she was innocent. God would prove her innocence. She would be a testimony to Him, and He would be a testimony of her innocence.

Scanning the various faces, Sam realized they were all talking, all but the detective, but she had missed the majority of the conversation. It was probably for the best. If she listened, she might find herself becoming anxious and Sam didn't want to go there. For the next ten minutes, she sat back against the couch, closed her eyes, and whispered prayers to the Lord. He was the only one who could save her, and while He did what she couldn't do, she wanted to wait in peace. His peace.

When the back screen door slammed, Sam jumped.

The detective stepped over to the swinging door and glanced into the kitchen. Returning to his original place, he leaned against the wall again. "They're moving the search outside, ma'am. It looks like we're almost through. Sorry for the inconvenience." Detective Barnett gave a slight nod.

"Can we move to the kitchen? I'll fix us some cool glasses of lemonade," Sam said. "How does that sound?"

"Like a great idea," Claire said as she followed Sam's lead to the kitchen.

"Let me make it, Sam." Margaret said as she hurried around the line walking into the kitchen. The detective was the last one in line.

Everyone fell silent as they stopped in their tracks.

Margaret let out a squeak as she covered her mouth with both hands. Dropping them slowly, she said, "Oh my gosh!"

Sam looked around the room. "What have they done?"

Things had been pulled out of every cabinet. Stuff was strewn on the floor and stacked on the counters. It was a mess.

Picking the gallon pitcher up off the countertop, Sam blew out a breath of agitation. "I was going to say, let me do it. I need to stay busy, but it looks like there is enough work here to keep us both busy for a while. So for now, Margaret, help me make the lemonade. Grab two cans out of the freezer. Everyone sit. Ignore the mess. I am." She forced her focus on finding the big spoon to mix the lemonade.

Everyone sat, except the detective. He remained standing with his back to the swinging door. His face showed almost as much displeasure as Samantha felt, but she wasn't going to give in to it. That would make Jones too happy when he came back inside with nothing to charge her for. At least he would have the satisfaction of knowing he ruined her home. She could only imagine what the rest of the house looked like. For the time being, she wasn't going to think about it, because she was not going to give him the satisfaction.

Cover me in peace, Lord, and let it be real.

In no time, the lemonade was mixed and ice filled five glasses. Sam poured them as Margaret passed them out. When it came to the last two glasses, Sam grabbed them both. She extended one toward the detective.

"I really don't need it. Thanks."

"Please? For me. Just take it. I didn't poison it," she said with a smile. "I promise."

The detective returned her smile as a slight chuckle

slipped past his lips, making Sam's smile deepen. She knew he believed in her innocence. He took the lemonade she offered.

Holding her glass, she joined the three at the table. After taking her first sip, she sighed. "I hope they finish soon. Marty will be out of school shortly. I don't want him coming home to them or this mess."

"Don't worry. I'll help you and Margaret. We'll have everything shipshape before he gets home," Greg said.

"It shouldn't be much longer, ma'am. How many storerooms do you have outside?" the detective questioned.

Looking at the detective, she thought for a brief second. "Only two. One attached to the carport, my laundry room, and the other back in the corner of the lot."

"That's the one I stored the poison in," Margaret added.

The detective smiled at her.

"This lemonade sure hits the spot, Ms. Cain." Claire set her glass down on the table after swallowing another sip. "This is just part of the investigation, you know. It will be over soon. Eventually the police will get on the right trail and leave you alone. I'm sure. But if not, still don't worry. You're innocent. It will work out."

Claire sounded very sure of herself today. The other day at her office she sounded like she would do her best. But today, the woman sounded more confident. Apparently she'd done a little of her own investigating—or she'd been listening to Greg singing Samantha's praise. Either way, Sam was glad to hear her sound so confident.

The back door slammed again and every head turned in the direction of the sound. "I need your keys, Ms. Cain. Now."

Standing, Sam moved to the counter and picked them up.

Pulling out the key to the ignition, making it stand separate from the rest, she handed the lot of them to the detective. "My car is the Camry under the carport." Sam smiled knowingly at the man. They hadn't found anything. That was why they were still looking, and it was killing him. His grim expression told her everything she needed to know.

Yes! She smiled.

He turned and walked back outside without saying a word.

Greg and Margaret both laughed as Sam strutted back over to the table and returned to her seat.

"That man is ridiculous," Margaret said. "He looks upset that he hasn't found anything to throw you in jail for. What is his problem?"

"I wish I knew," the detective said in a very low whisper. Not low enough, though.

"You and me both, sir," Sam said to the detective and his eyes opened wide as if he didn't realize he had spoken his thoughts aloud. She liked that. Proved even further, he was a man out for the truth, not ready to hang her just because his partner wanted to.

Detective Barnett focused swiftly on the floor, keeping his gaze away from the people at the table. He was probably berating himself for speaking his thoughts aloud. Sam almost felt sorry for him, but he didn't need to worry. His partner didn't hear anything and he, for sure, wouldn't hear it from any of them.

The next few minutes were spent in silence. No one had anything to say, but it was all right. Everyone knew what was going through each other's mind. Sam just wished it would all be over soon.

The screeching of the back door pierced Sam's ears as Detective Jones yanked it open and stepped inside. He dropped the keys on the counter, looked at his partner, and gave a nod. "We're going now." Turning his sour face toward Samantha, he said, "Ms. Cain, it's not over yet. I hope you understand we don't take murder lightly."

She rose from her seat and moved closer to the overconfident man who was speaking. "I hope you understand, Detective, I too do not take murder lightly. Nor do I take the invasion of my home lightly. I've done nothing wrong and the sooner you figure that out and get your mind in the investigation, the sooner you'll find the true killer, because it isn't me." On that, she turned her back on him, looked at the other detective, and gave him a short nod. Hopefully he understood her silent words. She couldn't afford to lose someone who was on her side.

"Detective Jones, before you go," Claire said as she rose to her feet, "I need you to e-mail or fax me a copy of the final ME report. By the warrant, I see the ME changed his preliminary findings." She pulled her business card out of the side pocket on her purse and extended the card toward the detective.

His brown eyes darkened, and he snatched it from her hand. "I'll send it to you when I return to the station." The two left out the back door as the screen door slammed behind them.

Margaret moved over to shut the wooden door, not making a sound. Quietly, she turned back toward everyone and said softly, "It's over. Right?"

"For now, Margaret." Greg moved next to her, rubbing her

forearms gently as if trying to reassure her, and then draped one arm over her shoulder, pulling her next to his side.

Sam grimaced. "Unfortunately that man believes I'm guilty, and he's going to keep digging, trying to find something to make the courts agree to arrest me. But he won't succeed. My God is bigger than he is."

"That's right," Margaret said, smiling sweetly.

As bad as it seemed, Sam knew she could only take one day at a time and wait on the Lord to direct her and Greg in their next step to clear her name. She smiled, filled with hope for her future. "Claire, thanks for coming on such short notice," she said as she led her to the front door.

"I'm only a phone call away. Don't panic, and don't let that bully torment you." She patted Sam's shoulder as she headed out the front door.

Closing the door behind her, Sam turned back to her friends, whom she considered like family, and said, "Let's get busy. We have less than fifteen minutes to turn this place around before Marty gets home."

Chapter 18

Mark listened to Ben Jones' grumbling all the way back to the station. The young detective couldn't wait to get out of that enclosed space. So many times he wanted to open his mouth to his senior partner and try to correct his statements, but deep inside, he knew he'd be wasting his breath. Ben Jones didn't want to look at the truth. He had it in his mind to condemn this woman, and Mark had no idea why.

Although he had tried several times to get Jones to admit his accusing notions about Samantha Cain were ludicrous, the detective would not agree. He stood by his convictions that he was following the evidence. Mark knew better but couldn't turn that hardheaded man's thoughts around, so he accepted defeat quietly. He planned to continue his pursuit in finding the true evidence that would point toward the real killer.

Standing on the sidelines as Samantha Cain, the retired

detective, and the woman they called Margaret talked among themselves, Mark couldn't help but notice the belief they had in Ms. Cain's innocence. He thought so, too. His gut told him that he and his partner were chasing the wrong scent, but he couldn't get Ben to believe him, believe his instincts. Mark needed to learn more about the victim. Whom did the man cross enough to be killed? Besides, usually you looked to the spouse, and Ben hadn't even given that woman a first glance, let alone a second.

If we don't investigate the man, we'll never find the truth, and that is our job.

So Mark was going to do just that. Ben could follow his take on the evidence found so far, even the planted evidence in Mark's opinion. He felt certain there was more evidence to be found, and, given a little more time, he'd find the right trail to follow to find the guilty party.

Besides, he didn't read the crime scene evidence in the same light that his partner had read it. Although the crime scene had blood spatter and blood pooled around the wound and on the floor, it didn't show major blood spatter as you'd normally find in a stabbing. And, besides, how could that little woman get close enough to take such a big man down with one swing of the letter opener?

Luck? I don't think so.

The poison in the blood could help explain things a little better. Maybe she gave him poison in a cup of coffee, and then, while he was close to passing out, she stabbed him and left him there to bleed out. But in the back of Mark's mind, he still felt the crime scene lacked signs of a struggle. No furniture was overturned. His desk was neatly organized.

Nothing was out of place. Not even one of his many pictures was knocked over. As far as the blood spatter was concerned, one jab wouldn't spray much, but something still boggled his mind. How would she know the one exact spot to jab with the letter opener? No.

Was she aiming for the heart? Or for the lung? Both would kill him. Puncturing the lung would be a slow death, as well as bleeding out, unless, of course, she sliced his throat, cutting the carotid artery. He would have bled out with every pump of his heart. Now that would have sprayed and pooled some blood.

With his lung punctured, oxygen would have to be cut off from the brain for about five minutes for him to die. It was an odd way to asphyxiate the man, but it would work. What Mark needed to do was read in full the final report on the cause of death. Was the COD poison? Loss of blood? Or loss of oxygen? Someone truly wanted this man to die, and it looked like they wanted Samantha Cain to take the rap for it. That to Mark was obvious. Why couldn't Ben see it, too?

Inside the station, Mark watched Jones walk straight to his desk and, from that moment on, he didn't open his mouth again. That suited Mark just fine. Instead, Jones plopped himself in his chair and logged onto his computer.

Now that was a strange sight. . .a man who didn't like the computer going straight to it.

Mark couldn't help but wonder what the man was up to. Surely, he wasn't going to dig for more information on the victim or look for other clues surrounding his death. Things he should be doing. No, not Ben Jones.

Mark smirked as he fought to hold back the laughter

that wanted to bubble up from within. Then he turned his thoughts, as well as his computer, on to the things he was checking earlier. Glancing back over the things he had copied and pasted from Ken Richardson's chatter from his different media sites, Mark was more convinced than ever that some of these chats meant more than what they seemed to mean on the surface.

As quick as his computer dinged, telling him he had a new message, Mark checked his e-mails to see if his favorite geek from IT had responded yet.

Seven new messages. Yes. And one was from Kevin. The real names would be a great help; if the geek wonder could have gotten those, it would make Mark's life easier, or at least his investigation. Kevin was a smart dude. He knew how to get around walls, find hidden passwords and messages and get into places most ordinary users didn't even know existed. If there were any hidden messages or secret codes, he would find them.

Clicking on the message, it appeared, and Mark started reading.

All right.

Instantly he saw that Kevin, too, thought it was coded messages. The "boy wonder" couldn't break the code, not yet anyway, but he felt certain the conversations dealt with a product being available and setups to meet at various times and places for selling or buying the product. Kevin managed to find IP addresses on most of the chatters. Some of the addresses piggybacked so many times going to so many places all over the world that it made it difficult to find the origin. For those, Kevin was not able to find all the owners. . .yet.

But Mark wouldn't lose faith in his Computer Genius. Most of the people Richardson communicated with on his media sites, thank God, weren't smart enough to hide like the ones who hopped around the world.

By attachment, Kevin sent him a list of names and addresses he had gathered so far.

Pulling them up, Mark printed the list off. After retrieving the paper, he started checking for rap sheets on any of them. Two had records. One was arrested several times on petty misdemeanors while another one was arrested for distributing drugs.

Oh, this is good. Maybe the victim was selling drugs. Mr. Innocent, I knew he wasn't. Now I just need to find proof of whatever he was doing.

The two people with priors was where he would start his investigation, but not with Detective Jones. He had to do this on his own. When he found something concrete, something that could open Jones' mind to other possibilities, then he would start sharing. It was for the best. Normally Jones was a good cop, but for some reason he wasn't on spot with this investigation. Mark really needed to find out what was messing with the detective's mind. If he could find that out, maybe he could help his partner look beyond his nose. He quickly jotted down the addresses of the two parties of interest, as well as their job sites and their parole officers. This was a great start.

He glanced across the desks. Jones was still messing with his computer. Must be playing games.

Mark sighed. This case was going to take them a long time to solve at the rate they were going. The first forty-eight hours, when the trail was really hot, was usually the best time to solve a case, but this wasn't going to be one of them.

With confidence, Mark looked back through his copy of the paper file. He didn't have a copy of the completed autopsy in his file yet. Glancing back at the other six messages, he found a message from the ME he was copied on. Quickly he pulled it up. It was the latest report on the Richardson murder. After hitting the print button, he scanned the report, already knowing the final COD was poison.

Why stab him? Hurrying up the death? What was the point? In his gut he felt this, too, was more of a setup to make Samantha Cain look like the guilty party. When the machine quit making a whirling sound and the paper shot out, he grabbed the hard copy and added it to his folder. Glancing through the rest of the pages, including notes from the interviews, he felt a gnawing in his gut, but what?

Something kept tugging at the back of his mind. He knew there was something that wasn't right but couldn't bring it to the front. Clasping his fingers, he turned them down and out, cracking his knuckles. His thoughts kept flipping the pages in his mind.

Finally he sighed and shook his head.

He'd start with the leads he had just found and hopefully that nagging feeling would surface soon with the answer on what was missing or bothering him, or at least with the right question to ask.

Mark needed to get a warrant so he could pull the info from the telephone company. He needed the erased messages on Richardson's texting as well as any deleted phone calls. Mark turned a few more pages over and found the victim's cell phone information.

He dashed off an e-mail to Patricia Reynolds, ADA, a friend of his in the District Attorney's office, and gave her the case file number, victim's name and address, and the home phone and cell numbers. He asked to get a warrant to get copies of incoming and outgoing calls from the home number, as well as erased numbers and texts from the cell phone. He made sure he covered all aspects of what he needed. Mark didn't want anything to backfire down the road, keeping him from being able to use what he would find.

In the e-mail, he explained that it was only him asking because his partner already believed he'd found the guilty party and wouldn't look any further. He gave her what he had so far to back up his reason for pursuing this line of investigating so she could get the warrant, and Mark explained to Patricia how he really believed they were going down the wrong trail and needed her help desperately, but to keep it on the QT.

After sending his request off, he didn't worry in the least about Patricia ignoring his request. She knew how Jones worked. The man believed in old school still being the best way—letting gut override evidence. Sure, they did great things in the old days and took down many a criminal, but also some innocent people went to prison when a cop tried to go purely by his gut instinct.

About the time Mark's computer dinged and a box popped up, saying "new message," Jones rose. "I'm going for lunch. Are you ready to eat?"

Mark glanced at his partner and then back at the box on his screen. It had to be Patricia. Scrunching his face, he said, "I'm not really hungry. I have something to take care of, so if it's okay with you, I'll do it while you go do your lunch. How does that sound?" Mark figured he could swing by Mickey D's and that would do him just fine. Eat on the run; he did it all the time.

"You kids today. You never eat. No wonder you stay so skinny." Grabbing his rumpled jacket off the back of his chair, Jones said, "Take your time. Nothing's really going on today. I've got to figure out our next move. We've got to find the poison and link it to Cain, or something more concrete to get that woman. To connect her to the crime."

Sitting back in his chair, Mark said, "Jones, let me in on your secret. Why are you so dead sure she did it?"

The man's eyes darkened. Pinning his gaze on Mark, he said, "You know who she is, don't you? I know you weren't here when her husband was killed, but go do a little detective work. You'll see why I believe she's guilty. People don't change." Turning his back on his partner, Jones headed toward the exit as he stuffed his arms into his jacket sleeves and tugged it on.

Yeah, Mark knew who she was. She was the woman engaged to a fellow police officer. A great cop. There was no way Matthew Jefferies would fall in love with a cop killer, had she truly killed her husband—and Mark knew that was what Jones was insinuating. He'd look it up, but he doubted what Ben Jones was thinking was reality.

"Enjoy your lunch. I'll see you later," Mark said as his partner was stepping out the door. He had other things to do at the moment.

Scanning the e-mail from Patricia, he found she had his warrant.

That was quick.

Reading further, he noticed she was not on this case so the QT worked both ways. The warrant would be on legal record showing the policeman who requested it and the attorney who got it, but that was not important. The important thing was not to talk about it, drawing attention to what they had done. If it ever came out, it would be after it helped catch the true culprit and then no one would care who requested the warrant. In fact, Mark was pretty sure Ben would gladly take the credit.

Great. She got it. That was all that mattered.

Mark had no plans of telling anyone who helped him get the warrant. As his hopes heightened and a smile touched his lips, Mark decided he would slip by her office and pick it up. Afterward he would grab a bite to eat. He could chow down on his Mickey D's on the way to the telephone company.

His heart pounded as he rose. Mark knew he was finally starting to get somewhere on this case.

Grabbing his blazer and slipping it on, he hurried out the door.

Today he was going to get the lead that would take Jones' fixation off of Samantha Cain and turn this case around.

Chapter 19

All three hustled around the house, setting everything in its place. Greg took Marty's room, since most were toys to throw back in his toy box, clothes to realign in the closet, shoes to set straight, and refold some of the clothes in the drawers. . .an easy job compared to the rest, and then he ran out back to check the storage room, making sure it was locked up again.

Meanwhile, Margaret and Sam tackled the kitchen together, and then each ran off to straighten their own bedrooms. The bathrooms followed that and were another easy fix, refolding and stacking towels back on the shelf, followed with straightening and organizing the medicines in the cabinet.

When finished, all three collapsed in the living room.

Moments later, Marty scurried through the front door. "Hey, hey, hey," he shouted as he raced across the living room toward the kitchen. "What's my snack for today?" The whole time he was wiggling out of his backpack, getting ready to toss it down at his convenience.

Sam smiled to herself.

Margaret held up her hand to Samantha. "I got this. You rest. I'm sure the two of you need to talk." As she spoke she looked from Samantha to Greg.

The room grew quiet as Sam's thoughts tumbled out. "Greg, what about the terminal manager who was let go just before they replaced him with Ken? Or even our chief dispatcher, who was passed—"

The phone rang, cutting off her words.

"Passed over for terminal manager when they hired Ken." She reached out to grab the phone. "Hello."

"Sam. Hey, it's me, Pat."

Her stomach dropped as she heard the voice of the dispatcher who relieved her every morning. She stood quickly, holding the phone so tightly her hand hurt. What was he calling for? As concerned as she was, she tried not to let it sound in her voice. "Hi, Pat. What's up? Someone got sick and they need me to fill in?"

"No. I wish." He sighed.

His tone twisted a knot into her stomach. She saw in her mind's eye Pat stroking his dark beard as he tried to form his words. What was going on? She held onto the receiver with both hands, attempting to stay steady.

Apparently Greg saw the movement because he jumped to his feet and stepped to her side.

"Oh no, Pat. Something is wrong. I hear it in your voice. What happened?"

Greg stood silently next to her.

"I'm sorry to be the one to tell you, but you know how it works. All the bad news to share they dump on us in the dispatch office. You'd think the chief dispatcher would be calling you, but no. He passed it on to me." He chuckled. "And we always thought it was just Ken who did that. This comes down from the main office. They have suspended you, without pay, while you're under investigation for Ken Richardson's death."

"What?" She drew in a short breath. "That's not fair." Her knees wobbled.

Quickly, Greg caught her by the elbow and gently helped her sit down.

"But, Pat, I didn't do it. I wouldn't. You know that."

"We all know that, honey. No one here thinks you're guilty. In fact, all the drivers and mechanics keep asking about you—how you're doing through all of this. None of us have called, 'cause while you're off, we're hoping you're getting a break from all of this commotion at work dealing with his death."

"Oh, Pat. Will this ever end? Please tell everyone I miss them and I wish I was there. Also tell them to keep me in their prayers and stand strong on believing my innocence."

"Honey, you know we will. Everyone around here loves you. Take care. And if we can do anything, don't hesitate to ask." Encouragement poured out of Pat's voice.

"Thanks so much. You don't know how much that means to me." On those words they said their good-byes.

"More bad news?" Greg asked.

After she shared with Greg that her job had given her

an unlimited time of personal leave, Margaret walked in and caught the tail end. But she heard enough to cause a reaction. "They did what? That's not fair! How could they? You, who stand true to your friends, your boss, and your company, even when faithfulness is not deserved. Your company should be standing behind you." She gritted her teeth, seething with anger.

"It's probably for the best, Margaret. When I'm at work, everyone wants to talk about it, and I'm wishing I was home trying to help clear my name." Reality clicked, and she looked at Greg. "Well, now I can."

Greg smiled slightly. "Everything always works out for the best."

"Now I can do what I was in the middle of suggesting to you when the phone rang. What do you think about us going to see TJ Perry together? I know where he works. Maybe he knows something that could help us. Or maybe he knows someone who could give us some helpful information."

"That's not a bad idea, Sam. When the main office let him go and put this guy in his place, he probably did a little research on his own. I know I would."

Margaret laid her hand on Greg's shoulder. "I knew you two would figure out something. Don't you worry about Marty. I'll see he does his homework before playing. If y'all are a little late, I'll shoo him to take his bath. We'll be fine. And don't forget, steak and gravy. Dinner will be ready when you return."

When Greg's gray eyes flashed in Margaret's direction, her face flooded in a haze of red, but her smile showed her pleasure.

"I also thought we might try to catch Dean at home to-morrow. As Chief Dispatcher, he works Monday through Friday and is off every weekend. Ken was the one who hired him. We didn't have a chief dispatcher before. Those two were pretty tight without obviously crossing the line in front of all of us at work. They never let on that they saw each other after hours, nor did they talk like they knew one another beforehand. Dean Smith does a good job, so I never thought foul play there, even though I thought the job should have gone to Pat. But Dean might know more and be able to shed some light on Ken's life. I think he likes my work, so he probably wouldn't have a problem talking to you in front of me."

"Let's have a cup of coffee and then hit the road," Greg suggested. "Clearing your calendar just opened up some doors, don't you think?" He lifted his brows up and down like Groucho Marx.

The women laughed, and Margaret hustled out, leading the three of them to the kitchen.

"The cookies were good, but how long before we get fresh baked again?" Marty said as they entered. He threw his napkin in the garbage, then placed his empty glass in the sink.

"Oh you," Sam said as she roughed up his hair. "Be thankful you have a snack. There are kids around the world who don't even get three meals a day."

"Aw, Mom, I wasn't complaining. I was just asking. Can't a kid ask a question without hearing about the problems around the world?"

They all laughed. The boy was such a little grown-up for only being in the third grade. What he said was sad but true, but with the problems they had in their own backyard, she couldn't help herself. She was probably trying too hard to find something else to keep the focus off the troubles at hand. Squatting in front of him, she hugged him tightly. "I love you, Marty. I hope you always know that."

"Gee. Women." Marty looked to Greg and rolled his eyes.

Greg almost doubled over in laughter. Between bellows, he said, "He's so young, but already he knows there is no understanding women." The laughter spread around the room.

Marty looked about, as if to say the whole roomful of adults had gone crazy. Shaking his head and shrugging, he asked, "Can I go play outside?"

"Homework first. And, sweetie, I'm going to be leaving with Uncle Greg for a little while, but Margaret is here for you. Be good and mind her." She winked at him as he nodded. "Thanks, buddy."

~❧~

An hour later, Greg turned his car into the parking lot of Big Truck Services, a competitor of the company where Sam worked. When she called TJ, he told them to come on over, and he would talk to them.

TJ met them at the door garbed in a neatly pressed white cotton shirt, with the company's logo embroidered in dark blue thread across the pocket, and a pair of navy blue chinos. Sam remembered him well. He worked hard and always did a wonderful job. His country-boy smile and accent won the hearts and trust of many customers, as well as drivers over the years. "Hi, Samantha. Good to see you, honey. Sorry for all the trouble you're having." His bald head reflected the overhead fluorescent lights while his snow-white, neatly trimmed goatee made him look distinguished.

"I appreciate you taking time to see us, TJ. Greg, my friend here, is going to ask you a few questions that might help me clear my name," she said as she shook his extended hand. Truck drivers shared gossip like women; it was no wonder he already knew what she was going through.

After shaking Greg's hand, TJ said, "I hope I can help. Follow me." While leading them down a hall and into what looked like a conference room, he said, "I can't believe anyone would think you'd kill that man—or anyone for that matter. Don't tell me you're not the same sweet Sam you've always been." He chuckled slightly. "I warned you before moving into the dispatch office that those drivers and that job would change you." He winked. "But into a killer, no less. I never thought it would change you that much." He grinned and shook his head.

She knew he was only picking at her and trying to make things a little more comfortable for all three. She smiled. "Yes, you did warn me. And don't you worry one little *pea-picken* bit. I'm still the same old me." Sam imitated his country twang and tossed her hair behind her shoulders one side at a time.

Both laughed heartily as Sam tilted her chin in the air. When the laughter settled, TJ motioned for them to take a seat. "Would either of you care for coffee?" Both declined. The man fixed himself a cup and then joined them at the table. "Now, what kind of questions can I help you with?"

Greg pulled a small tablet from his inside jacket pocket and snatched a pen from his shirt pocket. *That was probably how he did it in the old days,* Sam thought. He looked in-charge and ready for business.

"Can you give me any personal things, assumptions, known facts, anything overheard or told to you about Ken Richardson? Do you have any idea what the man was doing before Bulk hired him?"

"First, let me say, I did not know Ken Richardson at all. He wasn't a local Terminal Manager with any of our competitors, so I never met him at plants when the carriers called us together for their company meetings that meant we had to change something or they had changed something. The kind of meetings where they tried to play us against one another, but in a hushed way, to bring us down on our charges."

Greg nodded, letting him know he understood what he meant.

"Anyway, I heard he was fired from his last job. He was Terminal Manager for a trucking company in Mississippi for about three years. It burned my innards that they ran me off to replace me with someone who had lost his job. I wondered what was up. It was so convenient. They let me go at the same time he became available. Then reality hit and I remembered I was 'technically' fired, too." He made quotes with his fingers. "Well, I was given a choice to resign or be fired. I knew I didn't do anything wrong, so I chose the former. Maybe Ken was innocent, too, so I chose to give him the benefit of the doubt and just believe the company was ready for someone new."

"Our loss," Sam added softly.

"So you never did any research on the man?" Greg asked.

"No. But so many different Operational Managers of different plants Bulk was connected to let me know how much they missed working with me over there. But my loss was Big Truck Services gain. I'm not trying to pat myself on the back, but they got their foot in the door, so to speak, because they hired me and those guys at the plants I mentioned liked working with me. So a little here and a little there, BTS now services some of the same plants. Sure, we're a smaller company, but I kind of like that. So does my wife. I'm not nearly as stressed when I go home at night, and I go home at an earlier hour."

Sam smiled. "I'm sure Helen loves that."

Greg twisted his lips from one side to the other. "So it sounds like you don't have anything that would help me. I mean, help Sam."

TJ's lips disappeared as the edges turned up slightly. It was almost a haughty look, but in a helpful sort of way. Sam knew immediately he knew something but was hesitant about sharing.

"Tell us, TJ. Please. We never know what is going to help."

"I don't like to talk about people or spread rumors, but I can tell you something I've been told by more than one Operations Manager, so there must be a little truth to it."

"That's what we're looking for," Greg said. "We just need to show the police that Ken Richardson was no saint and other people might have had motive to kill him. Everyone has him pictured as a saint, and I believe that's why the police are looking so hard at Samantha instead of looking elsewhere. They need another lead to follow. Right now she's all they've got."

TJ glanced around before speaking, then lowered his voice. "According to a few of the plant managers who make the decisions as to which company gets the haul, he's made some under-the-table offers to them. A chance for them to receive kickbacks or some extra side benefits, if you know what I mean."

Greg and Samantha both looked at him and then at each other.

"Really?" Sam was shocked. This was big, and she knew it. Hopefully there was still enough time to find something. . .a deal gone wrong maybe?

"Don't get me wrong. It hasn't been all of them who have told me such things, but it is more than a couple."

Greg's brows shifted slightly. "The ones who haven't said anything might be the ones who went in cahoots with Richardson's offer. You never know."

Silent looks were exchanged among the three at the table.

They talked for a little longer as Greg tried to get some names from TJ. Of course, he couldn't and wouldn't expose them. Some may have taken the offer for all he knew and he wasn't going to get any of them in trouble. They trusted him, and he couldn't afford to lose their trust. And that was why everyone liked TJ. A man of honor.

On the ride back to Sam's, Greg said, "Cheer up. It may help us. At the least it's a start, if I can get a little proof to back any of the rumors or gossip."

Sam leaned her head against the headrest. *Yes, but where do we start looking?* She shook her thoughts out of her head. It would be okay. It would all work out. "I'm not worried, Greg. I trust you. And more than that, I trust God. We'll get through this and the true culprit will be convicted. Not me."

She spoke boldly, but in her mind she whispered, *Lord, You know my true thoughts and even though I do trust You and*

Greg, my flesh is still a little shaky. Show us where to start. Please don't let this drag out too long. I'm not sure I can bear it—and I know Marty doesn't need the added tension, either.

Chapter 20

The smell of steak smothered with onions and garlic, simmering on a low heat, led their steps straight into the kitchen. As they reached the table, Sam and Greg saw that their plates were filled and ready for consumption.

"I heard you drive up and the car doors slam. I hope you two don't mind, and I hope you're hungry."

"You'll hear no complaints from me, dear one." Greg kissed her cheek as he found his place at the table. "A man could get used to this, Margaret. You best beware." He cocked his head slightly.

She giggled, and Sam smiled. She was glad to hear a little joy spread through the room.

"Oh, Momma, did you hear that? I think Uncle Greg likes Ms. Margaret." In his elementary ways, Marty picked up on the romance in the air mingling with the smell of some good old home cooking.

"Marty," Margaret squealed as her face turned ten shades of red.

Everyone laughed. "I think the boy is reading my mind." Greg's smile deepened as he winked at Margaret.

After everyone calmed down, the blessing was said and all started filling their mouths with the delicious food.

Margaret cast a glance toward Marty and then settled her gaze on Samantha. "So, how did it go. . .if you don't mind me asking right now? It can wait, if you want."

"I think the meeting was productive. Although he didn't give us a lot, TJ gave us something to check into, a place to start. Don't you think?" Samantha directed her question to Greg.

Chewing the morsel already in his mouth, he finished it quickly so he could answer. "It went great. I think tomorrow we'll drop in on Dean, like you suggested. And tonight, when I get home, I'm going to make a few calls to some friends in high places, so to speak, and see if I can find out anything to back up what TJ shared with us. Sometimes Big Brother's watching and sees things we try to hide." He stirred the rice around in the gravy and said, "Pass the salt, please, little buddy."

Marty handed it to him.

Greg went on to say, "Big Brother is always watching. People think they are getting away with things, when in reality, most of those under-the-table deals are being noted. And sometimes they jump on them right away. Other times they wait until it's convenient to help Big Brother in something they are doing."

Sam's lips curled upward as hope started to rise a little higher.

~~~

The next day, Marty planted himself in front of the television set with cartoons spilling out and said, "Are you going to watch with me this morning, Momma? You look like you're dressed to go to work, but it's daytime."

Laughing, she said, "No work today. After we eat breakfast, Uncle Greg and I are going to run another errand together. Maybe tonight we can go see a movie, or rent a movie and pop some popcorn. What do you say to that?"

Jumping to his feet, he scurried over to his mother. Wrapping his arms around her waist, he said, "You are such a fun mommy. Thank you."

Holding him close and pressing her fingers against his curls, she leaned down and kissed the top of his head. "Of course I am. I have such a wonderful boy, what else could I be?"

He laughed and dropped his hands, then plopped back down in front of the TV. Within seconds he was lost in his make-believe world.

Thank You, Lord, for protecting him through all of this, she thought as she made her way to the kitchen. Coffee was already brewing and three empty cups sat fresh and clean on the counter waiting for their recipients. Margaret was standing by the stove, steadily cooking breakfast. Sam smelled the sizzling sausage and watched her slowly stirring the scrambled eggs as they cooked.

"Greg must be already on his way," Sam said as she noticed the table was set for four.

"If he doesn't want cold eggs, he better be pulling—" A knock on the back door interrupted Margaret's words. "Ah, great. He's here. Will you let him in please?"

Opening the door wide, Sam said, "You were about to miss out on hot eggs, but you made it just in time."

"I have a good feeling about today," Greg said as he walked into the kitchen. "I wouldn't dare mess it up by starting my day off wrong. Thanks for the invite, Margaret dear." He flashed her a wink.

"Greg called while you were in the shower. I told him if he hurried, he could be here in time to eat with us." Margaret opened the oven and pulled out a tray of piping hot, lightly tanned biscuits.

"I'll get Marty. It looks like breakfast is served." Sam stepped to the swinging door and held it open slightly. "Come on, Son. Breakfast is ready."

Sam didn't have to tell him twice. He jumped to his feet and dashed through the swinging door before it even came back on the first swing.

Greg had poured three cups of coffee and was carrying two to the table, so Sam grabbed the third one and joined them. She said grace and then they all dug into their food.

"I'm going to get fat if I keep hanging around here for all the meals," Greg said as he stuffed another bite of sausage and egg into his mouth.

"If?" Sam said as she picked up a buttered biscuit and spread a teaspoon of strawberry preserves in the middle. Out of the corner of her eye, she noticed Margaret silently watching Greg for his response. The poor woman seemed to be holding her breath as she tried not to appear to even notice anyone around the table.

"Okay, ladies. *When* I keep hanging around. I just didn't

want to be so bold."

Sam giggled softly.

Quiet relief spread through Margaret's facial features. Sam had known her long enough to know that Greg could be bold, but Margaret wouldn't dare. "Greg, the door is always open to you. And it's kind of nice to have a man around, right, Margaret?" Sam said.

"What about me?" Marty cried out. "I thought I was your little man."

Everyone chuckled and Sam said, "Sorry, buddy. I wasn't thinking."

After the plates were empty, or close to it, Sam started clearing hers.

"You two go take care of business," Margaret said. "I've got this. It's the least I can do to help. Let me." She reached out for Sam's plate.

"Thanks." She handed over her plate and then turned her eyes on Greg. "Give me one minute, and I'll be ready."

"Take your time. I'm going to have one more cup of this delicious brew." He cast a smile to Margaret as he rose to help himself.

"Let me," she said softly as her lashes fluttered downward.

Sam slipped to the back to brush her teeth. At least for the time being everything seemed to be as it should. Her heart felt light.

❧

Within the half hour, she and Greg were driving to Dean's home. "You sure you didn't want me to call him first?"

"And give the man a chance to slip out or make up an excuse why he can't be bothered with you today? Not on your life."

Glancing his way, Sam said, "So what did you discover last night that gives you great expectations today?"

With no music on and the air down low, the steady hum of the tires rolling on the street sounded louder than normal. Sam wasn't sure if it was her nerves exaggerating things or what. Part of her thought Dean might be willing to be helpful, but in the back of her mind she had always believed he and the boss had a special connection and he might not be so willing to share.

"Turns out there's an ongoing investigation at one of our major gas plants right outside the city." Greg's words grabbed Sam's attention. "The plant manager contacted local authorities, and Ken Richardson's name is in the mix. That's really all I can tell you. Don't know if it has anything to do with his death. Maybe. . .maybe not." Greg swiftly glanced in Sam's direction, then just as quickly returned his gaze to the highway. "But I'm thinking your number one dispatcher who was hired directly by Ken Richardson himself might know more about Richardson's personal life and maybe something about this other situation—not that we can mention it, because it's an ongoing investigation. And, truthfully, we shouldn't know anything about it, not that I know much. In case he is involved in some way, we don't want to tip him off."

"You got that from your inside help? It sounds to me like you still have some pretty significant connections. That's great." She watched his maneuvering, turning one way and then the other. He knew exactly how to get to Dean Smith's home. Sam hadn't even thought about directions, even though she'd never heard of the subdivision. Dean wasn't one of the coworkers she cared to befriend, not that she would treat him poorly. That wasn't her way. "I just hope he has something to tell us that will help us find the police another lead."

"Don't worry, kiddo. If he doesn't, I still believe we'll find more on what TJ Perry told us. Your boss was in too deep with too many things not to have a few enemies. If that head homicide detective wasn't so bent on putting the blame on you, they might have another lead on their own by now." Turning left into a subdivision, Greg slowed down his car. "Watch for 12469 Trailing Pines. This is his street coming up." He took a right, and they continued down the street.

"It'll be a couple blocks down on the left," Sam said as she eyed the first address on the right. It ended with an even number, 12202.

In minutes they were standing at the front door. Greg pressed the doorbell.

A woman in her midfifties with bright red hair, dressed in a tailored suit and light green pumps to match, opened the door and said, "May I help you?"

"We're here to see Dean. Is he around?" Greg did the talking.

She frowned as she turned toward the stairs. Hesitantly she said, "Yes he is, but. . .he's getting dressed. We need to be somewhere in the next hour."

"No problem," Greg said. "We'll only take a few minutes of his time, but it's important we talk to him today. May we come in?"

She backed up slowly. "Please do." Her manners took control as she directed them to the formal living room. "May I get you a cup of coffee?"

They refused the offer but both said thank you as they took

the seat she indicated. If Samantha wasn't mistaken, she felt certain the woman's lips turned up into a smile as they turned down the coffee. This emphasized to Sam that the woman was merely being polite but never meant the offer. Oh well. It didn't matter. Sam didn't want to be there any more than the woman wanted them there. She hoped the discussion they had with her husband would be fruitful but also quick. Dean was still a man she had no desire to know on a personal level. Something about him had kept her at arm's length from the beginning.

As footsteps descended the stairs, the redheaded woman called out, "Dean, you have company. They're waiting in the living room. He'll be right with you," she said as she made her exit. They passed shoulder to shoulder at the arched entryway, eyes locking for a mere breath.

Dean's bright blue eyes turned on Greg and then shifted to Sam. "Samantha," he exclaimed, almost with excitement, "what on earth are you doing here? And how are you? I hate what I'm hearing at work."

His face seemed sincere.

Greg and Sam rose. Greg reached out to shake the man's hand while Sam made quick introductions. "We're sorry to bother you at home, Dean, but I'm hoping you can help shed some light on some things."

"Sit. Sit. Please, by all means. Ask away." He pointed to the settee and then sat in the chair that was positioned at a 90-degree angle from the couch. "Anything I can do to help."

He sounds friendly enough. I just hope it's real. "Greg, you go ahead and ask the questions." Sam wanted him to take the lead, because she truly didn't know what to ask. The only thing she could think of was, "What do you know about our boss that would have gotten him killed?" That was a little too obvious. She figured Greg had a better way of approaching this.

"As you know, the police have focused all their energies on proving Samantha to be the guilty party."

Shaking his head, he agreed. "That's absurd." His words were directed at Greg, but his eyes rested on Sam. "The woman gives over 100 percent of her life to the company and has a life of her own. When would she find time to be a killer, too? You know it takes a special trait, and not a good one, in a person to actually kill someone else?"

Greg sat a little straighter at that remark. "I agree Sam isn't capable of killing anyone, but it's a well-proven fact anyone pushed hard enough can become a killer. But this wasn't the case with your boss. I'm hoping, you being the—"

Cutting his own words off, he looked to Sam for help on the wording, and she instinctively knew what he was looking for. "Chief dispatcher," she inserted.

"Yes. You, being the chief dispatcher, would have a little closer relationship with the boss. We're hoping you knew of someone who might have a little more reason to kill him."

His eyes opened wide. "I assure you, I know nothing of the kind."

"Mr. Smith, surely you know of his goings-on with some plant managers. Don't get me wrong. I didn't get any of this from Samantha, because she had no idea. But I have my sources and have connected with enough of them to know Ken Richardson was making money other than through his normal paycheck."

"But, but—"

Greg held his hand up as if in reassurance. "I'm not here blaming you or saying you are involved in any way. But he was your boss, and you were in on all the big deals. You know more about his business ways than anyone, as well as you know a little about his personal life, too. Right?"

Shaking his head, Dean rose to his feet. "No. Emphatically no. I assure you I don't know anything about Ken's goings-on outside of work. And as far as any business dealings that were unethical, if he did those, trust me to say, I knew nothing."

"Dean," Sam assured him as she snatched his hand, "we really aren't accusing you of anything. We were hoping Ken confided some things with you, to you." She tightened her hold on his hand.

He grabbed hold with his other hand and held on as if his life depended on it. "The only reason that man hired me instead of promoting within was to stir up agitation. He lived to aggravate. Ken wanted everyone to not trust anyone. Sam, I promise. I know nothing. I knew he was a cruel, evil man, but the pay was good, is good. I need the money, so I work hard and keep my nose clean."

She squeezed one more time and then dropped her hand. "I understand, Dean. We were hoping," Sam said, her voice revealing her disappointment. Suddenly she heard a noise coming near—a steady slapping followed by a thump. Turning toward the sound, Sam saw a cute little girl with red ponytails wobbling into the living room, propped up on her crutches.

"Hey, Daddy. Are we still going to the show?"

Greg and Sam stood as the little girl talked to her father.

"Yes, Princess. Daddy has company, but they are about to leave. Amanda, this is Samantha Cain. Daddy works with her.

And this is her friend, Greg." Turning his eyes on Greg, he added, "Sorry. I didn't catch your last name."

"No problem. Greg Singleton, ma'am. Nice to make your acquaintance." Greg dropped to one knee in front of the little girl as he spoke. He bowed his head as if she were royalty.

"Tee-hee-hee. He's funny, Daddy." Turning her cheerful face back on the company, she said, "It's nice to meet you two, too." Then she giggled again.

Greg rose. "You have a nice time at the movies, Ms. Amanda. We won't keep your daddy any longer." Turning away from the little girl, he thanked Dean for his time. Sam added her thanks, and the two headed toward the front door.

Following them, Dean stopped them as they exited his home. "I can tell you, Ken was into a lot of things. Nothing I have proof of, but conversations I've overheard tell me the man had his hands in many pots, if you know what I mean."

Greg nodded.

Sam reached out and hugged Dean. . .something she'd never done before, but she felt led to do. She whispered, "Thanks so much, Dean. I'm sorry I listened to rumors. I've had the wrong idea about you all along. Take care. And God bless you." Sam fought to hold back the tears. The man had a lot on his plate, and unfortunately rumors made him out to be sinister and out to get each employee. Sam was glad to learn different today.

On the drive home no talking was done. Sam's eyes had been opened to a new way of perceiving the chief dispatcher. Talk had always made the boss and the chief dispatcher out to be best of friends. Well, she already knew rumors were just that. Rumors. She was glad to know the truth and prayed

God would pour out his blessings on the Smith family.

When Greg turned into Sam's driveway, he said, "I'm not going to be coming in this time. I have a few things I need to check on."

Opening the door, Sam climbed out. "Margaret will be very disappointed that you won't be coming in. Can you come back in time for supper?"

He shrugged. "I'm not sure, kiddo. I'll call if I can make it. Plan on not seeing me until tomorrow. Y'all are going to church, I presume?"

"Yes. We'll be there."

"I'll see you three then. Save me a seat."

On that, Greg put his car in reverse and backed out of the drive. He must really have a hot lead. Sam couldn't figure out what that could possibly be. If anything, they hit a dead end today. As she headed to the front porch, she heard in her spirit, *I will never leave you nor forsake you. Trust in Me and stay in peace.*

That was the best advice she'd heard in a long time and she felt her spirits lift as she opened the front door. She would cast her cares on the Lord. Worry about nothing and pray about everything with thanksgiving. That was what the Word told her to do, and it had been her motto or direction every day for most of her life. No time to stop now.

"Marty, Margaret, I'm home," she called as she stepped into the living room.

Chapter 21

Mark Barnett stuffed a couple of hot fries in his mouth as he pulled out onto the street. With every bite of his Big Mac and sip of his Coke, he drew closer to the telephone company. The stirring of excitement stimulated him with each passing mile. The answer, the truth, was around the corner, and he would find it.

A short time ago, Mark had shoved the warrant in his top jacket pocket. "I appreciate the help. This should assist us in connecting to the real killer. In my gut, I believe this was a well-thought-out murder. Definitely premeditated. So well planned, the killer even set it up for someone else to take the fall. Finding Samantha Cain guilty is just too easy, if you know what I mean."

Nodding she said, "You already convinced me, Mark; now convince Ben." Patricia smiled as she walked him to the door. "I'm here if you need anything else. And please keep me posted how it goes."

Riding down the elevator, he laid his hand on his jacket's lapel. Folded neatly below it was all the help he needed at the moment. Anticipation started growing.

In no time he pulled into Richardson's phone carrier's parking lot. Inside the building he found the manager. After flashing his badge and his winning smile, he introduced himself. With fingers pinching the warrant, he knew the power this little slip of paper held. With confidence, he handed the warrant to the petite woman. After glancing it over, the manager led the way to the back of the store, where she stepped into an office. Apparently the woman decided they needed privacy for this transaction.

It worked for Mark. Whatever it took to get the info he needed.

"Now, Detective Barnett, what can I do for you? What exactly is this?"

"That's a warrant for Ken Richardson's cell and home phone activity. This also includes the text messages to and from that number," he said as he pointed.

Holding the paper in her hands, Mark could see her eyes moving as she rescanned the document. Her brows flickered occasionally as she read. A few minutes of silence filled the office. Finally she lowered the paper and locked her gaze on him. She nodded ever so slightly as she appeared to be thinking things through.

Finally a smile touched her lips. "I want to help you, but I have to get approval from the main office first. Give me a minute, and we'll see what they say."

"You don't really need their approval. That warrant gives

you all the permission you need."

She tucked her head slightly, batted her lashes, and flashed a seductive smile his way. "Detective, you wouldn't want to see me lose my job now, would you?" She reached her polished nails out and laid her hand gently on his arm and gave it a squeeze. "It's procedure. We have to."

He sighed. "Go right ahead." He glanced at her nametag as he added, "Miss Lynette. I wouldn't want you to lose your job."

"Have a seat, please." Lynette motioned toward the chair sitting to the side of her desk and then sat down behind it. She made the call to her supervisor and then faxed the main office a copy of the warrant. Afterward she flipped her long blond curls behind her shoulders, flashed him another smile, and then proceeded to key in the information she needed for the warrant. When she finished, she dipped her shoulders one at a time and then said, "You see. I'm here to serve. Oh wait." She chuckled as she tossed her head back slightly, then pointed one of her manicured fingers in his direction. "That's your job." Her smile deepened as she searched his face, waiting for him to get her little joke.

Mark nodded. "Right. My job is to serve and protect. Cute." *Just get me what I need, woman.* He wanted to roll his eyes and show his irritation but instead kept his gleaming smile pasted in place.

A whirling sound from her printer started up and papers started filling the holder. In less than a minute it stopped. She tapped a few more keys and the noise of the machine started up again. When the noise quieted again, she grabbed the pages from the printer, separated them in two stacks, stapled each stack, and then handed them to Mark. "There you go, sir. All nice and neat." She rose and walked around to the side of the desk. Leaning slightly against it, she laid her manicured hand atop of her chest and said in a breathy voice, "If I can do anything else to help you, just let me know." Her smile said more than her words dared to say.

Mark stood. He thanked her for her time and walked out. With his looks, flirting women were at every turn. But his mind was strictly on business.

By the time he returned to the office, he found Ben back at his desk, sitting in his chair skimming through his computer.

"Something up?" Mark asked, hoping the answer would be no.

Ben shook his head, never looking up. "Things are kind of dead at the moment. I'm doing a little background check on our Little Miss Innocent."

The sarcasm in his voice made Mark want to laugh, but the only thing funny was Ben doing research on the computer. Nothing about Ms. Cain and her innocence was funny. Mark believed it was fact even though the circumstantial evidence said otherwise. If only Ben would do research on Ken Richardson instead. Shaking his head, he knew it wasn't worth the breath it took to tell him so.

"Did you look up her history with Officer Cain like I'd suggested you do? It wouldn't hurt to get you on the same page I'm on. In fact, it would make things a heck of a lot easier." The old man leaned back in his chair. "We'd probably have her behind bars right now if you'd do your little magic on the computer. I bet you could find all the backstory that could bring this case together so we could hand it over to the DA."

Mark shook his head slightly, wanting to tell his partner he was insane. Instead, he took a deep breath, then said, "I'm checking into things. I want to close this case as much as you. And then move on to the next. You know I don't like murders to drag out. The longer we take solving it, the harder it becomes to solve."

Ben's gaze darted from Mark's face to the paperwork he was pulling from his breast pocket. "Whatcha got?"

Not ready to share yet, Mark said, "Nothing yet. But I'm looking for connections like you said. Something that will bring it all together." Mark laid those pages on his desk, sat down in his chair, and flipped on his computer.

"That's my boy." A grin spread on the old man's face as he turned back to his own computer.

Let him think what he wanted. At least that would keep him off Mark's back for the time being.

Grabbing the folder tucked away neatly in his locked drawer, he set it next to him and then started reading Ken Richardson's texts—those he sent and those he received. Mark didn't go back the whole year as the warrant called for. He only went back one month. He figured if nothing jumped out at him in the last month of the man's life, then he would go back another month.

The next thirty minutes he spent perusing page after page, focusing on one contact person at a time, reading the texts back and forth for the entire month. It turned out he texted thirty individuals on a regular basis, five being family members. Nothing too interesting on the home front, but there were ten different people where the conversations sounded questionable—with some possibly buying and others possibly selling. One even sounded like a possible love interest.

Now that's something we haven't thought of, or should I say, something we haven't looked into. So far everyone has painted him as the perfect family man. Normally the wife is the first one we look at. I'll go back to that angle later.

Trafficking drugs usually gave motive for a lot of killings. Mark felt certain that was the lead to follow now. A more powerful motive. Money was almost always a big factor in murder.

It looked like he had another job for Kevin, the IT expert. Making two copies of the last month of texts, he slid one into his file folder and the other he slipped into a manila envelope. Slipping his file folder and the original copy of the year of texts and calls on Richardson's cell, as well as the copy of the home phone calls, incoming and outgoing, inside his middle desk drawer, he glanced around. No one seemed to be watching, especially Ben, and while the coast was clear, he quickly locked the drawer shut.

Sliding the keys back into his pocket, he rose. "I'm running upstairs. Be back shortly. If something comes up and we need to hit the road, beep me."

Ben grunted in agreement but never took his gaze off of his computer screen.

Mark took the steps two at a time. It was quicker than waiting on the slow elevator. Opening the door, he stepped out into the hallway and turned right, heading for Kevin's office. The hall was quiet, but he knew when he walked through IT's door, he would hear the humming and buzzing of all the computers that kept everything up and running throughout the department.

He stepped in and closed the door behind him. *Just as I thought.* How people worked with the steady whirring all day long, he would never know. It was enough hearing the energetic activity from the copiers and desktop computers they had running in homicide's room.

His shrewd friend's face was buried in his computer screen as his fingers flew across the keyboard. Mark didn't want to interrupt, but what he had was very important. "Kevin, my man. You got a minute?"

"Just a sec. I'm almost done here." His fingers tapped a little more on the keyboard as the light from the screen mirrored in his glasses. A rainbow of colors flashed in the reflection.

What in the world is he doing? Mark didn't want to sound impatient, but all the rushing colors made him wonder if Kevin was just playing around or what. *Let's take care of business, man.*

"Okay. Whatcha got?" Kevin pushed his glasses back up on his nose.

Mark passed the envelope to Kevin. "You remember that list of names you found from the various social networks Ken Richardson had tapped into? I need you to go through these. I highlighted ten names of interest. I'm hoping you can get me real names and addresses to go with the contact names. And I'm hoping some of these match up with the other list you gave me. I'm hoping we find some sort of pattern. I have his financials, so I'm going to double check that against what you find—if it appears to you buying and selling is for sure what is going on."

"That shouldn't be a problem." Kevin opened the envelope

and slid the pages out.

"You'll notice a lot of strange conversations that I'm sure are similar to the conversations on the social networks. You know what I mean, where people will mean things other than what they are truly saying. Because what they are saying doesn't really make sense. At least I hope you find the same thing. I need a break. . .a lead. . .something."

"I'll get on it right now and call you as soon as I finish."

"Oh. One more thing. The one name highlighted in pink might be a love interest. See if you find anything that can confirm that—and who it is."

"Gotcha."

"Thanks, man. I appreciate your help." Mark gave a slight wave as he left Kevin's office.

Running down the stairs was a whole lot faster than jogging up, and easier. On the way back to his desk he took a second to pass by the break room and get a Coke. As he dropped the three quarters in the machine and pushed the button, he murmured, "Please, Lord. Open the door. Point me in the right direction." He knew Ms. Cain's future depended on it, as well as her son's. A single mom raised Mark, and he knew how hard it was—but to be raised by a stranger would have to be worse. At least in his way of thinking it would.

A peace swept over him as he grabbed the soda can out of the machine drop. "Thanks," he whispered to the Lord.

With confidence he strode back into his office and plopped into his chair.

Ben looked up at the sound. His brows drew together, forming a deep V as he darted a glance in Mark's direction but said nothing. It was obvious that Ben wanted to know where all the confidence and vigor had suddenly come from. He wanted to know if Mark had found something that would drag him away from the trail Ben was running down full force.

But since the man truly didn't want to be redirected, he looked away quickly.

That worked for Mark, because he didn't want to tell Ben anything either—at least not yet.

Chapter 22

Sunday morning, as Sam's car curved around the lake following the two-lane road, she shivered.

"You should have worn a sweater. The weather is starting to cool." Margaret's voice was fueled with concern. "And I doubt the heater will be on in the sanctuary yet."

Sam nodded as she glanced in the rearview mirror. It wasn't the weather that left goose bumps lined up on Sam's arms, but dare she share her concern? A black SUV with dark tinted windows was behind her. SUVs were very popular, and although it had been said windows could only be so dark, it didn't stop people from going to the extreme. Seeing the vehicle shouldn't bother her, but for some reason it did. Was someone following her?

She turned right on Stanford Avenue and then left on Highland Road. When she glanced again, the same dark car stayed steady on her tail, about two car-lengths behind. She shrugged it off. She had to. Samantha didn't want to start suspecting everyone and everything. *Big deal.* So the black vehicle was going in the same direction as she was driving. They may even be going to the same church. That was what she told herself anyway. Her body didn't listen as her grip tightened on the steering wheel. Was it a coincidence?

To prove how silly she was being, instead of waiting until she got to Lee Drive to turn left, Sam decided to cut left a couple of blocks earlier on Stuart. Pinning a glance in the mirror, she didn't see the SUV behind her anymore. A quiet breath of relief seeped from her lips. *Great. They didn't follow us.*

"You okay, Momma?" Marty asked.

Straightening her back, she sat up in the seat and tucked some fine strands of hair behind her ear. "Sure, baby. I'm fine."

Margaret reached across the seat and patted her hands. "Relax. Things will get better. You know God's going to take care of you."

Glancing down at the steering wheel, she saw her knuckles. They were white from clenching the steering wheel. She loosened her grip and mouthed at Margaret, "Thank you."

A glance over her shoulder revealed Marty's worried eyes fixed on her.

"I'm okay, baby. Really I am. Smile and don't worry." *I just have an overactive imagination.*

Turning the car down a few more side roads, she made their way back to Lee Drive and then steered the car toward the side road of the church, directing the car to the parking lot behind it. When she stepped out of the car and shut the door, she heard the triple slam as each door closed simultaneously.

"See ya," Marty said as he dashed across the parking lot to the stairs that led up to his Sunday school class.

Taking a few extra seconds to look around, Sam double-checked, making sure it had all been her imagination working overtime.

"Sam, what's going on?" Margaret said from right next to her.

Sam jumped. She'd been concentrating so hard that she hadn't even noticed Margaret had walked around the car to join her.

"Your face is white like you've seen a ghost. And I saw a look of fear in your face as you were driving over here. You can talk to me, you know. Any time."

"Too many late-night movies, Margaret. You know me and my crime shows. It has my mind seeing things that don't exist." She tried to laugh at herself, but it came out weak.

"Shake it off and get into class then. You'll feel better after you spend some more time with the Lord and your fellow believers."

"You're right, Margaret." Sam couldn't help but grin. "And by the way, Greg said when we get into church to save him a seat. So if you get in there first, save three, not two, seats."

A slight blush touched Margaret's cheeks.

Their little romance seemed to be cultivating quite nicely, which made Sam happy. These were two people she loved very much, and the thought of them being attracted to each other made Sam's apprehensions slip to the back of her mind.

Margaret nodded and then went on to her class on the bottom floor, to the right of the stairs.

Glancing at her watch, Sam realized she needed to hurry

or she would be late. She dashed across the parking lot and ran up the stairs. At the top, she peered out to the street one more time to reassure herself that it was only her imagination.

Instead, she caught a glimpse of a black SUV with dark-tinted windows rolling slowly down the side street of the church. Was it the same one? She bit her bottom lip. The darkness of the tint on the windows confirmed it in her mind. It wasn't her imagination after all.

Why would someone be following her?

Detectives drove dark, plain, nondescript vehicles, and policemen drove cars with the bubbles on top and their name written everywhere in plain sight for all to see. Who would be following her in one of those big fancy SUVs where faces were hidden behind dark windows? In the movies, FBI and Special Forces drove those types of vehicles, but what would they be following her for? Her heart hammered.

Help me, Lord.

❧

Almost three hours later, the four of them were sitting around the kitchen table chomping down on a pot roast Margaret had put in the slow cooker that morning before leaving for church. The wonderful fragrance of roast, onion, garlic, rosemary, green beans, and bacon peppered the air, keeping the focus on the food.

"If I keep eating like this, I'm going to gain twenty pounds in no time. I think I've already added an inch to my belt line. And it's entirely your fault, woman." He darted a light gaze in Margaret's direction, all the while a half smile etched his face. "You cook better than anyone I've ever known. Who can resist?"

Laughter surrounded the table as Marty said between laughs, "Oh, Uncle Greg, you haven't gotten fat. I know you're like Matthew. You work out all the time."

Suddenly a hush blanketed the air. It was the quick memory that quieted everyone, but Sam wanted it to be okay to talk about Matthew anytime.

The more, the better.

She loved him and wanted to always remember him. And she wanted the same for Marty. She didn't want her son to feel he had to watch what he said or for him to think talking or thinking about Matthew was a bad thing. No. It was a great thing, because Matthew was a great man who instilled a strong sense of courage into her young son.

A smile touched her lips. "You know, Marty. I think it's because Uncle Greg is working so hard tracking down the truth on Mr. Ken's death that he hasn't had time to do his daily exercises. You are right. When he does his normal routine like Matthew, Greg stays in great shape. . .for a man his age."

"Watch it!" Greg pointed his fork in Sam's direction.

Chuckles filtered the air around the table.

"All I'm saying is you better look out, Greg. You and I both know Margaret's the best cook in the world. Right, Son?"

"Right."

"And pounds can slip on easily when you're not paying attention."

The older woman blushed as the compliments rained around her. "Eat up, people. The food is getting cold." She jabbed her fork in a piece of the meat and stuffed it in her mouth.

Sam noticed that Margaret's eyes softened as they rested on Greg. He filled his mouth with her cooking and then a satisfied look covered his face. Conversation and eating continued around the table. A nice family-feel filled Sam's heart as she soaked in the atmosphere.

After everyone finished and Margaret and Sam were clearing the dishes, the men went into the living room to relax and let their food settle while the women stayed behind to clean up the mess.

"Are you going to tell Greg about what happened this morning on the way to church? Tell him what you thought you saw? You never know. It may be important."

As Sam placed the leftover roast in a plastic container and then poured the gravy over it, she said, "Yes. Unfortunately it is important. I'll tell you, too. I saw a big black SUV following us this morning—all the way to church." Popping the lid on top, she placed it in the refrigerator.

"Who would follow you?" Margaret rinsed the dishes as she started sticking them into the dishwasher.

Those were all the same questions Sam had already asked herself. She still had no answers, but maybe Greg would. When the table was clear and clean, Sam busied herself making a pot of coffee as Margaret finished filling the machine with the dirty dishes.

Within fifteen minutes they had the kitchen shining like new, and then they joined Greg and Marty in the living room. "Coffee will be ready in a minute or two."

Tom Sawyer and Huck Finn were keeping Marty entertained as everyone watched with him. Sam wasn't sure who laughed the hardest at some of their pranks, Marty or Greg.

When Margaret started to rise, Greg caught her arm and held her motionless. "I'll get it. You relax. I know how you take your coffee. Let me wait on you this time." His hand slid down her arm, and he gently held her hand for a moment.

Margaret rested back against the couch. A delighted smile touched her lips. "Thank you," she murmured.

He rose and jabbed a glance Sam's way. "I'm getting yours, too." His voice spoke with authority.

She smiled.

As he left the room, she stood and said, "I'll be back in a minute. Now's a good time to tell him," she whispered to Margaret, trying not to disturb Marty's concentration.

Pushing the door open, Sam stepped into the kitchen.

"I thought I told you, I got it," Greg said as he pulled three cups down from the cupboard. "What's the matter? You don't trust me?"

"Go right ahead and fix the cups of coffee. I'm here to watch. I love being waited on. There is no way I'm going to stop you." She grinned, but then let it fall. "I'm only here to talk."

A serious look crossed Greg's face. "What's the matter? Did something happen that I don't know about?"

Sam told him about her suspicious mind that morning. Then once she decided it was her imagination working tirelessly, unfortunately she saw the car again. "So who would be watching me? And why?"

"By the way you described the vehicle, it sounds like someone who doesn't want to be seen. I think of drug dealers. . .hardened criminals. . .killers. You know the kind of people I've dealt with over the years." Pouring the third cup, he continued sharing his thoughts aloud. "But what would any of them want with you? That's the question to ask. If it were the real killer, they wouldn't want to give any excuse to the police to start checking around for another suspect. I think it was coincidence. Don't dwell on it, but from now on, keep your eyes open for what is going on around you."

"So you don't think this SUV has anything to do with Ken's murder?"

"I didn't say that. I don't know. I hope not. It's like I said with the police already thinking you are the guilty party, why would anyone want to shift suspicion on them? They would be foolish. Right now the detectives think they have this case solved. The true killer wouldn't want to give them any cause to look elsewhere." Stirring all the cups, he grabbed one and handed it to Sam. "Here. You take yours."

"That makes sense." She took a sip of her coffee. Perfect. He did know how she liked it. The man paid attention. As she sipped the brew, Sam let his words sink in. Greg made sense, true, but if that was the case, why was someone following her this morning? She knew what she saw. And that didn't make sense. She sighed. "So Greg, what are we going to do next? Do you have a game plan for us?"

He picked up the other two cups. "Today is Sunday. We're going to take it easy. Tomorrow we'll start bright and early. You and I are going to go meet with an FBI agent I know. I'm hoping he can help us dig a little deeper into Ken's gambling. See if maybe Ken Richardson got in a little too deep with a bookie or two. And I have my friend in the corporate world checking on some of his under-the-table deals. See if any of them went sour," Greg said as he pushed the door open with his elbow and waited for Sam to enter the living room first.

"Thank you," she said as she passed him by.

Sam sat in Matthew's chair and leaned back. Pulling out the footrest on the recliner, she let her mind drift. Greg was right. Today was Sunday, the day of rest. Closing her eyes, she prayed, *Give us strength and direction for tomorrow, Lord. Lead us where You'd have us go.*

Her eyes popped open to a room full of laughter. She glanced from one to the other and thought all was right with the world—at least, her little world.

She smiled.

Thank You, Lord.

Chapter 23

Sure it was his day off, but Mark knew today was a good day for him to accomplish his task without the watchful eye of his superior. With what all he discovered Friday, Ben seemed to keep a close watch on his partner. Maybe it was Mark who had an overactive imagination. Who knew? Maybe it was Mark's guilt talking to him, guilt of working behind his partner's back, but he felt certain Ben was trying to see if he could figure out what his partner was up to, at the same time working diligently on his own trail he was following.

Saturday another case had dropped into their laps, with the death of a white-collar worker. Was it suicide or murder? It wasn't uncommon to work more than one case at a time. Unfortunately that was the norm—to work several—due to the number of crimes versus the number of officers.

After following the leads in the death and the evidence at

the scene, both he and his partner felt certain it was suicide by the end of the day. Yes, there was a note, but that didn't always mean it was the real deal. However, everything pointed that way. There were a few loose ends they would tie up Monday, and then they could put that one to bed quickly.

Today he was going to follow the leads he had on the Richardson case. Hopefully one of them would pan out to be the one both he and his partner should be pursuing. But Mark had to get all the evidence, all the facts, before he could present it to his lieutenant.

The first thing he did was touch base with a friend of his, a narcotics agent. Jim met him at the precinct downtown where Jim was stationed when the man wasn't working undercover. At the station, the man always dressed clean, sharp, and neat. Undercover, you'd never know it was the same person.

Greetings were friendly, and after they caught up on one another's lives in a few sentences, they sat down at Jim's desk.

"These are the conversations I found texted on my victim's cell phone," Mark said as he handed a couple sheets of paper to his friend. "And these are from conversations Richardson had with other people in cyberspace. I found them on two different social media networks that Richardson frequented. And when my computer geek tracked the IP addresses, I found they led to two known users. I'm hoping this will help me find a reason for the man's death. Right now, the only direction this thing is going is this little piece of woman, an employee of his, a third his size, who supposedly killed the big guy without disturbing any furniture. No commotion whatsoever at the scene. We have it all: motive, means, and opportunity, but you really have to stretch the imagination to believe it's true."

Jim, interlacing his fingers, laid them behind his head as he rested back in his chair. "It's every cop's dream to have it laid out in front of him like that. Why are you so sure it's not true?"

"She was engaged to a fellow officer who always spoke highly of her. I find it hard to believe she could kill this big guy. Especially now that it seems he's involved with some very seedy characters. It makes more sense for it to be one of those guys. Besides, it's more circumstantial evidence against her than anything. I believe she's being set up."

Cocking his brow, Jim said, "You have to follow your gut. That's what makes a good cop—One who follows his instincts as well as the evidence. Let me look at this." Jim reached out and took the pages Mark had handed to him and started scanning them.

"I found Richardson's bank statements reflected some set patterns that coincided with the texting. The day before the person texting Richardson, the one highlighted in orange, met him, Richardson had removed a large sum of money from his account. A week after the texting from other parties, conversations marked in blue, I found large deposits made to Richardson's account—totaling almost double what he withdrew the week prior. Same with the social media notes. Looks like he's dealing to me. I thought with the names I have for you, you might be able to shed some light on the matter for me. Hopefully confirming my suspicions."

The pages drew Jim's undivided attention. After he studied the names and conversations, and looked at the connection with the bank statements, he asked, "Do you have a picture of your victim?"

Mark had brought his complete folder with him. Digging through it, he pulled out a single sheet. "Here's a good one."

Nodding, Jim said, "I've seen him with the biggest distributor we have in the city, but my guy wouldn't do business with him. Look what he missed out on." Handing back the papers, he said, "I think you're on to something. But the question you have to ask yourself is if he's selling, making money for the big dealer, why would the head of the drug ring want to off his money train?"

Mark sat back and blew out a gush of air. Jim was right. Why would anyone making money from the chump want to kill him? He raked his fingers through his tight curls of brown hair. "Thanks. I didn't think of it that way. I just know the woman we're chasing for the crime isn't the killer. I have to find the right trail to follow." Stuffing the papers back into his file, he closed it, and then extended his hand.

As Jim shook it, Mark said, "I appreciate your time and your insight."

"No problem, Barnett. But I didn't say don't look in that direction. There are reasons people kill people in the drug business every day. They may not make sense to us, but drug users don't always think. They are too focused on their next score. And drug dealers. . .it's all about the money. Maybe Richardson shorted his supplier. Maybe one of Richardson's buyers came up short and thought it was easier to off his dealer than come up with the money he owed him. Either way, there are always reasons. Good luck on finding your perp."

Mark climbed back into his black pickup and headed to his apartment. Turning the music up loud on his radio still didn't wash away all his doubts.

What if he couldn't find another suspect? What if she did it, like Ben thought? Why did Mark believe so strongly in her innocence? What was it to him?

All those questions raced through his mind. But no matter how many questions hit him, he knew down deep in his gut that Samantha Cain was innocent.

Help me, Lord. Help me find the true guilty party. Don't let an innocent woman take the blame.

Chapter 24

The first thing Monday morning, Sam and Greg talked with Todd Holmes, Greg's friend from the Bureau. He had the intel on the top controllers of the big gambling rings. Unfortunately, Ken Richardson was only involved in a small way. The man was addicted to gambling—on everything. But in the insignificant ways he gambled, no one officially bothered to look at him twice.

Todd gave Greg a list of bookies. "One may have been Richardson's, but unless the man didn't pay up after a loss, they wouldn't be going after him. And if he was a regular who paid when he lost, they definitely wouldn't want to kill him. Break his leg, maybe, if he was late paying up, but that wasn't the way things played out in today's world. Bookies got their money, and as long as their customer found ways to pay off their debts, everyone was happy. In fact, they loved losers who could pay. That was how they made their fortunes."

They thanked Todd for his time and headed to the car.

"I'm sorry this lead didn't pan out," Greg said as he opened the door for Samantha. "But the good thing is, we can cross off the gambling addiction as a motive and focus on his bad work ethics."

Sam's shoulders sagged.

Slamming the door closed after she got in, he walked around to the drivers' side. As he climbed in, Sam said, "Are we ever going to find out who set me up?"

Silence was Greg's response. What could he say? Of course he planned to find this guy, whatever it took. She knew that, but waiting and wondering was wearing her down.

"I don't understand why I was picked as the patsy. Ken and I were never close, so why me?"

Greg reached across the front seat and covered her hand with his. "Because you do have a connection to the man through work, and apparently the killer knew of the discord between the two of you."

"Whoa. Then that raises another question." Her voice grew in volume as the questions mounted. "How can they know about me, when I don't know about them?" She scratched her head for a split second. "I don't get it."

Pinning his eyes briefly on Samantha, he returned his gaze to the road in front of him and deliberated. "That's a good question. Maybe it's something we need to look at a little closer." As he kept the car between the lines and continued toward Sam's home, he said, "We need to make a new list. We'll work on it as soon as we get to your house."

Sam sat up taller in her seat. She thought she heard a glimmer of hope in his voice. "What are you thinking?"

"Let's make the list and then I'll tell you. Your words just gave me a thought, one I should have thought before now." He glanced her way again, this time with a big grin.

Back at the house, they gathered around the kitchen table one more time. Margaret brought the cups of coffee and Sam pulled out a notepad. Opening it, she flipped pages until she found a fresh sheet. "Okay. What kind of list are we making this time?" Sam asked as Margaret set a cup before each of them.

"I want you to think hard. List everyone you know who also knows Ken."

"That's easy, but it will take forever to write. Everyone who works for Bulk, all across the nation. It's a long list." She laughed, her disappointment filtering through her tone as she dropped the pen on top of the tablet. "I don't think I even want to go there."

He shook his head. "No. No. We know you both know all the employees at your company. I'm talking about outside the company. Don't even list names from other businesses connected to Bulk that you two know in common. I want names away from the trucking industry."

She straightened her spine as she sat up in her chair. "Humph." Her brows lifted. "Sounds like you've come up with something, even though I don't get it." Lifting her cup, she took a sip of the dark brew, then set her cup back down. "That will be a short list." Lifting the pen back up, her hand hovered over the blank page as she thought.

"As long as it's complete."

Margaret's eyes sparkled. "Oh Greg. It sounds like you have an idea who killed Ken Richardson."

Greg reached over the table and laid his hand on top of Margaret's. "I do believe I might. Not the person, mind you, but the type of person we may be looking for. Let's just see who she lists."

The older woman turned her hand up and cupped his, then squeezed.

Sam could feel the excitement in the air. She hoped she had the answer, the right name. A few names flittered through her mind. Snapping the button on top of the pen, exposing the point with ink, she touched it to the paper and started scribbling.

The only names she could come up with were his two best friends, who she knew but not well, and then his wife and his mother. She started to list his children but then scratched that idea. Truly she knew of them, not the girls themselves. She'd only known them by what Ken had said about them in passing and that was in the early days of his employment, when Sam was on the day shift. She tried to think of any other name she could add to the list, but drew a blank. "I don't know how this will help, but here you go." She tore the piece of paper from the tablet and handed it to Greg. "The names listed are all people who cared about Ken and barely knew me at all."

His eyes scanned the short list and the smile returned. "That's what I thought. If it's not work-related, or gambling-related, it's like what you said. It had to be someone who knew the bad vibes between the two of you. Someone personal. Who better than his best friends or his wife? We need to look closer at them. I know they seemed helpful when we talked in the beginning, against better judgment I suspect, but that could have been a front so they wouldn't be suspected."

Testimony of Innocence

His friends seemed helpful, maybe, but Dorothy didn't seem one way or the other. It has to be one of his friends. How could she not have thought of that before? His buddy from Arkansas, the one who flirted on the phone with her when he called to find out where his buddy was that night. . .to see if she knew. Timothy Tyler.

"Greg, I know we talked to his fishing buddy, Jerry Connors, who lives here. But we never talked to Timothy Tyler, his friend from his hometown. They grew up together. I know they live over a thousand miles apart, but they've been friends for over fifty years. I know they used to talk all the time. Every year they took a vacation together. Could they have had a falling out? He has called several times over the past few months asking me what Ken was up to, like I would know. At the time, I always thought it was because maybe Ken didn't answer a call and Timothy assumed he was called out to an accident somewhere, or I'd called him to the terminal for a problem."

"I had talked to him before, but only a very short conversation that at the time seemed forthwith, but I think all three make great candidates. In fact, I think we should start with his wife."

"What?" Sam shook her head. "I don't think so. There is no way Dorothy could have killed Ken. She's smaller than me. Besides, she loves the man." A chill swept her body from head to toe. "How could anyone find that man loveable?"

"You *think* she does, and maybe she does. But people don't always know what goes on behind closed doors. Besides, usually that is the first place police look and no one has looked that way as far as I know. I know we didn't. So it needs to be looked at."

Sam sighed. Her head was pounding. If that was standard

procedure to police, they probably checked Dorothy out quickly and then moved on to Sam because they couldn't find anything. She couldn't believe Dorothy had anything to do with Ken's death. It just wasn't in her nature. And then to blame it on Sam? No. Not Dorothy. Sam rubbed her temples, trying to chase away the headache.

"It's okay, sweetie," Margaret said gently. "Nothing makes sense. But Greg knows what he's doing. You should trust him."

Dropping her hands to the table, she nodded slightly. "I do trust him. I just know Dorothy, and I can't believe she would do this to him or to me."

Greg finished his coffee and set his cup back down. "If you're that sure, we'll start with," he looked at the list and then said, "Timothy and Jerry first. Do you know what town Timothy's from? Where he lives now? Do you know if he and Ken have been together lately? And are Jerry and Timothy friends? Do they know one another? Jerry was helpful, but it could have been a front."

"I don't know. I can only remember Timothy coming to town maybe twice. Usually Ken and Dorothy went up there." Sam wrote down the name of the city Ken and Timothy were from. Other than Timothy's name and the town he lived in, Sam didn't know much about the man. Over the few years Ken had been her boss, she had only talked to him on the phone maybe ten times a year tops, if that many. Usually the man joked about his friend and always made Sam laugh. She remembered thinking, why couldn't her boss be as nice to her as he was? But it never changed anything between her and her boss. Ken probably didn't know that Timothy was so nice to her over the phone. He would have stopped it, I'm sure. Who knows? Maybe Ken never told Timothy about the problems between the two of them.

"Greg, I just had a thought. Maybe Timothy didn't know about our conflicts. Maybe Ken never talked about me to the man." She explained to him quickly the thoughts that had just crossed her mind. "To him, our indifferences were of no consequence, so why would he even think about me when he was hanging out or talking with his best friend?"

"It's possible Ken never mentioned the rift between the two of you, but some men like to talk about women—especially if they have a power over them. Some even like to embellish on their relationships, even when there isn't one. He probably enjoyed putting you down to his buddy, and he probably bragged about the power he held over you. It's a man thing. Not a good thing, mind you, but people like Ken Richardson enjoy bragging about a sense of power they feel they have. It's a control issue, as well as an ego booster."

"What about his kids? Didn't you know them, too?" Margaret asked. "You talked about the way they reacted when you showed up to pay your respects, and it sounded like you knew them. Or at least they knew you."

"I know of them, but I don't know them personally. I'd only met the youngest daughter once and knew of the three girls from when Ken bragged on them to me. It happened sometimes, but not often. He didn't share his personal life with me or with any of us for that matter."

Finishing her last swallow, Margaret asked, "Can I fix either of you another cup? I'm about to make tuna salad for lunch. Greg, would you like to join us?"

He darted a grin her way. "I'd love to, but I'll have to pass this time, Darlin'. I'm going to go see what I can dig up on Timothy Tyler and Jerry Connors. Thanks for asking."

After Greg left, the girls made the tuna salad then sat down to enjoy a bite together. Margaret talked up a storm about Marty. Sam knew it was an attempt on Margaret's part to keep Sam's mind off of the trouble at hand, and she was grateful for it.

When lunch was over and their little mess cleaned up, Margaret said, "I'm going to take a trip to the store. We're out of milk and a few other items. Can you think of anything you'd like me to pick up for you while I'm out?"

Sam thought for a second but couldn't come up with anything.

About five minutes after Margaret left, Sam picked up her Bible. She stepped into the living room and looked out of the big picture window. Memories flashed of times before. She would stand looking out and Matthew would come up behind her, holding her. Memories of watching the sparkles flashing across the lake as he held her in his arms. That brought more peace and serenity to her than one could fathom. She sighed. With Bible in hand, she turned and padded to what was now her favorite chair—Matthew's.

Quietness filled the house like Sam had never heard. At times the sounds of silence could be deafening, but right now it was welcomed. Reading the Word helped the tension flow out of her, relaxing her. She let the stress of life slip off her shoulders as she closed her eyes and bowed her head. Taking time to thank the Lord for all her blessings, she then asked him to continue to direct their path in this investigation. She admitted to the Lord she had no idea as to how to bring the guilty party to justice, but she also knew from His Word that was what He did.

Vengeance is mine, saith the Lord.

When she finished her prayer, she thought aloud, "I don't want vengeance. I only want the guilty to be brought to justice. And that is what the Lord does." As she spoke those words, she reminded herself to leave it in His mighty and capable hands.

Breathing a sigh of relief, she started to relax as the phone pealed out a loud ring in the silent house. She jumped, then chuckled to herself for being so silly.

"It's only the phone ringing," she scolded herself as she rose to answer it.

Stepping near the sofa she reached for the receiver. Pulling it to her ear, in a soft voice, she said, "Hello."

"Samantha. Hi. It's me, Dorothy. I know you haven't been able to work lately so I felt sure you didn't know about the arrangements I made for Ken's funeral."

"Hi, Dorothy. Thank you for calling. You're so right. No one has told me anything lately. Everyone seems to be staying as far away from me as possible. I'm taboo. I have to admit your call surprises me. I hope this means you know I didn't do it."

"Of course, dear. I never believed you had anything to do with it from the beginning. I'm so sorry that one of those detectives seems so bent on pinning it on you."

"That means so much to me, Dorothy. Thank you." A heaviness lifted off of Sam's shoulders. Had she been that downtrodden? Apparently so, and now relief gently invaded her heart.

"Samantha, you are the sweetest person I've ever met. I know Ken rode you hard. That was something I never understood, except maybe because you are a woman. Anyway, I know you wouldn't have done such a thing." The female voice sounded friendly to her ears.

"I wish the police felt the same way. I would have never hurt Ken." Sam wrapped the telephone cord connecting the receiver to the phone around her finger and then let it loose again. Freedom filled her heart, as Dorothy sounded so reassuring, believing in Sam's innocence.

"I know, dear. I've expressed to the police I felt they were way off track going after you, but they didn't want to listen to me."

Jones, she thought. "Sorry your kids don't feel the same way you do. Your girls believe what the police are saying, so they think I'm a killer. I felt the tension when I stopped by. I'm so sorry."

"As for my kids, I've tried to reassure them as well, but that's their daddy, and they don't want to hear me defending the person the police think is guilty, so I can't say much. Anyway, I wanted to tell you the arrangements have been made. You may or may not want to come to the wake, but I'm sure if you want to make it to the funeral itself, and watch him being lowered in the ground, surely everyone would understand. After all, you've worked for the man several years."

Sam frowned but didn't say a word. Surely she would look more guilty if she only showed up to watch him being buried. It would be like she wanted to make sure the man was dead and gone.

A chill swept over her.

"Aahh. . ." She tried to think of the right words to say, but nothing came to mind.

"Are you okay, Sam? I didn't call to upset you, dear. I know your life is in a mess and, after last year, that serial killer, and then Matthew's death, I wouldn't think this would be easy to bear. Is someone with you? You don't need to be alone."

"No. No one is here at the moment, but Margaret won't be gone too long. I'm okay. Thanks for caring. It's I who should be offering aid to you, Dorothy. If there is anything I can do, please don't hesitate to ask me. I'm here for you."

Dorothy conveyed the details of the arrangements, and then they said their good-byes.

Sam sat back down in Matthew's chair and clutched her Bible to her chest. "Thank You, Lord for helping Dorothy realize that I didn't kill her husband." She lay back in the chair and closed her eyes, waiting for that peace to overtake her again.

But it never came.

Chapter 25

Mark whipped his truck into the parking lot of the station. Disappointment consumed him. How could he not find the killer? He just knew it had something to do with the man's dealing drugs. All the signs were there. All the coded messages and texts. The money trail proved the man was dirty, but it didn't lead him to the killer.

Jamming the gears into park, he jumped out of his truck with his file in hand and dragged himself into the precinct. He always found his desk a great place to think, especially when he and Ben were on the same trail. They would bounce ideas off one another. It worked. Just not now, because Ben had his mind made up, and there was no changing it.

Mark hauled himself to his desk, dropped the file on it, and plopped down in his chair. For days now he had been going over and over his file, but to no avail. Lacing his fingers behind his head, he leaned back and closed his eyes. *What now?*

Flipping his file open one more time, he wanted to look anew, hoping something would pop out. As he glanced over the report of the first policeman at the scene, he heard the door of the homicide division open. He felt a tight squeeze on his heart as he believed Ben had just walked in the door. Any minute he'd find out what Mark had been up to, yet he still had nothing concrete.

Turning slightly as he looked up, Mark's eyes spread in surprise. It wasn't Ben.

"Can I help you?" Mark asked.

"I sure hope so," said the other man who also believed in Samantha Cain's innocence. "Can we talk?"

"Have a seat," Mark said reluctantly. "Greg, is it?"

Should he discuss this ongoing case with an ex-cop? A man who believed the opposite of what his partner believed. Should he? Maybe this was what he needed to do. Maybe the two of them could bounce ideas back and forth. The beating of Mark's heart started to race.

Hold on, boy.

He had to slow himself down here. He was getting ahead of himself. Let him see what the man had to say.

"Greg Singleton," he said as he sat. "I've been doing a little investigating on my own. First, I want you to know Samantha Cain does not know that I am here. I hope I'm making the right choice. When I left her house this afternoon and was heading home to follow up on a few new ideas, your face flashed through my mind. When it did, I took a chance coming by here, hoping to find you."

"Well, it's your lucky day. I don't usually work on Sundays and Mondays, but I happened by here a short time ago.

What do you need?"

"I need to prove to you Samantha Cain is innocent." Greg's fist pounded Mark's desktop.

"Hold on, buddy. Don't get all riled up on me. First, I have to admit, I believe she is innocent also."

Shaking his head, Greg's fist relaxed. "I knew it. I knew it. You are nothing like your partner. I believe I can talk to you. Trust you to listen. Trust you to do the right thing."

Sticking his right hand up in the air, palm facing the man at his desk, Mark said, "Don't get carried away here, man. Know whatever you share with me, I will be sharing with my partner if I feel it is pertinent to the case."

Clearing his throat, Greg said, "No problem. I'm not asking you to keep secrets. In fact, I believe if I can tell you what I've found, maybe it will help you two find the real killer. . .that is, if you are looking past Sam."

"I can't discuss an ongoing case with you. You're free to tell me what you've found out, but don't expect me to share with you what we know. You were a cop. You know how this works." Mark quietly, and hopefully unobtrusively, closed the open file on his desk. He didn't know if the man knew how to read upside down or what. Cops always had their own specialties. Right now Mark was open to hearing what Greg had to say, but not so ready to spill his thoughts to the man. His partner would never understand. And Mark didn't want to do or say anything that would jeopardize the case.

Greg pulled a little notepad from his pocket and flipped through some pages. "We've been talking to people who work or worked with Ken Richardson, trying to find out more about the man himself."

Mark nodded but didn't interrupt. That was what he had tried to get his partner to do; so right now this guy seemed to be going in the direction Mark believed the case should go. . .looking into the victim.

"We've found out that Ken Richardson wasn't quite the innocent man everyone tried to picture him to be. Sure, he and Sam never got along and all the evidence at the crime scene looks to be pointing in her direction, but to any good cop, which I believe you are, they would see it was a setup."

"Possible setup," Mark said in a correcting tone. His thoughts exactly, but again he didn't want to share that with Greg Singleton.

"Right. In talking with ex-employees and coworkers and even some people at the plants the company worked with, we found out some interesting things about Ken Richardson."

"I'm sure you did, but the question is, are the things you found out fact or opinion?" Mark wanted to hear him out, but he wanted the facts, not supposition. He had enough of those on his own.

"Facts. I checked some of this out with some official people I can still talk with. At the present, I don't want to name names. I'd rather just tell you what I have. What we have."

"You and Ms. Cain?"

"Yes."

"I'm still listening. Try to get to the point. This is my off day, if you don't mind." Mark didn't dare tell him he was spending his off day trying to prove her innocence. If the man had something, Mark wanted to hear it, and he needed him to spit it out.

"Richardson did some under-the-table deals. Some of

them or one of them could have gotten him killed. Also the man was addicted to gambling, which could also put his life in jeopardy."

"All of this still sounds like supposition to me," Mark said. "I love all the hypotheses you're sharing with me, but what facts do you have?"

Greg sat forward in his chair and leaned in the detective's direction. "We know for a fact he was in to all of these things and we believe one of these things got him killed. He was a dishonest man. Dishonest people get caught, make wrong choices all the time, and things backfire. I have plans to talk some more to his two best friends because I believe they know more about the man than anyone. And I'm hoping they will tell me. Who knows? Maybe he shafted his best friend and then he had him killed. I don't know. The only thing I do know is Samantha Cain is innocent and if you two don't start chasing the right leads, you'll never find the truth." On those words, with chest puffed up, Greg stood. His eyes bore down on Mark.

"Sit back down, Mr. Singleton."

After a moment, the man did as he was told.

"Truth be told, I believe Samantha Cain is innocent also. I'm here today trying to find the one piece we are missing." Mark didn't mean to open his mouth to this man, but once he started, he couldn't stop. "Something has bothered me from the get-go, and I can't seem to bring what it is to the front of my mind. I was hoping one of your facts would do that—joggle it loose, but it didn't. I know Matthew Jefferies believed in Samantha Cain, and that was enough in the beginning for me not to believe everything my partner said. Unfortunately he was one of those policemen who believed she got away with murder. He believed she killed Martin Cain, her husband, years back. He keeps saying people don't change."

Greg shrugged and then nodded. "I believe people don't change easily. I believe situations change people. I just don't know enough of the facts on the case to know who is the guilty party. I do know it's not Samantha. I've even found proof of infidelity on Ken Richardson's part." Pulling his pad out of his pocket, Greg flipped a couple of pages over and then said, "Elizabeth Brumfield. Lizzie to her friends. Did y'all ever check out the wife? Did y'all find out if she knew anything about his girlfriend? Usually the spouse is the first person of interest, and the first to know when a husband is fooling around."

Instantly, something shot through Mark's mind, and he turned over the file cover, exposing the first report in the folder. Was it that simple?

The first policeman on the scene stated something in his file that pricked at Mark's brain. Using his pointer finger as a guide, he scanned down the report. Flipping the first page over, he came to the notification of next-of-kin. Jabbing his finger on the paper, he said, "That's it!" He smiled at Greg.

"What's it?"

"That was what bothered me from the get-go. When Mrs. Richardson was told about her husband's death, she told the officer Samantha Cain had called at midnight. Said he was needed at the terminal right away. And when we questioned Ms. Cain, she said she never called him. That should have thrown up red flags all around for us, but for some reason it was pushed to the side."

"Because your partner didn't want to hear the truth."

"Don't go there, Mr. Singleton. Let's stay on track here. If Samantha never called at midnight, the question is, who did?" Mark flipped the pages over in his file until he came to the phone records. Glancing at the records of the office phone, he saw there was no call made to Ken Richardson's home or cell phone at midnight. Just like Ms. Cain said, but she could have used her cell phone. Quickly, he flipped a few more pages over and glanced at Ken Richardson's home phone. He found one incoming call at midnight and jotted down the number.

"What did you find? I see you are on to something. Can you tell me?"

"Hold on, Mr. Singleton." Mark flipped through the home calls, seeing if that number had called before. No such thing. Next he glanced through the phone calls to Richardson's cell phone. There it was. Fifteen minutes long. Again, five minutes. Again and again. He kept finding a repeat of that same number calling. Each day there were a couple or more incoming or outgoing calls to that number, and each time it lasted from five minutes up to thirty. This was someone they needed to talk to. They, as in his partner and himself. But would Ben follow up with him? Should he go by himself? It was always best to have backup. This could be the killer.

Mark glanced at Greg Singleton. *Take him with you.* Blowing out a spurt of air but shaking his head, Mark said, "Okay. We're going to go for a quick ride. . .if you want to go with me. It's sort of your lead, so I'm inviting you—but not officially. You are not a policeman."

"I do carry a gun, you know. I work to protect the governor."

Mark nodded. "I know. I checked into you. That's why I'm making this offer to you." He punched a couple of keys on his computer, typed in the phone number, and then jotted down the name, Elizabeth Brumfield, and her address. Tearing the top page off of his notepad, he rose to his feet. "It looks like your suspicions may be true. Are you coming?"

"You couldn't leave me here if you tried."

That was what Mark was hoping he would say. As much as he hated doing this without his partner, as long as they got to the truth, he felt sure in the end Ben would understand and agree with him. Right now, his partner was wearing blinders so thick he couldn't see the forest for the trees, as the old saying went. But Mark knew the older detective was a good cop, and in the end he would want true justice.

"Let's go."

Chapter 26

The doorbell rang, and Sam's eyes popped open. Who could that be?

Laying her Bible on the end table, she rose. As she stepped toward the door, her eyes glanced toward the window, hoping to recognize the car. Nothing she could see in the driveway. Well, she knew it wasn't the detectives. They would have pounded on the door. That was Jones' way of announcing himself.

The bell rang a second time as her hand reached the doorknob. Opening the door slightly, she was surprised. "Dorothy! Come in," she invited. "I didn't know you were so close when we were on the phone a few minutes ago."

"Yes, dear. I realized it only moments ago myself and thought, why not stop by? You sounded so distraught. I wanted to come cheer you up." Her sweet words practically embraced Samantha as Dorothy entered the living room.

"Thank you so much. It's so sweet of you to be thinking of me at a time like this. It's I who should be there for you. Let's go in the kitchen, and I'll fix us some coffee. You do drink coffee, don't you?"

"I'd love a cup," her voice rang out. "Thanks."

After closing and locking the front door, Sam led the way to the kitchen. Dorothy followed closely on her heels.

"Has your housekeeper made it home yet? I know Marty won't be home from school for a couple more hours."

Sam slowed in her steps as she noticed a slight shift in Dorothy's tone. Turning, she glanced at her guest, and the woman flashed a sweet smile in her direction. It must have been Sam's imagination.

"Margaret is so much more than a housekeeper," she said. "Over the past year she has become more like family than anything." Sam pushed the swinging door and stepped through to the kitchen.

Dorothy followed. "That's wonderful. Does she live with you all the time?"

"As a matter of fact, she does." Stepping to the cupboard, Sam opened the door and took down two cups. Glancing at the pot, she saw it was practically empty. "I'll make a fresh pot. Do you have enough time?"

Her guest didn't answer, so she turned toward Dorothy and froze in her step, almost dropping the empty cups.

"Sit down." The command came in a deep, angry voice, and the strength came from the gun pointing in Sam's direction. "Now."

Keeping her eyes on the gun, Sam set the cups on the counter and then pulled out a chair. Quickly she slid into it.

"What's going on, Dorothy?" *I thought she believed me. Why is she doing this?* The look in the woman's eyes brought chills to Sam. Icy fingers played havoc with her neck and shoulders and then slid down her back. "Why are you doing this?"

"You should already be in jail for killing Ken," Dorothy spat at her.

"But I didn't do it. I thought you believed me?" Sam's heart broke, seeing so much pain in Dorothy's face.

Waving the gun in Sam's direction, Dorothy said, "Don't be so stupid, girl. I know you didn't do it—but you were supposed to be blamed for it. Everything pointed toward you. Why are you not in jail?"

Sam wasn't sure how to answer that, or even if she was supposed to answer Dorothy. She seemed to be more talking out loud to herself than she was to Sam.

"I had it all worked out. Everything was going as planned. You should have already been arrested, case closed, and Ken buried. But no. You're still running around free, asking questions, visiting *my* home, and upsetting *my* girls. I can't let this go on. They were trying to figure out a way to take revenge on you. I don't want my kids to end up in jail because their father was a no-good piece of garbage."

Dorothy's eyes stared straight at Sam, but the woman seemed to be miles away.

Her girls planned to harm me? Sam couldn't believe it. "What are you saying?"

"I'm saying you've ruined everything. I can't let my girls kill you, thinking you killed their precious father. They would end up in jail, and with the way they are feeling now, they don't care. But I do."

The Bayou *Secrets* Romance Collection

Sam wished she knew what she should do. Call the police, of course. But how could she? The woman had a gun on her. Greg wouldn't be coming back over today. He was gone until tomorrow. And Margaret, Sam had no idea how long she would be gone to the store. She definitely didn't want Dorothy to still be here when Margaret got home. The woman was acting crazy. She could hurt her. Sam couldn't be responsible for that. She had to figure out a way out of this.

"What do you want, Dorothy? How can I help you?"

"If you only knew. My husband used to come home complaining about the snip of a girl who worked a man's job, who thought she knew so much. He hated you. I could tell. He hates strong women. He likes women to be submissive to their man, in every way. I was his doormat for so many years, I was sick of it. His little girlfriend was the last straw." Shaking her head, she said, "I have to go to plan B. I wasn't going to do this. But it's the only way. If they would have arrested you, you could have gone to jail and maybe got a light sentence because of the way he treated you. You could have said you snapped. Everyone knew. You have so many friends at that company they would have all come to sweet Samantha's aid."

Plan B? What was plan B? Surely the woman wasn't going to just shoot her. Then the police would know something wasn't right. *Think. Think. What can you do to distract her and get to the phone?*

"Get a pen and paper. Now!"

Sam scooted out her chair and stepped over to the junk drawer. Pulling it open, she grabbed the little notepad she had used to write possible suspects on for Greg. The one name she didn't want to put on it turned out to be the one who did it.

But how? Dorothy was smaller than Sam.

She grabbed a pen and sat back down at the table. "What are you doing, Dorothy? You know I didn't do it, so tell me. Who did?"

"No one you know. I hired someone. A professional."

"You hated him that much?" Sam truly felt sorry for the woman.

"Look who's talking. You hated my husband, too."

"But I—"

"Shut up. I want you to write a letter to your son. Tell him how sorry you are for having to leave him. Tell him you couldn't live with the guilt. However you want to say it. Remember, it will be the last chance you have to talk to your son."

"This is crazy!"

"Do it!"

Dear Lord. Help me out of this. What do I do?

"Start writing, or I'll write it for you. I'll print. No one would be the wiser."

Drawing in a deep breath, she glanced at the gun and then at Dorothy. "I'll write him a note, but tell me what you plan to do."

"Don't be so foolish. I plan to kill you, of course," Dorothy said, as if it were the only natural thing to do.

Sam tried to think of ways to stall her. But when she glanced at Dorothy again, she noticed the woman's hand was starting to shake. That gun could go off by accident if she wasn't careful.

Pretending to start writing, Sam looked down and scribbled slowly on the paper. "You know, no one is going to believe that I killed myself here and left a mess for my son to come home and find me dead on the floor. I've been too much of a loving mother. Everyone will know something else happened—"

A ringing phone interrupted Sam. Automatically she rose to go answer the phone.

"Sit down. Let it ring. I need to think, but I know I'm not going to let you talk on the phone." The ringing continued. "Keep writing. Finish the note to your son. Remember, it's your last words to him so you better make them count."

On the fifth ring the machine picked up. As usual, the sound was turned down, so Sam had no idea who was calling or what was being left on the machine for her. Would she ever get to hear it? Would she ever get to see her son again? Would Dorothy have enough decency in her not to leave Sam dead on the floor for her son to find? That would scar him for life.

Finally, to be safe, she did write something on the paper. She wrote, *I'll always love you, Marty. Forgive me.* Dropping the pen on the table, she rose, shoving the chair back with her legs. It screeched across the floor. "I'm finished. Please don't kill me here."

"Toss me the paper. I want to read it for myself."

Sam shoved the tablet across the table. Turning it around, Dorothy glanced down at it but kept the gun aimed on Samantha. "Ah. How sweet. Yes, this is perfect. Where is your car? I think it would be for the best if I take you away from here to do this. You're right. No one would believe you'd kill yourself and leave it for your boy to find. I'm glad you're thinking."

"My car is in the carport, out back."

"All right. Grab your key and let's go. You first."

Sam moved over to the counter quickly and Dorothy hollered, "Slow steps. I'm watching you, and I will shoot you here if need be."

Moving slower, Sam grabbed her key ring off of the counter and held it up for Dorothy's inspection, then slowly made her way toward the back door. She could hear her killer's feet shuffling in her direction, closing the gap between them.

Suddenly the swinging door flew open. A scream filled the air as a gun fired.

"Margaret!" Sam cried out as she turned toward the door.

Chapter 27

Lizzie spilled her guts in no time. She talked about her affair with Ken Richardson. She stated everything was going well—until this big threatening man who knew of the affair approached her. Someone she didn't name, but she revealed his threat. "The only way to protect myself was by following his orders. I didn't know he was going to kill Ken."

Mark couldn't believe how quickly she gave herself up.

"The man was going to kill me," she cried. "I had to do it. I had no other choice. Then I had to keep my mouth shut. It was the only way to stay alive!"

"You have the right to remain silent. Use it." Mark had a squad car coming to pick up Elizabeth Brumfield for accessory to murder. The woman couldn't give him the name of the one who did the actual killing. Mark needed that man to identify who hired the killer. But the way Lizzie described the killer, he sounded like a professional hit man. If he was, why didn't he kill Lizzie after she did what he needed her to do? *Surely she could recognize him, if we ever brought him in for questioning, which is exactly what we plan to do.*

Shaking his head, the truth hit Mark in the face. The killer was a professional. The man only killed whom they paid him for—a sick man, but a lucky break for Lizzie. The pro must already be out of the country. So now Mark needed to discover who hired him. It had to be Mrs. Richardson, because of the girl. Why else use her?

When the squad car arrived and took Lizzie out in hand-cuffs, Mark said, "At least now I can go to Ben, and he'll have to believe Samantha is innocent. Maybe he'll figure out a way to catch Mrs. Richardson for hiring a hit man."

They followed the policeman out the door.

"I know y'all will get the true killer now." He pulled his phone out of his pocket, hit a button and pressed the phone to his ear.

"Who are you calling? Do you know something I don't?"

"I'm calling Sam. She has a right to know. It's going to break her heart to find out it's probably Dorothy Richardson who killed her husband. Sam just knew she was innocent."

Mark shook his head. "Usually it's the one you least expect. Glad that it didn't turn out to be Ms. Cain."

Greg snapped his phone shut. "I knew it wasn't."

"No answer?"

"No. And I know she's home, unless she and Margaret went by the store. She lives just a few blocks from here. Would you mind us rolling by there so I can tell her right away? Or better yet, you tell her. I'm sure she'd love to hear it from you. It would be more believable. From me she'd think it was wishful talking."

Mark nodded. "No problem. I'd love to bring that woman some good news for a change."

They got into the car and Mark fired up the engine.

"I'm glad I was led to your door, to trust you'd do the right thing."

"I'm glad you were willing to share your findings with me," Mark said. "It helped unlock what was stuck in my mind and wouldn't come out. Have you ever had a case like that, where you knew something was important and it was staring you in the face, but you couldn't get it to come to the forefront?"

Greg chuckled. "I sure don't miss those days. Trying to solve a crime can give you ulcers, so be careful, lad."

Mark turned the wheel and into the drive. "You know it's a passion. . .a calling. You were a cop, so you know what I'm talking about."

As the car came to a stop, Greg climbed out. Mark was right behind him as they headed up the sidewalk to the front door. Suddenly a scream pierced the air, and a gun went off. Both took off into a run and rushed up the steps. Turning the knob, Mark hoped the door was unlocked. It was, so they both rushed in. The commotion was going on in the kitchen, and the swinging door was barely swinging. Greg caught Mark by the arm, the one not holding a gun already extended and ready for action.

Mark turned his gaze on the older man and watched him motion with his hands. Understanding, he moved slowly toward the swinging door as Greg shot around in the other direction, but moving ever so quietly.

As Mark eased up to the kitchen door, he heard a woman

say, "You shot her. Let me help her."

"You just keep heading toward the back door. We're going for a little ride. They'll think you shot her. I'm not worried about her."

~⊚~

Sam watched as Dorothy stepped around Margaret's body, moving closer to Samantha. Using her gun, she motioned for Sam to move. Out of the corner of her eye she saw movement as the swinging door moved toward the living room but never made it back into the kitchen. Fingertips held it in place and then she saw a brown eye peek around the edge.

Help is here! She hoped so anyway. Who was it? Greg had blue eyes. It didn't matter. As long as they did something quickly so Margaret didn't die.

"Keep your hands where I can see them. Now move. And remember, I won't mind shooting you. I just don't want to. I want to clean this up quickly so they'll arrest you for Ken's murder." Dorothy took another step toward her.

"Police! Freeze!" a voice shouted.

The door from the hall and the door from the living room slammed open at the same time. Sam spun around on her heel, but Dorothy didn't freeze. She lifted the gun higher, pointing it straight at Sam. She saw Dorothy's finger start to squeeze the trigger. Just as quickly, Greg knocked the woman to the ground, and the gun flew from her hand, skidding across the floor.

The detective moved quickly and picked up the gun. Using his cell, he called for backup.

Greg flipped the woman facedown and jammed her hands behind her back. "Cuff her, Mark. She is your killer." Looking around, he said, "Sam, are you okay?"

Sam rushed past him, close to the swinging door. There, crumpled on the floor, was Margaret. "Quick, Greg. Call 911. Margaret's been shot!"

Greg pushed himself up on his feet as Dorothy hollered out in pain, "Watch it, mister. That hurts."

"You're lucky I don't kill you myself. Margaret better be all right, or you'll wish I had." He pulled out his cell and punched in 911. As he gave instructions over the phone, Mark took control of the prisoner, placing her in cuffs, and Greg moved over to Margaret's side.

Sam had her cradled in her lap, holding her head, whispering to her, trying to wake her. "You'll be okay, Margaret. Help is here. Greg is here. He's not going to let anything happen to you."

Her eyelashes started to flutter. "What. . .what happened?" she asked as Margaret started coming to her senses.

"It's over. Everything is over. Right, Greg?"

Laying his hand gently on Margaret's cheek, he smiled down at her. Lifting his gaze, he looked Sam in the eyes and said, "Yes. Now we all can start living again."

"For sure," Sam said, knowing Greg was speaking not only of Sam and her family, but he was including his plans for a future for him and Margaret.

Sam couldn't wait to be the one who told Marty.

Epilogue

S am stood, staring out of the big picture window. After a month of red tape and various things, all was right with the world again, at least her little world, as the rain dribbled from the sky, dropping rhythmically across the lake, causing a steady pitter-patter. She took in a deep breath and then released it slowly. She had been thinking on her future and her life for the past several hours. Thoughts she couldn't believe she was thinking but thoughts that had great potential for her and Marty. Was it okay to be thinking about her future when people she'd known for a long time were in such horrid times in their own lives?

Dorothy Richardson was in prison waiting to stand trial for her husband's murder. Sam's heart broke for the woman. . .and her children. How would they survive?

Help me, Lord, to be all that You called me to be. Help me be the mother You'd want me to be. Help those three girls forgive their mother for what she has done, and most of all, help Dorothy to forgive herself as well as her husband in her heart so she can heal from this awful situation. Thank You for clearing my name and allowing my innocence to be made known. Help me be a testimony to You.

As Sam finished her prayer, she knew that a new day was upon them.

"Can I interrupt?" Greg said as he joined her in the living room.

"Be my guest. I'd love the company."

"I want your advice. Now that you've been cleared of all suspicions, I wanted to get to know Margaret a little better. I think I want what you and Matthew had, and I believe I could have that with her. She has taken me by surprise. I truly never thought I would fall in love, but when I'm around her, my heart perks up. In fact, I feel like a schoolboy around her. Do you think I'm too old to have these thoughts? Do you think it would be all right for me to pursue her?"

"I think I'm the wrong one to ask, but since you did ask, I'm going to say—go for it! I think you and Margaret will make a dynamite pair. I love you both. And you have my blessing."

The swinging door opened and Margaret stepped in, holding the door with one hand. The yellow and purple shades of coloring to the left of her eye had almost faded completely away while the scar was still prominent from the flesh wound she'd received when shot at by Dorothy. Thank God it was nothing more serious and the woman was a lousy shot. Had Margaret not hit her head when falling down, she would have witnessed the whole incident. . .including Greg coming to her rescue. "Would either of you care for a cup of coffee?"

"Now's as good a time as any." Sam nudged Greg toward the door.

Margaret's eyes jumped from one to the other as she said, "What are you talking about?"

"Ugh. I was, ah, talking to Samantha about possibly taking you out to dinner. . .just you and me. Maybe even dinner and a movie," Greg said as he edged his way over to the door.

About that time, Marty came running into the room from the hallway looking for the remote. Picking it up, he stopped for a moment. Turning toward Greg, he said, "What about me? Can I come to the movies with you two?"

"Marty!" Sam started to correct him, but Greg cut her off.

"It's okay," he said holding his hand out toward Samantha as if saying wait a minute. Turning to Marty, he said, "Not this time, little buddy. I want to take Margaret out on a date." He grinned at the boy, exposing his teeth, and lifted his brows like Groucho. "Is that okay with you, Marty?"

"Boy-o-boy. You two on a date? Like Mom and Matthew did? Way cool! Isn't it, Momma?"

Greg shrugged. "It all depends on what Margaret says. I think we have something there. And at this time in my life I don't want to mess around. . .I'm not looking for a good time."

"You hurt my feelings," Margaret said as she punched Greg in the arm. "If you don't think we'll have a good time, then why are you asking me out?"

"You get me wrong, dear," he said as he took her by the hand. "I know we'll have a good time wherever we go and whatever we do—but if what I'm feeling is the real thing, like I think it is, I want us to have a good time. . .for the rest of our lives. You and me. Do you know what I mean? I mean, at our stage in life, if this is love I'm feeling and you find you feel the same way, I don't want to play around. I want us to get married and live together. . .forever."

Margaret's eyes widened as Sam's mouth dropped.

"Am I rushing things a bit?" Greg questioned, looking from one to the other, holding his hands up in the air. "Sorry."

Margaret's eyes brightened, and a smile illuminated her face. She shook her head. "I know exactly what you mean, and I'm with you 100 percent."

Greg matched Margaret's grin as he opened his arms. Margaret slipped right in. Closing his arms around her, he lowered his face, closing the distance between them, and pressed his lips to hers for a brief moment. Then he whispered, "What a perfect fit!"

Marty squealed with excitement.

Quickly Sam covered his mouth, trying to stifle his exuberance, not wanting to disturb the couple. He shook his head back and forth until he freed himself from his mom's hold. "Oh, Momma, does that mean Greg is going to live here, too? Oh, boy." The little boy was jumping up and down, unable to hide his joy.

Overhearing the dear boy's question, they both started to laugh. Greg, not letting loose of Margaret with his right arm wrapped around her waist, turned toward Marty. "Sorry, little buddy, but when we marry, I'll bring Margaret home to live with me, if she'll have me."

Marty's smile faded quickly.

"But don't think you're going to lose us. I hope you'll think of us as grandparents. We're family. . .and don't you forget it."

"Oh, Greg. How sweet. Thank you." Sam's heart felt like it was about to explode.

Sam and Marty rushed to the couple's side, and the four fell into a group hug as tears streamed down Margaret's face—tears of joy.

While the four embraced, Sam wondered. *Is now the time? It's perfect timing.* As Sam broke free, she said, "While we're making plans for your future, I have something I want to throw in the pot, but I think we have to talk about this sitting down."

"You're looking serious, Sam. Should I go make a pot of coffee now?"

"Thanks, Margaret, but no. I think the four of us should sit down right here in the living room while I share some thoughts that have come to me in the past few hours."

Greg slid his arm from Margaret's waist and caught her by the hand. "I like this. Our first family meeting." A smile spread across his face as he tugged Margaret's hand and led her to the sofa. They sat close, holding one another's hand.

Sam, slipping into Matthew's chair, said, "Marty, you grab a seat. This includes you, too."

"Oh boy, oh boy." He jumped on the other end of the sofa. "I'm all ears."

Greg stole a peck on Margaret's cheek, and then said, "You've got my full attention, Samantha. What's up?"

"During the time I was a suspect in the death of Ken Richardson, I was forced to wonder if that was the end of my life as a mother, as a friend, and as a dispatcher. I started thinking, I know God's got a special plan for me, and I don't think it is working at the trucking company anymore."

Glancing at each of their faces, she said, "You know how I say everything happens for a reason?"

Greg and Margaret nodded in unison as Marty said, "Yes, Mom. We know. That's your answer to everything that goes wrong."

For a brief moment, laughter filled the air.

When everything settled, Samantha continued, "Well, I truly believe it. I believe it so much that it hit me a few hours ago: the serial killer, my time with Matthew, and now this ordeal, what has come from it? What purpose did it serve? For what reason did all of this happen? Then it hit me, we may not have Matthew anymore, but he set us up for life. I don't have to work to support us. He did that. We have enough money to take care of us, so I think it's time I, we, take care of others."

Greg frowned as he glanced at Margaret and then to Sam. "What do you mean? You're going to start taking people in and take care of them? We're not married yet, and you really don't have that much room."

"Don't be silly. I'm going to have to learn how to take care of Marty and I now that you're stealing away our lovely caretaker, friend, and grandmother." She laughed as she spoke. "With our blessings, I might add."

"I'm glad to hear that." Margaret flashed Sam a smile of love.

"But seriously. I think God has shown me other people go through situations that put their lives in jeopardy and get accused of things they didn't do, but aren't as lucky as me to have dear friends who know the ropes, know the law, know how to help them. I'm quitting the trucking company and, if you're game," she said pointing to Greg and to Margaret, "I'd like us to start our own business, trying to help others. You know, like a private investigator service. You being the head PI, of course. You are retired, you know, even though you keep working. And I will train and learn and get a license, but in the meantime, I can do some things to help."

Greg squeezed Margaret's hand. Looking at this woman, as love seemed to be pouring out of his eyes, he said, "I was going to tell you, Margaret, I plan to resign my job as bodyguard to the Governor. I've only worked all this time because I had no life—no one I cared to be with. I have a monthly pension that would more than take care of us, as well as a great deal of savings. I mean it's not like I owe on my house or have any bills. So since I haven't been spending, it's been piling up. Now I am hoping to enjoy the rest of my life with you."

Turning his eyes on Sam, he added, "So I am free to start working on the side. . .if Margaret agrees. But mind you, I don't want to work all the time. I want my honey and me to do a little traveling and just plain enjoy life while enjoying one another. So if she agrees, and God is behind everything, you can count me in."

"Me, too! I think you both have grand notions, and I'm ready for both. I've always wanted to travel. And in case you didn't know it, Sam, I didn't take this job Matthew offered me because I was in need of money. My husband left me quite well-off, too. So it sounds like money won't be a problem to get your new business off the ground." She laughed as she reached around Greg, hugging him. "I can't believe we're about to start living at our age."

"You and me both," Greg whispered. "I never thought I'd

find true love. And look what I've got—love, family, and a new life. Wow!"

If Sam didn't know better, she believed she saw tears materializing on the rims of Greg's eyelids. Was he about to cry? She knew she was on the verge of tears.

Sam jumped to her feet and rushed over to the happy couple. Wrapping her arms around them both, she said, "Thank you so much. It just feels so right, doesn't it?"

Before they could answer, Marty, with arms spread and a puzzled look on his face, said "What about me? Where do I fit in?" He had sat quietly listening to all the adults through this whole ordeal, but now he seemed to feel left out.

Samantha rushed to her son's side and knelt down before him as he was still seated on the couch. "Sweetheart, you are in all of this! My question to you is, will you be able to handle having your mom home almost every day? And I'll be cooking, or should I say fixing you something to eat—I'm still not the best cook in the world. Margaret can teach me if she will. But I'll be fixing all of your meals. Can you handle a momma 24-7?"

This time Marty was the one jumping up off the sofa. "All right, Momma." He wrapped his arms around her neck, as she was still down on her knees by the couch. "This sounds great! Count me in, too!"

About the Author

Deborah Lynne, beloved inspirational romance, mystery, and romance-suspense writer, has penned eight novels: *After You're Gone*, *Crime in the Big Easy*, The Samantha Cain Mysteries (*Be Not Afraid*, *Testimony of Innocence*, *The Truth Revealed*), *Grace: A Gift of Love*, *All in God's Time*, and *Passion from the Heart*.

 She is an active member of ACFW, RWA, and HEARTLA. She enjoys sharing her stories with her readers as well as the knowledge she gains as she grows as a novelist with other writers who share the same dream—of becoming a published author. She and her family enjoy their relaxed life in Louisiana.

http://www.author-deborahlynne.com
www.oaktara.com